CAINE'S MUTINY

CHARLES E. GANNON

BAEN

CAINE'S MUTINY

This is a work of fiction. All the characters and events portrayed in this book are fictional, and any resemblance to real people or incidents is purely coincidental.

A Baen Books Original

Baen Publishing Enterprises
P.O. Box 1403
Riverdale, NY 10471
www.baen.com

ISBN: 978-1-4814-8317-9

Cover art by Bob Eggleton
Maps by Charles E. Gannon and Robin Szypulski

First Baen mass market paperback printing, April 2018

Distributed by Simon & Schuster
1230 Avenue of the Americas
New York, NY 10020

Pages by Joy Freeman (www.pagesbyjoy.com)
Printed in the United States of America

With boundless love and appreciation to my entire family (my wife Andrea and living children Connor, Kyle, Alexandra, and Pierce), whose patience was matched only by their willingness to have me absent for so much of their lives during the completion of this book.

And in memory of I. F. Clarke, whose friendship, scholarship, and raucous, cackling laugh are always with me as reminders and inspirations as I apply his beloved concept of "future-think" to exploring the shape of warfare in the decades and centuries to come.

CONTENTS

Interstellar shift links
(max human range: 8.35 ly)

(Biogenic worlds are labeled in **BOLD FACE**)

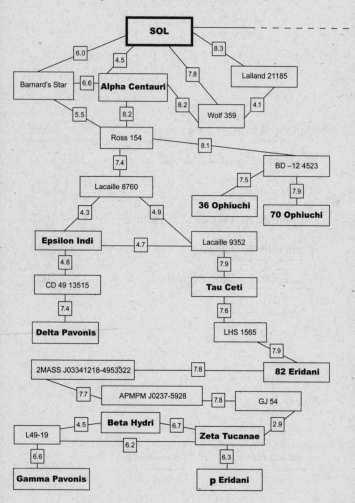

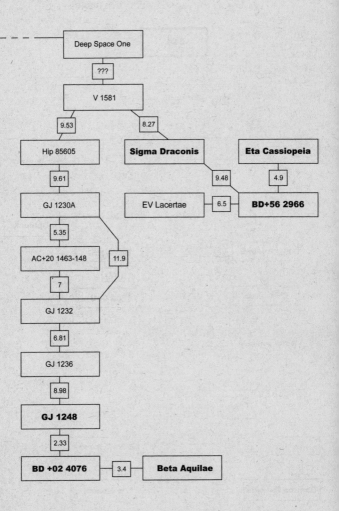

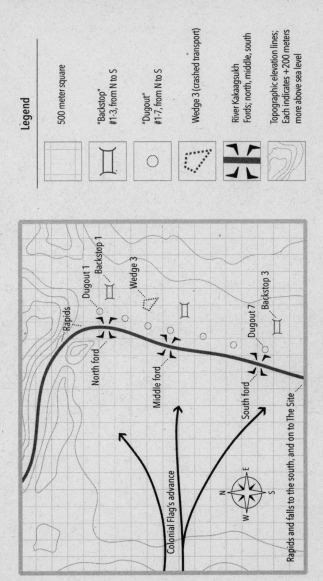

Legend

500 meter square

"Backstop"
#1-3, from N to S

"Dugout"
#1-7, from N to S

Wedge 3 (crashed transport)

River Kakaagsukh
Fords; north, middle, south

Topographic elevation lines;
Each line indicates +200 meters
more above sea level

Dugout 1

Backstop 1

Wedge 3

Rapids

North ford

Middle ford

Backstop 3

Dugout 7

Colonial Flag's advance

South ford

Rapids and falls to the south, and on to The Site

N E W S

PART ONE
May 2121

APPEARANCES

Species decepit
(Appearances deceive)

Chapter One

Cold.

Icy, bone-cracking cold. Like the winter he was nine and fell through the ice rimming a backwater inlet of the Chesapeake. Only one of his legs had gone in all the way, but the ache in his femur and tibia seemed ready to explode out through his skin, even as the frigid water burned down into its nerve endings...

But this time that burning was entirely inside him, running the length of his skeleton, running in and out of his heart, his brain, his groin: conduits of fire that made him flinch, groan—

—groan as loud as the voice which said, "We are sorry, Caine Riordan. But we have no choice. You must awaken."

Riordan struggled to move, to turn his head, to open his eyes, to fight up through layers of subzero molasses. Perhaps his eyes had already been open, because suddenly there were lights. But too bright. With multiple halos around them all.

He reached to either side, discovered he was in a

3

bed. Or in a pit. Or maybe a coffin. None of which made any sense.

Nothing made any sense, Caine realized as he scrambled to escape the claustrophobic box. The wheeling lights and surging sounds around him were unsteady, indistinct. His thoughts were a jumble of images that had nothing to do with each other: a ruined Grecian temple; then another half its size; explosions in jungles and massacres in cities; creatures and plants that seemed half vision and half nightmare; and finally, the head of a child's doll, rolling out of a roiling mass of smoke and debris in a war-torn Indonesian *kempang* . . .

Whether it was that last image, or the abruptness with which the fire streaming along his arteries changed back into debilitating icewater, his attempt to clamber out of the box-coffin was derailed by a fit of shivering . . . which quickly amplified into shakes so profound that his teeth did not merely chatter but clacked together convulsively.

His fingers weakened, his grip slipped, and he tumbled out of the box-coffin, catching himself unevenly. He swayed on his knees, still half-blind, discovering that the deck—or whatever was beneath him—was not only hard, but was even colder than he was.

Hands steadied him, kept him from falling over. But no, they weren't hands. They were clusters of prehensile tendrils, wrapping around his arms, his torso. He flinched away, horrified. "What—? Get off! Get the hell off—!"

"Caine Riordan, it is I, Yiithrii'ah'aash. Do not fear. You are safe. My fellow Slaasriithi will help you in every way possible. But we had to awaken you swiftly. We have employed drugs that accelerate your metabolism and heavy doses of chemicals that mimic your body's own epinephrine and endorphins, as well as neuromodulators and neurotransmitters. We apologize for the discomfort, but we had no choice."

Yiithrii'ah'aash: the Slaasriithi ambassador. The one who had snatched him from death's door after humanity's first diplomatic mission to his species ended in a furious firefight on the world known as Disparity. Images and ideas started swirling slowly into logical alignment; currents of order began surging up out of the frigid chaos. He realized he was clutching the side of the cold cell in which he had been placed when they had departed Delta Pavonis. "This mix of chemicals; are you sure it's safe? It's—very painful."

"We feared it would be." Yiithrii'ah'aash leaned into Caine's steadying field of vision, his tetrahedral head tilting downward as the tendril clusters at the end of his long, tightly furred arms gestured for the other Slaasriithi to resume assisting the human. "But our mission is in jeopardy. Human skills may be required to ensure its safe continuation."

No longer disoriented, Riordan discovered himself surrounded by the slightly shorter but even more lanky-limbed Slaasriithi that had been specially bred—or "engendered"—to dwell and work in low- and zero-gee environments. Now glad for their steadying "hands," Caine rose slowly. "What kind of jeopardy?"

Yiithrii'ah'aash straightened. Whereas his assistants resembled thick-bodied lemurs with emaciated extremities, the Slaasriithi ambassador was more akin to a tall, digitigrade gibbon with an ostrich neck. His pupilless mauve eyes, arrayed in equilateral triangles on each surface of his tetrahedral head, considered the larger human for a long moment. "We are in danger of detection."

Caine's pain didn't fade, but suddenly, he was only distantly aware of it. "Where are we?" He realized that his teeth had stopped chattering.

"At our destination: Turkh'saar. Or as your catalogues list it, system BD +56 2966."

Riordan started. "What's our situation?"

"We shall brief you as you recover. It is essential that your companions see that you are well."

"Well?" That's a pretty relative term right now . . . Caine's vision cleared enough to reveal his surroundings. He was in the navy-issue cryobank module, lined with the cold cells in which they had been conveyed from human space. He also realized that he was naked. "Ambassador, I should be wearing clothes when I rejoin my crew."

Even as he said it, one of Yiithrii'ah'aash's assistants— subtaxic members of the *pastorae* taxon—laid a folded navy duty suit over Riordan's sweat-slick left forearm. Flipping the unipiece garment open, Caine discovered the underwear he'd been hoping to find. The Slaasri- ithi were quite observant and were usually excellent at recalling and anticipating human customs, but found clothing particularly baffling, having no nudity taboos or particular need for covering. He began pulling on the regulation briefs, discovered they were a size too big as he scanned the rest of the module.

Shallow alcoves lined either bulkhead, each filled by a large white cold cell flanked by medical gear. The nine bays closest to Riordan's own were scenes of considerable activity. The lids of the cold cells were open. A sweat-shining human form was fumbling and shivering out of each high-tech sarcophagus, attended by clusters of the space-bred *pastorae*. One or two of his team began retching.

Alarmed, Caine began pulling on the lower half of the duty-suit at the same moment he started forward at a trot. "Are they okay?"

The *pastorae* did not exactly restrain him, but their hands slowed his progress enough that his concerned haste did not result in yet another fall. "Your companions are well, Caine Riordan. Be at ease." Yiithrii'ah'aash's voice was soothing, backed by a faint purr. "They had less concentrated therapeutic infusions than yourself. It was essential that we awaken and orient you first, that you may provide suitable guidance and leadership to them."

Riordan glanced at Melissa Sleeman, who, having recovered from her momentary nausea, discovered that she was staring at Peter Wu's short, nude body. She blinked. He blushed and stared back—which was the moment that Sleeman discovered that she herself was unclothed. She gasped in alarm.

"There are medical gowns in each alcove," Riordan mumbled to the ambassador. Yiithrii'ah'aash's sensor cluster fixed on him in what might have been quizzical regard. Caine suddenly recalled the confusion the term "gown" had occasioned the last time it was used in reference to medical garb. "I mean a cover, a wrap," he explicated.

"Ah. Yes, of course." Yiithrii'ah'aash sent a stream of liquid syllables down the length of the cryobank module, prompting quick, efficient searches by the *pastorae*. Pale blue gowns were promptly offered to the various humans, who fumbled them on with what seemed to be palsied hands. Lithe, muscular Dora Veriden cursed her unsteadiness in a sulphurous mix of Spanish and French profanities.

Although the Slaasriithi ambassador's familiarity with human idioms and customs was incomplete, he was evidently expert at reading Caine's pensive expressions. "I assure you there is no cause for concern. The cold cells are manufactured by your Commonwealth bloc and are quite reliable and robust. Also, we have been able to refine your reanimation cycle. Our modifications reduced the possibility of medical complications and enabled your accelerated return to awareness."

Caine exchanged nods with his almost fully dressed executive officer and friend, Bannor Rulaine, before turning back to Yiithrii'ah'aash. "When did you commence our reanimation?"

"Six hours ago."

Well, that was certainly impressive. It usually took thirty-six hours for awakened cold-sleepers to become ambulatory, another twelve to twenty-four to become fully functional. Whatever methods the Slaasriithi had used to shorten this cycle would be extremely interesting and valuable to the people in exosapient technical intelligence. Assuming that Caine could get the Slaasriithi to share the details ... "Ambassador, although I'm sure this unusual process was warranted, you *did* circumvent our own reanimation protocols and systems. Did you seek permission to do so?"

Yiithrii'ah'aash was still for a moment; his neck twitched in surprise. "I did not consult the human that your superiors left in waking oversight of your care. There was no time. It also seemed unnecessary, since our collective interests are served by your swift reanimation."

"I don't disagree, Ambassador. But in my role as acting ambassador plenipotentiary, I must point out that my government's medical experts will want to review the procedures and substances you used. Otherwise, the issue of quarantines between our species could arise again."

Yiithrii'ah'aash was still for a moment, then his neck contracted slightly. His verbal response rode over a series of clicks and a rough buzz: grudging compliance and a hint of amusement. "You shall have the protocols and samples of the compounds we used." The clicks subsided, the buzz slid into a faint purr. "It is good to see that your resourcefulness is unimpaired."

Riordan responded with a lopsided smile. "As you say, your reanimation methods are extremely effective. Now, you mentioned a human who remained conscious during our journey?"

Nods and waves greeted Caine as he and Yiithrii'ah'aash moved slowly down the module's center aisle. The Slaasriithi continued his explanation. "Your superior, Richard Downing, assigned a human to watch over you and, I presume, to brief you upon reanimation."

"Brief us? About what?"

"New information has come to light about our destination and how recent events upon the system's main world, Turkh'saar, may be amplifying political tensions in the Hkh'Rkh Patrijuridicate. Furthermore, Mr. Downing was able to provide some additional forces for this mission."

"Then why not send them instead of us?"

"Because they too are in cryogenic suspension and have been for some time."

Riordan heard the extra emphasis that Yiithrii'ah'aash had placed upon the final phrase. "Just how long have they been in cold sleep?"

"Their last memories date from before your species became aware of what you label exosapients."

Caine stared at the Slaasriithi. "You mean, before the Convocation and the invasion of Earth?"

The ambassador's sensor cluster inclined slightly. "I infer they were part of the ground forces that your late strategist Nolan Corcoran put into cryogenic suspension as a counterattack force to accompany the fleet that you named Relief Task Force One."

Good grief, the amount of disorientation those sleepers will experience upon awakening—"How long has it been since we were cold-slept and left Delta Pavonis?"

"Just over three of your months."

Riordan did the mental math, back-calculating along the calendar of frenzied recent events. "So they've been asleep at least two years. Possibly more."

"That is consistent with what Mr. Downing intimated. It is also why we did not feel safe waking them. They do not know of our, or any other, species. We feared that their reactions to our unexpected appearance might be—unpredictable."

Well, Yiithrii'ah'aash's tact remained as extraordinary as ever. "I think that's a fair assessment, Ambassador. I revise my initial reaction: you certainly made the right choice leaving them in cold sleep. But you said that Downing left someone in charge of the mission?"

The Slaasriithi stared at Caine. "Yes. You."

"No, no. I mean, someone who stayed awake to oversee the welfare of those of us in cold sleep?"

"Yes. A Mister Duncan Solsohn. As I understand it, there was some tenuous personal connection between him and Mr. Downing. It was a distant familial connection, I believe. I confess that the more nebulous human associational matrices continue to elude my understanding."

"That's okay, Ambassador; sometimes, they elude my understanding, too."

"I beg your pardon: such relationships also elude *your* understa—? Ah, now I perceive: you speak ironically. I am sure that if I were human, I would find your remark witty."

Caine was glad his self-worth was not vested in comedic aspirations. "Or maybe you wouldn't." They had arrived at the docking hatchway that provided ingress to the corvette that had seen Caine and his team through more than a few battles and tight spots: the UCS *Puller*. "Now, since you say it's an emergency and there's no time to waste, how about you tell me why you felt it necessary to jolt us out of cold sleep?"

Standing just beyond the gangway tube into *Puller*, Riordan double-checked the data that Yiithrii'ah'aash had downloaded to his palmcomp while synopsizing its operational significance. Hearing noise in the access tube, he looked up. Two of the starved-limbed, fireplug-torsoed lemur-Slaasriithi were approaching, followed at some distance by his team.

As the two space-adapted *pastorae* approached, Caine leaned toward the ambassador. "I didn't think you'd want to risk your personnel on this mission."

"While we prefer to avoid risk, that is not our reason for asking you to perform this task. Rather, success probability is maximized by the innate proficiencies with which your species' evolution has equipped you. These two *pastorae* are accompanying you in order to ensure that your personnel master the replacement systems with which we have finalized the repairs to your corvette."

"Which systems have you replaced?"

"We only made one entire replacement: the power and drive components. But we suspect your two engineers will readily comprehend our technology. Other partial replacements and upgrades—for instance, those we made to your life support systems—will be less familiar to your technicians. In particular, we use a radically different approach to recycle air and water."

Riordan's flesh cooled suddenly. "I presume you use specially 'induced' biota for that?"

"Of course." The Slaasriithi ambassador studied Caine's face for a second. "Ah. I see. I assure you, there are no microorganisms in those biota other than the ones which will freshen your environmental resources."

"I see." *And although I like you, Yiithrii'ah'aash, and even trust you to some degree, I'll let the experts on Earth be the judges of your biological adjustments.* "And what about the other damaged systems? I'm guessing you had to replace our avionics and sensor suite."

"We did."

"Great—but how? Our systems use different electric current, different data links and protocols. Or are you using tailored biots to—?"

"No, Caine Riordan. We understand your reluctance to accept any biota from us without complete screening of them. However, it was also illogical to provide you with replacement systems that depend upon biota that you could not restore or regenerate, should they be destroyed or damaged. Our ability to blend our technological systems with your own is a product of our opportunities to familiarize ourselves with your devices, even before your species asked for membership in the Accord."

Further evidence that we were under observation for years before we knew there were other intelligences; I'm not sure how that's supposed to be reassuring, but—

Riordan's team was drawing close, led by Dora, who was securing her palmcomp to a wrist-adapter commonly referred to as a bracer. "Thank you for the explanation, Ambassador," he concluded. "We hope to have completed the mission in half a day, at most."

"That would be prudent, Caine Riordan. As you have no doubt surmised, when the stimulants in your body have worn away, you will experience fatigue." Yiithrii'ah'aash moved to depart, then looked back. "*Profound* fatigue," he emphasized.

"Thank you for the warning, Ambassador, and I— hey, Dora. On this mission, that earbud isn't going to be anything but jewelry."

She slowed as she passed him, her hand stilled where she was affixing the device in question. "Whaddya mean?"

"An earbud means wireless. Wireless means signals. And our mission requires we run silent and undetected as long as we can."

She scoffed. "Hell, the RF signature coming from

our bridge controls will be putting out more EM junk than our portable commo."

"Yes, but we *can't* run the ship without the controls. So regardless of how convenient wearables are, they come with a signature—and any unnecessary signature could be the difference between us getting spotted or not."

She started toward the airlock. "Huh. So, any idea what we're up against?"

"Not much, but I'll share it as soon as everyone is on board and squared away."

Dora left with a nod, Flight Officer Karam Tsaami right behind her. As usual.

"We'll be working in duty suits," Riordan called after his pilot. "And we'll need to fit them with EVA liners."

"I'm on it," Karam shouted back, detouring to the ship's locker.

"While you're there, see if we still have the pony tanks for extended ops."

Karam's reply was muffled by the dogleg in the corridor down which he had turned. "They're still on board, Boss. Locker is fully stocked."

The ventilation system kicked on. The cold, stale air deeper inside the hull came rushing out the passageway, pushed from behind by a blast of hot air.

"Christ, that's nasty," Miles O'Garran muttered as he hustled past.

"Won't be once you get your liner in your duty suit, Miles. Hey, on your way aft, check the armory."

"Heading there now," replied the short, broad SEAL.

From much deeper in the ship, Dora's voice was shrill with amused amazement. "The armory? I heard our job was to intercept something in space."

"That's correct," Riordan shouted into the ship.

Her head poked around the nearest bulkhead. "*Mierda*, Caine, are you planning on plinking at the bad guys from the airlock?"

"No, but do you remember what happened on Disparity because we didn't have all the necessary gear on all of our ships?"

For the first time in Riordan's memory of her, Dora's face blanched. "I'll go help Little Guy check the armory," she muttered as she went aft.

"No need," O'Garran shouted. "Armory is full up. And don't call me Little Guy."

"Sure thing, Little Guy," Dora replied as Caine turned to face back down the boarding tube—

And discovered that the next person approaching was a stranger: a man in his thirties, maybe six centimeters shorter than Caine. "I'm guessing you're the official helping hand sent along by Richard Downing." It took more than a little effort not to sound sardonic; any person assigned by Downing was likely to be more of a monitor and a snitch.

"Guilty as charged. Hey, I couldn't help overhearing: what *did* happen to you guys on Disparity?"

"We didn't have the time to sort out our gear. So some of us had to kill alien monsters and enemy soldiers with survival rifles chambered for old-fashioned pistol rounds."

The man's eyes widened. "Well, I'm guessing *that* didn't work too well."

"Didn't work at all, half of the time."

The newcomer put out his hand. "Duncan Solsohn. And I know who you are."

So much for keeping a low profile. "Caine Riordan,"

he said anyway, offering his hand in return. But Solsohn was already shrugging into a navy-issue duty suit, fitted with an EVA liner. "Mr. Solsohn, exactly what do you think you're doing?"

"I'm coming with you."

"No. You are staying here."

Solsohn paused, his right arm halfway into the suit's sleeve. "Er, Mr. Downing gave me explicit instructions—".

"Unfortunately, Mr. Downing relayed no such explicit instructions to me. And if they are buried somewhere in a special orders packet, I haven't had time to catch up on my reading since I was awakened. So you stay here."

"But, Commodore, I—"

"You just uttered the magic word, Mr. Solsohn: 'Commodore.' Which is what I am. Are you?"

"Er, no."

"Then you follow orders and keep your head down." Caine leaned closer and lowered his voice as tall Tygg Robin and diminutive Melissa Sleeman slipped around and past them. "Listen, Duncan. Unlike me, you clearly know the updated operation orders for this mission, and have reviewed the other assets Downing sent along with us. Which means, at this point, you're more essential to the success of this operation than I am. So, for now, *this* is your post." *Besides, I don't know you from Adam, and if you were sent by Downing, your first loyalty is to him, not us. So until I sort you out*—"I want you to stand by on the radio, though. I need another barbarous human interpreting our encounters and reactions for the Slaasriithi. They don't perceive confrontation the same way we do."

Duncan grinned ruefully, may have been on the verge of rolling his eyes. "Yes, I've noticed that, sir. Anything else I can do to help?"

Riordan thought. "One thing: do you believe the Slaasriithi are overreacting, or is there a genuine threat out there?"

Duncan's steady gaze faltered a moment. "Wish I could say they were just starting at shadows, but no, sir, there's reason for them to be concerned. And for you to be careful."

"Thank you, Mr. Solsohn. Now, one more thing, if you please."

"What's that, sir?"

"Step back. We're casting off."

Chapter Two

As soon as Karam Tsaami had maneuvered far enough from the Slaasriithi ship—improbably named the *Tidal-Drift-Instaurator-to-Shore-of-Stars*—to lay in a course for the after-fringes of the most trailing of the debris fields, he turned to Riordan. "We're clear to commence transit, Skipper."

Riordan turned to Dora at the comm panel. "Ms. Veriden, please signal the rest of the crew to strap in. We'll be pulling a decent portion of a gee in a few moments."

Dora nodded, made the announcement over the hardwire comms.

Riordan turned back to Karam. "Get us under way, Helm."

Tsaami adjusted the thrusters, prepared to engage—and stared. "Holy shit," he breathed. It sounded more reverent than profane.

"Problem, Helm?"

"Anything but, sir. Good thing I checked our power levels before kicking in the juice. The Slaasriithi didn't just replace the power plant. They must have swapped in something a whole lot more muscular than the old nuke unit."

Tina Melah's voice was suddenly on the open channel. "That's a big affirmative," she said, almost breathless. "There's an honest-to-god fusion plant down here. Inertial. Pulse fusion. Fits in the engine room of this little corvette. How the hell do they—?"

"Ms. Melah, let's consider the technological ramifications later. Is the plant's function nominal?"

"If you want to call this kind of output nominal, well, yeah, I guess so. And Commodore?"

"Yes?"

"Did Yiithrii'ah'aash happen to mention that he replaced our drives, as well?"

"He did."

"And did he happen to mention that these are not patterned after our standard MAP drives at all?"

Well, damn. "He did not."

"Looks like he put in a highly advanced version of what we call an H-MAP thruster: a heavy-particle magnetically accelerated plasmoid drive. I think this is the Slaasriithi standard, and what our egg-heads are trying to monkey-copy back home."

"Well, then, we're fortunate enough to have the first in the fleet. Estimated increase in thrust?"

The silence on the line was profound. It was the other engineer, Phil Friel, who broke it. "Conservative guess would be two point two times more thrust, sir. Conceivably as much as two point five. And there's only a fraction of the radiation, shielding, and coolant headaches we're accustomed to. In a smaller, lighter package."

Riordan glanced back at Karam, whose face was no longer the careful, cynical mask he usually affected; he looked like a kid at Christmas. "Helm, do you think you're up to the challenge of flying with this new system?"

Tsaami spent one second looking offended and then saw the slow smile that Riordan could not keep back. "Oh, yeah, sir, I think I just might be able to handle it. Strap in, thems of you what ain't, 'cause here we go!"

And indeed, they did go—fast enough to push everyone back in their couches.

After several minutes of two-gee boost, Riordan gave orders for Karam to bring the thrust back to .8 gees constant. Tsaami looked like his Christmas present had been abruptly transmuted into coal.

"Signature," Riordan explained. "We don't want to look like a roman candle coming in."

"Understood, sir, but it's nice to know we've got that in reserve. It was a nice test-drive."

"It truly was." *And besides, we needed to put the new drives through a fast shake-down run. Wouldn't be smart to count on that thrust until it was a proven value.* Riordan adjusted his hardwire comm set. "Major Rulaine?"

"Here, Commodore." Bannor's voice had a slight echo. He was in the gunnery bubble: a sealed, spherical station amidships that allowed for weapons control using intuitive motions within a 360 by 360 virtual representation of the battle-space.

"All weapons green?"

"They are, sir. And I believe our hosts upgraded the cooling systems on the railgun."

"Any guess why?"

"Yes, sir. Because they've doubled the power supply to the weapon. Advantage of having that fusion
plant: juice to spare."

"What about our load-out?"

"All the missiles we had after Disparity are still
in the rotary launcher. The larger systems, including
our independent point defense platforms, are in the
midship ventral munitions bay. However, the Slaasriithi
have added some of their own toys. I'm going over
the specs now."

"Did they give us one of those drone fighters we
saw at Disparity?"

"No, sir; we wouldn't have the room in the bay
for anything else if they had loaded up one of the
cannonballs."

Logical. "Did they give us any PIPs?"

"Yes, sir. Two Slaasriithi Point-defense Independent
Platforms are in the soft-deploy bay."

"Very well, Major. When you and the rest of the
crew are done squaring away your action stations, head
back up here. It's time you find out what we're facing."

As the rest of his team filed on to *Puller*'s bridge,
Riordan smiled. "You know, even though you've had
almost three months of sound sleep, you all look
like hell."

"Yeah? Have *you* looked in a mirror, yet?" Dora
Veriden had sounded testy when she began the retort,
but her tone ended on irony, not annoyance. Caine
smiled more widely. She almost smiled back.

Karam Tsaami, who was returning from the ship's
locker, passed close to her—a little closer than strictly
necessary—and grinned as he fell into his pilot's couch.

"Okay, so I saw the cold cells' reanimation data; the Slaasriithi got us out of cryo in record time. Impossible time, I would have said before today. Of course, the more we learn about what some of our exosapient neighbors can do, the more I hesitate using the word 'impossible.'" His stomach rumbled and he stifled a belch; Caine could smell the geneered glycerin that would take weeks to fully work its way out of all their systems. Genetically reverse-engineered from the same compound that kept Arctic cod from freezing solid in blocks of ice, it retained a faintly fishy undertone. "Pardon," Karam offered as half of the team waved hands in front of their noses.

Not that it would help much. They all stank of the glycerin in addition to the antiseptic reek of the other chemicals that would slowly leach out of their bodies. But one sensation was new to Caine: a coppery taste in his mouth. Probably stimulated by the near-overdose of hormones and neurohumors that the Slaasriithi had pumped into them.

Miles O'Garran, a former tunnel-rat like Peter Wu, folded his arms. "So what's the big rush? Something's up or the Slaasriithi would have followed the standard reanimation protocols."

Riordan nodded. "We're in the Turkh'saar system. Outer reaches." Caine activated the holotank—just before he realized it was not of human manufacture: another refit, courtesy of the Slaasriithi.

The holotank, although much smaller, projected a breathtakingly detailed and faithful display of the system. Caine looked for a plasma stylus to change the view, didn't see one, tried manipulating the view with his hand.

Accordingly, the representation zoomed in, the rest of the system falling outside the view as it centered on the seventh, outermost planet. "We're here. A gas giant, about half the size of Saturn, just over three AUs from the primary."

Tina Melah, one of the two engineers, frowned. "Why the hell are we out here? Turkh'saar is the colony world, so we should have shifted in near the habitable zone. Which can't be more'n half as far out as Sol's goldilocks girdle, given this star's a K3 V."

Riordan nodded. "True, but we're trespassing in what could be a hostile system. And the Slaasriithi are nothing if not careful."

"That's one way of putting it," grumbled Tygg Robin. Even when speaking under his breath, the tall SAAS soldier's broad down-under accent was unmistakable.

Riordan shared a rueful grin. "Here's why they woke us up." Caine put his hand into the holoplot near Planet Seven, stretched his fingers further apart. The view zoomed in even more. Four small moons appeared, moving slowly about the gas giant. Two faint rings, one located beyond the orbit of the innermost moon, were slightly askew from the system's ecliptic plane. "Show debris," he ordered the computer; since it was not in emergency operations mode, it could still process voice commands. A litter of red specks appeared in a ragged half-wreath around the planet, scattered liberally in the rings as well as near the orbital tracks of two of the moons.

Bannor Rulaine raised a single eyebrow. "So who's been shooting at whom, out here?"

"Slaasriithi raiders came through shortly after the Arat Kur and Hkh'Rkh attacked us. They hit the Arat

Kur refueling facilities, as well as their automated sensor and defense assets."

Peter Wu stepped closer, examined the distribution and density of the red flecks. "Then they must have had very extensive facilities around this planet. The amount of debris is consistent with a much larger engagement."

Riordan nodded. "That's one worrisome mystery. Here's another: according to Yiithrii'ah'aash, the final scan by the Slaasriithi who hit this system showed a different picture." Caine waved away the current display, summoned the postbattle readings with a slow raise of his palm. The red wreath in the new image was slightly thicker. In several places, debris clusters predominated where there was now clear space.

"Someone came through to clean up the rubbish?" Melissa Sleeman's tone indicated she didn't believe her own speculation.

Riordan smiled. "In a manner of speaking." Karam Tsaami rolled out of the pilot's couch, came over to scowl down into the holotank. "What do you think, helmsman?"

Karam's scowl deepened. "Hell, you already know what I think—and what Yiithrii'ah'aash thinks, too, I'll bet. The Arat Kur returned and reseeded the planet with new sensor and defense assets. No other reason to clean up the junk."

Dora, who had less spaceside experience than most of the others, squinted at the holoplot as if that might help her see it more clearly. "I don't get it. Why not leave the debris in place, as cover and hiding places for your new robots? They'd be invisible to our sensors if they were snugged up tight against that junk: same materials, same temperature, same size. Or smaller. Great spots from which to mount ambushes."

Riordan nodded. "All true, and they've left plenty of those hunter's blinds for themselves to hide in. But, if the junk is too dense, it becomes an obstruction for their own sensors and maneuver. Too many small objects tumbling along at different velocities, on different vectors. An ambusher needs to groom the ground—or in this case, the space—between themselves and their prey."

Veriden's squint intensified. "Yeah, that's what they've done, all right. They've thinned out the debris in a couple of places. And gotten rid of a couple of larger objects as well."

Engineer Phil Friel moved forward. "Actually, I'm a wee bit puzzled about those missing larger objects."

Karam made a troubled noise. "Me, too."

Riordan grew concerned. "What's worrying you?"

Phil shrugged. "Well, the biggest of the missing bits were so shockin' large that any ship that's been here before—or that can compare the current sensor readings to these older ones—is sure to see they're gone. Rather spoils the surprise, doesn't it, calling attention to the changed debris field, that way?" Karam grunted approvingly.

Damn it, they're right. And damn me for not seeing it, myself. "Okay, but then *why* remove those bigger pieces? Unless that large debris was not debris."

Karam looked at the large red flecks again. "You mean, you think the missing chunks might have been intact systems that were lying doggo when the scan was made, then moved off on their own power later on?" He cocked his head. "Zoom in some more, will ya?"

Riordan complied. Now, at maximum resolution, each debris field looked like a funneled storm of large ragged ice chunks being spattered by a faster blizzard of hail and fine snow—all bright red.

Karam shook his head. "See that? If any craft tried weathering that storm as it waited for a safe window in which to move, it would get holed. Or worse." Karam peered more closely. "I'm guessing the smallest of the junk is still massing close to ten kilos. At those velocities, any hit would be serious. If it smacked any of a craft's critical systems, it would be disabling. And with all the big pieces still colliding, spinning off on new vectors and generating new debris, there are no reliable eyes of calm in that storm."

"Okay, but we haven't gotten any closer to knowing why the larger objects were removed," Melissa Sleeman pointed out.

"And I doubt we are going to, Doctor. At least not from this distance," Peter Wu observed respectfully.

Miles O'Garran stared around the group; his deepening frown was impatient, almost angry. "Okay, so do I have to ask the obvious? Why the hell did the Slaasriithi wake us up for *this*? I mean, are we supposed to go out and collect the garbage because it makes them nervous? I know they flee from conflict whenever possible, but Christ Almighty, this is—"

Riordan held up a hand. "You asked a question, Chief. Wait to hear the answer."

O'Garran stopped in mid syllable, mouth open, looked away. "Yes, sir."

Riordan waved away the older sensor survey of Planet Seven; the current, slightly less crowded one reasserted. "Show emission sources," he instructed the computer. Three faint, lavender spheres superimposed upon the view, each one straddling a different debris field. "Each of those areas are possible locations of Arat Kur platforms, sending intermittent pings to each other."

Tygg Robin (whose first name was actually Christopher, and thus spawned a steady stream of Winnie-the-Pooh jokes), shook his head. "So, you mean, we already know where the targets are, Commodore?"

"You'll note I called them 'possible' locations, Lieutenant. Whatever enemy systems are hiding in those spots, they're hardly pinpointing themselves. In fact, if we hadn't laid hold of all the Arat Kur stealth and covert operations protocols when they surrendered, the Slaasriithi would probably never have found these telltale signs at all. The signals rotate frequency and transmit only when the gas giant itself sends out a wash of solar-induced static. So, if you don't know exactly where and when to listen, their pings just sound like part of the background noise. Unfortunately, the objects sending out the pings are probably not the ones we need to worry about."

"That's covert SOP for us, too," Karam agreed with a sharp nod. "The pingers are tiny, expendable. The business platforms—weapons and sensors—will be nearby. They'll be lying doggo, maintaining line-of-sight connection to the little repeaters, which only exist to poll the more distant parts of the autonomous matrix, confirming readiness and position."

"Which means, even if you home in on and close with these pingers, they're really just bait," Bannor concluded with a nod.

"And that's why the Slaasriithi are spooked." Riordan

swept a hand through the Slaasriithi holo; it flicked off. "They are used to cat-and-mouse games, but not when the clock is running."

Sleeman nodded. "Which started ticking when we arrived, because of our immense in-shift signature."

"Exactly, Doctor. Yiithrii'ah'aash tells me that, under normal Slaasriithi rules of engagement, the current circumstances warrant withdrawal."

O'Garran scowled. "What? Because of a few hinky signals?"

Riordan shook his head. "Miles, the Slaasriithi philosophy is to work from stealth and at great distance. They don't like fighting, particularly not up close and personal. Nor do they like starting an engagement that they can't be sure of winning."

"Then, with respect, sir, how do they expect to win *any* fight, much less a war?"

"They don't. That's why they see us as essential allies."

"You mean, so we can die instead of them?"

Riordan did not allow any change in expression which would suggest just how much he sympathized with O'Garran's last, irritated outburst. "No, Chief. So we can succeed at tasks for which their evolution has made them singularly ill-equipped. And succeeding at those tasks is exactly what we are going to do. Is that clear?"

"Clear, sir. What now?"

"The Slaasriithi have replaced a lot of *Puller*'s systems, particularly those compromised after she went into the drink on Disparity. Yiithrii'ah'aash only gave me a brief overview of the major changes before we detached. So you'll need to survey your action stations for any alterations and familiarize yourself with any new toys. There are two of the space-adapted *pastorae* on board; call them for assistance."

"Or we cán ask the computer," Tina Melah put in.

"Not anymore, at least not vocally." He glanced at Dora. "I'm instructing Ms. Veriden to take the computer's voice-command option off line. Immediately."

"Why?" asked Veriden, even as she complied. Staring at Caine, she missed how the eyes of the military personnel hardened as they began edging in the directions of their various action stations.

"Because," Caine answered, "you can't trust voice recognition when you're operating in a combat zone. Which we've just entered."

Chapter Three

Caine watched as Peter Wu moved to occupy the bridge console next to Melissa Sleeman's sensor panel. "Remote ops manned and ready," he announced.

"Very good. Ms. Veriden, have the Slaasriithi responded yet?"

"Just now. They acknowledge reception of our final transmission and advise that they are going dark, too. We have an automated check-in lascom ping set for every thirty minutes, with a three minute maximum plus-or-minus randomizing element built in."

Riordan nodded. Now two light-minutes distant from the shift-carrier, *Puller* was about as alone as alone could get. If something happened, there'd be no way for *Tidal-Drift-Instaurator-to-Shore-of-Stars* to intervene in a timely fashion. "Dr. Sleeman, what are sensors revealing about the debris?"

"Easier to show you than tell you, sir."

"We'll all take a look. Main display; use faux 3-D."

Sleeman complied. The three major debris fields appeared on the large screen above the piloting couches. The innermost field was the longest, located between the orbit of the planet's closest moon and its slightly skewed belt. The other two debris traces were slightly more dense and slightly less attenuated. Riordan frowned. "Mr. Tsaami, I'll bet you've got some recommendations at this point."

The former Survey and Settlement Office pilot glanced down at a small screen reprising the view in the larger one located just behind him. Even from his oblique rear vantage point, Riordan detected a hint of a smile raising the outline of the helmsman's cheek. "Why do you ask, sir?"

"Don't be coy. We've got enough data now to decide where we're going to make our first sweep."

"Yes, we do. So what are you thinking?"

"I'm asking you." *And you know why; because I'm pretty much a newb and you've been doing this so long you could do it in your sleep.*

Tsaami seemed pleased as he answered. Whether that was because he was gratified to show off his profound experience or because his skipper was neither too proud nor too insecure to seek expert opinions freely from his crew, was impossible to tell. "We want to start with the nearest one. And I think you already know why."

"The attenuation of the debris and proximity to the moon."

"Yeah, and the fact that any heavies which send refueling drogues to scoop up deuterium from the gas giant's exosphere would have been easing in from that orbit. And would want to keep that moon within reach."

Commenting over the comm, Little Guy sounded

puzzled. "I thought it's SOP to avoid moons, to stay away from their gravity wells and the debris around them."

Before Karam could reply, Tina Melah's voice jumped in. "True in a lot of places, but not always true around a gas giant—particularly not one where you're going to conduct frontier refueling. You can get all sorts of bad 'weather' if you get in close to a gas giant. There was one time near Epsilon Indi when we—"

Riordan cleared his throat. "Thank you, Tina. Karam, please finish your recommendation."

"Happy to do so if people let me," grumbled Tsaami. "As I was saying, sir, that inner moon is a likely way-point for ships initiating a refueling run. First, as Tina mentioned, it gives you hard cover against the crap you encounter near gas giants: higher radiation levels, ionic irregularities due to solar wind variations, and rings of frozen volatiles that clutter up any equatorial approaches. In the latter case, a moon tends to work like a vacuum cleaner, sweeping up a lot of that junk, making normal navigation easier.

"So a proximal moon can work like a waystation as you make your way in closer to a gas giant. It's a good sensor object, too, so it's friendly to navigators looking to plot courses. And it's easy to eyeball if instruments break or get sketchy. Lastly, if something really goes wrong and you need to wait for help, you can usually find a natural feature—like a crater with ice—that is a better long-term choice than floating in free space. It gives you some hard cover and some volatiles: helps you live off the land if rescuers aren't nearby."

Riordan nodded. "So of the three debris trails, the one close to the moon was probably the site of any permanent or semi-permanent facility that the Hkh'Rkh or the Arat Kur might have built."

"So, do I set course for that debris trail, Commodore? ETA would be"—Karam checked his instruments quickly—"forty-two minutes."

"That's the course we want, Mr. Tsaami. Dr. Sleeman, let's bring the rest of our passive sensor array on line. And Ms. Veriden, keep the command channel clear from this point forward and pass the word: all crew is to strap in."

She moved to comply, smiled sardonically in the direction of the helm. "Why? Are you gonna give Tsaami another chance to test out his new ride?"

"No, Ms. Veriden, I am readying us for combat. Stand ready to sound general quarters."

The bow view in the main screen was unlike any Riordan had seen before. In space, you usually never came close enough to other objects to eyeball them. They were sensor blips until right before you docked with them or they came at you with lethal intent. But as *Puller* angled in toward the inert, frost-dusted moon low off their port bow, space ahead winked and flickered intermittently: tumbling debris or ice chips that caught and flung off the primary's light. There weren't many such twinklings—maybe a dozen scattered across the whole forward panorama—but to be able to see so many with the naked eye indicated that they were in a very densely littered section of space.

"Dr. Sleeman, distance from the mean center of the object cluster we delineated fifteen minutes ago?"

"Just under two thousand kilometers, sir."

"At what point along our trajectory will we begin passing the outermost objects of that cluster?"

"Approximately three hundred kilometers further along, sir."

"Current relative velocity?"

"Four hundred thirty meters per second."

Riordan did the math, frowned. "So if there's anything here to jump us, it will do so in the next ten or twelve minutes."

The back of Karam's head cycled through a quick set of nods. "Once we begin moving past their hiding spots, the robots will consider the possibility that our sensors will get a peek into the sensor shadows in which they've been hiding. They'll start the party before that happens."

Riordan rubbed his index finger across his upper lip. He leaned his mouth closer to the mic. "Gunnery."

"Rulaine here."

"Bannor, have you digested the specs on the Slaasriithi Point-defense Independent Platforms, yet? We'll need to deploy them soon."

"Well, Slaasriithi don't seem to organize specs the way we do, but I can tell you this: their PIPs are way beyond ours. Their lasers have more endurance and better focal performance per meter of focal length. They're UV weapons, so they have better energy delivery on targets in vacuum. I can't figure out what their cycle rate is, yet; the translation of their data tables is far from perfect."

"Have you consulted one of the *pastorae* advisors?"

"Not on the PIPs. They were helping me with the *Puller*'s own lasers and then got called back to engineering. Again."

That made five visits to engineering by the Slaasriithi. Not surprising: many of their systems were not simply more advanced analogs of *Puller*'s original hardware; they were devices without human precedent, and so, completely beyond the experience of Tina or Phil. "Give me your best guess on the PIPs. Then tell me what's wrong with our own lasers."

"I think the Slaasriithi PIPs can engage roughly three times as many targets per minute as ours do, and they are more likely to generate a mission kill when they hit. They could be better than that, but I can't figure out their targeting specs. They use terms and metrics that have nothing to do with any gunnery software I've ever heard of."

"Are they partially biological systems?"

"Maybe. I don't know. I *do* know that, in the aggregate, their PIPs do the job of about four of ours. At least."

"Okay. Now what's the problem with *Puller*'s onboard lasers?"

"Well—they're not *Puller*'s onboard lasers. Not anymore. They're Slaasriithi replacements."

"What? But our lasers weren't damaged."

"Right. But, according to the *pastorae*, when the Slaasriithi were running live trials, they miscalibrated the feed from our new monster of a power plant and fried our own laser's capacitor. So they had to replace the whole system."

"You mean, the capacitor?"

"No, I mean the laser itself. All of it. The splitter-blisters weren't affected, but the main laser is all theirs, from power input all the way to the primary centerline firing housing at the bow. Yiithrii'ah'aash didn't tell you?"

"No, he didn't." *But maybe it's not so odd that he didn't want to announce it when we were still*

*in human space. The Slaasriithi Great Ring isn't
comfortable giving us access to their technology. On
the other hand, a lot of them—Yiithrii'ah'aash in
particular—seem glad to find excuses to slip us a few
more crumbs whenever possible...* "So does this laser
substantively change our combat profile?"

"You bet. This isn't a tactical laser for PDF and
small craft engagement, Caine; this is one of their
dual purpose lasers. Cannibalized straight from the
Shore-of-Stars's own defense batteries. It puts ten
times the energy on target and has five times the
effective range of our old laser."

Riordan managed to suppress a surprised gulp
that would have been wholly inconsistent with anything resembling "command image." "That's—pretty
impressive."

"There's more. It's variable wavelength. UV is the
primary setting but it can range most of the way down
the spectrum. Loses a lot of hitting power doing so,
of course, but it's an option. Gives you deeper reach
into an atmosphere. It may have other uses I can't
even guess at."

"But how the hell do they even do that?"

"I'm even less of a physicist than you are, Caine. But
right now, I'm not looking a gift horse in the mouth."

"Good philosophy. Are our gunnery controls recalibrated for it?"

"The Slaasriithi technical advisors say so. At least,
I think that's what they said. These guys—or gals,
or whatever—are relying on their translators. Which
don't seem very reliable."

"Understood. Prepare to transfer control over the
PIPs to Peter. He'll be handling them along with our

scout drones and phased sensor arrays. I want you to stay focused on the ship's laser, as well as any missiles or offensive drones we have to launch. If they have any bigger systems out here, I don't want you distracted by swatting down their small stuff."

"Roger that. Rulaine out."

Riordan tapped off the mic, turned to Melissa Sleeman. "Anything yet?"

"All quiet out there, sir."

"That wreckage up ahead, bearing fifty-seven by three-thirty relative: it looks fairly intact."

"Yes, sir. Fuel tanks and the remains of a ship. Well, half of a ship."

"Type?"

"Rotational cross section matches it with a Hkh'Rkh modular hull. Designated as type Yankee-Whiskey Three. Can be fitted out as a transport, tanker/tender, or construction auxiliary. Fuel tanks are both Arat Kur and Hkh'Rkh." She turned. "Milspec all, sir."

Yes, and lots of it. Too much.

Dora was frowning over her computer panel. "I thought the Hkh'Rkh were only permitted access to the colony world, Turkh'saar, and that the rest of the system belonged to the Arat Kur."

"It's a little more complicated than that, but encountering Hkh'Rkh milspec vehicles and tankage out here is strange." *More than strange; it violates their codominium agreement with the Arat Kur. But maybe they mutually set that aside some time before the Slaasriithi showed up and crashed their party.* "Dr. Sleeman, what's the local density of frozen volatile particles?"

"Erm . . . eight percent above system normal for open space, sir."

Karam's voice was low. "If you're thinking about detecting their point-to-point lascom transmissions by reflected or refracted light, those numbers still won't cut it."

"No, but I think we can boost the numbers a bit. Lieutenant Wu, ready our scout drones for active launch. Include micrograin particle dispensers in their modular payload bay. Image makers as well."

Tsaami turned briefly from the helm to grin back at Riordan. There was nothing disrespectful in the helmsman's expression, but even so, Caine felt as though he'd been patted on the head. "You wish to add something, Mr. Tsaami?"

"Uh, no . . . no, sir."

Riordan nodded, turned back to Peter. "Coordinate with Dr. Sleeman. Look for areas in the wreckage where there are sensor shadows. Plot logical line-of-sight telemetries between those areas. Aim the scout drones to intersect those lines."

"Sir, that will scatter our scouts across a ninety-five-degree frontal cone. Their sensors will probably be too dispersed to coordinate upon potential targets."

"That's fine, Mr. Wu; we only need them to flush out the game. Our second launch tier will be phased sensor arrays, and behind them, our two PIPs."

"The Slaasriithi models, sir?"

"No; our own. We're saving the two new ones for terminal defense of our own hull."

"Do you expect the enemy systems to get that close?"

Riordan gazed calmly at Wu. "I do, Lieutenant. Because I suspect they already *are* that close. Commence launching our three waves of remote platforms."

❖   ❖   ❖

The scouts had closed half the distance to the mid-point of the wreckage when Melissa Sleeman straightened abruptly. "Pings, sir. The ones the Slaasriithi heard. But... a whole chorus of them. Up ahead; all within five hundred kilometers of the mean center."

"Well, I'd say they've seen us. Signals analysis: are they Arat Kur or Hkh'Rkh, Dr. Sleeman?"

"I can't tell yet if—no; a mix of both, sir. But mostly Arat Kur."

Figures. "Watch carefully for small thermal blooms, Dr. Sleeman. They might not be in our line of sight, and will be very faint, barely above background."

"Low power electronics coming on line as the systems wake up?"

"Exactly. And the Arat Kur systems are too advanced to show up at all. But the entire matrix will start coordinating for an attack as soon as they've reconfirmed each others' locations. Lieutenant Wu, I need you to sprint our scouts forward at max gees to get one hundred kilometers closer to those possible line-of-sight telemetries we plotted earlier."

"Yes, sir. And once they get there?"

"Discharge the micrograin packets. Send those seeding coordinates to Dr. Sleeman so she can watch for any LOS emissions cutting across the local sleet or the reactive particles we're adding to it."

"Boosting scout drones now, sir."

Riordan turned to Dora. "Ms. Veriden, signal the crew: bogeys detected. Engagement imminent. Stand to all systems."

For the first time since meeting her, Veriden's reply was neither gruff, snarky, or sardonic. "Yes, sir." She might have even sounded anxious.

Riordan considered saying something reassuring—she was used to having her threats up close, personal, and directly susceptible to her lethal skills—but he suspected that would have annoyed her.

Karam Tsaami cleared his throat. "Orders for the helm, sir?"

"Steady as we go, and no additional thrust. I want to remain as dark as we can, for as long as we can."

"Understood, sir . . . but thermally, we still stand out like light bulb in a dark room."

"Which is why I'm going to give them something brighter to look at. Mr. Wu, deploy image makers and engage."

"Deploying and activating, sir."

Up ahead, visible to the naked eye, at least a half a dozen bright, blue-white stars ignited, moving very slowly, despite the fact that they were now travelling several hundred kilometers per hour faster than *Puller* itself.

"Will the enemy systems really get fooled by those?" Dora wondered aloud. She sounded more worried than dismissive.

"Not if there were living, breathing beings in the command-and-control loop," Caine replied with a shrug. "But automated systems, even the Arat Kur's, are always weaker when they are on their own. Right now, their drones are calculating the likelihood that those are in fact decoys which we just lit up, supported by image makers. And the Arat Kur systems are almost certainly deciding that our decoys are probably just that: decoys. But only *probably*. So they won't ignore them entirely; their programming won't allow them to. So they'll dedicate some assets to counteracting the decoys. Probably starting just about—"

"Commodore!" Sleeman's voice was a mixture of raw excitement and incompletely suppressed fear. "Lascom light refraction coming off the micrograin particles we seeded at suspected telemetry intersection coordinates three and five. One Arat Kur lascom system, one Hkh'Rkh."

Here they come. "Assess LOS beam directionality; interpolate vector of origin. Relay that to drone control. Mr. Wu, activate passive phased array components of the second wave of sensor drones. Have your scouts send detection and triangulation data back to that array directly; *Puller* needs to be out of that loop to accelerate the overall threat-reaction time."

Which turned out to be a prudent decision; enemy contacts popped up so quickly in the holoplot that Sleeman did not have the time to call them all out. "Multiple bogeys all across our front cone—and beyond its edges, sir. Cone of engagement is one hundred ten degrees. Multiple sprint-mines inbound, most targeting our image makers. A few still hanging on our scouts. A half dozen enemy drones as well. Two are deploying a phased array."

Given the paucity of highly autonomous systems in the Hkh'Rkh inventories, most or all of the drones were certainly Arat Kur in origin. "Mr. Wu, evasive thrust on all decoys and scouts so that their mines have to light up active sensors: it will take them a few more seconds before they sort out their own phased array. Have our PIPS engage any mines that are homing on our scouts."

"What about covering our decoys, sir?"

"They'll be done fooling anyone in another twenty seconds. Better they each take another mine out of the game."

Out in space, several small, bright stars—thermal decoys—flared and winked out. "We are eliminating their mines, sir, and several elements of their phased array. But their drones are now reciprocally targeting ours."

"PIPs to evasive. Bring our phased array on-line for active targeting. Relay the firing solutions directly to the PIPs. After they've neutralized their first target-set, they may light up and use their own arrays."

"Executing, sir."

In the holoplot, the number of bogeys was dropping off sharply. Enemy missiles and drones sought where the evading PIPs had been moments before, overshot them, spent what little thrust they had left to come around, activating their own sensors to reacquire the targets. Which gave the PIPs flawless firing solutions; they sent short laser bursts right back up the active sensor pathways. But the Arat Kur drones had been waiting for that, began firing at the newly rediscovered PIPs in a spastic dance of death.

"Good thing we got to look at the Arat Kur play-book when they surrendered," Dora breathed grimly. "Looks like we're beating them."

Riordan hated to ruin her attempt at self-reassurance. "No, we're just taking their bait." He almost missed her worried glare as he tapped his mic on. "Major Rulaine, soft deploy the Slaasriithi PIPs. Lieutenant Wu, soft deploy our other phased array sensor drones. Keep them in a local security footprint."

As Wu complied, Bannor asked, "I presume I'm watching our flanks for the real hammer coming down?"

"Our flanks, maybe even our rear," Riordan affirmed. "And be ready to shift our laser blisters to PDF mode."

"You sure you don't want me to do that now?"

"We still can't be sure that there aren't a few threats larger than conventional drones out there, Bannor. So we can't afford to reduce our beam output by shifting the laser to the splitters. Not yet."

"Got it. Is Karam ready to tumble *Puller*?"

Before Caine could reply, Tsaami muttered into his own commlink. "I know the drill, too, genius. And don't get cocky; remember who held your hand during the gunnery simulator."

"That's enough," Caine ordered. "You two can snarl at each other later. Right now, just stand to your stations. When they spring their trap, we won't have a lot of time to spring ours."

As Peter Wu managed the human PIPs that were dueling with the Arat Kur laser drones and slapping down the last of the Hkh'Rkh mines—which were actually swift, short-ranged missiles with large warheads—Dora muttered, "What do you mean, 'when they spring their trap'? Haven't they just done that?" She waved a hand at the flashing discharges beyond their bow.

"This is not a knife fight, Ms. Veriden; this is chess. Ploys within ploys. The enemy system is trying to focus our attention ahead, but that's not where the danger is. They're like a magician waving a bright wand in one hand: it's a good bet they're just trying to distract us, keep us from anticipating just where they're going to pull the next rabbit out of their hat."

"Which we've probably already passed, on our flanks or behind us."

"Exactly. But we know that trick. And we have a few of our own."

"Commodore," Sleeman shouted, "multiple bogeys registering behind our relative midship plane. Relaying data to Rulaine."

"Bannor, it's your show, now. Call the ball."

Rulaine's voice was utterly calm. "Peter, light up the second phased array: give me active targeting." A split-second pause, then: "Good. Engaging—"

In the holoplot, more than a score of bogeys—all identified as having Arat Kur thrust and communication signatures—had illuminated, closing on *Puller* and the phased array and Slaasriithi PIP drones that were covering her.

"You knew they'd save the Arat Kur drones for their Sunday punch," Dora murmured, as much to herself as to him, "because the Hkh'Rkh units were just there to make us look in the wrong direction."

"Yes, but we could still have some unpleasant surprises." *Such as: what if the Arat Kur left behind a drone fighter. That would be big enough to force* Puller *to keep her laser in its bow-aimed ship-killer mode, rather than the split-beam PDF flyswatter mode.* If that happened, and if the Slaasriithi PIPs were not able to take on twenty or so enemy drones in time... well, the outcome would be in doubt. Very much so.

At which point, another dozen Arat Kur drones came swarming out from behind one of the rapidly tumbling fuel tanks.

"Damn," Bannor breathed over the tactical channel. "Caine, I don't think the Slaasriithi PIPs can—"

Riordan assessed the number of bogeys, their rate of approach, the rapid coalescence of their active scans upon *Puller*. "Shift laser to PDF mode. And soft deploy four standard missiles from the rotary launcher."

"Complying . . . but why the missiles?"

"In case they pull something even bigger out of their hat. If they do, then the deployed missiles can keep their other platforms busy while you shift our laser back into the role of ship-killer."

"Works for me," Bannor mumbled, distracted.

Riordan glanced into the holoplot, studied the forward edge of the battlespace. "Mr. Wu, update."

"A draw, sir. We shot each other into rubbish. I've got nothing to send back to help Major Rulaine."

"Then soft-deploy a laser drone."

"Sir, that's our last one—"

"And hopefully we won't need it, but if we do, it could buy us the seconds we need to survive. Karam, tumble us; I want our bow laser one hundred and eighty degrees about."

"Thought you'd never ask. Hang on."

Dora snapped on the open channel, shouted, "Brace for maneuver"—and just barely grabbed her shoulder straps in time to keep from flying free as *Puller* turned a half-somersault, bringing them face to face with the new wave of attackers.

The Slaasriithi PIPs had made short work of the leading Arat Kur laser drones. That appeared to prompt the enemy's defense net to reassess the relative danger of the enemy targets. If left unengaged, the Slaasriithi defense drones might erode the remaining Arat Kur attack platforms so rapidly that they would not be able to swarm and overwhelm their adversary. Their automated response: to shift their targeting. One of the blue motes in the holoplot—the relative portside PIP—flashed once, became yellow-lined.

"PIP two is compromised; function unreliable,"

Peter reported when Bannor did not do so himself; he was probably preparing to swat down the remaining drones before they got too close.

The deck thrummed lightly. An irregular tattoo of vibrations rose up through their acceleration couches, shimmied their organs slightly.

"What the hell was that?" Veriden asked, wide-eyed.

"That," answered Caine, "was our new laser getting charged and dissipating heat as it fires. In very rapid sequence." He pointed into holoplot.

The gradual reduction of the enemy drones suddenly became a wave of annihilation. No longer were they being disabled every few seconds; they were being vaporized in a seamless cascade, the nearest first.

In thirty seconds, the holoplot was clear.

Dora Veriden leaned back in her seat. "Well, that was exciting."

"Wanna do it again?" Karam asked impishly.

"Go to hell, Tsaami," she muttered. Although they had become involved in some kind of semi-romantic relationship that no one else could fathom, this time she didn't add a reassuring smile to the end of her exhortation.

"Unfortunately," Riordan interjected, "Mr. Tsaami was not kidding. We have two other debris trails to scout and clear."

Melissa Sleeman, who had more than her share of nerve, grew pale. "Commodore, we don't have as many assets as we did going in this time. We've spent all our image makers, our own PIPs are reduced to rubbish, and one of the Slaasriithi's is none too well for the wear."

"Which is why we're going to bring their PIP on

board to see if our exosapient technical experts can effect repairs to it while we move on to the next survey point. And although this was a far more extensive ambush than we anticipated, there's reason to hope that the other two debris trails will not present us with the same challenges. They do not offer the enemy the same level of concealment or close-range surprise, nor are they traffic hot spots. So they are unlikely to warrant the same level of defense." He unstrapped, rose from the couch, stretched. "All things being equal, this should prove to be the worst of it."

"And if it's not?" Wu asked.

"Then, Lieutenant Wu, we have a harder job ahead of us." He tapped his mic. "Lieutenant Robin, Chief O'Garran, prepare to go EVA to collect the damaged Slaasriithi PIP. Then everyone takes five to eat a light lunch while Mr. Tsaami brings us around. We shouldn't go into battle again on empty stomachs."

"Well, that wasn't so bad," commented Bannor as he drifted back on to the bridge, prepackaged dinner in hand.

"Speak for yourself," grumbled an ashen-faced Dora, whose lunch of several hours ago had not agreed with her. Or, more accurately, the strain of additional combat had not agreed with her lunch.

Riordan understood Veriden's reaction. They had all been lulled into the collective hope that the lack of enemy presence at the second debris trail foretold a similar lack of danger in the third and final one. Instead, they were greeted by an all-Arat Kur ambush.

Granted, the ambush had been small by comparison to the first: a dozen platforms, all told. And because the debris was less dense, the range of engagement had been considerably greater and had come from fewer points of the compass. With no large chunks for the drones to hide behind, *Puller* had more time between detection and combat, which worked very much to the favor of the humans.

However, with fewer remote assets, *Puller* was also more vulnerable to being swarmed by Arat Kur drones if too many approached her simultaneously. So Riordan had fought them in a sequence of fundamentally separate engagements. He had kept Tsaami moving *Puller* aggressively about the battlespace, eliminating each group of targets before any others could draw within effective range. But those tactics had necessitated several close calls and dramatic, high-gee maneuvers.

That had taken a heavy toll on Dora Veriden's nerves. She was a seasoned operative, highly trained, resourceful, tough, and brave beyond belief on occasions. But all her work had been on planet, at close quarters. Her fate had always been firmly in her own capable hands and decided in environments akin to those in which she had grown up. However, in space, automation and unappealable physics held sway, trumping her skills, creativity, and shrewdness. She had made her career, and her life, about maintaining control in all ways, at all times. But in this airless, weightless battlefield, she was no more a master of her fate than anyone else—arguably less, because she had fewer spaceside skills. Having lived the truth of that several dozen times in the course of a few hours had clearly rattled her.

Peter Wu turned around in his couch, food wrappers a neatly crumpled square in his left hand. "I was surprised at the ease with which we defeated the Hkh'Rkh platforms in the first engagement."

"Coulda told you that would be the case, Pete," Karam drawled as he punched in the last burns and corrections for their automated return to *Shore-of-Stars*. "Hkh'Rkh tech is easily fifteen, twenty years behind ours. More, in computers and material science. So when it comes to drones, their robobrains are stupid, their structures are heavier, and their engines have poorer thrust-to-mass ratios. Piss poor, in fact. The Hkh'Rkh may like to build things tough and with lots of redundancy, but they can't when it comes to spacecraft: to be fast enough, they have to be extremely light. But that means no redundancy and reduced range. That's why you could knock them out of action with love taps."

"Thank you for the lecture, Karam," Wu deadpanned, "and do not call me 'Pete.'"

Tsaami nodded. "Sure. Forgot you were sensitive about your first name . . . Pete."

Wu sighed, toggled his ROV command panel off. "I think today, I will break with habit and have a bulb of coffee, rather than tea."

"Same here," Phil Friel chimed in from engineering. "I won't deny I'm feeling a spot of weariness coming on."

Melissa Sleeman nodded. "We all will, before long. That Slaasriithi wake-up cocktail is wearing off. And if we don't sleep when that happens, we're going to feel awful. And have a longer recovery period."

"I'll make a second pot, then," Tygg called from the galley. His voice was loud enough that he didn't need to resort to the open channel.

"Sounds like java all around," O'Garran commented.

"We could pop some stimulants, if we have to," Tina Melah mumbled as she drifted on to the bridge as well.

Karam shook his head. "No, you don't want to do that." Bannor nodded in silent, glum agreement. "If you extend drug-induced wakefulness with more drug-induced wakefulness, you start going down a rabbit hole of decreasing reaction time, misperception, testiness, even downright schizoid behavior if you take it too far." He patted the helm. "Besides, we don't have to. *Puller's* going to take us home all by herself."

Tina Melah crossed her arms. "Huh?"

Caine rubbed his eyes. "As soon as we burned down the last Arat Kur drone, we boosted into position for reestablishing line-of-sight contact with *Shore-of-Stars*. We set rendezvous coordinates and got under way toward her. We tumble at midcourse and counterboost so that we arrive there at relative all-stop. Then they scoop us up and Duncan helps them dump us in our berths, if we're too exhausted to do it ourselves."

Melissa Sleeman stifled a yawn. "Did they get any word from your contact on Turkh'saar while we were clearing the approach?"

Riordan shook his head. "No, but there was some more of the strange radio traffic that Downing told us about."

"More archaic rock music?" Tina asked.

"No. That wouldn't have been so bad." He nodded at Dora, who shrugged and tapped her dynamic console. The speakers crackled a bit before a voice emerged from a thin wash of static. It was a Hkh'Rkh, apparently trying to speak English. "Respond. We are

here no soldiers. Workers, young, and females. Only.
Do not—"

There was a sudden raucous up-dopplering of rotors,
more akin to the open type of old-style helicopters
rather than the sound made by a vertibird's ducted
fans. Heavy automatic weapons stuttered, came closer.
Cries of pain, dismay, anger—not human—rose, then
were cut short as a dull crump resounded very close
to the pick up. More rotors *whup-whup-whupped* in
the background, punctuated by small arms fire—and
then silence.

"What the hell was that?" Tina Melah breathed.

"I don't know," Riordan answered, suddenly feeling
much more tired than he had five seconds earlier,
"but that's what we've got to find out."

Chapter Four

The band leader serving as his adjutant and de facto radio-bearer looked up, black-bead eyes half-retracted beneath their protective bony ridge. "Flag Leader Yaargraukh, the scoutband reports that the den is empty."

Yaargraukh could not entirely suppress the annoyed phlegm-warble in his foot-long nostrils. He reached up for the dioptiscope which was fixed atop the sheath-helmet of articulated plates covering his snoutlike head. He flipped it down, adjusted it until the lenses were snugged against his eyes, and scanned the entrance to the den. Dug into a rock-face, as were most Hkh'Rkh habitations on Turkh'saar, the opening showed no sign of forced entry or damage. Two of his Warriors were roving back and forth in front of it, their large-bore scatterguns at the ready, their torsos stooped and tails slightly raised: a cautious, prowling posture. They were large, even for honor-guards; two and a half meters when they rose erect from their digitigrade crouches, their pony-necks widened to stretch almost entirely across their broad, sloping backs. The tufting that followed the crest of those necks ran down between their muscle-bulging shoulders, along their spines, and all the way to the ends of their slowly swaying tails. Yaargraukh wondered at their unwillingness to wear a kevlar warhide like the rest of the troop. Though they were the two mightiest melee fighters in the group—both *halbardichers* of the Great Clan Gdar'khoom—even their immense barrel-chests were not proof against bullets or shrapnel. But then again, their oaths of fealty might well require them to believe, or at least act as if, they were invulnerable.

"No sign of other casualties?" Yaargraukh asked, pushing the dioptiscope back up on the undifferentiated slope that ran from the top of his long head to the beginning of his neck.

"None, Flag Leader."

"The body spotted out among the herpeculture ditches: is there a report on specifics, yet?"

"Just coming in, Scion. A male, presumably the clan's Voice. Who was also its Fist, I believe."

"They are so small a clan as that?"

"Yes, Scion. They *were*."

Yaargraukh was tempted to reprimand the radio-bearer, but paused. It was possible that his adjutant's correction was not measured impertinence but a subtle attempt to underscore that among the Old Families, the loss of a clan-head was not so manageable as in a New Family, where relationships were more fluid and practical. In any Old Family moiety, the loss of a clan head without scions to replace him portended the dissolution of the clan itself: no guardians were appointed to the dependents, no property was kept in trust for them.

But even if the adjutant had intended no insolence, it was best to remind him that Yaargraukh had more familiarity with the formalities of Old Families than did most of those who belonged to them. "Band Leader, having been in the invasion fleet yourself, you should recall that I served on First Voice's staff in the late war against the humans. I am more versed in the protocols of Old Families than thee," he finished, moving to the archaic informal pronoun to remind his adjutant to remember his place. "It is yet possible that this slain clan-head had a litter-mate who will reinstate the line, come the time. Or do you know otherwise?"

"I do not, Flag Leader," the radio-bearer replied, dipping his head and keeping it low for a brief but respectful interval. "But Fringelanders usually come out here to seek their fortunes because they have no bloodbonds in the Clanlands, none upon which they may rely for support or sustenance."

Yaargraukh nodded his agreement and his acceptance of the apologetic bow. "Let us hope this clan is more fortunate than that. Any sign of other family members?"

"None, Scion, but the scoutband estimates that the attack occurred within minutes of the radio summons we received from this place."

Yaargraukh studied the surrounding terrain again: craggy uplands to the east, a sprawl of clusterwoods to the north, lichen plains to the south. The dirt track by which they had approached from the west wove in between long, low, scrub-covered hillocks. If survivors had run, they would have made for cover: either the northern woods or the western hillocks. But Yaargraukh's five vehicle convoy had come in from the west and would surely have spotted them. So if there were survivors, they were probably deep in the woods. Capture was the least likely possibility; the raiders had shown no inclination to take prisoners—so far.

The attack had almost certainly come from the north or the east; the woods and the uplands blocked the horizon at both those compass points, providing excellent screening for the raiders' rotary aircraft, right up until the final approach. And once they emerged from that cover—

"Adjutant, I require information: what manner of weapon was used to kill the clan-head?"

After a brief, muted exchange over the radio, he looked up. "His wounds were inflicted by both human weapons and our own."

Yaargraukh nodded. "This was to be expected."

"You mean, some of—of our own people have sided with the humans?"

Yaargraukh fluttered phlegm in disgust. He could almost hear what the radio operator had really meant to say: "You mean, some of the New Families have sided with the humans?" And the adjutant need not be a determined bigot to believe so; there was no dishonor that scions of the Old Families put beyond those of the New, largely because it fit the narrative of disdain that they reserved for that lower class. From which Yaargraukh himself was descended. "No. This simply confirms the earlier, unsubstantiated reports that the humans have been salvaging our weapons and ammunition for their own use."

"But Scion, Great Fist Jrekhalkar has dismissed this as impossible. The humans are too small to wield our weapons effectively. Their recoil and weight—"

"—are of no consequence if the humans mount them on their vehicles or on bipods or tripods. Which they are certainly capable of fabricating. Besides, their attacks have changed in recent months. They no longer kill indiscriminately, but they now steal all useful equipment, even from the smallest dencote."

The radio-bearer bobbed deference. "Yes, Flag Leader. As Fist Jrekhalkar points out, they began simply as murderers. Now, they are behaving as invaders."

Yaargraukh rounded on the radio-bearer, who was easily ten centimeters taller than he was. "If that is so, then why have they reduced the number of casualties they inflict? How does Fist Jrekhalkar explain that?"

"He—he is not beholden to explain his reasoning to those of my station," the adjutant blurted.

How convenient for Jrekhalkar that none may question his dung-witted conclusions. "Has the scoutband identified any other damage inflicted by the attackers?"

"There is evidence that they hastily removed a great number of fish from the edible aquaculture tanks closer to the dencote. They also entered the dencote itself and apparently inspected its contents."

"And they took nothing?"

"Nothing, Scion."

Yaargraukh waited for the radio-bearer to become aware of and correct what was almost certainly his oversight, but when that did not occur, he began to have misgivings. "And the den's radio?"

"Present and intact, Flag Leader."

Yaargraukh felt his eyes retract behind their protective folds, then under their bony ridges. *The radio—left behind?* The humans never failed to take radios or fuel. Ever.

He rose from the passenger seat in his command vehicle, uncertain and unsettled for the first time since he had left Iarzut'thruk in an attempt to locate, and possibly make contact with, these perplexing invaders. If that was in fact what they were. *Time to leave. And maybe, not a good time to tarry too long in any one place.*

He waved and then crossed his long arms twice, resumed his seat in the four-wheel-drive scout car. The other vehicles—one like his, the remainder large-wheeled troop carriers—were already in motion, picking up their dismounted teams and swerving round to form up on him. "We must return to Ylogh at once," he muttered to the driver. "Something is amiss."

Halfway back through the winding hillocks and rolling plains of lichen and runner-shrubs that separated his convoy from the large clancote of Ylogh, Yaargraukh called for a general stop and then commanded his driver to move forward an extra five kilometers. From there, he sent signals—in English and German, the two human languages with which he was familiar—on the frequencies that the invaders used as tactical channels during their attacks. There was, once again, no response.

Reaching around the pintle mount of the scout car's tri-barrel gatling, Yaargraukh replaced the radio's handset slowly, resisted the urge to outwardly vent his frustration. He had been trying intermittently to find these humans for months now, tracking them from one raided community to the next, but never in time to encounter them or raise anything on the radio except for static.

He had hoped that the summons to Ylogh might be different, partly because he had been much closer to this settlement than he had been to the others when they were struck. His large-wheeled vehicles had arrived only four hours after the raiders left, the smoke still rising toward the low clouds. What he found resembled no prior attack. There had been few casualties and no seizure of goods. Indeed, the humans had fired only desultory bursts from their automatic weapons until Ylogh's Voice had activated the clancote's long-range radio: first, to alert Yaargraukh and the leadership back in Iarzut'thruk and then to ask the humans to cease their assault. Instead, the humans had focused an intense stream of fire at the source of the transmission until they silenced the radio and its operator. After which they had left. Abruptly.

Then, hours later, a desperate call from the name-less den out in the Fringeland. Yaargraukh had not wanted to split his forces, but the humanitarian and morale values of allowing half of his task force to remain in Ylogh had been compelling. So leaving one troop of his tassle behind to secure the town, he had taken the other east to investigate the more recent strike on the den.

Now he was headed back toward Ylogh again, with nothing to show for chasing to and fro other than the vague and ominous feeling that he was being toyed with. Before his convoy began returning through the hillocks, he had called his executive officer, Troop Leader Hshwaarn in A carrier, to seek a perspective other than his own. But that had been unprofitable. Hshwaarn was an upright and dependable Warrior, but he was merely a Fringeland hunter turned militia leader for the duration of the current crisis. His thought largely reprised that of the others in the unit, and of the leadership back in Iarzut'thruk: that the humans had come to Turkh'saar to follow up their victory over the Hkh'Rkh and Arat Kur invaders of Earth to exact some vengeful reciprocity.

Of course, to the best of anyone's knowledge, the human "invaders" had not landed in spacecraft, were comparatively few in number, and equipped with decidedly outdated weapons. However, these facts did not concern the other Hkh'Rkh populating the politically significant echelons of society on Turkh'saar. Their resolute disinterest was surprising not merely because the data they disdained was tactically important, but because it was highly inconsistent with the presumed human motive of invasion. An intent made even more improbable by the fact that Turkh'saar was unreachable by Earth's shift-carriers.

But in concluding that the humans were here for vengeance, his fellow Hkh'Rkh were merely projecting their own behavioral reflexes upon the invaders, and so, needed no further explanation. Indeed, any data which problematized that narrative were unwelcome. Why seek facts or motivations that would only lead to uncertainty? Much better a clearly understood conflict with clearly demarcated sides and objectives for all parties involved.

Yaargraukh took up the handset, entered the coded channel-breaks that signalled the convoy to catch up. His executive officer contacted him on the private tactical command channel. "Since the invaders may still be operating in this area, should we perhaps travel with greater separation, Flag Leader?"

"Hshwaarn, your caution is admirable, but we must maintain a formation that allows for mutual support. Our rocket launchers have an anti-air engagement envelope of less than three kilometers. Visibility among these hillocks is often well less than that, particularly once we approach the plain and begin descending through the clusterwoods. If we spread out further, we can be picked off one by one."

Hshwaarn sounded embarrassed. "Apologies, Flag Leader. I do not have your knowledge of these weapons and vehicles. I meant no affront by my suggestion."

"And none was taken. While I was on Earth, I had much opportunity to become familiar with similar equipment." *As well as their limitations; it is a fortunate thing that the humans with whom we are currently contending do not have the weapons of contemporary Terran militaries.*

If they had, it would have been folly to engage them with the colony's militia-grade matériel. If any of the Great Voices of the Patrijuridicate had given thought to surreptitiously establishing a true military garrison on Turkh'saar, they had taken no discernible steps in that direction. And who among them would have perceived any need to more openly violate the nonmilitarization agreement with their partners in the system, the ever-anxious Arat Kur?

As his scout car topped a ridge, Yaargraukh turned to look back along the vehicles of First Troop. Excepting the other scout car, they were three six-wheeled armored carriers. Blocky, diesel-powered conveyances, their hatch-rings sported the venerable fifteen-millimeter machine guns that Indonesian guerillas had dubbed "autocannons." Compared to the humans' lighter weapons, Yaargraukh understood the inspiration behind the label. One of the carriers was also equipped with a heavy, pintle-mounted rocket launcher, its tube locked in the slightly elevated ready position.

But despite their fearsome appearance, this model of APC had been decommissioned from front-line military service forty years ago, and lagged almost a century behind human APCs—those which were still wheeled or tracked, that is. Confronted with a true invasion, this vehicle, like the other equipment of the small Colonial Militia, would have been reduced to smoking wrecks within the first hour. Possibly within the first five minutes. They began descending into the next narrow vale that separated the washboard-ridges of the region.

Yaargraukh's radio-bearer gestured for his attention. "A call, Scion—no, I was mistaken. Or perhaps it was the distortion of a growing solar storm. Or—" He stared at the overcast skies. There had been some distant thunder on the drive out to the isolated dencote, but the clouds had dissipated.

Yaargraukh nodded. "Or it could be jamming. Was there a consistent pattern?"

"I could not discern one, Flag Leader. The signal only lasted a moment, right as we crested the last rise."

Yaargraukh conveyed his understanding with a sweep of his hand. With true military commo gear, even that brief sample would have been sufficient to discriminate between jamming and meteorological effects. But the militia's radios were no better than those used by the upland rovers of the New Families, whose livelihood depended upon an uneven mix of hunting and prospecting. Indeed, that would have

been Yaargraukh's lot in life, had he not been chosen
by the Rectorate to study on Rkh'yaa.

"Are the human *s'fet* truly capable of jamming?"
his adjutant wondered aloud.

"They are; the humans have done so several times.
And I shall correct you only once more; the humans
are not *s'fet*. They are beings." *More than that, they
are* persons, *but you are not ready to hear that. You
may never be.* "If you label them as animals, you will
think of them as animals, and so you will underestimate
them. As we did, repeatedly, during our invasion of
their homeworld."

"I remember, Flag Leader."

Yaargraukh clacked the opposed thumbs of both
hands as the scout car started its descent of into the final
defile that separated them from the plain dominated by
Ylogh. Hearing that sharp warning sound—one which,
from first steps onward, signaled the almost-exhausted
patience of a parent or teacher—the radio-bearer
spun around to face his superior with lowered head.
Yaargraukh waited a long moment, forcing the other
to hold, and reflect upon, that position of attentive
compliance. "You remember what you *heard* about the
invasion, Band Leader. You remained in orbit; I was on
the ground. From the very first hours. So, learn this as
if your life depends upon it, for it very well may: if you
underestimate the humans, that will be your undoing. I
cannot count how many times I saw that demonstrated,
on both the smallest and largest scale.

"In part, I chose you to be my adjutant and radio-
bearer because you know what we suffered on Earth,
and, as a communications-intercept specialist, you
learned two of the human languages. But now you

must learn to see the world through their eyes, if only for the briefest glimpses. Otherwise their methods and reasoning will remain dark to you. And I assure you; your death waits in that darkness."

The driver's small, triangular earflaps were tight against his head, snugged just under the lower rim of his sheath-helmet. He was trying very hard to act as though he heard none of the exchange. In part, that was simply common courtesy during a comrade's reprimand, but it was exacerbated by an ardent desire to shut out Yaargraukh's notorious and, to some, disloyal opinions regarding the humans. *Well, so be it. Today we only have time for the truth. Battles are won by facts and physics, not self-congratulatory ideology.*

As they started up the back slope of the last ridge, Yaargraukh clacked one set of opposable digits, releasing his adjutant from the submissive posture. "Begin scanning for coded signals from Troop Two. Only send a squelch break in reply. We need to alert them to our imminent return to Ylogh, yet maximize radio silence."

"Do you expect the humans to still be in the vicinity, Scion?"

"I do not *not* expect it, Adjutant."

"Even though they already struck Ylogh once?"

"Even so." *Their first strike on Ylogh was peculiar, as was the one upon the Fringeland den. Something is not right here, and where humans are involved, that is reason enough to remain wary.*

As they began rising out of the radio shadow of the ridgeline, and the following vehicles of the column began emerging over the top of the prior bluff, the radio began spitting and hissing, bursts of a voice-grade message struggling to be heard between the waves of static.

"What frequency, Adjutant?"

The radio-bearer looked up at him, his eyes starting out from their recessed sockets. "Fist Jrekhalkar on the command frequency. Sending from back in Iarzut'thruk."

What idiocy is this? "Do not respond, even in code. We must not betray our location by transmitting."

The radio-bearer was halfway through an affirming nod when the signal cleared suddenly. He listened, turned back toward Yaargraukh with tightly retracted eyes. "Scion, it is the Fist himself. He demands to speak to you. At once."

Yaargraukh kept himself from blinking. It was difficult to believe that the *de facto* leader of this world—the meager gem in the shabby colonial crown of the Hkh'Rkh Patrijuridicate—had so little understanding of communications protocols. "You are to reply in coded channel breaks only. Send the cyphers for 'cannot comply,' 'observe battlefield protocols,' 'will recontact soonest.' Execute."

The adjutant did so, waited, turned back toward Yaargraukh the same moment that the scout car topped the ridge. "The Fist is insistent—and waiting on the line."

Yaargraukh took the handset, checked to see that the scramblers were synced before speaking. "Fist, this is unwise. We should—"

And then, between the parallel trunks of the cluster-trees through which they were descending, he saw long, black lines of smoke rising up from the vicinity of Ylogh. "Fist, I must clear this line. Ylogh has been attacked again. I fear Second Troop has been heavily attrited."

"It has. And you will remain on this line, Flag Leader."

There is no stupidity like that of a pampered Old Family second scion. The eldest usually has more innate confidence, less to prove. "I must send instructions to my executive officer; then I shall return." *And give the humans an easy opportunity to triangulate upon my signals and blast me out of existence, if they are still in the area.*

"Do so quickly."

The radio operator needed no prompting. As soon as he heard Jrekhalkar's agreement, he switched the channel to the secure tactical frequency. Yaargraukh flicked over to a new encryption setting. "Hshwaarn, reply."

"I am here, Flag Leader."

"Ylogh has been attacked again. You will coordinate our Troop's approach. Use coded squelch breaks only. Presume there are hostiles in the area and that once we break from the clusterwoods, we shall be under immediate observation and that the enemy will seek and rapidly achieve firing solutions. Make for the cover of Ylogh swiftly."

"And what will you be doing, Flag Leader?"

"I will be conversing with the Fist on a long-range, voice-grade channel."

"You say this in jest."

"I wish I was."

"Be careful, my friend. He is painting a target-circle upon you."

In fact, I wonder if that is precisely what he is doing, since he has not been able to silence me any other way. "Be careful as well, Hshwaarn. I shall head across the plain first. Watch for enemy reactions. Flag out."

The driver's ears had gone rigidly erect at his instruction, "Watch for enemy reactions." He knew what that really meant: the command car would attempt to draw enemy fire so that the rest of First Troop could locate and hopefully suppress any human attackers. Wherein the key term was "hopefully."

As his adjutant changed the frequency and encryption back to the one used by Jrekhalkar, Yaargraukh surveyed Ylogh. There were four black plumes curling skyward: almost certainly vehicle fires. Not a good sign.

The radio operator glanced back, "Fist Jrekhalkar is impatient, Scion."

Yaargraukh thumbed the handset. "I am on the channel, Fist. From your last message, I infer that you have been in contact with Second Troop since they were attacked."

"No, I was in contact with them *when* they were attacked—"

—Meaning your lack of discipline almost certainly led to them being targeted and destroyed, you dungspawn—

"—and subsequently lost contact with them. Report their status."

"Destroyed by your incompetence." But what Yaargraukh actually said was, "I am assessing that now." He snapped down his dioptiscope and panned across the low, angular skyline of Ylogh. "All three carriers have been hit and disabled, probably destroyed. One scout car is fully aflame. I have no visual on the other. I believe I see casualties lying in the streets, but we are still too distant to be certain. However, if those are bodies, their number is significantly less than Second Troop's full complement. It is likely that many have survived, are sheltering in the buildings."

"Any sign of the *s'fet* invasion force?"

Yaargraukh resisted retracting his eyes in frustration. "I see no sign of the attackers. I see no new damage to Ylogh itself, although a building near one of the tracks also seems to be burning."

"Has the clancote itself been attacked?"

Yaargraukh swung his head in the direction of the various openings that had been carved into the face of the largest rock spur that jutted up from the flat, empty plain. "No sign of attacks against any Unhonored."

Jrekhalkar's phlegmy snort was audible through the connection. "I think that more a consequence of fortunate laxity rather than an increase of conscience among the invaders."

"It may be as you say," was the most agreeable reply Yaargraukh could bring himself to utter. Humans had no concept of the complex Honor Codes that bound and dictated behavior in Hkh'Rkh society. And yet, they were not without their own version of it. Although human soldiers did so for different reasons and with less reliability than true Warriors, they usually attempted to spare "civilians," their analogous but far more malleable term for the Unhonored.

Jrekhalkar did not sound happy with Yaargraukh's reply. "It is *exactly* as I say, Flag Leader. And it is your good fortune that the humans have not yet attacked Ylogh's females, young, elderly, and infirm, for their blood would be on your digits."

The radio-bearer and driver both started. Even though they were Old Family sons themselves, the Fist's imputation of responsibility for the unfolding situation was not merely beyond justification, it was beyond reason. It was Jrekhalkar himself who had ordered Yaargraukh to explore the signal from the isolated Fringeland den, thereby necessitating the splitting of his force.

Yaargraukh waved away their surprised stares; he had expected no less from Jrekhalkar. After all, if a New Family officer could be blamed for a defeat, it was almost obligatory among the Old Family scions to do so. "It is indeed fortunate that the Unhonored have been spared."

"And what are you going to do to ensure their continued safety?"

Yaargraukh had not expected that. "I stand ready to intercede, should the humans return."

"You are finally close enough to strike, and instead you show the timidity that First Fist Graagkhruud saw in you during the invasion of the *s'fets'* homeworld. You plan to wait in safety while Unhonored huddle, terrified, in their clancote? You will go at once to their aid!"

Yaargraukh flipped back the dioptiscope, surveyed the plain they were rapidly approaching, the thickest of the clusterwoods behind them. Almost two kilometers across at its widest, the flatland upon which Ylogh squatted was completely clear in all directions, except for occasional, lesser spurs of scrub-covered rock. The eastern hillocks from which they were approaching climbed higher as they wound southward and became less wooded. Conversely, they tapered to the north, where the clustertrees grew higher and even thicker, sending out a long green and yellow arm that dominated the northern horizon as well. To the south, the land sloped down to the distant Okhrek River, which ultimately wound its way to the Equatorial Sea. The west was a mix of gently rolling country, and scattered hills: the only useful cover for attackers approaching from that direction.

"Fist, hear me. We will soon arrive at the edge of the last stand of clustertrees. Once there, we will have a commanding view of the plain and the advantage of cover. We shall dismount weapons and personnel to set up a broad base of fire with which to protect the clancote and ancillary structures. If the humans return it will be we, not they, who shall enjoy the advantage of attacking from ambush. And given the human doctrine of surprise attacks, they will withdraw, even if they detect our—"

"Enough. Do as you are ordered. Move immediately to Ylogh. Reinforce the remaining Warriors of Second Troop and assure the Unhonored that those who bear Honor shall protect them, as is their first responsibility—despite any personal fear that might make some of our commanders seem to be cowards."

The radio operator and the driver turned slowly to gaze at Yaargraukh. Only by the thinnest of semantic margins had Jrekhalkar's mention of cowardice remained a generalized imputation rather than a personal accusation. It was within Yaargraukh's right to ask for a clarification that would preserve his Honor. If Jrekhalkar did not provide it, Yaargraukh would have to give Challenge or be much diminished.

But since Jrekhalkar seemed more focused on Honor and Challenge than the execution of his own orders, Yaargraukh gambled that a disorienting shift of topic might allow him to salvage a potentially disastrous command situation. "Fist, I presume you mean me to advance upon Ylogh according to standard battlefield doctrine?"

Jrekhalkar balked. "I—what? Well, yes, of course."

"Excellent. I am executing that directive. Going to radio silence until we have reached Ylogh."

"What? I—?"

But his baffled voice snapped out of existence as the radio operator obeyed Yaargraukh's hand signal to terminate the comm link. The two Hkh'Rkh in the command car looked at their leader. "What now?" asked the driver, slowing as they neared the last, sparse edges of the clusterwood.

"Now, you accelerate and hold this car to all its speed."

"Scion, that will put us in the open—and alone."

"That is correct. Do it—and drive well, lest you wish to sup with your Greatsires tonight."

Chapter Five

The scout car's engine roared as the vehicle broke from the treeline. The sudden rush of wind—and sudden possibility of swift death—were exhilarating, if not exactly for the best reasons. But a Warrior lived to embrace risk and Yaargraukh reached out to it.

"Shall I signal the others to follow as they may?" the radio-bearer shouted above the howling engine and whipping wind.

"No, Ezzraamar," Yaargraukh shouted back, using his adjutant's given name since they were facing death together, now. "They are to halt at the treeline and spread out. Fifty meters separation at least. Up to one hundred, if possible. Driver, how are you called?"

"Kaazhkul, Flag Leader."

"Evasive action, Kaazhkul. A shallow serpentine. No more than five seconds between turns, and never the same interval twice in a row. Execute."

Kaazhkul did as ordered.

Up ahead, Ylogh seemed to rise up out of the plain before them. Unlike the human settlements Yaargraukh

71

had seen during the invasion of Earth—from the smallest Indonesian *kempang* to the sprawling warrens and lofty towers of Jakarta—most Hkh'Rkh habitation was below ground. However, on Turkh'saar, it was necessarily dug into the side of rock. Most of the flora, the vast majority of which reproduced asexually and was therefore biochemically aggressive in protecting its ground, transmitted much of its irritation through the soil into which it decomposed, making earthen cotes painful to both skin and lungs.

But now, the rock-cut warrens were also traps; they lacked escape tunnels, which were much easier to dig in typical soil. So the Unhonored of Turkh'saar had no way to retreat or even defend multiple fall-back positions, which often gave Warriors enough time to effect a rescue.

But Ylogh was no longer just a clancote; it was evolving into a town. Whereas the Hkh'Rkh dug their dwellings into slopes or hills or cliffs, larger businesses and activities were conducted in open air. Consequently, the workshops, warehouses, stores, and refectories of Ylogh had grown up into a loose tangle of buildings among which Warriors might hide, and from which they might strike.

Yaargraukh snapped his dioptiscope back down, swept the horizon again. No movement. No exhaust plumes, either, although that was hardly a definitive observation: many of the human rotary-wings were relatively quiet when they were hovering or if they were grounded in a clearing, waiting for a call to action. But so far, they had not appeared and there were only three hundred meters remaining between Yaargraukh's command car and the outskirts of Ylogh.

Lying athwart their path, one of Second Troop's APCs guttered and smoked: a blackened shell with several carbonized corpses hanging out the back hatch. A ragged hole in the right side of the vehicle was mute testimony to where a human antiarmor missile had struck it. "Steer closer to it, on the southern side," Yaargraukh ordered the driver.

"I obey, Scion."

The driver demonstrated that he understood tactical subtext of Yaargraukh's command. Angling out of a serpentine swerve, he put the APC's plume of black smoke between the scout car and the northeast horizon: the area from which the missile had apparently been launched.

Yaargraukh scrutinized the tops of the clusterwoods lining that part of the horizon: no movement.

"One hundred meters," announced Ezzraamar. He almost sounded calm.

At this range, it was clear that Ylogh's buildings had been hit by a second deluge of small arms fire, most of it ominously grouped around windows of the sturdier buildings. The other vehicles of Second Troop smoldered alongside those structures, their crews hanging out of the hatches or slumped over their pintle-mounted machine guns. They had done all that conventional tactics would have told them: snug up against buildings for both concealment and cover, use dismounted observers to keep apprised of the approach of enemy craft and then direct fire.

But if they had inflicted any losses upon the humans, there was no sign of it. The plains were free of rotary-wing wreckage. But that was fairly typical of these raids. Even the humans' outdated rockets had admirable range and destructive power, and their pilots and gunners were surprisingly skilled. They had also made a careful study of Hkh'Rkh heavy weapons and, after one or two losses, discovered how to stay well beyond their effective range until they were silenced by those rockets.

But most of the Warriors had apparently dismounted before or during the attack; although some of them lay sprawled in the streets, they accounted for less than half of the Troop. Unfortunately, there was no way of knowing how many more had been killed returning fire from the various bullet-riddled building hardpoints, or who were hiding in the shadows, incapacitated by their wounds.

The scout car swerved around the corpse of a Warrior sprawled near the main refectory's aquaculture trough and entered the wide, meandering streets. Yaargraukh, knowing the layout, pointed the driver toward a storage shed. "There. Slow as you approach it."

The driver sped across the dusty expanse that was Ylogh's pitiable equivalent of a town square, then braked as he eased off the gas. As the car's speed dropped beneath ten kilometers per hour, Yaargraukh leapt off, hit the ground running, reached the shed, and threw open the doors a moment before the vehicle swerved inside.

Yaargraukh closed the doors, giving orders without looking at the two Warriors. "Kaazhkul, seek out and determine Second Troop's remaining numbers, equipment, ammunition, and positions. Return with the senior surviving Warrior to make your report. Ezzraamar, dismount the radio; you are on me."

Shouldering the transceiver, Ezzraamar followed his superior out the smaller, south-facing door of the shed. Yaargraukh quickly checked his surroundings, pointed to a cinder-block building that had a half-finished second floor. It did not look as though it had been a primary target, although stray rounds had left a drunken trail of pockmarks climbing up its western wall. In combat crouches, they slunk across the street to the structure, found the stairs, crept up to the roof. Yaargraukh positioned them where they could observe Kaazhkul's progress.

No sooner had they found a place to hunker down and get a better view of the town's defensible positions—of which there were few—than the radio hummed. Ezz-raamar put a hand up to cover and better listen to his earbud, answered into the linked neckcom, "We are, Fist. He is here by the radio." He held out the handset toward Yaargraukh slowly, the retractile folds around his eyes wrinkling in regret and apology.

Yaargraukh, amused, let his serpentine black tongue lick out briefly before taking the handset and speaking. "I attend, Fist Jrekhalkar."

"You have reached Ylogh?"

"I have. Given what we have seen thus far, it is my intent to wait out the humans. As I have indicated in all my reports, they avoid night attacks, probably because they lack or have few night-vision systems. The other vehicles of First Troop are in dispersed formation at the edge of the treeline to provide cover fire. Once night falls, they should be able to safely rejoin us here in—"

"Am I to understand that only you and the crew of your scout car are in Ylogh presently?"

"That is correct, Fist."

"I ordered a general advance."

"You did—in accordance with doctrine. Which stipu-lates that if possible, a recon element is to assess and report prior to committing the main body of the unit. Since the other vehicles of the Troop were still several minutes off, that reconnaissance role fell to my command car."

During the long pause that followed, Yaargraukh imagined Jrekhalkar fuming beside the radio in his command center back in Iarzut'thruk. "Your willful misinterpretation of my order is quite evident, Flag Leader, and shall figure in my determination of your future here on Turkh'saar. However, for now, you will immediately order the balance of First Troop to reinforce the town and reassure its people."

Yaargraukh felt his eyes retract slightly. "With respect, Fist, I must ask: will it reassure the people if First Troop is destroyed trying to make its way across open ground?"

"Your polite speech does not conceal your intolerable insolence. Your Warriors would be there now had you not disobeyed my order—"

"Again, with respect, I interpreted that order differently than you might have intended, Fist." *"Interpreted" it according to standard practice and official doctrine, you imbecile.*

"You will not interrupt me again, Flag Leader. However, your disobedience did prove what you evidently hoped it would: that the enemy is no longer in the area."

By the generative polyps of my dead Sires—! "I shall endeavor to explain my purposes more clearly, Fist." *Since you are clearly too dungwitted to understand basic military practice.* "Determining whether the enemy is or is not still in the area of operations was not what I hoped to ascertain by crossing the

plain to Ylogh. Rather, having no radio contact with
the surviving defenders, it was imperative that I learn
more about the numbers, equipment, and tactics
employed by the attackers during our absence. It was
also essential that we determine how many of Second
Troop remain combat effective, how many support
weapons remained operational in the buildings of the
settlement, and if any hardened positions had been
established. Taken together, that determines the base
of fire we may provide to cover the APCs of First
Troop when they eventually cross the open ground.

"I further reasoned that the humans—if they are
still nearby—would not reveal themselves to eliminate
just one scout car. On the other hand, if they did, that
would have been a small price to pay to locate the
enemy and determine the response of the rest of First
Troop. That I was not fired upon proves only one thing:
if the humans *are* still out there, they are waiting for
better targets." *Or they are after some entirely different
objective. Which eludes me. Because, had they wanted
to destroy both Troops, they would have ambushed us
outright, not played this unnecessary back-and-forth
baiting game. Something is still not right—but this
st'kraag-wit will not understand the potential significance
of such an anomaly, nor do I have the time to educate
him enough to see it. If that is even possible.*

Jrekhalkar was proving himself to be exactly what
Yaargraukh believed him to be: myopic and stubborn.
"You prate about the humans' actions as if they conceal
a careful, mysterious strategy. What nonsense. It is
perfectly clear what their two objectives are."

And of course you're going to tell me.

Which is exactly what Jrekhalkar did. "Firstly, they

mean to slaughter our people, destroy the town, and seize as many of its goods as they can. Secondly, they are trying to draw you into an ambush."

"Our two Troops hardly seem worth the effort of—"

"You are not listening, Flag Leader. I said they are after *you*. Personally."

That gave Yaargraukh pause; it was an odd suggestion, but, to Jrekhalkar's credit, it wasn't the product of blind conventionality. For all his limitations, was it possible that the Fist had perceived something in the human attacks that Yaargraukh himself had missed? "How would they even know of me, personally, Fist?"

"Not by name, of course. But by activity? You have been chasing after them for weeks, trying to learn more about them, hoping even—Sires forbid!—to talk to them. Perhaps they have discerned that. Perhaps they simply believe you are trying to gather tactical intelligence on them. Either way, they are after you. Why else would they draw off so quickly after the first attack on Ylogh, where they did almost no damage and were careful not to eliminate its long-range radio—until *after* it had sent a summons for help?"

"This is an interesting hypothesis, Fist, but again, why would they want to kill *me*? If, as you have long averred, the humans care for nothing except our destruction, and have no tactics other than wanton slaughter, why would they change their course of action simply because one Hkh'Rkh became interested in talking to them, or analyzing their intents and methods? Logically, that would not concern them." *Unless, of course, they perceived my attempt to gain intelligence on them as a threat. And so they decided to mount a counterintelligence strike to eliminate the* one *Hkh'Rkh that might evolve new tactics against them. Whom they extrapolated was not present during their second attack on Ylogh, since there were no attempts to contact them when they reapproached* . . .

Jrekhalkar was becoming both angry and impatient. "I do not have the time to consider answers to these imponderables. These humans are nothing more than amoral marauders. They do not wish to talk to you; they merely wish to kill you. Why would you expect their actions to be consistent or logical? As you yourself have said, they are perverse and cruel. They target females and young in their own wars, use them as hostages, as shields, as bearers of suicide bombs. Their species is twisted, sick to the core, brutally insane by its very nature."

Yaargraukh felt a vague sense of disappointment. Whatever spark of insight Jrekhalkar had used to shed a new light upon the inscrutable intents of the humans' current attack was now smothered beneath his bigoted rage. "I agree that there is no point to such a discussion at this time, Fist." He detected movement down in the street; Kaazhkul was returning with an officer in tow. He waved to them as he concluded, "I shall receive a report on the town's defenses and circumstances within the minute. I shall recontact you shortly with a report and my recommendations."

"Do not keep me waiting, Flag Leader." The line cut out abruptly.

Moments later, Kaazhkul emerged from the partially walled staircase, a young, weary-looking squad leader with him. "He wishes the honor of making the report to his superior," Kaazhkul muttered from deep in his thorax; it was a sympathetic, even regretful sound.

There was indeed something poignant about this inexperienced militia officer doggedly following protocol.

"Report, Squad Leader," Yaargraukh said with a full nod of acknowledgement.

The young officer listed the remaining Warriors; there were twenty-three, fifteen of whom were combat-effective. With the exception of a single AA missile, their only remaining weapons were personal arms. They still had ample ammunition. The enemy hadn't come close enough to be taken under effective fire, except with the now-destroyed heavy weapons. Consequently, they no longer had much decisive use for the hardpoints they had reinforced with rubble and construction materials.

Yaargraukh listened without interrupting, noticed that the sun was now well into its descent toward the horizon. In just four hours, their best ally—night—would end the engagement. He gazed at the young officer frankly. "Tell me: did they land troops?"

"Scion?"

"Did any of the human rotary-wings approach and deploy troops?"

"Not in Ylogh, Flag Leader."

Yaargraukh sighed. *Patience, with this one.* "I am not just asking about here in town. I am talking about any place that you had under observation." With a sweep of his left arm, he gestured at the plains surrounding Ylogh.

"I . . . we cannot be sure, Flag Leader. The fighting was intense here among the buildings, and we were focused on the enemy's approach from the north."

"Did you not have observation posts watching the other directions?"

"We had one, Scion. In the high gantry of the water tower, but—" His eyes strayed to the west. Yaargraukh followed them, saw the water tower—or rather, what was left of it. The top of the structure was a blackened ruin of twisted steel. If the observers there ever sent reports, they had been lost in the same infernos which had killed the radio operators that would have received them in the now-gutted APCs.

Ezzraamar glanced up. "Fist is recontacting. He is irate."

Of course he is. Yaargraukh took the handset. "I have just finished gathering the report."

"What have you found?"

Yaargraukh told him.

"So, you still have almost three quarters of your Warriors left. And all the heavy weapons from First Troop. You can mount a credible defense. Order your remaining vehicles into the town to take up positions."

Did he really not understand? "Fist, in four hours we could do so without incurring any risk of further loss. Or, I believe, any risk of further attack."

"What do you mean by that?"

"Fist, the humans could have annihilated Ylogh in either of their first two attacks but did not. I suspect your surmise to be correct: today, they are not motivated by supplies and matériel, but intelligence objectives. Perhaps they do wish to eliminate me, or—"

"Your arrogant self-importance is complicating your perception of what is a very simple matter. The humans wish to destroy Ylogh. They are behaving in a somewhat atypical matter, but whatever the cause of that, it does not change our objective: to defend the town. To do that, the carriers of your First Troop must be in the town itself. Summon them. Immediately. They are ready to move."

"They—? What?"

"They have remounted their weapons and are ready to cross the open ground. I contacted them myself while you were being briefed on the conditions in Ylogh. Your executive officer, Hshwaarn, provided me with a comprehensive report on his Troop's readiness."

Yaargraukh could not help himself; his eyes yanked back tight beneath the long, bony prominence that was his skull. *You ordered my XO to give you a lengthy verbal report from his hidden position at the edge of the clustertrees. Because you had to take charge, because you had to meddle with the command of a New Family flag leader who had the luck and gall to serve as a direct advisor to the First Voice of the Patrijuridicate in the last, disastrous war. And because of your combination of arrogance and suppressed jealousy, you've now ensured that if our enemies are waiting, and are capable of triangulating our radio transmissions, they had ample time to pinpoint exactly where Hshwaarn and the rest of First Troop is hiding.*

Jrekhalkar had tired of waiting for a reply. "You will reinforce the town as ordered."

"Fist, since the humans are not hastening to secure the town and its supplies, it is unlikely they will press an attack if we wait until the cover of night. We could then regroup and evacuate the Unhonored while it is still dark. We can be back among the major towns of the colony before dawn has—"

"Order your carriers into Ylogh. This is your last warning, Yaargraukh. Repent this craven inability to act."

"Craven?" *Well, you either mean to Challenge me or*

try me in court. "I do not refuse to act out of fear. I refuse because it is both wrong and profitless to order Warriors to deaths that serve no purpose. Troop One is now at high risk: they have sent strong, persistent radio signals. However, they are still hidden, and if they stay so until—"

The radio-bearer started, pointed at his set. "Scion."

Yaargraukh glanced over. The light indicating a live connection to Iarzut'thruk was dark. "What has he—?"

"Flag Leader," the driver began in a tense voice, pointing toward the eastern horizon.

The APCs and second scout car of First Troop were emerging from the clustertrees at high speed, rooster-tails of dust kicking up behind them as they hit the dry flatlands.

"He ordered them himself." Ezzraamar said it through a gulp deep in his throat.

"Change to tactical, secure channel," Yaargraukh ordered harshly. "Now!"

His adjutant hastened to comply, nodded after a long moment.

"Hshwaarn?" Yaargraukh shouted.

"Here. What manner of—?"

"No time. These are your instructions for approach and entry into Ylogh. Maintain as much speed as possible while using a limited serpentine. Do not brake as you approach the edge of town; come straight in. Park in the southern lee of buildings—the south-east if you can."

"What? Why should we—?"

"The humans won't come out of the open lands to the south, and they won't have been following behind us as we drove out of the east. We have to expect attack from north, possibly the west. As soon as your carriers stop, the infantry must abandon the vehicles as per evacuation protocols. Crews remain behind long enough to dismount heavy weapons, including launchers. Everyone regroups in the building next to which they parked. But do not stay there; each squad must move to the next building. Keep spreading out. Do not bunch up."

Out on the plain, the bulky APCs were doing their best to begin an evasive slalom. However, being somewhat top-heavy—a design aspect that was a consequence of Hkh'Rkh body size—they were at risk of spinning out, or worse yet, rolling, if the turns were too abrupt or performed at too high a speed. B carrier, the one to the rear right flank of Hshwaarn's command vehicle, had popped the security lock off its remote-pintle rocket tube, which was now swinging toward the north—

Slightly to the west of the rocket tube's protective aimpoint, there was a disturbance above the distant treeline, merely a shimmer at first—before it resolved into what looked like a hovering, upright rectangle. From either side of the rectangle, there was a brief flash and then two pencil thin lines of dense white smoke streaked across the intervening two and a half kilometers, accelerating as they came.

The tactical channel erupted with shouted warnings, azimuth bearings for intercepts. The APCs' heavy weapons slewed around to concentrate on the barely visible threat vehicle, the B carrier slowing to give a better shot to their missile operator—

One of the two streaking rockets from the strange rotary-wing slammed into the side of B carrier: a sharp explosion, a gout of flame and then smoke rose up. Warriors were abandoning the right-listing vehicle by both the top and rear exits as the other carriers swung around to put their slightly thicker glacis plates toward the enemy aircraft.

But with B carrier disabled, and its missile tube sagging limply in its pintle mount, there was no way for the Hkh'Rkh to effectively counterattack. The fifteen-millimeter machine guns could not reliably reach the odd, narrow rotary-wing, which was already dipping back down behind the trees, a distant hum the only audible signature of its rotors. The big Hkh'Rkh autoweapons certainly had the range, and their impact was legendary, but—manually engaging pop-up targets at twenty-five hundred meters while rolling along in a large-wheeled, hard-suspensioned vehicle? That was the equivalent of trying to hit a small bird flying over your den with a hand-thrown rock; success would ultimately have more to do with luck than skill. Even at full stop, any hit would be a gift from one's deceased Sires.

But the Warrior reflex to strike back was powerful. To a one, the APCs were braking, their commanders resolved to give their machine gunners stable firing platforms. "No," Yaargraukh shouted into the handset, "do not stop to engage!" The humans would never come close enough for the fifteen-millimeter machine guns to hit them. The only viable tactical option was the one toward which Hkh'Rkh were instinctually, reflexively opposed: to flee at high speed for the cover of Ylogh. Not all would make it, but some might—and some was better than none. But the carriers had already swerved and slowed to face their now-vanished attacker, machine guns sweeping the horizon. Questions and doubtful grunts started clogging the tactical channel.

"No," Yaargraukh shouted over them. "You must—"

Whereas the first rotary-wing had emitted only a distant hum as it faded from sight, the next ones were preceded by a monstrous growl—which was appropriate for the two airborne behemoths that came lumbering over the low, well-forested ridge line two kilometers to the northeast. Bulky, slow, brutish, the rotary-wings' weapons pylons seemed to droop with the weight of their ordnance. Each one fired a rocket from the outermost tip of its starboard pylon.

The APC machine gunners swung their weapons in that direction, the jackhammer sound of their fire commencing even before they were zeroed on the new targets. Outgoing tracers showed the streams of fire arcing low. The gunners began to adjust—

But before they could correct their aimpoint, the human rockets were among them. One struck the front quarter of C carrier, blowing the lead right wheel clean off the chassis and holing the hull beyond it. The other narrowly missed A carrier. Its commander, Hshwaarn, had been bringing it about to lead the rest toward Ylogh, but now it swung over to B carrier, ready to take survivors off as it began to burn fiercely.

Yaargraukh's cry of warning died in his long, rough throat as each of the immense rotary-wings fired another missile. One struck the middle of A carrier's deck, just as survivors from B carrier were swarming up on to it. The first explosion was relatively small; evidently an antitank rocket, it entered the vehicle's troop compartment through the top-opening troop hatch and detonated inside. The burst of smoke and debris obscured the Hkh'Rkh Warriors who had been helping pull the survivors of B carrier up onto the deck.

But even as their silhouettes convulsed within the smoky veils of the first explosion, a blast of flame shot up out of A carrier's exposed guts. The missile's HEAT warhead had evidently sliced through the interior deck into the fuel tank. The force of the blast sent the survivors of B carrier toppling off the back of their would-be rescue vehicle, some missing limbs, one missing everything beneath the waist. Several more writhed on the ground, wreathed in flame; other bodies burned and were still.

The great, beastlike rotary-wings closed in, their chin-mounted gatling guns emitting sharp, rough coughs as they came. The Warriors who were exiting C carrier sprawled in all directions; the machine gunner shuddered and slumped halfway down into the disabled APC.

Yaargraukh closed his eyes for one moment. In fifteen, maybe twenty, seconds, the entirety of First Troop had been destroyed—no, slaughtered—by the humans. Opening his eyes, he saw that the second scout car had survived so far, swerving to avoid a rocket fired by one of the slowly approaching rotaries. He hoped it reached the outskirts of Ylogh, but he could not afford the time to watch its progress; he had to prepare the defenders of Ylogh to face the onslaught of these two flying tanks.

Even as he turned to give orders to the young troop leader who stood transfixed by the scene of destruction out upon the flatlands, Yaargraukh heard a chorus of higher pitched engines crescendoing, of faster rotors slicing the air—from the opposite direction. He turned.

Rising from behind one of the wooded hillocks to the west, five smaller but faster rotaries were skimming low and lethal toward Ylogh, troop compartments overflowing with humans, their rifle muzzles angling forward in something like eagerness.

There was only one tactic left against such overwhelming odds. Yaargraukh turned to the three younger Hkh'Rkh clustered around him. "Seek the other defenders. They must obey three orders." He took a breath, spoke slowly and clearly through clenched grinders:

"Run. Hide. Now."

Chapter Six

"Rise and shine, Commodore."

Caine Riordan swam up through cross-currents of dreams, memory-fragments, and a repetitive nightmare of checking the holoplot for a one more Arat Kur drone, the one that always seemed ready to emerge from behind wreckage that there hadn't been time to check, that was too close to intercept, that was sure to cripple *Puller* and pave the way for the other killbots to swarm in and—

"Commodore, are you all right?"

Riordan sat up quickly, noticed that the hair on his forearms was slicked down with sweat. "I'm fine." He blinked, looked for the source of the vaguely familiar voice.

Duncan Solsohn. With that same congenial smile on his face. Which was probably an accurate reflection of his general disposition; it was too easy a grin to be a sham. But Solsohn was also a creature sent to do Downing's bidding, to be his watchdog, maybe even his button-man, if push came to shove.

Solsohn gestured for Riordan to lay back. "Take it easy, sir."

That was when Caine realized that he was in a bunk instead of on *Puller*'s bridge. Disoriented panic pulled his mind in several directions. "Where am I? What's happening? Is the crew—is *Puller*—?"

"You're back on *Shore-of-Stars*. *Puller* made the preplotted rendezvous just fine, although the two Slaasriithi technical experts were the only ones aboard who were still awake by the time you reached us."

Riordan nodded, part acknowledgement and part thanks. He leaned back, looked around his stateroom in the hab module. Who would have ever thought this small, austere compartment would ever look like "home?" "How long have I been out?"

Solsohn handed him a glass of water. "The better part of two days. You guys looked like hell when they brought you in. Had to hook you up to IVs to get more carbs, protein, and electrolytes into you."

Caine started, glanced at the other man. "Were those *our* IVs, and *our* personnel, or—?"

Solsohn smiled. "All from Mother Earth. I figured you guys wouldn't want to have the Slaasriithi messing around with your biochemistry."

Riordan relaxed again. *Well, not any more than they already might have.*

But what he said was, "Thanks. So you were our angel of medical mercy?"

"Well, I had help. The Slaasriithi provided the hands—well, tendril-clusters or whatever they call them. I provided guidance and watchful eyes. And not just in here."

"What do you mean?"

"They were fiddling around with *Puller* again, shortly after you came back."

"Yeah, we took a few hits. Nothing major, though."

"That's not what they were fiddling with. Seems like their technical advisors reported that the wiring wasn't sufficient to handle some of the peak loads of the systems they put in to replace the original hardware."

Caine nodded. "The laser they put in was pretty energetic."

"Well, Commodore, I guess that's why our hosts decided to put in some auxiliary power couplings to manage power overflow."

"Got it. And 'Caine' is a lot less of a mouthful than 'commodore.'"

"Kind of you to offer that first-name basis, sir, but I don't think it's a good idea on this mission."

Riordan held Solsohn's gaze. "Why?"

"Look, sir; you're the commodore, so you're going to call me whatever the hell you want. But I don't think the security forces Mr. Downing sent with us are going to be comfortable with the kind of informality you permit among your team-members. Most of these troops don't even want to be part of a unit, let alone an unofficial family." He considered. "On the other hand, that might be just what they're looking for. Hard to tell, at this point."

"Mr. Solsohn, that was about the most cryptic and convoluted explanation I've ever heard."

"Sorry, sir. Details, then. You remember that Mr. Downing had attached a short section of security to us for the mission?"

"They were scheduled to make rendezvous with

Shore-of-Stars half a day after we entered cryogenic suspension."

"Right. But they didn't. Mr. Downing found some better security assets closer by. Twice the number and far better trained. About five squads of worth of seasoned troops, a lot of them from tier three units and better."

"Get to the bad part, Mr. Solsohn."

"Like I said sir, they're not a unit, sir. They are a—a classification category."

"I don't even know what that means."

"Commodore, I'm pretty sure you know that the best Commonwealth and Federation troops were sent out to Delta Pavonis before the war, to counterattack the anticipated invasion of Earth." Solsohn punctuated his last comment with a small, respectful nod. He, too, was a member of the Institute of Reconnaissance, Intelligence, and Security, the covert organization that had used Caine as an unwitting weapon in the final defeat of the invaders. "What you might not know is that some of the troops in cold sleep did not return to Earth with Relief Task Force One. It was decided that a small reserve had to be held back as a hedge against failure and as a means of staffing a variety of post-defeat contingency operations."

Riordan nodded. "Insurgency. Cadre for resistance. Security for a diaspora to further systems."

"Exactly. But that reserve force had to have some special characteristics. They had to be good working alone or in small numbers. They had to be tough as nails and deadly as hell, because there were never going to be a lot of them. And they had to be willing to stay on the job for—well, for a very long time."

Solsohn's tone changed, became more careful, perhaps regretful. "That's where the classification category comes in, Commodore. You see, when these troops signed up for that tour of duty, they checked a box accepting what was termed 'open-ended cryogenic deployment.' Checking that box got them triple combat pay for the length of their tour and a ticket into the future, destination and duration unknown."

Riordan leaned back. "So they didn't know when or where they would wake up."

Duncan nodded. "The only thing they knew was that, whenever they defrosted and stopped puking glycerin, they'd be in the shit again."

Riordan stared. "Damn. What kind of people take a job like that?"

Duncan shrugged. "All kinds. But all of them knew it was a one way trip, as far as their lives back in The World were concerned. The few that had families or spouses or significant others have almost all been dear-johned or dear-janed by now. Most of the others volunteered for the job because they had no families to miss them. Or they had families who wouldn't miss them. If you get my drift."

"So none of them are even from the same unit?"

"They don't know each other at all. Records indicate that two of them were boots at the same time in the same camp. Another two went through B.U.D.S right after each other, so they were probably tortured by the same instructors." Solsohn sighed. "The only thing they have in common is that these are boys and girls who didn't care when, or if, they were going to see home again."

Riordan leaned back, trying not to feel nauseous.

"So are you telling me Downing sent us out here with a bunch of—literally—suicide squads?"

"No. More like the French Foreign Legion. They're not looking to cash it all in; they just don't care about leaving it all behind. Their files tell a lot of sad stories, if you read between the lines."

Riordan nodded but thought. *Yes, and they have one other thing in common. No one will miss them. If they learn or see something they shouldn't, if they have to disappear, who will look for them?* That was more likely to motivate Downing's superiors than anything else: a force with no loose ends, from which any surviving operators could be shuffled quietly off to some isolated safe house for people who had seen or heard too much.

Riordan drained the glass of water, sat up straight. "Thank you for the update, Mr. Solsohn."

"My pleasure, sir. I was wondering if I could trouble you to return the favor."

"You'd like me to brief you? On what?"

"Well, I could use a little perspective on the Slaasri-ithi, sir. Since you didn't have the opportunity to brief Mr. Downing before we left, he couldn't brief me."

"Fair enough." *But still a problem; Downing is cleared to hear everything I learn or suspect during a first contact. Hell, it's his job to know all of that. But Duncan?* "Mr. Solsohn, it would help if you tell me a bit about yourself, first. Starting with your role in IRIS."

"Yes, sir. Until shipping out with you, I was part of the cell responsible for downstreaming crucial IRIS field operations to the Central Intelligence Agency. During the war, I worked the other side of the street. I tapped

Agency data to collect the pre-strike intel we sent up the pipe to IRIS's braintrust at the Naval War College."

So, Solsohn had extremely high clearance and had been entrusted with slipping IRIS's operational mandates into the hit-lists that the Agency was farming out to its strikers: mostly SOG operators, probably. No doubt Duncan had handled a lot of politically radioactive—and in some cases, bloodstained—documents in his career. Which had not been very long, apparently. "How old are you, Solsohn?"

"Thirty-six, sir."

"Married?"

"Was, sir. When I got tapped for IRIS, things got . . . complicated."

Riordan nodded slowly, kept his eyes on his empty water glass. *That was either the most understated and poignant truth I've heard since Downing reanimated me three years ago, or Solsohn is an expert at playing on heartstrings while looking and sounding like a choir boy. Because everyone who gets snagged in IRIS's web seems to have a sad tale just like his.* "And your significant other: did she or he know about your new . . . work?"

"'She,' sir. She didn't know exactly what I was doing, but she knew my job description had changed and that I wasn't in a position to take early retirement. And I wasn't disposed to, either."

"What do you mean?"

Solsohn looked up. "Sir, why did *you* say 'yes' when they defrosted you and asked you to help? And why have you *kept* saying yes?"

Riordan couldn't keep the smile off his face. "I take your meaning."

Duncan shook his head, as if trying to dislodge the pained expression that had crept onto it. "I got married to a talented, beautiful woman, started planning a life that allowed us to split the year between our respective homes—St. Louis for me, Copenhagen for her—and then along comes a mission that can't be disclosed to anyone. And which sounds so insane that, if you did blurt it out, they'd lock you up in a loony-bin. 'Aliens might be out there! Gotta get prepared!'" He shook his head once more, sharply. "And some of the stuff we had to do along the way—" He fell silent.

"Like what?" *Might as well get a look at the nastier parts of Solsohn's resume.*

Duncan looked down, shifted in his seat. "My family—we fish and shoot. I wasn't a big fan of standing in cold boots, in colder streams, waiting for trout that went after everyone's lures but mine. But I was pretty good at the shooting."

Solsohn looked up. "None of that counted for anything when I joined the Agency as an analyst; those were not the skills they were asking me to bring to the game. They always had plenty of ex-military people on tap for the wet-work, the field expediting, the strikes. But when Mr. Downing tapped me for IRIS . . . well, my clearance had new implications. Implications that put me in the field. There always has to be someone on very sensitive ops who knows what the real objectives are, but there weren't a lot of strikers with that kind of clearance. But if you go into the field without training, without a skill that gives you a solid reason for being there as an operator, they know you're the company watchdog, the suit-in-commando-clothing who probably needs babysitting—and so you're ignored whenever and wherever possible. And that couldn't happen. So IRIS trained me. For the field."

Riordan nodded. "Sniper?"

"Yeah. And comms and backup pilot. Dad used to rent a plane when we flew to Idaho for the fishing and hunting, so I knew my way around a cockpit and a radio. Toughest stuff was the endurance training. Damn, I was only twenty-eight at the time, but I'd been piloting a desk too long, even back then."

If the story was a fabrication, then Solsohn had missed a career as the preeminent method actor of his era. If it was not, then Solsohn's story was not entirely unlike his own. *Of course, that's exactly the way Downing would play it: choose someone who was a kindred spirit so that I'll be a little bit more sympathetic, a little easier to manipulate.* There was only one way to get some preemptive control over that possibility. "Let's cut to the chase; you're Downing's eyes and ears here too, aren't you?"

Duncan blinked, then leaned back and laughed. "Well, that didn't take you very long. Yeah, I'm afraid I am." A congenial smile. "Sorry."

Well, if Downing has chosen Duncan Solsohn for his ability to be amiable and disarming, he had certainly chosen well. But at least the issue was on the table, now, and Solsohn knew that Caine was on the lookout for being managed or massaged by IRIS's overseer-in-place. "Well, I guess you have the clearance, so what do you want to know about the Slaasriithi?"

Duncan scratched his head. "Well, to be honest, pretty much everything. But since we're short on time, I'll settle for this: how the hell does their social order work? Do they have a caste system, like the Arat Kur?"

Caine shook his head. "No. Stranger than that. They're polytaxic." Having anticipated Solsohn's bewildered look, Riordan continued without pause. "They're one species, but comprised of numerous subspecies. Each subspecies, or taxon, serves a set of predetermined functions, for which their physiotype and temperament is optimally suited."

"And Yiithrii'ah'aash is a...a leader?"

"Yes, and more. He belongs to the *ratiocinator* taxon, the least numerous of the seven taxae. He's also a Prime Ratiocinator, which is kind of a cross between a senator, ambassador plenipotentiary, policy advisor and colonial field manager. The Slaasriithi don't run things the way we do."

"Yeah, I've noticed. And they organize information so differently that I can't always figure out what they're getting at."

Riordan nodded. "Since they grow up in task-defined groups from birth, information streams are tailored with the anticipation of prespecialization. There are no real generalists among them." *Well, not anymore.*

"And no soldiers either, from what I can tell."

"That is correct." *And that's where your "need to know" clearance runs out, Mr. Solsohn. I doubt more than fifty people are aware that we are also helping the Slaasriithi reclaim a lost taxon—the* indagatorae—*who were once their species' pioneers and jacks-of-all-trades.*

Duncan rose. "Well, that makes things clearer. Sort of. Don't understand them any better, but at least I understand why I don't." He checked his wristcomp. "Sorry to rush you, sir, but we're needed on *Shore-of-Stars*'s bridge."

Riordan was suddenly aware he was only wearing

underpants. "How did Yiithrii'ah'aash even know I'd be awake?"

"He didn't, Commodore. I've been waiting here for an hour. Or more. I was to bring you aboard the Slaasriithi ship as soon as you awoke."

Caine threw off the sheets, looked for and found his duty suit. "What's the rush?"

"Wish I knew, sir."

Riordan started climbing into the unipiece garment he'd worn on *Puller*, smelled the sickly mix of fear-sweat and glycol, cast it aside, pulled another suit out of the compartment's narrow locker. Only when he kicked one foot into a pants leg and felt no imbalance from coriolis effect did he realize that the gravity equivalent he felt was not coming from rotation: they were under thrust. A lot of it. "What are we pulling, half a gee constant?"

"Closer to a full gee, sir. Been boosting for almost three hours now."

So the Slaasriithi really are *in a rush*. "They're not exactly staying inconspicuous that way."

"No, sir, doesn't seem so." Seeing that Riordan was about to close the locker after slipping on his regulation footwear, Duncan shook his head. "Sorry, Commodore, but Yiithrii'ah'aash requested that you report with your gear. All of it."

Riordan stared. "That sounds ominous, Mr. Solsohn."

This time, Solsohn's smile was clearly forced. "Yes, sir. It does."

Chapter Seven

As Yaargraukh led the way down from the roof of the half-finished building and activated the camera in his dioptiscope, the survivors of Second Troop emerged from their hidden positions throughout Ylogh to fire at the approaching human rotary-wings.

The enemy's response was immediate. Machine guns peppered every window, every scrap of cover from which they had drawn fire. The narrower rotary-wing that had disappeared behind the far treeline rose into sight again, accompanied by another of the same type. And still further back, one that was much larger and thicker hove up into view, its rotors sending out a heavy bass *thrupp-thrupp-thrupp* like the drum that was said to announce the return of the ghostly Ancestral Host at the Final Battle.

Reaching the ground floor, Yaargraukh and the other three Warriors prepared to spread out, but had to leap back against the wall of the building they had just exited. The second scout car from First Troop swung past in a blast of sand and grit, the driver swerving when he saw them at the last moment. The Warrior manning the pintle-mounted eight-millimeter tri-barrel peered through the mist, clearly recognized Yaargraukh, opened his mouth to shout in the driver's ear—

A distant sputter of heavy machine guns cut through the sound of the approaching rotary-wings. The driver's head went sideways on his shoulders as if it had been slapped by a pile-driver. Bullets punched through the right side of the vehicle and flattened the front tire, the self-sealing compounds unable to compensate for the multiple punctures. The driverless scout car lurched heavily; the sudden resistance of the naked wheel against the ground brought the rear of the vehicle up at the same moment it started slewing sideways. It flipped into a short barrel-roll, ejecting the gunner before it came to rest on its side in a cloud of dust. The driver was a mangled body still strapped into his seat; the gunner was motionless, blood gushing out of an almost severed leg at a rate that assured exsanguination within the minute.

One of the big flying tanks growled overhead, elevating sharply to pull away from any possible ground fire.

"Our Warriors will be slaughtered if we cannot cover their retreat with heavy weapons," Yaargraukh muttered. "Ezzraamar, Squad Leader; you will spread the orders to flee and hide. Kaazhkul, you will assist me in securing the necessary weapon."

A Warrior with a splinted leg stepped out of a rooftop shed fifty meters north of them. He raised a disposable rocket launcher to his rounded shoulder, began tracking the large attack rotary that had passed them—

Yaargraukh waved Ezzraamar and the junior officer on their respective ways, hooked a claw at Kaazhkul to follow, hoped against hope that the Warrior's rocket would find its target—

Out on the flatland, notched in a pair of rock spurs that emerged like gray teeth two hundred yards from the edge of town, there was a brief sparkle: a muzzle flash or the glint of a scope. The Warrior with the rocket staggered. Yaargraukh detected a quick, cyclic arm motion out in the rocks; probably a sniper working the bolt on a rifle. Best move while his attention was riveted elsewhere.

He gestured sharply to Kaazhkul and, sprinting low, led him back to the shed where they had hidden the command car. Yaargraukh pulled open one of the doors; the driver rushed through. As the sound of the rotary faded, Yaargraukh heard another small, spiteful crack from the direction of the rocks. The Warrior with the rocket, who had swayed back into a steady position, went limp and fell over, the launcher clattering as it rolled down a pile of rubble.

Yaargraukh stepped into the shed, closed the door. "Dismount the tri-barrel," he said.

Kaazhkul promptly lifted the weapon off its pintle mount. Yaargraukh lifted out the ammo-cassettes by their shoulder straps and helped settle them on Kaazhkul's broad back.

"Where shall we set up, Flag Leader?" the driver asked.

"Close by," Yaargraukh answered. "We must act swiftly if we are to take the attackers' attention off our Warriors." It wasn't much of a plan, but in a scenario as desperate as theirs, there was neither sufficient time nor information to optimize their actions. They would be lucky to be set up and commence firing before they were overwhelmed, judging from the approaching roar of a rotary.

"They are upon us," Kaazhkul said loudly, striving to be heard above the thunder of the human engines.

"But they will not land right away. They will send down three or four rapellers to clear and secure their landing zone against ambush, if they follow their customary doctrine." Yaargraukh took the heavy gatling gun from Kaazhkul, looped the straps and brace over his left arm. "Can you carry my scattergun?"

"Of course, Scion. But should I not bear the tri-barrel, as it will attract enemy—?"

"No. I will wield it." Yaargraukh leaped down from the rear deck of the command car, made for the side exit of the shed. "We must move quickly, if we—"

The side door flew open. Two humans entered, alert for hidden enemies—and stood, stunned, when they saw those enemies standing directly in front of them, overburdened and as surprised as they were.

The lead human—who was wearing what looked like a towel wrapped around his head—brought up his weapon first, largely because Kaazhkul was struggling to carry his own twelve-millimeter assault rifle, Yaargraukh's short-barreled scattergun, and several ammunition cassettes for the eight-millimeter tri-barrel. The human's weapon began a staccato barking as the driver moved to get in front of his commander, who had no ready access to a personal weapon.

Yaargraukh tossed the tri-barrel aside, started reaching for his shortsword, realized that Kaazhkul was already falling backward; his armor had not absorbed every round of the long burst that had been fired by the human's AK-47.

*—an AK-47: one of the invaders' preferred weapons—
and a weapon which cannot possibly be on Turkh'saar.*

Yaargraukh dove for the scattergun tumbling from
the driver's nerveless hand. He caught the weapon,
spun it around to get his quadrilaterally arrayed digits
on the pistol grip—

—as the towel-hatted human tried to track Yaargraukh with the barrel of his stuttering gun. Which
abruptly fell silent: out of ammunition. Meanwhile,
the other human was pushing around his comrade,
bringing up a heavy-framed submachine gun with a
large drum magazine—

—just as one of Yaargraukh's thumbs flicked off the
safety, the opposed digit pushed the scattergun's setting
to full automatic, and the calar claw hooked behind
the grip to steady it. His fourth and final opposable
thumb slipped into the trigger guard and squeezed.

The twenty-four-millimeter autoshotgun sprayed out
a hail of .28 caliber balls as its muzzle swept across
the two human torsos at a range of three meters.
The one in the lead—already slapping another magazine into the AK-47—shuddered, his chest suddenly
pocked by red eruptions. The other one's entire torso
was riddled, and the small, thick man staggered back
under the impact: not a common effect when hit by
gunfire, but he had been hit by a blizzard of at least
fifty projectiles. The human sprawled back out the
door into the rotor-churned dust.

Yaargraukh scrambled to his feet, already resolved
to abandoning the tri-barrel. Although he might be
able to carry, fire, and even load it, the weapon was
dangerously cumbersome unless a Warrior stood at
least two-and-a-half meters and had a heavy build.

Yaargraukh just barely topped two meters, and had a typical Upland rover's build: leaner, less top-heavy. And now that he was on his own, he would not be able to carry enough ammunition to mount a meaningful counterattack.

His only remaining option was to follow his own orders—run and hide—and the only weapon that made sense in the tight quarters of Ylogh was the scattergun. Holding it at the ready, Yaargraukh sprinted out the door behind the command car, crouched over for speed, his tail up for stability and balance.

He emerged into a street swirling with dust. One rotary-wing—vaguely familiar from his study of human military history—was descending to the ground not more than thirty meters to the north. Another, different model rotary had already landed further to the south; the whole vehicle was shimmying as the pilot pulsed its engines in preparation for a rapid lift back into the sky. The last of its soldiers were leaping out into the spirals of dust and taking up their spots in a defensive perimeter. In another few moments, the air would clear, the humans would be oriented—and Yaargraukh would be detected.

The only nearby cover was the partially completed building from which he had watched the attack begin. He darted toward it through swirling veils of grit and sand. A rifle spat several times, perhaps at him, perhaps not.

He plunged into the darkness of the building, sprinted for the other end, cautiously leaned out the doorway that overlooked the eastern perimeter of Ylogh: no humans or Hkh'Rkh in sight. He heard some of his own force's weapons, but every time they spoke, there was an answering chorus of large-caliber automatic fire: support from the perimeter-circling rotaries. He scanned for shelter, for a hiding spot further beyond the humans' expanding tactical footprint. There were a few storage sheds, a prefabricated office module which served as a community affairs building, and the town's herpeculture refectory and refinery. *Yes, that.*

He stepped into the street, crouched low, looked for humans: none visible, but he could hear their voices, drawing closer even as the gunfire tapered off. He sprinted across the street, raced through the door into the refectory.

Once inside, he rose slightly to increase his speed; the long, narrow tables of the dining chamber flashed past on either side of him. He leaped the serving counter at a bound, bashed through the plastic pleating hanging between the eating and preparation facilities.

He looked around quickly; it was functionally identical to every other herpeculture refectory on Turkh'saar. Cookers and cupboards lined the wall which separated this preparation chamber from the dining hall, along with sinks for washing utensils and trenchers. Beyond them was a broad walkway with separation tables placed at regular intervals. And further still, near the far wall, were the herpeculture tanks themselves.

Yaargraukh recoiled at the sight of them. Herpeculture was the euphemism by which Turkh'saar colonists referred to their primary source of protein: worms. Sometimes this meant eating local worms themselves, but that was not the most frequent source of nourishment.

Turkh'saar's most plentiful indigenous creatures were worms that were thoroughly infused with the local plant life's toxins. However, they were also a preferred food source for various larger worms that did not retain, but excreted the toxins. Those larger worms, although only marginally edible, were raised in bulk to feed palatable local eels and a few species of fish which had been successfully transplanted from Rkh'yaa.

The steps whereby these processes were carried out was anything but pleasing to the snout. The local worms were rank to begin with. But when raised by the thousands in vats filled with the swamp algae and wastes upon which they subsisted, they were revolting in the extreme. The tubs in which they were separated and then reduced to mush or pellet-feed were even more vile.

The edible worm tanks were, on the other hand, somewhat less odorous and markedly safer, so it was toward one of them that Yaargraukh now headed. Even so, he would have been happier facing machine guns at point-blank range. That, however, held out no chance of survival. The tanks, on the other hand, did.

Crossing to the closest, he grabbed several of the large-gauge hoses used for cleaning and filtration, then a handful of heavy latex workgloves from a nearby tray. He closed the slide of his scattergun, sleeved one glove over its muzzle, used another to tie the first tight against the barrel. The gun at the ready, he slipped into the tank. But slowly. His volume, added to its contents, might cause it to overflow.

Fortunately, the water was already low. Unfortunately, it was also cold. The first attack on Ylogh had knocked out the power, so the tanks' heaters had been off for the better part of a day. It also meant the filters had stopped operating, so the water was already becoming foul and slimy. On the other hand, it also made the plexiglass-sided tank murkier, which was good for hiding.

Yaargraukh grabbed the sensor float, slipped an auxiliary water hose through one of its four retaining clips. One end thus held above the level of the water, he fixed the plastic tube's other end over his snout, cinching it firmly in place by using a shorter length of hose and a latex glove to fashion a rough tourniquet for further tightening, in case liquid started leaking in.

Running one last tube from the surface directly into the long, rough audial canal that was his outer ear, Yaargraukh submerged and tested his makeshift snorkel apparatus. Although the tube smelled faintly of bleach, it presented no danger or discomfort; Rkh'yaa was a harsh homeworld, a highly volcanic planet where sulfur compounds were common and other more immediately poisonous gases had to be tolerated if a species was to survive.

Yaargraukh sank to the bottom of the tank quickly. Not only did his armor and gear weigh him down, but his body had much less natural buoyancy than a human's.

Hkh'Rkh tended to avoid water, particularly full immersion. It was not part of their evolutionary legacy and they were poorly adapted to it. Their bodies were ill-shaped for swimming and if their lungs were not filled with air, they sank like stones. But Yaargraukh had been determined to learn the ways of humans, since they were his particular topic of study.

Accordingly, he had accustomed himself to immersion in water and attained some swimming skill. This had prompted many alarmed stares and partially heard slurs about the eccentric scholar whose actions revealed that New Family scions were not merely barbarous, they weren't fully Hkh'Rkh. Their deranged actions— like Yaargraukh's self-immersion in water—proved it.

Yaargraukh pushed himself closer to the edge of the tank so that he might watch for the inevitable human sweeper team. Not too close, though: if he put his long head too near the plexiglass sides, he could misgauge the distance and bump against it. If so, a human might notice the perturbation in the otherwise uniform mass of worms that filled the steel-framed reservoir—and if that happened, it was his death.

As Yaargraukh waited in the dark water, and felt the worms begin writhing their way inside his armor and across his heavy hide, he finally had the luxury of a few moments to ponder why the humans had baited his forces into Ylogh with the apparent intent of splitting them.

Could that mud-packed moron Jrekhalkar be correct? Could they have been after me*? But why? And if that was their purpose, how could they be sure not to kill me in these attacks?*

Unless, of course, they were not after me personally, but simply determined that they needed to capture a military officer for interrogation. Which would be difficult, since it seems they have not yet learned our language.

But . . . I have been signalling to them in their language. And just because they did not answer did not mean they were not listening. It simply means that they were not willing to talk to me—at least not over the radio.

The pieces fell into place. From their perspective, the Hkh'Rkh who had been signalling to them was their best—possibly only—source of useful intelligence. And since he spoke their language, they reasonably deduced that he would be better educated and at least somewhat familiar with their culture. What more enticing target could they have been given?

But in order to get information without imparting any in return, they had to secure that target, control it without destroying it. Which, in turn, explained why they had been so atypically skittish in their attacks on Ylogh, why they had taken such extraordinary measures to split Yaargraukh's forces, to avoid destroying the primary source of radio transmissions: they needed to separate his Warriors into such small groups that, in the end, it would be almost as easy to subdue them as kill them. And so, gave them the best chance of capturing the one Hkh'Rkh who spoke their language.

Yaargraukh kept watch between the steel bands that braced the plexiglass against the outward pressure of the water, but was only half aware of what he saw. If only his critics from the Clanhall in Iarzut'thruk were here. If only they had seen the human attack, had watched those small yet lethal bipeds leaning far out of the open sides of their rotary-wings, eager to get on the ground. They did not exult in battle the way Hkh'Rkh did, but once they were committed to it...

Yaargraukh had seen considerable action against insurgents in the jungles of Java. The great majority of the Indonesians had been highly motivated, many of them startlingly savage. But they did not work together like these attackers did. These humans were more akin to the elite units that seized the Arat Kur headquarters in Jakarta after the final bombardment subsided, their shadowy silhouettes pressing stubbornly closer, their advances swift and tightly coordinated. Unlike his Warriors' excited eagerness for battle, the humans' elite teams waged war like quietly furious automatons. Indeed, the anger they held in check was the engine that drove them on their relentless errands of death to invaders and collaborators alike.

Yaargraukh was recalling how the insurgents dispatched traitors with knives rather than guns when the back door to the loading bay—the one door he could not see—opened with a sharp crash.

Chapter Eight

Humans swarmed past the tank, maintaining the careful, erect crouch that was intrinsic to their species. Lacking tails for counterbalance, they would have fallen on their hideously flat faces had they tried to lean any further forward.

They advanced in two waves, the rear rank aiming through the widening gaps in the first as the point men fanned out through the room. Yaargraukh was only indirectly aware of their sharp professionalism; he was too startled by their numbers. This was not a routine security sweep of the building. That could have been managed with three, maybe four men, at the most. No, this looked more thorough, more focused. Had one of the humans seen him enter the refectory? Were they searching for him? Were they trying to—?

A short, heavily-built human wearing fatigues with a rough, lateral camouflage pattern reached the pleated plastic sheeting that separated the kitchen from the dining hall. He peeked sharply around the corner, waited out a two count as he rose slightly to change the position of his head. He glanced around the door jamb again, but longer, surveying the other room. He glanced back, took one hand off his unusually long rifle, and spread his fingers, waving twice toward the front of the building.

From behind his tank, Yaargraukh heard a mutter. "Rear is secure. Team One is in position. Team Two, you are go for front entry in five, from my mark. And...mark."

Yaargraukh reasoned he had at least five seconds to observe the humans around him without much possibility of being detected. He moved slightly closer to the side of the tank. What he saw amplified his growing perplexity.

Several soldiers were wearing loose-fitting fatigues of the strange greenish color that human militaries labeled "olive drab." Two were in the tiger-striped pattern that their eyes read as effective camouflage. All of those were armed with the long, vaguely familiar rifle. Like the AK, its magazine was mounted in front of the trigger guard.

Three soldiers had slightly darker and greener fatigues and were armed with more of the anachronistic AK-47s. Two others, wearing slightly browner uniforms and hanging toward the rear, carried bolt-action rifles; although antique these weapons fired bullets of sufficient mass and velocity to kill a Hkh'Rkh with one shot. Granted, that outcome was unlikely unless the hit was in the head or the cardiosac, but still, it was enough of a possibility to earn the weapons a healthy measure of respect.

The camo-striped soldier at the entry stood, waved in

the group that had evidently swept the dining hall: five soldiers, also carrying AK-47s. Their clothes appeared too big for them and the smallest was a female. They resembled Indonesians at first glance, but Yaargraukh's practiced eye picked out subtle differences in physiotype and facial features. The hurried, non-English words they exchanged with the tiger-striped man at the doorway confirmed Yaargraukh's hypothesis; they were definitely not speaking Javanese *behasa*, although this tongue had some of the same sounds, and moved with the same liquid fluidity. However, he had only learned English and German and had no better guess at their language than, "not *behasa*."

These new troops and the others glanced toward a point over Yaargraukh's head. From behind the worm tank, a final group approached: five human males, two in the camouflage fatigues, two others in olive drab, and the last and oldest in what looked like a dark blue flight suit. The latter nodded to the larger of the two soldiers wearing camouflage. "Signal the CP secure, Rich. Break squelch, only."

"Yes, sir," the rangy soldier replied. He began manipulating the dials on an unusually large hand radio.

The silver-haired male in the flight suit nodded toward the closest of the handling tables. "Okay, gentlemen, let's clean that off and take a look at our situation."

The immediate shift into well-rehearsed actions demonstrated that this group had performed these tasks many times in similar surroundings. Two soldiers cleared the table and wiped it down with rags they seemed to be carrying for that express purpose. Half of the initial entry team left, followed by the five East Asians who had cleared the front of the building. The remaining members of the entry team took up posts at the various doors into the kitchen, except the camouflaged one who had signaled the all-clear on the doorway into the dining hall. He joined what appeared to be the group of officers gathering around the table.

One in slightly greener olive-drab and carrying an AK-47 produced a long tube, snaked out several maps, spread them flat. The camouflaged door-checker leaned in toward the silver-haired leader. "Orders, sir?"

"Yes, Sergeant Owen. Pull in our scouts and dress our perimeter to protect this building. Then signal the chopper jocks to reposition the slicks to the freight lot at the rear entry."

"You want them to power down, Colonel?"

"No, they're to keep the rotors turning. We'll be dusting off in less than ten minutes. Once you've passed those orders, send out the search teams. They are to keep their eyes peeled for any easy, worthwhile salvage."

"Sir, we have not secured the 'ville beyond the perimeter. Those teams will need security against ambushes."

"You were makvee sogg, Staff Sergeant. I'm pretty sure you can make those security assignments on your own."

Sergeant Owen smiled. "Yes, sir."

The tiger-striped officer let the radio dangle in his grasp. "Report from Kresge. Greek Nick has gone missing, along with another salvage scout."

"What?"

"No more info than that, Colonel. But the pilot on

Nick's Huey, Captain Turnbull, dropped him near the last observed position of the first scout car we saw enter town. That was the last anyone saw of him or his partner."

"Damn it. Who's the next senior scout after Greek Nick?"

"Rating Koruda," supplied the man with the AK-47, using its stock to hold down a map corner that kept trying to curl up. "He is also senior automobile mechanic in ell zee. Is most competent." His English was strongly accented: Polish or Russian.

"That means putting Koruda in charge of today's greasemonkey gang—from the *Scorpion*," countered Sergeant Owen.

"*Bozhe moi*," muttered the officer in the brownish uniform.

"You said it, Arseniy," the blue-suited colonel affirmed with a nod. He glanced at the tiger-striped sergeant. "Will the greasemonkeys cooperate with Koruda, Emmett?"

"Well, they're submariners, sir—but I think so. No promises, though."

The colonel straightened, hands on hips, head slightly forward. His voice confirmed· what Yaargraukh had conjectured from the posture—annoyance. "In that case, Sergeant Owen, you will *personally* see to it that *Scorpion's* crew cooperates. Completely and respectfully. All our people have to work together. Even the ones who still dream about killing each other. Hell, even the slopes· take orders from me, now."

"Sir," said the officer with the AK-47, "Colonel Paulsen's policy regarding derogatory language—"

"Damn it; yes, you're right, Alexander. I meant to

say 'even the *Vietnamese* take orders from me now.'
But you get the point, Emmett?"

"Sir, yes, sir."

"Then get about your job." He wagged a lazy salute
at Sergeant Owen, who responded with a far more
crisp one before leaving at a trot.

The taller of the two tiger-striped soldiers who'd
entered along with the colonel scratched his ear.
"Emmett's going to have his hands full with those
greasemonkeys, Colonel Rodermund."

Rodermund hung his silver-maned head. "Good
God, not you, too, Robert."

He was about to reply, but not before the tiger-
striped officer holding the radio interceded abruptly.
"You know how it is, Colonel. Personnel may snap-to
when the brass announces new directives, but it's hard
for NCOs to enforce them in the field."

Rodermund raised his head. "Rich, I know perfectly
well that out in the mud, good intentions and theory
break down in the face of gut reactions and reality.
But look deep into my one good eye, Captain, and tell
me if you see any indication that I give a damn about
what the men—er, persons—of this command *like*."

"Not the faintest sign of that, sir."

"Good. I'd hate to think that your vision is going,
too. Now, what's our best guess at continued enemy
presence here in the AO?"

"Half a platoon, at most. But the opposition isn't
making it easy to get a headcount. Their survivors
have gone to ground."

"Gathering for an attack?"

"Doubtful, sir. We're not detecting any radio chatter
on other frequencies, and we shot up all their support

weapons and hardpoints on the way in. Best guess is that they're just hoping to wait us out."

"Damn, isn't that just like the A Shau all over again. Where do you figure they are, Rich? In their burrows?"

The officer named Rich frowned. "Well, sir, we can be pretty certain that's where their civilians are. But I'd say most of their troops have holed up in the town." He paused. "Having our search teams combing through those buildings could get pricey."

Rodermund nodded sharply. "Good point, Captain Hailey. Runner!" he shouted. One of the olive drab security personnel peeled off from his position near the side door and ran to the colonel. "New orders for Lieutenant Kresge and our search teams. Do not engage enemy infantry directly. In the event of contact, Kresge's infantry is to identify, isolate, contain, and mark with smoke for our gunships to suppress. Kresge is to follow up with gas if the enemy remains active and refuses to surrender. He is not to kill any enemy soldiers."

"Colonel Rodermund, sir, the lieutenant's gonna wanna know what to do if they come straight out after our people . . . sir."

Rodermund paused, then: "Shoot to immobilize. If possible."

The runner turned pale. "Sir—?"

"Son, if Kresge gives you any flack, you tell him to come see me after this op. I am fully aware that his troops are nervous and don't want to take any chances. But we need to take one or more of the snorkelheads alive, so those are his orders."

Despite all the implications of what he had heard,

the increasing probability that the humans were indeed trying to capture him, and the constant threat of discovery, Yaargraukh's reflexive thought was, "*Snorkelhead?*" *Is that really what they call us?*

The humans had resumed their council of war. The officer named Alexander checked his watch. "Sir, I point out there is not much time. Taking prisoners may require a more direct method."

"Such as?"

The tiger-striped sergeant named Robert leaned forward. "Assuming that some of enemy have retreated to their caves—well, we're all small enough to work in them like tunnel rats. Better than." The Russian named Alexander nodded.

"God, no." Rodermund leaned away from the makeshift map table. "I'm not sending any men down those holes. Kreuzer tried that on the second op—and look what happened."

"Just a suggestion, Colonel," the tall, tiger-striped sergeant disclaimed, hands raised in that peculiar human gesture that signified either an assertion being retracted or an exhortation being diminished. "I just figured that, if you're still looking for the snorks' cadre, they might have ducked in there. Hidden among the females and junior snorks."

Rich Hailey looked at his subordinate, shook his head. "I doubt it, Bob. Their males always come out for a straight up fight."

The officer named Arseniy shook his head. "They are all *duraki*."

"No, Lieutenant," the colonel said slowly. "I don't believe they're stupid. I think the snork soldiers are doing what's expected of them. By coming out into the open, they draw the battle away from their non-combatants."

"Or it just keeps them out of the way," the American sergeant offered with a shrug.

Rodermund stood straight, a gesture which even Yaargraukh could read: the discussion was over. "Whatever reason the enemy has for refusing to hide among civilians, we're not going to figure it out here. And we don't need to. Whether they're noble, stupid, or both, I'm not sending men into one of those dens. Costs too much, even if we were to gain the intel we need."

Alexander's voice was as carefully oblique as his comment. "On other hand, casualties have been light—very light—over last two months."

Rodermund frowned. "Yes, Lieutenant Shvartsman, and I intend to keep them that way, as much for morale as force preservation. Or do you have access to a reserve regiment of which I have been kept unaware?" Rueful, gallows-ready grins crinkled most of their faces. Shvartsman's own smile was more stiff, as if he was not amused but merely fulfilling a polite obligation. "Now," the colonel continued, his own grin fading quickly, "what's the bigger tactical picture, Alexander?"

The Russian lieutenant gestured toward the maps. A few aerial photographs were strewn among them. "Naturally, all is guesswork. And I am not photo reconnaissance specialist. Was only trained in bomb damage assessment for our flight wing."

"That's more expertise than the rest of us, Lieutenant Shvartsman. Continue."

"*Da*, sir. So far, all is as expected. No enemy activity seen along western road. Radio traffic during and after our attacks was brief and not extensive; not enough

to signify enemy coordination for a major advance."
He pointed to the largest of the maps. "Road network
suggests that mechanized platoons we engaged today
came from here." He tapped his rifle's cleaning rod
on the map, then one of the aerial photos. "A larger
town. Likely to be motor depot and garrison here, in
fenced lot outside limit of buildings. Long structures
inside compound are, we think, garages." He moved
the pointer further away on the large map. "Here is
largest community we see on map or photographs
from captured intelligence. Two days to drive, given
speeds we have now observed of their APCs."

Rich Hailey leaned over the maps, scanning. "Still
no evidence of air assets?"

Alexander Shvartsman waved a dismissive hand at
the table. "None. But lack of evidence does not mean
lack of air assets."

Rodermund nodded. "Point well taken. I've been
particularly concerned about this feature." The colonel
pointed to one of the photographs. "This could be
some kind of short airstrip. Maybe a heliport."

Shvartsman nodded. "I agree, Colonel. But even if
enemy has STOL or VTOL craft, we shall be gone
before they can arrive. And again I stress: unless their
technology is much greater than ours, this base lacks
evidence of necessary infrastructure for jet aircraft.
Unless these photos are outdated."

Captain Hailey craned his neck, twisting his head
to get a closer look at the photos; he did not seem
as familiar with them as the other two. "These don't
look like surveillance photos."

"They do not," Shvartsman agreed. "They resemble
prospecting or, er, survey pictures. Before satellites,

KGB often acquired photographic intelligence of other nations by, eh, 'commissioning' surveys though false businesses."

The sergeant named Robert leaned closer to get a look, too. "So you think these might be satellite images?"

"Possibly, Sergeant Lane. Some pictures from orbit have distortions that are consequence of altitude of observation, cannot be fully corrected by optics. These?" Shvartsman shrugged. "Maybe."

Sergeant Lane crossed his arms; his black brows pulled together into a shallow, bushy vee. "So if the snorkelheads do have satellites, why haven't they found us yet? Satellites did a pretty good job of that during the Cuban Missile Crisis—no offense, Lieutenant Shvartsman."

"I take none. We all survived. That is good outcome. But I have same question about satellites."

Colonel Rodermund leaned away. "Maybe they don't have many. Maybe this photo was snapped by a high altitude recon flight."

Captain Hailey scratched his ear. "Which only changes the puzzle, since we haven't seen any aircraft, either."

"We haven't seen any *intact* aircraft," the colonel amended. "We did find that weird delta-shaped wreck that looked like a refugee from the scifi late late show, five weeks back. And that didn't just fall out of the sky; those holes were combat damage."

Sergeant Lane nodded. "Yeah, and it had at least a year's worth of growth covering it. Which might explain why we haven't seen planes and why they might not have satellites."

The Russian lieutenant named Arseniy glanced around at the rest of the nodding HQ staff. "What do you mean by this?"

Rodermund smiled. "Robert means there might have been a shooting war upstairs." Seeing Arseniy's baffled expression, he added. "All the way upstairs, Lieutenant Pugachyov. In outer space."

"Space combat?" He looked around the group, smiling and stunned at the same time. "What have you all been drinking? Or"—he glanced at the Americans—"smoking?"

Robert Lane smiled back. "I didn't say it makes much sense, Arseniy. But then again, none of this does."

Rodermund held up a hand. "We can fret about all the mysteries later. Right now, let's assume that the snorks have airmobile assets similar to our own, say twenty percent faster. What's their minimum reaction time?"

Shvartsman pursed his lips, scanned the largest map. "It would take them minimum three hours to reach this town."

"More than enough time for us to finish our salvage operations and be long gone," Hailey nodded.

Yaargraukh wished he could point out that the captain's assumption was only accurate if the Patrijuridicate had kept its promise to keep Turkh'saar demilitarized. Which now seemed increasingly unlikely: the only delta-shaped atmosphere vehicles in the entirety of the Hkh'Rkh inventory were military. And the only other two species which had visited this system—its Arat Kur co-owners and the Slaasriithi raiders—did not have any delta-shaped craft at all. So, if Jrekhalkar and his sire's Old Family backers on Rkh'yaa had broken the rule against militarization, there was no certainty that they did not have more vehicles of that type in storage. Or attack jets. Or missiles for space, air, or even ground defense. And if they did, today's attack on Ylogh might have provided Jrekhalkar and his local allies what they had wanted for so long: a target that loitered long enough to be attacked. Suddenly, Yaargraukh wondered which was the greater immediate danger: the human guns around him or the possibility of inbound Hkh'Rkh missiles and attack planes?

"Doc coming in," called one of the door guards.

The group at the map table turned toward a very different figure who came through the side door. He was even taller than Rich Hailey, had very dark skin, and was dressed in camouflage fatigues that had an almost pixelated appearance. His head protection surprised Yaargraukh momentarily; at first he mistook it for the iconic helmet of the German Wehrmacht, with its somewhat flattened crown and neck-protecting rear extension. But a second glance told him that although it was patterned after that "sallet style" helmet, this was a much later piece of technology. In addition to the fabric outer surface, it did not bounce on its wearer's head like the Germans' original, heavy metal helmets. This was lighter, probably made of a ballistic compound more akin to plastic. Furthermore, it was adorned by clips and rails typical of modern, modular armor systems that mounted various sensors, comms, and other support implements. As the darker human approached the table, he snapped a salute at the colonel.

Rodermund returned it. "What's the word on casualties, Lieutenant Franklin?"

"Not as many as we feared, sir. Two WIA. One

just a through and through, another we'll need to medevac ASAP. Two KIAs."

"Who?"

"Greek Nick from the *Scorpion* and Wally."

"'Wally'?" muttered Hailey, frowning. "Sorry, Isaac. I don't recall anyone named Wally."

Lieutenant Franklin shrugged. "That's just what the greasemonkeys nicknamed him. They didn't mean anything by it; they liked him. He was a good mechanic and handy with an AK."

Rodermund nodded. "Wally was one of the Pashtuns, wasn't he?" Shvartsman stiffened slightly.

Franklin pulled off his helmet, scratched at his hair, which was shorter than most of the others', and had a tightly curling texture. Yaargraukh placed his features: subsaharan African. "Yeah. Wali Fahim. He's going to be missed by a lot of people, not just the other mujahideen."

"Also Greek Nick will be missed," Arseniy added, making a brief crossing gesture: from forehead to belly, then right shoulder to left. "He told good jokes. Was a good cook."

"Yeah," Lane agreed. "And he was one of Clive's best scroungers. That's going to hurt."

Rodermund's voice was so low that Yaargraukh almost didn't hear the words. "Every one of them hurts."

The silence that descended over the humans would have been strange to other Hkh'Rkh, but Yaargraukh had learned that the humans mourned their battle-dead immediately and lauded them later, rather than lauding them immediately and mourning them later, as was the Hkh'Rkh way.

It was the newcomer, Franklin, who glanced quickly past the colonel's shoulder, toward shadows approaching through the plastic pleating that led to the dining hall. "Looks like an update, sir."

"'Bout damned time," muttered Rodermund with a fast glance at his watch.

A new human appeared, wearing a flatter, panlike helmet covered in some sort of mesh. His uniform was the heaviest yet, and a deeper, almost forest green with some brown in it. Upon entering, he saluted, but with his hand turned up and palm fully outward. He stomped his foot slightly as he adopted the strange, rigid posture that humans called "at attention."

The colonel couldn't keep a smile off his face as he returned a salute which waved away the one proffered by the new arrival. "Don't sprain yourself, Clive. What's the haul?"

"Everything but Christmas pudding, sir. More fuel and food than we've ever seen before. Fourteen of their giant shotguns, twenty-one of their assault rifles. Three of those rotary guns. Some grenades. Got a few of your lads nicking the baby-Bofors from the snorks' carriers, but at least half of those will only be good for parts. Hull fires weren't kind to 'em. Destroyed a lot of their ammo, too. But the teams on the plains haven't reported back yet, and those carriers were more intact. And the dead snorks in the open—well, we can be sure of getting all their kit."

Rodermund thought, turned to Sergeant Lane. "Bob, head out back and see if you can wave one of the Jollies toward the plain. I don't want to lose any of that gear."

"On it, sir." In a few long strides, Lane was out the wide, bay door behind Yaargraukh.

Rodermund had already turned back to Clive. "What else?"

The wiry human blew out his cheeks: a startling behavior that, in any other creature, would logically have been an aggressive body-enlargement display. But among humans it simply signified exasperation or momentary perplexity. "Too long a list, sir. A lot of little electric devices. Tins of what might be food or chemicals or paints; can't read the labels, naturally. Water purification plant, but it would be hard to move."

"And taking it would be hard on the civilians, given all the toxins that leach into the water. We'll leave it. What about the scout cars?"

"Find of the day, sir," Clive beamed through the grime on his face. "Koruda found one good as new where poor Wally and Greek Nick snuffed it. It was equipped with what looks like a long range wireless, but that took some rounds. Now it's only good for the tip.

"The recce car that raced into town just ahead of us wasn't far off. The bonnet and front right wheel are in rough shape, but it's otherwise right and ready. Good for parts, at least.

"The third took a little longer to find. It was on the western edge of town, lying on its side. Apparently it ran off the road when our lads bagged the driver. Looks a bit shabby now, but all the bits are there and working."

Rodermund nodded. "So, two functional scout cars and a third for parts. Excellent. Give Rating Koruda my compliments. Now, can we get them on the Chinook?"

"Just barely, sir. I'd recommend breaking up the disabled one, load the parts by hand. There isn't room for all three vehicles on the after-ramps in your big whirlybird, Colonel."

Rodermund and Hailey looked at their watches at

the same moment. The colonel frowned. "How long will it take the greasemonkeys to break it down, Corporal Strather?"

Clive Strather didn't blink. "Ten minutes, sir. Maybe five. We found power tools that we can run off the car's battery, so long as we keep the motor idling."

Rodermund looked at Strather as if worried for his sanity. "Son, five or ten minutes? That's just not possible."

Strather's steady gaze broke, wandered sideways. "Well, sir, that's true, of course—if we were to be starting *now*."

Rodermund appeared to be trying very hard not to smile. "I see. And exactly when did you start the breakdown?"

"Soon as we found the bloody thing, sir." The corporal swallowed; the strange, vulnerable bone that humans called the Adam's Apple cycled once, quickly. "Sorry for acting without orders, Colonel. But time was wasting and we—"

"Son, in my military, we call that 'taking the initiative.' But still, ten more minutes is longer than we hoped to be here." He summoned another runner. "Find Lieutenant Kresge and inform him that we are dusting off in fifteen minutes. He is to commence collapsing our perimeter back to this building. Leave a triangle of three listening posts fifty meters beyond the line. NCOs are to coordinate plans for a fast, staggered withdrawal to the choppers. I want our men on the slicks and unassing this AO as soon as Corporal Strather is done. If we've found Colonel Paulsen his intel prize by then, great. If not, we're gone. With the additional cloud cover rolling in from the west, the light is fading fast—and we are *not* going to start flying in the dark. Too much risk."

There was a commotion in the dining hall: loud shouts, a momentary struggle, and then a cluster of figures burst through the plastic sheeting. At first, all Yaargraukh could see were a half-dozen humans, struggling to drag a large, resisting figure into the room—and then he had to discipline himself not to inhale so sharply that the snorkel's intake might whistle.

His radio-bearer Ezzraamar staggered into the room, one leg bleeding heavily. Behind him, the American sergeant, Emmet Owen, kept his long rifle trained on the wounded Hkh'Rkh. "Look what we found," he said. Although the phrase was jocose, his tone was anything but.

Rodermund stared. "Son of a bitch."

Captain Hailey raised his rifle slightly, but the expression on his face was one of caution, not hostility. Isaac Franklin, on the other hand, began drifting toward Ezzraamar in what appeared to be a state of distracted fascination.

Hailey jerked his head in the direction of their prisoner. "Have you checked him for bombs? Bugs?"

Owen nodded. "He's clean. Trust me, Cap'n, he was genuinely trying to escape. Took three shots to that leg to bring him down."

"They're tough," Rodermund agreed.

The wiry, pan-helmeted human named Clive put his head back in the side door. "We haven't made a pretty job of it, but we've got the car in parts. Ready to go, Colonel!"

Rodermund nodded. "Very good." Then to his command staff. "Start loading the slicks. Any man who lags will be cleaning latrines for a month—and his NCO will be in boo coo shit with me. Move!"

As Shvartsman started rolling up and returning the maps to their tubes, and Emmett Owen began overseeing Ezzraamar's limping progress to the rear bay door with a six-man security escort, Yaargraukh felt his breath grow short. *I cannot leave a fellow-Warrior to such an uncertain fate. I must—* And then the half of him that was an officer retorted: *what you must do is report what you have seen and heard, back in the Clanhall in Iarzut'thruk. That is your first duty. Besides, this information may sway Jrekhalkar, might even stop the fighting. You cannot assume that Caine Riordan will arrive in time to help. Indeed, he may never have received your message.*

Yaargraukh settled back into the depths of the tank, tried to ignore the worms that were winding deeper into the longer fur that covered the juncture between his shoulders and torso. To even the most jaded observer, it was clear that these humans were not part of an officially sanctioned invasion force. The physical evidence had always indicated to the contrary; their own speech now proved it.

But bigotry was not only invulnerable to the appeals of logic and deduction; it was often blind to counterproofs such as those Yaargraukh had just witnessed. And furthermore, there was one missing puzzle piece, without which Jrekhalkar might yet dismiss the new evidence as inconclusive, and potentially misleading:

If humans of the Consolidated Terran Republic had not brought this strange, ill-equipped group to Turkh'saar, then who had? And when? And, above all, *why?*

Chapter Nine

Nezdeh Perekmeres waved her hand over the belt-com on her night table. The paging tone terminated in mid peal. She rolled toward the unit, grabbed it, murmured, "Here."

"Nezdeh," said her distant cousin Brenlor's voice, "the Slaasriithi shift-carrier is moving further in-system."

"In response to the new radio activity on Turkh'saar?"

"Very possibly so." In his excitement, Brenlor's dialect slipped out of High Ktoran, slurred down into the street-speech of his youth. "The scenario is unfolding as I predicted; the tactical communications of the low-breeds from Earth are drawing in trespassers."

"Yes, but are they the right trespassers? We need a response from the Terrans, not the Slaasriithi."

"We may have both. Sensors have confirmed our earlier suspicions: the Slaasriithi ship's thrust signature is a match for the one we drove off eight months ago at BD +02 4076, and she might still be carrying human diplomats."

"The same ship?" Nezdeh sat up, rolled to her

131

feet, padded away from the motionless form lying on the other side of her bunk. "It is not possible." She immediately regretted the implicit weakness of indulging in hyperbole; the Progenitors rightly taught the Elevated that "clarity in every moment is the foundation of mastery in every moment."

Brenlor used her slip to reemphasize his marginally superior position. "Are you suggesting that I am in error?"

"I am suggesting that the odds of it being the same ship are far smaller than the odds of a sensor error," she replied, congratulating herself on recontextualizing her surprised disbelief into a genuine, prudent doubt. Because to admit that her personal mastery had slipped, even for one second, was out of the question.

If Brenlor detected her subtle redirection he gave no sign of it. "I had Sehtrek replace the Aboriginal sensor officer who first discovered the matching drive signatures. Sehtrek confirmed the finding, ran a diagnostic and recalibrated the instruments, then scanned again. Again, a match. It is the same ship." A pause. "They cannot have tracked us here." It was a statement of the obvious, but Nezdeh knew that Brenlor's assertion was also an indirect request for reassurance.

Which Nezdeh provided. "That is not possible. There was never any sign of pursuit after we shifted out from BD +02 4076 and left no spoor along our path to this system." Where they had mostly lain doggo for nearly six months, occasionally harvesting volatiles, but primarily training and bringing the six new huscarles up to readiness.

There hadn't been time to do so during their retreat— well, rout—from BD +02 4076 and its main world,

Disparity. They had lost two shuttles, half a platoon of Aboriginal clone-soldiers, two reasonably skilled Aspirants to Elevation and an irreplaceable Intendant even before the Slaasriithi reinforcements arrived to rescue the Terran delegation. Worse yet, all those losses had been incurred planetside, meaning that they had left the Terran Aboriginals and the Slaasriithi a rich, if confusing and inconsistent, forensic trail. Unfortunately, being but one shift away from the Slaasriithi homeworld, it would have been unmitigated suicide to remain in the system any longer than absolutely necessary. They had out-shifted as soon as possible, their plans more thoroughly ruined than the Wolfe-class corvette—the UCS *Puller*—that had been instrumental in preventing the slaughter of the delegation's survivors.

A long string of hurried shifts followed. There had been no time to do anything other than approach each system's most congenial source of volatiles—usually a gas giant—and begin harvesting and converting them to antimatter as quickly as possible. Since the largest of their three ships was a laughably "state-of-the-art" shift-carrier that had been the pride of the humans' megacorporate fleet, this meant that fuel skimming and initial processing proceeded at a glacial pace. Accordingly, they spent the first month of their "strategic withdrawal" figuratively staring over their shoulders, painfully aware that if they were caught in the midst of refueling operations, they were all as good as dead.

Yet Nezdeh recalled that fearsome period with gladness, and with an additional emotion she knew the Breedmothers would decry as not merely foolish and contrary to the imperative of dominion, but dangerous. According to their wisdom and that of the Progenitors, it was an emotion that might cloud her judgment, her ability to retain the self-interested utilitarian edge that was the guarantor of success as a Ktor.

Yet the glance she cast over her shoulder was not one of fear, but fondness. The broad back of Idrem's blanketed silhouette cycled slowly through the expansion and contractions of deep sleep. He would, when the time came to declare it, be acclaimed a wise choice in a mate. Brenlor was too close to her own genecode and was not merely obsessed with dominion, but delighted in pursuing it with unnecessary brutishness. He no doubt conceived that as a sign of his strength. Nezdeh, having listened to the Breedmothers' wise words about men of his type, recognized it for what it was: a weakness, a need to reassure himself of his dominion. That did not make a man—or woman—their own master; it committed them to posturing, rather than true power and efficacy. And nothing was more important than power and efficacy.

The early weeks of their small band's flight had been tense, but she and Idrem had spent and exhausted their tension upon each others' bodies. And had shared more, besides. They had not addressed the growing bond between them—the words for it were all but forbidden—but they knew it, could feel it. And sharing it as an unspoken, growing secret somehow made it both more exciting and more precious, even as it blossomed in the shadow of possible destruction.

Ultimately, throughout those eight weeks, the Progenitors had smiled upon them (according to those who believed in such mythical nonsense), and they had reached their next objective: Turkh'saar. Where, it was now confirmed, the same Slaasriithi ship they had attacked at Disparity emerged from shift just three days ago. The oldest Autarchs often declaimed, from their lofty peaks of many centuries, that the universe was a surprisingly small place, and that the older one became, the more it seemed to shrink. Well, perhaps they were right. She said as much to Brenlor.

He uttered the snarling coughs that were his equivalent of a laugh. "Let us hope our House is restored so that we may say the same thing from the heights of our own Autarchal chairs."

"Indeed," Nezdeh said, but she thought, *The day I must consign myself to the near-dotage of a seat on the Autarchy is the day I shall purposely overreach in one last great act of dominion. I shall not be a slave to anything, including the customary ambitions of my own race, nor the decline of my own body.* "Are the Slaasriithi making for Turkh'saar?"

"They are. They are crossing our orbital track now."

All three ships of their ragged flotilla—the Aboriginal shift-carrier *Arbitrage*, the small but lethal patrol hunter *Red Lurker*, and a two-century-old Ktoran shift-tug that they had dubbed *Uzhmarek*, or "Lord of Loads"—were following along in the sensor shadow of the sixth planet of the system. The Slaasriithi craft would cross its orbit almost a quarter of an AU in front of them: an excellent place from which to maneuver in behind it. "So, we will allow her to pass and then enter the asteroid belt between us and Turkh'saar to avoid her sensors."

"As discussed," Brenlor confirmed. He paused. "I must now inconvenience you in one further way. There is an urgent matter with which I require your assistance."

"And what is this urgent matter?"

"I need you on the bridge of *Arbitrage* to ensure that our chief collaborator Kozakowski remains alive."

*Well, so much for returning to my bunk. And to
Idrem.* "Kozakowski? He is in danger?"

"Yes."

"What from?"

A pause. "From me. Hurry."

Escorted by one of the indoctrinated Optigene
clones, Nezdeh entered *Arbitrage's* bridge. Her apprais-
ing glance at Brenlor—who was standing off to one
side, ostensibly studying the sensor returns—shifted
over to Kozakowski. The somewhat pudgy Aboriginal
was in a stooped, cringe-ready posture; he seemed
ready to wring his hands.

He nodded at her. "Srina Perekmeres, Brenlor was
good enough to inform me that you would soon be on
duty here and might answer a—a question of mine."

"To what does it pertain, Kozakowski?"

"The morale of my—eh, of the original crew of
this vessel."

He still thinks of them as his *crew?* "An appropriate
change of description, Kozakowski." *And it is probably
just such egoistic slips of the tongue that has Brenlor
ready to cut yours out. Right along with your heart.*
"You were wise not to trouble Brenlor with this matter. Explain how morale among Aboriginals should
necessitate a question to him, or to me. You are to
oversee and report on them, as you have done since
we commandeered this ship. None of us Evolved are
to be troubled with such mundane matters unless you
have detected mutiny. Have you?"

"No, Srina Perekmeres. Not yet."

*Ah. And there is the ham-handed attempt to inveigle
my concern, and so, manipulate me.* The ploy was as

pathetically obvious as it was devious. "Well, since you clearly *foresee* a possible mutiny, you have my leave to retain the services of half a dozen of the clones, in combat gear, so that you may eliminate the crewpersons you suspect of being traitors. Does that answer your questions?"

"It is *an* answer, Srina Perekmeres, but I hope my more humble query makes it unnecessary to employ such extreme measures, and thereby preserve your resources."

An appropriately obeisant entreaty, but without the genuine humility that should give rise to it. Small wonder that Brenlor had been ready to kill the unctuous rodent. "Ask swiftly."

Kozakowski spread his hands in a gesture of self-deprecating supplication she associated with helot merchants. "The crew of the *Arbitrage* knows we are lying in wait for an enemy craft, that we mean to ambush it." Seeing her stern look, he hastily added, "Since they perform half the bridge functions, how could they not be aware of this? They also believe that if they are obedient and helpful in achieving this objective, they may hope to remain in your service. But they become restless over one particular: they do not know why you wish to ambush this craft, or whose it might be."

Nezdeh allowed herself a slow smile that was not in the least amused or amicable. "I do not think this makes the *crew* restless, Kozakowski. I think it makes *you* restless. And attempting to wheedle such information out of me again could earn you a reward you do not expect—such as an unsuited stroll out the airlock."

The Aboriginal's hands stretched wider, more desperately. "Nezdeh Srina Perekmeres, I ask your indulgence. I admit that I too am curious regarding our mission here, but please understand: I have learned your ways well enough, even before I came aboard this ship, to know the danger of asking questions. But the rest of the *Arbitrage*'s crew still does not understand how your methods and expectations of dominion differ from analogous terrestrial customs."

"Then teach them the distinctions."

"I endeavor to do so, Srina Perekmeres. And I know that if you are pleased by their behavior, that signifies that you are satisfied with my efforts to educate them in your ways. But since we have, at your behest, minimized the contact between your people and the human crew, there are few opportunities for practical observation or correction. I labor to explain the variances between your dominative actions and their interpretations of them to the best of my still-imperfect understanding. But it is a slow process. Far slower, at any rate, than the mounting curiosity about their future prospects for survival and for service with you."

"And for profit too, no doubt."

Kozakowski shrugged. "They do not understand that even having the presumption to entertain hopes of profit is an affront to your dominion."

Well, at least Kozakowski himself seemed to be starting to understand the rudiments of interacting with Ktor. But that did not mean his query about morale was genuine. Indeed, Nezdeh was relatively certain that it was merely a back-handed attempt to worry her about the dependability of the *Arbitrage*'s crew, and thereby, to reinforce his position as the indispensable liaison to them. Of which it was time to disabuse him. "Kozakowski, you have understood much of us, but have not understood as deeply as you must if you hope to survive in our service. Firstly, if you ever again attempt to make yourself important in my eyes, as somehow holding any measure of power over the other Aboriginals of which you were once master, I will kill you on the spot. And do not deny that this was your intent in raising this topic. That would be lying: another transgression which will earn you instant death. Do you understand that my words are not a threat, but a promise?"

Kozakowski, eyes bulging, nodded. His lips tried to form words, but he did not manage to speak.

Unconcerned—Kozakowski was least offensive when he was silent—Nezdeh continued. "We owe no person an explanation, and shall execute any who are disgruntled over being denied one, much less protest it openly. Communicate this to the other Aboriginals in the same words I have used. They should know who their masters are and that we will destroy an asset rather than stoop to negotiate or compromise with it. Do you believe you can remember those words, and convince the other Aboriginals that these, too, are not threats but promises?"

He nodded again.

"Of course, if you, and they, serve us well, we may ultimately return you to Earth." She saw an eager light in his eyes. "No, not as a free agent. You are our creature and shall remain so in perpetuity. Or until you become a liability."

He frowned. "I do not understand."

Nezdeh stepped closer to him; he seemed to shrink into himself. "Think, low-breed. Our influence upon your megacorporations back on Earth has been almost completely exposed. What will we need to do, therefore, in the years and decades to come?"

"Reinfiltrate?"

"Yes—happily for you. You have been recorded as lost with this ship, presumed dead. So, with appropriate 'modifications,' you could be reintroduced to Earth. Perhaps many of this crew can be retained as operatives; their service and yours will determine that. However, suffice it to say that once there, the depth of your involvement with us shall grow with each passing day, making it increasingly suicidal for you to ever confess your betrayal to your own peoples.

"And lest you entertain the hope that you can somehow purchase their forgiveness by revealing what you know of us, be warned: your actions on Earth will be completely compartmentalized, so you will never be aware of enough of our operations to be useful to your planet's intelligence services. If you are discovered, you will have nothing with which to bargain. Do you understand?"

Kozakowski's reply was a parched croak. "Completely, Srina Perekmeres."

"Excellent. Begone."

Kozakowski left the bridge so swiftly that he stumbled over the lower rim of the main hatchway's coaming.

The only other person on watch was one of the clones who had shown an aptitude for piloting, and, through a rigorous program of both positive and negative reinforcement, had attained the qualifications necessary for normative station-keeping. "Summon the first pilot to the bridge," Nezdeh ordered, "and report to your quarters; you are given the remainder of this shift to rest."

"Yes, Srina Perekmeres."

When the clone was gone, Brenlor turned toward her and away from the sensors that he hadn't been studying at all. "Is that obsequious Aboriginal serious?

Does he actually think he can extort, however subtly, higher regard from us by indirectly calling our attention to his greater knowledge of the systems and personnel of this wretched ship?"

Nezdeh shrugged. "In truth, I do not fault him his instincts to seek power and dominion however he might. Those are the instincts the Progenitors teach us, after all."

"Agreed, but to see that will to power in an Aboriginal with the intellect of a substandard Intendant and to the cowering self-abasement of the lowest helot: it is akin to beholding a hideous deformity."

Nezdeh nodded. "I do not disagree. But in this matter, let us concede that although Kozakowski overreaches, he is merely mistaken in his actions, not deficient in his intellect. He does have valuable familiarities that we lack."

"Such as?"

"Brenlor, I know you contemn him, but let us be frank. Even though we have spent months familiarizing ourselves with this hull and its primitive technologies, Kozakowski has access and common context with all the original crew, and has overseen the revivification and indoctrination of the additional personnel we have chosen to awaken. Similarly, he is far more familiar with the capabilities and limits of this ship's four landers, remaining tanker/tender, fuel scoopers, locker contents, and manifest. To say nothing of his knowledge of the training and oddities of its nearly two battalions of clones. And let us not forget that we unavoidably emboldened him when we asked him to brief us on the best ways to minimize the security risks intrinsic to this hull, particularly its reconfigurable torus."

Brenlor snorted in disgust. "A ring of flexibly linked modules that can rotate so we are feet-down when under thrust, and feet-out when the ring is in rotation? An imbecilic design. One significant hit by a tactical weapon and the whole structure will come apart."

Nezdeh nodded. "But it was Kozakowski who saved us much time, and possibly error, in choosing which modules to shut down, which to guard, and how to emplace monitors—both overt and covert—to ensure that there were no places hidden from our eyes and ears, places where mutinous conversations might begin."

Brenlor nodded. "Do you think he suspects, though?"

"That House Perekmeres has been Extirpated, and that we are alone, without family, patrons, or power behind us?" Brenlor merely nodded and glowered as Nezdeh catalogued their dire circumstances. She shrugged. "Our choice is between silence and lies. If Kozakowski is clever, he will have already begun to wonder why our discussions are devoid of any references to what power we wield beyond these ships. Logically, he would expect us to openly mention those resources as de facto evidence of the full depth of our mastery, and so, further reinforce the Aboriginals' submission to us. That is another reason why we must keep him from presuming to ask questions: so that we need never give evasive and weak answers. If Kozakowski ever suspects that we are not answering his questions frankly, he is likely to wonder if that is because we dare not do so. Consequently, we must make certain that he continues to construe our dismissal of his queries as a sign of our indifference to his concerns, of our assured dominion."

Brenlor leaned upon the sensor panel, rested his

blunt chin on his fist as he stared out the small cockpit window, frowning at the bright orange speck that was the system's primary. "It is a demeaning path we are upon," he muttered.

"It is a prudent path, and only a leader of great self-mastery could have accepted our short-term subterfuges as the price to be paid for the long-term glory of our House's resurgence." Brenlor's frown retreated. Nezdeh congratulated herself on soothing him yet again, on keeping both his faith and focus fixed upon his own false-flag scheme. "But we must still exercise great caution. Being only one shift from the Arat Kur homeworld and the Accord's Convocation station at EV Lacertae, we are carrying out this ploy upon the very doorstep of those who would slay us."

Brenlor frowned again, this time in perplexity. "I understand your concern with EV Lacertae. The Custodians, and possibly the entirety of the Dornaani Collective, would exult in our destruction. But the Arat Kur? After their defeat by the Aboriginals, they are all but crippled."

"Although I refer to their home system, Sigma Draconis, my concern is not with the Arat Kur themselves."

"Ah. So you believe that the Aboriginal conquest fleet is still there, hovering above their planet?"

"Since we have no way to ascertain that they are not, we must presume that they still are. And if the Aboriginals are still orbiting the Arat Kur homeworld, it is because the peace treaty has not been signed. In which case, Tlerek Srin Shethkador and *Ferocious Monolith* are still there as well, meaning that the elect of the Ktoran Sphere's Autarchs and the favorite son of the House that most hungered for our Extirpation is near at hand with a ship that could obliterate us effortlessly."

Brenlor nodded. "As you say, we must be cautious."

"And prudent." Nezdeh waved at the navplot. The archaic Aboriginal display, a faux 3-D flatscreen, flickered to life. The orange mote that denoted the Slaasriithi shift-carrier was still making for the belt.

Brenlor stared at it fixedly. "Once the trespassers are engaged on Turkh'saar, events may evolve rapidly. We must be close, lest we miss a pivotal opportunity to destroy the Aboriginals and thus indebt the Patrijuridicate to us for having protected their interests."

"Agreed." Nezdeh studied the concentric rings of the planetary orbits, the current trajectory of the target, the courses they might use to intercept, trail, or evade its notice, respectively. "It will be at least a day before we can follow. More before we can deploy our own forces."

"Yes, but the enemy's course and actions will tell us much about what they intend, and how best to lay our trap for them."

Nezdeh nodded, added, "And to carefully consider the timing of it, for if we move too soon, we may ruin our chance to achieve the best possible outcome."

"To destroy the Slaasriithi and any humans with them?"

Nezdeh shook her head. "Better yet, to catch them embroiled with the locals on Turkh'saar. And timed so that the Hkh'Rkh will need us—*ask* us—to aid them by delivering a final, unexpected blow."

Chapter Ten

Duncan led Caine out of the module that had been reserved for the human passengers aboard the *Shore-of-Stars*. They made excellent time, since the Slaasriithi ship was still under acceleration and therefore, with the thrust providing gravity equivalent, the rotational habitats and interchange slideways were still.

They entered the shift-carrier's heavy keel-boom and slid into one of the waiting transit capsules that travelled its length. Solsohn smiled like a kid at an amusement park. "These things are pretty fast."

Riordan nodded. "So are we meeting with the whole security detachment?"

"Just the six officers and senior NCOs. They know the basic mission, but I expect they've still got questions, given all they've missed since they went into cryo."

"And what exactly do we call this unit that isn't a unit? 'All you military folks'?"

"Well, in my logs, I've been referring to them as the Guard."

145

"The Guard?"

Duncan grinned a bit sheepishly. "A shorthand label, sir. And a pun. Most of the way out here, they were still in cryosleep. So I started calling them the Cold Dream Guards."

Caine tried to figure out the significance of the name, then shrugged. "Sorry. I don't get the reference."

Solsohn looked faintly disappointed. "The old British unit, The Coldstream Guards? The one that fought at Waterloo and the Somme?" When Caine just shook his head, Duncan sighed. "Well, that's what I get for being a history buff who likes puns. I was partial to the name because of the Scottish connection; that's where the unit was first formed, back during the English Civil War."

Solsohn's explanation trailed off diffidently, as if he was leaving the door open for a remark, for further conversation. *Probably worried after I pinned him to the wall about being Downing's proxy. So if that was the stick, this may be a good time to offer the congenial carrot.* "So, Solsohn doesn't exactly sound like a Scottish name."

"Well, the family came over to the States pretty early. The original name was Solisson, or something like that."

"But wouldn't that be uh—Scandinavian? Maybe?"

"Well, if it was, I'm Scandinavian by way of Edinburgh." Duncan shrugged. "Probably."

Riordan dangled another carrot. "Well, either way, I don't have a better name for the unit than the one you've come up with."

Solsohn smiled. "That's because you haven't had any time to think of one or hear anybody else's ideas."

Riordan couldn't keep from grinning in response. "Well, there might be some truth to that. But the name is unique, has some history to it, and it's one less thing we need to think about." The car stopped, opened, revealed a corridor that terminated in what looked like a fusion between a hatch and a sphincter.

Solsohn jutted his chin at it. "We're here." Seeing Riordan stare at the strange portal, he added, "Yeah, I know. I had the same reaction. It's mostly mechanical, but according to the Slaasriithi, more reliable due to its biological elements."

Riordan approached it cautiously. "How so?"

"Because it has reflexes of its own and the ability to operate even in the event of power or control interruption. It's also got better security; even if you can hack the mechanical part, you've got to get past the biological part as well. Which would be more like trying to fake your way past a suspicious guard dog."

Opening, the portal revealed the rest of *Puller*'s crew, sipping what smelled like honest-to-god coffee. All except Dora.

"Welcome back to the world of the living," Karam said, raising his mug. "Want a cup of awake?"

"Don't mind if I do." Riordan smiled at the faces surrounding the coffee dispenser, which looked like a cross between a storage tank and a centrifuge.

Tina Melah breathed in the vaporous wisps floating up from her mug. "Real beans. Nice."

"Nauseating," Dora countered defiantly, sipping at her cup of water.

"*De gustibus non est disputandem,*" muttered Bannor.

"Eh?" asked Miles O'Garran.

"Latin," murmured Tygg to the surprise of the

entire group. "'In matters of taste, there can be no argument.' Or words to that effect."

"I didn't know you spoke Latin," Sleeman said, eyes wide, a smile growing as she brought her own cup to her lips.

"Well, I speak *some*." Tygg's qualification did not seem to diminish her admiration.

Riordan was tempted to take a swallow himself, but for now, found the warmth of the mug even more pleasant than the anticipated taste. "So, where are the Cold Guards?"

"The what? The who?" asked Miles.

"Mr. Solsohn's nickname for our security detachment." Seeing the curious looks, he waved his free hand as if shoving the label behind him. "The story can wait. I thought we were meeting them here."

"You will," said a new voice from the doorway. "But I wished to speak with—and thank—all of you first." Yiithrii'ah'aash entered, a very faint purr riding underneath his words.

Riordan noticed a subtle change in the team's reaction to the Slaasriithi Prime Ratiocinator. Yiithrii'ah'aash moved into their midst with greater ease, and they made room for him not the way they would for a dignitary, but a personal acquaintance. *So, is this new, casual familiarity an outgrowth of our shared experiences or due to a slow-acting variety of their Amity spores?* That was the kind of question which was going to plague every interaction with the Slaasriithi for the foreseeable future, maybe forever. Since they possessed biological agents that Earth couldn't detect, there was no way to be sure if feeling positively toward them was natural or "induced," to use their word.

"You wished to thank us? Why?" Melissa Sleeman asked.

"For clearing our path of dangers and obstacles."

"Which I suspect you could have done more easily yourselves." Dora set down her glass of water with a punctuating clack.

"As it turns out, that may be a correct assessment, Ms. Veriden. But I assure you, the process would have taken longer and involved far more destruction. We would have used drones, controlled from distant standoff. Locating the automated defense systems would have been a slow, painstaking process, which would have greatly increased the likelihood of our detection."

"That doesn't wash," Veriden insisted, keeping her distance from Yiithrii'ah'aash. "You have your own small ships. Better than *Puller*, I'm sure. Maybe not built for war, but faster, stealthier, and able to control dozens more drones with more firepower. You just didn't want to go right up to the threat and get your hands dirty." She glanced at the Slaasriithi's tendril clusters. "Uh—no offense."

"I perceive that no insult was intended in your use of that common idiom. But I do perceive anger and resentment. Which must be addressed. You are right, Pandora Veriden: we did not wish to be proximal to the threat. And yes, we are fearful of such situations. But that is not why we asked you to act in our stead."

Phil Friel crossed his long, thin arms. "You're unaccustomed to close conflict. You feared you'd make mistakes."

Yiithrii'ah'aash trailed two tendrils like streamers in the wind. "Yes, but our reason runs far deeper than that. It is a matter of instinct—and our instinct is to flee."

"Well, so is ours," Tina Melah commented. "But we resist it."

The ambassador's tendrils froze in mid flow. "You do not merely resist the impulse to flee, Ms. Melah; you replace it. Your species possesses what you call your 'fight-or-flight' reflex. You will do one, or the other, in crises. But let me ask you this: what if you had no 'fight' reflex at all?"

Riordan nodded. "We'd never attain a stable mindset for dealing with a crisis. We'd constantly be resisting the impulse to flight, because we'd have no alternative reflex that takes over when we decide to stand and fight."

"Exactly. This is our limitation." Yiithrii'ah'aash extended one tendril from either cluster. "We have measured our reflex times. Neurologically, ours are slightly better than yours: a consequence of our arboreal origins, I suspect. But our crisis reactions are far slower. And it was from you that I learned the axiom that is so pertinent to this metric; in war, there are two kinds of combatants: the quick and the dead." He folded his tendrils into a tight—embarrassed? regretful?—knot. "In war, we are not quick. You are. And you invariably demonstrate the instincts that prove it. You doubtless recall the situation when *Shore-of-Stars* had begun preaccelerating to flee back to our homeworld and summon reinforcements to rescue you on Disparity."

"Of course."

"Then you will also recall that you instantly perceived that, in our absence, the Ktoran ship would commandeer our automated antimatter refinery and use its fuel stocks to gain the freedom of action to ensure your destruction, and then their escape, before we returned."

"And you couldn't reason that out for yourselves?" Karam's voice veered toward a sneer. His eyes dropped when Caine shot a hard look at him.

Yiithrii'ah'aash turned toward the pilot. "It is not a matter of reason, Mr. Tsaami. It is a matter of how innate reflex exerts influence on all thought. In this case, we would certainly have arrived at such a strategy eventually, but we needed to make a *rapid* decision. And just as our natural instinct is toward flight, our thought processes habitually move away from destruction as a means of solving a problem. You have analogs in your own species. But they are outgrowths of cultural taboos rather than evolution, which make them less determinative of your behavior and thought."

Miles crossed his short, thick arms. "Name one."

"Cannibalism," Yiithrii'ah'aash answered promptly. "There are many accounts of stranded humans who, faced with insufficient nourishment, have not even thought of acquiring the necessary sustenance from dead bodies. In many cases, the bodies denatured to the point of unuseability before the survivors realized that they must act to preserve their food value, let alone resolve to consume them."

"That's because only a monster would think about people as . . . as food," Tina Melah blurted out, hugging herself.

"That's his point," Phil said, laying a hand on her arm. "We are so deeply trained, consciously and subconsciously, to resist seeing other humans as nourishment that, even in a life-and-death crisis, it may not occur to us until it is too late."

Yiithrii'ah'aash's sensor cluster dipped slightly; a Slaasriithi bow. "It is as Mr. Friel says. We suffer a similar blindness with regard to the reflexive thoughts and actions that make one successful when perpetrating violence, and, to a lesser extent, preemptive destruction."

Caine could feel that his smile was brittle. "Whereas we excel at them."

"You do, although your species has also tempered those reflexes more than others. The Hkh'Rkh, for example."

"There's an artful shift of topic," Bannor murmured.

Yiithrii'ah'aash's neck skin rippled slightly. A... chuckle? "We are entering the asteroid belt, which affords the best cover from any automated sensors which might still exist. So we must swiftly settle upon our collective course of action."

Riordan crossed his arms. "Because this is where you intend to cut us loose."

Yiithrii'ah'aash's tendrils flexed once, sharply. "Yes. We will steer toward a cluster of larger asteroids along our path. Once concealed among them, we shall launch your expedition."

"And I assume you have now received a message or other coded signal from our Hkh'Rkh contact, Yaargraukh?"

Yiithrii'ah'aash's tendrils became very still. "Unfortunately, we have not."

"Then how do we know where to go, and how to assure the locals that we are not simply another bunch of marauding humans?"

"I regret that I have no counsel to offer on these matters."

Karam took a step closer to Caine, his widening

eyes upon the Slaasriithi. "We've heard the recordings of their tactical radio chatter, Yiithrii'ah'aash.
Based on that, the Hkh'Rkh colonists aren't going to
be eager to welcome another bunch of humans. So
I doubt it's a good idea—or healthy—for us to go
down to Turkh'saar without some kind of invitation,
first. And besides, any humans who'd be crazy enough
to attack the Hkh'Rkh in their own space might be
insane enough to draw down on us, too."

Bannor nodded. "The people we heard on those
transmissions didn't sound like they were hoping to
be rescued. Unless singing along to classic rock and
machine guns is some new form of distress signal."

If Yiithrii'ah'aash had discerned the sarcasm behind
Bannor's deadpan delivery, he gave no sign of it.
Rather, he seemed to resist a reflex to back away
from the group. He put out his tendrils in a writhing flare, instead. "I understand your reluctance, but
you accepted this mission knowing that Yaargraukh
did not speak for the Old Families of the Hkh'Rkh
Patrijuridicate. Indeed, if they become directly involved,
it is likely that they will claim to have been actively
invaded by the Consolidated Terran Republic and
declare war. Yaargraukh's request presents the only
reasonable alternative: to extract the human raiders
before that can occur. Unfortunately, because time is
very short and the Old Familes are very reactionary,
overtures through legal channels would be futile. It
could take years—if ever—for both the Arat Kur
Wholenest and the Hkh'Rkh Patrijuridicate to formally allow your military units to enter their space
and remove the human interlopers from Turkh'saar.
By that time, the ongoing violations would have given

the Old Familes the pretext they need to break off the minimal diplomatic relations that exist and begin reequipping for war."

Miles's grin was not pleasant. "Fat lot of good that would do them. They got their asses kicked so bad, they're not going to be able to return the favor for ten years. And by that time, we'll have—"

"There's a more pressing problem," Caine interrupted. "The leader of the Patrijuridicate, First Fist, has still not been located. He went missing during the liberation of Jakarta. Hkh'Rkh conspiracy theorists and warmongers are milking that for all it's worth. They claim that First Fist is dead, or that he's our prisoner and we won't admit it, or even that he's leading some kind of ongoing guerilla resistance on Earth. All of which have the same effect: the remaining Hkh'Rkh leaders are on the brink of fighting to succeed him."

"Civil war," breathed Melissa Sleeman.

"Yes," Yiithrii'ah'aash concluded. "Which, in all probability, would be blamed upon Earth."

"You mean," Tygg said, frowning, "that whichever rival won, they'd unify the survivors behind the idea that Turkh'saar was a human attempt to stir the pot and increase their need for a leader, and so plunge them into a succession war. To weaken them even more."

Yiithrii'ah'aash's sensor cluster bobbed slightly. "That is what your Mr. Downing and his superiors fear. I concur with their projections."

Phil Friel smiled, stuck his hands in his pockets. "And yet, that doesn't quite answer the original question now, does it, Yiithrii'ah'aash? Which, if memory serves, was: what makes it a good idea to land on Turkh'saar without an invitation, or even local contact?"

Riordan smiled at Friel. *Leave it to Phil to never lose sight of the* real *issue.*

Yiithrii'ah'aash exhaled forcefully through the slits that flanked the mouth in his "chest." "I did not say it is a good idea. But it has become essential, even though there is no way to ascertain if Yaargraukh is in this system or still alive. During our voyage here, Mr. Downing arranged to have us updated by secure communications as we passed through systems under human control. The last message reported that the negotiations with the Arat Kur have still not been completed."

"Damn conniving roaches," Tina muttered.

"They were indeed duplicitous in both their attack upon your space and your homeworld," Yiithrii'ah'aash agreed. "But your own communiqué indicates that it was your negotiators, not the Arat Kur, who were the source of the delays. They pressed for considerable wartime reparations and arrogations."

"Arro-what?" asked Miles.

Peter Wu cleared his throat, then spoke with great precision. "Arrogations are enemy matériel or possessions that are seized either during the course of a conflict or afterward, which become the legal property of the victor."

"D-damn," sputtered Karam, "when did you swallow a law dictionary, Pete?"

"It was part of my training in Taipei. And remember to call me Peter, please."

For once, Karam did not bait him by calling him "Pete" yet again. Instead, he turned to the Slaasriithi. "So our diplomats started getting greedy?"

Yiithrii'ah'aash did not reply immediately. "Let us say they realized, in the course of negotiations, that the Arat Kur were more desperate to comply than originally thought. Also, some national leaders back on your homeworld were under considerable pressure to cripple the Arat Kur economy and interstellar capability for at least twenty years. They ultimately took possession of almost half of the Wholenest's shift-capable craft and were still pressing for occupation concessions in a number of systems.

"Just as the negotiations were concluding, however, word arrived of the Ktoran attempt to ambush this very ship and your diplomatic delegation at Disparity. Ktor ambassador Shethkador, who had insisted on remaining in the Sigma Draconis system until the negotiations were concluded, denied that the Ktoran Sphere had any hand in such an action. Of course, we know differently."

Riordan shook his head. "We know that some of the attackers were Ktor. That's not the same thing as knowing that they were operating at the behest of the Ktoran Sphere."

Yiithrii'ah'aash's sensor cluster jerked back slightly. Then: "That is true. However, we know this: it was not the Hkh'Rkh. They cannot reach our planets. It was not the Arat Kur; their ships have all been accounted for. It was not my own people attacking ourselves, since that is anathema to us. It is not the Dornaani or the Custodians. They would have destroyed us so completely and swiftly that there would have been no evidence of a battle. We would simply have disappeared."

"So that leaves the Ktor and Earth itself," finished Dora. "And if the report that reached Sigma Draconis includes the interesting little detail that the attackers' planetary landings were carried out by shuttles registered to the missing SS *Arbitrage*, that gives the Ktor an opening to accuse us of sabotaging our own mission. Internal power struggle or some such bullshit, probably."

Caine smiled. "Except that everyone, the Ktor included, knows that no human ship has the shift range to get to Disparity. The distance between the stars along the only possible path are well beyond our eight point three three light-year maximum range. Which means the *Arbitrage* got a lift from someone who has much greater range—which brings us back to the Ktor, a couple of whom left their bodies on Disparity."

Karam snorted. "Yeah, along with a couple of CoDev-Co's black-market Optigene clones."

Yiithrii'ah'aash passed a ripple of tendrils in the air. "It is not clear to me if all those details have been shared with the other parties at Sigma Draconis. However, the consequent accusations and aggravations have caused heated diplomatic exchanges, with the Ktor refusing to discuss the ambush at Disparity except to reiterate their denials of involvement."

"Yeah, well—screw 'em." Miles seemed inordinately pleased with his simple, and Caine felt completely understandable, proposal for resolving the situation.

Yiithrii'ah'aash replied in a measured tone. "I understand your idiom and impatience, Chief O'Garran. But the last communiqué intimates that your government believes the situation on Turkh'saar could be used to weaken accusations of Ktoran wrongdoing on Disparity."

Riordan nodded. "By ostensibly implicating humans as the source of the sabotage in both places. So we have to complete the mission here before that can happen. Even though we have no contact or invitation to intervene."

"Unfortunately, this is what is required of you. As I'm sure Mr. Solsohn will confirm."

Riordan saw that his weren't the only eyes that rotated toward Duncan.

Solsohn nodded. "He's right. Mr. Downing made it quite clear: we might not hear from this Yaargraukh, or from anyone on Turkh'saar. But that didn't change the objective: to clean up whatever mess our species is making down there and bring home the perpetrators."

Riordan nodded back and smiled. "Sure. But that isn't all Downing wants, is it?"

"Not sure I know what you mean."

"Duncan, if you start lying to me now, we're not going to have a pleasant relationship. Downing knows perfectly well that what these supposed raiders are doing isn't one tenth as mysterious as how they managed to reach Turkh'saar to do it. Our ships can't get here unless they take a two-year voyage through mostly unprospected systems. Which means they would have had to be on their way out here before we even knew the Arat Kur and Hkh'Rkh existed. The answer to that mystery is worth its weight in gold to the strategic analysts back home."

Solsohn shrugged. "Probably, but that's way above my pay grade and my clearance level. What I do know is what's spelled out in the operations orders: that we proceed even in the absence of a contact from known or friendly Hkh'Rkh personnel. We are to remove the humans trespassing upon sovereign Hkh'Rkh space as quickly as possible and by any means necessary."

Tygg started, then leaned toward Solsohn. "'By any means necessary?' So, if the raiders refuse to leave, we have to kill them—kill our own kind? That's why we're going to Turkh'saar?"

Duncan sighed. "If it comes to that, yeah; I guess so."

Chapter Eleven

OUTER SYSTEM, BD+56 2966

Tygg's face reddened and his shoulders came forward: he seemed to expand ominously. "'You guess' we might have to slaughter other humans? What the hell kind of—?"

Riordan put up a hand. "Look. If those humans are in fact pirates and raiders, it shouldn't matter to us whether they're targeting our own civilians or the Hkh'Rkh's: they have to be stopped. And we should be ready to use the same methods we use when dealing with pirates on Earth and in the Epsilon Indi system. We apprehend if possible, kill if forced to."

Tygg's posture was no longer threatening; the fury was out of his voice. "And if they're *not* murderers?"

Caine shrugged. "Then why wouldn't they want to get the hell off Turkh'saar as quickly as possible?"

Tygg stared, then looked away. "None that I can think of."

"Right. So let's not put ourselves on the horns of dilemmas that probably don't exist. Besides, judging from Yiithrii'ah'aash's posture, I doubt we have the time to worry about anything but commencing the mission."

The Slaasriithi Prime Ratiocinator shifted slightly, attempting to imitate a more casual human stance; it was arguably the most awkward position that Caine had ever observed in him or any of his species. "You are quite right. A more productive, and essential, use of time would be to become acquainted with the peculiarities of the stellar system in which you will be operating."

Melissa Sleeman's question had a hopeful lilt at the end: "You mean, physical peculiarities?"

"No. The system, which you designate as BD+56 2966 in your stellar catalog, is quite conventional. There are five very hot inner planets of reasonable size, several of which are tidally locked to the primary. None have any development or notable features.

"Turkh'saar itself is somewhat colder than your Earth, with extensive polar ice caps. The atmosphere is breathable, but from what little relevant intelligence we extrapolated from the satellites and communications relays captured by our wartime commerce raiders, much of the indigenous biota is either marginally or significantly toxic to humans. Prolonged epidermal contact is not advisable. Consumption is potentially fatal unless the biota in question has been properly treated."

Sleeman frowned. "Then how can the air be breathable? Some of the spores or pollens would doubtless be inhaled."

"An excellent conjecture, Dr. Sleeman. However, the dominant reproductive paradigm in the indigenous biota is evidently parthenogenesis, or other asexual modalities. There seems to be little airborne flora."

"Paradise for hayfever sufferers," quipped Karam, adopting a bad parody of an advertising voice-over.

"I doubt any of your species would define Turkh'saar as a paradise. Which does, however, touch upon the peculiarities I initially referred to: its awkward status in both Hkh'Rkh and Arat Kur politics."

Peter nodded. "That is inevitable when a single region's political control is divided into a codominium."

"Quite true, Lieutenant Wu. But those complexities are especially problematical in the case of Turkh'saar. It is the only habitable colony world that the Hkh'Rkh can currently reach with their maximum shift range of seven point four light-years. And even once they achieve longer range, their allotted region of space has far fewer green worlds than others."

Riordan nodded. "Yaargraukh explained that to me when he was our Advocate to First Voice. Given the Hkh'Rkh monomania for expansion, the lack of green worlds makes the Patrijuridicate a political pressure cooker. The Old Families don't have new room for competition, and the rapidly growing New Families have no place else to go, other than back into servitude."

"Exactly. Unfortunately, the Hkh'Rkh technological limitations make Turkh'saar a difficult world for development. In political terms, this means that Turkh'saar has ceased to be, to extend Commodore Riordan's metaphor, a useful release valve for the political and population pressures that are growing on Rkh'yaa. It doesn't help matters that their cryogenic suspension units have a failure rate of just over four percent."

Dora's eyes widened. "*Coño!* That is not a means of transportation; that is suicide."

Yiithrii'ah'aash turned toward her. "And yet, they

risk it. By the thousands. Nothing demonstrates the pressures within the Patrijuridicate more profoundly, or poignantly, than that statistic."

"And having to get Arat Kur permission for half of their routine activities must gall a species like theirs," Bannor observed.

The Slaasriithi's tendrils pulsed an amplification of the human's assertion. "That was one of the greatest objections to the codominium model adopted for this system: that if the Hkh'Rkh were compelled to keep their development of Turkh'saar wholly nonmilitarized, they would ultimately find that constraint unbearable."

Riordan knew the smile on his face was bitter, but did not care. "Well, now I understand why the Arat Kur were willing to ferry the Patrijuridicate's Warriors to our worlds: so that the Hkh'Rkh could scratch their lebensraum itch someplace else. If they had remained bottled up here, they would have eventually broken the agreement and flooded over the border."

"This was indeed what the Arat Kur feared. However, the outcome of the war has worsened the situation. What hope the Hkh'Rkh had for additional expansion is gone."

"Damn," muttered Tina, "what a nightmare."

Caine considered his now-lukewarm coffee. *Speaking about potential nightmares*—"Yiithrii'ah'aash, we need to establish one last thing before we get under way."

"And what is that, Caine Riordan?"

"If my people are injured, we need a formal guarantee that no Slaasriithi will treat us with anything other than our own medicines, fluids, or biologically based products. This includes placing us back in cold sleep for any reason. And if at all possible, you will summon a qualified human to observe and oversee any interactions you have with our biology."

"You do not trust us, still."

Riordan shrugged. "As someone once said, unclear contracts are blueprints for disaster. I'm trying to make sure everything is clear."

"Yet the basis of your concern is a lack of trust. Which is profoundly ironic. You naturally realize that we may have biological methods of influence that are so subtle, so undetectable, that we could employ them without your ever becoming aware that we had. So logically, if you do not trust us, you cannot fundamentally be sure of your safety even if we overtly agree to the limitations upon which you are insisting."

Pandora Veriden stuck her hands in the pockets of her duty suit. "Great. So this all boils down to a line from one of the archaic action movies my Grandmama rigged for me to watch as a kid."

Caine heard the cue, decided to play the straight man. "And what line was that?"

"'So, do you feel lucky—punk? Well, do ya?'"

Caine shrugged. "I don't see that we really have any choice. If we're going to go ahead with the mission, these are the only precautions which we can reasonably take." He turned back to Yiithrii'ah'aash. "Do you agree to the restrictions on treating us?"

"If you wish, yes. However, it may critically, even fatally, restrict our medical options if you are seriously injured."

Caine looked around the group; heads were nodding slowly, gravely. "We understand that. Now, where do we go to meet our security forces?"

Yiithrii'ah'aash began moving toward the portal

through which he had entered. "I will have them sent in as I depart."

Dora glanced up suspiciously. "What's the matter, Ambassador? Not sure they'll be friendly?"

"No, Ms. Veriden, I am concerned that if I am present for your initial meeting, they might suspect that I am there to censor your comments, that your race's autonomy has been compromised. So, I shall absent myself." With a rolling, radial wave of his tendrils, he exited.

A moment later, the portal at the other end of the compartment paged softly.

Caine put down his coffee mug. "Come in."

The door, evidently computer controlled, took an extra fraction of a second to translate the command. When it opened, half a dozen humans came through, eyeing it suspiciously. Their uniforms were not bloc-standardized but nationally distinct duty suits of different design and color: the norm before the short-lived World Confederation of 2118 and its successor, the Consolidated Terran Republic.

Several of them caught sight of Solsohn. The tallest male in the group—a captain wearing a Canadian uniform with a CSOR insignia—nodded and offered everyone a wide grin. "Well, at least there's coffee."

Riordan smiled. "Grab a cup." He was going to add, "—and a seat," but there were no chairs in the room. A typical Slaasriithi oversight: being digitigrade, their most common resting positions varied between a legs-locked crouch and a rigid squat, sometimes supported by a piece of furniture that was half box, half bench. "Looks like we're going to be standing."

"Yeah," agreed a short, muscular woman whose

Israeli semi-chameleon suit identified her as belong-
ing to the Sayeret Matkal. "The Ostrichimps aren't
much for sitting."

O'Garran barked out a surprised laugh. "Ostrichimps? Oh, that's good."

She glanced at him, eyebrows raised. "I just have
trouble saying Slaal . . . er, Slaasir . . . damn it." She
closed her eyes and concentrated. "Slah-sree-thee."
She opened her eyes. "I must have some mental
block on that word."

"You and me both," Miles grinned. "What's your
name?"

She glanced at his field patch. "Well, Master Chief,
I'm *Lieutenant* Thon."

Riordan elected to accelerate the introductions to
cover over the awkward silence that threatened to
follow in the wake of O'Garran's equally awkward
attempt to fraternize with an officer on sight. "And
the rest of you?"

The last officer in the group—spare, dark, long-
faced—hung back, smiling. "I'm waiting to see if my
friend Peter Wu will recognize me."

The usually unflappable Wu started in surprise,
peered at the speaker, and then rushed forward to
shake both of his hands at once. "I wondered what
had happened to you after Singapore, Newton. There
was so much chaos on Earth, in Indonesia, even once
the invasion was over—"

The much taller man smiled slowly. "I was never
there. You didn't hear from me because I was in a
cold cell at Delta Pavonis. Have been since 2017."
He turned to Caine, saluted. "You must be Commodore Riordan."

Caine saluted, saw faces among the newcomers either flush or blanch as they hastened to snap their own salutes. The Canadian captain stammered. "S-sir, we thought—I'm sorry. We were told there were civilians in the command group, and we hadn't been given—"

Riordan turned the end of his salute into a waving away of concern. "Since we're not part of a larger unit, we have no reason to wear ranks. So unless you have the power of precognition, Captain—?"

"Captain Bjorn Hasseler, sir."

"—then you can hardly be blamed for not saluting. Besides, given all the officers in this room, we'd be saluting for days. So let's keep this an informal gathering."

"For now," Solsohn added with a hint of caution.

Riordan remembered Duncan's warning about being casual with these troops, wondered how justified it was, and waited until the ragged round of introductions had finished. "So is this your whole command staff, Captain?"

"Yes, sir. We were pretty light on senior NCOs; apparently most of them were sent on to the Earth. Sergeant Major Ippolito is our only armorer, Top Sergeant Fanny is the only person we've got with quartermaster experience, to say nothing of scrounging."

Tygg's eyes and cheeks bulged as he labored to suppress a laugh. "I'm sorry. I hadn't caught your name the first time"—he almost snickered—"Sergeant Fanny."

Tina Melah glanced at Tygg, surprised, as Newton Baruch did his best to hide a small grin. "Oh come on, there's worse names. Like yours, maybe."

Matthew Fanny sighed. "Ma'am, you sound like a fellow American. If so, then Fanny doesn't mean what you think it means. Not to an Aussie. Or a Brit." He jerked a head at the carefully oblivious Newton.

"Then what—?"

Riordan folded his hands. "Tina, in the U.K., a fanny is not one's, er, backside."

She stared. "No? Then what is it?"

Caine cleared his throat quietly. "On a woman, it is the—the other side." A puzzled stare. "The *front* side. If you take my meaning."

At first she didn't. Then, eyes widening, she clearly did; one hand started reflexively toward her groin before she snapped it away.

"Yeah," Fanny sighed, nodding. "So now that we've had that special moment, can we move on?"

Gladly, thought Caine. He nodded toward the sixth member of the group, a slender woman with very dark skin and very green eyes. "I'm not familiar with your uniform or service badges, Chief Warrant Officer Gaudet, but from where I'm standing, it looks like you're wearing some wings."

Her smile was small, careful. "Yes, sir. Caricom Defense Forces, originally from Guadeloupe. MOS in transatmospheric transports, sir. I'm the senior pilot."

Riordan resisted the reflex to raise an eyebrow. A young warrant officer was the senior pilot for the landers that Downing had given them? That was not a good omen. "Chief Gaudet, how many other pilots are there?"

"Two, sir."

Riordan turned toward Solsohn, who shook his head. "I know; a total of three pilots for three landers. Zero redundancy. I pointed it out to Downing."

"And?"

"And that was all they had left out at Delta Pavonis. Everything else had been pulled back to Earth to kick the Arat Kur back where they belonged."

"Okay, but that's more than a year ago."

"Roger that, sir, but from what I heard, the big landgrab is stretching everything pretty thin."

Captain Hasseler shifted slightly. "Beg your pardon, sirs, but—landgrab?"

Riordan nodded. "After we defeated the Arat Kur and arrogated a lot of their shift-capable ships, we chose not to join the Accord just yet. That means we are still not bound by the accords themselves. So we weren't required to obey the territorial limits that had been established for us. As I understood it from Mr. Downing before we left, the overwhelming sentiment on Earth was to go on a flag-planting spree with most of those Arat Kur ships."

"Why exosapient ships, sir?" asked Hasya Thon. "Why not our own?"

"Because the Arat Kur have a shift range of about nine point five. That allows us to reach many more systems, much more rapidly. Also, they have portable antimatter production facilities that cut the time required for frontier refueling by a third."

"The imperialist impulse is alive and well," Dora commented.

"So is the survival imperative to build a buffer around our home systems," Bannor retorted in a flat tone.

Caine motioned for silence. "Regardless of the advisability of the initiative, it is not violating the direct rights of any Accord species. We are scrupulously avoiding areas that belong to, or have been expressly reserved for, other races."

Hasya Thon frowned. "Yes, sir, but these, er, Custodians can hardly be pleased that you are doing this."

"Doubtless. But compared to the violations perpetrated against us by two member races—the Arat Kur and the Ktor—and one other provisional member—the Hkh'Rkh—our violations are the equivalent of a speeding ticket versus premeditated murder. And since the Custodians and Dornaani failed to protect us when they were supposed to, they have little grounds for complaint. So far, they have not done anything other than lodge protests."

Duncan nodded. "Pretty weak ones."

This time, when Duncan spoke, Riordan noticed a slight posture change in several of the half of the new group: was it a shadow of distrust? If so, it wasn't hard to reason through. They were all from select, even elite units and had missed being included on the most important mission in the history of humanity: the rescue of Earth. Instead, they had awakened to find that an undisclosed international intelligence agency had rounded up their cold cells and sent them off to the ass-end of nowhere with such poorly defined objectives and such thin support that it hardly merited the label of being a "mission." And Solsohn was left holding the bag without any formal military service or rank to his name, yet assigned as their immediate CO. Riordan understood the officers' reaction, but also understood that it needed adjustment. Immediately. "Your unit has no name."

Captain Hasseler looked up quickly, a bit startled. "Uh . . . that's correct, sir."

"A unit has to have a name. So here's yours: the Cold Guard. Borrowed from the Coldstream Guards.

One of the oldest standing units in the collective history of our bloc, and with one hell of a reputation. Gives you a name to live up to."

Newton Baruch nodded. "And our table of organization, sir?"

"You report directly to Major Solsohn; he reports directly to me."

Hasya's voice was not entirely respectful. "Did you say that Mr. Solsohn is a major"—the pause was too long—". . . sir?"

Caine hated using her as the example, but she'd put up her head. "If your hearing is impaired, Thon, then get it checked. And you will stow that tone or I'll bench you. Understood?"

Hasya Thon blinked as if struck. "Sir, yes sir!" She visibly worked at getting out a second, more difficult sentence. "My apologies, Commodore."

Before she finished, Riordan moved his hard stare over to Captain Hasseler. "Clearance levels make it necessary that Major Solsohn not disclose his prior assignments. As for my team, some of us are cleared to talk about our service records; some are not. You will instruct your personnel to be courteous and respectful if they must go fishing around for unit gossip—which they will." Riordan allowed the hint of a smile to curve one side of his mouth. "They are soldiers, after all."

Fanny nodded. "The army marches on beans and scuttlebutt," he recited in a monotone. Riordan gestured toward his team. "My command staff is charged with overseeing this mission, aspects of which are also above your clearance. Rank comparisons are thus suspended when it comes to us. Master Chief

O'Garran may be an NCO, but if necessary, you take orders from him, too."

Riordan was pretty sure that O'Garran flashed a quick, triumphant grin in Thon's direction. Caine resisted the urge to roll his eyes. "Now, before we give you the final mission brief, any questions?"

Gaudet cleared her throat. "Any mail for us, sir?"

"I'm sorry, Chief, but no."

The others didn't even look disappointed. Evidently they had not expected to get any mail or would not have been interested in it if they had. Or were such hard cases that they were unwilling to admit to themselves that they gave a damn about any reality beyond their immediate surroundings. And the rest of the unit was probably in the same boat—or worse. Well, again, no time like the present for finding out.

Caine checked his wristcomp, put down his cup. "We don't have a lot of time left. Time to muster the Guard."

With the Cold Guard loaded upon the three wedge-shaped transports, Riordan was preparing to order *Puller's* airlock hatch sealed and to retract the boarding tube when the trooper on anchor watch announced Yiithrii'ah'aash's arrival. Caine had the Slaasriithi piped on board. Twenty seconds later he was on the bridge; *Puller* was a very small ship.

Riordan and the rest of his bridge crew stood. "To what do we owe the honor, Ambassador?"

"What honor there is, is mine. I come merely to wish you safety, a swift resolution of your task, and to impart information you might wish to keep among your closest staff." The Slaasriithi's speech was somewhat rapid, for him. "We have located a large asteroid behind which we can deploy your landers and our automated tugs. We estimate that it should take you no more than fifteen minutes to mate the tugs to the landers and commence a high-energy transfer to Turkh'saar."

"*Puller* will be able to keep up?"

"Caine Riordan, in its new configuration, the *Puller* could easily outrun the tugs if it had to. You shall be able to maintain excellent speed. We estimate it will be just under thirty-six hours travel to the point where you shall commence planetfall."

"Have you been able to get a better scan of the near-space conditions around Turkh'saar?"

"Better, yes, but not precise. You will want to continue to improve the data during your approach. What we have been able to determine is that while there are still orbiting masses, they are not emitting any radiant energy and are in vigorous three-axis tumbles."

"So debris, then."

"Yes, but various small systems, particularly monitors such as you encountered at Planet Seven, could easily be hidden behind, or seeded in among, that detritus. Once you have ended the human intrusion on Turkh'saar, we shall maneuver in to retrieve you and your craft. From that time onward, speed, not stealth, becomes our most important attribute. We shall pick you up and immediately commence preacceleration. If we move with sufficient alacrity, we should be able to shift to Sigma Draconis and report our findings here—and the end of human raiding on Turkh'saar—before any rival reports can lead to further awkwardnesses and delays in concluding the negotiations."

"I thank you for the update, Ambassador. However,

I've been wondering about one other piece of data, something that might impact our operations near or on Turkh'saar."

"And what is that?"

"The debris elsewhere in the system. Specifically, the amount and diversity of it. On the way back from the gas giant, I had Dr. Sleeman start running real-time analysis of what we were encountering."

"And what did you find?" There may have been the faintest hint of caution in Yiithrii'ah'aash's voice.

"Well . . . more than we should have. According to the reports of the forces you sent into this system, the only appreciable infrastructure was for refueling and cargo handling, almost all of which was out at the seventh planet, correct?"

"That is correct."

"Well, the war taught us what Arat Kur and Hkh'Rkh infrastructure looks like and what their doctrine instructs they should have in place. But what we found out there"—Riordan waved beyond the bulkhead toward the distant gas giant—"goes way beyond what we would have any reason to suspect. Most of the wreckage should have been tankage, plus a few support modules. Almost all the thrust-capable platforms should have been robotic or remote-operated vehicles.

"We found plenty of that debris. But we found at least as much debris that shouldn't have been there. Hab mods, mostly stuck in torus clusters; that would have indicated long-duration stations with rotational gravity. We also detected clear outlines of a variety of smaller warcraft and transports: not the type that would be used for refueling, repair, or refinery operations. So I'm wondering: why were they here?"

Yiithrii'ah'aash's neck bobbed once, very slowly. "I have noticed the same types and proportion of wreckage and am perplexed. However, I am not overly concerned. There are other possible explanations. If enemy craft moved through the system after our strikes, it may have been ambushed by automated systems we left behind, creating the debris you mention."

"Then where are they now? No surviving units?"

Yiithrii'ah'aash's neck rotated slightly. "That question occurred to me, also. However, it may be that the enemy forces, despite taking losses, accounted for all our units before shifting on to another destination." He trailed a limp tendril. "But this is all conjecture. And you must make haste."

"Indeed we must. Thank you for seeing us off, Ambassador."

Yiithrii'ah'aash lowered his sensor cluster in regard, then left the bridge with O'Garran escorting him.

Solsohn leaned toward Caine. "I guess we're not going to get any better answers than those, Commodore," he murmured.

Still staring after Yiithrii'ah'aash, Riordan shook his head. "No, and if all his guesswork is wrong, then we'll be getting the real answers in the worst possible way."

"Which is?"

"On the job. Mr. Tsaami, prepare to cast off."

Chapter Twelve

"They have destroyed a whole town of the Hkh'Rkh, from the sound of it," Brenlor announced as Nezdeh entered the bridge of *Red Lurker*. "My father's legacy is bearing the fruit we hoped."

Nezdeh peripherally watched the current pilot, the *Arbitrage*'s former XO Ayana Tagawa as Brenlor spoke. She had not reacted to the Srin's oblique but injudicious explication of how the groundwork for the current unrest on Turkh'saar had been laid long ago, and by whom, but that meant little. The small Japanese woman was not only far more clever than most of the other Aboriginals; she was far more composed. Had she heard and understood the significance of Brenlor's exclamation, it is unlikely she would have shown it.

Nezdeh focused her attention on Brenlor, "This is excellent news, my cousin. And it means we must now determine our next steps." She turned to Ayana. "You are dismissed, Tagawa. Send the second pilot forward, but instruct him to wait in the crew lounge.

We require privacy until we are ready for him to assume his station."

Ayana stood smoothly in the microgee imparted by their slow rotational rate. She made the slightest perceptible—and permissible—bow. "Yes, Nezdeh." She kept her eyes down—*but still, not quite submissive*—as she exited *Red Lurker's* bridge.

Brenlor glanced after her, then at Nezdeh. "What concerns you?"

"Tagawa is too clever, infers too much from our speech. It is best not to make any comments regarding our strategies or our origins in her presence."

Brenlor crossed his arms, tried to act dismissive but was not up to the task of ignoring Nezdeh's steady, assessing stare. "And who would she tell?"

"At this time, no one. But fate is a fickle mistress and we cannot be sure what strange chains of events might take Ayana from our control and put her into the hands of rival Houses. Or back into the arms of the Aboriginals."

Brenlor Srin Perekmeres frowned. "Even if that were true, so casual and cryptic a reference to 'my father's legacy' provides her with no useful intelligence to share."

"Not on its own, no. But she is no fool. She knows that the human radio transmissions we have been monitoring from Turkh'saar originate from older Terran technology, more than a century in her homeworld's past."

"And how could she discern that?"

"She has shown great interest in the callsigns and slang used by the forces your father planted on Turkh'saar as a dormant false flag option. She has noticed certain physical peculiarities in the transmissions themselves. I suspect she knows they are characteristic of radio technologies particular to what they label their twentieth century. With the added context furnished by your comment, she is certainly capable of deducing the truth: that House Perekmeres seeded these humans on Turkh'saar, thereby violating the oath and duties Ktor had accepted in becoming assistants to the Custodians. And once Tagawa arrives at that conclusion, it is simplicity itself for her to conjecture why it was done: to sow discord and confusion between species whose eventual invitation to membership in the Accord was undesirable."

Brenlor's frown deepened before he blanked his face of any expression—but not before Nezdeh had seen each one of her deductive arrows find its mark. "There is some merit to your caution regarding Tagawa, but even she cannot discern our actual purpose in having activated this sleeper cell now."

"Probably not," Nezdeh allowed, "but if her knowledge is combined with that of other Aboriginals—for instance, those who know of our failed attempt to eliminate the envoy to the Slaasriithi homeworld—then together they may be able to reason it out: that these acts have actually been attempts to undermine Shethkador and the Autarchs, to illustrate how ineffectual their passive stratagems have been. They might then correctly conjecture that our intent on Turkh'saar is to place the Hkh'Rkh in a position where they will solicit our help and alliance against 'further invasion' by the so-called 'Terrans.'"

"These would all be significant concerns," Brenlor agreed, "if it were not for one small, contrary fact."

"And what is that?"

"That we will kill Ayana Tagawa before we would allow her to pass from our dominion."

It was a hollow boast concealed as a self-assured statement, and Nezdeh was fairly certain that Brenlor was aware of that. But he was unwilling to admit to the inadvisability of his first, unguarded words, even to his near-peer Nezdeh. Who simply replied, "We should summon Idrem."

Brenlor nodded sharply. "Agreed. His counsel is wanted at this stage."

Taking her cousin's cue, Nezdeh touched one of the top studs on her beltcom. After a moment, it vibrated beneath her finger. Idrem had received her summons and was on the way. "What is the Slaasriithi's status?"

Brenlor waved the holoplot into existence. "Four small craft have commenced a high speed transit to Turkh'saar." He smiled humorlessly. "One of them is an Aboriginal Wolfe-class corvette."

Could it be true? "So not only is this the same Slaasriithi ship, it is still carrying the same defense craft that the human envoy to Beta Aquilae was using?"

"At this distance, we are unable to delineate its thrust signature in sufficient detail to establish a match. Besides, from what you reported, the human craft that disrupted our operations on Disparity—"

—*"Disrupted?" Ruined, rather*—

"—would likely have needed extensive repairs to its engines. That could change its thrust profile."

Nezdeh stared at the four green motes that had emerged from the clutter of the asteroid belt. They were angling in toward the sixth orbit to rendezvous with the blue, brown, and white sphere that represented Turkh'saar. "There are other ways we might identify it, later." She nodded at the tactical plot. "No sign of the Slaasriithi shift-carrier itself, though."

"No, and that is a concern. It could have paused behind any of several larger asteroids that it passed on its way into the belt. It might have cut loose these craft on a parallel course either before or after its final disappearance from our scans, could have shielded them in its sensor shadow as long as they continued together without expending thrust."

"But the shift-carrier's last known position should give us an idea of its general location."

"Possibly. But the Slaasriithi were sly. When they went into the sensor shadow of the last asteroid they used to conceal themselves, there were several other large objects in that vicinity. It is quite possible that they could have repositioned themselves behind any of those others by engaging a short, maximum burn while they were still hidden, and then simply coasting along that trajectory until they drifted into the shadow of one of the other rocks."

Idrem's voice came through the hatch. "And if they apply a similar tactic sequentially, they could significantly alter their position before we see them again."

Nezdeh turned toward Idrem and reminded herself, *I must not let my emotions show on my face.* But that seemed to make the swelling knot behind her sternum grow larger and tighter, as it if was trying to rise out of her to get to Idrem.

Brenlor was nodding at Idrem's summary. "You said, 'before we see them again.' How can you be sure that we will? The Slaasriithi ship might simply have deposited a team to deal with the 'human invaders' on Turkh'saar, and await their return in the belt."

"They might, but I doubt it." He moved past Nezdeh without a glance, but she detected a slight softening of his expression in the instant that he was abreast of her. Idrem pointed into the tacplot. "If the Slaasriithi wait for these four small craft to return to the belt on their own power, they incur needless risks and delays. Firstly, if enemy has presumed that hostile craft could be in the system—and they are too competent not to—the mission detachment will be at its most vulnerable when making their return. They will not have the high velocity that they begin with now. Rather, they will have to boost up from the bottom of a gravity well and beyond orbit, meaning they will be exposed much longer than on their way in. Consequently, the Slaasriithi would be fools not to advance to provide cover and effect the earliest possible rendezvous."

Brenlor nodded. "Yes. But if they are so concerned with concealment, why would they be willing to forego it at that juncture?"

Idrem stuck his index finger into the holoplot approximately midway between Turkh'saar and the last indicated position of the Slaasriithi shift-carrier. From there, he drew his finger slowly toward the edge of the holoplot, which expanded in an attempt to keep up with the trajectory he was tracing. "This is their logical path once they decide to preaccelerate for out-shift. They will want to commence that thrust as soon as they receive word that the mission is complete. However, once their mission craft departs Turkh'saar, any observer would rightly suspect that their return vector points to their ultimate point of rendezvous with the shift-carrier. So that is the effective end of the Slaasriithi's concealment." He stepped back; the line denoting the preacceleration trajectory glimmered once and faded out. "From that point onward, speed is their only ally."

Brenlor nodded, and Nezdeh felt a sense of grow-ing well being. Originally hesitant to take Idrem's counsel, the Srin had come to regard him as a trusted counselor. And since Idrem was not of the prime progenitorial geneline, he was not a potential political rival like Nezdeh.

Idrem had, for his part, adapted smoothly to his role, showing a marked facility for suppressing the head-butting dominance challenges that would have elicited a similar, competitive response from Brenlor. Not all Ktoran males were capable of that measure of self-control, but Idrem was truly Elevated in that he did not require nor seek the opinion of others as a means of informing his opinion of himself. Many of the other males did not understand this, but they understood his expertise, his intelligence, and cold-eyed readiness to respond to the faintest of their challenges. What he might lack in charisma, he accrued in respect and regard, and that made him doubly valuable to Nezdeh as a potential lifemate.

She forced herself away from that thought and the daydreams of pleasure and joint dominion that inevitably followed, nodded at the plot instead. "It seems that we shall need to employ our contingency plan, given the enemy movement."

Brenlor's voice was a loud grumble of unwilling consent. "I suppose we must. I do not like separating into two forces."

"Nor do I, but our whole body may not advance without revealing our presence. The *Arbitrage*'s sensor profile is enormous, and our shift-tug's antimatter drive will show up on their instruments like a signal flare on a moonless night. But if we wait to move until the mission craft has landed on Turkh'saar, they may be able to conclude their operations before we can arrive. We must be there at the crucial moment, to rescue the Hkh'Rkh from potential enemy devastation, thereby placing the Old Families directly in debt to our House."

Brenlor nodded. "Agreed. If we do not achieve that, our ploy here will have failed. Only the unwavering support of the Hkh'Rkh will protect us against our own Autarchs, compel them to reaccept us as the price of securing a firm alliance with the Patrijuridicate." He leaned back. "I am decided. *Red Lurker* is the only craft with both sufficient stealth and combat capabilities to approach Turkh'saar and remain undetected until we may intervene." He gestured at the plot. "It is also the only hull which may hope to engage and defeat all these small craft. Our other ships would be more of a hindrance than a help."

Nezdeh nodded. "I concur. Before you and Idrem depart, I recommend—"

Brenlor straightened slightly. "Idrem is not coming on this mission. I shall take Tegrese Hreteyarkus as my executive officer. Ayana Tagawa will be the pilot. The rest of the crew will be drawn from the *Arbitrage*'s complement."

Nezdeh and Idrem exchanged glances, and from the look in his eye, she could tell that this, a policy matter rather than a tactical decision, could not be his fight. A challenge to Brenlor's prerogative as Srin, as House leader, had to come from his peer: the House's only surviving Srina. She stepped forward. "This is not as we decided, Brenlor."

"It is not as we *discussed*, Nezdeh. I made no

final decision when we considered the many possible scenarios months ago. I have given much thought to this matter since then, more often since we detected the in-shift of the Slaasriithi a week ago." He put his head back slightly. "It is imperative that I lead the mission, that the Hkh'Rkh know that they are indebted to me, personally, as the head of the resurgent House Perekmeres."

"None have debated that," Nezdeh conceded. *Although I would have, had it been possible.*

"Similarly," Brenlor continued, "Tegrese's geneline, that of the vassal-House Hreteyarkus, must also be amplified by deeds, which indebts the Hkh'Rkh to more of our genelines. We know that, like us, they think in terms of family and inherited obligations. So it is necessary that we spread the recognition of their indebtedness to include our other, subsidiary Houses."

"With respect, Brenlor, there is an even greater necessity."

"And what is that?"

"The success of the mission." She hated what she was about to say, wanted to send Brenlor off with Tegrese of House Hreteyarkus and keep Idrem uninvolved with this unpredictable mission, but Idrem himself had pointed out why he had to be the executive officer. And against the surging of the knot in her chest then, as now, she could not find a flaw in his logic. "Tegrese's skill set is focused on combat, as is yours. However, your executive officer must compliment, not *duplicate* your abilities, must have expertise in sensors, engineering, communications, astrogation." *To say nothing of subtler tactics and cool, level-headed judgment.* "And as we discussed, an Intendant cannot be your executive officer, cannot simply replace Tegrese in your crew equations. You cannot risk being the only Evolved on that ship. In the event that you should be incapacitated, you must not be the only person capable of exerting dominion and speaking for our House. And other than myself, Idrem is the only one of the remaining seven of us who possesses all these traits, and has proven himself in combat multiple times, besides."

Brenlor's face had darkened, despite his obvious attempts at controlling his flush response. His autonomous physiological control disciplines had never been very good, for much the same reason that he had been an indifferent student, particularly when it came to more complicated subjects. Patience and equanimity were not his fortes. "Tagawa is broadly capable, as well." His voice was more than a mutter, but barely so.

Nezdeh was careful to keep her tone respectful as she checkmated Brenlor. "Yes, but she is an Aboriginal. Surely you can't mean that you would abase yourself by soliciting her counsel?"

And so Brenlor was trapped; he had indirectly conceded that broad technical competencies were required on the mission, but could hardly propose resorting to an Aboriginal for command-grade advice. Nezdeh would have found it both gratifying and relaxing to breathe a sigh of relief, but she dared not even exhale, yet.

Brenlor glowered at her, then nodded. "I had considered sacrificing my pride for the good of the mission, but you are right; as the Progenitors' axiom has it, 'dominion cannot abide compromise.'" He straightened. "Idrem is with me, then. And the balance of the crew shall be from the *Arbitrage*."

Nezdeh slowly released her breath, did not glance at Idrem, tried hard not to mentally replay the conversation they had had almost a month ago in anticipation of this very moment. The conversation in which Idrem had taken her face in his hands—gently, surprisingly gently—and explained, "There must be a person on the bridge of *Red Lurker* who can challenge Brenlor's decisions effectively, to whom he is likely to listen. And he listens to me now." Then seeing the look on Nezdeh's face, Idrem had smiled, one of the few times she had ever seen him do so, and amended, "Well, most of the time."

In the present moment, Idrem was nodding. "Very well. I shall ready my gear and alert Kozakowski that we shall want the first crew assigned to *Red Lurker* for the mission." He glanced at the holoplot again. "I presume you will want to boost hard so long as we are still within the belt ourselves, and then coast under thermionic-assisted stealth as far in as we may."

"Correct," Brenlor agreed with a nod. "We have no reason to get too close to the enemy." He stared hard at the four green chevrons in the holoplot. "Yet."

Nezdeh stared at her empty, still-unmade bunk aboard the *Arbitrage*. The bunk from which she had risen when Brenlor had called from the bridge. From which Idrem had risen when she summoned him. And to which he would not return until *Red Lurker* had completed its mission.

The oddly musical door chime interrupted her reverie; the Breedmothers and Progenitors would have approved, no doubt. Reflection was only useful in considering new ways in which one might improve one's dominion. When focused on emotions, it could only be deleterious, a weakening of the absolute will to power and to self. "Enter," she ordered.

The crude Aboriginal hatch swung inward. Tegrese Hreteyarkus stalked into the room, stopped in front of the desk at which Nezdeh was working. "Nezdeh Srina Perekmeres, I come to speak to you frankly."

Nezdeh leaned back, considered Tegrese's tone and posture. Like Brenlor, she tended toward impulse rather than analysis, and was too rash to ever become politic. Nezdeh had wondered if she and Brenlor might become mates at some point, and it seemed that Brenlor had diffidently wondered the same thing for a while. But over the passing months Tegrese had shown no interest in such a union and Brenlor's disappointment had been as tepid as his interest. Perhaps he had possessed enough wisdom to realize that they were both too rash and willful to ever become a stable pairing.

Standing before Nezdeh's desk now, and chafing at the implicit subordinacy it underscored, Tegrese radiated a temper that was different from her typical fiery variety. She was cold and focused and prepared—but for what? "Be seated, Tegrese. And unless you have come to challenge me, you may dispense with formal titles and family names."

Tegrese's eyes wavered; she clearly had not expected so reasonable a response. Which led Nezdeh to wonder: *then what* did *she expect? And why?*

Tegrese sat, remained rigid, stared. "What do you have against me, Nezdeh?"

"Whatever prejudice you believe you have deduced, Tegrese, you are mistaken. What I hold against you this moment, though, is your apparent willingness to leap to unwarranted and insulting conclusions." She lowered her tone, made it less aggressive in order to temper the words she was about to speak. "You should have care both for your professional reputation and the limits of my patience, Tegrese Hreteyarkus."

"Then tell me why I am being excluded from the mission to Turkh'saar, Nezdeh."

Ah, now it was clear. And it was also clear that Brenlor had either spoken to her earlier about his intention to include her on the mission, or just before he and Idrem had departed in *Red Lurker*. Which was exactly why Brenlor remained a problematic leader: he acted without due consideration of how those actions would impact others in his command. "The decision was taken collectively," Nezdeh answered.

Neither Tegrese's rigidity nor stare altered. "Brenlor intended to make me his executive officer on this mission. But then he met with you and Idrem and now I am forced to remain here, nurse-maiding huscarles on the *Uzhmarek* and disciplining Aboriginal dolts." She leaned forward, her eyes brightening, her tone low and tense. "I did not join this desperate gamble to restore House Perekmeres only to be sequestered, safe in the rear, as a reserve womb. And I never thought I would have to explain that to a woman, certainly not a Srina renowned for her own boldness."

Nezdeh frowned as she spent a moment inspecting Tegrese's smooth oval face, a shape which was reprised by her eyes and her lips. Prior to the Extirpation of House Perekmeres, Nezdeh had always been careful before approving women for wet-work, or any field missions whatsoever. Frankly, the Breedmothers' galling axiom was usually true: greater power was to be cultivated—and wielded—from their positions of power within the walled precincts of the Hegemonies. While men went out and expended themselves in the perpetually internecine, and often pointless, strife between the many Houses of the Ktoran Sphere, and their fortunes rose and fell correspondingly, the power contests within their citadels invariably rewarded women's superior calculation and patience. In the field, men might give a few more orders than the women, but women ultimately held more strategic trump cards than men.

But Tegrese eschewed the wisdom of the Breed-mothers since her youngest years, and had risen to the call when she heard of Brenlor's quest to restore House Perekmeres and destroy House Shethkador in so doing. Nezdeh remembered her wide-eyed, impassioned rationale for inclusion in their piratical band. "If we do not succeed, our genelines are lost anyhow. If we triumph, we liberate all those of House Perekmeres who still remain. Desperate times call for desperate measures. What does my sex matter?" And who could disagree with the simple logic of that?

But Nezdeh could not share the actual reason that Tegrese was not shipping out on *Red Lurker*: she and Brenlor together were too rash to be trusted with such a delicate mission. Saying so would undermine Brenlor's authority, and Tegrese would no doubt report the implicit insult to him. "Brenlor's leadership must be bold, direct, aggressive," Nezdeh said crisply. "Consequently, we required an executive officer who is willing, even temperamentally disposed, to advise restraint, patience, and assessment. This mixture of personalities makes for the best combined leadership. Effective command is a balance of the traits of aggression and caution. You and Brenlor both excel at aggression—but then who was to provide the caution on this extremely sensitive mission?"

Nezdeh had meant Tegrese to hear the question rhetorically, but she didn't. "Ayana Tagawa is—"

"—Is an Aboriginal. She must remain in abject servitude. She cannot advise, nor exhort actions, from such a position. Besides, although she has both the skills and the caution that would make her suitable for the role you suggest, she is the Aboriginal whose loyalty I trust the least. So she is the one I am least willing to send on a mission that involves her own, under-evolved kind."

Tegrese folded her arms, sounded sullen. "If you feel she is such a risk, then why do you not rid yourself of her?"

Nezdeh raised her chin. "If I could, I would. But we cannot afford to lose her skills. Not at this point."

Tegrese displayed the other trait she had in common with Brenlor: stubbornness. Rather than admit that her objections had been refuted, she slid sideways into a new complaint. "So this is how we are rejecting the caution and self-neutering evasiveness of the Autarchs—by adopting their methods, by refusing bold action in favor of subterfuge, by refusing the blood-drenched sword for the shadow-hidden dagger?"

Nezdeh rose, silent and aloof, looked down at Tegrese for what she hoped were the longest ten seconds of her subordinate's life. Judging from the other woman's sudden need to shift position in her chair, Nezdeh felt it might have been. "You have the right to question if you are the target of prejudice." *Even though you do not have the right to an answer.*

"But if you question the judgment and orders of your superiors again, you will be executed. According to the Precepts of the Progenitors. Do you understand?"

Tegrese nodded, looked away. "I apologize, Srina Perekmeres. I did not intend to question your judgment or orders. But I do not understand why we have adopted these indirect tactics. When I first learned of the quest to restore our House, and then heard Brenlor speak, I believed that not just our goals, but our means of achieving them, were to be an act of defiance against the Autarchs, not a continuation of their conceits."

Rash woman. "Your thought is dangerously simplistic." Nezdeh glanced at the holographic mission clock on her desk; Idrem had only been gone an hour now, but it felt longer. Much longer. "We defy the Autarchs selectively. The deeper objective of our mission is not to unseat, but to embarrass the Autarchs of those Houses that called most ardently for Perekmeres' Extirpation. In so doing, we create an advantageous political climate for our old allies, that they might help us rise up once again.

"In contrast with your expectations, we pointedly do *not* want to irritate the Autarchs, or the Houses—yet. If we do, we will find ourselves on the brink of yet another internecine war, and if that occurs, we can be sure of their first action. They will decide that it is in their collective interest to exterminate us and so put aside those tensions along with our ashes." She paused to give her concluding sentence more emphasis, more finality. "If we press too hard, Tegrese, we shall bring about our own destruction." She turned her back on her subordinate, walked leisurely back to

her seat, and began scanning through the reports she
had been reviewing when the door chimed. "However,
that is not the point of this conversation. You wished
to know why you are not selected as the executive
officer for the mission with Brenlor. Now you have
your answer. Return to your duties."

Tegrese exited without a word.

Nezdeh looked up, saw what she longed to see,
and yet hated to see:

Idrem's half of their unmade bunk—but empty.

Chapter Thirteen

Tlerek Srin Shethkador's new first officer, Zharun Ptaalkepsos was announced to be passing the inner security check to the Srin's quarters just as he finished ordering his notes for the Reification contact that he had promised to the Autarchs a week ago. They were eager for news regarding the state of negotiations between the Aboriginal humans and the Arat Kur; Shethkador was loath to share it.

He also knew that Ptaalkepsos would, once again, have no pleasing developments to report. Hardly a surprise: having no official standing in the peace talks, Shethkador could do nothing more than communicate separately with the parties, attempting to sow discord and doubt between them by misrepresentation and intimation. However, the diplomats of both sides were evidently accomplished enough that they had proven mostly immune to such attempts at manipulation. The Arat Kur delegation had stopped replying to his messages at all; he could not even be sure they were receiving them.

The humans were led by a canny *krexyes* of an admiral-turned-diplomat named Vassily Sukhinin who had proven far more troublesome. He actually responded with leading questions of his own. And so Shethkador had determined that this bearish Aboriginal was attempting to gather data on Ktoran policy and strategy indirectly. No doubt the hoar-headed Russian had a team of intelligence personnel examining all their exchanges, trying to deduce what Shethkador had been trying to achieve with his queries and assertions, what useful misconceptions and presuppositions he was trying to inculcate in the Aboriginal leadership. The Srin now kept those exchanges quite brief. That did not make them any more useful, simply less likely to impart intelligence to the Terran enemy.

The entry chime sounded. Shethkador sighed, rose, stretched. "Enter."

Zharun Ptaalkepsos entered briskly. "Honored Srin, what is your bidding?"

"Have you decrypted the latest communiqués from our informers in the Terran Fleet?"

"I have."

"Summarize."

"Yes, Fearsome Srin. One of our agents in the enemy fleet came across a report indicating that an Aboriginal remote sensor may have detected the out-shift of the destroyer *Will Breaker* under the command of Olsirkos Shethkador'vah, thirteen weeks ago."

Shethkador prevented himself from starting. Was that truly possible? *Will Breaker* had not shifted until she was over fifty AU beyond Sigma Draconis's heliopause, too distant for Aboriginal sensors to detect such a relatively subtle anomaly. "Are you sure they were not simply projecting the point of shift, based upon *Will Breaker*'s preacceleration track?"

"I am certain, Dominant One. The report included exacting measurements of the neutrino bursts and gravitic distortion pulse in the precise location of *Will Breaker*'s shift. And at the precise time, as well."

Shethkador frowned. Could the humans have planted passive sensors out that far, to be able to detect an out-shift? Unlikely, although they had been in system for many months now. *Or could they have received the information from someone else—?* "Does the report identify the platform that collected these readings?"

"No, Fearsome Srin. And the delay between the time the readings would have been collected and the relative tardiness of the report is strange."

Yes, it is strange, unless the sensor readings were not collected by the Aboriginals at all, but by the meddlesome Dornaani Custodians. Who could easily have been far enough out in the system, or have sensors powerful enough, to detect and analyze the shift signature of *Will Breaker* as Olsirkos had taken her to observe and report on the apparent human incursion at Turkh'saar. And who might have delayed relaying the sensor readings to the humans. Or perhaps the humans received them immediately, but elected to hold them secret for some time, hoping that they would then fail to attract any special attention when included in routine reports. And if that was the case, then the Aboriginals were clearly aware of how deeply Ktoran collaborators had entwined themselves into the intelligence and communications apparatuses of their fleet.

Either way, this was not a complexity that Shethkador wished to bring before the Autarchs. They were impatient and disgruntled enough. Besides, until there was more concrete intelligence on the source of the Aboriginal sensor data, it did not warrant report.

Shethkador stood. "I am finished with you," he pronounced in the general direction of his first officer. "Now escort me to the Sensorium. I must confer with the Autarchs."

Chapter Fourteen

Caine Riordan studied the rapidly growing disk in the upper left hand quadrant of *Puller*'s main viewscreen. Hoping against hope, he asked the same question he'd been asking every hour for the past day. "Mr. Solsohn, update on Hkh'Rkh communications activity?"

"Nothing significant to report, Commodore. After that surge of high-power radio chatter during and after the attack we heard, they've gone pretty quiet. Certainly no commo meant for us. If your contact on Turkh'saar is trying to put out a welcome mat, I'm not hearing it, sir."

Riordan acknowledged the report. He'd had enough of quiet, both on the radio and on his ships, over the past thirty-four hours, particularly in contrast to the frenzy of activity that had surrounded their departure. To ensure command-grade presence on every craft, the members of Riordan's staff had been split up. Bannor Rulaine, Pandora Veriden, Christopher "Tygg" Robin, and Peter Wu were aboard Wedge One with the majority of the Cold Guard. They were set to make

the run dirtside behind *Puller*. Once in orbit, the last
two wedges were to remain on station while *Puller* and
Wedge One neutralized any Hkh'Rkh air defenses, and
then descended to mount a preliminary search for the
purported human raiders. Miles O'Garran had been
left in nominal oversight of Wedge Two, whereas Phil
Friel had been assigned to the not-quite-spec Wedge
Three. Friel had spent most of the journey trying to
figure our why that transport's MAP thrusters were
falling short of their impulse rating.

Puller had taken on Top Sergeant Matthew Fanny
and eight of the hardest cases among the Cold Guard
as a combination security/strike team. All were career
soldiers, most of whom should have been senior NCOs,
but had never managed to hold on to more than
two stripes for very long. Also, they had apparently
forgotten there was a life beyond the service, or had
completely turned their back on it.

Unfortunately, none of them had much in the way
of useful shipside skills. One—Lance Corporal Kather-
ine Somers—could perform routine sensor operations
in a pinch. But the others had nothing to do except
checking their gear and cleaning their weapons. There
was always make-work to assign, but Riordan had
reservations about that option; it kept enlisted ranks
busy, yes, but experienced ones like those on *Puller*
would simply roll their eyes at the "keep 'em busy"
ethos. Often, what was advisable for new recruits was
almost an insult to seasoned professionals.

So, instead, he had assigned double PT and furnished them with all available news reports of what
had happened since they entered their cryocells. They
still grumbled, of course, but never within his earshot.

Besides, grumbling was the true anthem of every military unit that had ever existed. And their current grumbling was simply aimless grousing about the food, the cramped quarters, and anything else that struck them as modestly annoying. It was, in summary, both a harmless and timeless bonding ritual.

Melissa Sleeman turned halfway in her couch. "Commodore, our current angle gives us some decent surface visuals."

"Thank you, Doctor. Show us the pretty pictures."

Sleeman complied. Turkh'saar magnified dramatically, its half-lit disk stretching from the top to the bottom of the main screen. Riordan noticed that there was some green and yellow mixed in with the equatorial brown. "Dr. Sleeman, have you been able to localize the source of the raiders' tactical comms?"

She nodded, picked up a screen-linked stylus that worked like a laser pointer. "Working with the other ships, we've confidently mapped the footprint from which the human radio traffic has emanated since we arrived." Her stylus pointed carefully to a band of green hills near the northern shore of the equatorial sea. "All of it came from this one-hundred-fifty-kilometer diameter circle."

Riordan stared at it. "Did the signal sources move within that circle?"

Sleeman checked her data. "Difficult to tell, but there is a suggestion that toward the end of their most recent attack, the transmission points were moving steadily east."

"Back-calculate the time of day when that was occurring."

Sleeman raised an eyebrow, turned to her panel,

tapped at the dynamic screen several times. "Sundown at that longitude, or just after."

Riordan nodded. "They were moving eastward into the dark after completing their attack."

Behind him, Solsohn's voice explicated the conjecture. "They were heading back to base. Meaning we're probably going to find them bunkered in someplace to the east of that transmission footprint."

Riordan nodded, raised his chin. "Mr. Tsaami?"

Karam answered over his shoulder. "Let me guess: you want to know if we can come in against rotation at high altitude to the west of the footprint. That way, we can descend over it as we cross over the terminator into the dark."

"Correct." Riordan stared at the globe in his holoplot, estimating. "Looks like our velocity is just about right for that trajectory."

"We'll need to kick out a little thrust to get beyond the western end of that landing track before the sky goes completely dark."

Riordan considered. More thrust now might be spotted this far out if the Hkh'Rkh still had some decent satellites watching the approaches to Turkh'saar. But if *Puller* began its descent any later, it would be a bright, moving object in the night sky. That meant anyone with an eyeball could potentially detect their intrusion. Riordan sighed. "Give us the delta-vee we need to keep our planetfall timed for early dusk in that part of the sky."

Tsaami nodded. As he made the announcement to strap in and expect a few minutes of thrust, Solsohn came alongside Riordan. "What's in those western extents, do you think?"

"Probably the Hkh'Rkh's primary settlements. Look at the debris in geosync over that spot. It's still more dense than any other point, despite almost two years of drift and attenuation. Also, the best analysis of the radio signals intercepted by *Shore-of-Stars* suggests that the raiders don't venture further west. It also suggests something about how far they're likely to be based from the areas they've struck. Certainly not more than a thousand klicks. Probably less than five hundred."

"Well, that narrows the search area some—but not a lot."

Riordan smiled. "Well, at least it's a start. Dr. Sleeman, have you completed the planetary summary?"

"Yes, Commodore. I confirm the gross astrophysical estimates collected by war-time Slaasriithi reconnaissance drones. Gravity is .96 gee, length of local day is 24.37 terrestrial hours, and length of local year is 153.15 local days. Turkh'saar's average temperature is 9.6 degrees centigrade, placing it at the cooler extremes of a garden-planet classification. It is heavily glaciated through to the edge of the subarctic, with year-round snowfields extending well toward the tropics. The equatorial regions, such as the area in which the raiders seem to be operating, are what climatologists label cool temperate. The local weather is moderated by prevailing warm air currents running in from the tidally energetic ocean, which evidently has relatively high salinity, probably because of halite freezeout that ultimately leaches down from the seawater permanently water bound up in the polar caps."

Solsohn shrugged. "Doesn't sound so bad if you bring a jacket."

Sleeman smiled faintly. "And if you're not dependent upon unshielded electronics."

"A flare star?"

Sleeman nodded. "Yes. The Slaasriithi measured peak REM intensities that would significantly erode lifespan. The planet has a strong magnetic field, which helps, but doesn't help us if we stay in orbit."

Riordan brought up the mission cumulative exposure statistics. "Our numbers don't look that high. Has there been a recent trough in stellar activity?"

"Possibly, but we don't have periodicity data on this star, except for the intervals between the flares that were strong enough for us to observe from Earth. Unfortunately, a lot of flare stars have almost constant, low-grade activity: a grumble of stellar irregularity. It only rises to a shriek—a flare—occasionally. But others are completely silent until they blurt out a coronal mass ejection. We're not sure which BD+56 2966 is, because we don't have sustained local observations to draw upon.

"However, it's reasonable to assume that it's been relatively quiet since we arrived in system. It's also reasonable to anticipate that will change."

"Which means it's also reasonable to anticipate that no matter how hardened our electronics are, we could lose some of them if we get unlucky."

"Yes, sir. Best way to preserve systems is to observe the same protocols you would for imminent tactical nuclear attack."

Solsohn sounded worried. "That means keeping most of our sensors in sleep mode until they're needed. That's going to make any Hkh'Rkh forces hard to detect and the human raiders harder to find."

Riordan nodded. "Harder to pinpoint, yes. But since

the raiders are still operating radios and helicopters, I think it means we can further shrink the search area."

Karam's smile was evident in his voice "Yeah, they must have learned the hard way that they need to keep their missions brief in order to minimize the risk of being airborne during a flare. Which means they have to live closer to their targets."

Riordan nodded. "Or they have a main base and a forward operating base. But even so, finding one will lead us to the other; none of the operating ranges will be too great."

Solsohn's eyes were unfocused as he did the mental math. "So what, about two hundred kilometers from the target? At most?"

"Sounds right," Riordan agreed. "About an hour to spin up and fly to target. About an hour for operations, including whatever spoils of war they're grabbing, then an hour home. And still, each attack means a three hour operation without sufficient hardening. They're rolling the dice every time."

"Sounds like a crappy environment for raiders or pirates," Karam commented, "since they traditionally hate risk even more than they love profit."

"I agree, but we don't have any more time for hypothesizing." Riordan stuck his hand in the holoplot, widened his fingers. The view expanded, showing their landing trajectory and its terminus at a spot on the planet soon to be swallowed by the creeping black tide of the terminator line. "Dr. Sleeman, anything else we should know about Turkh'saar?"

"It's got to be a hardship world. A shorter growing season due to the cold and the extreme axial tilt. If there are mineral resources, they are not evident;

most of the mountain ranges are half-buried under ice sheets. However, there is one area located somewhat to the south of the recent transmission footprint that is a distinct anomaly. It looks like it may have been heavily developed in the recent past."

"And now?"

"No radiant emissions, no sign of habitation. The remaining structures appear to be in advanced states of decay, but I will get better data as we descend; we will pass almost directly over it."

Riordan thought for a moment, then said, "Flight Officer Tsaami."

Karam's answering tone was invariably less jocular when Caine addressed him that way. "Commodore?"

"I want you to give that anomalous area a wider berth. Say, two hundred kilometers more than our current trajectory would give us."

"Very good, sir. To the north or the south?"

"South. An equatorial approach is easier and both puts us out over the ocean and further away from the western regions. Less likely to be spotted."

"We're going to have to perform a last-minute sidestep in order to hit the same landing zone, sir. That will require additional delta-vee."

"Understood. Do it. And Dr. Sleeman, send your findings to the other ships. And tell Wedge One to stay twenty kilometers behind and above us. When you're finished, I need you to add our gunnery relays to your panel's dynamic controls." He turned to Solsohn. "Major, you will now oversee remote platform operations." Caine sat down slowly, drew the straps across his torso. "As soon as you're ready, deploy our tacsats."

"All of them, sir?"

"Have to. Any lower and we won't be able to insert them into a stable orbit." Riordan looked at the landing telemetry, hoped against hope that Yaargraukh's voice might growl out of the speakers at this last possible moment. But this moment was no different from all the others Caine had spent listening for that message since entering the BD+56 2966 system: empty, expectant static of open channels. "Commence descent."

The equatorial sea rolled underneath them like a vast, ragged roadway of glinting blue-black. The glints diminished in size and number as, aftward, the sun sank swiftly down behind the curve of what Riordan had come to think of as Turkh'saar's western extents. As it did, the black arc of the terminator loomed closer in their forward view.

They had seen no ground lights nor detected any significant power emissions, staying well south of the northern plains in the hope that they would remain invisible to the suspected epicenter of Hkh'Rkh habitation. Likewise, there had been no challenges by radio, no radar sweeps. In short, the Hkh'Rkh seemed wholly unaware of the two closest human craft descending toward the atmosphere.

Until a wave of almost three-dozen missiles streaked upward at them.

Karam managed to sound bored. "Evasive, sir?"

Riordan stared at the rising red lines in the holoplot, measured the rapidly diminishing time and distance metrics glowing in the air beside them. "Not yet. Mr. Solsohn, patch the fire control for the Slaasriithi PIPs over to Dr. Sleeman's console and deploy them. Then activate the tacsats' image makers."

Karam's voice was slow, measured. "We could lose all of our orbital eyes, if we do that."

"Unavoidable. We have to draw off the first wave of missiles while the three Slaasriithi drones get into an intercept formation beneath us. Major, order Wedge One to climb away; they don't have our defensive capabilities. Dr. Sleeman, I need to know the moment the drones are available to commence point-defense fire against the Hkh'Rkh missiles. Main screen to ventral view."

The flattening curve of Turkh'saar was replaced by a flat expanse of the dark equatorial ocean below. Faint smoke trails crept upward. Two jinked sideways. A small, sharp flash and the trails ended at a point of final intersection.

"One tacsat gone, sir," Solsohn reported. "The remaining six are in enemy target lock. It looks like some of rearmost missiles are ignoring the image makers and pushing higher."

Which indicated that either their onboard or ground-based active arrays were no longer significantly distracted by the tacsats and were boosting toward the only other target on their scopes: *Puller*. "Major, undertake evasive actions with all remaining satellites. Let's wiggle the bait."

"Mimicking evasion protocols, Commodore." In the holoplot, the six remaining tacsats—cyan dots—began swerving in different directions. Perhaps a third of the missiles that had fixed upon *Puller* altered course to chase the newly enticing alternatives. But that left almost a score of missiles still on target.

Sleeman's announcement came out in a tense rush. "The Slaasriithi drones are now ready to engage, Commodore."

Riordan gauged the blood-red lines reaching up from the planet toward the tiny blue triangle that signified *Puller*. "Not yet, Doctor."

"Sir, we have them all in range."

"That's not my concern. When our Slaasriithi PIPs start burning them down, those missiles may shift their targeting to the drones themselves, if they can. We can't afford that; we need to keep our defensive shield, especially now that we know the enemy has a missile inventory."

Sleeman stared at the holoplot for a moment. "So you're going to wait until the missiles have committed to a course that makes it impossible for them to retarget on the drones when they open fire."

"That's why I'm hoping. And they should be reaching that point right about... now. Drones to PDF fire mode, Doctor, and engage."

The missiles had almost reached the lighter blue pinpricks of the three drones when they started winking away in twos and threes. The Slaasriithi PIP technology was, once again, startlingly swift and accurate. In the viewscreen, small blossoms of flame sparkled against the dark backdrop of Turkh'saar as they crossed the terminator.

Sleeman seemed to force herself to speak slowly. "All targets destroyed."

Riordan nodded, hid a smile. The only real civilian in his team, Melissa Sleeman was still not as accustomed to suppressing panic as the rest, but she was learning quickly. Hardly surprising; learning quickly was arguably the doctor's most outstanding talent.

Solsohn shook his head. "Lost all but one of the tacsats, sir."

Riordan realized he had been leaning forward throughout the engagement. "That's one more than I thought we'd have left. And if we leave it at this altitude, they'll probably try to hit it again. If they can."

Duncan frowned. "Sir, with respect, it certainly seems that they have demonstrated that capability."

"They have, but take a look at this." Riordan poked a finger into the tacplot, traced the red launch trajectories of the missiles to the surface of Turkh'saar. "They came from three sites arranged in an equilateral triangle around the anomalous area Dr. Sleeman detected."

Karam half-turned his head. "So you think they fired everything they had because they thought we were making a reconnaissance pass?"

"Possibly. Or these may be automated launchers. It's odd that the Hkh'Rkh didn't use these missiles against the Slaasriithi commerce raiders. Unless, that is, these particular missile batteries are part of a dedicated, autonomous defense network."

Sleeman nodded. "That's consistent with what looked like their swarm-intercept programming." She sniffed. "Pretty poor automation, if you ask me."

"Which is why the Slaasriithi PIP system knocked them all down so swiftly." Riordan stood. "Bow view." The mottled darkness of the night-side surface beneath them was replaced by an onrushing tableau of space, cut in half by a curved mass of lightless black: the planet occluding the stars behind it. "Major, send to Wedge One: we will be nosing down and crowding thrust for a steeper, faster descent. I also need you to find me a hiding spot for our one remaining tacsat."

"There's some junk big enough to hide it behind,

but that means we'll only have use of it twice a day. For two hours at a time."

"Understood. If you can, try to place it so that one of those two-hour intervals falls between midnight and dawn in our approximate landing zone. I want to be able to see well beyond the light of our campfires."

"And the Slaasriithi PIPs, sir?"

"Leave them deployed. Same orbit, same hiding among the debris. Space them evenly along that orbital track, if you can."

"That will give us access to only one drone at a time, and at very high orbit, sir."

"One at a time is better than complete gaps in our coverage. And if we need to regroup them, they've got decent thrusters. Assuming we have enough warning."

"Risky, sir."

Karam sounded impatient. "If you leave them any lower, Major, what makes you think that the Hkh'Rkh won't start taking potshots at them? If they do, and if they splash one, then we've got a coverage gap. Through which they'll probably launch a barrage at us when we're on the ground."

Solsohn leaned in the direction of the pilot. "Not sure I like your tone, Flight Officer."

"Not sure I care, sir—and I'm not sure I'm under you on the T.O.O."

Caine kept his tone crisp. "That's enough, Mr. Tsaami. You'll show Major Solsohn the same respect you show Major Rulaine."

Karam turned in his seat; his smile was like a hook waiting for bait. "I thought you'd want me to show him more respect than *that*, sir."

Riordan felt a grin trying to pull at the left corner

of his mouth. He turned to Solsohn. "Major, I'll task Mr. Tsaami to remember you're not part of our dysfunctional family."

Duncan nodded almost wistfully before adding, "Sir, besides the lost tacsats, something else bothers me about the engagement: how did they detect us? We weren't maneuvering, weren't broadcasting, weren't even sending lascoms anymore. And they never ran active sensors. So how the hell did they see us at all?"

Karam's tone was almost as dismissive as his one-shouldered shrug. "We dumped out a bunch of tacsats. Major."

"That was before our last burn, well before any long-range passive sensors could have detected us. And our own sensors never spotted any dirtside power generation consistent with that kind of orbital watchdog system."

This time, Karam gave no sign of discounting Solsohn's assertions.

Riordan nodded. "I don't like that mystery any better than you do, Major, but we can be sure of this: the Hkh'Rkh know we're here and where we're heading. So any chance of making an undetected planetfall is gone. Mr. Tsaami, take us down as quickly as our hulls can handle." He tightened his straps. "There's now a fuse burning on this op. Let's hope we can be back in orbit before it blows up in our faces."

PART TWO

May 2121

IGNORANCE

Timendi causa est nescire
(Ignorance is the cause of fear)

Chapter Fifteen

"May our chants speed your way to the Ancestral Host," hooted Jrekhalkar, "and may you be surrounded by banner-bearers on the Final Day of the Final Battle." He raised the shallow, double-handled funereal bowl, fashioned from the top of a *st'kraag's* domelike skull. "We drink your blood to carry your valor forward in our own veins, brother."

At which ritual pronouncement, Jrekhalkar dipped the end of his snout into the bowl and sucked deep. Yaargraukh, holding a simple mug, did the same, but was careful to take up only a modest amount of the *zhyzh'hakz*. This was not the time to let the dark blue syrup affect his thinking or behavior. The timing of this council was particularly unfortunate; tempers would be short, passions high, and veins afire with the musky stimulant. In ages past, *zhyzh'hakz* had been used before battle as a combat drug, albeit in more concentrated forms. Of course, in times before, they had also quaffed the actual blood of the deceased.

213

But ritual gatherings such as this were connected to another sacred tradition the Old Families still revered: to combine affairs of state with Family and clan rites, whether of Mate-making, Warrior-naming, or Pyre-burning. It hardly mattered which of these rituals preceded a meeting. The consumption of *zhyzh'hakz* and elevated emotional state of the attendees assured that bold claims and Challenges were more likely than wise words and decisions. And at this meeting there was a further complication: the mortally wounded father of the dead Warrior whom they honored.

That worthy sucked in long and hard at his own bowl, which was slightly less traditional: shaped like a cup, it was a drinking vessel for the young, the wounded, or the infirm. With one's snout dipped to the bottom, even a frail Hkh'Rkh could drink long and deep without much effort.

As the haggard head of O'akhdruh the Silent Voice rose up again, his eye folds were less wrinkled by the heavy bags that were one of the diagnostic precursors of death. The *zhyzh'hakz* was doing its work, restoring vitality briefly but probably hastening the former Voice's demise by an equal margin. Invigorating to a healthy Hkh'Rkh, *zhyzh'hakz* taxed the system of a badly injured one—and O'akhdruh's wounds were beyond the art or tools of the doctors on backward Turkh'saar.

However, the patriarch's damning glare was undimmed as, in its sweep of the room, it ran across Yaargraukh and those few other scions of the New Families who were in attendance. They were representatives of the upland rovers and Fringelanders who otherwise had no voice in the affairs of the colony, which was dominated by the Old Family clans that populated its towns.

Jrekhalkar's eyes followed his father's, narrowed. "If
you wish, I will clear the Clanhall of these—"

"No," O'akhdruh interrupted. "It is their right to
be here. Besides, I have need of information from the
former Advocate." He nodded solemnly at Yaargraukh.

Who knew, although the gesture was superficially
congenial, that the crippled and dying Silent Fist was
far more dangerous than his second, and only surviving, Scion.

Jrekhalkar's massive shoulders hunched at the word
"Advocate." "He came by his title naturally enough."
Rumbles of assent rose among the Old Family scions who
had gathered in response to Jrekhalkar's summons, his
first as both Fist and Voice of his Family on Turkh'saar.

But it was still O'akhdruh who commanded, clearly
vexed by Jrekhalkar's lack of instinct for his new, dual
role. Jrekhalkar had been a reasonably able Fist during the war-time absence of both his sire and older
brother, and had not taken the title Voice: whether out
of respect for his father or silent acknowledgement of
his own limitations was unknown.

But with his older brother Uzkekh'gar on his pyre,
and his sire soon to follow, he had no choice but to
take on both roles and lead his family. All his remaining siblings were females, and none of them had the
spirit and drive that the New Families encouraged in
their daughters. Not a one of them was a physician, or
a scribe, or a technologist; they had been bred to be
Mates and nothing else. And that was just what they
were: vessels for the sires of other Clans. It was fortunate that Jrekhalkar was large and personally fierce,
otherwise he could have anticipated many Challenges.
With him defeated, the entire moiety of his Clan and

Family on this planet would become the property of the victor, whose right to those gains would be easily solidified by Mate-making any of O'akhdruh's daughters.

The Silent Voice raised his long, scarred head to glance at his surviving son. "Well? Why do you tarry?"

Jrekhalkar's smaller-than-normal eyes flinched back into their folds before emerging again. "Sire, to what do you refer—?"

"You are Voice and Fist, now. Who is to call this council to order other than you?" The old Hkh'Rkh almost spat the words; a phlegmy warble of disappointment was loud in his snout.

Jrekhalkar stepped forward—*too fast, too anxious,* Yaargraukh observed—grabbed his clan's ceremonially-pennanted *halbardiche,* and rapped it down against the paving stones of the Clanhall three times. The gathered scions quieted, but their obedience did not radiate commensurate respect. The old Voice was too experienced and canny not to discern the council's reaction to his son's accession: decidedly underwhelmed. At best.

His son continued. "Scions, as Voice and Fist of the Family Srenshakh of the Moiety and Great Clan Gdar'khoom, I have called you to Council in the shadow of my brother's waiting Pyre. As embers, his body shall rise to join the stars. As smoke, his blood shall rise to join with that of Departed Heroes."

"He joins Departed Heroes," the gathering chorused in loud ritual affirmation, Yaargraukh's voice no less than the rest. Old Family or New, death in battle was death in battle. Or in this case, upon revivification: Uzkekh'gar's ghastly wounds, revealed when the lid of his hibernaculum rose up, had come as a terrible shock.

"But he needn't have joined them at all," Jrekhalkar

continued. "That was the result of human cruelty."
Jrekhalkar's eyes flicked over toward Yaargraukh.

Who thought, *Or was a consequence of their ignorance and our intransigence.* But to say so aloud would
seal his fate and whatever chance there was to end
the human raiding in the west and avert a potential
confrontation with Earth.

But it seemed that holding his tongue was not
enough. Z'gluurhek, a troublemaker since the day
he was whelped, spiked his crest provocatively. "Of
course, there are those who would make excuses for
the humans in this matter...as in most others." He
considered. "Well," he said, now looking directly at
Yaargraukh, "there is at least one."

Careful now. "I made no excuses nor accusations
in the matter of Uzkekh'gar's hibernaculum. I merely
pointed out inconsistencies."

Before wily O'akhdruh could interrupt—and thereby
prevent Yaargraukh from presenting evidence that
would reveal his son's overly dramatic accusation to
be irresponsible or even misleading—Z'gluurhek thrust
his head forward into the open circle that defined the
Council space. "What inconsistencies?"

"Inconsistencies in the human handling of our
hibernacula. It is true that there was no resuscitation
warning icon upon Uzkekh'gar's unit, although the
humans did mark it with our own sigil for indicating that the recipient had received some measure of
medical treatment. But from the reports I have read,
the humans also did not understand that our cardiosac
is a diffuse structure, rather than a single, coherent
organ such as their own heart. It is likely that they
believed their intervention had stabilized his condition

enough for routine treatment upon reanimation."

"And here is the professional human apologist at his labors once again," sneered Z'gluurhek. "Has no one told the Advocate of the Unhonored that he is their advocate no longer?"

"I am quite aware of that," Yaargraukh said quickly, to stifle any laughter that might make it necessary for him to respond to Z'gluurhek with a Challenge. "But I am also aware that my own hibernaculum—and that of our revered O'akhdruh—were both clearly marked as containing severely injured occupants who might require resuscitation when awakened. They also included passable attempts to describe the nature of our wounds in our own language. It would be strange for the humans to be so inconsistent in their handling of our wounded if they were, as you suggest, so determined to be cruel to all Hkh'Rkh. Indeed, if they meant to slay us without exception, how is it that I, and the Silent Voice, stand here at all?"

Almost in unison, the heads of the gathered scions turned slowly to where Jrekhalkar and O'akhdruh stood stolidly before the Uzkekh'gar's funeral bier. Conspicuous in the failure to do so were Z'gluurhek and several of his cronies, who stared at Yaargraukh as if they meant to attack him. And they probably would have, but for the proprieties imposed by both a funeral and Council.

O'akhdruh waited for Jrekhalkar to speak, but only for a moment. He clearly discerned that his second son was not up to the task of forming an effective response swiftly. The former-Voice's once-towering form buckled further under the paternal disappointment before he took the tack that Yaargraukh had anticipated. "Fine words . . . and many of them may be accurate. But this explanation does not bear upon the burning buildings and slaughtered Warriors of Ylogh, or upon the two human spacecraft—for whose else would they be?—which have landed just to the west of that shattered clancote. If there are tolerable, responsible humans somewhere in the reaches of space, that is of no matter to us in this place, at this time. We know the nature of the humans on Turkh'saar well enough; they are invaders, wanton destroyers with an insatiable appetite for inflicting misery wherever their cadaverous, blood-smeared fingers might touch." His eyes returned to Yaargraukh. "Do you deny *this*?"

Yaargraukh noted, from the corner of his eye, Z'gluurhek and his cronies edging forward, hands slightly raised, claws tilted up.

In all probability, Yaargraukh conjectured, his answer to O'akhdruh's pointed question would either be among the most artful of his career as a Warrior-diplomat or his last. He did not speak until he was sure that his voice was not merely calm, but casual. "I deny none of the things you have said about the humans, Revered O'akhdruh. But conversely, while I have seen the destruction the humans have caused, and it is grievous indeed, I think it hasty to presume that they are best understood as invaders. Specifically, I find it strange that the Terran Republic would send an assault force equipped from their museums."

O'akhdruh waved a silencing hand before Z'gluurhek could fumble out a reply. "I do not understand this. What do you mean, the humans are equipped from their own museums?"

"I apologize, eldest. I was unaware that you have yet to be briefed on the specifics of the humans' equipment and tactics. Specifically, the weapons and vehicles employed by the humans are illogical to the point of bafflement. If I may give you an example of—"

Jrekhalkar stepped forward. "You may not."

"He may," O'akhdruh countermanded irritably. "I require complete information if I am to make a sound decision. And as this decision shall be my last, I wish it to be prudent and well-remembered."

"My sire, your condition is not so grave that—"

O'akhdruh glared at Jrekhalkar. "Do not dishonor me or yourself with such fantasies. All gathered here know I cannot survive the week, probably not more than three days. The damage to my organs is too great. Had I been sent on to Rkh'yaa and its medical facilities, then, perhaps—" He shook his crest as if casting off a nagging parasite. "What is before us is all that matters. These humans are a grave threat, but I have no specific knowledge of the particulars or history of their operations. So I will hear what the former Advocate has to say of them. And be certain, Jrekhalkar, that I am not so enfeebled that I shall fail to separate partial truths or wishful thinking from the facts of Yaargraukh's report. Now, Yaargraukh Onvaarkhayn of the Moiety of Hsraluur, I bid you speak of the humans and their strange equipment, leaving out no pertinent detail."

Yaargraukh felt talons of wariness claw lightly at his bowel. This injunction to speak freely was a singularly fortuitous opportunity. Too fortuitous to be entirely safe. "I shall, Revered O'akhdruh, but the strangeness of their equipment and actions are but a hint to deeper contradictions in their presence and purpose."

"So you say. But I shall judge. Impart the facts, as you know them. Then I shall hear your hypotheses."

Chapter Sixteen

Duncan Solsohn glanced around the bridge again, not wholly accustomed to the communications panel on the UCS *Puller* and wondering if anyone else had noticed. Apparently not, since their eyes were all still fixed upon the main viewscreen and the lightless surface of Turkh'saar.

All except for Dr. Melissa Sleeman, who was leaning low over her sensors. Solsohn found her a bit intimidating. Not because of her personality—she was arguably the cheeriest of the group, and disarmingly open—but she was also that kind of scary genius who mastered just about every piece of technology at first touch.

By comparison, Karam Tsaami was, or at least affected the demeanor of, a wise-cracking cynic who also happened to be an extremely seasoned pilot. Engineer Tina Melah spent most of her time back in the drive section, but mounted occasional forays into the tiny crew lounge next to the head, always waylaying one or more of the Cold Guards to do something back-breaking or noxious involving the new engines. Initially disposed to grouse before complying, they had learned that behind Tina's ready smile was an easily irritated hellcat with the imperious rage of an older sister, annoyed to be left in charge of such lazy siblings. They had shaped up within the first three hours of the voyage and had even begun to express a gruff fondness for her when she wasn't around to hear.

Their behavior toward Riordan was, in contrast, respectful, careful, and uncertain, and Duncan had the impression that was exactly what the commodore had wanted. Whereas Caine was decidedly casual with his own team, he maintained a measure of formality and distance with the Cold Guard. His interactions with them were firm, frank, and scrupulously fair, but Solsohn couldn't exactly call them friendly. Not yet, anyway.

Duncan turned to look at Caine—who he discovered was already looking at him.

"Major Solsohn, we're descending through twenty-five kilometers altitude now. As we start nosing around for an LZ, I'm going to need fully encrypted lascom for terminal coordination with Wedge One, and for operational updates to the other ships. Constantly." He paused. "And I notice you're a big coffee drinker."

"I am, sir."

Riordan waited. "I also know that the after-effects of that habit can make it uncomfortable for you to, well, sit in one place for long periods of time. And from about ten kilometers onward, we'll be tied to our stations. That means I need your focus at one hundred and five percent from the second we start our approach until our fans are spinning down."

Duncan took the hint. "Thank you, sir. I think I'll hit the head."

Riordan smiled. "That sounds like an excellent idea. We'll be running a detailed passive sensor sweep, looking for our optimal landing point, so you've still got some time."

Rising into the mild, rearward force of the thrust, Duncan made his way through the bridge's aft-leading hatchway and past the commons room, where five of the security/strike team were lounging, sitting feet braced against bulkheads to ensure that their posteriors remained in their seats until they were sent to strap in.

He didn't expect them to rise, but still, their significations of respect were faint. Three of them nodded, the unofficial substitute for a salute during unpredictable maneuvers—which was not the present case. The other two murmured, didn't even look up.

He continued on without pausing. This was neither the time, nor the place, to snap them up by their short hairs and dress them down. But the real problem was that it probably wouldn't do much good, because he'd started out too informal and too solicitous. And damned if he probably wouldn't make the same mistake all over again. He'd personally thawed out all fifty-six members of the Cold Guard, had seen what they were going through. Not only was it physically debilitating, but they were returning to a world in which they were fundamentally alone. So Duncan Solsohn had offered a helping hand and a friendly face—and that had been his fatal mistake.

Solsohn reached the head, opened the diminutive hatch, frowned at his situation as much as at the cramped space and poorly repaired walls. *Hell, in what kind of screwed up reality do you lose respect because you were kind to a bunch of sick soldiers who've been given a shitty job by a distant homeworld that doesn't remember their existence except as serial numbers?* The answer came at him in a rush: *in any reality where you always have to project strength and superiority. It's stupid, unwashed, primate bullshit, but in the military and particularly in the field, everything boils down to that. You were too damned civilized; you were too busy trying to be their friend to realize that even when they are as sick as dogs—or maybe especially then—you have to be their leader first.*

There was something bitterly ironic about having these revelations in the head. About seeing how the Southern-inflected congeniality and easy affability he had learned at his deceased parents' knees, and which had helped him ascend the ladder at the Agency, had given him exactly the wrong instincts for dealing with this scenario. Which only went to prove that, no matter where you were or what you did or how carefully you planned, some mistakes were just out there waiting to be made. It reminded him of what a pararescue jumper had told him as they were inserting into a then-disputed part of Asia Minor: it's not what you don't know that will punch your ticket; it's what *you don't know* you don't know. Ironically, she was the only person who had ever been killed on one of his field ops for IRIS—and she never saw it coming.

Just as Duncan sealed the small hatch behind him, he heard his name, muffled by the non-bulkhead wall separating the head from the crew commons. "—Solsohn hasn't. I mean, he may have been shot at and shot back, but he's never served. Not with a unit. He's cupcake, man." The voice was that of Baker, whose legal first name had been changed to "Two-Gun" some years back. Baker wasn't a bad guy, but he was the most mouthy of the Cold Guard and had proven to be touchy about inquiries into his original given name. *And now I get to listen to his unfiltered opinion of me; just great.*

But Baker wasn't the only ward-room pundit, apparently. "Yeah," agreed another, "Solsohn's still in the wrapper. But the new guy, the commodore, he's harder to figure." The speaker was York, a private who'd never managed to hang on to even one extra stripe. Although he gave his *nom de guerre* as Sundog, Duncan had seen his dossier and knew that his improbable legal name was Yehuda ben York. He was reputedly excellent on the battlefield, but not so good at getting back to base at the end of his leave. He frequently missed that deadline by days, not just hours.

Charles "Chucky" Martell, the heavy weapons specialist from Force Recon, answered in a broad, urban drawl. "Oh, no, the new CO's a very diffren' story, allgens. A very diffren' story. He has looked the gator in its eyes. Got the 'follerme' in his own. Quiet, like some officers do. The good ones, I mean."

A few muted chuckles, cut through by a sharp, disagreeable voice; it was Bettina Fajari, the youngest of the bunch, the best educated, and attached to a dossier that had more entries redacted than present. "So why are you such a fan of our Fearless Commodore Whatsisname, Martell? No one's ever heard his name before. And it's not like he's been able to tell us about any astounding naval accomplishments."

"Not like he's allowed to tell us much of anything,

it seems." That was Katie Somers. She was as sharp as she was preemptively watchful—and resentful—about being teased for her Scots-trademark fire-red hair.

Baker sounded perplexed. "Huh? Whaddya mean?"

"Donna Gaudet let me play around in the computer updates. Riordan's in the database. First listed as Navy only a few months before the war."

"And he's a commodore now?"

"Aye, an' that's my point, eh? An' there's this, too: he commissioned at Lieutenant Commander. On the same day and at the same base where the Arat Kur started the war." The wall creaked as, apparently, Somers leaned back against it. "This fella's like Solsohn: a spook. Nae doot of it."

"Yeah," agreed York, "but Riordan is a spook who totally fell off the grid. Until he popped up again in Delta Pavonis, just before we got shipped out. And it seems he knows these aliens—"

"Exosapients," Fajari corrected.

"Yeah, whatever—he knows the *aliens* who brought us out here. Scuttlebutt is he was in the shit with them."

"Yeah?" Fajari's voice was an annoyed challenge. "Where and against whom?"

Sundog York was getting impatient. "If I had that info, I'd have shared up front. But I will tell you what: the CO has some graveyard hombres behind him. That Special Forces major, Rulaine? He is serious shit, allgens, serious shit."

"A bunch of 'em are." Two-Gun Baker's voice cheated down a decibel. "That little SEAL chief? He's got those smile-as-I-choke-you eyes. Like my DI at Paris Island. Except I don't think I've ever seen a DI—or a SEAL—that small."

Chucky Martell's response was slow, sagacious, amused. "Well, if he's anything like the top who busted *my* ass at Paris Island, you better not let him hear you talking dat shit."

Steps in the corridor, then a new voice intruded: Bernardo de los Reyes, the Ranger career-corporal whom everyone just called Bear. "So, you're not fans of the new bosses, huh?"

Katie Somers sounded evasive. "Well—they're like to be pretty hard on us."

De los Reyes sounded like he was smiling. "Just us?"

Chucky Martell's question was careful. "Whatchoo mean, Bear?"

"I mean, yeah, so some of the commodore's crew are hardcore. But they're hardcore professional. And I want hardcore when I'm heading into the shit."

There was silence, a few mumbles that usually went along with nods, in Solsohn's observation of this group.

"That scans, sib," murmured York.

"I guess I can live with it," Fajari muttered.

"Hell, you may live *because* of it," Bear muttered back. "Now get your gear taped and wires checked. They're saying this is going to be a soft op, but I'll believe that when we're back on these boats, outbound."

"Amen, sib," agreed Martell.

Duncan's collarcom paged: a long, low tone, one that would not carry through the thin wall. Probably. The carrier tone in his earbud was abruptly replaced by Sergeant Fanny's voice, toneless but clipped. "Corporal de los Reyes and Private Martell, report to the bridge. Before we hit dirt, the CO wants a full brief on nonstandard ToE elements, and he wants it ten minutes ago."

De los Reyes's voice was just as uninflected as he responded, which Duncan heard both in his earbud and muffled through the wall: "On our way. Out."

The modular chairs in the crew commons squeaked and screeched as bodies pushed out of them. "This is always how it starts," Fajari complained loudly. "The first sign that your CO is an armchair general is when they start bean-counting. Particularly when it comes to how many prophotabs we've got left."

"Why that?" York asked.

Fajari triumphantly sprang her sardonic quip-trap. "Because he wants to know how soon he can fuck us over."

Martell's voice was quick and a bit dark. "Word to the wise, wiseass: if you don't stow that, I 'spect the CO or that little chief will stow it for you."

"Why? You gonna report me?"

"No, but someone will. And we don't know how this ship is rigged for sound, do we, sib?"

An extended silence followed. Duncan could imagine all of them, but particularly Bettina Fajari, staring around the commons with worried eyes.

"Besides," de los Reyes said, his voice already starting to recede toward the bridge. "The CO's got good reason to see how the standard table of equipment squares with what we actually have on hand. The Rag Tag Fleet picked over a lot of the gear when they were outfitting the reinvasion force. Left everything in a mess, too; word from the wedges is that they've spent the trip out here sorting through it. So, even though the commodore is a navy puke—er, officer, he's smart enough to know that since we don't have our standard load-outs anymore, we're gonna have to reshuffle what we've still got."

There were pronounced, if muted, kissing noises.

"Fajari, stow that crap or *you'll* be kissing *my* ass just to make sure I don't permanently put you on point or make you our designated door-kicker. That scan?"

"Scanned, Corporal. Sorry."

If de los Reyes made any reply, Duncan didn't hear it. He smiled to imagine Fajari's nervous agitation— right before his earbud came alive again, but this time, with the subtler hum of a private channel. Riordan's voice was very quiet, for comparative privacy. "Mr. Solsohn, at your earliest convenience, we need you on the bridge."

"Yes, sir," Duncan replied, resealing his duty suit. "On my way."

Chapter Seventeen

Solsohn was just behind the others as they entered the bridge. Riordan, inspecting the sensor data scrolling alongside the holoplot, waved them toward the acceleration couches which were fixed in the upright position. Sergeant Fanny remained standing beside him, tilted into the lateral quarter-gee at a sharp angle, a dataslate cradled in the crook of his left arm.

Once they were belted in, Riordan turned away from the holoplot. "Corporal de los Reyes, you're here because, from what I've seen, the troops don't give you much trouble and their ears perk up when you pass the word. So you will acquaint the Cold Guard's rank and file with the challenges we might face as a result of our nonstandard ToE."

"Sir, yes, sir."

"Private Martell, you're to do the same thing."

"Me, sir? I'm not what you'd call an authority figure—"

"Not by your rank, perhaps, but certainly by reputation. Scuttlebutt says that in your old units, you had a knack for keeping spirits up and in-fighting low. I'm counting on you to be this unit's social glue. And from what little I've observed, you're already beginning to fill that role."

Martell tried very hard to keep his eyes from widening in surprise. "Well, sir—no reason for folks not to be friendly. But that jus' comes natural. I'm not really needed at a special meeting about—"

"Private, the more you know about our state of play—where we're well-equipped and where we are substandard—the more authoritative you can be in shaping opinion and reaction among the troops. And since none of them could have anticipated a mission like this when they entered cryosleep, there could be a reflex toward anxiety and rumors—the kind that lowers morale. You're here to get information that will assist you in knocking down those rumors with hard facts."

And to let all those enlisted personnel know that Martell has some pull with the CO, which also makes his job easier—but also pushes him out of the sibhood of being "just another grunt." Which could make him uncomfortable, too . . . Riordan waited for Martell to mount another respectful protest, but the private nodded slowly, somberly.

Riordan turned to Matt Fanny. "Top, tell us what we're facing in terms of changes to the individual load-outs, then work up the line: squad, section, platoon-level shortages or overages."

"Yes, sir. Individual changes mostly involve commo and wearables. Armament is still the same: eight-millimeter CoBro liquimix modular assault system, currently configured as battle rifles and squad support weapons. Only two ten-millimeter Remington M167s, though."

"Configured as assault guns or sniper systems?"

"Currently as assault guns, Commodore."

"Swap 'em to sniper rifles."

"Sir, you might want to wait until you hear about our heavy weapons mix, and if—"

"Your concern is duly noted, Sergeant, but I'm guessing that the Remington 'longs' are the only option we have for reliably lethal three-kilometer accuracy. Am I correct?"

"Yes, sir."

"Then my order stands. I need those configured as sniper systems. Next item."

"Yes, sir. Our electronics are a bit old school. I'm guessing they didn't want to risk broadcast comms or less hardened electronics when they were facing off against the Arat Kur on Earth. So the Relief Fleet's quartermasters grabbed most of the personal lascom rigs. We only have enough for NCOs and officers. Less, if we're going to set any aside for your command staff."

"My staff will need at least six."

"Then we'll be tight, sir. Very."

"With any luck at all, we will not be highly dispersed. However, if it turns out we need to cover more ground, I'll make sure that at least half of my command staff is embedded with your squads. Their sets will function as command relays for the units they've been assigned to. How are we on encryption tech?"

"Fine, and more than we can use when it comes to electronic warfare. I guess the brass presumed we'd be so outclassed by the Arat Kur that they didn't bother to lug more than a third of it back home."

Duncan shrugged. "Actually, that could be a lucky break. Our postwar tech intelligence indicates that we have as much of an edge on the Hkh'Rkh as the Arat Kur had on us. Our broadcast comms should be almost as safe as lascom—but no reason to give them a lot of signals to analyze until we have to. So we stick with lascom until they can't support the traffic or the line of sight is compromised. That's when we shift to encrypted broadcast."

Riordan nodded. "Fine. Back to personal weapons. Do we have enough rocket-assisted projectiles for the underslung tubes on the CoBros?"

"We have lots of RAPs, sir, but not enough of the ones we need. We're light on both the antipersonnel and the dual-purpose warheads. We have only a few of the antiarmor stik-RAPs."

Riordan nodded. "Makes sense. That's what the counterinvasion force would take to maximize its hitting power. What about flechettes and suppressives?"

"We have a normal draw of flechettes, sir. You could shoot gas rounds all day and not run out."

De los Reyes's grin had no humor in it. "Guess they weren't planning to use crowd control tactics against the invaders."

Riordan matched his grin. "Guess not. What else, Fanny?"

"We have no external armor shells for our duty suits, sir, and we're short on ballistic liners. From the specs in your database on the Hkh'Rkh personal weapons, I don't know how much good they're going to do our people in a firefight, particularly at close range."

"Agreed, but they could still make the difference when it comes to shrapnel and fragmentation grenades. What about night vision?"

Fanny shook his head. "Goggles, not visors. Another pain, sir."

Riordan leaned toward the inventory entry at which Fanny was pointing. "At least they're combo goggles: light intensification and thermal, both. But no eye-triggered designators."

"Nope, sir. Older American and Aussie models. As with everything else, they left us the stuff about to be redesignated for the reserves or decommissioned. Even when it comes to the juice bottles for the guns."

Martell sat up a bit. "Don' mean to interrupt, sir, but what's wrong with the juice? The allgens are gonna wanta know if they can't shoot as hard or far as they're used to."

Solsohn explained before Fanny could pull up the relevant notes. "It's the same juice that you remember, Martell. But that means it's already being decommed from front-line service. Just after you hit the cryo-pods, they managed to make a slightly better liquid propellant. The Relief Fleet snapped all of that up."

Riordan nodded at Fanny. "Anything else, Sergeant?"

"Special and support equipment, sir. All of us were trained to make drops, but we don't have any parapods. Oddly, we do have enough heavy weapons. Twice the normal issue of MULTI rocket launchers, probably because they were too heavy to drop."

Riordan frowned. "Possibly, but I suspect there were tactical considerations, also. MULTIs are good in the direct-fire role, but they're really designed for indirect fire. So they usually set up behind the lines.

Not right for the highly mobile operations which the counterinvasion force had to anticipate. So, conversely, I suspect they didn't leave us many autonomous systems."

"Correct, sir. They snapped up all the latest lascom relay and control microbots. We have a reasonable number of broadcast quadrotors and creepers, but only a few of the larger, dual-commed hover-drones."

"What about armed RoVs?"

"Just one anthrobot, a Proxie. And that's a training frame, so it's beat to hell."

Martell leaned back. "Allgens not gonna be too happy to hear that, either. RoVs and anthrobots take a lot of fire that would otherwise be aimed at us."

Riordan frowned. "Not a thing we can do about it, Private. Besides, ROVs, drone weapon platforms, Proxies: they all require a lot of combat support elements, rear-area C4I and full-body InPic control bubbles. We don't have any of those."

"So we can't even use the Proxie, sir?" It was the first time de los Reyes sounded worried.

"I don't see how, Corporal. We don't have a remote-operator rig."

Duncan glanced up. "Commodore, I might be able to cobble one together."

Riordan raised one eyebrow. "How?"

"By converting this ship's full-body gunnery inter-face."

Karam Tsaami had evidently been listening to the conversation. "Major, with all due respect, I don't want to have this hull's primary weapons offline so that you can drive a tactical anthrobot around. Not while we're in a potential ship-to-ship combat zone."

"*Puller*'s primary weapons wouldn't be offline. They

just wouldn't be controlled by a gunner in the interface globe. Primary fire direction would come from the bridge's gunnery station, just like in the landers."

"Major, those landers only have to control ground support weapons. *Puller* has the only real battery weapons, so if we wind up tangling with—"

"Officer Tsaami, I'm right with you: if we have to tangle with another ship or spaceside drones, we yank the Proxie controller out and the gunnery globe is restored to being the primary interface for *Puller's* weapons."

Riordan nodded. "Sounds good in concept. But how do you make it work?"

"Well, sir, I've put together a similar system. Last time, I had to adapt a remote gunnery globe stored in the bay of a drop shuttle. If I could make that damn kludge work, I can sure as hell manage it here."

De los Reyes's voice was slow, as if grudgingly intrigued. "Where did you get the tech training for that, sir?"

"They sent me to Coronado."

De los Reyes's eyes opened very wide. "Wait. You were trained as an *operator* . . . sir?"

"That and field tech for the system."

Riordan felt his other eyebrow rise. "How many hours as an operator?"

Solsohn looked away, seemed to be running through mental math. "About twenty-five in actual field ops, sir. Probably about ninety training and refresher."

Riordan glanced up at Fanny. "How's that compare with your best operator?"

"Actually we only have one person qualified for Proxie ops: Graceless Grace Obajou. She's got six

hours in live-fire exercises, about a dozen live training, about forty in the simulator."

"Combat experience?"

"None, sir. We haven't had a shooting war in a
long time."

Caine let a smile emerge. "Looks like you're going to
be wearing the sensuit in the gunnery globe, Duncan."

Solsohn managed not to stammer. "Sir, with all due
respect, I belong in the field. Personally."

Riordan shook his head. "Your desire to lead from
the front and in the flesh is noted and appreciated—"

—a point which was also noted and appreciated by
de los Reyes and Martell, evidently—

"—but the bottom line is that, if we have to mount
ground operations, our one Proxie is too crucial a
resource to put in any hands other than those of
our best operator: you." Riordan nodded to the three
enlisted men around him as he reached for his couch's
restraints. "Dismissed. We'll be nosing down into our
final descent soon. So get on lascom to update the
people you trust on the other wedges and then strap
in. We can't be sure of what kind of reception we're
going to get."

Chapter Eighteen

Riordan turned toward the screen as the enlisted men filed off the bridge and Solsohn resumed his station. With any luck, the Cold Guard's opinion-leaders would now have a greater appreciation for Solsohn as their immediate commander and would spread that impression, along with what to expect about equipment shortages and how that might affect operations. *Which could be commencing any minute now, depending upon what the passive sensors are telling Melissa about the situation on the ground.* "Mr. Tsaami, what are our landing options?"

"Spoiled for choice, sir. Got a lot of suitable clearings, decent cover in about half. I just need the Doc to tell me where we won't run into the locals."

Riordan nodded. "Dr. Sleeman, what's looking good?"

Melissa Sleeman was frowning. "I wish I knew. There's unusual activity down there."

"Show me on the main screen."

Sleeman complied; a topographical rendering popped up, with darker splotches indicating woods of some kind, and small lakes scattered liberally throughout the region. Yellow markers were crowded into two main clusters: one small and dense to the north, one large and diffuse to the southwest. The latter was configured as two parts: a thin, ragged bow wave moving generally northward in front of a curved blob of larger trailing icons. They were all angling in the direction of the tighter, smaller cluster to the north. "Are those vehicle or individual biosigns, Dr. Sleeman?"

"A mix, sir. The triangles are individual vehicles. The circles are groupings of individuals. The larger the circle, the larger the group. The specks are individuals at considerable distance from any others."

"So what we're looking at is a wide sweep of vehicles moving up from the southwest. Different kinds of vehicles, too. Judging from the variation in heat signatures and size, it looks like the leading vehicles are smaller, lighter."

"That is correct, sir. And before you ask, I've tried to get a visual on LI. Nothing usable. Most of them are moving under the cover of light vegetation."

"No surprise, Doctor. Any Hkh'Rkh near a radio has probably been warned about our planetfall and death-dance with their missiles."

"Then, if they already know we're here, would it do any harm to try to contact them, Commodore?"

"Doctor, our OpOrd is very clear. Even if we are detected making planetfall, we wait for communications to be initiated by Yaargraukh or some other Hkh'Rkh official."

"But maybe, if we communicated with those nearby to reassure them that—"

"Dr. Sleeman, we have not been invited here. Yes,

we're trying to clean up an apparently human-made problem, but we don't have the Patrijuridicate's permission to do so, or even enter their space. In short, they are within their rights to declare our intrusion an act of war. But there's also the chance that we might unwittingly establish contact with a renegade group of Hkh'Rkh: New Family outcasts, let's say. That would open the door to accusations that we were willfully interfering with the sovereignty of the Hkh'Rkh Patrijuridicate and inciting rebellion against it.

"So, unless we receive permission from Yaargraukh or some other Hkh'Rkh official who has been given the authority to interact with us to help solve their 'human problem,' our sole job is to extract any humans that are on Turkh'saar, along with their matériel. Quickly."

Melissa Sleeman's frown seemed to bend her entire face downward. Her precise Anglo-American accent broke for a moment, slid into a Temne and Indonesian sing-song rhythm. "This is a very shitty job."

"No argument, Doctor. Now, if I am reading your results correctly, those faint biosigns out in front of the lead vehicles look like individuals on foot: advanced scouts or a skirmish line."

"Maybe both," Solsohn suggested.

"Could be," Riordan agreed. "Doctor, I'm having a harder time making out the signatures to the north."

"That's because they're more tightly clustered, Commodore. It's very hard to separate them. I think some vehicles are there, too, but I suspect that they are not operating currently, so their heat signatures are residual. Probably not much above the biosigns that look like individuals dismounting and reentering them intermittently. And you should also see this."

The image seemed to plummet away from them as a zoom-out expanded the ground scale by an order of magnitude. At the far eastern edge, there were a few spots that were brighter than the pinpricks of local wildlife which dusted the entire sensor map. Riordan leaned forward. "What do you see when you zoom in on that easternmost clump of signatures, Doctor?"

"Hard to say. They appear and disappear without warning. Here. Take a look."

The map recentered to the area in question, then zoomed in to the earlier, more intimate scale. Within the first five seconds of observation, one of the regularly spaced signatures moved slightly—and then vanished. "There. That's what I mean."

Riordan was pretty sure he knew what he had just seen. The stare exchanged by Solsohn and Tsaami confirmed it. "I believe we are looking at perimeter guards, moving in and out of underground positions of some sort."

"You can be sure of it, sir," Duncan muttered. "I've seen that kind of sensor return plenty of times during prisoner rescue or exfiltration ops. But I don't think it's a perimeter post. Not exactly."

Riordan squinted, nodded. "You're right. Those outposts are not protecting a central position. They're just following a slightly bent frontage."

Karam nodded. "Because they're guarding a large underground facility located behind them."

Duncan sounded impressed. "Yeah. How'd you know?"

"Lissen, Major, I've been the airborne wheel man for more than a few getaways in my time. Every time I saw that kind of deployment without any discernible rear security, our folks ran into a subterranean facility. Which usually meant more body bags."

"Both observations duly noted." Riordan kept his increased concern out of his voice. "However, we can't be sure that any of that activity is military, or that any of it is ours. Or theirs."

"In short, we don't know squat."

"Correct, Flight Officer."

"Yeah, but we've still got to land someplace, and we are now descending through the three-thousand-meter mark. At two thousand, I'm going to be losing airspeed because I've got to starting edging the fans upward into vertical mode for landing. I'll need an LZ site selection by one thousand if we don't want to start zigzagging around a potentially hostile countryside."

"Understood. Dr. Sleeman, can you get any better definition on the mass or temperature of the biosigns in our target area?"

"No, sir. The low power passive sensors are not capable of that resolution from this altitude. Besides, differences in clothing, thermoflage, and exertion levels could all compromise our ability to distinguish humans from other biosigns, if that was your intent."

"It was. Any sign of roads?"

"Not here. We passed over what look like dirt roads well back to the west. All the vehicles below us must be designed for cross-country driving."

"Buildings?"

Sleeman shook her head. "I'd have to ask Karam to go higher again to be sure, but certainly no substantial construction."

"Unless you really want to call attention to us, sir," Tsaami added, "I don't recommend boosting back up."

"Agreed. Besides, according to the self-reference they gave us at the Convocation two years ago, the Hkh'Rkh rarely construct buildings except in larger communities. They're ground dwellers."

Duncan looked up. "Really? I though it was the Arat Kur who were the diggers."

"They are, and seriously so; they're fully subterranean. The Hkh'Rkh are descended from open plains creatures, but prefer living in burrows."

Karam's tone was grim. "For a moment, I thought you said they live in barrows."

Solsohn's answer was equally sardonic. "Could work out that way for an attacker."

Caine adjusted his straps. "Enough gallows humor. Sensors are not showing us a clearly superior LZ. So we've got to go with our best guess."

"Which is what, Skipper?" asked Tsaami.

"Which is that the two rough lines approaching from the south are laid out in the shape of raiding or search teams, closing in on the smaller, denser cluster to the north. I'm guessing that is more likely to be the humans, with the Hkh'Rkh trying to quietly close in on them—or just find them."

"Or," countered Sleeman, "the vehicles to the south are being used by the humans and they're creeping up on a small Hkh'Rkh community to the north."

"Entirely possible. But that northern cluster is in pretty tight formation. Even in urban areas, groups don't clump up that tightly without more gradual diffusion at the edges. They're ganged up like that for a reason, whatever it is."

Karam, still watching his instruments and smaller bowcam monitor, nodded. "So what do we do, boss? Go to the one further to the north?"

"Yes, but not directly. You're going to skirt all these blips by sweeping around here"—Riordan swept his own interactive stylus at the map; it drew a bright red line that stuck to the left side of the display until it reached the top and then angled sharply to the right—"so that we can come in behind the compact group by landing even further to the north. I don't want to get in between any of the clusters. That would be a great way to scare or piss off everyone in the neighborhood."

"And once we're in that position?"

"Well, by then, our sensors should have given us results we can act upon."

Sleeman's voice was quiet. "And what if we discover that what we've been watching is humans creeping up on a Hkh'Rkh town, about to attack them?"

"That doesn't change anything, Doctor. We're here to remove our people. But until we know what they've been doing here, the jury is out on how gently we do that. However, since we don't know who's who down there, our immediate objective is to prevent conflict, no matter who's trying to bring it to whom." He pulled his straps tighter. "Altitude, Mr. Tsaami?"

"Five hundred fifty meters, sir. I've got your LZ locked in. Ready to go nap of the earth when you call for it. We can approach on low fans the last four kilometers, to keep us as quiet as possible."

"Excellent. Mr. Solsohn, just in case, have our strikers report to the ventral bay."

"Will do, sir. Anything else?"

"Yes, Duncan. You are on gunnery. And you are weapons free."

"Weapons free, sir? We don't even have a target, yet."

"And hopefully, we never will." Riordan jutted his chin at the screen. "On the other hand, judging from all those sensor returns, we might have hundreds of them. So until we know...weapons free, Mr. Solsohn. Mr. Tsaami, take us in."

Chapter Nineteen

Silent Voice gestured Yaargraukh forward into the circle, who kept his head bowed as he complied, thereby signifying that he was not putting his words up to the proof of a Challenge, but was responding to the request of the convenor of the Council to make a report to all its members.

Yaargraukh began without the customary salutations and preamble. "Half a year ago, just months after our hibernacula were returned from Earth, strange reports began filtering in from Turkh'saar's far northeastern Fringelands. Several rovers disappeared without a trace in the same week a dencote was found abandoned and rifled. The reports were brought here to the Clanhall. The events were deemed to be related. It was conjectured that a few of the missing rovers had gone rogue, possibly after killing the others in a dispute, and had resorted to living Out-Law and raiding. Your son Jrekhalkar took the prudent step of recruiting several Warders from among the ranks of the local families, who were sent to investigate the matter and locate the missing rovers.

"They did not find any Hkh'Rkh living Out-Law, nor did they discover any trace of the rovers. However, they did hear rotary-wing vehicles in the far distance on several occasions. Since none remained in the colony after the Slaasriithi raids targeted all our aerial vehicles from orbit, it was supposed that last year's shift-carrier from Rkh'yaa had landed some troops and vertibirds covertly."

O'akhdruh may have glanced briefly at Jrekhalkar. "And why would forces from our homeworld not announce themselves to the colonial authorities, Yaargraukh?"

"It was conjectured that they might be under orders to remain unannounced, if their mission was to surreptitiously monitor and guard the Site."

"And did you agree with this explanation?"

"I did not disagree with it. There seemed no alternative explanation at the time. But I was at pains to point out that, even if unannounced Warriors from our homeworld had eliminated the Out-Law rovers, the other matter of the stripped dencote remained a mystery."

"And what reply was given to this exception?"

"That while anomalous, it was still explicable. Perhaps the Out-Law rovers had stripped it before they were found and dispatched by the Warriors."

"But you felt this unlikely?"

"I felt it wanting of further investigation."

"Why?"

"Firstly, if the Warriors were ordered to both guard the Site and to remain unnoticed, they would not have been conducting unnecessary security missions more than one hundred and fifty kilometers north of their areas of operations. Secondly, it made no sense that the dencote was stripped so clean by rogue rovers. They would not have burdened themselves with every unattached object they found in the warren. Those who live Out-Law must live and travel as lightly as possible, or they will be caught."

Neither O'akhdruh's voice nor posture suggested that he considered these conclusions dubious. "And did you point out these peculiarities to the leadership here in Iarzut'thruk?"

"I did."

O'akhdruh did not look at his sole surviving son, but his pause suggested that he had to gather himself again before continuing. "And no action was taken?"

"None."

"And did you not press your concerns?"

"My observations were not always welcome. Besides, in defense of those who heard them, there was no logical path of subsequent inquiry. We were confronted with peculiar disappearances and circumstantial evidence, but it did not point at any other hypothesis. And I had none of my own to offer."

"So you did not suspect a human invasion at this point?"

"No one did, Revered O'akhdruh. There was no reason to. However, that changed approximately a week after our upland Warders returned. A significant attack was made upon the easternmost clancote, Gad'aglahkh. Its Voice reported the attack by radio, including mention of rotary-wing vehicles before his transmission ended abruptly. Those of us with military or militia experience moved quickly to reach the site, but it was still a three day drive.

"As we feared, there were no survivors. Like the dencote, the settlement had been completely stripped of removable objects. However, the most striking after-action discovery was the massive use of unfamiliar small-bore weapons. Both our Warriors and Unhonored were riddled with such wounds." Yaargraukh paused, remembering. "The others in our team were perplexed. But I had seen these gunshot wounds before."

"On Earth," O'akhdruh murmured. It was not a guess; he had been there, too.

"Yes. It was also evident that a wide variety of such weapons had been used, ultimately confirmed by post-mortem removal and examination of several bullets."

O'akhdruh started. "Why was that necessary? Were there no shell casings?"

"Almost none. The few we found had slipped through cracks or fallen into herpeculture ditches. The attackers had collected the spent casings."

O'akhdruh's eyes half-disappeared into leathery folds of consternation. "To conceal their identity."

"Perhaps. Or to facilitate reloading."

"You suspect they were short on ammunition?"

"In a manner of speaking. Frankly, I am surprised they had any ammunition at all, considering some of the calibers we discovered."

"I do not understand the significance of your comment."

"Revered O'akhdruh, you were on Earth. You saw the weapons that the insurgents used in the last hours: tens of thousands of the assault rifle that the human history books designate the 'AK-47.'"

"I recall. You found those cartridge casings at this site?"

"Those, and others even more peculiar. A British round called a .303. A German round that is designated the 7.98-millimeter Mauser."

O'akhdruh's eyefolds puckered even more profoundly. "I have never heard of these."

"Nor would I have, had I not made the study of human military affairs my specialty. That was the primary reason I was selected as Advocate: so that I might also serve as an advisor regarding Earth's military doctrines and technologies."

"And so, this ammunition: are they specialized rounds of some kind? Hunting or sniper calibers, perhaps?"

"No, they are relics. Museum objects, originally developed for early machine guns and bolt-action rifles almost two hundred fifty years ago."

O'akhdruh leaned back slightly, then glanced at his son, none too pleased. Evidently, Jrekhalkar had not had the time, or heart, to fully explain these inconsistencies to his sire, who had now been put in the compromising position of appearing surprised. "Although the weapons whereby the humans perpetrate their atrocities against Turkh'saar are immaterial to their guilt and our response, I perceive why you feel it prudent to make note of these . . . oddities. Did you conduct further research into them?"

"We did, and unfortunately, we did not want for opportunities. Within the week, the human attacks mounted in scope and savagery. They utterly despoiled the clancote of Sysh'khmar and then twice attacked the town of Haakh'haln. My team arrived four hours after the second strike, which was the most anomalous of all their attacks to date, and marked a change in the character of their operations."

"How so?"

"It is easier to show you the answer than explain it. Please flip down the monocular playback lens of your dioptiscopes, Scions. I will share scenes retrieved from our casualties' helmet cams."

As O'akhdruh pawed feebly at his dioptiscope, he pony-nodded. "It was fortunate, indeed, that our slain Warriors were equipped to record the events."

When Yaargraukh didn't say anything, Raakhshaan of the Moiety of Ukhvurashn, one of his few friends in the Clanhall and a fellow Fringelander, hastened to "help" him. "It was not good fortune, Revered O'akhdruh, but good planning. Yaargraukh sent word to all the eastern communities that their Warriors should wear video-capable dioptiscopes whenever they were on duty, with the feed relayed to a central recorder. That way—"

"Yes, yes." O'akhdruh muttered, eyes closed against the awkwardness of having to allow what amounted to testimony of Yaargraukh's foresight. "That way, even if the Warriors were stripped of their equipment, the central recorder would still show what transpired."

In an attempt to diminish the irritation his friend's addition had sparked among the more bigoted Old Family scions, Yaargraukh qualified the claim. "Unfortunately, as you will see, the scenes recorded were not especially long or detailed."

The first clip was very short. The scene began with the wearer of the dioptiscope running; the long loping glides between camera-jarring footfalls and the slight downward angle of the view indicated that the Warrior had been moving in a sprint posture: tilted forward at the waist, tail up, head and neck an outstretched column of muscle and bone. From over a ridge topped by a ragged expanse of clustertrees, four rotary-wing aircraft arose. They were old designs: boxy with a single, top-mounted set of rotors, rather than contemporary variable-attitude VTOL nacelles.

But the view was not on them for long. It swiveled about, picking out several other Warriors following in the same posture, assault rifles cradled at the ready as they made for an earthen berm of fresh dirt—

The lichen beneath their feet started jetting upward, pocked by violent divots. Two of the Warriors sprawled, their hide armor suddenly spattered with the light mauve blood of their species. A third Warrior swerved aside, making for a low stone wall, but never reached it. A flash cut across the screen, dug into the ground just beyond him, unleashed a soil-spewing explosion that blasted him sideways like a rag doll.

The perspective began slewing back around toward the approaching rotary-wings . . . but ended abruptly.

"That recording of the machine gun and rocket fire from the human rotary-wings is all we have from the first source-camera," Yaargraukh explained to the hushed Clanhall. "The source of the second was almost certainly a Warrior in the ready room on standby, possibly overseeing communications."

The feed began on a drunken tumble up a narrow staircase cut into rock. It was ascending toward a brightening, looming rectangle of light—a doorway—which seemed to explode as the camera-carrier reached it. The automatic light level kicked in, darkening everything for a moment.

Contrast restored, the perspective was now looking between the narrow-slatted blinds of a long, high window. The interior was familiar to all of them; it was one of Turkh'saar's ubiquitous civilian office modules. In the middle distance, a human rotary-wing had lowered itself to the ground, doorguns sweeping protectively as humans poured out of it. They carried a bizarre combination of weapons: bulky submachine guns, AK-47s, larger battle rifles, and a crude rocket-propelled grenade launcher, possibly an early Russian design. None mounted the various electronic sensors and sighting aids that had been routine human equipment for the past century.

Most wore fatigues of varying shades of green and deep-bowled helmets that recalled those used by both the Russian and American forces in the conflict that Yaargraukh had studied most intensively: Earth's Second World War. But there were exceptions. Several humans were in light blue shirts and slightly darker trousers, wearing white caps.

As this first group of humans spread out in a protective circle around the still-gyrating rotary-wing, four more individuals dismounted from it, two of them carrying a weapon that Yaargraukh had, until his first viewing of this tape, never seen beyond the scratchy images digitally reconstructed from Earth broadcasts: a belt-fed machine gun of German manufacture, dating from the Nazi era. Its designation had been *Maschinegewehr Zwei und Vierzig*, or MG-42, and it had had a fearsome reputation. Yaargraukh shared that fact with the silent scions as the gun crew set it up with cool precision, their field-gray uniforms and sallet-helmets distinguishing them from the rest of the human troops.

"It was a fearsome weapon, you say, but it is now an antique?" Z'gluurhek sounded doubtful.

"Yes." Yaargraukh confirmed. "We shall return to that conundrum later. For now, I call your attention to the other two individuals who exited the rotary-wing with the gun crew."

Jrekhalkar squinted more closely into his monocle. "You mean, the ones who seem to be giving orders?"

"Yes, them. Note their uniforms, particularly the insignias worn on the right side of their collars."

"Those two flashes: are they signs of rank?" O'akhdruh sounded dubious even as he hazarded the guess. The two men did not look to be of the same rank at all. One was in a plain gray uniform, whereas the other's was more cut to follow the form of his flat body, and he wore a strange, peaked cap rather than a helmet.

"Actually, their signs of rank are on their shoulders or sleeves," Yaargraukh explained. "Those collar markings mark a special branch of service: an elite, or at least, lavishly equipped, unit within the Germany armies of the Second World War. The two flashes are frequently misconstrued as lightning bolts. In fact, they are ancient, tribal renderings of the Roman letter *S*."

"And these signify what?"

"The term *Schutzstaffel*, which translates roughly as 'armed-' or 'protection-squadron.'"

"You seem to attach great significance to this, Yaargraukh."

"I do, but now, the footage concludes. Please watch."

The camera-wearing Warrior spent a few moments assessing the general pattern of the human attack: a shock assault at the western end of town followed by a flanking, vertical insertion into the sparse, widely scattered buildings just north of the community's central square. Then the Warrior shouldered his assault rifle and pushed its muzzle between the shutters. He sighted it on the MG-42, which had started gunning down fleeing Hkh'Rkh, without regard to their age, sex, or social station. A number of the humans looked away. Several others spat casually, yet markedly, in the general direction of the gray-uniformed soldiers.

The view began to shake wildly; the Warrior was firing his assault rifle on full automatic. The crew of the MG-42 was shredded by the ten-millimeter hollowpoints. They, and their weapon, were momentarily obscured by a dull red fog consistent with the color of human blood.

But before the tattered bodies had even hit the ground, the point of view was changing. The Warrior obviously expected return-fire on his position and was abandoning it with all speed. He crashed against the thin metal walls of the office module as he made for a small back exit, rather than the larger one which led toward the town square. He hit the narrow door at a run, burst into the light—

—and was looking down the barrel of a strange gun with a side-mounted magazine. Another gray-uniformed human held it braced against his hip, leaned into the weapon as its muzzle shudder-flashed through a long burst.

The view wobbled, then toppled heavily to the left, the camera coming to rest at a right angle to the ground. The world appeared to be lyying on its side as booted human feet ran back toward the town square.

Yaargraukh turned off the video feed. "I arrived at Haakh'haln a day after this attack. We encountered survivors before entering the town itself, asked what they knew of the aftermath of the slaughter. They imparted a strange story: approximately an hour after the humans had secured the town, gunfire broke out once again. Human gunfire.

"Entering the town, we found the Hkh'Rkh dead that we had expected: Warriors, females, young, old, all scattered about. But then we found something that we had never encountered before: human bodies. However, their weapons and equipment were gone. Only their clothing remained. I recorded what we saw."

The new video was of far better quality, having been shot through a military-grade dioptiscope. Among the low, burning buildings, humplike corpses of Hkh'Rkh predominated, but as the view moved toward where the rotary-wings had landed, the strangely flat bodies of humans began to appear. Many had been torn into tatters, a fairly common outcome when hit with the larger-bore Hkh'Rkh weapons. But off to the side of what looked like a marshalling area—possibly where spoils of war had been collected for loading upon their aircraft—there was a dense tangle of decidedly pale-skinned human corpses. Almost half had the light-colored fur that was common only in certain of Earth's northern latitudes.

O'akhdruh's next inquiry emerged as a resentful grunt, as if duty compelled him to pose a question he would rather not have asked. "You clearly attach signal importance to this particular group of dead humans. Explain."

It was the request that Yaargraukh had been waiting for, as O'akhdruh had no doubt surmised. "Every one of the gray-uniformed soldiers who participated on this raid is in that pile of corpses. They are all Northern European, at least in general genotypic origin. Not only was their now-missing gear overwhelmingly consistent with that of Nazi Germany, so too is the language and lettering on their garments. All of their bodies showed a pattern of careful personal grooming and many bore evidence of primitive, yet meticulously executed, dental care. Both would be consistent with the upper or elite classes of the German-speaking nations of that era. Together, these forensic details point toward a historical anomaly that defies any ready explanation."

"This is madness," Jrekhalkar muttered before his sire silenced him with a look.

"I agree the conclusion beggars belief," Yaargraukh answered with a single, deep nod, "but I can find only one explanation: that these humans are indistinguishable from a group that last lived almost two centuries ago."

"So is that how you conjecture the humans have invaded us?" Z'gluurhek shouted, his long, black tongue thrashing about in a fit of hilarity, "By sending an army of their own ghosts across great expanses of not only space, but time?" Phlegm rolled richly in his snout. "The campaign on Earth may have wounded more than your body." Although his tone was sardonic, his eyes were eager and alert, shiny black marbles that waited, hoped, for a sign that he had struck enough of a nerve to elicit a Challenge from Yaargraukh.

Who turned slowly, deliberately away from Z'gluurhek. "Revered O'akhdruh, it does me no honor to advance such a strange hypothesis. If I could offer another in its place, I would gladly do so, both for the sake of our people and to preserve their opinion of me. But you have tasked me to make a full report. I cannot in good conscience gloss over these inconsistencies, since they may be of prime strategic and tactical importance."

Yaargraukh had hoped that the former Voice would ask him how such a situation was possible, but O'akhdruh merely folded his claws together in contemplation, refused to give him the opportunity to explicate what these strange facts might signify about the so-called invaders—and conversely, what they might preclude. "Have you other pertinent information on the human operations or equipment to share, Yaargraukh?"

"I do. It appears that, except for the four slain during the attack on the MG-42, these humans died from wounds sustained solely from their own species' firearms. And since none of our Warriors commandeered human weapons, nor have digits small enough to employ them without modifications, it seems certain that these humans were slain by their own kind."

"Perhaps it was an execution over a disciplinary matter?"

"Unlikely. As I mentioned, the senior-most officer we saw in the footage of the raid was among the dead. Furthermore, the wounds were not consistent with execution, which, in humans, usually involves several wounds to the front of the body, or a single one to the rear of the skull. In this case, the wounds were distributed widely and from various angles; they were close-quarters combat wounds. Lastly, although they had full control of the town, the humans were evidently panicked and in a hurry to depart. They reclaimed equipment from the dead, but did not spend any additional time gathering spoils. They did not even stop to retrieve their cartridge casings, which they had invariably done before and have continued to do since."

"Their obsessive concern with the cartridge casings

might be a clue to why they are using what you call 'antique' weapons," interjected O'akhdruh with a quaver in his voice. "Because these older firearms still utilize brass cartridges, the humans can generate new ammunition locally by reloading the spent rounds. Therefore they are less dependent upon resupply."

And in trying to explain away those peculiarities, you have opened a door that leads to still greater ones, you old bigot. "I concur, O'akhdruh. But is it not strange that an *invasion* force, dispatched on so provocative a mission, by so formidable an opponent as the CTR, is not provided with the most effective modern arms and sufficient ammunition? By what logic would the Terrans so willfully undercut their own chances of victory with uniformly outdated equipment?"

O'akhdruh's long, narrow lower jaw closed with a sharp, upward snap. "War compels strange choices, Yaargraukh. Perhaps they were uncertain of their ability to reinforce this expedition promptly, and so equipped it with simpler gear, that it might more readily preserve its own battlefield readiness if it became isolated."

"However," Yaargraukh rebutted carefully, "their primitive dentistry, uniforms, and needlessly absent electronics, all remain unexplained."

"We need not explain every anomaly to know that our people are being killed by these human invaders," O'akhdruh snapped in return, and was then visibly irritated by having thus lost his composure. "Quickly: what else have you to report?"

"After the raid on Haakh'haln, the indiscriminate killing of our Unhonored stopped. If I correctly understood the conversation I overheard while spying upon the human cadre in Ylogh, their commanders now attempt to minimize *all* casualties, wherever that is practicable."

"An account for which we have only one source: you," Z'gluurhek pointed out.

"Which is why I present it last, and merely as support for data I have already advanced through more objective sources." *Besides, half of what I heard while listening to the humans in Ylogh I dare not mention here, not without courting accusations of perjury, treason, or both.* "Lastly, there is no longer any report of human invaders wearing the gray uniforms I conjecture as being German. Some still wear the helmets, but repainted and with all insignias removed. This, I believe, is highly significant."

O'akhdruh straightened, painfully, to his full height. "I do not deem it so."

And so he shut down the key point toward which Yaargraukh had hoped to build and that he had suspected now for months: these were not merely Germans, were not merely connected—inexplicably, impossibly—to Earth's twentieth century. More importantly, they had been executed by their fellow humans who, immediately afterward, had rejected their barbarous tactics and even erased their insignias in what seemed like a frenzy of repudiation. Which was not entirely surprising to Yaargraukh, because of all the military units in human memory, none was more reviled and hated than the Nazi *Schutzstaffel*.

Or, as commonly abbreviated, the "SS."

Chapter Twenty

O'akhdruh waved a dismissing claw at Yaargraukh as if he was attempting to telekinetically push him back out of the circle. "I have heard all I need to hear. I consider your report complete."

"You have the data, Silenced Voice, but you have yet to hear my hypothesis—as you assured me you would."

"I suspect we already know what that hypothesis is, but I give you leave to share it—as one, short, declarative sentence."

Dung and folly: one *sentence?* To do that might be worse than silence, if Yaargraukh's statement seemed too simplistic or implausible. But he who dares nothing gains nothing, so—"Given the many inconsistencies and inexplicable peculiarities of the operations and technologies of the humans, I consider it extremely unlikely that they came to Turkh'saar with the intent of invasion." He waited for O'akhdruh to ask him what reasonable alternative explanation there might be.

But the shrewd old Silent Voice did not open the

door to that topic. Rather, he nodded faintly, and stood forth from his son's side—who kept a supportive hand near the frail Hkh'Rkh as he advanced, and then spoke in a surprisingly strong voice. "I have heard much counsel. And I have arrived at a conclusion: that the human raiders who have been on this planet for some months are merely a pathfinder force. Their strikes against our outlying communities had a hidden purpose: to serve as both a practical reconnaissance and a clearing of the landing zone for the ships which violated the sovereignty of Turkh'saar tonight, and which may be but the first of a much larger wave of invaders."

The mutters around the circle grew into growls and grunts of affirmation. Yaargraukh estimated he had about three seconds to make a statement—as provided for by tradition—between the time that a Voice pronounced his determination and his plan of action. From that point, the scions' approval would carry the Clanhall forward on a confrontational path out of sheer social impetus, regardless of defects in logic. Unless those defects were exposed boldly and fearlessly.

Yaargraukh bowed his head. "Silenced Voice O'akhdruh of the Moiety of Gdar'khoom, if these humans were charged with carrying out a military invasion of this planet, why did they not commence their operation by shattering Iarzut'thruk, our main citadel and settlement, with a rain of munitions from what we must presume to be the invisible ship that brought the first group of raiders? Since they would have been undetectable until they attacked and we are clearly without defenses against bombardment, what would have stayed their hands?

"Today's events are equally confounding. Specifically,

after eliminating almost forty interception missiles that—apparently—were secretly arrayed in defense of the Site, why would the humans not simply continue to orbit until their weapons came to bear upon us here, and so destroy our hub of political exchange and action? For surely they know that this is the place where we will mobilize and project a counterattack against their ground forces."

O'akhdruh swayed, cast off his son's proffered arm, steadied himself, waved a negating hand that seemed to carry Yaargraukh's objections away like fading cobwebs. "The presenting of data and discussion is at an end. My son called this Council that I might hear the many perspectives that exist upon this matter, and the report of those who have seen the humans' handiwork firsthand. His counsel and that of many of your Clans has become known to me." O'akhdruh's eyes travelled around their circle, which stood before the large pedestal bearing his son's bier. "Now I have heard from Yaargraukh Onvaarkhayn of the Moiety of Hsraluur, as well. I shall now presume upon my son's role as Voice and Fist of my Family to speak for it one last time, for my hours are short and my wounds weigh heavy upon me.

"My eldest's death and the attack upon Ylogh made it necessary to wake me. It is fortuitous that the human ships have landed in this last hour, for now I may counsel you with a full understanding of their intents.

"Their recent changes in raiding could have been optimistically construed: that the humans were reconsidering and relenting in their initial savagery. Until, that is, their new invasion forces landed tonight, in a region that has now been well-scouted and cleansed by their advance group. And we may rightly understand the inconsistencies of that first group as no longer puzzling, but shrewd: theatrics meant to give us pause in our response, to waste precious weeks gathering evidence and attempting to discern what strange manner of raider was besetting us."

And because in this one instance he was neither allowed nor able to quickly and conclusively rebut O'akhdruh's hypothesis, Yaargraukh felt the last shreds of tenuous credibility he had built among the scions dissolving from under him like tidal sand being carried out by a greedy, receding wave.

"So," O'akhdruh continued, "we spent months failing to mount what should have been our first response: a direct counterattack with all our force.

"But, unbeknownst to you, my friends and scions, you did not have access to the maximum force at your disposal. Indeed, that could not be achieved without awakening my eldest son, and then, given his unforeseen mortal wound, myself."

Z'gluurhek's unusually broad, short-snouted head waggled in perplexity. "Revered O'akhdruh, I do not understand your words."

"And you would have no reason to, loyal Scion. My son and heir Jrekhalkar was not so deaf to your entreaties for action as you may have thought. And he did not awaken me primarily for my counsel but for knowledge—knowledge that only I possess."

"Knowledge of what, O'akhdruh?"

The Silent Voice collected himself, looking more pasty by the moment. "Nearby, there is a well-hidden cache of decommissioned military equipment, enough to arm two Tassles, along with some light armor and mobile artillery. Knowledge of its presence, location, and access codes was entrusted to a mere handful of this colony's most senior leaders, long before most of us were called away to war against the humans. The three who possessed the knowledge and remained behind died when you sent our few transatmospheric interceptors up in an attempt to repel the Slaasriithi raiders. They were to have entrusted the information to Jrekhalkar before gambling their lives thusly, but I am told that duty called upon them so quickly that they lacked the time to observe that precaution—"

—Or they were already well-acquainted with the intemperate nature of O'akhdruh's second scion—

"—And so the ability to access the hidden equipment was lost. Not wishing to risk Uzkekh'gar's and my own life, having no clear data on the severity of our wounds, Jrekhalkar delayed rousing us as long as possible. His decision to do so was a greater sacrifice than most Warriors are ever called upon to make. For the good of our colony, he had to awaken his older brother, and then his own sire, into losing battles with mortal wounds.

"But he did what he had to, and now so must you. But your choice is far easier than his was. You have but to resolve to expunge this alien pestilence from our planet, our home. And as swiftly as possible. Every day invaders are left unopposed, their strength and preparedness grows greater."

"But, my lord O'akhdruh," Z'gluurhek almost groaned, "those few of our brothers who were foremost in readiness, who had trained frequently with the militia, were slain during the Slaasriithi raids or at Ylogh. There are but a handful who remain."

"And they shall train you as best as they may as you move to engage the enemy. Any who have militia training shall report to former-Advocate Yaargraukh. Despite his excess of caution, he is a flag leader of the Patrijuridicate Great Host and served acceptably not merely on First Voice's staff, but in the field. He will organize the training and exercises the others shall conduct over the next forty-eight hours."

"Do we dare leave the adversary unengaged for so long?"

"We shall not do so. As we speak, our scouts north of the Site-lands are preparing to rendezvous with a larger strike force closing from the west. It is equipped with the remainder of our militia gear, and although most of its Warriors have only rudimentary training, they are officered by several band leaders with sufficient experience. The scouts shall locate the anticipated human beachhead, then both forces shall advance to contact and fix the invader in place, or at least delay him and keep him engaged. Then the more numerous, heavy forces we are readying here in Iarzut'thruk will arrive to destroy the invaders." He raised a calar claw high; his voice was surprisingly strong: "We will carry human heads to the Accord as evidence of their invasion."

Yaargraukh appreciated the expert manner in which Silent Voice had maneuvered him into a trap from which he could not escape or even continue to mount objections. Now honored with a prominent role in the coming battle for Turkh'saar, the former-Advocate no longer had the freedom to express his doubts and disagreements. If he uttered those views now, they would be tantamount to treason, to aiding and abetting a foe that was ravaging the world of his birth. But if

the ships that had brushed aside the missiles earlier
in the evening had in fact been human, then it stood
to reason that they might be bearing an envoy—Caine,
perhaps—who could shed some light on the origins
and intents on the first group of intruders.

And perhaps those missiles, realized Yaargraukh, were
the key to arresting the headlong rush to war. "Revered
O'akhdruh, if I am to ready our Warriors for all tactical
eventualities, there is a crucial datum I lack."

O'akhdruh nodded slowly, wary. "Ask."

"What other missile defenses do we possess, and
what is the nature and location of their support infrastructure?"

Although almost all Hkh'Rkh males were Warriors,
most of them had no formal military training. Consequently, a majority of the heads in the circle first
swiveled toward Yaargraukh in surprise, then back
toward O'akhdruh in curiosity.

The Silent Voice was silent for three full seconds.
"We have no additional missiles. Those were the only
ones we possessed."

"Then I must broaden my question: What other
unrevealed military assets are at our disposal?"

O'akhdruh's voice was slow, his eyes watchful. "Why
do you anticipate further assets?"

"Because the Patrijuridicate has apparently seen fit
to provide various military resources surreptitiously,
thereby evading the constraints of the nonmilitarized
codominium of this system." *I won't say "violation
of our treaty with the Arat Kur," but I hardly need
to; the broad wings of that stooping ut'hakash hover
ominously over every word spoken today in this Clanhall.* "Firstly, there were the interceptors with which

Turkh'saar defended itself against the Slaasriithi raiders. Just now, you have revealed that there is a cache of weapons and armored vehicles which, in number and type, clearly exceed the expected legal limits. And lastly, the Site's defense missiles imply a deeper investment in useful communications and sensor arrays."

Jrekhalkar's digits flexed anxiously as O'akhdruh, who remained very still, explained. "These missiles were left as a precaution to prevent unauthorized reentry to the Site. To my knowledge, they were left behind long ago, and depend upon no additional systems."

Ah. Now I have you. "Indeed? But then how were the missile batteries alerted and the weapons targeted?"

O'akhdruh eyes wavered. "They were self-seeking."

Yaargraukh allowed his genuine perplexity to show, while carefully concealing his dubiety. "I confess some confusion, Silent Voice. As one of First Voice's tactical advisors on Earth, I know something of our self-seeking missiles, particularly those used for surface-to-low-orbit intercept. They are self-seeking only during the latter third of their flight. Without external targeting sensors to guide them until they enter the terminal intercept phase, it would be blind luck for them to hit a target at all."

O'akhdruh's response was halting. "Our electronics specialist informed me that evidently, one of our satellites is still working, at least intermittently. It was probably roused from its post-battle lurk mode when the human craft entered the Site's defensive airspace. The satellite acquired the target's general trajectory and relayed that by lascom to a ground receiver, which automatically launched the missiles."

The Silent Voice's explanation, while careful, seemed

hobbled more by uncertainty than prevarication, almost as if the missile launch had taken him by surprise, as well. But for now, that was immaterial. Yaargraukh had to make the scions uncomfortable with the scenario, enough so that they would demand more knowledge before taking action. "And are these batteries furnished with multiple missiles per launcher? And, now that we know of its existence, can we access the satellite's autonomous control system to activate it for our militia's tactical needs as we—?"

O'akhdruh's voice sounded brittle. He was feeling weary, cornered, or both. "I am unfamiliar with the details of these systems and have no further information on them." That answer confirmed that either O'akhdruh was either suspiciously ignorant or lying. "Your questions are valid, but we no longer have the luxury of time to seek answers that are not available to us. We must be comforted by our knowledge that the enemy has encountered these missiles and therefore must expect he will encounter more."

Yet isn't it strangely convenient that our one remaining non-geosynchronous satellite just happened to be at that brief part of its orbital track to both detect the approach of the human ships and initiate an attack against them? One glance at O'akhdruh's smooth and expressionless snout told Yaargraukh that the patriarch had thought the same thing, but was unwilling to reveal or voice it. Such improbably serendipitous help could not be admitted without potentially distracting, and thus derailing, the rush to decisive action that O'akhdruh meant to put in motion before he was placed atop his own pyre. Accordingly, he was determined to eliminate any further obstructions. His sustained stare at Yaargraukh was both a mute testimony to that resolve and a pointed warning.

Studying the increasingly ashen Silent Voice, Yaargraukh understood more, still: that in following this course, O'akhdruh was preserving not only the authority, but the continuity, of his line. When the campaign against Earth commenced, Jrekhalkar had still been too young to go to war. The sire's second scion had not trained in military matters, not even in the militia; his focus had been the *halbardiche* and attaining the physical prowess to wield it decisively. It had been the logical course for him. His elder brother had both the birthrank and innate talents to succeed their father as Voice. Accordingly, it fell to Jrekhalkar to be the Fist. Besides, although no one would tell him so, he was roundly considered too rash to go to war unless it was one in which the engagements were ritually limited to melee weapons.

But now, with his Clan's Sire and First Scion dead, how long would it be before some shrewd scion of another Family baited Jrekhalkar into issuing a Challenge over some trifling slight? And since the Challenged has the right to choose the means whereby the Challenge is settled, Jrekhalkar could be compelled to undertake any one of a number of mental competitions at which he was unlikely to win—and so, lose all his property and all control over the fate of his own family.

But if O'akhdruh was able to emphasize that it had been Jrekhalkar's sense of communal duty and foresight that had compelled him to awaken, and thus sacrifice, his father in order to acquire the weapons necessary to repel the human invaders of Turkh'saar, he would be a popular and honored leader. Wiser heads among the scions would offer him their counsel out of gratitude and respect, and so protect him from his own rash excesses.

It was a masterful ploy and necessary, since Jrekhalkar had not been allowed to make a name for himself in the invasion of Earth, a lack that the Second Scion obviously felt keenly. After all, a Hkh'Rkh who does not go to his species' first great interstellar war will not be remembered in the hero-lays of his generation. Unless, that is, he accrued renown and regard as the savior of his race's one productive colony world: that he alone had met and decisively defeated the humans in battle, and in so doing, redeemed the honor the Hkh'Rkh had lost at Earth.

And so, O'akhdruh had no choice but to hold fast to the claim that this was an invasion, even if he knew it to be otherwise. The grim set of his eyes told Yaargraukh that the evidence placed before him had, in fact, brought the Silent Voice around to the former-Advocate's own belief: that these humans were at most distaff raiders, and were possibly something even less threatening and more unusual than that.

Jrekhalkar had come to stand beside his sire, who seemed to shrink into more stooped decrepitude. O'akhdruh looked around the circle one final time, his eyes ending upon Yaargraukh, unblinking. "I presume all questions have been asked and that preparation and training may commence."

With the rest of the scions, Yaargraukh bowed slightly from the waist, his tail in contact with the floor as the ritual show of respect required.

When he looked up, the Silent Voice was doddering

back to the side of his eldest's bier. Almost as an afterthought, he spoke over his palsied right shoulder. "Make haste. You shall be judged by how the days to come reveal your honor and your bravery—or not."

Filing out with the others, Yaargraukh could not shake the impression that the now truly Silenced Voice had meant that warning especially for him.

Chapter Twenty-One

Idrem turned away from the sensors and discovered that Brenlor was nodding. "This was well done, Idrem. We could hardly have created a more disastrous situation for the Aboriginals than if we had been physically present ourselves."

Idrem elected not to point out that, because of his sensor artistry, they virtually *had* been there. "The Hkh'Rkh show no signs of doubting that the signals came from one of their own satellites. They are primed to rush headlong into battle."

Brenlor only leaned forward slightly, but was unable to conceal his eagerness. "What else can we do to push events along faster?"

Idrem considered. What was the best way to show Brenlor how foolish that request was without saying so openly? "As the Progenitors remind us, profound correction is best reserved for profound errors. In this case, the more we intervene, the more the Hkh'Rkh are likely to begin questioning the source of these 'fortuitous' relays from their supposed satellite."

Brenlor started. "You said that the methods you used would ensure that the Hkh'Rkh remained unsuspecting of our interference."

"And so they will. The relay which our remote-operated orbital vehicle emplaced on their disabled satellite mimics the signals and results they would expect to see from their own platform. However, it might arouse suspicion if we activated the system too frequently, or at times too perfectly convenient to their needs. They would begin to wonder why a supposedly dead satellite not only reawoke when an intruder passed it, but then continued to provide extraordinarily timely updates on their adversaries' equipment, numbers, and deployment.

"It may, therefore, be best not to overuse this asset, but hold it—along with our other options—in reserve, to be used only when clearly needed."

"Yes, there is wisdom in that," Brenlor relented, frowning as if he were a child whose favorite toy had been snatched away. "Just so long as we can reliably monitor the Hkh'Rkh communications."

"We can, and shall do so most successfully if we remain unobtrusive. We will even have some ability to monitor the Aboriginals' communications with the Slaasriithi, thanks to the nanosensors we seeded into low orbit months ago. The Terrans have false confidence in the security of their lascom sensors, a conviction of which we should not disabuse them."

Brenlor's frown was still present, although diminished. "Unfortunately, the nanosensors are so broadly dispersed that they will only intercept signals occasionally and partially."

"At first, perhaps, but given time, they will swarm

to provide amplified coverage along active comm beam telemetries. We can at least expect to detect any lascom communications that pass through the low and medium orbit regimes of Turkh'saar."

Brenlor shrugged. "I find it hard to believe that the Aboriginals remain unsuspecting of our ability to tap into their lascoms."

"Their understanding of the relevant physical theory is extremely rudimentary. They have yet to discern that microgram particles can form a phased array to pick up lascom diffusions, or detect back- or side-scatter from particles that lay along the beam's trajectory."

Brenlor pushed against the backrest of the conn, as if trying to shove it away. "And everything else is in readiness?"

Idrem nodded carefully. "*Red Lurker* is impossible to detect now that we are housed within this shell of a derelict Hkh'Rkh hull. Our railgun is preranged on the anticipated area of engagement. We have firing solutions for all grid coordinates."

Brenlor frowned. "The flight time of the railgun projectiles concerns me. The Aboriginals still have two landers in a nearby orbital track. They will detect our fires, track back to the source."

"Be at ease regarding that variable. They will have to bring down all the landers to effect extraction, which will be a political failure if it is not complete. Consequently, the Aboriginals will no longer have any craft in orbit when we commence our intervention. And they will be stuck at the bottom of Turkh'saar's gravity well."

Brenlor closed his eyes, breathed out slowly. "Yes, I remember the logic—and your and Nezdeh's careful

repetitions of it. I am merely—eager to begin." He
glanced up, a smile hinting at the left corner of his
mouth. "I may not have the patience for statecraft,
but I am not unobservant: either of the situations in
which we find ourselves, or of the value of my best
counselors. Idrem."

Idrem was not frequently surprised, and having
schooled himself to readily mask any reaction with
a look of somber reflection, he did not betray his
momentary disorientation. "I am honored to be thought
of so highly by you, Brenlor Srin Perekmeres."

Brenlor stood, stretching his limbs. "As well you
should be." The same grin still played at the cor-
ners of his mouth. He stared around the bridge at
the humans who were crewing *Red Lurker*. "These
Aboriginals have learned their duties well enough."

"You have been exacting in their drills."

"Yes." He stretched again, seemed to be trying to
twist out a kink in his neck. "Speaking of drills, we
have not refreshed our combat skills since departing
the *Arbitrage*. We should do so."

"Now?"

Brenlor glanced around the quiet bridge. Nothing
had changed in hours, and it was unlikely that anything
would for many hours more. "When better? Besides,
if I sit here waiting for each uneventful minute to
creep into the next, I might be tempted to use one
of these Aboriginals for a sparring target."

Idrem elected to deliver his response in a deadpan.
"Brenlor, you know very well that we cannot afford
to dispose of a body. Opening the airlock could give
away our position."

Brenlor's grin finally surfaced; it was both feral and

wistful. "Always the cautious one, eh, Idrem? Come, let us go."

Idrem twisted sharply, just in time to dodge Brenlor's long, flying kick. The heavier Ktor shot past the rangier one, heading for the aft bulkhead.

Just before reaching it, the Srin tumbled—like a swimmer executing a racing turn—and pushed off from it, heading back at Idrem.

Who was no longer where he had been. Anticipating the fast reversal, Idrem had used his twist to catch at the wall and tug himself sharply toward the deck and forward. In consequence, as Brenlor came rocketing off the aft bulkhead, reorienting out of his tumble, Idrem was passing under him. He jabbed the practice dagger into the torso that flashed overhead.

The lights in the compartment flashed red. "Mortal," intoned the hand-to-hand subroutine that was monitoring their practice.

Brenlor's head jerked around. Idrem saw the Srin's trademark temper flash hot, before he groomed it back to mere self-annoyance. "You are crafty, Idrem."

"I am fortunate, my Srin."

Brenlor stopped himself against the forward bulkhead. "Do not patronize me. Yes, I anger easily, but I am not a child."

Idrem managed to look somberly thoughtful yet again. It was odd that Brenlor should be so willing to admit personal failings. "A child could not own their anger as you do, Srin." A refreshing truth. "I did not intend to patronize you." A flat out lie. "However, while I may have a passable command of the tactics of zero-gee melee, I am distinctly your inferior when it comes to the correct reflexes. So I maintain that, thus far, I have been fortunate." A careful mix of truth and deference.

"Your tongue is as smooth as a serpent's, Idrem," Brenlor said without any detectable heat. "I count that a singular asset to the future of this House. I wonder. When the time comes for us to negotiate with other powers that, like us, do not have a seat in the Sphere's House-Moot, would you feel it below your station to oversee those conversations?"

Idrem was becoming more accustomed to the sensation of surprise with every passing minute. "Srin Perekmeres, I would be honored. Of course, it will be quite some time before any of the other Houses will be so open in their alliance with us that they would accept direct speech."

Brenlor pushed off the forward bulkhead casually; it was not a combat move. "Very true. In all likelihood, we will need to identify disaffected Aboriginal groups, black market helots, and of course, Voices of any number of Hkh'Rkh Old Families. I would, of course, be the first to meet with them and would be either their host or honored guest of record. But when discussion was wanted, I presume that they will pass off the details to a subordinate. I will match that move by putting you forward in my place. And in so doing, I will be leading with our best asset." He paused. "Those who mostly command lesser beings never accrue the same honor as those who devote themselves solely to the exercise of dominion. I would not set you on such a potentially demeaning course without your consent, Idrem."

"That is most generous and most wise." And Idrem

meant it. He drifted toward his would-be Hegemon. "But for now, the most important consideration is that our House employs every one of its scant assets to its best advantage."

Brenlor nodded. "Excellent." Without warning, his slightly bowed legs flexed, hitting the deck at an angle and launching him forward with considerable force. The Srin's shoulder smashed into Idrem's diaphragm, driving the wind out of him as it also drove him back. Idrem tried to parry, tumble, but to no avail. Brenlor had dropped his practice knife, had wrapped his arms around Idrem.

Who, forearms pinned to his side and his own practice knife trapped low, could only roll his wrist to score partial hits. "Graze. Graze. Graze," announced the sepulchral voice of the training subroutine, indicating that while blood was being drawn by the feebly shortened slashings of Idrem's weapon, they were not landing any hits that degraded his opponent.

As they drifted closer to the wall, Brenlor's smiling—or was that smirking?—face was close to Idrem's own. "The match is not over until we so signal," he observed. Then his eyes widened slightly: the aft-bulkhead was coming up quickly. Brenlor's grip released slightly, his arms moving, probably to brace against the impact.

Idrem waited for his knife arm to be free, then drew back to slash—

But never landed the disemboweling cut he had intended. Brenlor was not where he was supposed to be. He had pushed off Idrem in such as way that he was now rolling over the top of his subordinate's head, twisting as he went. Idrem slashed with the knife, cut air, and then, with a sickening certainty particular to the inevitable physics of zero-gee combat, felt himself pulled sideways by his own sudden cutting motion.

Which was clearly what Brenlor had been counting upon. The Srin finished his tumble just as his feet grazed the aft-bulkhead. *Nicely timed*, Idrem admitted as he tried to pull himself around to face his opponent. But being out of contact with any surface, his ability to change vector was extremely limited. And he only had a second, before—

In fact, he had well less than a second. As soon as Brenlor's feet had sufficient contact with the bulkhead, the Srin kicked hard. That motion sent him crashing into Idrem's left side at murderously close range. With a twist like that of a predator using its momentum to bring down prey, he dragged Idrem forward, managed to get behind him. One arm was around Idrem's throat in a moment, the other slipped into a viselike half-nelson that pushed his windpipe against the opposing forearm. Idrem's weapon arm was cinched high and sideways, stuck in a useless position, no matter how he thrashed with it.

Brenlor did not speak until they drifted down to the deck. "Mortal," the automated referee announced.

But Brenlor did not let go. "You are greatly prized by this house, Idrem Perekmeresuum," he murmured. The words were reassuring; the tone was not. "I presume you realize that."

"I do."

"Excellent. I require one simple clarification before we end our chat. Is your loyalty fully and solely to this House?"

"It is. Why would you even ask?"

The forearm came up slightly more snug against

his windpipe. "Firstly, I may always ask, because I am not merely the Srin but, soon, the Hegemon. It is my right to ask any question I wish of those in my House, whenever I wish it. And questions which ascertain the loyalty of those around me are the most logical and crucial of all, yes?"

"If their loyalty is in doubt, yes, Srin."

"Ah, but one can never be too sure, Idrem. Particularly not when it comes to a trusted advisor who is shrewd, keeps his own counsel, rarely displays emotion, and has a gift for shaping a Srin's moods and decisions with soft and subtle speech. And who has caught the eye of that Srin's cousin—and second-in-line—as well."

Ah. So that was it. "Brenlor, if I may—" Idrem moved to exit the choke hold, but the Srin held him firm.

"You may speak, but not leave. Not just yet."

"I have little to say. Brenlor Srin Perekmeres, you have observed me closely, which is indeed the action of a wise Hegemon when it comes to those they must trust. So I ask you this: have you ever detected ambition in me, the kind that would covet the Hegemon's chair?"

"None. But you are the consort of a Srina, now. And unless I miss my guess, her intended mate. No, do not deny it," he emphasized with a momentary constriction of his forearm. "I may not have your or her skills in the sciences and complicated disciplines of space combat, but I understand the passions that move our people. I have seen you together, even when you try your hardest to purge your glances, and your tones, of anything that might betray the nature of your relationship. I know what is transpiring in my own House, my own precincts. And I know that Nezdeh is as ambitious a Srina as a Breedmother ever trained. So I need to know one thing with absolute clarity: is your first loyalty to me, or to her?"

Idrem knew that too hasty an answer would be suspect, would seem a product of fear rather than reason. But to wait too long—"Brenlor, are you the rightful Hegemon of House Perekmeres?"

That gave the Srin a moment's pause. "You know I am."

"Then know this: I am loyal to House Perekmeres. And so I am loyal to you. And thus, so is she. And should one of our enemies accomplish the unthinkable and slay you, then I shall still be loyal to House Perekmeres and its rightful Hegemon. And shall continue to do so until I am no more."

Brenlor's arm remained around his throat, but the tension on the back of his neck from the other arm relaxed. Two silent seconds passed. "That is not the answer I expected. Or the one that I hoped for." Another second passed. "Indeed, it is better."

Brenlor's hard, heavy arms unwound from Idrem's neck and throat. They faced each other. "Idrem, the worst threats to a Hegemon are the ones that might arise within the walls of his own precincts. I would put another mantle upon your shoulders: that of House Perekmeres' High Sentinel."

Idrem managed not to blink. "The security of our House has long been my first concern. I am proud that you confer this highest honor upon me." Which was an understatement. High Sentinel was one of the most powerful positions in any House. And, since it blended the roles of chief diplomatic strategist and internal security chief, it was the one Idrem had most coveted.

"Then I am well-pleased and well-served." Brenlor braced himself against the bulkhead with one hand and stood erect. "And with your aid, and Nezdeh's, I shall surely realize my lifelong dream."

"Which is?"

Brenlor might have even forgotten that Idrem was there, his eyes were so distant. "To wear the flayed skins of all the Srinu of House Shethkador. After ascending to the Autarch's dais on a ramp made of their bleached skulls."

Chapter Twenty-Two

Ezzraamar Laarkhduur of the Moiety of Nys'maharn stared out between the bars of his makeshift cage toward the humans standing around their map table. The amount of time that these small, wiry, patch-furred bipeds discussed plans was mind-numbing. They could argue for hours over the advantage of using one model of machine gun rather than another, even though the only difference between them was reloading logistics. He wondered if they also debated among themselves when they felt the urge to excrete their wastes; perhaps they felt there were two sides to that matter, as well.

But Ezzraamar had to allow that the humans were shrewd and that their less hierarchical social organization had some tangible advantages. The most obvious was how it made the exchange of ideas and alternatives both broader and faster. That would have been a detriment on a battlefield, but from what Ezzraamar had seen, and as Yaargraukh had informed him, humans were able to set aside their reflex for interminable discussion during crises. The result was that they were excellent and thorough planners, leaving far less to chance than the average Hkh'Rkh leader of any comparable rank, yet were able to give and execute orders swiftly in the field. No wonder their raiders had been so successful for so long.

What was most puzzling was their lack of significant dominance displays. They promptly corrected any hint of disrespect with stern words, but they never had to resort to physical violence or compulsory subservience rituals. The "lesser officers" which he had heard called *ensee'ohs*—or perhaps it was an acronym, NCOs?—maintained discipline in a manner somewhat more reminiscent of what transpired among the ranks of Warriors. However, they too were far more casual in their interactions and occasionally seemed to be sympathetic to soldiers who had displeased an officer. It was all quite confusing and quite illogical.

It was also confusing and illogical that, to the best of Ezzraamar's understanding, the humans had not moved him to their main base, the one where the majority of the rotary-wings, or "helicopters," had gone. Instead, a relatively small unit, no more than forty or fifty, had remained behind with two helicopters and the two intact scout cars that the humans had commandeered during the raid on Ylogh.

It was further baffling that they spoke openly in front of Ezzraamar. That would never have been permitted among the Hkh'Rkh. They would have completely isolated human prisoners, even if it was known that they were incapable of understanding a single word of Hkhi.

The humans were demonstrating this extraordinarily

lax prisoner protocol now, having just brought Ezzraamar his (rather tiresome) supper of small, edible worms mixed with their version of another staple of Turkh'saar: a mash made of an edible root. Well, it was "edible" after going through multiple rounds of chemical treatment and leaching. However, the human variety of the dish was even pastier and less tasty than the Hkh'Rkh. The root had been more thoroughly cleansed and denatured. Not surprising, he reflected, since the human gut was far more sensitive than the Hkh'Rkh. Of course, that was true of pretty much all other intelligent species.

The human who had brought him the food, Sergeant Emmett Owen, was joining the others at the map table which they kept here at the rear of the cave. "So, sir, is it grubs and groats for us, too?" he asked.

"Nope," answered Lt. Colonel Rodermund. "Special night. C-Rats."

"Hot damn!" Owen exclaimed. "Bullets and dicks!"

The Russian who was in charge of Ezzraamar's minimal guard detail seemed startled. *"Shto?"*

Rich Hailey, the soft-spoken American captain who seemed to get along with everyone, from the often-irritated Rodermund to the lowliest soldier—some of whom were from nations that had apparently once hated his—laughed. "Beans and franks, Arseniy."

"Ah. That is relief. Although even real bullets and dicks might be better than worms and roots." He stared quietly down at his hands.

Rich Hailey followed his eyes, may have noted what Ezzraamar had been observing since he had been captured: although they ate frequently and in reasonable quantities, the humans looked thinner than the specimens he had seen in the briefing materials and later news videos of Earth. They also spent a great deal of time excreting their solid wastes and complaining that they had exhausted their supplies of something they called *tee pee*. Which Ezzraamar had thought he remembered as a word signifying a portable shelter used by more primitive humans, but in this case, apparently meant some fibrous wadding they used for postexcretive hygiene. The human body was oddly dependent upon external tools and products to remain clean and functional: a strange species indeed.

Some were greedily opening cans which they had briefly heated over low flames. Rodermund was already half finished with his. "In point of fact, boys, this isn't a treat. It's a precaution."

"Sir?" asked Emmett.

"Everyone's gotta be up at 0400 so we can fly out at first light. And I want to be back at Base Camp in time for breakfast. So we're having human food tonight so no one has the trots come sunup."

Sergeant Owen wagged his head in Ezzraamar's direction. "Wish we could handle the local grub as well as they can."

"Well," sighed Rodermund, "they ought to handle it just fine. After all, they're *from* here. Wherever the hell 'here' is."

Ezzraamar always had to be very careful not to react to the humans when they said such patently incorrect or absurd things, although in this case, he was struck by the unusual nature of the human's ignorance. Colonel Rodermund, reportedly their second in command, clearly believed that Hkh'Rkh were native to Turkh'saar. Which made no sense, since the encyclopedic self-reference that the Hkh'Rkh had distributed to the other Accord races at the failed Convocation clearly indicated that they were from Eta Cassiopeia. How, then, could these humans believe...?

But he would have to ponder that oddity later. The humans were speaking again, and their tone was less jocular, more serious. Meaning that, he had to listen as carefully as he could. If, by the intercession of some Fate-smiling Ghost Sire, he was to escape from the humans, he would need to remember all the details he could in order to debrief the colony's leadership.

Owen was shaking his head as he scooped around the inside of his now empty can with great care. "Yeah, well I know someone who's going to drop a brick and bust a gut no matter what he eats tonight. Clive. He's not gonna appreciate our leaving the snorks' cars here. Certainly not unattended."

Hailey was carefully finishing his "bullets and dicks" with a spoon. "He might not like it, but those vehicles won't do us any good unless they're already prepositioned close to our AO."

Rodermund nodded. "And 'unattended' is the only safe way to leave them out here, Sergeant Owen." He shook his silver mane. "The alternative is to establish a fixed forward base, tasked to radio silence. Hell, we could lose everyone before we even knew they were in danger On the other hand, if the enemy comes snooping around and finds these cars while we're gone, then the worst that happens is we're back to relying on our choppers for everything. I can live with that; I can't live with leaving our people out in the boonies."

Owen shrugged. "To say nothing of the intel the snorks might be able to squeeze out of them."

As Owen finished, Lieutenant Franklin strolled in,

nose aloft, mimicking sniffing for food. "Oh, you mean the way we've been able to squeeze intel out of our pal in the cage?"

"Yeah, well, we've been pretty damned friendly about it."

"More to the point, we haven't really tried," Captain Hailey added. "That's for Colonel Paulsen and the specialists to deal with."

"Wasn't aware we had any specialists in monster debriefing, Captain," Owen said mischievously.

"Sure we do. They're here so we can debrief *you*, should that ever become necessary."

The two humans exchanged what they called smiles, which—for all the wisdom of the Greatsires—looked as though they were exchanging bared-teeth aggression displays.

Franklin wandered closer to the cage they had built for Ezzraamar. He knelt down, looked at the Hkh'Rkh's wrapped leg.

"How's that wound of his doing, Lieutenant? He lost a lot of blood on the way here."

Franklin stared at Ezzraamar, who stared back. "Those wounds won't kill him. These snorks are damned tough. Judging from the old scars we've seen on some of their dead, I suspect they have much better recuperative and regenerative powers than we do. I've seen some indications that they might have the capacity to regrow lost digits, even limbs."

Ezzraamar labored—successfully—to conceal his surprise; Franklin was extremely observant. It was unclear if, over the entire course of the Patrijuridicate's Jakartan occupation, any of the humans ever realized what he had just hypothesized.

Sergeant Owen was circling the cage, now, inspecting him closely. "Y'know, I still say this one's in uniform. Those markings on its armor: they're insignias of some kind."

Rich Hailey nodded. "Yep, and he's very alert, even though he tries to act like he's disinterested in what we say and do. Watch his eyes, how he is assessing, noting details."

"Yeah," breathed Franklin, "almost like he understands us, what we're saying."

"Understands us?" Arseniy barked out a harsh laugh. "That is crazy, my friend. I will show." The Russian spun, stepping close to the hulking Hkh'Rkh. "YOU! Do you understand us?"

Ezzraamar flinched and blinked, then leaned ominously toward Pugachyov, unleashing a stream of his own harsh, guttural language. Which translated as, "As if I would ever admit to such an ability, you imbecile!"

"Okay," Rodermund shouted, "that's enough. He might not understand us, but he's responsive, and he's military or something like it. And even if he isn't Radio Snork—hell, he'd be talking his snout off in English and German if he was—Colonel Paulsen could still be right: he could provide us with the common context by which we can establish communication."

Ezzraamar surveyed the room, affecting wary surliness. Regardless of what these humans hoped or thought, they would not be "establishing communications" with him any time soon.

"Can't say I'm too optimistic about the chances of learning his lingo," Rodermund was continuing. "You ask me, it's a long shot. And the benefits are too damn intangible. Not like getting our hands on those recce cars, as Clive calls them. Finally we've got some easily repairable mobility that doesn't gobble fuel like these damn helos. But trying to find, isolate, and grab Radio Snork?" He shook his head. "Frankly, I don't understand why Pat Paulsen, and the two of you"—he shot a hard glance at both Isaac Franklin and Rich Hailey—"all thought that taking *any* captive was worth the added risk of the last mission. That was nuts. But rearranging our whole operation to optimize the chances of getting Radio Snork himself? That was certifiable."

Franklin produced a small, slanted, maroon cap with a shield insignia on the front, smoothed it over his hair. "Well, sir, I think Colonel Paulsen made a pretty sound point when he observed that 'the only folks who have answers to all our questions are the ones we're fighting.' And he's probably right in guessing that even if we didn't bag Radio Snork, then someone in their military is likely to think at least *some* of the same ways we do, have some of the same concerns and culture—"

"Really? And how will we find out if they do?" Rodermund jabbed a finger toward Ezzraamar. "He shows no interest in cooperating." The silver-maned human kept staring at him through the bars of the cage. "And then there's their annoying tendency to shoot first and ask questions later. Or never."

"Well, that's kind of how *we* started this whole show, Colonel."

Rodermund rounded on Franklin. "'We?' *We* started this? None of us who are left have any reason to take the rap for starting these hostilities, Lieutenant. As for what happened during those first miserable weeks, well—yes. Although once we were set on this course, it's not like we've had much choice in the matter."

Rich Hailey smiled what seemed to be his characteristically crooked smile. "Seems to be our lot in life, sir: messing around uninvited in someone else's back yard. And in the shit because of it. At least we don't have to keep saluting the assholes who sent us *here*."

Rodermund grunted. "Well, I guess that makes it better than Laos. Sort of."

"Somalia, too," Franklin added. "But at least there we mostly knew who we were fighting, and why. We need a better sense of that here." He looked at Ezzraamar; the human's strange two-colored eyes— tinted irises swimming in seas of white—were not hostile. At all.

"Well, Pat Paulsen certainly agrees with you," Rodermund allowed. "And it's making my hair turn gray. Well, it would, if it wasn't already white." He sighed, rubbed his eyes. "Frankly, the only reason I agreed to go on that back-and-forth baiting spree he concocted was because he is absolutely, inarguably right about one thing: we can't do this forever. Not without all eventually winding up the way Greek Nick and Wally did in that last town." He stared into his empty c-rat can. "I give us a year."

"You really think we've got that long, sir?" Rich Hailey's face was still bent by the same lopsided smile.

Rodermund shrugged. "I am ever an optimist, Captain. And I have to be, just to keep going every day. We've done our best to keep caching captured supplies, but we still don't have enough. We'd have to hit five more towns like that last one before we managed to become self-sustaining."

"And if we did, then what?" Franklin sounded surprised, as if this topic was new to him.

Rich Hailey glanced at Rodermund, who nodded: a permission to share information. Arseniy and Emmett Owen came closer as the captain gestured off beyond the edge of the map, at someplace far to the south and west. "We leave the gameboard. We deedee mau for the equatorial islands, Ike."

"Except everywhere is the gameboard, now," Franklin replied, frowning. "It's not like the locals are ever going to be cool about all the bodies and raided towns we've left behind."

"That's why I wonder if it makes any sense grabbing one of their soldiers," Rodermund added with a sigh. "Seems like we're way past talking. Hell, it always seems like we're past that point—first 'Nam, now here."

There was noise at the mouth of the cavern: loud, agitated mutters and the clack and rustle of gear being readied. The humans reached for their weapons, had them in hand and safeties off by the time another of the striped-camo soldiers came rushing into their rearmost alcove: Sergeant Robert Lane. "Snorks on the way. They'll be in the tangle-foot within five minutes, and that single-strand wire won't hold them for long."

Rodermund pounded a small, white fist on the table. "Damn it, this is—"

"Sorry, sir; not done. Airmobile of some kind is flanking us to the north. Thought it might be fast movers at first, but now I'm thinking something more like a jump jet. A big one."

"Guess they've got air assets, after all." Owen drawled, checking the grenades on his web-gear and moving closer to the cage, his weapon coming up slowly.

"What are you doing?" Franklin asked.

"Nuthin'." Owen said in the same odd, slow tone. "Securing the prisoner."

Rich Hailey cut a sharp glare at the smaller man. "Take one step closer to that cage and I will have your ass, Sergeant."

"Don't mind me, Captain." Owen seemed personally injured by the rebuke. "I'm just getting ready to do whatever turns out to be necessary."

Rodermund banged his hand on the table. "That prisoner is the least of our worries right now. Our base here, those recce cars: it's all foobar, now."

"Boo coo foobar," Owen agreed with a nod. "Time to spin up and sky out?"

Rodermund shook his head. "Can't. Too risky, now that they've got air assets."

"But—"

"We saw the wreckage of a goddamned spaceship that wasn't much bigger than a Phantom. So anything they've got in their inventory will probably junk our birds like slow-moving tin foil." He glanced at Hailey, who was already activating their perversely large radio set.

Owen sighed. "So, the choppers and our other gear: destroy in place?"

"Not destroy," Rodermund corrected. "Abandon. I'm not wasting time and risking lives to blow material that the snorks can't use anyhow." He turned to Rich Hailey. "Captain, you've passed the word?"

"Base Camp has been informed that we are withdrawing. Contingency Papa Two."

Rodermund nodded, turned to the others. "You officers split the men into teams of three. Any bigger and they'll make too much noise, leave too much of a trail. Give them the compass heading for waypoint two, and get them going, one NCO or officer per team. Teams reaching waypoint two are to dig in and wait for the eagle flight from Base Camp."

Arseniy frowned. "We do not simply regather at waypoint and march back to Base Camp?"

Owen was already dumping various components out of his rucksack—they appeared to be related to hygiene and grooming—and was replacing them with additional magazines and water containers. "If we go back to BC Dante directly, we're leading the snorks straight to where we live. So we rendezvous at a groupment point and then wait for the cavalry, which will clear the surrounding area and then extract us. Textbook recondo."

Rodermund looked up from his own hasty preparations. "Make sure it happens that way, Sergeant. You and the other lurpers share what pointers you think valuable before you cut everyone loose."

"Copy that, sir. One question: fighting rearguard. Do we ask for volunteers?"

"Negative, because there will be no fighting rearguard. Everyone bombshells out of this place ricky tick. We can't afford heroes; there aren't enough of us. Now get the men moving." Rodermund turned to Franklin, gestured at Ezzraamar, who had spent the last three minutes no longer wondering if he was going to die, but simply when. "The snork: your recommendation?"

Franklin swallowed. "Let him go, sir."

Rodermund shook his head. "Rich?"

Ezzraamar had the distinct impression that whatever the ever-calm human captain suggested would be the course of action followed.

Captain Hailey shrugged. "Cut him loose, Colonel. We don't speak their language, but it's our one opportunity to send a clear message: that we'd rather not kill them, given the choice."

Hearing this, Ezzraamar was stunned, so much so that he was certain he could not experience a greater sense of surprise. But that assumption was disproven in the very next moment: Rodermund nodded, his silver mane waving. "I agree. But we're going to leave him in the cage. That way, he can't run to his pals and cut down our lead time. Now, let's move."

And, Hailey shouldering the radio and Franklin scooping up the map, they ran for the cave mouth, beyond which, when Ezzraamar strained his ears, he could detect the faint whine of approaching high-speed turbojets. In vertical mode.

Someone was coming. And soon.

But whom?

Chapter Twenty-Three

"Commodore Riordan, something's—It has gone crazy down there, sir."

"Put it on the main screen, Doctor. Duncan, lasers in PDF mode, railgun at the ready."

"Aye, sir."

The treetop view of the clearing toward which they were descending was abruptly replaced by an overhead plot of the biosigns in the region. The slow wave of approaching signatures to their south, and the tight cluster of signatures nearly beneath them, were becoming frenetic churns of disparate activity, as if some invisible foot had kicked this collective ant's nest and sent all its denizens scurrying madly about.

"Dr. Sleeman, I'm going to need to you take over all remote sensor assets as well."

"Aye, sir. What do you need?"

"Four of the semiautonomous light-duty quadrotors."

"Deploying, sir."

"Are we close enough now to distinguish between Hkh'Rkh and human biosigns?"

"Crudely, sir. Mostly based on the size of the thermal outline due to mass differential, but I'm starting to get outlines, too."

"Good. Sort those biosigns."

"Sorting."

The thermal smudges on the map became blue triangles and red dots.

"You're using blue as human elements?"

"As per our prior conversation, sir."

"Doctor, just to be clear. I don't—*I can't*—presume the humans on Turkh'saar are friendlies." Riordan studied the patterns of distribution and movement, which made slightly more sense now. The human signatures were in the process of abandoning what appeared to be a small base, fanning out as they moved rapidly north and east.

"Our extraction targets are not moving directly toward their main base," Karam observed.

"Probably, because they're professional enough not to lead their enemies straight to it."

Duncan's voice was slow. "Could it be a trap, that their retreat is a ruse to draw in the Hkh'Rkh?" Several of the easternmost red spots were veering toward the fleeing blue triangles. In all probability, they'd caught some hint of hurried movement ahead, were making for it. Other red dots were pushing forward aggressively, but in an ever-widening and irregular pattern. They knew they were closing in on something, but didn't know exactly what or where it was, and eagerness was eroding their careful patrol intervals.

Riordan rubbed his chin. "That doesn't look like a trap. The humans would be holding a tighter formation, trying to lead the Hkh'Rkh into a finite kill zone. They just bolted."

"Maybe because they heard our thrusters and fans," Karam put in sourly.

"Probably, but there was no helping it: we had to attempt to swing around to deploy our ground teams close to the objective. Otherwise they would have been walking right into the middle of that trainwreck down there. Major Solsohn, tell Sergeant Fanny I need his people ready to go."

"They're standing by."

"Doctor, what are the quadrotors picking up?"

"Not much, sir. Comms are infrequent, I don't have eyes on anybody yet, not with all the trees and their weird canopy."

An interesting phenomenon worthy of investigation—assuming they survived to do so. "Send two of the quadrotors after the humans. Keep them slightly to their south. Try to get me visuals."

"That will put our 'rotors between the humans and the advancing Hkh'Rkh, sir."

"That's the idea, Doctor. Place the other two 'rotors half a klick south of the abandoned base. I want to have eyes on any Hkh'Rkh who might be closing in on it."

"Aye, sir. I'm getting queries from Wedge One. They want to know if they should land or continue to hover?"

"They hover and hold. Karam, when I call for it, I want the fastest NOE course down into the base's clearing."

Tsaami's reply was a mutter. "Already prepared to execute."

"Dr. Sleeman, any sign of reaction from the Hkh'Rkh vehicles behind their skirmish line?"

"They've slowed. No active sensors, if that's what you're watching for."

"It is indeed. Keep our laser-sensors wide-eyed, Doctor. If they detect us at long range, that's what they'll use for targeting."

"Yes, sir. One anomaly of interest."

"Go ahead."

"There were two, maybe three Hkh'Rkh biosigns that charged ahead and reached the base. But they've disappeared."

Karam twisted to look back at Caine. "Bunker? Cave?"

Riordan shrugged. "Guess we're going to find out. Time for us to skip across the treetops and see what's going on."

"We might lose LoS commo with Wedge One when we hop into the other clearing, sir."

"That's unavoidable. If Wedge One has enemy contact, she is authorized to use broadcast. Now, let's go, Mr. Tsaami. Major Solsohn, stand to your weapons."

"Haven't taken my fingers off the relays, sir."

Puller lurched forward. The rush pushed them back in their couches. Karam turned. "You want me to land right away?"

"No; bring us up short, just over the clearing's northern tree line. I want a look at the LZ before we commit."

"Roger that. Coming up on line of sight...now." As the words were leaving Tsaami's mouth, Sleeman snapped the mainscreen over to a bow view with light intensification and thermal imaging.

Riordan saw the two vehicles the humans had left behind—and, for a second, was unable to maintain a cogent stream of thought: both were twentieth-century helicopters. As a defense analyst with decent historical knowledge, he'd seen plenty of photos of one of the models, had watched it *whup-whup-whup* across the screen of old films. It was a UH-1, officially labeled the Iroquois, but commonly known as a Huey, or—if not fitted with various weapons or other outboard systems—a "slick."

The other helicopter was a Russian design: a workhorse of the Soviet forces, but not an epochal icon. But most importantly—and improbably—they were not wrecks. The surrounding gear, fuel drums, and flightline parapharnalia indicated that they were not merely operational, but on standby. Or at least, they had been until a few minutes ago.

"Biosigns?" Riordan's query came out as a croak. His throat had gone suddenly dry.

Sleeman shook her head. "None in the clearing, but do you see behind the...uh, the helicopters? There's a pile of rocks. I think I caught a glimmer from there. Reflected heat, nothing direct."

"Biological?"

"Impossible to confirm. But with that ghostlike waver and disappearance—yes, I think so."

"Hkh'Rkh?"

"Can't tell. I suppose some humans could have holed up in there, not come out yet."

Caine felt two instincts tugging at him. The correct one, inculcated by both recent training and experience, was to remain on *Puller*'s bridge, coordinate activities, manage resources, stay focused on the big picture, and be ready to react swiftly and effectively. But on the other hand—

If the biosigns were Hkh'Rkh, they would be small in number. Probably just the two or three who had sprinted ahead of their forces. And no one but he had experience contacting them. If the objective was to avoid a firefight, to keep this from becoming a conflict between legitimate CTR troops and the local Patrijuridicate colonial forces, then he needed to be present in order to maximize those chances. Unless—

He toggled his collarcom. "Sergeant Fanny?"

"Yes, sir?"

"Do any of your personnel have experience with the Know-It-All add-on?"

"The what, sir?"

Well, that doesn't sound promising. "Are you familiar with the NOAH system?"

"Oh, that. Um . . . yes, that's the, uh, the . . ."

Duncan filled in. "NOAH is a Network Overseen Automated Helper: an automated personal assistant. NOAH-ITAL is the military model: 'Independent Tactical Augmentation Link.'"

"Yes, sir. Heard of it, sir. Never used it. None of us have."

Solsohn turned toward Caine. "But I have, sir. Many times. And I think I see why you're asking. I've worked with the 'culture coach' subroutine. We had to use it on field ops, particularly when we were in AOs where we didn't speak the language, or—"

"I'm glad to know that, Major, but like me, you're not leaving the bridge of this ship. You're needed at gunnery, so we don't have the time for you to boot up the Know-It-All, make sure it supports the new

Hkh'Rkh interface, and then outfit you with the wearable. For now, we'll do this old school. Mr. Tsaami, take us down. Sergeant Fanny, prepare to deploy."

Riordan watched Fanny lead his team out in a widening search pattern. On smaller screens, their individual helmet cams showed their crouching progress past the helicopters and toward a gap between the upthrust rock spurs behind them: evidently a cave mouth. "Sergeant, a quick word about dealing with the Hkh'Rkh at night. Their unaided dark vision is significantly better than ours, but the LITI goggles you're wearing give you an immense advantage. However, they've got some rudimentary ocular IR sensitivity as well, so engage your thermoflage liners."

"Engaged, sir. Cold cans are smart-compensating at lowest rate, sir."

"Good. Now, let's get a little more advance warning. Have Somers deploy your creepers. Two into the cave, the rest on walkabout."

"You want us to set their patrol circuit, sir?"

"Negative, Sergeant. Dr. Sleeman will control them. The creepers will fan out and help the quadrotors maintain a perimeter watch five hundred meters out from your current position."

"Copy that, sir. Letting the creepers go."

The small robots—shaped like spider-centipede hybrids—streamed around the upthrust stones and toward the scattered copses behind. "At the first sign of a Hkh'Rkh approaching that picket line—"

"I'll let you know immediately, sir," Sleeman interrupted.

Two of the clockwork insectoids disappeared into the

dark maw of the cave, their passive sensors intensifying the light and searching for heat sources. It wasn't long before they detected three Hkh'Rkh biosigns: two creeping carefully toward the rear of the cave, a third, no more than a dim haze disappearing.

"That third biosign: how sure are you that it is Hkh'Rkh?"

"Over ninety percent, sir. It would require two large humans to put out that much heat. And one would have to be carrying the other piggyback for the motion of the two sources to look so unitary."

"Are any of them putting out radio signals?"

"None that I'm detecting si—wait; yes. One of the closer two, but it's faint, degraded by the cave walls."

"Likelihood that other Hkh'Rkh will receive it?"

"Uncertain, sir. Not knowing the geological properties around the cave, it's entirely possible that—"

Riordan stood. "Sergeant Fanny, secure both the mouth of the cave and your present six. I'll be there in two minutes."

"You, sir? Coming out here?"

Riordan felt all three pairs of eyes on the bridge upon him. "I say again, I will be joining you. Hold the creepers in position, out of sight. I want two of the personnel you have covering the cave to swap out their lethals for suppressive rounds. Low juice feed, high rate of fire. And gas grenades for your tubes. If possible, we are going to keep this from turning into bloodshed. Keep me updated. Riordan out."

"Sir—" started Sleeman and Solsohn.

"No time," Caine interrupted. "And no time to equip a Know-It-All rig."

"Even so, sir, protocol in this situation—"

"Does not encompass the variables here. Of which, one is paramount." He was already at the ready locker just beyond the valve to the bridge. "Who here speaks Hkhi?"

Silence.

Riordan grabbed a duty suit already fitted with a ballistic liner. "I speak about four hundred words. That's probably at least three hundred ninety-nine more than they've heard from a human so far. So if there's a chance to talk our way out of a fight, this is the moment. Once blood is spilled, it becomes an Honor issue. Finding a way back to a parley would be difficult and highly unlikely."

"Yeah, I heard about that crap," Karam muttered. "Scuttlebutt is that once Honor is involved, they become bushido bear-aardvarks beating their horse chests and making much ado about nothing."

Caine pulled a CoBro 8mm liquimix rifle out of the ready-rack. "It's life and death to them, Karam. Talking to them, rather than shooting at them, in the next five minutes could mean the difference between getting our people out of here peacefully, or going to war. But if if comes to shooting, I'm going to need to know if our suppressives will work, Dr. Sleeman."

"Right. I'll get on the research. With the eye that's not watching the sensors."

"Commodore," Duncan murmured. "Protocol says you must be wearing an armor shell—a cuirass, at least—before you—"

"Major, you are correct to quote the regs. I am exercising commander's privilege to disregard due to extenuating circumstances. And if those circumstances become more extenuating than we hope, you are in charge of *Puller* in the event of my—my prolonged absence. You will also inform Major Rulaine that he is brevetted to lieutenant colonel and to carry on as the mission CO." Riordan grabbed a helmet, moved toward the ventral bay.

Duncan cleared his throat. "Good luck. Sir."

"You save that luck. Major. This situation is well in hand," Riordan lied with a smile, then resumed his short jog to the bay.

Through the combo goggles, Turkh'saar didn't look different from any other biogenic world. The outlines of the plant life were so repetitive in form as to be interchangeable and there was no color, not even of the corrected variety. Since the atmosphere on Turkh'saar was an unknown as far as humans were concerned, Riordan was running with a sealed helmet, the filtration set on maximum. The fact that other humans had already been operating here didn't prove much. For all he knew, they were using filter masks. But, glancing at the Huey again, Caine was coming to doubt that more and more.

The rest of the team showed up as blue triangles on his HUD display, located just ahead, three aiming into the cave, three aiming outward, one hunkered down in the center. Riordan headed for that central triangle, overrode the voice-activation of his tac-set, made sure the external speaker was on. "Coming in on your six," he said quietly.

The external audio pick ups crackled as Fanny responded. "We see you, Commodore." If he noticed that Caine was not armored to protocol, he didn't say anything.

Riordan crouched low as he approached, staying well out of the threat-cone defined by the cave mouth. He took a knee next to where Fanny was keeping his attention divided between the two fire teams. "Sitrep, Top."

"No movement in the cave, sir, but when our audio pickups are on max gain, we get what sound like voices."

"Human or Hkh'Rkh?"

"Too faint to say. This cave probably goes back a way. Forty meters, probably more. No further thermals, but we can see inside the first ten meters or so: abandoned sentry posts, noncombat load dumped all over the place. Everyone left in a hurry. Funny they didn't take these two helicopters."

"Not if they heard *Puller.* They probably figured us for Hkh'Rkh and that we'd shoot them out of the sky the moment they took off. What have the creepers found?"

"Solid rock in there, sir. If I send them in further, we'll lose line of sight and have to resort to broadcast. And that might not be much better. Creepercam shows us what look like some sharp switchbacks. That'll baffle-block the hell out of their weak broadcast units."

Riordan wasn't about to try a blind advance into a cave for which he had no ground plan. "Top, who's your best with comms and remote ops?"

"Lance Corporal Somers, sir. Head and shoulders above the rest."

"Okay. When we go in, she's going to keep one creeper advancing so that it remains just within LoS of our point man. I don't want to send them an automated greeting card in advance, but I'm not about to charge in there blind, either."

"And if they tweak to the creeper?"

"Then we'll have already closed to within ten meters or so."

"That could get messy, sir. Hand grenades?"

"That's our last recourse, Top. I'm here to talk to the Hkh'Rkh, not splatter them."

Fanny required an extra second to process that. "Understood, Commodore. Who do you want on entry?" He was already checking his weapon.

"I appreciate your eagerness, Top, but I need you back here, protecting our backs and maintaining a clear route of withdrawal to *Puller*. I need the calmest folks you've got. I'm guessing two of those are de los Reyes and Somers."

"That's my read on them, sir. 'Course, I haven't known 'em much longer than you have."

"No, but you eat and bunk with them, so you've had more face-time—and not in officer country. Tell me: can you spare Martell?"

"Sure, sir. Securing the mouth of the cave with a friendly corvette in immediate fire support isn't exactly a scary job. Not even for green recruits, and we don't have any of those in the Guard."

"Okay, then Martell is coming with me also. Have York watch the cavern mouth, just in case something happens to us and the OpFor comes boiling out at you."

"Roger that, sir. Anything else?"

"I'm going to get some last second info. Then we execute." He reactivated the tactical channel. "Dr. Sleeman?"

"Commodore, when are you going to start calling me Melissa?"

"When we don't have military discipline to maintain.

What have you found out about using our suppressives on the Hkh'Rkh?"

"Nothing promising. They shrugged off tear gas. CNDM was, at most, an irritant. More to their mood than their membranes."

Damn. "What about tranq rounds?"

"Not much better, sir. Their armor deflects nonlethals like ours, so you'll need hits on exposed flesh. You'll also need multiple hits, at least two to slow them down, four to drop them. But then, there's a tendency to go downhill quickly from there."

"You mean, the sedative becomes toxic at those levels?"

"That, and a possible allergic reaction. Our database still doesn't include much about their biology. It hasn't been updated since Downing was last on Earth. These early reports speculate that their allergy analogs have much more gradual onsets than ours, but if you hit them too hard with a substance, there's apparently a toxin/immuno-modulation response that gets overloaded and starts to cascade. Exponentially."

Great. So the line between knocking them out and sending them into cardiac arrest or a coma is a dangerously fine one. And probably varies from individual to individual. "Thank you, Doctor. What are you seeing on the sensors?"

"Threat vehicles are becoming active again, sir. The heavier ones in the second rank are moving, collecting into three groups. The lighter vehicles are advancing, but staying at least one hundred meters behind their scouts."

"Range?"

"The closest Hkh'Rkh team is within three hundred

meters, sir, and advancing slowly in your general direction."

"ETA if they maintain pace?"

"Five to six minutes, sir."

"Duncan, if I need those lasers for suppressive fire—"

"I can override their PDF function and use them in tactical mode, sir."

"Excellent. Riordan out."

Fanny had evidently heard the chatter, despite it being muffled by Caine's sealed helmet. He had silently rearranged his rump squad. De los Reyes, Somers, and Martell were waiting near the cave opening. "You don't have a lot of time, sir."

"You have a talent for understatement, Top. Somers, you're at the back with the ROV and comms gear, controlling the creepers and making sure we have LoS back to the cave mouth. Drop a relay each time we come to a blind corner. Martell, I want you to swap out your CoBro's expanders for tranq rounds. De los Reyes, from what I hear, you are among the Guards' best when it comes to seeing while not being seen. You've got point—but you are not, I repeat not, weapons free. If you detect anything, you wave me forward."

"Sir, with all due respect—"

"Corporal, trying to talk our way out of this means we've got to lead with a mouth, not a muzzle. That's why you're in the lead until we know contact is imminent—or we get a rude surprise. Either way, you're the best for those jobs."

Martell leaned forward. "So you want me as the slackman, Commodore?"

"No, I'm taking the number two spot until de los Reyes waves me forward. You will advance with me past de los Reyes if we are moving into final contact, because we're loaded for tranq. Set your weapon for five hundred rounds per minute, lowest juice. We want lots of hits, so low recoil."

"We won't get any penetration."

"With tranqs, it won't matter. Either we hit skin or we're just pissing 'em off. Everybody clear?"

"The plan scans, sir," de los Reyes nodded.

"Then let's move out."

Chapter Twenty-Four

Ten meters in, Caine pointed at the abandoned gear: some old-style military fatigues, sleeping bags, a few shelter-halfs rigged as hammocks, rations, water containers—but no sign of masks or spare filters. Judging from the abandoned utensils, no one had been eating through the cheek-mounted ration packets that CTR troops had nicknamed "feed-bags." Riordan popped the full seal on his helmet, opened the earplates.

"Yeh reck that tae be safe, sir?" Somers asked.

"Mostly, and at this point, I want to be listening with my own ears rather than those damned pickups."

"Bear" de los Reyes nodded emphatically. "Copy that, sir."

They all adjusted their gear.

Faint sounds came from up ahead. Then a sudden sonorous hoot.

"What the hell—?" breathed Martell.

"Hkh'Rkh expression of surprise," Caine explained.

"Happy or nae?" Somers whispered.

312

"Can't tell." Riordan put a hand over his mouth to signal for silence, nodded to de los Reyes. They resumed their advance.

Ten meters further on, staying as close to the cavern's sides as the irregular surface allowed, Riordan watched one of the two small blue dots in his HUD—a creeper—inch forward. It revealed a low side cavern filled with stores, mostly of unfamiliar manufacture and purpose. The creepercam cycled through vision options until it arrived at maximum-gain thermal imaging. Ghostly footprints were revealed, both entering and exiting the chamber. Somers panned the view around the chamber: no biosigns of any kind.

De los Reyes held up, took a knee, gestured with his off hand toward the main branch of the cavern, checking if it was permissible to bypass the storage area. Riordan nodded and gave a forward wave. De los Reyes nodded back, rose, resumed their approach.

Somers moved the second creeper beyond the first, performing a kind of remote-operated leapfrog advance deeper into the cave. Some thermal afterimages came into view: faint, but over two meters tall. Hkh'Rkh had passed recently. De los Reyes slowed his advance. If he made any noise, Riordan could not hear it.

Five meters further on, the lead creepercam showed the cavern becoming far more irregular: sharp turns and cuts and dips. More thermal afterimages, but almost fully faded. On the other hand, the creeper's audio pickup was becoming far more active. There was clearly an excited conversation in Hkhi taking place. Hard to tell how far away given the twists in the passage, though.

"What are they saying, sir?" Somers asked.

"Can't tell. The ones I knew spoke a lot more English than I ever spoke Hkhi. The local dialect and this cave's acoustics don't help. But they're excited; trying to figure something out." *So we'd better hurry.* "Corporal de los Reyes, we've gotta pick up the pace. Now."

"Bear" de los Reyes waved once and began moving with long, gliding steps. He entered the cave's chicane section with fast, waist-snapping motions as he covered each new bend with his rifle. But his feed, as well as that from the creepers ahead of him, was starting to break up.

"Commodore," Somers whispered tensely, "I'm losing contact with de los Reyes. And our signal back to the cave mouth isn't—"

Riordan shook his head, kept moving forward. The switchbacks in the cave were causing more trouble than anticipated. *Well, no plan survives contact with reality and today is no exception.* He looked back at Martell quickly, very deliberately took his gun off safety; the private did the same.

De los Reyes held up the same moment that the lead creeper went swiftly around a corner and suddenly found itself on the threshold of a large, higher-ceilinged chamber. And behind a small outcropping of rock to the right, were two Hkh'Rkh. But they were only partially visible, and their actions had them moving into the line of sight and out again.

"Double-time," Riordan ordered Martell. "De los Reyes, we're going past you."

"Copy that."

Riordan discovered his armpits were suddenly as damp and cold as if he'd climbed out of a pool. He wondered what his pulse and BP looked like, refused to spare them a glance. His focus was rapidly contracting down to a single point: the large, thermal Hkh'Rkh silhouettes that came into view in his own combo goggles at the end of his third step past de los Reyes...

Which was the same moment that the larger of the two silhouettes raised a darker object. It had the boxy outline of a Hkh'Rkh assault rifle. Its wielder aimed it at something hidden by the rock outcropping, snarled something about ugly or monstrous humans.

Riordan tensed. Had they discovered humans hiding back in the cave? Maybe not—but reflex took over, because he had to beat a tightening trigger finger.

Riordan stepped forward, shouted "No!" in Hkhi. Then "Friend!" and "Honor!"—as the Hkh'Rkh spun and aimed the gun in his direction, albeit somewhat uncertainly. Then, a split second later, the aim steadied.

Damn it. Caine dropped, locking his CoBro's smart tracking system on the approximate target area, and squeezed the trigger.

The cave amplified the rebounding reports into a deafening, spastic thunder. The sharp twelve-millimeter barks of the Hkh'Rkh weapon sent a spray of rounds snapping over Riordan's head, snarling and whining as they chewed at the rock wall behind him. Riordan's CoBro uttered a simultaneous rippling cough, a byproduct of the high rate of fire and low velocity projectives. A few of which may have hit, thanks to the gun's automatic area engagement system and gyroscopic stabilization.

A second stream of CoBro fire added to his own: Martell, firing from behind the last turn of the rocky chicane.

The Hkh'Rkh's thermal outline staggered under the impact of the combined fires, recovered slowly.

"Friend. Stop," shouted Riordan. "No kill. No fight." He had already spent forty of the sixty tranq rounds in his heterogenous magazine. After that, he only had standard penetrators.

The upper torso of another Hkh'Rkh silhouette popped around the blind corner, raising a shorter, but heavier weapon: a scattergun.

"Commodore?" de los Reyes yelled over the tac channel as the first Hkh'Rkh resumed firing, albeit unsteadily. Splinters of shattered stone started jetting up in front of Riordan.

Damn it. "Go lethal." He swapped over to his magazine's left-hand stack, cut the rate of fire to two hundred rounds per minute, upped the hot juice to fifty percent, and aimed at the further silhouette.

By that time, Martell had unleashed the rest of his tranqs at the lead Hkh'Rkh, who wavered, his aim wandering away from Caine as he staggered back toward cover—and straight into Caine's and de los Reyes's line of fire.

The echoing, much-magnified sound of the CoBros had changed; each now emitted a stuttering hiss. The fleeing Hkh'Rkh's silhouette sagged almost as soon as the ugly duet commenced, and a moment later, de los Reyes's rounds were chewing into the cover used by the other Hkh'Rkh, who flinched back.

"Sound off," yelled Caine, who scrambled to the side of the chamber, getting out of the second Hkh'Rkh's line of sight. Martell, de los Reyes, and Somers all answered.

"Now what?" Martell asked. In the background,

Riordan could hear him reloading and making adjustments to his CoBro.

The second Hkh'Rkh popped out briefly. The twenty-four-millimeter shotgun roared like a stone-gutted cannon. As de los Reyes's CoBro replied, a moment too late, Caine made sure his voice was steady. "Martell, get up here with me. Move after his next pop out."

"Sir, how do you know he'll—?"

Riordan grabbed an abandoned boot, tossed it back toward his prior position.

The Hkh'Rkh evidently leaned out, blasted at the sound. De los Reyes returned several shots: came closer, but did not hit the big exosapient. Under the cover of that targeted fire, Martell rolled around the final corner of the chicane and scrambled over to join Caine, out of the enemy's field of vision.

"Somers," Riordan said, "sacrifice a creeper. Keep the other in overwatch. De los Reyes, we'll be going in low and close."

"Yes, sir," they answered in unison as the Hkh'Rkh leaned out and blasted away again. Apparently at nothing.

In his HUD, Riordan watched the newest creeper skitter forward. The other fanned out to the left, courting the shadows and moving slowly, ultimately achieving a flanking view of the large exosapient, who had just finished reloading his weapon.

The other creeper reached the blind side of the corner, just two meters closer to it than Riordan and Martell.

Somers's voice was sharp. "I'm in position."

"Go."

The flanking creeper emitted a short chirp, skittered

back. The Hkh'Rkh started, swung its weapon uncertainly in that direction—just as the other creeper scuttled around the corner.

As it rounded the bend, its feed zoomed in on the Hkh'Rkh's digitigrade left leg, painted brief crosshairs on the joint most analogous to the ankle. The exosapient became aware of the closer creeper, swung his weapon down sharply—

Less than a meter away, the creeper launched itself with all limbs. Its appendages stretched out, grabbed hold, and tugged its body tight against the boot-greave of the exosapient.

It was the other creepercam which showed its small mechanical twin explode, taking the Hkh'Rkh's leg out from under it, the large being slumping abruptly into the sheltering wall.

"Go," muttered Caine.

He and Martell swept around the corner. Caine went wide and low, Martell tucked close and kept his weapon high.

"Stop!" Caine yelled in Hkhi. "Stop now!"

The Hkh'Rkh, holding his ruined joint with one gore-drenched hand, was so surprised that the scattergun slipped in his grip; he grabbed after it, started bringing it up—

Probably just reflex, Caine thought bitterly. *But if I'm wrong—*

He squeezed the trigger of his CoBro the same moment that Martell did.

At two meters range, two five-round bursts of eight-millimeter CoBro penetrators were the equivalent of industrial mining lasers going through a plywood sheet. The Hkh'Rkh's armor was peppered with holes,

none particularly big. Even the exit wounds were
not especially gruesome; they only varied from the
entry wounds because the smart rounds knew when
to start allowing flanges to widen out from their tails,
thereby increasing drag and imparting more energy
to the target.

The Hkh'Rkh fell back against the covering wall,
already limp, and then slumped over, leaving a dull
mauve smear behind him.

Caine rotated, swept his weapon across the back
of the cave, searching for what the first Hkh'Rkh had
been threatening with his assault rifle.

And discovered that it was, improbably, another
Hkh'Rkh, crouched in a cage just large enough for
him to stand in. *What the hell—?*

Martell came up alongside him, saw the imprisoned
local. "Sir, are we clear? Or not?"

"That, Martell, is an excellent question." Riordan
panned his helmet cam slowly. "Are the rest of you
seeing this?" There were murmured affirmatives.

Martell stepped closer. "Were they going to shoot
him, sir?"

Riordan swept the room with his goggles at max
gain. "Somers, does your last creeper show anything
in here with us?"

"No, sir. I've had it scoot around the perimeter.
Except for that caged bugbear, ye're clear."

"Understood. Corporal, you head back to where
you can regain LoS to Sergeant Fanny."

"But, sir—"

"Martell, you follow her far enough so that you
and she can still read each other *and* you've either
got LoS to me, or can shout and be heard."

"Got it, sir."

De los Reyes came alongside Caine as Martell departed. "And me, sir?"

"You keep your rifle trained on this Hkh'Rkh. Semi-automatic, expander rounds, go for a leg if you feel you can do so safely. I need a prisoner, not a corpse."

"Yes, sir. I'll do what I can." Bernardo de los Reyes did not sound enthusiastically committed to his new assignment.

Riordan turned toward him, raised his faceplate. "Corporal, if you can't curb your animosity and follow your orders to the letter, I will have your stripes in my hand and your ass in hack. Within the hour."

De los Reyes's eyes opened a little wider. He nodded. "Sir, yes, sir. I will only shoot to subdue. Unless you are in imminent mortal danger, sir."

"Excellent." Riordan stepped closer to the cage. The Hkh'Rkh's small, black-pebble eyes followed him warily, but he did not move. Caine studied the dimensions of the cage. *Probably can't shift position even if he wanted to.*

Studying the Hkh'Rkh further, he was struck by another difference: the exosapient's apparel. It was different from those of the two that had been killed; it looked more finished, as if it was part of a uniform. A closer look yielded more evidence for that conjecture: there were insignias of rank on his shoulders, where epaulets would be on a human uniform. Riordan recognized the rank; he was a senior band leader. Roughly equal to a sergeant, but with overtones of being both a warrant officer and a lieutenant-in-training.

But the wide-legged shorts that were the typical Hkh'Rkh lower garment were not of the same manufacture. Wait; no, they were, but they had been damaged, torn.

No: shot. There were two bullet holes near the cuff. Crouching down, Riordan inspected that leg: it was still wrapped. One wound, mostly healed, was uncovered. Caine stared at it, quickly glanced up at the Hkh'Rkh.

Surprised, it flinched away its eyes, unsuccessfully trying to conceal its reciprocal interest.

Caine stood slowly, toggled the tactical channel, hoped the relay through Martell and Somers was working. "*Puller*, can you read me?"

"Aye, sir," Duncan's voice answered, "and glad you're on the horn. You don't have a lot of time left. The Hkh'Rkh are closing in on your position. Not a lot of them, but if we want to keep this bloodless—"

"We're past that. I don't know if my Hkhi was incomprehensible, they were worried about being tricked, or they just didn't give a damn. But I blew our chances to keep this from going sideways. I've got two dead in here and . . . are you seeing this?"

"Yes, sir," Sleeman replied. "We've seen high-speed playback of the whole encounter. There's nothing you could have done, sir."

"That's not my focus, now. Run the playback from the creepercams and time it. How long do you estimate the two Hkh'Rkh scouts were in this rearmost chamber before we arrived?"

There was a pause. "Maybe twenty seconds, sir. But I repeat, don't blame yourself—"

"Doctor, I'm not concerned with that right now. Twenty seconds. They must have found him here."

"Stands to reason," Karam said in the background.

Riordan scanned the area around the cage, discovered a drinking vessel, a honeypot, some food that was definitely not of human origin. He studied the cage more closely. It had been fashioned from thick wooden shafts, and the door was secured with a distinctly human padlock of massive proportions. *An old one*, Riordan realized, and upon leaning closer to it, discovered that the manufacturer's information was written in Cyrillic.

Riordan leaned away. "He wasn't being threatened."

"Then why did they level a gun at him?" Somers asked.

"They weren't aiming at him. They were trying to shoot off the lock."

De los Reyes sounded skeptical. "Sir, do you really think it would take them that long just to shoot a lock?"

"I do, Corporal. Look at the size of that cage. He couldn't get out of their field of fire. He probably had to fold himself over like a contortionist to be safe. At which point, we enter the picture."

Duncan's voice was eager. "So you think he was their—the humans'—prisoner?"

Riordan rubbed his lower lip. "Well, let's find out." He approached the cage. The Hkh'Rkh did not move. Caine stared meaningfully at his symbols of rank, then some other markings on his armor's midriff, which usually denoted lineage, status, other data of a personal nature.

Riordan inclined his head slowly, bending it further forward as he did so in order to best emulate the Hkh'Rkh gesture of respectful greeting among equals. "Honor," he pronounced carefully in Hkhi.

The exosapient did not react. But that in itself was

odd. The prisoner certainly spoke Hkhi, so he should have been shocked to hear it coming out of a human. "You know that word. And you're not surprised."

Still no response. Well, that was to be expected. This Hkh'Rkh was on the horns of a dilemma and was sticking with the best path for interviews or interrogations by an enemy: no response.

But Caine was facing his own dilemma. "I also suspect that you know English, or possibly *du kannst die Deutsch*," he finished, shifting into the tongue that Yaargraukh had told him was the second most common human language studied by the Hkh'Rkh. No response to either. But the lack of response confirmed what Caine now perceived as a careful lack of all expression.

He's in Patrijuridicate standard livery. He was probably in, or prepped, for the invasion. So he's likely to know a little English. Maybe a lot. And it had better be the latter because we're down to three minutes, at most.

Riordan sighed. "Normally, I'd like to take this slowly and carefully, to learn of your lineage and your Sire and Greatsires. But you are not talking and I don't have a lot of time, so here's how it's going to go. I can't afford to leave you here, and I'm pretty sure you know exactly what I'm saying. I'm sure because I was at the Convocation and know how many of your people speak one or more of our languages. So, to me, you are either a source of intelligence or an intelligence risk. And if I can't tell which, I have about thirty seconds to tranq you and stick you in our brig. Of course, if your forces retake this cave first, that means you'll die alongside us. Or, if you want to help both our peoples, you could talk to me. You have ten seconds to decide."

Eyes still on the Hkh'Rkh, Caine chinned his commlink to *Puller.* "Any radio activity?" And then, hoping against hope at this last possible moment: "Any word from Yaargraukh?"

As Duncan started to detail the limited enemy radio chatter, the prisoner's small black eyes almost ejected themselves from their leathery protective folds. "You—know Yaargraukh?" His English was heavily accented, but thoroughly understandable.

"I do. I was with him at the Convocation. I was with him on Earth. He is a friend. He will know me."

"What name are you known by, human?"

"Caine Riordan."

The Hkh'Rkh's eyes yanked back into their covers. "This name is an ill-omen. It is said you are an oathbreaker whose lies led to the deaths of many of our Warriors."

"Is that what Yaargraukh says?"

"No." The prisoner's eyes returned hesitantly, the folds sagging around them: sadness, frustration, futility. "I believe he holds you in esteem. But he is almost alone in that opinion. And he is too shrewd to make public statements on your behalf. He would be branded a traitor."

Riordan nodded. "I understand. What are you called?"

The Hkh'Rkh looked at the two human rifles. "I am Ezzraamar Laarkhduur of the Moiety of Nys'maharn, senior band leader of the Patrijuridicate and in present service to the Colonial Militia of Turkh'saar. Why do you ask?"

"To do you honor, no matter what you decide. Your ten seconds are up, Ezzraamar of the Moiety of Nys'maharn. Tell me: what do you want to do?"

"I want you to fire your tranquilizing rounds into me, but to leave me here."

Riordan frowned. "Why?" Duncan was counting down the seconds to probable enemy contact with increasing tension in his voice. Caine tuned it out, focused on Ezzraamar's answer.

"I cannot go with you. I do not know if you mean to harm or help us."

"We are here to remove the humans on Turkh'saar."

"Are they your raiders?"

Riordan shook his head. "Absolutely not. Not authorized by the Consolidated Terran Republic, at any rate. We are here to find and extract them. That is all."

Ezzraamar's head wagged slowly from side to side. "Puzzling, yet your uncertainty of their origins recalls Yaargraukh's own confusion—and now mine—regarding their purpose here. What I have heard since becoming their prisoner is not consistent with the speech or motivations of raiders. That is why I am willing to speak with you at all."

Duncan's voice was becoming louder. "Commodore—"

"Hold position, Major. Fire if you must." Riordan turned back toward Ezzraamar. "I have to leave in sixty seconds. Tell me why I should tranq you and leave you here."

"Because if you take me with you, I could share some information, but then I will be utterly useless to you, and the other Warriors will not trust me once I have been your prisoner. But if you tranq me and leave me behind, I can explain that you found me just moments before our own forces arrived, and that you subdued me after your failed attempt to tranquilize the two Warriors you first encountered in this chamber. They will see that you are trying not to kill us. Hopefully, they will take me back to our capitol, Iarzut'thruk, to debrief me. I will be able to surreptitiously inform Yaargraukh that you are on Turkh'saar now. This is the best hope for both our peoples."

Damn, this guy's sharp. "I agree. But I could start trying to contact Yaargraukh right now, since—"

"No. Do not attempt that. There are political tensions of which you are unaware. Contact from you could easily be construed to mean that Yaargraukh is your confidential agent, and hence, a traitor. Contact must come from him. If it is permitted at all."

Riordan knew that five minutes more would give him all the information he needed to massage the unfolding scenario into a better, maybe peaceful, outcome. But it was five minutes more than he had left: Duncan was shouting in his ear. "Just had to use the lasers on their scouts, sir. No helping it. Couldn't see if they were packing missiles, or something else that might cripple *Puller*."

"Acknowledged," Caine replied. "We're coming out. De los Reyes, start back and tell Somers to retrieve her creeper and unass this cave." De los Reyes left, making disapproving sounds. Riordan switched his CoBro back over to feed from his magazine's tranq stack. "Ezzraamar, these tranq rounds are a major risk. Three probably won't put you out. Five or six could kill you."

"Then I suggest you use four and wait to see if I fall over."

"I would, except I don't have the time to wait."

Ezzraamar's head swung from side to side. "Then fire five and we shall hope for the best—for both our sakes."

Admiring the unflinching courage of the Hkh'Rkh, Riordan leveled the CoBro at Ezzraamar's unwounded leg and fired four rounds into it.

The exosapient staggered, blinked, slurred, "Yooo zhud fire mawr than faw . . . fawr. To be shurr . . ." He slumped over.

"You need to be sure of survival," Riordan answered as the Hkh'Rkh's eyes slowly retracted fully into their folds.

He turned and ran, shouting for Fanny to prepare for a leapfrog retreat back across the clearing to *Puller* and for Tsaami to be ready to boost as soon as they were in the ventral bay.

Chapter Twenty-Five

Some of the clustertrees were smoldering when Riordan followed de los Reyes out of the cave mouth. Twenty meters away, Fanny had the balance of the security team hunkered down behind some crates. They were scanning the southern half of the perimeter constantly.

The cave entry team had crossed half the distance to the crates when a patter of small, scree-flinging explosions erupted, paralleling their path ten meters to the west.

"Cover right!" Fanny shouted over the tactical channel. "The CO is under fire—"

"Belay that." Duncan's interruption was sharp. "That fire is intended for *Puller*."

"Pretty weak effort," Riordan remarked as he threw himself down behind the crate next to Fanny's.

"They probably don't know what they're shooting at," Solsohn explained. "Our passive track-back indicates that burst came from one of their light vehicles, almost four hundred meters away. They don't have any units closer than that."

Fanny scanned the solid walls of interconnected trees around them. "How the hell do they know where to shoot? Er . . . sir."

"There's a pipe-thin sight line from their position to ours. My guess is they can't see us, but they'll have passive sensors, too, and *Puller*'s engines must stand out like flares on their thermals. I could use the laser I kept in PDF mode to intercept the rounds, Commodore."

Riordan considered. "Negative, Major. Intercept requires active sensors. If they've got any missiles waiting for us, we might as well paint a bull's eye on the hull."

"Just trying to keep down the local bodycount, sir."

"Acknowledged. But we're going to need to take out that vehicle before we can cross the rest of the clearing."

"I could maneuver closer—" began Karam.

"Negative. Don't give them anything new to detect and aim at. Duncan, can you align the railgun back down that line of sight to the enemy vehicle?" Another patter of autocannon rounds tore up a strip of ground near the two helicopters, leading toward *Puller*.

"Already there, sir. We rotated *Puller* to take the enemy under fire if necessary."

"Then I say three times: you are weapons free. Engage the target."

Puller, still hovering at the far edge of the clearing, rose up slightly. A sharp flash near its bow—so quick that Riordan wondered if he had actually seen or imagined it—was accompanied by the characteristically flat crash of a railgun discharge. An instant later, deep in the woods, there was a sharp explosion.

"Target neutralized," Duncan reported.

Riordan rose, waving the others up. "Let's go. Straight into the ventral bay. No rear security element. Move."

Riordan knew that there were no Hkh'Rkh within visual range and that the only enemy that had weapons bearing was now a flaming wreck. But that did not reduce Riordan's eagerness to get across the clearing and up *Puller*'s ramp. As soon as the last Guard was on board, he leaned toward his helmet's audio pickup. "We're aboard. Boost." Then, to the troopers around him: "Hang on."

They did—just in time to get slung about like rucksacks dangling from single straps.

Karam's voice was calm, almost amused. "Where to, sir?"

"I'll tell you as soon as I get a report from Dr. Sleeman on enemy movement."

There was a pause, during which *Puller*'s flight leveled off. Then: "Commodore, this doesn't make sense."

"Details, please, Doctor."

"Yes, sir. I'm piping it to your HUD. Faster that way."

The view through the helmet visor grayed as it went into display mode. An aerial view of the same region blinked into existence, but the positions and activities of the Hkh'Rkh sensor contacts were radically different from before. Rather than reversing away from the clearing, the local vehicles, both light and heavy, were converging on it rapidly. Further to the right, or east, the Hkh'Rkh scouts who had apparently caught the scent of the fleeing humans were now overtaking them. Video feed from the quadrotors sent to that area showed that two light vehicles had swerved to join the pursuit.

"Typical," Riordan murmured.

"What's typical?" Karam asked. "That the Hkh'Rkh are crazy?"

"No. When faced with aggression, they don't stop to assess. They just respond with even more aggression. I suspect their evolution hardwired them for it."

Solsohn's voice was flat. "Tactically stupid, though."

"I saw plenty of that in Indonesia," Riordan agreed. "But in the long run, it helps them, too. Anyone they fight knows that when a Warrior is coming at you, it is not a threat, it's a promise—and either you or they will die in the process of their keeping it. If anyone's morale is shaky, they give up—and the Hkh'Rkh spare them. They never kill or torture prisoners, even though they may have utter disdain for them. It's part of their code."

Sleeman sounded distracted. "A bit like the Mongols. Surrender, and your life goes on as before. Resist, and you're exterminated."

But Riordan's attention was on the vehicles converging on the clearing they had left. *Damn it, if they keep coming on at that pace, I won't have any choice but to . . .* "Karam, we need to get between the Hkh'Rkh chasers and the humans we have to extract."

"Sir, if I do that, I can't guarantee the Hkh'Rkh won't eyeball us."

"Acknowledged. But tell Wedge One to stay north of the objective. We need to keep them out of the fight."

"Roger. Executing."

The deck swayed as *Puller* began angling in a different direction.

Fanny stood. "What about us, sir?"

"Restock ammo and consumables and rest if you can. I don't think the day—well, the night—is over just yet."

Riordan arrived on the bridge just as Karam Tsaami was slowing *Puller* and easing her down closer to the trees. "One of those vehicles saw us, sir. Took a pot shot. Missed by a mile. Literally."

"No target lock? No guidance systems?"

"It was cannon fire. Not even laser targeting. Amateur hour."

"Local militia," Riordan corrected as he slid into his acceleration couch. "They've probably got hand-me-downs, and even the frontline Hkh'Rkh matériel was pretty rudimentary, by our standards." He studied the regional overview. "But they've got lots of it, and it's all over the place."

Karam nodded. "So what's the play, Skipper? Hovering on fans isn't something we can do all day."

Riordan started forward. "No, it isn't, and not just because of fuel consumption. Look."

As the larger blue delta signifying *Puller* settled to the south of the fleeing human icons, and Wedge One began paralleling them on the north, their activity became frenetic.

"What the hell—?" began Solsohn.

"They've heard us. They're getting spooked."

Duncan nodded. "And they think we're the Hkh'Rkh, just like they did back at their camp."

Riordan glanced at the diminishing distance to the scouts and light vehicles approaching from the south. One of the quadrotors gave him a brief glimpse of what looked like an armored car with a large, shielded machine gun. If its crew had seen the human sensor platform, it gave no sign of it.

"Caine..." began Karam. It was one of the few times Riordan could remember the pilot sounding worried.

"Okay. Here's the bad plan—which is the one we're following because all the alternatives are worse plans. We're going to land and redeploy Fanny's team to take out those vehicles. We're going to cover their rear from those"—he flicked his laser pointer at the converging mass of vehicles to the west—"which have just pushed through the old clearing without stopping. Otherwise, they're going to be on us within a few minutes.

"Dr. Sleeman, orders for Wedge One. They are to get within two klicks of the northernmost humans and land a squad. The squad is to attempt to make contact directly and secure the cooperation of the humans."

There was silence on the bridge. Duncan cleared his throat. "Those are pretty ambitious orders, sir."

"They are. On the other hand, our other two alternatives are to eliminate all the pursuing Hkh'Rkh, which I'm pretty sure that they—or any other self-aware species—will interpret as an act of outright and unrestrained war. Or we can stand back and let a bunch of humans who do not seem to be here of their own volition get slaughtered. I'm open to alternatives."

There were two seconds of silence.

Right. "Major Solsohn, see to the deployment of Sergeant Fanny's squad in that rocky high ground just a klick north of their oncoming scout line. We have a MULTI system onboard, correct?"

"One, sir. But in those rocks, a MULTI is going to have line-of-sight problems."

"That's not a problem at all; Fanny's team is going to

use it in the indirect launch mode. Have them pull at least a dozen of the overhead-attack antiarmor rockets to add to their standard load. Also, all line personnel are to be given double loads of flechette RAPs.

"Fanny's mission is to halt the Hkh'Rkh, not to inflict maximum casualties. So his first job is to take out the vehicles with the MULTI. After that, the CoBros have significant range and lethality advantages over the Hkh'Rkh shoulder arms, and should be able to keep the enemy infantry at a distance. The plan is to extract Fanny's team five minutes after they engage, if not sooner."

Duncan was already talking to Fanny. "I'm on it, sir."

As *Puller* began decelerating and angling toward the cluster of rocks that Fanny's squad was going to use as their defensive position, Sleeman looked up. "Commodore, Major Rulaine on command channel. Private and scrambled."

Riordan nodded, toggled the circuit open. "*Puller* Actual."

"Caine, we're landing Wedge One now. I'm just not sure how we're going to make contact with our targets. These guys are rabbiting out in every direction. And they don't know that we're friendlies—if, in fact, we are."

"Understood, Bannor." *Puller* tugged to a halt, settled quickly; Duncan was talking Fanny toward the battery position for the MULTI. "Tell your ground team that self-protection is first priority, making contact is second. Shadow them and be ready to extract."

"Already there. But there's a deployment issue."

"Which is?"

"Caine, experience and doctrine both say that I shouldn't drop any element smaller than a 3-sib team into a hot LZ. But that's going to give us a maximum of four search elements."

As *Puller* lurched aloft again, Riordan spent two precious seconds considering the alternatives. "Send them out in teams of two. Maximum separation of one hundred meters between teams."

Rulaine punctuated his answer with an affirming grunt. "I can live with that. Wedge One out."

Melissa Sleeman cleared her throat. "Commodore, to the west—"

Riordan glanced, nodded. "I see them." The lighter vehicles had, if anything, accelerated their approach. Almost half of the heavy ones had stopped in a fairly open formation.

"Targets, sir?" asked Duncan.

"As soon as I know what we have to shoot at," Caine answered. He circled one of the stationary vehicles with his pointer. "Doctor, can you angle one of our quadrotors to give me a visual of that?"

"I'll try, sir."

Karam's voice was almost bored once again. "Look like full-sized APCs."

"Yes, that's their chassis. But these stopped and they don't seem to be dismounting troops."

"So you're thinking—?"

"I'm thinking they're—that." Riordan leaned forward as the image from the quadrotor cut into the overhead. The vehicle was indeed a wheeled APC chassis, but the passenger compartment had been converted into a spacious bay, protected by top-folding doors that were opening as they watched. Once fully out of the way, they could see what was in the bay: a single muzzle, angled toward the sky.

"Mortar," Karam breathed.

"Or a rocket launcher," Riordan added. "But I'm thinking you're right, Flight Officer. I see no vents for launch exhaust to get out of that bay."

"It's a mortar," Duncan averred. "Look. There's a gun crew climbing around back there. No signs of remote operation systems, so the bay has to be safe for the Warriors tending the weapon."

Melissa Sleeman glanced back at Fanny's team: the small blue triangles marking his personnel were less active now. They had evidently settled into their positions. "Sir, once Sergeant Fanny starts firing his MULTI—"

"Yes, Doctor. We've got to assume that the Hkh'Rkh will range him and start counterbattery fire." *Which means I have to take another escalatory step, damn it.* "Major Solsohn, get firing solutions for all six of those halted vehicles."

"Already calculated, sir. Awaiting fire orders."

Riordan would have liked to close his eyes. Or take a stiff drink. Or vomit. "Engage all targets, starting with the northernmost. Walk your fire down the length of their formation."

"Engaging targets, sir."

On the one hand, Riordan was simply grateful and relieved for the immense superiority of technology and firepower resident in *Puller*. On the other, there was a sickening frustration that, despite possessing such an immense advantage, he had no way to convert it into a bloodless solution, a stalemate. But there was no way to communicate his actual intents, and the Hkh'Rkh would have probably disbelieved him, anyway.

Puller jolted as its railgun discharged. With almost

light-speed suddenness, the northernmost mortar carrier flared brightly in the thermal imaging overlay. As
Duncan shifted his aimpoint, and *Puller* swung slightly
to port to acquire that firing vector, the stricken
vehicle continued to fulminate furiously, sporadically;
its ammunition hoppers were cooking off. Riordan
saw a wheel—massing at least a quarter of a ton—fly
off the chassis as if some child was flinging away an
unwanted donut.

Duncan fired again. The result was less spectacular,
but just as swift: the vehicle seemed to cave in on
itself, with a bright glowing line running down its
longitudinal axis.

"What's that?" Sleeman asked.

"That," Riordan muttered, "is where the projectile
sliced through and severed the metal of the chassis
along the vehicle's centerline. The edges are probably molten."

As Solsohn engaged the third vehicle, Sleeman
glanced at her sensor panel. "The remaining vehicles
are firing, sir."

Riordan acknowledged with a nod. "Flight Officer
Tsaami, take over PDF. Engage the rounds if needed."

"Looks like they're firing blind, sir. They're not
running active sensors, and they haven't had enough
time to range us for counterbattery fire."

Not that it would matter if they did. A mortar
round hitting the hull of *Puller* was like a spitball
splatting against a suit of medieval armor. "Continue
to monitor their fire." *For the twenty seconds that
they might still be alive.*

Actually, it was only another twelve seconds before
Duncan Solsohn had walked the railgun projectiles down

to the southernmost vehicle of the mobile battery. Not wanting to see their grim handiwork, but resolved to the necessity, Riordan nodded at Sleeman. "Those burning vehicles are giving us a lot of thermal smudge. Bring the quadrotors a little closer to the lighter vehicles. I need to see how they, and the infantry, are responding."

Sleeman complied. The quadrotors' cameras showed what Riordan had expected: hurried confabs between vehicle commanders and individual scouts, gesticulations, aid teams running back toward the burning mortar carriers in what both they and Riordan knew were futile missions of mercy.

"Radio activity, sir," Sleeman reported. "But they are not using any of their wartime codes. This is a simple transposition cypher, Commodore."

Riordan nodded. "Homegrown, probably. After their invasion failed and we captured all their equipment, they'll presume that all their codes are compromised."

Duncan turned round in his seat, his face grave, his eyes unblinking. "Sir, since they are transmitting..."

Riordan sighed, waved his hand. "Lock on their signals. Fire as soon as you acquire each target." He rubbed his eyes.

Sleeman's voice was low, almost horrified. "Sir—is that absolutely necessary? They are no longer advancing toward us, and—"

"—and they could resume that advance any second, Doctor. Besides, we need to teach them that they cannot operate their radios without giving us a free target lock on that transmitter. If they can't use their radios, they can't coordinate tactically or send reports back home. Both of which slow them down and buy us time."

"And make it all the more unlikely that they might try to talk to us. Sir."

Riordan did not look up, waved his hand at the sensor overlay while further jolts from *Puller*'s railgun announced the bright, sudden deaths of even more Hkh'Rkh vehicles. "I think we're already past that point, don't you?"

As *Puller* maneuvered back toward Fanny's squad, there was one final MULTI launch from the ring-fort of rocks. The ten-by-seventy-five-centimeter missile arced upward, trailing rapidly cooling exhaust, then pitched over sharply and flashed down—and straight through the glacis plate of yet another light APC which had come to support the uncertain advance against the Cold Guards' position. In the overhead view, the vehicle sagged, and vaporous heat—smoke—started leaking out from a thermal smudge up near its bow. Several Hkh'Rkh silhouettes bailed out, but far fewer than were the typical crew and passenger complement of such vehicles.

Riordan nodded at Solsohn. "Tell Fanny to prepare for extraction in ninety seconds. Dr. Sleeman, give me a last sweep. Any enemy scouts in the area?"

"The closest is three hundred meters away. The range is increasing."

Retreating. At last. "Very good. Karam, take us in as close to those rocks as you can, and no longer than it takes to scoop up Fanny's squad."

"Aye, aye, sir."

As *Puller* began slewing around on its fans to back into the LZ and give the Guards a straight run up into the ventral bay, Sleeman looked over at Riordan.

"Sir, Major Rulaine reports his people haven't had any success approaching our extraction targets to the east. And most of the Hkh'Rkh scouts have remained in that area. It's a total jumble."

Riordan sighed. "Zoom out, Doctor. Give me an overview of the AO."

The bridge screen showed that the Hkh'Rkh scouts to the south had not been deterred either by Fanny's elimination of the light vehicles supporting them, or his team's sniping at those individuals unfortunate enough to wander within half a klick of his position. Instead, the Warriors had simply flowed further eastward, skirting the Guards' position and coming into direct contact with a number of the southernmost human icons. Judging from the intermittent, abrupt, movements, it now appeared to be a running gunfight, with the humans getting very much the worst of the engagement.

"Damn it," Duncan muttered. "They're going to be slaughtered."

Karam agreed. "Without night vision, they'll never have a chance. They're getting picked off at ranges over one hundred meters." As another cluster of Hkh'Rkh icons angled to cut off the humans' route of retreat, his head hung slightly. "Worst case scenario, all around."

Riordan settled back. "Sadly, it may actually turn out to be a blessing in disguise."

"Sir?" Sleeman's carefully controlled tone did not quite mask the shock beneath it.

"Doctor, we've not had an opportunity to make our intentions clear to anyone so far. Except for Ezzraamar, who we had to leave tranqed and locked up. But now,

we have an absolutely clear means of communication."
Riordan reached for his couch straps. "Flight Officer
Tsaami, as soon as we have Sergeant Fanny's team on
board, get us moving east. Best speed."

"Sir, 'best speed' means no NOE, and that means
maximum exposure to enemy counterfire and detec—"

"Screw their counterfire and detection. We need to
get there five minutes ago. So boost. Now."

Chapter Twenty-Six

Riordan gripped the armrests of his command couch. *Karam certainly knows how to fly—and scare his passengers to death.*

Tsaami had not followed the treetops after *Puller* retrieved Fanny's squad. He had boosted up hard, rolled and come back down almost nose-first, just beyond the easternmost blocking force with which the Hkh'Rkh had cut off much of the human retreat. At only one hundred meters altitude, he now half-flipped *Puller* into a belly-down attitude, fans groaning as they snapped into vertical mode.

The stomach-plunging plummet ended with an abrupt, gag-inducing jerk that sent every loose object on the bridge smacking up against the ceiling before raining back down. They were hovering at eight meters altitude.

"What now?" Karam asked.

"Hold us steady," Riordan answered. "Doctor, I want target lock on all the enemy between us and the humans."

342

"Target lock—on individuals? Sir, I'd need active sensors in order to be one hundred percent certain of hits and of discriminating between human and Hkh'Rkh—"

"Engage active sensors. Get those locks. Major Solsohn, how many discrete targets are you reading?"

Solsohn sounded reluctant. "I assume you are referring to the Hkh'Rkh only, sir?"

"That is correct."

The major half-turned toward Caine. "Sir, I am compelled to point out that, according to the operation orders and rules of engagement, we have not yet conclusively determined that—"

"You are free to lodge a complaint regarding my orders and leadership after this engagement, Major. Right now, the Hkh'Rkh are sure we're the enemy and we can't convince them otherwise. So they are the targets. How many?"

"Eleven, sir, across a two-hundred-meter frontage. They were faced away from us originally, but some seem to know or suspect that we've landed behind them. However, I do not have clear sightlines to three of them."

"About those three: will the lasers overpenetrate and mission-kill the target, anyhow?"

"Likely, sir."

"And if you two-tap them?"

Duncan swallowed. "A sure mission-kill, sir."

"Then you know what you have to do. Commence firing."

Puller quivered as one of her forward laser blisters shifted out of PDF mode into tactical and jerked through a rapid set of retargetings. The air ionized, sparking and snapping, along the otherwise invisible laser beam's swiftly changing trajectory.

In the scattered copses to their front, a few small fires sprang up.

"Dr. Sleeman, report."

Her voice was small, yet thick. "All enemy either dead or incapacitated. Most likely the former; thermal and biosigns are fading."

"And now what?" asked Solsohn hollowly.

"And now," said Riordan, "we wait for the humans to resume their retreat as soon as they realize that the enemy blocking force is no longer active." He undid his straps, rose, moved toward the bridge portal.

Karam turned around. "And where are you going?"

"To meet them when they arrive. Set *Puller* down behind the copse just aft of us. Major Solsohn, tell Fanny I want him, Martell, and Somers ready to debark with me in three minutes. The rest of the squad is under de los Reyes and on standby."

"Any specific orders for de los Reyes, sir?"

"Yes: stand ready to save us."

Martell leaned away from the scope of his CoBro. Its LITI had better range and resolution than the goggles he was wearing. "Company still coming our way, sir. Range is now two hundred meters. Looks like a few are moving with help. They've just come across the Hkh'Rkh you lasered."

Riordan swung his own rifle around to observe, watched as several discernibly human figures stood over a rapidly cooling Hkh'Rkh corpse. The barrels of the humans' weapons were brighter than their bodies.

"They sure are taking their time checking out a deader," Martell added.

"It's not the body that's making them hesitate, Private Martell. They're trying to figure who did the killing. They know it's not one of their people." Which was why the grim slaughter of the Hkh'Rkh had been necessary. Riordan toggled to the secure command channel. "Bannor?"

"Wedge One Actual. Go."

"Any further Hkh'Rkh movement?"

"Actually, they've all started backing up, Caine. The APCs are withdrawing without dismounting their troops."

"So a full retreat?"

"I wouldn't go that far. They're leaving behind scouts, best as I can tell. I'm guessing that they're setting up a string of observation posts while their main body pulls back to lick its wounds and debrief. This must have been a pretty confusing engagement for them."

"True enough for everyone, tonight." Riordan watched the bright human silhouettes resume their advance. They were traveling in an offset delta formation, the wounded following the point of that wedge by about twenty meters. "Are the two creepers we left at the clearing showing us anything?"

"A few Warriors retreating. Want them to follow?"

"No, let's leave the creepers in place, for now. The humans you've been tracking: how are they doing?"

"The northern half of them seem to be converging on a low hillock. I'm guessing it's a fall-back or waypoint."

"Concur. Keep me posted on any changes."

"Roger. You do likewise, Caine—and keep your head down."

"Don't worry about me; I'm safe and sound."

"With all due respect: bullshit. I can hear the night sounds behind you every time you send. Which means you're on the ground and damn near the point. Again. Bad habit. Sir."

"Scold me later. This is not about 'lead from the front.' This is about making sure we get to talk to the humans here, rather than shooting them."

"Understood. But still, keep your head down. Rulaine out."

Matthew Fanny gestured for Riordan's attention. "One hundred meters, sir. Time to let them know we're here?"

"Yes, it is."

"We've identified the frequencies they use, sir. You could have Dr. Sleeman search and see if—"

"Not likely they'll be using radios right now. And comms could be faked, even voice-grade. The Hkh'Rkh could record, and now play back, a wide variety of statements."

"So then how do we start the dance, sir?"

"*We* don't, Sergeant. I do." Riordan rose up on one elbow and spoke loudly. "I am a human and I am coming out where you can see me."

Fanny grabbed his arm. "Damn, are you nuts? Er... sir? And how the hell will they see you in the dark?"

Riordan held up the emergency flare he had been carrying in his left hand. He shouted into the dark. "I am now lighting a flare so you can see me. I will carry it as I come forward." He leaned toward Martell. "What reaction?"

"They've stopped cold, sir. Gone to ground."

"Numbers?"

"I make out fourteen, including the wounded."

Riordan nodded, raised his head and voice. "I will not come out until you give reply."

There was a very long silence. Then, in English, "So, if you're a human, why are you showing up now?"

"We just arrived. We came as soon as we learned you were here."

"Are you at war with the snorks?"

The snorks?—oh. "Not anymore. But they still don't like us. And there are more of the—er, 'snorks'—approaching from the rear."

"Are you the ones who killed their blocking force?"

"We are. We tried to contact you in your camp, the one with the two helicopters. But you ran before we could reach you."

Another long pause. "Okay, human, so tell me: if you're color-blind, are you more likely to be a male or a female, and what colors do you have the most trouble distinguishing?"

"Male. Red and green."

"And tell me what that had to do with Caesar losing the battle of Waterloo."

"It had nothing to do with it—particularly since Caesar died more than eighteen hundred years before Waterloo was fought."

"All right, come out. Only you. No weapons. Hands where we can see them."

Riordan popped the flare. "You can see me?"

"I can."

Fanny almost growled. "This is insane." Somers nodded vigorously.

Riordan ignored them. "I am standing up." Then he turned to the Guards. "If we don't do it this way, we'll still be playing twenty questions when the Hkh'Rkh scouts reach us. Besides, I doubt their weapons can get through this armor insert at one hundred meters."

"Unless they've adapted some Hkh'Rkh weapons for their own use," Somers added. "In which case, ye're pretty much a dead man. Sir."

Riordan tried to ignore the sweat that sprang out along his brow and the cold-gravel feeling in the pit of his stomach. "I'm guessing Hkh'Rkh weapons are too heavy for humans to carry. They're more likely to mount them on their helicopters."

"Ye're sure aboot that, sir?"

"Corporal Somers, I'm not sure about anything."

The human voice from the darkness shouted. "So, are you standing up or what?"

"Here I come." Riordan stood.

"Stay where you are," the voice from the darkness shouted.

Fanny's warning was an urgent hiss. "Lining you up for a head shot, now that they can see you."

"Or just checking me out, making sure I am what I say I am before they let me approach."

The voice from the darkness sounded a little less hostile and a lot more curious. "Advance slowly. Follow my voice."

"It's all right. I can see you."

"You mean, through those goggles?"

"That's right. You're familiar with them?"

"Some of us are. Keep on coming. And keep your hands away from your sides."

Riordan complied, walked for what seemed like half a minute.

"Stop," the same voice ordered.

Riordan could now tell which of the thermal outlines the voice was coming from. He chin-toggled to LI only: the light from the flare illuminated his surroundings as if it were high noon in the desert. The speaker was in an old style of camouflage pattern that had been called "tiger stripes." He was holding a vaguely familiar battle rifle, immediately post-World War II in design. Riordan did not dare turn his head yet, but several of the men—all men—were similarly armed, but had different uniforms and helmets. A few others were in old naval deck wear and carrying one of the iconic submachine guns of human history: the .45 caliber Thompson. They were all fitted with drum magazines. *So. All of a vintage with the helicopters, more or less.*

The speaker stood, and now Riordan saw the insignia of rank on his uniform: two vertical bars. Still a symbol used by the United States. "Pleased to meet you, Captain."

The soldier's gun came up slightly. "Who the hell are you, and how do you know my rank? Were you one of the people who dumped us in this hellhole?"

"My name is Commodore Caine Riordan, I'm a citizen of the United States of America, and I am familiar with the symbol of rank you are wearing. And I am most definitely not connected to the people who dumped you in this hellhole, which is actually called Turkh'saar. But we have to get you and the rest of your people out of here as quickly as possible."

"Yeah, well, assuming I believe everything you're

saying, that last part is going to be difficult. We all didi—um, retreated through these woods, so we're all split up. Hopefully, the others can make it to the rendezvous point, but that's as much as I'm going to tell you about where—"

"Captain, I am going to hazard a few guesses. You are to rendezvous at a small hillock about six kilometers northeast of our current position. It is a waypoint or extraction site only. You will either make your way to, or anticipate rescue coming from, your main base approximately fifty-three kilometers further to the east."

The captain's weapon edged higher. "And how the hell do you know that?"

"Captain, we have excellent sensors on the aerial vehicles from which you ran. They allow us to see individual thermal signatures at considerable distance. While I presume that your main base must be underground or otherwise sheltered from overhead observation, there were still thermal blooms from its perimeter outposts. So before you worry too much about whether you can trust us, consider this: if we had come to harm you, wouldn't we have just allowed the Hkh'Rkh to finish the job here and headed straight for your main base, instead?"

Although the captain and his men were less than ten meters away, this was the longest silence yet. By far.

"So, assuming we believe you, we've still got a problem."

"The rest of your command. On the run from the Hkh'Rkh—um, snorks."

"Yeah."

"That won't be too much of a problem. We're

tracking all your personnel and all of theirs. Currently, yours was the only group actively engaged with the enemy. Which means we can use one of our aerial vehicles to scoop up the rest of your people and use our other one—the one I have just over there—to provide cover in the event of any attempted interdiction."

The captain stepped forward into the light of the flare. Riordan pushed the goggles up on his forehead. "That sounds like a plan," the captain said, "but I need to ask for one more guarantee."

"If I can make it in good faith, I will."

"My men who—who didn't make it." He glanced back into the dark woods behind. "I don't want to leave them where they fell."

Riordan nodded. "I'd ask for the same consideration. We can't retrieve their bodies tonight, but we'll mark them on our scans. In my experience, the Hkh'Rkh do not deface our dead. They leave them for us to dispose of as we will. And I doubt they're going to be here that long. Their APCs are pulling back and they're setting up a string of observation posts well to the west of your base."

The captain nodded. "Disengaging but not losing track of us." He stuck out his hand; it was muscular, but somewhat wiry, as if he was slightly malnourished. "Captain Richard Hailey, United States Army—which I guess still means something. Because between what you've said and how we got here, I'm pretty sure we weren't just lost in space; we've been lost in time."

Riordan shook the captain's hand. "I suspect that is correct. And I suspect I know how that happened. But there's something I need to see before I can be sure."

"What's that, Commodore?"

"Your main base—which is, I suspect, where you started out on this world."

Hailey looked at Riordan through narrowed eyes. "It was. Okay, then"—he waved to his men, who helped wounded comrades gather around—"how do we start?"

Riordan activated the multichannel option that connected him to *Puller*, Wedge One, and Sergeant Fanny. "We start by getting you and your men on board my ship. Karam, lift on low fans and come as close as you can. We've got wounded."

Chapter Twenty-Seven

BASE CAMP DANTE, BD+56 2966 TWO ("TURKH'SAAR")

Caine Riordan checked his wristcomp, one foot tapping in his eagerness to be off *Puller*'s bridge. He was due to meet Rich Hailey in less than five minutes, but before he did, there was one last detail he had to double-check, because if he was right, the mission to Turkh'saar was about to evolve in a very strange, and potentially dangerous, direction. And in order to be sure how best to handle that change, he had to get a crucial piece of information from...

Peter Wu, out of breath from sprinting to his face-to-face meeting with Riordan, fetched up short against the hatchway into the CO's stateroom. "Sir," he panted, "I came...as fast as...I could. Wedge One just landed."

Riordan nodded, motioned to a seat. "I know. Sorry about the rush, but the clock's ticking and there's something I have to know."

Peter nodded. "Certainly, sir. Anything that I can—"

Caine leaned sharply toward Peter, interrupted in a low tone, "So what can you tell me about the Guard officer you know, Newton Baruch? Other than his being in IRIS, that is."

Peter's eyes opened wide. "Sir, what makes you believe that he is—?"

"Lieutenant Wu, you might recall that I am very familiar with your dossier. If you last saw Newton in 2116, that means you and he were friends when you were already up to your hips in IRIS operations for Downing and Nolan Corcoran. Newton is SAS. But he was in Singapore five years ago. When you were. The likelihood that you got so chummy with another operator in that kind of environment with whom you did *not* share equal clearance levels—well, that's a long shot." Riordan waited.

"Well...yes, sir. He is IRIS. He is also an excellent surgeon. And a very good and conscientious man." Peter frowned. "Perhaps too conscientious."

"How do you mean?"

"As I understand it, Newton was recruited even before I was, but was kept very much out of contact with other IRIS operatives. He is quite learned and was valued for his ability to research, observe, and submit actionable reports on evolving...situations."

"So his work kept him isolated."

"Yes, sir. In more ways than one."

"You mean, in his personal life, as well?"

"Yes. He was concerned that he would never be able to fully reveal the nature of his work, and his duty, to a significant other. And he is a very serious person. Not the kind for casual dalliances."

Riordan almost smiled. Out of the entire team, only Peter Wu would use the term "casual dalliances." It was strangely endearing. "You respect him a great deal, don't you?"

"Indeed I do, sir." Wu was more earnest than

Riordan had ever seen. "You can trust Newton absolutely. I would wager my life on it." He reflected. "Actually, I already have, years ago."

"Well, that's good enough for me. Now, I've got to run. Thanks, Peter."

Matthew Fanny stood at the edge of the lowering bay door that led down from *Puller*'s belly, his CoBro eight-millimeter in an assault carry. "I don't like that you and Major Solsohn are going in there alone, sir."

Riordan shrugged as he shed his sidearm and helmet. "No helping it, Top. If we want this to go smoothly and quickly, we meet on their terms. After all, in order to get them off this planet, they're going to have to trust us enough to march onto the wedges, unarmed."

"And besides," Duncan added, "they've now had reports of what *Puller* can do. And she's sitting right outside their complex."

"All the more reason for them to think that you two might be awful useful as hostages, as bargaining chips."

"Well, Matt, I made sure Rich Hailey was standing right next to me when I turned command over to Major Rulaine for the balance of our visit. Who is under strict instructions not to jeopardize this command for our welfare, for any reason. Remember: Hailey is military, too. He knows what that meant, Sergeant." Riordan started down the ramp.

"Yeah, well—let's hope Captain Hailey's superiors get the message as clearly as he did."

"Matt, I suspect that if their cadre has managed to keep this weird patchwork unit alive and functional this long on Turkh'saar, they're professional enough to understand that threatening us would be the very worst thing they could do." Riordan stepped off the ramp, blinked against the rays of the local primary, which was just cresting the foothills behind them. "We'll be fine, Top."

Fanny nodded but did not look convinced. "I hope you're right, sir. And *we'll* be right here if you need us." He stepped back as the warning klaxon shrilled and the ramp began rising up to smooth itself into *Puller*'s ventral surface.

Duncan looked at Caine, looked at the massive rock overhang that sheltered a flightline of more than a dozen helicopters. Just back from its edge, small dirt-berm pillboxes had been constructed, each sprouting a mix of heavier human weapons—mostly historical .50 cal M2 machine guns—and modified Hkh'Rkh assault rifles. "Well," he said.

"Well," Caine echoed. "It's showtime."

They walked toward the bristling array of weapons and war machines.

As they reached the perimeter of the outer defenses, Rich Hailey emerged from a large shadowy gulf behind the flightline. Scans indicated it was the entrance to whatever cave network was housing the forces of which the captain was a part.

Hailey came to a halt just two meters away. "Sirs, are you able to provide the documentation my superiors have requested?"

Riordan nodded, handed over a courier pouch. "Our commissions and supporting materials."

Hailey nodded his thanks, opened the pouch, popped open the two folders, scanned their first pages quickly. "Thank you, sirs." He returned the documents to their folders, the folders to the pouch, sealed it, signalled three waiting guards to approach.

Perhaps because Riordan's undergraduate degree had been in military history, and because of his work as an analyst since then, he was able to place all three with fair certainty.

The one in the lead had wide, winglike chevrons on his dark green-brown uniform, and a broad, shallow helmet: almost certainly a British infantry sergeant of the World War II era. Next to him was a short, olive-skinned man in camouflage fatigues with a deeper, bowl-like helmet: almost certainly an American of the decades following World War II. And the last was Asiatic, probably Southeast Asian, in what looked like thick black pajamas: he could have come from any one of a number postcolonial insurgent groups, but Caine was guessing Viet Cong.

Hailey nodded to the man in the British uniform. "Sergeant Seedman, please take these documents to the command group."

The sergeant snapped to with a slight stomp, answered, "Very good, sir," quite a bit louder than necessary, turned smartly, and moved for the cave mouth at a trot.

Captain Hailey faced Riordan again, and with a glance that included Duncan, came to attention himself and offered a crisp salute. "Sirs, thank you for presenting your credentials, and welcome to base camp Dante."

Riordan saluted casually. "Inspired by the Inferno?"

"There's some debate as to the label's origin, sir. Some claim it's more a reference to the Purgatorio. Can't say I'd know. Didn't have time to read a lot of classics between electrical engineering and ROTC. Now, if you'd please follow me, sirs."

Riordan did so, noticed the leisurely pace. "Since we don't seem to be in any rush, I take it we're to get a casual look around as your senior officers go over our documentation."

As the last two guards fell in behind them, Hailey turned to smile at Caine. "The more things change, the more they stay the same, eh, sir?"

"That's certainly my experience. And you don't need to keep calling us 'sir.'"

"Actually, I have strict instructions to maintain all due respect in best military tradition, sirs."

To say nothing of retaining maximum formality until your COs know we can work out a modus vivendi. "Well, I won't encourage insubordination, Captain. Mind if we ask a few questions as we walk?"

"Sorry, sir, I've been instructed to keep our conversation to a minimum until we get to HQ. The rumors are flying fast and furious as it is. Any chatter about who you are could potentially have some of our guys wigging out."

Duncan frowned. "'Wigging out'?"

"Uh . . . yes, sir. That is, going bonkers."

"Going where?"

"Well, damn it—sir—uh, vernacular sure has changed. Let's put it this way: the men would get very upset."

They had passed beyond the helicopters, most of which were UH-1s, and were approaching the cavern opening. It was at least five meters high and ten meters wide, and opened into a chamber so expansive that Riordan immediately thought of it as a cross between a marshalling area and a warehouse. Crates stenciled in either U.S. block-lettering or the Cyrillic equivalent climbed toward the shadow-hidden ceiling. The top layers, covered in tarps, shed droplets that seeped down from the rough ceiling. Guards—mostly carrying AK-47s or the larger battle rifles that Rich Hailey had identified as M14s during the inbound flight—were omnipresent, and comprised of groups at least as heterogenous as the guard detail that was escorting them. They only had one thing in common: each of them stopped whatever they were doing to stare as Riordan and Solsohn walked by. Very few of them blinked. Or smiled.

"Y'know," Duncan muttered, "I could do without being the center of attention right now."

Hailey chuckled. "Well, we got used to anticipating all sorts of things arriving here in this camp, most of them after our blood. But you two? No one imagined anybody like you would show up." He grew somber. "Wouldn't have allowed ourselves to believe it, even if we had."

"Say again?" Duncan asked.

"Sir, every man on this base knows two things when they see you and that scifi gear you're wearing. First, it means that we just might have a ride back home. But second, it's like the song says: you can't go home again." He shook his head. "As long as we were busy trying to stay alive from day to day, with nothing but empty guesses to go on—well, you can't spend a lot of time worrying about anything else. But when—no; *if*—we get off this rock, that might be the start of our real battle."

Riordan took a longer step, drawing abreast of Hailey. "Captain, I can't promise you that the path forward will be easy for you and all these men. But I can promise you this: you won't be left without help. We've acquired a lot of experience dealing with the aftermath of postwar trauma; we have a lot of institutions and support systems to work with you, to assist you as you find your way back into the world."

Hailey glanced over; amiable but a little dubious. "You have experience with this? With people who've been gone as long as we've been? I saw the dates on your commission papers, so, for me, the cat's out of the bag."

Riordan nodded. "As we knew it would be. And no, we haven't dealt with folks who have been ... away ... as long as you have. But there are some precedents. Hell, just four years ago, I returned after losing thirteen years of my life. I worked with another person who had lost damn near sixty. It's not easy adapting to the changes, but it's not impossible. And you won't be alone. I promise you that."

Duncan emitted what sounded like a cautionary grunt.

"You seem less optimistic, Major," Hailey observed with a wan smile.

"Well, see, I don't have the commodore's rank, but I *do* work closer with the government. Makes me leery about making promises. You know how governments are."

Rich Hailey laughed. "Do I ever. See, some things don't change at all, do they?" Having wended further back into the hillside, passing through one makeshift barracks or armory after another, they came to an imposing inner checkpoint. A drop gate, fashioned from what looked like multiple layers of steel roofing, hung suspended like a sword of Damocles across the four-meter-wide passageway. Three meters in front of it, five meters beyond it, and cresting the elevated pulley apparatus on either side, were essentially welded-steel machine-gun nests. Riordan and Solsohn stared at the weapons: MG-42s. Another World War II icon.

Duncan's voice was sardonically animated. "Well, you don't see those every day."

Hailey glanced at them. "No," he mused, "I don't suppose you do. We're almost there, sirs."

This section of the cavern complex—what Hailey had referred to as the "inner compound" during *Puller*'s flight to the main base—was more labyrinthine. Twists and turns vied with dips and sudden inclines. Alcoves and galleries erupted off the sides of the rough passages without warning. Some had been turned into storerooms, others into armories, still others into workshops. In one of the larger ones, water dripped from stalactites into a wide, still pool that was only visible because the ripples from each drop faintly caught and reflected rings of light from beyond the entrance.

"Quite a complex," Riordan commented.

"Yeah, almost as extensive as the biggest VC undergrounds, but with better headroom."

Duncan, whose knowledge of history tended to be more specialized and less broad than Caine's, wondered aloud, "VC?"

"Viet Cong. The Communist guerilla forces in South Vietnam."

"Oh. Right."

Rich's smile looked like it cost him considerable effort. "Ancient history, now, huh?"

"Not ancient," Solsohn corrected, none too convincingly.

Riordan intuited that it was time to change the topic. "Captain, did you find this complex ready to use, or did you have to do some of the excavating and finishing?"

"For reasons you'll soon understand, I'm not sure any of us will be able to give you a definitive answer to that, but none of the stonework seems recent. Everything is pretty evenly weathered, and there's no sign of spoor from either digging or demolition. But you can ask the brass yourself, now. We're here." Coming to a vee in the passage, Hailey swerved to the left, which brought him into a small, capsulelike chamber with a four-man guard detail. Signs and countersigns were given, and they were admitted into a large room with a long table fashioned from cut-up crates. Against the side walls, smaller platforms—some for maps, some for sand tables—shared space with crude benches and a few field chairs. Everything was illuminated in the same fashion as the rest of the cave complex: a single strand of overhead lights.

The five men seated at the table rose as Riordan and Solsohn entered. Two were younger than Hailey. The other three were considerably older, one of whom was missing his left leg below the knee. Judging by the bandages, he had lost it on Turkh'saar.

Rich Hailey had steadfastly declined requests for detailed information about the base or personnel. Consequently, Riordan had no idea how he was going to address a room of unknown military personnel from various nations and, possibly, epochs.

But he never got the chance to work out a suitable

introduction. A spry, flight-suited man with leathery skin and a hawklike nose resembling those seen in portraits of early frontiersmen, came to attention and slowly presented a salute. The others followed his example. "Commodore Riordan, Major Solsohn, I'm Colonel Patrick Paulsen, USAF. On behalf of the rest of the senior officers, I want to say that we are very glad to have you here. We are happy to report that, to the best of our ability, we have ascertained your credentials to be authentic. Although"—there was a sudden twinkle in his eye—"I must confess that while I have heard of some personnel being commissioned while at the Pearl, that always referred to our base at Oahu, not at a space force facility located at someplace called Barnard's Star IIc."

Riordan returned the smile. "Well, Colonel, reaching Barnard's Star would have required a bit more in-flight refueling than was typical for your air force."

Smiles—at the surreality of the moment, rather than the forced witticisms—arose briefly, were pushed aside when Paulsen backed up to clear a path for his colleagues. "Commodore, Major, I'll let my other senior staff and specialists introduce themselves before we get down to business."

The others came forward like awkward guests at a wedding reception line: silver-haired Steven Rodermund, a Lieutenant Colonel from the U.S. Air Force in Vietnam; crutch-wielding Lieutenant Colonel Ivan Zhigarev of the Soviet Army from the Second World War; U.S. submarine Commander Carlisle Hansell from that same conflict; First Lieutenant Alexander Shvartsman of the late era Soviet Army; and Lieutenant Isaac Franklin, a pararescue surgeon from the very end of the twentieth century and very much the youngest of the group.

Indicating the crude stools and benches around the table, Pat Paulsen gestured back toward the core of the cave complex. "We're missing a few of our senior officers, but someone's got to watch the shop while we're meeting. I invited Lt. Shvartsman here because, given his particular experience with coordinating airmobile special operations, he brings a unique skillset to the table when it comes to integrating recon and intel data. And Ike is here because he's more educated than any of the rest of us, and too damned smart for his own good."

And they sat, looking at Riordan and Solsohn.

Caine leaned forward. "Gentlemen, I'm going to propose that we leave two areas out of our discussions for now: what's happened back home, and any detailed chronological accounting of your time here. My reason for putting those two topics aside is purely practical. We could talk about them for days, but we have just a few hours. At most. On the way here, we polled our only remaining satellite. The mechanized infantry force we repelled last night has withdrawn back across a north-south river approximately seven kilometers west of your forward operating base. However, there is a much larger unit heading into the region. Together, they would comprise a reinforced regiment."

"That is a sizable force," Paulsen allowed. "But from what Captain Hailey—who is our senior tactical commander—told us of the weapons on your, er, 'ship,' you could very possibly blast all of them to smithereens."

"That might be true, sir, but it touches upon one of

the many unknowns in this situation. We arrived here expecting that there would be no remaining orbital defenses after the recent war. We were wrong. The Hkh'Rkh sent a sizable flight of missiles up to shoot us down as we began planetfall. Our ship, UCS *Puller*, is adequately equipped to respond to that kind of threat, but not our transports. In a similar vein, we have no way of knowing if the Hkh'Rkh—the exosapients you call 'snorks'—have more advanced weapons available that they haven't wanted to deploy just yet."

"Why would these Hkh'Rkh refrain from using their best weapons?" Shvartsman asked.

Solsohn folded his hands. "Because this planet is, to use parlance from your era, the equivalent of a demilitarized zone. For a variety of reasons, some of which we are privy to and some not, the two species which border each others' region of space at this point elected to split rights to the system. It creates a kind of two-way buffer zone.

"This world, having a biosphere, was of special interest to the Hkh'Rkh. Although the other species, the Arat Kur, are their technological and military superiors, they elected to give the Hkh'Rkh full and free use of Turkh'saar in exchange for a treaty stipulating that they may not have any military-grade weapons here. The Hkh'Rkh have clearly violated that in a number of particulars. And they may have violated it much more than they've been willing to reveal, thus far."

Rodermund leaned back, frowning, pulling his lower lip. "And you're thinking that with you dropping out of the sky and ruining their little attack last night, that they'll bring their bigger guns out of hiding when they come after you. And us."

Riordan nodded. "So we don't have a lot of time. They're on their way and my forces may not be enough to hold them. Best case scenario: we're all out of here before they arrive.

"Let me be quite clear on this point, gentlemen: I did not come here to fight. And although that part of our objective has already been shot to hell, it's imperative we keep our violations of local sovereignty as minimal as possible. Otherwise, we could wind up starting the war we came here to prevent."

"By which you mean," Pat Paulsen said, "that our actions on this planet have created a political crisis."

Solsohn nodded. "Right now, this is the most dangerous flashpoint in known space, according to the Joint Chiefs back on Earth."

Ike threw back his head and laughed, attracting alarmed stares. He returned them. "Really? Am I the only one who finds that phrase—'the Joint Chiefs back on Earth'—not only surreal but funny? I mean, when were the Joint Chiefs ever really 'down to Earth' at all?"

Riordan smiled, but not as widely as the others. All except Shvartsman, who seemed a bit vinegary, a bit careful, and very observant. He radiated the aura of *junior spook* so strongly that he would have looked more natural in a fedora. "Well, Lieutenant Franklin, the Joint Chiefs may be no more Earthbound in their thinking than they were in your day, but at least now they have good reason for looking at the truly big picture. Which we don't have time to even sketch out for you until we're off this planet. And that is our first order of business."

Zhigarev straightened. "You mean, removing us from this planet?"

"Yes, but there are two preliminary steps we need to take. Firstly, I need to ask you, formally, whether the documentation we've presented regarding our *bona fides*, including the legitimacy of the political entities which have evolved from those you served, is something you recognize as official."

The command group paused, several drawing back; on their faces, puzzlement vied with wariness.

Duncan leaned forward. "Allow me to clarify. You all took oaths to, and hold your military authority via, your home nations. However, not all those national entities still exist in the same forms. If you and your men accept that our authority is directly derived—you might say 'inherited'—from the authority of those older states, then we have passed the first hurdle: that you'll follow the orders we issue pursuant to effecting your extraction."

Paulsen nodded. "I see. Well, frankly, I'm pretty sure that our commands have been officially stricken from the record. So we are not going to question the authenticity of your credentials, or your assertions regarding the current conditions back home. And you don't have enough time to get the separate approval of each different nationality's senior officer or NCO. We're a pretty diverse bunch."

Riordan smiled. "I've noticed."

Duncan glanced briefly at Caine, asked, "Just how many different groups are we talking about, Colonel Paulsen?"

"Well, let's see: the largest group are us Americans. A bunch of us from World War Two—mostly Pacific submariners—and a smaller group who were serving in Vietnam. Plus Ike here who was running some kind of snoop-and-poop in Somalia when he got his one-way ticket to this madhouse."

"We are next largest group," Zhigarev announced, his chest coming out. "Both from Great Patriotic War and putting down later rebellion in Afghanistan."

Rodermund pushed back his silver hair. "Then you've got Brits from Crete, Filipino insurgents, Israeli freedom fighters, Poles from a submarine, some of the Pashtuns who were fighting Lieutenant Shvartsman in Afghanistan, and a handful of dinks—er, Vietnamese. Viet Cong, to be specific. Oh, and a few Japanese."

"From World War Two?" Duncan asked.

Brief, uncomfortable glances ping-ponged between the officers at the table, came to rest on Pat Paulsen, who nodded carefully. "Yes, the Japanese are from World War Two."

The sense that there was an immense, but invisible, elephant in the room was overpowering.

Riordan thought about World War II—about units which, like these, would have never been missed if they disappeared without a trace—and realized that one nationality was conspicuously absent from the list. An absence which might explain their discomfort at mentioning the Japanese and how it might be connected to the otherwise inexplicable presence of the MG-42s in the hardpoints defending the inner passageway.

Riordan sat very straight. "Where are the Germans?"

Chapter Twenty-Eight

BASE CAMP DANTE, BD+56 2966 TWO ("TURKH'SAAR")

Zhigarev blurted out a response before Pat Paulsen could intercede. "I will show you mass grave. I go often. To spit on it."

The following silence was deafening. Riordan looked around the table; not all the officers met his gaze. *Carefully now.* "I said earlier that there were two steps we had to take before we could commence extraction. The first was that you recognize our authority for the duration of that operation. The second concerns the nature of your presence and actions here. Specifically, how and why you came to Turkh'saar, and why you attacked the Hkh'Rkh." He held up a hand against the indignation he saw growing in the faces around him. "Understand: Earth will have to answer for your actions, voluntary or not. So, in order to establish your legal status, I need to understand your actions in the context of the conditions here. I naturally suspect that will be connected with the dead Germans. So perhaps you should start by explaining—in detail—how you came to Turkh'saar and what happened after you arrived."

Carlisle Hansell, possibly the oldest of the men there, pursed his wrinkled lips. "If you are asking about the specific means of our conveyance, none of us know. We weren't awake for that part of the process, or we can't recall it."

"Well, let's back up a step, then. What is the last thing that you do remember, Commander?"

Hansell lost what little animation was on his face. "Depth charges off the bow. Hull shaking. Sprung a leak up near tube two. Then all the electricity went off. I figured we'd had a short or plant failure and were pretty much as good as dead. Last thing I remember.

"Surprised to wake up. Given some of my early years, I figured I'd been sent to hell. Woke up, found a Nazi with SS collar tabs staring down at me. Seemed to confirm my suspicion."

Solsohn stared around the introspective faces. "Is everyone's story pretty much a version of that?"

Zhigarev shook his head. "No. Some of us were given choice."

"By whom?"

Hailey himself leaned forward. "If you're hoping for a description of some little green men, I'm sorry to disappoint. I was shot up—pretty bad—in Salavan Province, Laos. I sent the rest of my team to the fall-back extraction site. We didn't have more than an hour's lead time over the NVA, and I doubted I'd live long enough to get shot again."

Duncan's jaw sagged slightly. "And they left you?"

Rich Hailey's eyes became very, very patient. "Major, it probably doesn't mean anything to you, but we were MACV-SOG. For officers and senior NCOs, part of the job description is that you don't tie down your team and get them killed. But you don't ruin their morale by eating a bullet, either. You go out fighting, buying them time. You owe them that. And it sets the necessary example for those who rise up in the ranks after you. In Laos, sometimes all you had was your faith in each other."

Riordan nodded, let a second of silence pass. "So, you were contacted after the rest of your team left."

"Yeah. Came out of the bush so fast I didn't see him do it, and I'm not half bad in the bush, sir. Asked if I preferred living to dying. I told him that with my wounds, I was pretty sure that choice was out of anyone's hands but God's. He found that amusing, told me that his hands were not tied by God's. I asked him where he was going to take me. He said he couldn't tell me, but I would arrive there healthy—and that I had ten seconds to decide." Hailey shrugged. "And here I am."

"Was he a local?"

"Hell, no. Dressed like he was from back in the world ... er, the U.S. We called it 'the world,' back when there was only one we knew about. I figured him for an Eastern European. Or maybe a Russian. I asked him about that as he started toward me with some gadget that looked like a watering can with a pistol grip. He just smiled and said he wasn't from anywhere near Russia. Guess he was telling the truth."

Pat Paulsen put his hands flat on the table. "Commodore, I will ask you to take my word for it when I say that with the exception of two groups, Rich's story is consistent with those of the others who had contact with our abductors. Indeed, his is one of the most detailed accounts. I would prefer that you do not debrief the men individually."

Duncan leaned forward, a hint of suspicion in his tone. "Why not?"

"Because, as you might gather from the captain's account, a lot of our soldiers have very mixed emotions about what they now see as having cut a deal with the devil. They expected they were being given the opportunity to accept imprisonment instead of certain death."

"That outcome seems a little implausible, wouldn't you say?"

"I would not," Shvartsman responded archly, each syllable crisp, controlled. "I was approached in similar manner. My men and I, we were wounded, isolated, no rescue possible. In such circumstances, you have no time for deep thought. You have ten seconds—it was same with all of us—to decide to live or not. You do not have time to assess if it is implausible. You have just enough time to choose to survive. We did. Perhaps others did not. If so, they are not here. They are in graves on Earth. Where some of our men now think they should have been."

Riordan nodded. "Because of what you were brought here to do."

"*Da*. You know expression, 'dogs of war'? That is us, with Nazis holding leash. I have no love for snorks—what you call 'Hkh'Rkh'—but I had no wish to kill them, either." It seemed as though Shvartsman was ready to say more, but instead, he leaned back, his jaw suddenly retracted and tense, his cheek muscles clenched and bulging.

Riordan nodded his thanks, turned toward Paulsen. "Colonel, you said that when it comes to contact with your abductors, Captain Hailey's story is the most detailed, but you added the caveat, 'with the exception

of two groups.' Would I be correct to conjecture that
those groups were the Germans and the Japanese?"

Paulsen frowned, like a father being compelled to
confirm that one of his children is a murderer. "That
is correct."

"And what was different about their contact with
the abductors?"

"They both indicated that they had slightly more
detailed conversations. But only slightly."

"Those details are potentially quite important,
Colonel, so if you could please—"

Zhigarev's face reddened suddenly. "As if *chudov-
ishniye* fascists told us anything. From them we had
orders or threats. Nothing else."

Paulsen looked ready to intervene, but Caine leaned
directly toward Zhigarev. "Colonel, I'm asking you to
help us against an enemy that clearly chose Nazis—SS,
no less—as the kennelmasters for their pack of enslaved
war-dogs. So I'm not asking for these details out of
idle curiosity; I'm looking for any scrap of information to fight an enemy who might still be watching,
an enemy that saw Nazis as their natural allies. To
put it another way, I'm asking for your help against a
common foe." He paused, held Zhigarev's eyes. "Can
I count on your help?"

Zhigarev, still trembling with rage, nodded sharply.
"*Da*. Apologies. Nazis killed my family, then my men.
First on one world, then another." He rubbed his leg
distractedly. "Is difficult to think clearly when I am
remembering them. I am sorry, Commodore."

Caine smiled, waved away the apology. "*Nichevo*,
Colonel. We are all on the same side here."

The Russian smiled, seemed pleased, as if until

this moment he had harbored reservations about the two newcomers.

Steven Rodermund leaned forward. "Well, I probably had the most contact with the Nazi and Japanese command staffs. Some of their people spoke fair English, and my Dad's side still spoke some German. Also, I guess I looked 'Aryan' enough for 'em.

"Didn't mean they trusted me much, though. I was almost the only officer they allowed into this part of the cave network."

Solsohn's eyes widened. "So the machine-gun emplacements near the gate: they built them. To protect themselves in here."

"Yeah, along with almost all the guns, ammo, food, and other consumables. And the well. They kept the Japanese with them, who they used as their chief technicians and scientists."

"That must have been a hell of a language barrier."

"Not so much," Hansell put in. "The bigger of the two Japanese subs wasn't an attack boat. It was a cargo carrier."

"Cargo?" Riordan echoed.

"Yep. The I-52, one of their Type C-3 class subs. Mid '44, she was sent to Europe to pick up some advanced Nazi hardware. Our sub-hunters caught her in the Bay of Biscay, sent her to the bottom. Or so we thought. Because of the technology transfer, she had a number of officers on board who were proficient in German and with appropriate science degrees. By the time we were awakened, they'd been set up as the Nazis' brain trust."

"You said you were 'awakened.' What do you mean by that?"

"I mean that they had us in some kind of hibernation. In machines."

Ike Franklin leaned forward. "The commander is referring to cryogenic stasis."

Riordan allowed his eyebrows to rise. "You sound familiar with the technology, Lieutenant."

"Well, if you count science fiction movies, I sure was. And I was pretty much the only other person they regularly permitted in their little back-of-the-cave country club. They didn't have any of their own physicians, and they didn't trust the Russian docs. Besides, none of them knew squat about computers and it was pretty clear that the 'ice-caskets' were automated."

"So you figured out how to open them?"

"Not exactly, but I figured out why they lost some of the first group that was reanimated, developed some basic protocols for the restoration process. I was familiar with cryogenics from surgical prolongation protocols being developed at the end of the twentieth century."

"Thank you," said Riordan, conscious of how carefully flat his voice had become. "It will be extremely helpful to inspect these cryogenic units before we return to *Puller*."

Franklin glanced at Pat Paulsen, who nodded. "Of course, Commodore. Now, best we let Steve finish telling you about how things started."

Rodermund shrugged. "Far as we can tell, the first of us were awakened at least four or five days after the Nazis had been roused. So we don't know exactly what they did before then. As Ivan said, they didn't fill us in on much."

"So you don't know if anyone contacted them after they came out of stasis."

"No, but if they had, I think we would have heard about it. Their colonel, Kreuzer, liked to brag about how he had been approached by a member of the *Zukunft Herrenvolk*."

"The who?" Duncan asked.

"The Future or Coming Master Race," Riordan replied flatly.

Rodermund nodded. "Yep. Came to them outside of Stettin, Poland in March of 1945. According to Kreuzer, Soviet artillery was dropping all around them, T-34s rolling in behind the barrage. And in walks this tall, calm, mysterious stranger, out of nowhere, who sits down, asks for a glass of their *schnapps* and tells them that they were to have the honor of carrying forward the mission of achieving a true master race, one which would transcend the impending loss of the Third Reich. Quite a speech, with 152s dropping around their ears."

Solsohn nodded. "And did they get a tour to go along with the speech?"

"You mean, a tour of whatever spaceship Mr. Master Race was tooling around in?" Steve sneered. "The Nazis didn't like to talk about the conclusion of their little Nuremburg Rally on the Eastern Front. I expect because as soon as they agreed to go along for the ride, they got handled the same way as the rest of us: lights out, and then wake up here."

Solsohn nodded. "Yes, but they were awakened first. So they must have known the condition of this facility, if there were any communiqués, what instructions had been left for them."

"If so, they must have destroyed it after memorizing— or deciding to forget about— it. Because we looked for it once they were, uh, gone. Zip, zilch, goose-eggs:

whatever they knew about the first few days here died with them. And before you ask, the Japanese didn't know any more than the rest of us. And they were less communicative than the Germans.

"First thing most of us remember is waking up wrapped in blankets, with some of the Japanese or Nazis pushing water at us, along with the rules of life here on Oz: obey them or die. They meant it, too. Shot a few of the Russians on the spot, the moment they got any lip from them."

"How many of them—the Germans and the Japanese—were there?"

The officers looked at each other for a few seconds. Zhigarev leaned back. "There were ninety-six fascists. We knew. We made careful count."

"And there were exactly eighty-four Japanese," Hansell answered. "Who were pretty upset at all the Americans that they found here."

Riordan frowned. "Why so many Americans, do you think?"

Steve Rodermund shrugged. "Mostly because they had two sub crews' worth of us, and when you rescue a submarine, it's pretty much all or nothing. And I'm guessing that Vietnam was the perfect conflict for picking us up in ones and twos. Easy to go missing in that bush, and a lot of it was pretty far away from help or anything like the Geneva Convention. The other large groups, the Germans and the Russians, were grabbed up as whole units—squads, even platoons—from the Eastern Front."

"Where thousands remain unaccounted for. Or did, when I was last there," Shvartsman added. "Whoever gathered us knew where to find desperate men who would be presumed dead, and so, not missed."

"Yes, it certainly seems that way," Riordan agreed.

"It seems like they had a pretty good idea of conditions here, too," Rodermund added with a bitter twist of his mouth. "Like Ike was quick to point out, it wasn't just chance that this planet had air we could breathe, water we could drink, and food we could eat—well, after we filtered and prepared it properly."

Rich Hailey tapped the table. "They knew more than that. They knew who we were going to be fighting against. I'm sure of it."

Solsohn nodded. "Because of the weapons they provided."

"Yup. Just take my group, for example: the Vietnam contingent. Standard weapon for us was the M16. Jammed like a sonuvabitch, sure, but there were tons of 'em, all over 'Nam. But what did they have here waiting in crates that had been coated in some kind of super-cosmolene? M14s. Chambered for .308: a much better round for punching through armor and taking down big targets. Like the snorks. Same with the rest of the rifles. All heavy caliber with maximum stopping power. The AK-47s are the lightest weapons they included. No carbines, almost no pistols, none of the dozens of submachine guns Ivan's people had when they were taken." Rich leaned away from the makeshift tabletop. "They—whoever they are or were—knew we were going to be hunting bear, so they equipped us for it. And only that."

Which, Riordan thought while nodding blankly, all coalesced into a terrible near-certainty that the Ktor had been behind these abductions, all of which had been carried out during the period when they helped the Custodians keep an eye on Earth. But why bring these "lost soldiers" here? And why start collecting them for this mission—whatever it actually was—almost two centuries ago?

Solsohn was murmuring, almost to himself. "Gotta wonder how they got so much gear for you guys."

"No mystery there," Pat Paulsen said loudly. "You gentlemen may not be familiar with our slang, but in my day, we called the Army, and the U.S., the Land of the Big PX. In Vietnam, that meant we were a black marketeer's dream. The amount of equipment— sometimes as big as tanks and APCs—that went missing or was mysteriously 'lost in transit,' is hard for most folks to believe. That's where a third of our equipment came from. The balance was mostly grabbed from Liberty ships."

Riordan vaguely remembered the term, but couldn't recall its significance.

Hansell must have seen the puzzlement on his face. "World War Two transport ships. Made in America. Cranked out in record time for sending matériel overseas. Some were good, some were awful. Lots were lost, particularly to U-boats. I'm guessing whoever grabbed us grabbed at least one of them. That's why so much of our equipment—particularly backpacks, spare clothing, helmets, radios, batteries—is American. And perfectly preserved, mind you. They must have done something extra special to the food, though. Should all have been rotten, but it looks like they froze it—really hard. Tastes like crap, but it's still better than the local mush." He and several others suppressed shudders.

Solsohn gestured deeper into the cave complex. "So is there a . . . a big refrigerator back here?"

Hansell shook his head. "Strange, but there isn't. 'Course, the Germans had unpacked all the rations before they woke us up. Conducted an inventory to figure how long we had before we'd need to find local food."

Riordan folded his hands. "So, you've got a ton of equipment, the Nazis are waking you up in what I presume are small, easily controlled groups, and if you want to live—and eat—you have to do what they say. What next?"

Rodermund picked up the tale. "Well, it was obvious we weren't in Kansas, anymore—which is why we nicknamed this place 'Oz.'"

Riordan shook his head. "I'm sorry. I don't understand the reference."

Rodermund looked like he'd bitten into a rotting lemon. "You don't understand—? Well, Christ, I guess that's gone, too. Wonder if I'll recognize Earth at all, anymore."

Riordan elected not to comment on the colonel's melancholy musing. "Is 'Oz' another reference to a place of damnation, like calling the base 'Dante'?"

Rodermund's sour expression continued for a moment, then lightened. "Well, I suppose some folks would have considered Oz to be another kind of hell . . . But no: it's a never-never land in a fairy story. Kid from Kansas gets whisked away to Oz—and like her, we realized right away that this was nothing like home. We had air and water and enough food to get by for a while, but no one had any idea where we really were, or how we'd gotten here. The Navy guys who remembered their celestial navigation were pretty sure they saw some of the same constellations, though."

Solsohn glanced toward Hansell. "How'd you figure that?"

The commander's leathery lips hardly seemed to move as he replied. "Different constellations' positional relationships to each other. Once we found the stars in Orion's belt, we looked for other nearby constellations. All present and accounted for. But they're warped or bent. As might be the case if you were spatially displaced. By a few dozen light-years or so."

"Did you share that with the Nazis?"

"Didn't have to. The Japanese had already seen it themselves. Weren't too pleased that we found it on our own. For the Emperor's more devoted servants, every task, every action, was a competition. Didn't like it if they didn't win. Particularly after all the postwar folks confirmed that we really *had* kicked their asses. But good."

Rodermund seemed impatient to resume his tale. "As with the food, the Nazis had already put all the weapons and ammo under lock and key. They did the same with a few key components from each chopper. In short, they had us all by the short hairs.

"They also had a clear plan of action for reconnaissance and gathering samples to ensure a local food supply. They were distant and officious, but they weren't lording it over us all the time. We Americans and the Brits had it the easiest; they tried to become our pals. But we knew what those double-lightning bolts on their collars meant, and what they were capable of."

Solsohn looked surprised, doubtful. "You mean none of your men...well, accepted preferential treatment?"

Rodermund shot him a hard look. "A few did, at first. But we put a stop to that. Right away."

"I'm surprised the Germans allowed your officers to intervene."

"They didn't—because we didn't," Rodermund answered with a smile.

Zhigarev's own smile was more wolfish. "American sergeants were excellent. They saw collaboration and stopped it. With help from their men." He looked sideways at Rodermund, his smile becoming more straightforward. "And without request from us."

Riordan nodded. "So the Nazis were less 'charitable' to the Russians in the group."

"That is understatement, Commodore," Zhigarev said, his considerable brows beetling. "We are to them—what is word?—*untermenschen*. Lesser beings. They treat us so at all times. And we do not forget. So they watched us carefully, never allowed many of us to have guns at same time, sleep in same place. Always mixed with others." His predatory smile returned. "That was mistake, though."

"It encouraged the different groups to learn each others' languages, share plans for a coup?"

"*Da,* that too. But not what I mean. They put us in other groups, but they fed us differently. We were—ah, my English is not good enough."

Rich Hailey leaned forward; Zhigarev nodded, gestured for him to speak. "It was the reverse of the 'separate but equal' racist crap we grew up with in parts of the States. Here, the Russians were mixed in with the rest of us, but were fed differently, treated differently." He leaned back. "A lot of us who had been in 'Nam or Laos, humping it through the bush, grew up thinking Russians were the enemy. But you can't spend too much time in the field before you learn the old soldier's truth: that the hate doesn't usually come from the people doing the fighting. It comes from the stuffed shirts and remfs who go around beating the drums."

"Remfs?" Riordan asked.

Hailey smiled. "Rear-Echelon Mother-Fuckers. Sir."

Riordan smiled back. "I see. Carry on."

"Yes, sir. Like I said, the Russians were being singled out for treatment as second-class—well, third-class citizens. Along with the Poles, the VC, the Pashtuns, the Filipinos, and the Israelis. But I think the Nazis were particularly worried about the Russians because there were a lot of them and the war was still fresh in their minds—even for Lieutenant Shvartsman, who was born long after."

"War's destruction does not end when peace is declared," Shvartsman said quietly. "I should have had four uncles and two aunts. Instead, because of Great Patriotic War, I had one aunt. And a father who woke up screaming at night."

"So," Hailey resumed gently, "the Nazis knew they had to keep the Russians in check. So they broke them up, made sure they were a minority in whatever group they were working, particularly when we started scrounging for food."

Rodermund nodded. "These weird runner-linked trees don't conceal a lot of wildlife, and what's there isn't very big. And none of what we tried was edible. Damn near killed a few of the VC the Germans tricked into trying it.

"So we started using the choppers to get a better idea of what was out there. Which was probably why the Germans treated us Americans so well: with the exception of three of Shvartsman's men, all the pilots came from our ranks."

Riordan leaned back. "And that's when you ran into the Hkh'Rkh."

"Yeah, on the second day. None of us in this room were there, but the reports were pretty consistent. It was some small 'ville, about eighty klicks to the southwest, near where the river widens and heads down to the sea. The Germans saw it, circled it once, landed inside of pistol range, swaggered out to 'meet the natives.'

"Well, the snorks didn't take too kindly to that. They went from surprised to upset to downright pissed in about a minute's time. We never did figure that out, why they weren't more cautious. But they approached the Nazi officer at a run, who started shouting at them and finally cut loose at them with an AK when they got too close. Turns out they had guns, too, and greased him and an adjutant on the spot. Two American submariners were killed in the firefight that followed, before everyone got back on the choppers and dusted."

Riordan waited. "But they didn't fly home, did they?"

Rodermund shook his head. "No. They didn't. They ignored all the protocols we had recommended in the event that they ran into someone. Damn Nazis ordered the flight to circle back in and hit them with the doorguns while hovering at a safe stand-off distance. Killed every snork they saw. Then they went back in, landed, led teams through the sheds, searching. Found the snorks' burrows. Shot everything that moved."

Riordan discovered his throat was dry. "Including the females and the young."

"Yeah. Once the adrenaline of the firefight, the deaths, and then the counterattack wore off, our guys started wondering about that. Particularly at the end, when they were gunning down snorks that were getting shorter. And then so short that—well, at the end, the Nazis were killing critters that could barely move under their own power."

"Just the Nazis?"

"Far as I know," Rodermund answered. "Why?"

"Because treatment of noncombatants—once you have identified which individuals *are* noncombatants— becomes an important issue in the determination of your status."

Paulsen leaned forward. "We thought as much. But I must make a few points here, Commodore. It's pretty hard to distinguish between a tall female and a slightly undersized male, even when we get up-close. And noncombatant is a term that doesn't quite apply. Once any given group of snor—Hik-Rik?—start coming at you, they are *all* combatants. More than a few of our men have been killed by claw-slashing females when they blundered into what was apparently a noncombatant sanctuary. We learned to avoid the tunnels, or 'dens,' as you call them, but apparently they have other designated safe zones that we never learned to spot."

Solsohn nodded. "And when exactly did you start trying to avoid the noncombatants?"

Rodermund leaned forward. "Right away, which got the Nazis pissed at us. And nervous. Which made them even more brutal. They didn't ever attempt contacting the locals again. They went straight to raiding and slaughter." Rodermund looked away. "First time I went out was with Kreuzer. In the first five minutes"—he paused, gathered himself—"Christ, bodies everywhere. I mean, it's not like we didn't see that in 'Nam. We did. Too often. But here, they weren't 'collateral damage.' The Nazis were gunning for them. Actively, like it was sport." Steve's jaw muscles bunched. "And that made us mad; real mad. We had no love for these Hikriks, or whatever you call 'em, but damn it, now they had every reason to hate *our* guts, thanks to Kreuzer and his pack of sadists.

"But he wasn't stupid. He knew, after two full raids, that we weren't just sick of these 'tactics': we were getting dangerously angry. That's when he decided to weaken us, but particularly the Russians."

Riordan felt a frown pulling down his brow. "Weaken you how?"

Rodermund pushed his silver hair back with a flat, broad hand. "Kreuzer saw how fast we were going through the supplies, so he shifted everyone but the Germans and Japanese to a fifty percent local diet. That—took some getting used to. Shits for days. Cramps for weeks. But then, he shifted the Russians to an all-local diet. That pretty much put an end to any thoughts Ivan and the others had about rebellion."

Zhigarev put a hand on his stomach. "It is hard to be revolutionary when insides are coming out."

Rich Hailey was staring fixedly at a spot on the table. "And that's how some of our enlisted men got flogged."

Solsohn leaned over to look down the table at him. "Who flogged them? And why?"

"The Germans and the Japanese. A lot of our guys started swapping rations with the Russians. We went halfsies with them, whenever we could swing it." He smiled. "In-country, we talk about being 'in the shit together,' but this put a whole new meaning on it."

Rodermund's was the first smile to dim. "So the tensions were already high between the Nazis, the Japanese, and the rest of us. And then—the other stuff happened."

"What other stuff?"

The American officers seemed hesitant. Zhigarev set his jaw and spat a single word: "Rape."

Chapter Twenty-Nine

Zhigarev looked from Solsohn to Riordan. "Surely, it is not surprise that fascists rape to show power. It is common habit for them. At least in my country."

Riordan cleared his throat. "Colonel, with respect, we were not even aware there were any women in your ranks. Until the late twentieth century, most nations had exclusively male combat units."

"Russia was exception, Commodore. But Russian women here were not soldiers. Our field hospitals were often staffed by women." He glowered. "And if you know Great Patriotic War, then you know rear areas quickly became front lines. Some Russians here were captured near Kursk. But my command was encircled defending hospital, our backs to Bay of Sevastopol. It was bitter end to bitter campaign."

"I see. And did you personally witness the rape or rapes?"

"*Nyet.* I was just released from hospital." He tapped his leg in annoyance. "Hit by giant shotgun of Hkh'Rkh." Which he pronounced quite accurately.

Evidently, the "kh" sound of Russian had prepared him reproducing its Hkhi phonetic cousin far better than his American colleagues.

Solsohn folded his hands. "So, who *did* witness the rape?"

Pat Paulsen shook his head. "Major, I understand that you and the Commodore need to establish our level of culpability for the many—almost innumerable—crimes that were committed by humans on this planet. And I think I understand the immediate significance: to determine whether it is proper to ship us home as free agents or in irons. Is that about right?"

Solsohn glanced at Riordan, who nodded. "That's the gist of it, Colonel."

"That's what we expected. So allow me to make the tangled events surrounding the rapes as clear as circumstances permit. Because we've had less than total success reconstructing the events of that night.

"From the outset, the Nazis and the Japanese had separated the women from the rest of us, keeping them in the inner compound. Probably as emergency hostages. But they were also forcing those who already had medical skills to teach the other women to function as, to use Ike's term, emergency medical technicians. They were well-treated at first. As least, better than we were."

"And then the Nazi policy toward the women changed?"

Paulsen shook his head: more resignation than negation. "We don't really know the answer to that. The Nazis and the Japanese started becoming more 'attentive' to the women, the Japanese showing particularly inappropriate interest in the Nisei infiltrator that Commander Hansell had been carrying aboard *Swordfish*. But they certainly didn't announce any official change in their treatment of the women; they'd have been damned fools to do so. Besides, at that time, all our attention was focused on possible repercussions over some Nazis we fragged."

"'Fragged'?"

"Killed on the sly. The last raid before the rapes was a bad one. The Nazis were worried about their authority and some of our guys were coming real close to crossing the line with them. While we were securing the town, we took incoming from one of their buildings. Tore the Nazi officer and machine-gun crew to pieces. An SS *feldwebel* named Hartmann goes nuts, orders our guys to spread out and flank the shooter. No cover fire, no leapfrog: just charge in and surround the building.

"Well, our guys pretty much ignored him. So off Hartmann goes, bags the snork—single-handedly, I'll give him that—and returns, lording it over everyone, including our senior officers. Accuses some of our guys of cowardice, then threatens them. They flip him the bird, and he brings up his light machine gun."

Rich Hailey nodded. "Which was the last thing he ever did."

Paulsen nodded back. "He got off a shot—killed Joe Parks, hell of a nice kid who'd been on *Swordfish*—before our people turned him into Swiss cheese. The other Krauts had been standing around, stunned, got gunned down by Thompsons before they could bring their rifles up."

Rich folded his hands carefully. "We didn't police

the brass, didn't take our dead, and didn't grab any food, because we knew the Nazis were going to grill us when we got back to Dante. And they did. But all we had to do was exaggerate and claim we left in a panic. After all, we could genuinely testify to seeing a lot German casualties inflicted by the snorks, and we'd lost a lot of our own. And since we hadn't even stopped to loot the 'ville, we figured that would convince them that we really had bugged out. And it did, for the most part. So we got docked two days rations and hoped that was the end of it. And for us, it was."

Paulsen sighed. "But in the wake of those losses, you could tell the Nazis were still suspicious. They started getting more twitchy, more nervous about proving who was in charge. So I suppose we should have seen it coming." He bowed his head. "A few nights later, there was a commotion in the inner complex. We heard shouting, then shooting, then two of our wounded came running out of the hospital, yelling about rape and that the Germans might kill Rachel, an Israeli, because she nearly tore one of their eyes out." He shook his head. "Then—chaos." After a moment, Paulsen nodded at Franklin.

The pararescueman folded his hands. "I was tasked to make some sense of how the violence had started. But there were so many deaths that it's been impossible to reconstruct all the events.

"After that raid that went south, some of the women made it pretty clear that they weren't going to miss the dead Nazis. A nasty, and constantly suspicious, SS bastard decided to take his anger out on Rachel. But she pretty much took out his left eye.

"There was another woman nearby, a Greek who

had been captured with the Brits on Crete, and she called in the others. Guards came running, but instead of stopping the rape, they joined it. The Greek resistance fighter, Kyma, tried taking one on and that fight turned into another rape or attempted rape; we really can't be sure. We think that's when the gunfire started. Either one of the nurses or one of the patients got their hands on a guard's weapon.

"All hell broke loose. The majority of the wounded in the med ward tried to intervene and died trying. Some others came running for us, opened the gates from the inside. Only two made it through before going down with bullets in their backs.

"But that gave the rest of us a way in. Those in the lead grabbed the guards' weapons, the machine guns out of of the hardpoints, and headed into the complex." Ike leaned back, rubbed his eyes. "In ten minutes, we humans killed five times as many of ourselves as the Hkh'Rkh have to date. There was blood everywhere, lots of wounded that needed immediate attention, lots who had to be triaged. We spent days sorting it all out. By then, it was clear that we'd never know what happened: whether Kreuzer tried to stop it or not, whether the rapes were sanctioned or spontaneous acts of violence, whether all the Germans supported their senior officers or not. It was just close-quarters carnage."

Riordan folded his hands. "How many dead?"

"Two hundred and eighty-four. About equal numbers of them and us. They had the advantage at first, but once our guys got to the armory, we had more weapons and better ones. At the end of the night, there were only half a dozen Japanese left. All the Germans had been killed. And so had Rachel and Kyma."

"And roughly how long ago did this occur?"

"About one hundred and seventy local days."

"And what happened after that?"

Pat Paulsen nodded his thanks to Ike. "We buried our dead. And stuck the Germans and Japanese in a shallow pit. Which was justice, of a sort: they got the same kind of grave they'd been putting innocent people in for years. It took the remaining Japanese seven days to dig it, too.

"The rest of us spent that time either recovering from our wounds or getting a handle on our supply situation. The Germans and Japanese kept anything having to do with logistics a closely held secret, and we never located anything that looked like quarter-master ledgers. Too many nooks and crannies in this cave network to do anything like a thorough search, although we did find a few booby traps the hard way. Besides, we weren't about to trust their record keeping. It would be just like their officers to hold back some secret stashes. So we took our own inventory.

"There was enough real food left for about seven months and we had accumulated an additional month's worth of local rations. So we looked at the towns that had been identified by recon flights and put together a raiding timetable. Meanwhile, we kept looking for opportunities to establish contact with the HikRik.

"The raiding was successful, but the contact was hopeless. I guess we looked as monstrous to them as they did to us, and we always came in superior numbers and with lots of guns. Couldn't risk it any other way; their first reflex was to attack—and those are some brave sons of bitches, let me tell you. They will keep coming at you when they should already be dead on their feet."

Caine nodded, remembering. "I know."

Something in his voice made Paulsen glance at him before resuming. "We put ourselves on about twenty percent real rations, eighty percent local: the most we could tolerate and remain functional. As it is, we're all about five to ten percent underweight.

"We tried to minimize their casualties, and I think we did a pretty good job once we learned that most of their females and young run for their dens as soon as there's any sign of danger. But they never seemed to learn—or never cared—that we were only after their food and some of their equipment.

"Then, recently, they started searching for us, sending out light armored columns to investigate where we'd struck. That was the first hint that they had a real military. We'd also run out of smaller, peripheral targets, so we had to strike larger settlements. That meant more casualties, but it also meant we found more intelligence that we could use: maps and other graphics. That gave us some new directions for exploration.

"Once we had a global map and some decent regional ones, we discovered a few places where we thought we might be able to relocate. We scouted them, decided that a few small islands well to the south would be best: local water sources, moderate climate, not heavily forested. We'd learned enough about how the locals produce food—some of which we can eat, some not—to realize that this was as good a shot as we were going to get at an isolated, distant, and defensible site to try to establish a self-supporting community. We didn't know whether it would work, but we knew we couldn't keep this up forever. And getting your daily bread by killing other sentient beings—human or no—is a lousy way to live. In every possible way."

Solsohn looked around the table. "It's not just a lousy way to live. It sounds like the kind of situation that would drive a lot of people into a hole, waiting for the end. On an alien planet, killing seven foot tall monsters to get enough supplies, trying to survive on food that wants to turn your guts inside out: how did you manage to maintain unit cohesion, morale?"

Ike smiled sadly. "Survival instinct, sir. Sheer, unadulterated survival instinct. That's not the whole of it, of course, but that was the bedrock. And beyond that, the shared resolve that you won't give up. I mean, one thing that everyone here has in common is that, when we were faced with a ten-second choice between certain death where we stood or possible life in a completely unknown place, we all chose life. So, although we come from different countries, I guess we're all members of the clan of survival. And that's a large part of what brought us through."

Paulsen nodded. "And there was hope that, one day, there might be a way out of this mess . . . if we could just hang on long enough. We knew that humans, or something that looked like them, had been the ones who contacted us and dumped us here. We examined the machines that they preserved us in: again, clearly made for, and possibly by, other humans. And the equipment and the base had clearly been left for a purpose: not one we welcomed, but a purpose nonetheless. It didn't make sense that someone wouldn't come back eventually, to see what we had, or hadn't, done.

"And all the troops in this group know how to hang

on to a thin thread of hope. It's something they've done before. We've got Israelis, Soviets from World War Two and Afghanistan, GIs from the Battle of the Bulge and isolated firebases deep in the Southeast Asian bush, the perpetually outgunned Viet Cong, Pashtuns who went into battle expecting to become martyrs. I may hate who put us here, but they had a pretty good idea of the kind of troops they were impressing: the kind that don't roll over and die."

Rich Hailey leaned forward. "I'll add one other factor that's pretty grim, but pretty important. The Nazis did us one, huge favor: they united us in hate. And that drove us together long enough and tight enough to realize that there were no political axes left to grind. Mujahideen and Russians; Viet Cong and Americans—what the hell did all that mean, anymore? We were lost in space, maybe time, and had some of the most insane, most sadistic bastards in all of history putting the whip to our backs. Literally, on some occasions. And when the pot boiled over and we got rid of them—well, we had the same blood on our hands. That bonded us, too."

The quiet that followed was almost like the one around a campfire late at night, when everything has been said and weariness is setting in. Riordan reflected that in the annals of military history, few units had ever had a better claim upon weariness. Each of its different groups had been in a losing battle less than half a waking year ago, usually in the midst of a losing war. Then they woke up on an alien world, being ordered around by Nazis at gunpoint and stealing what little they could eat from towering, warlike monsters.

Pat Paulsen folded his hands. "Commodore, maybe

your militaries now have precedents that bear directly upon situations like this. I can tell you I'm not aware of any from my time. However, I want to make it very clear that we officers were the ones who decided how to classify the local inhabitants in terms of their status as combatants. We possessed the best training and competence to understand the legal ramifications of those determinations, and it was our duty to set them forth for our personnel. So when official inquiries are made into the actions that led to the deaths of noncombatants, we want to make it crystal clear that the responsibility for those deaths is ours, and ours alone. Enlisted personnel were legally bound to follow our orders, which included accepting our classifications of the enemy and the rules of engagement. And I think it fair to assert that there were no precedents in the prior experience of our enlisted men—either as soldiers or simply as humans—that can be construed as having obliged them to question our determinations regarding the nature of our enemy or our actions against them."

Riordan smiled. "I know a prepared speech when I hear one, Colonel Paulsen. And for what it's worth, I agree with you."

Solsohn moved forward slightly, interrupting. "I should state, for the record, that we can't make any guarantees. There will probably will be an inquiry into your actions here. Nor can I give any assurances that it might not result in military tribunals, the outcomes of which are obviously uncertain."

Riordan, stunned, turned his eyes slowly toward Duncan, who was careful not to meet his gaze.

"I'm sorry to have to bring all that up," Solsohn

continued, still looking at Paulsen, "but that was my
own prepared speech—as per instructions from our
superior, Mr. Richard Downing. In part, he sent me
along to attend to legal details like this one. Accordingly, while Mr. Downing and I travelled to meet the
Commodore, who was returning from the field, I was
briefed on the legal posture the Consolidated Terran
Republic would need to take, as determined by the
different scenarios we might find here."

"You mean, whether we were a bunch of homicidal
maniacs, or a bunch of shanghaied castaways fighting
for our lives."

"Yes."

Paulsen glanced over at Riordan. "You seem a bit
surprised by this, Commodore. And rather quiet."

Riordan was still looking at Solsohn. "I am surprised, Colonel. But I really shouldn't be. I've worked
with Mr. Downing before. I should have expected
that he would compartmentalize this operation so
that I am able to focus on the military aspects while
Major Solsohn keeps track of its bureaucratic particulars." *And in so doing, kept me out of the loop
on what assurances we could and could not legally
make to whoever we found on Turkh'saar until we
were face to face with them. But just because I'm
learning it late doesn't mean I can't take additional
actions . . .* "However, Colonel Paulsen, you and your
command have nothing to fear. I give you my word,
as an officer of the CTR and as an individual, that
you shall not be remanded to higher authorities
until and unless the full particulars of your situation here have been made clear to those authorities.
And that they, in turn, publicly attest that you are

assured of maximum clemency, guaranteed by their tendering a statement of the most serious charges that they might bring against you. Unless, that is, they should learn that your report to us has been materially incomplete or untrue."

Solsohn's eyes widened. "Caine," he muttered, "you can't do that. You don't have the authority to—"

"Major, I do not have the authority to countermand any of the orders you received from Mr. Downing. And I am not doing so. I am simply adding conditions of my own." *And while it is bad enough that you did this publicly, it is wholly unacceptable that you did so in a setting and in a manner that undermines my authority. So you're going to lose this round: their faith in us depends upon that.*

Duncan glanced at the ring of unblinking eyes which were now watching their exchange. "You can't add conditions that constrain the actions of higher authorities."

"Not as a Commodore, no. But you may have forgotten, Major, that I came to you and Mr. Downing straight from a diplomatic mission in which I was given temporary powers as an ambassador plenipotentiary. I am acting in that role now, pursuant to resolving an interstellar dispute between our race and the Hkh'Rkh. If ending that dispute means promising these men fair treatment so that they may reasonably decide that their best option is to come peaceably with us, then I will commit to the necessary conditions and guarantees."

"Commodore, your diplomatic mission is concluded; you no longer hold those ambassadorial powers."

"Interesting, Major. I don't seem to recall sharing the details of my appointment with you. I wonder who did? At any rate, you are mistaken. The first diplomatic mission—that involving the Slaasriithi allies who brought us here—is technically not over until our joint operations are at an end. And what we do here will definitively shape their opinion of us, and furthermore, will color the way other species perceive their involvement with us in general. So yes, my powers still apply."

Duncan's eyes were pleading; his voice sounded as though he was suppressing nausea. "Commodore, *I* wouldn't object—but that interpretation of your ambassadorial appointment could be challenged."

"It certainly could, Major." *That was a possibility from the moment Etienne Gaspard saddled me with it.* "But no one here has higher military or ambassadorial rank, so it will have to wait until someone with greater authority is disposed to make that challenge." He turned back to Paulsen. "Do you consider my assurances acceptable, Colonel?"

Paulsen nodded soberly. "More than sufficient, Commodore. Maybe too much so. I may not be part of your military, but it sounds to me like you're sticking your neck way out on this one."

"Possibly so, Colonel. But since I'm asking you to put your trust in me, that means I have a responsibility to live up to that trust and see that you are all assured of fair treatment and safe passage. By the way, just how many of you are there?"

"Four hundred and thirty-two, twenty-eight of whom are women."

Riordan allowed his left eyebrow to rise slightly. "Thank you, Colonel . . . but why did you feel it necessary to break out the number of women, specifically?"

For the first time, Paulsen seemed surprised. He looked at his officers, who looked back, equally flummoxed. "Because they will require separate accommodations on the return, Commodore. Or, don't you—?"

Riordan smiled. "No, there are no sex-distinctions in terms of billets anymore, Colonel. Not in most nations, anyway."

Paulsen looked less surprised but more startled. "Then how do you—er, how do you prevent—?"

"We don't."

Paulsen frowned, rubbed the end of his prominent nose. "I see. Well, no, I don't see, really. That wouldn't work for us."

"I wouldn't expect it to. It's all a matter of what you grow up becoming accustomed to, I suspect."

"I suspect that's right. To be frank, those—matters— were of considerable concern to us as we tried to envision how to make a long-term community work. The balance between the sexes is, well, it's unsupportable. At least by our cultural standards and comfort. The consensus here was that we were headed for one hell of a hormonally fueled train-wreck."

"Well, I don't think you're going to have to worry about that anymore." Riordan set his hands on the table. "Now do any of you have questions related to the extraction?"

Paulsen shrugged. "Tell us what you need done, and we'll do it."

Riordan stood. "I'll let Major Solsohn go over the logistical particulars with you, but bear this in mind: we must not leave any trace of our presence here. That means no destroying machinery in place. We have to break it down and haul it away. All of it."

"And this cave complex?" Rodermund asked.

"Depends. How much has it been modified?"

He shrugged. "Not much, except for the power source."

"Good, then we may not need to demo it. Now, while you start organizing your unit to pull out, my people have to accomplish three things. They are, in order, to call down our other two transports, to sleep, and to assess an intelligence matter."

Paulsen looked up. "What intelligence matter do you mean?"

Riordan folded his arms. "The cryogenic cells in which you were conveyed and stored are concrete evidence of your impressment. They are also potentially destabilizing technologies. So too might be the power source your hijackers provided for this facility. We'll need a look at them to determine how to proceed."

"Of course. Rich, why don't you take Commodore Riordan back to the *sanctum sanctorum*?"

"It can wait a minute or two. I want to call in some qualified personnel from our lead transport to conduct the detailed assessment. I'm going to retrace my steps until I get a clear signal."

"Our guards will accompany you, Commodore."

"I will, too," said Solsohn, rising quickly.

"You will not," Riordan said quietly. "You need to coordinate with Colonel Paulsen and his staff." *And besides, our next conversation had best be in private—for your sake.*

Peter Wu and Newton Baruch managed to stay poker-faced until they reached the storage chamber where Paulsen's troops—or the Lost Soldiers, as everyone on

Wedge One was calling them—had been stored during their century-plus sleep. But the strange tableau overcame the two IRIS agents' apparent resolve to remain unaffected by their surroundings.

This cavern's ceiling was at least twenty meters high, reaching to thirty in some spots. Essentially an oval, it was sixty meters at its widest and more than one hundred thirty at its longest. Most of it was empty now, supply wrappings stacked in neatly folded piles at one end. Nothing manufactured, nothing from Earth, ever became rubbish for the Lost Soldiers of Turkh'saar. Everything was saved for repurposing, even if the form of that repurposing had not yet been envisioned.

But the cavern's arresting feature was on the right hand wall: a gridwork of heavy metal frames, like some immense skeletal array of mail slots or safety deposit boxes. Except that in each one of those long, narrow pigeon-holes was a coffinlike object: a cryocell. And there were hundreds of them.

But they were not all of the same type. Some were reminiscent of the best, recent models used by the CTR. Others were smaller, sleeker. A few seemed unusually large and bulky, until Riordan realized they were actually highly compact quad-cells. And then, further back along the racks, they came upon objects that hardly looked mechanical at all—and upon closer inspection, seemed not to be, except for some rudimentary controls which had been embedded in their dark brown and maroon surfaces. Their shapes were irregular, like cocoons of mostly opaque and discolored amber. Lights glowed and faded intermittently within them, changing tint and shape.

Newton's voice was very low as they stopped before

these final containers. "Commodore, what the hell are we looking at here?"

"I don't know, Lieutenant, but hell might very well be involved."

Peter had continued walking further down the length of the chamber. "There are more here. And I believe they still have occupants."

Riordan nodded. "Fifty-one. About twenty of which show warning lights."

Newton scanned the machines. "How did they learn which of the lights indicate potential failure?"

"By trying to reanimate some, whom they lost. They are not sure how many folks of each nationality are in these units, but evidently, whoever grabbed the occupants was looking for air force personnel: most of these cells are marked with a sigil indicating either a pilot or an aviation mechanic. Apparently, this model of cell is the one that most of the Vietnam era Americans came out of."

Newton nodded. "And what is my job here, Commodore?"

"To try to get a handle on this technology."

Newton looked up and down the grid of high-tech sarcophagi. "There is a lot of technology here, sir. I count at least eight distinctly different varieties of cryocell, not counting whatever these other containment units are. I have some reasonable experience in cryogenic medicine, but—"

"Lieutenant, you're here because you're the best we've got right now. I know you're not going to be able to give me a detailed briefing on each. And I know there are probably going to be aspects of this technology that you won't be able to figure out in time, maybe ever. That's fine. That's expected. I just want to know roughly how they work, how they're powered, if there are any marks or writing on any of them, and if there are any signs of foreign microbes or pathogens. Because we're taking these with us, and I need to know what I'm loading on our transports."

Newton, face long and solemn, nodded once. "Yes sir. I'll get right on it."

Riordan returned the lieutenant's salute and watched him walk further down the line of cryocells as Peter returned. "He's really quite brilliant," Peter commented, "no matter how much he claims otherwise."

Riordan nodded. "I figured as much. But that's only half the reason I gave him this job."

Caine felt Wu's eyes searching his face. "What is the other half-reason, sir?"

"He's IRIS. He's been vetted. He knows how to keep a secret. And this one—well, this may be the biggest one yet."

"You mean, because this might be the work of the Ktor?"

"Might be?" Riordan waved a hand at the solid wall of cryocells. "We don't have anything even approaching the sophistication of the most primitive units here. They're incredibly compact, apparently require little power, and they kept their occupants mentally and physically intact for over a century and a half. And who else is likely to build not just a few cryocells that humans can use, but so many of them and in so many varieties?"

"With respect, sir, your own report from the Convocation indicates that the Dornaani had cryocells that were adaptable for human use." His voice lowered further. "The same was true of the medical cryounit they used to save Admiral Corcoran's daughter after she was wounded in Jakarta. As well as you."

Riordan nodded, pushed back the memory of Elena Corcoran's face, her smile, her eyes, pushed away the persistent urge to drop what he was doing and find a way to get to Dornaani space, to find out if they had in fact saved her life, or if she was still suspended in their intensive care cryocell. "Yes, the Dornaani make human cryocells, too, but this isn't their handiwork. This is Ktoran. And not just because of the technology. Consider when they grabbed these people, and who they chose to grab."

Peter nodded. "At precisely the same time as their assistant Custodianship of Earth was coming to an end. And they sought out mostly elite units. Or at least, they all come from units that were both self-reliant and accustomed to a high degree of danger."

"Yes, but I think the Ktor preference may have gone even deeper than that. Everything we learn about the Ktor points to an obsession with genetics, with looking for and shaping the traits they want. Now, look who they impressed: individuals who, to their thinking, probably had the highest potential for being lone-wolf killers." Seeing Peter about to object, Riordan shook his head. "I know; not all of them are. MACV-SOG aren't the same thing as Nazi SS. Neither are dogged Soviet riflemen or determined Viet Cong irregulars. Or surrounded Brits or doomed submariners. But all those units stand out in history for their ability to persevere in the face of enormous danger. And not simply to build roads, or fly planes, or protect merchant ships: their mission was to kill the enemy, wherever and however they could. And to keep doing so, even in the face of staggering odds."

"So are you saying that the Ktor ultimately wanted to—to *breed* these troops?"

Riordan frowned. "I think we'd need to know a lot more about the Ktor before we can make a guess at that. But at the very least, their choices here do indicate their frame of mind, the kind of killer and soldier that they wanted for this mission. They selected for the traits to which they themselves aspire. That, almost as much as the technology and the ability to recruit and then preserve humans, is what convinces me that this must be Ktor handiwork. Nothing else makes sense."

Peter turned to glance at Baruch. He was crouching down to inspect one of the already opened cryopods that was most analogous to their own technology. "And that's why you asked me about Newton: you need to know if you can trust him." He shrugged. "In that case, I can assure you that he's an extremely lucky find."

Riordan shook his head. "I doubt it's luck. He was probably included in the Cold Guard as a covert observer. He may have been the only one the Rag Tag Fleet left behind. But I'll bet that Downing made sure to pull him for inclusion on this mission. Because Downing knew, or guessed, that this moment might come: when he'd be crouching down, looking at technology, at evidence, that could bring things crashing down if we're not careful."

"You mean, crashing down here on Turkh'saar?"

"No. I mean everywhere."

"Earth, too?"

Riordan turned to look at Peter. "Earth most of all."

Chapter Thirty

Idrem watched Brenlor Srin Perekmeres study the
various flight trajectories that had been relayed to
the holoplot. The curvilinear cat's cradle of white
arcs gathered and terminated at the same small spot
on the blue-belted brown sphere that represented
Turkh'saar. "And all the firing solutions are being
automatically updated?"

Idrem nodded, pushed away from his workstation,
glided toward the Srin. "Yes. It is not complicated. All
our targets are fixed ground points, not mobile objects.
Our relative position is not altering much, since the
debris concealing us is in very nearly geosynchronous
with our target points. We are maintaining hit confidence of ninety-seven percent or better."

"Flight time?"

"It partially depends on the particular munitions
we choose to launch from *Red Lurker*'s railgun. The
upper limit of launch to impact is sixty-four minutes.
The lower end is approximately fifty minutes."

"So any efforts to engage moving targets would require a round with a launch bus."

"Correct. The interval between launch and impact only allows us to put the projectile in a general intercept footprint. The projectile would then have to launch an independently propelled warhead for terminal maneuver to a moving target. But I doubt that will be our primary use of the railgun."

Brenlor nodded. "Conventional airburst over stationary formations."

"Yes, assuming that the enemy collects in any given area. Which it seems they must, if they are to halt the advance of the Hkh'Rkh forces now gathering west of the river over which they retreated. It is logical that the Aboriginals will choose the river as a line of defense, and their side of that river is now well-targeted."

Brenlor leaned closer to the holoplot, pulled at the edges of the image to expand that part, zooming in. "A great number of the trajectories are slightly further to the south, though. Why?"

"That is the approximate region from which Hkh'Rkh automated defenses launched missiles at the Aboriginal ships during their descent."

Brenlor frowned. "And why do you feel it necessary to target that? Logically, it would already be dangerous to them, and they will avoid it."

Idrem laid two fingers on the starboard bulkhead to steady himself in the zero gee. "That is the most logical projection. However, if the humans have the time and opportunity, they might wish to reconnoiter that region."

Brenlor's eyes narrowed. "Because it might give them concrete evidence that the Hkh'Rkh violated their treaty with the Arat Kur to keep the planet demilitarized?"

"Yes, but not just that. The area contains anomalous structures. Its very existence is anomalous."

Brenlor leaned away from the image, as if he did not wish to see it. His command—"Explain."—almost seemed to stick in his throat.

"Its shape is not unlike that of an asteroid impact site. Observe the tapered oval shape. Furthermore, the first Hkh'Rkh missions to this system, back when they were restricted to STL travel, evidently investigated this area extensively. The weathering of the abandoned buildings dates back further than their achievement of faster-than-light capability. So something here was of intense interest to them. I suspect the Aboriginals have noticed what we have, and will investigate, if given the opportunity."

Brenlor's reply was almost rushed. "And if they are foolish enough to go there, we have an appropriate welcome prepared for them. Which they will never see coming."

"Let us rather say it is very unlikely they will see it coming. Although the projectiles are extremely small, they are extremely swift, and will combust the surrounding atmosphere once they begin cutting through it. That might give personnel on the ground ten to fifteen seconds of warning. Active sensors would certainly detect the attack beforehand, but both the humans and the Hkh'Rkh seem unwilling to illuminate such systems."

Brenlor glanced at the ops screen. It was zoomed in on the region where the humans and Hkh'Rkh had clashed just hours before. "And they are almost as sparing with radio comms. I wish we knew more about what happened down there."

"Well, we know that over a dozen Hkh'Rkh vehicles were destroyed. Thermal imaging shows that clearly. The remaining vehicles withdrew to considerable range. While it was harder to assess casualties with any accuracy, the total for both sides must exceed one hundred. And given the speed with which the Hkh'Rkh reversal occurred, it is difficult to foresee a scenario in which the Aboriginals did not use the railgun of their own ship to break the attack."

Brenlor stared at the regional look-down. "If only the Hkh'Rkh had delayed their attack until their main force arrived. Their casualties would have been so heavy that we would have had all the pretext we need to 'save' the local government. But this way, they will tread carefully before making a broad assault. A tangled scenario, for us."

Idrem nodded. "Made more complex by the Terrans' restraint. They could have destroyed all the Hkh'Rkh vehicles. If they show similar restraint when the main body of their opponents arrives, it could create a drawn out engagement. A stand-off, even."

Brenlor shook his head. "But not for long. The Aboriginals need to leave this system as quickly as possible. So, once they accept that parley is useless, they will bring down their last two transports: a violation that the Hkh'Rkh will not be able to tolerate."

Idrem was impressed by Brenlor's ability to look beyond the frustrations of the moment. "That is almost certainly true, Srin Perekmeres." He elected not to mention the other, albeit distant possibility: that somehow the Terrans *would* be able to strike a truce and secure Hkh'Rkh permission to remove the raiders. But there was no benefit to perturbing Brenlor with that possibility, now. Although the likelihood of such a course of events was low, the Srin might perceive the need for preemption to be urgent, act peremptorily, and thus lose both a crucial military and diplomatic advantage: surprise.

Brenlor rose into the weightlessness. "Is there anything else that should be brought to my attention, High Sentinel?"

Idrem made his answer in the context of his preceding thoughts: "No, Srin Perekmeres."

"Very well." He turned to the former megacorporate employee who was manning communications. "Comms, ready the lascom. We are sending an update to *Arbitrage*."

Haddesh, the huscarle manning the *Arbitrage*'s technologically stunted communications station, signalled that the lascom pulse from *Red Lurker* had been successfully decrypted. He downloaded it into his beltcom, relayed it to Nezdeh's own.

Although three of the other Evolved aboard were present, it was Tegrese who could not simply wait for their leader and captain to relay the message in a time of her own choosing. Of course. "What news?"

Vranut Baltheker and Zurur Deosketer glanced sideways at Tegrese, who seemed oblivious to their disapproving attention.

Nezdeh finished reading the short message, reflected upon its significance before sharing those parts of it she deemed appropriate. "The Aboriginals landed in the midst of a Hkh'Rkh attack on the raiders. The attack was repulsed. A much larger Hkh'Rkh force is approaching, apparently to resume the attack. Oddly, the Aboriginal ship attracted ground fire from what is apparently a remote Hkh'Rkh missile battery."

Zurur's fine chin came up sharply. "That is not expected."

"No, it is not," Nezdeh agreed. She did not add that the anomalous impact site it was apparently emplaced to guard was even less expected. And was also vaguely troubling. She wondered if Idrem was experiencing the same misgivings that she was, given the reported age of the abandoned facilities around the site. "Also, Brenlor has selected Idrem as House Perekmeres' High Sentinel."

Nods and one murmur of approval answered this wholly expected announcement. Idrem was the logical choice, and although Nezdeh's relationship with him was in no way declared or displayed openly, there was no uncertainty among the crew regarding its existence. Which made his accession to High Sentinel that much more predictable.

However, the muted response was not indifferent so much as it was consistent with circumspect propriety. After all, they could not congratulate Nezdeh on Idrem's accession without implicitly presuming her relationship with him and that it was of sufficient seriousness that she had a personal stake in his selection. If anything, the Evolved of her crew seemed, well, not exactly pleased, but gratified: as if their small community had been made somehow more solid by this appointment, this filling of a traditional post which they associated with a true House.

Vranut glanced at the *Arbitrage*'s primitive *faux*-3-D

navplot. "I presume we are to hold position here, as per the initial plan."

"Yes. Nothing in this report signals a need to alter our present course of action. But we should be at full readiness. Events could unfold quite rapidly now. We shall return to fully manned watches. The crew has received as much extra rest as we may give them. Also, we need a new set of readiness checks and drills on all away-craft and munitions. Tegrese, Vranut: give the necessary orders. In person. That will let them know that our time of waiting is nearing the end, and that our exacting and unforgiving gaze is hard upon them."

The two Evolved nodded and floated out the portal connecting the bridge to the keel-following access tunnels.

"And I?" Zurur asked.

Nezdeh gazed at the navplot. "You and I shall—"

The senior human, Ayana Tagawa, looked up from her position at sensors. "New contact," she announced crisply.

Nezdeh managed not to start in surprise. Zurur did not have that measure of self-mastery; her eyes were wide. "Where?" Nezdeh asked. "Show me."

Ayana complied. The scale in the navplot shrank dramatically, so that it displayed deep space just beyond the orbit of BD+56 2966's most distant planetesimal. At the edge of the plot, an orange starburst icon floated and then faded. "Sensor readings indicate a gigawatt-level surge of mesons, high-energy particles, Cherenkov radiation. Surge duration: zero-point-zero-zero-two seconds total. Range: just over six light-hours."

Nezdeh leaned over the plot, her hands gripping its edges. "An out-shift."

"Yes, Srina Perekmeres."

Nezdeh glanced at the Asian Aboriginal. Generally, she trusted the competence of the genetically limited breed too little to rely upon their reports without double-checking. But Ayana was the exception: her skill and precision were unmatched. That is why, unless skilled piloting was called for, Nezdeh kept her on sensors: so that they would have as much advance warning, and accurate information, as possible. Still, she needed to be certain of this result. "You are absolutely sure?"

"I have played back the sensor readings twice now, looking for possible errors or inconsistent signatures. I find none. If it is not a shift, this phenomenon is a perfect mimicry of one."

Nezdeh nodded. The small Aboriginal female knew her life depended upon her reliability; she would have taken every precaution to be certain of the accuracy of her report.

Zurur came alongside Nezdeh. "The Slaasriithi shift-carrier: could it have—?"

"No." Nezdeh shook her head slightly, gestured at a small orange triangle at the inner edge of the asteroid belt in which they themselves were hidden. "We occasionally catch glimpses of their radiant energy from behind that planetoid. Besides, even if their stealth was the match of ours—and it is not—there is no way they could have withdrawn from their position and then preaccelerated without our detecting them."

"And even if they had," Ayana added, "the Slaasriithi craft only moved into that position three days ago. As we observed when we shadowed them on the way to Disparity, the Slaasriithi require at least nine days to preaccelerate. They have not had enough time."

Nezdeh glanced approvingly at the Aboriginal, but thought: *you are entirely too clever. We need your skills in this time and place, but I must expunge you as soon as possible. At some point, you will discover a flaw in our security protocols, or see an opportunity we do not detect in time, and you will either escape or destroy us—along with yourself, if necessary.* "The Aboriginal's deduction is correct."

"So what ship made out-shift, then?" Zurur wondered, her voice less firm and confident than was technically befitting of an Evolved.

"If we had *Red Lurker*'s sensors, we might be able to compare its shift signature with those we have on record. But lacking that, we can only conjecture."

But I know this much: we have seen no ship preaccelerate since we have been in this system. That means this was a ship with a short preacceleration period, one that could carry it out with its thrust signature largely concealed by the gas giant in orbit seven. A ship that suspected—or knew—of our own presence here and certainly knew of the Slaasriithi's. A ship that watched, waited, and shifted out within an hour of receiving transmissions signifying the commencement of new, amplified hostilities on Turkh'saar. So it is a Dornaani ship. Or—

—her mind momentarily ground to a halt as the only other alternative rose up—

—a Ktoran.

Olsirkos Shethkador'vah, Senior Tagmator and master of the Ktor destroyer *Will Breaker*, threw off his acceleration couch's straps as soon as the slight postshift disorientation had abated. "Communications, detect the pulse that will give us lascom coordinates for *Ferocious Monolith*. Sensors, what is the disposition of the Aboriginal fleet?"

"Mostly unchanged, Tagmator, although we are too distant from Sigma Draconis Two for detailed readings. If anything, there may be more ships here."

"Any sign of the Dornaani ship, the *Olsloov*?"

"None, but we will need to conduct a far more detailed scan before reporting with any confidence."

And even then, the confidence would be dubious. The Dornaani, and particularly the vessels with which they equipped their Custodians, excelled at one task above all others: not being seen unless they wished to be. Olsirkos turned to the navigator. "In-shift accuracy?"

"Nominal, Senior Tagmator Olsirkos: .9957 rectitude. We are well within the shadow of the gas giant you selected."

"Engineer, detach the shift-tug. The refueling shuttle is to commence operations. We may be ordered back to Turkh'saar within a few days."

"As you instruct, Shipmaster, but our protocols indicate that we should make a formal request of the Arat Kur authorities before refueling. It is possible that they might detect our violations of their sovereignty, that they may have seeded the upper reaches of this gas giant with microsensors that could detect our—"

"Then they shall detect us." He glanced at Weapons. "And if you detect any of their microsensors, eliminate them immediately. Comms, I require local jamming of their signals. You will find data on their secret frequencies in the emergency operations database."

The Intendant at Comms raised an eyebrow. "How complete is that data, sir?"

"Fully. We hacked their systems long ago. It is very easy to access even the most confidential information of so trusting an ally. Navigator, plot a course for the orbital track of Homenest, ten light-seconds to trailing of the planet itself. Pilot, heavy plasmoid thrusters only. We do not want to call undue attention to ourselves during our approach. Engage."

Tlerek Srin Shethkador checked his beltcom. Three minutes until Olsirkos was to commence his transmission. He rose, gestured to his first officer, Zharun Ptaalkepsos. "You have mastery of the bridge in my absence. Send the incoming lascom transmission from *Will Breaker* directly to my quarters: my personal decryption system is adequate." Swift, gliding, low-gee steps carried him toward the exit. "I am not to be disturbed unless there is a level three or higher emergency."

The end of Zharun Ptaalkepsos's reply, "Yes, Fearsome Sri—" was cut off as the bridge's iris valve sealed behind Shethkador. It was a relief that Olsirkos had returned. The possibility that *Will Breaker*'s mission had ended catastrophically had grown with every passing week. But, judging from the ship's unhurried approach, as well as Olsirkos's prudent decision to get within a few light-seconds before initiating transmissions, it seemed unlikely that his report was especially urgent.

As Shethkador passed from the main hull into the spin arm that led to the Evolved quarters, guards ritually presented their arms for inspection and their necks for slicing. He tumbled through a ninety-degree turn so that his feet faced away from the spine of his ship, extended his legs until they touched the broad platform that conjoined the doors leading to the four lift shafts at its compass points. He stepped toward the red-coded elevator; it opened, sealed behind him.

"Srin's quarter's." He leaned forward, let the biometric and live-retina scans catch up with the voice recognition.

"Recognized," the machine acknowledged. "Password required."

An archaic additional precaution, but better than allowing his genecode to be digitized and entered into a database, regardless of how secure it might be. "Kalamata," he replied.

The transport cell began its descent and he felt the pseudogravity increase as it moved swiftly outward from the center of the ship.

He tapped his beltcom, ordered, "Display confidential reports."

The holographic projector in the unit threw a bright screen up in front of him. Beyond the expected updates on the progress of the Aboriginal and Arat Kur treaty resolution, there was only one new item. A recently suborned junior officer within the ranks of the Russlavic Federation had committed suicide. It was a disappointment; she had been quite promising: intelligent, prudent, subtle. But she had also been deeply committed to her family back on Earth, and while that had offered the leverage whereby Shethkador's agents had turned her, it had also been the cause of her undoing.

Had he been less devoted to maintaining absolute dominion, even over his reflexes, he might have shaken his head in disgust and disappointment. And not just at her, but his own agents. It did not seem to matter how often he stressed that they discern *why* a potential traitor was interested in money. If the motivation was simple greed, then that was a promising target for development as an agent inside the enemy's camp. Greed was not only a predictable impulse, but was an indicator of the dependability of the individual being suborned. It was overwhelmingly associated with profoundly self-centered egos and values.

However, if the subject's interest in money was for other reasons, then complications could, and usually did, arise. As was the case with this pathetic Aboriginal. Her desire for money had arisen from a fierce resolve to better the situation of her family on Earth. There had apparently been an illness among her relatives, possibly related to hardships having to do with the late war's EMP damage to the power grid that served the squalid corner of the frozen Siberian waste in which she had been spawned. In short, she compromised her oath of service not out of self-interest, but out of dedication to a principle that she held even more dear: her duty to her loved ones.

Shethkador snapped off the beltcom irritably. Love. Even she—who had reportedly been as dispassionate an Aboriginal as his agents had ever encountered—had harbored that self-delusional rot deep inside her, so deep that even they could not detect it. It was difficult to comprehend that she could adopt the ruthless traits and reflexes expected of an intelligence officer aboard a Russlavic warship and yet not realize that they also exemplified the universal truth of all existence: that whatever did not contribute to one's own power and dominion was not merely extraneous, but dangerous. Had she realized that, she would also have realized that her hidden core of emotionality was not a secret strength or joy, but a corrosive parasite, consuming her from the inside out.

And it had done just that, had been the force that moved her to pick up her sidearm, put its muzzle in her mouth, and silence the anticipated moans of family and country that she feared would lament the imagined discovery of her betrayal. It was why so few of the Aboriginals were truly reliable agents. They were all infected with this repulsively primal reflex toward the pointless intangibles they called love, loyalty, selflessness.

But it was unreasonable to expect otherwise, Shethkador admitted to himself as the transport cell began emitting a steady sequence of tones indicating that it was nearing his chosen destination. Low breeds—Aboriginal or otherwise—rarely arrived at Ktor's pinnacle of dispassionate self-assessment, did not grasp that the locus of all things and all desire was, always and inevitably, the self. What the self wanted, thought, needed, was not only paramount, but the only useful way of structuring the universe: to place oneself at its center, and orchestrate all its components to comply or cooperate with one's will. Every other creature in the universe also placed itself at a similarly egocentric position, whether they were aware of doing so or not. But Ktor was dominant because it embraced no presumption of communal effort, of shared endeavor. There could not be both a unitary and collective center: that was as inherently contradictory as the claim that a supreme deity both did, and did not, exist. The difference between dominion and subordination resided strictly in being aware and accepting of the

422   *Charles E. Gannon*

inevitability of isolation, of the inescapable linkages between the power of self-interest, self-reliance, and self-determination. Alliances were possible—essential, even—and one could admire ability in a rival, but in the end, all self-determining creatures were rivals, and it was a step toward suicide of selfhood to think or believe any differently.

The transport cell opened. More guards; more proffered weapons and unarmored necks. He walked past them and into his quarters.

As he seated himself, his comm panel illuminated, indicated an incoming message undergoing decryption. He waved at the control sensor. After a second's delay, Olsirkos's voice emerged from the speaker. "Fearsome Srin, I bring news from the Turkh'saar system."

Shethkador permitted himself the luxury of a smile. Olsirkos's greeting was rather redundant—from what other location would Olsirkos be bearing news?—but was in the ancient, formal style, and heavy with respect. Adequate, overall. "Report."

There followed far more details than Shethkador wanted or required, but that, too, was a byproduct of his subordinate's awe-tinged respect: Olsirkos craved approval, but failed to realize that selectivity and succinctness were also virtues. After listening to endless specifics about *Will Breaker*'s maneuvers—canny ones, Shethkador allowed—that kept it invisible to the enemy as it monitored events, he called for a halt. "I require no further operational details. You did well to wait as long as you did. Having out-shifted any sooner would have risked missing the involvement of the Aboriginals and the Slaasriithi. About which: you are certain that the Slaasriithi craft was a shift-carrier?"

"I am, Potent Srin. Indeed, its drive signatures are virtually identical to those we recorded when monitoring the preacceleration of the *Tidal-Drift-Instaurator-to-Shore-of-Stars* when it left Sigma Draconis some months ago."

Shethkador was glad that the commlink was voice-grade only; his self-control wavered enough for him to frown momentarily. "You are sure of that match?"

"There is less than zero point one percent variance across all parameters, Imposing Srin." When Sheth-kador did not reply immediately, Olsirkos asked, "Is this a grave matter?"

"It is puzzling at least, problematic at worst. The *Tidal-Drift-Instaurator-to-Shore-of-Stars* carried the human delegation to the Slaasriithi homeworld at Beta Aquilae. It was commanded by one of their Prime Ratiocinators, Yiithrii'ah'aash. There has recently been some intelligence traffic on the Aboriginals' most highly classified distribution lists that intimates the diplomatic mission was compromised in some way. It is strange that this ship should have returned to this region of space already, and is carrying Aboriginal away-craft. It is further interesting that, according to your sensor returns, one of the craft was a Wolfe-class corvette. A ship of that class was among those dispatched with the delegation."

"How does this problematize our response to the situation, Srin?"

"It means that your application of force must be more selective than I initially foresaw." *And requires a more delicate touch than you possess, Olsirkos, meaning that I must be regrettably overcautious in my instructions, lest your actions do Ktor's interests more harm than good.* "Since we must consider it a

distinct possibility that the Slaasriithi ambassador is
still on that shift-carrier, you must avoid firing upon
it. Beyond the matter of attacking a ship so much
larger than *Will Breaker*, there would be diplomatic
repercussions. They could be severe enough to rekindle
the late war."

"I see, Potent Srin."

"I am not sure you do, Olsirkos, because I suspect
that is precisely what these Perekmeres fen-curs wish
to provoke. If your readings are correct—that it is
indeed the *Red Lurker* that you saw moving into the
asteroid belt one orbit out from Turkh'saar—then my
conjectures are correct: the renegades of that Extirpated
House are behind the otherwise inexplicable 'human
raiding' on that planet. And the only logical purpose
to instigate such a conflict is to disrupt the process
of postwar disengagement and decreased tensions. So
it is not merely to our disadvantage for your actions
to bring about that war in another way: it is playing
into the hands of Ktor's worst traitors."

"Esteemed Srin, I understand."

Yes, you probably do—now. "You will return to the
system as soon as *Will Breaker* is prepared to make shift.
You are to in-shift beyond the range of your sensors;
that will ensure that you are beyond the range of any
of theirs. This is imperative, since it is likely that they
detected your departure and now understand that they
have been under observation. If they see you return,
they will plan accordingly, making your job that much
more difficult. If they cannot be certain that you have
returned to the system, they may remain prepared for
your reappearance but time will erode their watchful-
ness. That is essential to your purpose."

"Which is?"

"To destroy both the Extirpated remains of House Perekmeres and the raiders."

"But, Fearsome Srin, the Aboriginal ships were landing when we departed. It seemed certain that they would rescue at least some of these raiders."

"Perhaps, but you must destroy all that you may. They are evidence, and we must eliminate as much of the evidence as we can."

"Evidence of what?"

Shethkador had hoped Olsirkos would be insightful enough to deduce what all this must mean, but was hardly surprised that he had not. "Evidence that Ktor is divided, that our dominion over our own Houses is not absolute."

"But—would it not be better to capture the Perekmeres curs, as well as the raiders, and so prove to the Accord that this was not Ktor's doing, but the actions of renegades? Who we will execute before their eyes?"

Shethkador forced himself to be patient. Olsirkos was a ship commander, a warrior, but would never be a statesman. "That would be disastrous, Tagmator. Firstly, to set the Perekmeres on display before the other races of the Accord would be to definitively demonstrate that Ktorans and humans are of the same stock. This would be a de facto admission that we joined the Accord under the false pretense of being a different species and could permanently weaken our position in it. It might even result in our expulsion. It would also indicate that there are elements of the Ktoran Sphere which do not answer to its nominally highest authority, the Autarchs, and that they have subverted its dictates for centuries."

The pause on the line was longer than could merely be explained by the two light-second reception delay. "For centuries, Potent Srin? What do you mean?"

Truly, you cannot see it? "Do you believe that these 'raiders' were just now deposited on Turkh'saar by the Perekmeres? How? Where would a few desperate Extirpates recruit so many disaffected humans? Besides, it if was a *modern* unit, would not the Aboriginals have already laid waste to the entire colony of worm-grubbing Hkh'Rkh brutes? Instead, your own sensors detected broadcasts from outdated human radios, using slang and references to vehicles and weapons that are equally outdated."

"Yes, Srin, but how—?"

"These raiders were brought to Turkh'saar at least a century ago, probably earlier. And if that is true, it means that the plots unfolding today were set in motion by the same rogue elements that, led by House Perekmeres, almost devastated Earth with what the Aboriginals call the Doomsday Rock, almost forty years ago." He leaned closer to the audio pickup, as if that would help it better carry his increased emphasis. "If any of the Perekmeres remain alive, they are evidence that Ktor kidnapped hundreds of humans from Earth in their twentieth century. That will show the Aboriginals that we have moved effortlessly among them. They will also learn that the Doomsday Rock was orchestrated by our species, since it will be shown that we had routine and easy access to their home system. So ultimately, the Ktoran Sphere will be compelled to either own these idiotic atrocities, or must admit that it is unable to control the actions of its own Houses, that our core dominion is challenged and imperfect, and that we are unable to assure it in the future. What dread, what terror, will we instill in other races, then, Olsirkos? How suitable, how worthy, how unchallengeable will we seem?"

The silence was long and deep. "I shall endeavor to make my perceptions more expansive, as unto your own, Fearsome Srin."

"For now, simply attend these instructions. The Perekmeres should be the easiest to destroy, since the Aboriginals and the Slaasriithi will logically be attempting to effect the same outcome. This is fortunate, since the destruction of the traitors is also the most crucial objective.

"If you can intercept the human craft without engaging the Slaasriithi, then destroy them as well, once they have taken the raiders on board their transports. If you do not have a reasonable chance of neutralizing all of them, you must ignore them. We cannot have any human survivors who report our attack upon them. If that occurs, we will stir the Aboriginals to a peak of readiness from which they might never descend, and so, the eventual war against them will be that much more arduous and costly.

"You must remain as undetected as possible when carrying out these objectives. It is your duty to sweep away the spoor left by the degenerate traitors of our race, and to do it without providing additional evidence of our transgressions and imperfections." He paused. "Can you do that, Olsirkos Shethkador'vah?"

"I shall do it, even if I must die doing so."

"Such an oath is fitting," Shethkador replied solemnly, as he thought: *and it may be an apt epitaph, as well.*

Chapter Thirty-One

The treads of the mobile multiple rocket launcher churned through the herpeculture ditches of the dencote. Or rather, what was left of them. The Colonial Flag's lead element, a mechanized infantry tassle, had already cut through the rows of worm-filled muck, untended since the steading had been struck the same day as Ylogh. Yaargraukh looked around the deserted expanses where he had hoped to contact the humans less than a week before. He had grown up in a cote almost as modest and primitive as this one, sixty kilometers to the north. He knew the daily rounds of those who had subsisted here: freshening and filtering the water in the ditches, trimming back the mostly parthenogenetic and moderately toxic growth, then opportunistic hunting in the uplands, always keeping an eye out for the signs of edible fungi, or more rarely, for a worthwhile deposit of sulfur or ore in the exposed rock. It was an arduous existence, one which physically broke his small family, sent the survivors back to Rkh'yaa shortly after he had been

428

sent there to commence his studies at the summons
of the Rectorship.

"Flag Leader, are you enjoying the view?" Z'gluurhek's
long black tube of a tongue fluted out of his nose,
twitched facetiously. The flat, ruined sward and half-
collapsed sheds were the very antithesis of an appeal-
ing tableau. "But I forget: this probably reminds you
of home."

Yaargraukh turned slowly. Z'gluurhek possessed
one mental skill worthy of note; he had a knack for
always being able to find a comment or observation
that teetered on the edge of insult, but never quite
fell over into it, never quite compelled a mortal Challenge in response. "Your unwillingness to insult me
directly does no service to the sophistication of your
wit," Yaargraukh countered. "It keeps you restricted
to tired and unimaginative gibes. Perhaps you should
try something a bit more—daring." Yaargraukh looked
into Z'gluurhek's eyes directly, unblinking, and waited.

Z'gluurhek, only a junior tassle leader among the
ranks of the Flag, leaned forward. Yaargraukh could
hear the cartilaginous rings of his gullet clattering
as they drew together in tight, constricting rage.
Z'gluurhek struggled for a retort, but a full second
passed without him uttering a word.

At which point, Yaargraukh turned away. "You must
strive to refine your skill at formulating extemporane-
ous retorts. The inability to do so customarily indicates
a lack of ready wit. Now, why have you come? Your
duties do not require you to report to me." Of course,
very few of the Warriors did report to Yaargraukh.
Although his rank was technically greater than any on
Turkh'saar, and he possessed more military experience,

he was necessarily junior to the colony leader, the Voice of its leading Family. His sidelining from active command under now-Voice Jrekhalkar, was attributed to the fact that Yaargraukh was deemed "too important" to be put in the field. Instead, his position as director of all training kept him out of the chain of command: an unspoken necessity, given his "dubious relationship" with humans.

Z'gluurhek had to audibly unconstrict his gullet before he could speak in a respectful tone. "You are summoned to the command track. The advance element has made contact with the survivors of the raiders' nighttime ambush and confirmed that the way ahead is clear. Final orders will be given by Jrekhalkar."

Yaargraukh dismissed Z'gluurhek with a wave. "I shall follow you momentarily."

"Jrekhalkar ordered me to bring you at my side."

Yaargraukh turned, allowed his tongue to emerge briefly, flip slightly in a display of ironic doubt and amusement. "Did he? And will he confirm having given that order, when I ask him?"

Z'gluurhek looked away after a moment. "He—used words to that effect."

"I'm sure he did. Return and report that I will attend directly." Yaargraukh kept watching the other Hkh'Rkh.

The rings of his gullet audibly contracting once again, Z'gluurhek lowered his head slightly and held that pose for half a second—the minimal amount of time required—before he turned and stalked back toward the laager of armored vehicles ringing the water hole at center of the herpeculture ditches.

❖   ❖   ❖

The scions of the Old Families—who had all been made officers, regardless of their level of military experience or aptitude—were arrayed in a rough council circle. Jrekhalkar stood on the glacis plate of his command track: a heavy-treaded APC with a small, turreted missile rack and half of the passenger compartment given over to communications gear. "Warriors and Scions, I come before you with two declarations."

The group fell to silence. "Declarations" meant that Jrekhalkar was issuing statements that were part official proclamation, part order.

"Firstly, my sire Silent Voice O'akhdruh has, this day, fallen truly and finally silent. His bier is being made ready. It shall be put to flame this evening, so that his embers may join the sparks of the Ancestral Host that adorn the night sky." Yaargraukh did not allow his reaction to show on his face. That ancient formulation, while poetic, had been eschewed by the New Families. They were less attached to the involved and ornate mythologies of Rkh'yaa's premachine era. Bowing his head in respect also allowed him to obscure the fact that he did not recite the traditional response with most of the other scions. "His embers adorn the night sky."

"They do so brightly. And now, speaking as both Voice and Fist, I make the second declaration: we shall make best speed for the rendezvous point west of the River Kakaagsukh. Once there, we shall wait until the next cover of darkness and attack the humans with all our force."

Yaargraukh started. "It was agreed that a small advance group would attempt to observe and confirm that the newly arrived humans are working to consolidate and expand the raiders' position, that they are not here for some other purpose."

Jrekhalkar's black eyes bulged in Yaargraukh's direction. "Do our dead and the vehicles destroyed last night make the humans' intents anything less than obvious?"

"First Voice, I must point out that it was our forces which were moving to ambush. And that while the deeds of the raiders are not in dispute, the intents and allegiance of the newly arrived human craft remain wholly unknown."

"Flag Leader, you would do well not to try my patience. It is a warning I will issue but once. I need not observe every *s'fet* I encounter to know that it, too, is yet another duplicitous and cowardly scavenger. So too with humans. Furthermore, we must not lose the current opportunity to strike them while they are at their weakest."

Z'gluurhek leaned forward eagerly. "They are weak, First Voice? How and when was this learned?"

"Minutes ago, we received a report from the communications center at Iarzut'thruk. The fragmentary radio transmission sent by the smaller human craft during its descent may have been a message to us, rather than their own forces. And if it was a message to us, was in fact an offer to parley, then it signals that they are not confident of their military ability to repel us."

"I have heard that their message was vague, First Voice."

Jrekhalkar's heavy neck wobbled through a single, slow oscillation. "It was too simple for us to be sure of its true intent. It is possible that they fear we will be unable to understand more complicated statements in their language. Or it might be a coded communiqué, instead. The words in their language were, 'Bridge-builder arrives.'"

—and suddenly, Yaargraukh was back on the Convocation station at EV Lacertae more than a year and a half ago. He stood gazing down at the human named Caine Riordan, whose white-rimmed eyes looked up out of the hideously flat face of his species as he said, "Sharing truths—particularly the dangerous ones—is how we will build a bridge of honor between us."

Greatsires and grassfires: a "bridge-builder arrives." It is Riordan! And, as requested, he comes to initiate communication, not combat. Jrekhalkar and the others were not likely to listen to or believe that, but for the good of Hkh'Rkh and human alike, Yaargraukh had to try to put the case before them. "First Voice, I believe I know who sent that message and why."

Jrekhalkar glanced at him. "Explain."

Yaargraukh did, succinctly.

Jrekhalkar did not respond immediately. Before he did, he took up the *halbardiche* of his office and gazed at Yaargraukh steadily, until all the other scions' eyes were similarly riveted on the former liaison to humanity. "Then tell us, former Advocate of the Unhonored: what do you propose?"

"To communicate, before we commit to combat."

"Communicate with whom, specifically?"

Yaargraukh knew, before he spoke the next word, that doing so might alienate him from his own race forever. "Riordan."

Jrekhalkar's surprise seemed affected, rather than

genuine. "Riordan? The humans' Chief of Liars? The one who has twice posed as a diplomat to work as a saboteur and an assassin?"

"In neither case was he an assassin. In neither case did he have knowledge that his presence as a diplomat would facilitate combat actions of others of his race. In my knowledge of him, he has never dissembled."

Jrekhalkar uttered a phlegm-clogged snort. "Let us say this is true. Then it seems that Riordan is not clever enough to preserve his honor from the lies and manipulations of the assassins who control him. And so, he might once again be similarly duped, even as he tries to contact us here."

"If he is being manipulated, then at most, he is guilty of the crime of poor judgment. Almost as guilty as I am."

Jrekhalkar had not anticipated that conversational turn. "You? Of what poor judgment are you guilty? Of believing humans to be creatures somewhat better than *s'fet*?"

"No. Of allowing my honor as a Warrior to be compromised by the bigoted blundering of those whom I served in the last war."

Crests rose all along the circle. Yet no challenge came. And after all, how could the scions make one? Had not the finest Warriors of their species lost? Had not all their Honors thus been smeared with the dung of a defeat inflicted when they had seemed on the verge of victory?

But still, Yaargraukh regretted his words: not because they were wrong, but because they were too accurate. The eyes surrounding him had been merely angry; now they settled into cold hatred. He had stated the unvarnished truth, and for that, they would never forgive him. He could try to continue to sway them—as unlikely as that was—but in fact, his objective in speaking changed. He would speak frankly so that the truth, and the longings and grievances common to the New Families, might at last have an unfettered voice in council. And if he did not survive this day, at least others, particularly those who existed outside the sphere of the Old Families, would hear the deepest truth of the late war.

Jrekhalkar uttered his next question in a low, dangerous voice. "Do you say that our elders' plans were not sound, that He Who Is First Voice—should he still live—was in error?"

"Yes. And no."

"Speak me no riddles, Flag Leader."

"I speak none. First Voice's tactics were sound. It was his strategy that was flawed."

Z'gluurhek forgot his place, speaking without first glancing at Jrekhalkar to be assured of his permission. His crest rose into a rigid spiky swath from his crown to the tip of his tail. "Flawed in what way?"

"Must I speak the obvious?" Yaargraukh swept his hand to the east, in the direction of the raiders. "Our crucial error was that we did not ally ourselves with the humans. They have true warriors among them. But instead we shared our talons with the Arat Kur: diggers, grubbers, prey animals. That was folly. Strategic folly and Honor-folly, both. And now we reap the rewards of that decision, of Old Family patriarchs that have evidently forgotten their forefathers' axiom: that choices which are Honor-wise usually turn out to be war-wise also, in the end. We turned our back on that wisdom when we allied ourselves with prey animals that lack any concept of honor as we understand it."

More than a few of the scions shifted uncomfortably; more than a few of their elders had made a similar point when news of an actual alliance with the Arat Kur had arrived almost two years earlier. Jrekhalkar, evidently sensing irresolution in his scions, banged the bottom of the *halbardiche's* haft against his APC's glacis plate. "The humans could have had the peace they wanted. They could have joined us rather than expecting us to court them, or later, could have acceded to our demands."

"Our demands." Yaargraukh's tongue snaked out as phlegm rippled in his main nostril. "Our demands were as foolish as our choice of allies."

"Foolish? You, of all persons, say this? Is it not the New Families who most cry out for new colonies, for green worlds?"

"Yes, but a war against the humans was not the way to get them. The Old Families think as they always have. They believe that there is but one pathway to success: to take what they need and cow the defeated. This was foolhardy. What we needed was not the conquest of human worlds, but their technological assistance, to expand our shift distance and our shift frequency. With a range increase of only ten percent, we would have been able to cross the gaps separating us from a new cluster of promising stars, beyond the system the humans call Iota Persei."

Jrekhalkar drew up in haughty disdain. "We need no technological assistance. Hkh'Rkh capabilities and engineering is unsurpassed."

Yaargraukh managed to keep his tongue from writhing

out in a spasm of grim hilarity. "I have heard others say the same thing."

"And your response to them?"

"That their empty rhetoric is delusional lunacy spoken as truth. Let me tell you what we all learned when we invaded Earth. The humans' weapons were better and more sophisticated than ours, and often nearly as effective as those of the Arat Kur. Their first shift drive had a greater range than even our latest, third generation system. Their computation and automation technologies outstrip ours. And our medical abilities, particularly in genetics, are primitive by comparison. And yet, not one of First Voice's advisors—or even he himself—could see and speak the truth about the cause of our inferiority."

"You mean, they were unwilling to demean themselves by professing a slavish, fawning belief that the humans are inherently more intelligent than we are?"

"No; of course not—because they are not. The truth behind their superior technology is simply this: the humans spend less time warring and destroying, and more time inventing and exploring."

The Council ring was very quiet. It was yet another truth that they had sensed but did not want to hear, probably because it articulated a problem for which there was no ready solution. If the humans were temperamentally better suited to the orderly development of superior technology, what could the Hkh'Rkh do? How could they behave other than was natural for them?

Jrekhalkar chose not to respond—a smart move, Yaargraukh allowed—but rather, to counter the assertions with another one of his own. "Here is the *real* truth the war taught us about humans, former Advocate.

They may have killers among them, but no Warriors, no creatures of honor. They do not have an understanding of that concept, regardless of what you contend. They fight opportunistically, assassinating and bribing where they may instead of engaging in fair combat. They are like *s'fet* and should be treated as such: vermin that cannot be reasoned with."

"They did not slaughter us when they might have, after the war."

"That is hearsay from the humans themselves and the Arat Kur, who proved themselves even worse by betraying us when victory was in our collective grasp."

"Which, since you were not there, is also hearsay... from scions eager to flatter their own species and to justify their own excesses of prejudice."

Jrekhalkar's eyes blinked once, hard, at Yaargraukh's word. "Do you call me a liar?"

"No," Yaargraukh responded earnestly. "You *cannot* be a liar, because you do not claim to have seen these things yourself. You are merely passing on what you were told, by our fellow Warriors who wished to believe that our species was the paragon of virtue and surpassing skill in all things. A perfectly understandable reflex. But, properly understood, it must give us pause when we consider the inaccuracy of the accounts it spawned."

Jrekhalkar's brow became a washboard of wrinkles. "Your gift with words cannot change present realities. We have invaders on our doorstep who have slaughtered our most helpless communities and frontierfolk with savage impunity. We will stop this. Our Honor requires no less.

"And as Warriors and scions, entrusted with the

safety of all our Unhonored, we must also see the human communication for what it truly is: yet another attempt to set us contending amongst ourselves. Every time we contemplate and debate a reply to them, we are not merely wasting time. Our transmissions mark the location of our communities and cadre, which they may then destroy at leisure from orbit, for our intermittent satellite feed has shown us that they have at least two other ships waiting beyond the range of the missiles that were fired at the first landing force."

Yaargraukh ruffled his crest in consternation and bafflement. "But what logical objective could be served by this handful of ships? To conquer all of Turkh'saar?"

"Why not?" Jrekhalkar retorted swiftly—so swiftly that Yaargraukh realized the new Voice had probably been waiting for this opportunity to dangle the spectre of extermination under the snouts of his scions. "They have taken the Arat Kur Homenest, have invested all of Sigma Draconis, and show no signs that they ever intend to depart. Should we be doubtful or surprised that the humans are extending their frail fingers into our systems, now? Is Turkh'saar not the inevitable stepping stone to the invasion of Rkh'yaa itself, being but one system away? And perhaps they hope to find sympathizers—or at least, less resolute defenders—on this colony, since so many of its settlers are of the New Families, who wrongly consider themselves to be undervalued by the greater Families of the Patrijuridicate. If so, if that is what the humans hope, then this is the hour when the scions of the New Families"—Jrekhalkar looked at the few such individuals who were part of the Council Circle—"may decisively show their loyalty by boldly leading the fight against these invaders. The humans have, after all, brought far more destruction to their outlying towns and cotes than they have to the central communities dominated by the Old Families."

Yaargraukh had to admit that Jrekhalkar, while not a stirring orator, had certainly given careful thought to the arguments most likely to sway other New Family members away from Yaargraukh's perspective and back to his own. It was difficult to see what kind of effect it was actually having. Scions of the New Families had long ago learned to let none of their reactions show in public.

Jrekhalkar's eyes moved from face to face around the Council, significantly skipping over Yaargraukh's own. "We were counselled to patience and we followed that advice." *A lie,* Yaargraukh reflected, *but one that's easily forgotten on the eve of battle.* "However, time is running out and our planet may be the price of our inaction. We dare not waste another moment considering details that may not bear upon the outcome in any way but one: they will distract and delay us from what we must do."

Z'gluurhek bobbed his head in deference. "As you order, so shall we do, Voice and Fist Jrekhalkar of the Moiety of Gdar'khoom. But without space or transatmospheric craft of our own, how can we hope to prevail? It is rightly said that those who are uncontested in the sky shall prove victorious on the ground."

Jrekhalkar regarded Z'gluurhek approvingly. "At last, a question worth asking." Z'gluurhek rose higher, black eyes protuberant and sparkling like onyx marbles. "And here is your answer. After his last declarations to the Council in Iarzut'thruk, my father entrusted me with information that only he possessed, since all his lieutenants perished against the Slaasriithi. Although we have no aircraft, we still have missiles. Following his words at the Clanhall, he brought me to a small, secure bunker. There we discerned a way to determine the number and disposition of the remaining missiles, as well as other equipment that might yet prove useful. When the human craft land, we shall be ready for them. If the human craft currently on Turkh'saar attempt to take to the sky to rain destruction upon our vehicles, we shall be ready for them, too. And I welcome—I long—for the humans to attempt either tactic, because when they see their spacecraft tumbling to the ground in flames, they will know their cause is lost and will already be beaten in their hearts." He rose to his full height. "At that point, we need merely slay their despairing bodies. My declaration is complete; discussion has ended."

Yaargraukh did not have to look around the Council ring to feel the many eyes on him. He was not concerned for his own sake, but understood that, with the blind bigotry typical of their class, the Old Family scions would not constrain their animosity to him. They would transfer it to the New Family scions and Warriors, would chastise them and give them the dirtiest—and most lethal—jobs and missions in the upcoming battle. In short, if Yaargraukh remained an irritant to the Old Family scions, it would be his own people who would be made to pay. Which meant he could not remain at all. And he was fairly certain he had a means to ensure that he was sent away. "Voice and Fist Jrekhalkar, I would. make a request. For myself, only."

"You may make it."

"Clearly, the task which your esteemed sire set me—to take charge of the brief training and familiarization of our Warriors with militia-grade equipment—is over."

"Correct. We no longer have time for preparing ourselves. Now, we move to battle."

"As I suspected. Therefore, my current post is no longer required. Consequently, I humbly request to serve in a combat command befitting my rank."

Jrekhalkar started. "I cannot grant that. Your standing rank in the Patrijuridicate is equal to my own."

Actually, it is higher. "I perceive the problem. Then how may I serve best? Perhaps as a deputy commander?"

Jrekhalkar was motionless for a moment. Behind his rapidly blinking eyes, Yaargraukh could almost see each realization spawning the next in a long, inevitable sequence of deductive foresight. If he retained Yaargraukh as a deputy commander, it meant that he might have a constantly contentious voice at his side, interminably asking for opportunities to parley with the invaders, to hold back from a fully committed attack. And if something were to happen to Jrekhalkar himself, the fate of the entire counterattack would be in the former-Advocate's allegedly appeasementist hands. Clearly an unacceptable set of circumstances.

O'akhdruh's less-than-brilliant son responded as Yaargraukh had anticipated. "Yaargraukh, you are to return to Iarzut'thruk and await instructions." Then he evidently realized that he could not afford to give the highest-ranking New Family scion freedom of action, either. "Once there, you must remand yourself into the protection of the militia."

Yaargraukh had expected this, played out his near-martyrdom with complete aplomb. "May I ask the Voice why I must be . . . protected?"

"Firstly, your expertise may be needed in the event that we take human captives and must interact with their diplomats. But also, given your predilection for wishing to converse with the human invaders, it would be imprudent of me not to assure that you remain without access to a suitable radio." And as he said it, Jrekhalkar clearly realized the shameful pit into which he was digging himself. He was placing a higher rank-ing military figure with vastly more experience under what amounted to house arrest in order to consolidate his own political power.

Yaargraukh knew his next question was the crucial one. "Shall I then depart immediately with a vehicle and an escort?" *And now you will realize that, hav-ing disgraced yourself by using your rank to dishonor me with insufficient cause, you must either reverse all your decrees or take a darker path.*

Jrekhalkar took the darker path. "You do not require an escort. You are a Warrior and your word to journey to Iarzut'thruk satisfies me. Besides, I cannot afford to spare a vehicle or Warriors to escort you there. It will suffice that you proceed back on foot."

Which Yaargraukh knew was his death sentence. He would never be allowed to arrive at Iarzut'thruk to bear word of the unjustified and suspicious ignominy in which he had been sent there. It would be far easier, and would justify everyone's suspicions of him, if, on his long walk home, it was discovered that he had strayed from his appointed path and attempted to defect to the humans. Of course, caution and good fortune would cause his path to cross with vigilant Warriors who would become his unwitting assassins. *So, Jrekhalkar, this is who you are at the core: a weak-willed disgrace to the title "Warrior," who will resort to dishonorable methods to save face.*

And judging from Z'gluurhek's gloating expression and the small tongue-wiggle that, in a human, would have been a dismissive snicker, he was delighted that—in his naive reading of the situation—Yaargraukh was being given an opportunity to hang himself, to show his true colors by betraying his own people to the humans.

Yaargraukh semi-bowed. "I regret that my skills are no longer needed here, but your words guide my deeds, Jrekhalkar. I shall commence my return to Iarzut'thruk at once."

And of all the statements Yaargraukh had made, only that one pained him, since it was flatly a lie. He wasn't going back to Iarzut'thruk, couldn't. Instead, he was going to do what Jrekhalkar would have eventually wanted everyone to believe he was doing, anyway.

He was going to find Caine Riordan.

Chapter Thirty-Two

Aboard Wedge Three, Phil Friel's customary calm and patience had apparently worn thin. "I think you need to hire a new engineer, Commodore," he muttered over the secure lascom link. "I'll be damned if I can suss out what's got the magnetic containment bollocksed on this bloody barge. If I push the MAP drive over eighty percent thrust, the bugger starts fluxing, triggers the automatic safety override against a breach, and drops me back to seventy-five percent. And I can't find anything wrong in the system. Not a blessed thing."

"Sounds like you'd need to tear down the thruster package and do a complete overhaul." Riordan nodded at the salutes from *Puller's* anchor watch as he strolled away from the corvette.

"Yeh, but then that has us needin' a fleet-grade facility. Which is more than twenty light-years away. I'm sorry, sir. I've failed."

Riordan smiled, even though Phil couldn't see him. "Mr. Friel, if you don't have the tools, you can't do the job. Just be sure that when you bring in Wedge Three tomorrow, you keep Wedge Two to the west, closer to the approaching Hkh'Rkh. She's got more speed, so more ability to dodge."

"And if the Hkh'Rkh have more of the missiles that they fired at you?"

"We've sent you a revised entry trajectory. Since we're not worried about stealth anymore, we can keep you well away from the missiles' launch site. You'll come in subpolar from the north and drift down toward the equator as you descend. That should put you well outside their intercept envelope until you're under their sensors and on final approach."

"Roger that, sir. We'll see you in time for lunch tomorrow."

"Don't get your hopes up regarding the food. Just get here safely."

"Will do. Wedge Three out."

Riordan paused a moment to take in Turkh'saar in the late afternoon light and with the improved perspective afforded by a night's sleep. The aquamarine sky had few clouds, but seemed less vibrant than those of other green worlds. The foliage was not as outré as the xenoflora of Slaasriithi planets, but nonetheless always registered as alien, even at a brief glance.

Alien and *dull*, if he was going to be honest about his gut reaction. There were no flowering plants to speak of; almost everything on Turkh'saar propagated by spores or parthenogenesis, leading to what could only be categorized as stingy, defensive plants. Half of the varieties had runners, often entwined with each other in an ultra-slow-motion death grapple as they fought over every patch of soil. Consequently, the borders between different species were often highlighted by brown or gray discolorations. Like lines in a coloring book, they traced how each plant was attempting to toxify the soil against its econiche neighbors. The arboriforms were variations on a similarly selfish theme: clustered stalks of vast, collective growths that struggled to smother anything beneath them and encroach on anything alongside.

He saw a couple of aviforms—small gliders, so far as he could tell—and not much in the way of insects. He'd seen pictures of the higher life forms, if you could really call them that: mostly hideous, flange-headed newts or spindly, spiky quadrupeds that would have made a defective opossum look like an evolutionary triumph. Turkh'saar was, all told, not much to look at.

His tac channel paged twice; a call on the encrypted lascom. He tapped his collarcom. "Riordan."

Dora Veriden's tone was almost civil. "You wanted to speak with me?"

"Yes." Riordan started walking back from the edge of the clustertrees to Wedge One, which was sitting well beyond the flight line, unable to fit beneath the long brow of rock that thrust out from the hillside. "I need your programming wizardry, Ms. Veriden."

"Jesus, when are you going to relax and call me 'Dora'?"

"Probably when we're not in the field. Now, I need you to put together a tactical interface and assistance program for me."

"What for? We're here to carry out an extraction, not a strike, right?"

Riordan walked past Wedge One, nodded up at Dora, whose face was peering down at him from the transport's narrow and currently unshielded starboard bridge window. "Extraction is our objective. But the Hkh'Rkh might have other ideas. If they do, we need contingencies. And since those contingencies will include dismounted personnel, then we have to anticipate embedding our troops with the Lost Solders."

"The what?"

"The Lost Soldiers. That's what Major Solsohn is calling them, anyway. They are all MIAs, presumed dead."

"What is it with Solsohn? Does he have some kind of naming fetish?"

"You'll have to ask him yourself."

"Thanks, but I'll pass on that. Don't want to know his fetishes. Or anyone else's."

Hell, for an innately contentious person, Pandora sure did like to chatter. "Understandable. Here's what I need. We've got to adapt our tactical automated assistant, the Know-It-All, to be able to advise mixed units, where some troops have data interfaces and some don't."

"You mean, so that our people can work alongside the Lost Soldiers?"

"Right. We need their manpower. But it's going to be awkward, given their differences in technology and training."

"So the Know-It-All has to integrate their skills and their equipment to give our leaders a usable tactical summary for the mixed units. And I'm guessing you need that yesterday."

"Pretty much."

After a moment of silence, Dora responded. "Okay, Caine. You need anything else?"

A quiet minute to recover from the shock of you agreeing with me that quickly about anything. But he said, "No. How's the loading coming along?"

"We're pretty much finished with noncombat gear. And there was a ton of it. Dozens of tons, actually."

"I'm glad that's done. We're going to need every minute, and cubic meter, to get those damn helicopters broken down and off this ball of dirt."

"Yeah, well, good luck with that. I'm going to start on the impossible project you've just asked me to complete in an unreasonable amount of time. Wedge One out."

As Riordan neared the flight line, a spry figure strode out of the cave entrance: Pat Paulsen. He slowed, hand raised, partially in greeting, partially to request that Riordan stop.

Caine complied. "Need something, Colonel?"

"Yes, Commodore: a minute of your time. I've compiled the equipment roster you asked for." He handed Caine an old style clipboard loaded with what appeared to be accounting sheets. "But I'm not sure you'll be familiar with all the items on it."

Caine scanned the sheets, saw that Paulsen's presumption was woefully accurate. "It's embarrassing to admit it, but I don't know what half of these things are."

Paulsen smiled, leaned to look at the items that had stymied Caine. "Oh, those are the helicopters."

"Okay, but those are just names. I need to know their capabilities."

Paulsen glanced at him, perplexed. "Is this just professional curiosity, or . . . ?"

"'Or,' Colonel. Until all our transports are making

for orbit with all of you and your equipment inside, these are still combat assets."

"Commodore, I've seen your spaceships and some of the weapons you're carrying. Seems to me our antiques wouldn't be much of a help."

"Colonel, if we find ourselves in a fight, every resource might turn out to be a help. So, give me a picture—in broad strokes, if you please."

"Very well. So, these are the utility helicopters: mostly for moving personnel, but some can also handle sizable equipment. These six are our workhorses, the UH-1 Iroquois."

Riordan was simply grateful that his ignorance was not absolute. "Those I know by name. Vietnam era, right?"

Paulsen nodded. "You'll hear my guys refer to them as Hueys and slicks. Solid, versatile machine. Can ferry an outsized squad and its gear. Reasonably fast. We left another one behind at the FOB and another was shot up enough that we've got her sidelined for parts."

"The other helicopter we left behind was an Mi-8. It's a Commie—er, Soviet 'copter. Same basic function, but a slightly larger carrying capacity. Not quite as fast or reliable, but serviceable. Only have one of those left, unless the one at the FOB is still working."

"These two are observation birds: OH-6 Cayuse. Very maneuverable, lightly built. But that agility comes at the expense of durability; they will not take a licking and keep on ticking."

Caine frowned. "Is that some kind of joke?"

Paulsen's smile was simultaneously abashed and ironic. "It was, once. Sort of. It was a commercial for a watch manufacturer."

"Okay," Caine replied agreeably but had. no idea what a licking would have to do with ticking. "What about these listed as H-3s? They seem to have a lot of footnotes."

"That's because they're some of our heavy lifters. We call them Jollies. Short for Jolly Green Giant."

"That's an odd name. Most of your helicopters seem to follow a Native American theme."

"Yeah, well, this one probably does, too. On some official papers, somewhere. But it was big and green so they named it after the Jolly Green Giant. Oh, right: that's another television advertisement. Um . . . canned vegetables."

Riordan stared. "Your . . . media . . . really advertised things like, uh, canned vegetables named after mythical monsters?"

Paulsen shook his head. "You wouldn't believe what our media did, on occasion. At any rate, the Jollies can lift half a platoon and carry more externally, if we have the slings rigged. But using the slings is not something you want to do under fire.

"And this last one is our big chopper, a CH-47 Chinook. It can fit two scout cars or a whole platoon. Unlike the others, primary egress and ingress is via a rear ramp."

Riordan nodded, having tallied the deployment capacity of the helicopters: almost five full platoons. Not that those spindly vehicles were likely to survive direct insertion into a modern firefight, but if used to ferry troops to a concealed rear area, it meant he had a lot of separate platforms for relocating light infantry around a battlefield. Good to know. "What's this next category of helicopter?"

"Attack choppers. Three Soviet Mi-24 Hinds. They came along after my time. For which I'm glad: damn things are flying tanks. Not fast, but they can absorb some heavy damage and even drop in half a squad. Not very sophisticated, but they are dependable and carry one hell of a weapons payload.

"The other two are AH-1/G Cobras. Pride of the fleet, you might say. Fast and nimble where the Hinds are slow and sluggish. They don't carry as much weaponry but the systems—and our pilots—can pretty much put the ordnance exactly where you need it. Every time."

So, I've got a fire brigade if I have to blunt an enemy advance or provide tactical air support. But again, it will have to be from stand-off. Even those Hinds probably won't fare well against Hkh'Rkh heavy weapons. "Thanks, Pat." Riordan let his eyes graze over the varied uniforms of the troops packing, moving, loading crates on Wedge One. Seeing the three-chevron symbol on the shoulder of one of the Americans, he jutted his chin in the direction of the busy soldiers. "One other question. Not about equipment."

"Sure. Ask."

"Your ranks look a little lopsided. Top-heavy with NCOs and officers."

Paulsen nodded. "Yeah, particularly those of us who were in 'Nam."

"How have you handled that, when you go into the field?"

Paulsen nodded at the question, as if approving of it. "We put our NCOs in charge of fire teams of our submariners. We try to have at least one guy who's good with a rifle. The others have tommy guns. They're good for holding the line, sweeping a ville, security, watches. But we use trained infantry for assaults."

"Good. We'll keep that structure, but I'll be adding at least one of my people to each of your squads."

Paulsen nodded. "I'll pass the word to my officers and NCOs."

Caine wagged a lazy salute at Paulsen who sent one back at him and trotted off, calling to crew chiefs as he went.

"Commodore?"

Riordan turned. Melissa Sleeman. Smiling. She and Tygg had managed to steal a few hours together, now that both *Puller* and Wedge One were on the ground and in the same spot. "Hello, Doctor. Can I help you?"

She nodded. "I hope so." And she waited.

Which was unlike her. Sleeman, while unfailingly polite, was also unfailingly direct. He smiled. "Doctor, some details would help."

She glanced away. "I have reservations speaking about this... matter."

The exchange was becoming more atypical with every passing second. "I can see that, Doctor. But I also know you would not make a request unless it was very important."

She looked back at him quickly. "I think this could prove to be more important than our primary mission."

"More important that saving these men and women and preventing another war?"

She looked him square in the eyes and nodded slowly. "Yes. Which is why I am reluctant to make this request. Because it could—no, it *will*—put lives at risk if you grant it."

Riordan was used to surprises, but not from Melissa

Sleeman. Which made this the biggest surprise of all. "Understood. Please explain what you have in mind."

"Commodore, I think it is important—no, imperative—that we survey that anomalous site to the south, the one that fired the missiles at us."

Suppressing objections—not the least of which was to point out that there could be more missiles and other defenses—Riordan leaned closer to her. "Why is that imperative?"

"Because, if I am right—and I might not be—I believe the Hkh'Rkh found something important there. Very important."

Riordan frowned. "I take it you mean something more important than a vein of ore, or some other natural resource."

She nodded. "Yes. I've been studying the images we took of that site. It's some kind of impact site. But I'm not sure that it is, well, natural."

Riordan recalled the outline of the area. "It certainly did not look like a meteorite crater."

"Exactly. The impact path was elongated, and there was no evidence that anything broke up before it hit the ground, like at Tunguska. Also, no sign of tree-fall or fires radiating out from the center. It looks more like—"

"—like a crash," Riordan finished, nodding. "And if the Hkh'Rkh built some kind of facility around a crash site—"

"—then it probably wasn't something of theirs that crashed." Sleeman's slow nod matched his own. "It could be Arat Kur, of course. They were present here centuries ago. Which is much longer than the Hkh'Rkh have had shift drive."

"If we can trust their self-report."

"We can, sir." Sleeman shook her head. "The Custodians were watching the Hkh'Rkh. Would the Dornaani have allowed a false date to stand?"

Well, damn. "Okay, Doctor, what do you need? Note my wording: *need*, not *want*."

Sleeman's features—an exemplar of the complete ethnic mixing toward which the globe was finally heading—were transformed by one of her wide smiles. "I was working as a researcher before I was out of my teens, Commodore. We never get what we *want*. So here's what I *need*: a security team, some of the Lost Soldier submariner officers to help me collect samples and data, and transportation."

"Doctor, we have two spacecraft on this planet. Tomorrow, we'll have two more. I might be able to detail one to you, briefly, if the Hkh'Rkh decide to stay away. Which is looking increasingly unlikely."

"I know. I've been monitoring it."

"Then you know it's a very large threat force: at least a hundred vehicles, many of which are tracked. I expect there are at least a thousand hostiles inbound. Maybe twice that."

Sleeman nodded through the whole unpromising report, her smile only dimming slightly. "Yes, sir. I understand. That's why I don't want to take one of our ships to the site. The wedges need to keep loading and *Puller* needs to stay on defensive overwatch. I'm asking to take two of the helicopters."

"You want to—?"

"Commodore, hear me out. There are no Hkh'Rkh in striking range yet. You don't need the helicopters, and you yourself said they're the last elements you're going to break down."

She sure has thought this through, but—"Dr. Slee-man, everything you've said is true . . . at this moment in time. Unfortunately, what's true right now might change drastically over the course of the next ten minutes."

"Yes, sir. I understand. But if there is a wreck out at that site, or even signs that one was there and then removed, that might tell our brain trust something about the strange technology gaps we've noticed in the Hkh'Rkh. And that might be strategically significant intelligence, would you agree?"

As if you have the slightest doubt. "Okay, Doctor, you've made your point. You'll get an Mi-8 and a 'Huey,' an escort pulled from the Lost Soldiers, and five or six sub officers."

She nodded. "I will gather my sensors and—"

"Don't rush it, Doctor. You're not leaving today. It's getting late and I am not putting anyone out beyond our perimeter at dark. Too many unknowns. Gather your gear and assistants today. Brief them tonight, then wake predawn, lift at first light, and get back in time for an early dinner. That's the deal; take it or leave it."

She nodded once. "I will take it. And sir—?"

"Yes?"

"Thank you."

No, thank you for being courageous and smart as hell. But he said, "Just make every minute at the site count and get back here safely. That's all the thanks I need."

She turned away with a smile, and over her departing shoulder, he saw Duncan Solsohn approaching.

Riordan grimaced. Given yesterday's dispute, it was possible that the first battle on Turkh'saar might be the suppression of an internal revolt. In which case—

—*Come get some.*

Chapter Thirty-Three

Surprisingly, the first words out of Solsohn's mouth were not a continuation of the civil war he'd initiated the prior night, but a peace treaty. Possibly a surrender. "Commodore, I apologize. Saying that is the first order of business, I figure."

"Apology accepted, but that doesn't correct the problem, Major. Granted, according to you, you were following orders. But I disapprove of how and where you carried out those orders. And if you ever again cut my legs out from under me at a meeting with—"

"Sir, you have my assurances: it won't happen again. But I—well, look: I let my emotions lead me, not my head."

"Your emotions? How do you mean that, Major?"

"Sir, these Lost Soldiers, they've been hanging on by a thread, physically and mentally. They want, and have every right to hope, that our arrival means that all their troubles are over.

"But they might not be. There's been some nasty inter-bloc crap going down back home, sir. And no,

457

you wouldn't have heard about it: it's all behind closed doors. But some of the blocs which were less involved in IRIS feel they've been kept in the dark, that we're operating with impunity and not really accountable to anyone."

"Not accountable? Damn, I wish they could see all the 'accountability' and 'control' straitjackets I've had to wear for the past two years."

"No argument from me, sir. I've worn some of those jackets myself. But from the outside perspective, we are evidence that the political equality of the blocs is a sham—until and unless all of them have an equal say in what we're doing, and when, and how. So Mr. Downing instructed me to make sure that if we found humans here, even if they hadn't gone to Turkh'saar of their own accord, that it would be unfair to let them get their hopes up. And sir, that's what was happening when I—er, interrupted, at the meeting."

"Fair enough. But why wait until then to tell me?"

"Mr. Downing knows you're, um, sensitive, to not receiving complete information. Says you've had a few particularly nasty surprises. So he advised me not to spring this on you until and unless it was determined that the presumed human raiders were victims rather than rogue operators. If we had to kill and capture rather than negotiate and extract, well, they were going to be swept under the rug anyhow."

Well, that's true enough.

"However, by the time we conclusively determined that the Lost Soldiers were victims, we were already in full tempo operations. No time for any explaining—particularly not Mr. Downing's special instructions to me."

Again, true enough. They walked on in silence for several very long seconds before Caine responded. "Major, I believe you will have a decision of your own to make."

"What's that, sir?"

"I am accustomed to how Mr. Downing operates. His job requires that he is always cautious and foresightful, regardless of whether or not he is happy or even comfortable with all the precautions and contingencies he has to put into place."

"Yes, sir." Solsohn sounded puzzled.

"So I know that Mr. Downing has probably anticipated that, if push comes to shove, I will not blithely hand these Lost Soldiers over to him or any other authority without assurances about their treatment, their fate."

Now Solsohn was conspicuously quiet.

"So, since I must presume he will anticipate such actions on my part, I must further presume that he decided to put an asset in place on this mission to ensure that I did not obstruct the final disposition of the Lost Soldiers, whatever that might involve. Such an asset would necessarily have sufficient proximity to me, and knowledge of the operation, to be able to assess when and how my potential 'interference' should be circumvented or removed. That asset would also need to have a high enough rank—and special clearance codes—to subsequently take charge of the operation, even over the authority possessed by my XO, Major Rulaine."

Solsohn was even more quiet, if that was humanly possible.

"Lastly, since the Cold Guard were awakened after me and my team, none of them could have been operatives for Mr. Downing. So that rather limits the field of possible persons that he could have assigned to this job. Doesn't it—Major Solsohn?"

Duncan's response sounded as though he was being choked. "Yes, sir."

"So as I see it, Major, if we get back home, and if the Lost Soldiers are not being given any reasonable, verifiable assurances regarding their treatment, you'll have a choice to make. And you'll have to make it swiftly, when and if that moment comes."

"What choice is that, sir?"

"Whether you stand with me, or against me. Now, there's something I need to show you in the inner compound."

The silence that followed was not broken by either of them.

The silence lasted until they entered what Caine had come to think of as "the mausoleum." In the middle distance, Newton Baruch was comparing data with Ike Franklin. They looked up at the same time, demonstrating the same species of perpetual alertness that was the hallmark of their shared profession, even though they had been born more than a century apart. "Sirs," they chorused, started salutes that Riordan waved away as he approached.

"Save your energy," he recommended. "What have you learned, gentlemen?"

Franklin grinned. "I learned that Newton here is a damned genius, with a hundred years of learning on me. I'm back to being just another grunt."

Riordan glanced at the folded maroon beret protruding from his cargo pocket. "Lieutenant, I've been learning a little bit about all the units represented among the Lost Soldiers. As I understand it, the personnel who wear that beret—pararescue jumpers—are the furthest thing from 'just grunts' that your century ever put into the field. And you were in your final year of a surgical internship when you joined, is that correct?"

Ike's grin widened. "I see that Colonel Paulsen has been telling all sorts of pretty lies about me again."

"So you deny it?"

"Well . . . I didn't say that, exactly."

Riordan smiled. "So I notice. Now, what have you found out about these?" He gestured behind him at the various cold cells.

"Not as much as I'd like," Newton said sourly. "The technology is not merely extremely advanced; it's also not developmentally consistent."

Riordan frowned. "You mean, not consistent with ours?"

"Or each other. They are all cold cells, but they don't follow—or even share—any discernible pattern of advancement." Evidently Duncan looked as perplexed as Caine still felt—and maybe looked—himself. Newton restarted: "Consider how most technology advanced on Earth once ships connected different cultures. Advances in one region influenced similar advances in other regions. The evolution of technology became more or less collective, even among rivals.

"But go further back into history, when centers of civilization had less contact with each other. Different communities frequently developed entirely different technological solutions to the same problems." He hooked a thumb over his shoulder, indicating the cold cells. "That kind of nonconvergent technological evolution is evident here."

Duncan frowned. "So, could some of these cold cells be Ktor and others, well, come from someone else?"

Newton shook his head. "No. What little writing I have found is not only from the same basic family of signification, but I've even found words—or parts of words—that are identical. If I had to guess, the maximum linguistic variation among the creators of these cryocells is analogous to the differences between German and Icelandic. Maybe less. Also, the quantitative notations are identical: all base ten, all the same character set."

"Even on those cystlike units?" Riordan gestured further down the gridwork toward the irregular brown-maroon cells that looked like acrylic art projects gone horribly awry.

"They're a special case. I'll get to them later." Newton ran a hand back over his widow's peak, smoothing the hair down against the sharply receding hairline on either side. "Some basic facts about the rest. They show very different levels of manufacturing sophistication. Some utilize alloys and batteries, and possibly capacitors, that I don't have any way to analyze here without risking an explosion or worse. On the other hand, many use materials, power technology, and biological support systems that are not too different from our own in principle, just vastly more advanced in terms of efficiency and elegance.

"Then there are the systems that use such revolutionarily different approaches to cryogenic suspension that I can only guess at what they're actually doing. Some seem to change the occupant's blood chemistry more slowly, increasing the level of glyceration while also triggering what might be an epigenetically coded hibernation reflex. That minimizes the need for quick perfusion of the glycerin, one of the biggest risks that our current cold-cell technology is struggling to reduce: that cells in a body's core have not been sufficiently saturated by the time their temperature reaches one or two degrees centigrade. That causes either decay of the unprotected tissue or, if the temperature variation is inconstant across the body, pockets of crystallization—which almost always result in brain death or fatality."

Riordan could feel his frown deepening. "Let's go back a step. Humans don't have a hibernatory reflex to activate, so how does that work at all?"

Franklin tilted his head slightly. "Well, sir, we don't have a hibernatory reflex *anymore*. And maybe hominids never did. But apparently, if you go deep enough into what we used to call our 'junk DNA'—before later research showed why that old stuff was being kept in the attic—you can find some, well, 'deactivated code' for hibernation."

"And this cryogenic technology finds and activates that code?"

"Apparently, sir," Newton murmured. "Although I don't have much evidence to support that hypothesis. But even with my crude instruments, it looks like the subject's DNA has undergone some kind of cascading trigger to reexpress various latent strings. Or maybe produced some compound that isn't native to our system anymore, but for which the recipe is lying hidden in our epigenetic matrix." He ruffled his thinning hair. "It's really just guesswork at this point, sir."

"Pretty impressive guesses," Duncan asserted under his breath.

"I agree," Riordan said. "Anything else jump out at you?"

"Lots. But I'll stick to highlights. A number of the cryocells also incorporate a mix of compounds—possibly synthetic, possibly natural—that maintain a very low theta rhythm in the brainwave. That avoids one of the other major problems that can occur during cryosleep: permanent impairment, or even total loss, of the ability to encode short-term memories."

"Don't our cold cells have a system which prevents that?"

"Yes, sir. But its electric: crude, unreliable, and the longer the subject is in cryosleep, the greater the chance of recollective impairment."

Duncan squinted. "Is that a fancy way of saying amnesia?"

"No, sir. Recollective impairment is when the subject can't add any new memories. The subject remains limited to the archive they have at the time they suffer the impairment."

Solsohn's face went slack with horror as Riordan asked, "But for this brainwave maintenance cocktail to work, doesn't the subject still have to be awake—or dreaming, at least? And doesn't that mean they are at temperatures too high to be considered functionally cryogenic?"

Newton shrugged. "Well, that's what I was taught and what I thought—until about four hours ago."

"Then how are these chemicals, natural or otherwise, making this happen?"

"My best guess is that the compound must also contain some kind of smart chemical or nanite that brings the necessary parts of the brain on line just enough to run a few of these pulses, then allows the cold to reassert for a certain amount of time. There is some evidence pointing to an underlying chemical mechanism: that the compound leaches out just enough glycerin to reprime the target cells, pumps in a little heat along with a bioelectric stimulus to get the wave going, then backs off and lets the baseline cryogenesis reassert."

Duncan's eyes widened slightly. "That's one smart nanite."

"If it is a nanite." Newton started walking fretfully along the row of cold cells, the others following. "Maybe it's a microorganism specially geneered to perform that function, triggered by conditions of temperature and chemistry, such as elevated glycerin levels. Or maybe there's a mini-lab inside the cryocell which maps the DNA of the subject and finds that part of their own latent code that can be activated to achieve this effect. And maybe that's why I'm not finding these mystery organisms in bulk storage: because part of what the compound does is trick the subject's body into manufacturing the chemicals that once supported this aspect of hibernation. And maybe it doesn't need to produce very much because those chemicals naturally gravitate toward and collect in certain regions of the brain."

Ike's stare was dubious. "I was working alongside you all night and I didn't see any of that. How did you get all that detail, man?"

"As I said, I'm only guessing. There is no way of *knowing*, not without extended analysis. But the Nazis did keep records which tracked the different reanimation sequelae particular to the different cyrocell types.

I compared that to the monitors and biointerfaces in the cryocells themselves, on the hypothesis that the nature of the controls and gauges would indicate the crucial data required by a trained operator. From that, I've come up with a few hypotheses about what each particular type of cryocell does to its subjects, and how, and why. For instance, the subjects who came out of the cells equipped with the kind of brainwave booster I was talking about had zero short-term memory loss and vastly decreased reorientation and neural restoration times. And there's no evidence of anything intrusive being embedded in or attached to them. So it's got to be systemic. And that suggests either biologicals or nanites."

They had arrived in front of the humans-in-amber cysts. "And these?" Caine asked.

Newton frowned. "The strangest and most unsettling of all the cold cells. Correction: this really isn't a cold cell. It's—call it a biococoon. No temperature reduction involved at all. Think of a fly trapped in living amber: slow moving, biomorphic sap or secretions that haven't become rigid, just very sluggish. Whatever that fluid or gel is, it gets inside the human body and takes it over. Slowly. First it renders the victim unconscious, then insensate, then begins changing body chemistry. Deactivates bacteria, and just about everything else. Then it goes dormant. When that biological medium is reactivated, it reverses the process."

Riordan stopped walking, found that he was staring at the biococoons, had to remind himself to inhale. "But how does it do that?"

"I don't have the faintest idea. Literally. I have no idea where the fluid comes from. No idea how the outer layer of it knows to harden. No idea how it interfaces with these control systems that are either embedded in it or which it grows around. All I know is how to make it release the occupant and which of the interior lights indicate that its operating status is nominal, compromised, or near failure."

Duncan stared up at the rows and columns of them. "So these are . . . living objects? Creatures, not devices?"

"Sort of. Maybe. Damn it, I just don't know."

Riordan had the urge to reach out and touch the nearest of them; he restrained that primitive impulse toward tactile exploration. "And is the chemistry of this, er, symbiopod natural or—?"

Newton raised his hands. "I can't even guess at this point. Not only don't I have the research facilities, I don't have the skill set to begin to know how to figure out the right questions to ask. Three years ago, there were—maybe—a dozen people on Earth who could tackle a project like this. Maybe, given recent events, there are more now. But this is a very specialized question. With some very profound implications."

"You mean, genetic implications?"

"Yes, that too, but the biggest impact would be upon our understanding of epigenetic interaction—still far from complete—and xenobiology. Because this thing, whatever it is, doesn't have much in common with anything we've ever seen, either on Earth or in any of the exobiomes we've colonized."

Riordan forced himself to look away from the eerie, inner lights that waxed and waned within the muddy amber objects. "Any more mundane data on the different varieties of cryopod?"

Ike nodded. "We found that the Nazis did have some code books stashed inside one of the empty units. The codes tell them how to start the reanimation cycle for each type of unit, detect either an impending system failure or excessive damage to the occupant, and reverse the process so that the reanimation can be attempted later."

"Are any of the remaining cryocells in a compromised condition?"

"Yessir: twenty-eight, only one of which indicates that the occupant is wounded. The other twenty-seven either have mechanical warning lights that came on when someone tried to reanimate the occupant, or had potential system failures before anyone tried."

Caine heard a slight hardening of Ike Franklin's tone. "Sounds like you have a personal stake in there, somewhere, Lieutenant."

"I do, sir. I wasn't put on ice solo. My buddy is in here, too."

"Another pararescue jumper?"

"No. Ground pounder. Special Forces. I was sent in to get him and the only other survivor from their five-man team out of Somalia. Up near the Ethiopian border. As dry and hot as hell and twice as ugly. Some of the locals spotted my drop. I'd jumped in, stabilized the other Green Beanie for medevac. But he was still in really bad shape.

"Our extraction was still thirty minutes out when we were surrounded by local clansmen. Fought them off, but we had next to no cover. Their fire killed the casualty, trashed the radio, badly damaged our ride home. Which had to abort.

"That was at dusk. We listened and watched for the weakest part of the surrounding forces, waited for night and hit them. Broke through, grabbed weapons, ammo, water from their dead, and booked. Kept ahead of the others until morning. But I guess they had radios. Just after dawn, we see dust on the horizon. Pickup trucks loaded with the local warlord's favorite flunkies, mounting heavy weapons. 'Technicals,' we called 'em.

"We didn't have any choice; we had to make for high ground. It's rough, craggy country out there, so no trucks could follow us when we left the flats. But we were also trapped on a hill of bare rock with no vegetation, no water, and damned little shade. A day later, my bro J.P. and I were down to half a dozen rounds each and our last mouthfuls of water. And we were already as dehydrated as old leather. We were slurring our words and promising each other a mercy bullet if we got wounded when this guy in a suit appears downhill, hands raised, carrying a white handkerchief. Like it was some movie or something.

"Not that we'd have popped him, anyway. No way he was a local. Hell, he looked like he'd just finished a few cool drinks before walking up the slope toward us. Don't know how he got past the Somalis, but I expect no one ever figured that out. They stopped making noise just a few minutes before he appeared. And then he gave us the same 'I'll save your sorry asses if you come with me' speech that everyone else heard. And here we are. Well"—he looked behind at a nearby cryocell—"here *I* am. J.P.'s cold cell has a red light where there ought to be a green one, so he's still napping. The lazy bastard."

"Does the light indicate that it's a mechanical failure, or is his body compromised in some way?"

"Malfunction. Looks like the Nazis tried to wake J.P. up, but the system signalled that the reanimation was going to go sideways. So they threw it into reverse, kept him in the bag."

Riordan nodded. "I'm sorry."

Ike smiled. "Hey, if you're going to waste some 'sorries,' waste them on me. I'm the one who's been awake, dealing with all the nasty shit on this planet. But it has been pretty reassuring working with Newt, here." "Newt" glared at Isaac. "Until he, and you guys, came along, I was worried I'd never see J.P.'s ugly cracker mug again."

"J.P.'s a 'cracker'?" Riordan asked.

Ike snickered. "A Southern boy. You know, a way-down-Dixie-bred son of the Big Easy." Apparently, Riordan's own face was as much a picture of bafflement as Duncan's. "Lieutenant Jean-Pierre Deveraux is from New Orleans, originally. A cracker was a term—a term I used to tease him. About his origins. Sir." Isaac looked away, almost like a truant kid. "It wasn't really appropriate, sir—but it was cool between us."

"Lieutenant," Riordan confessed, "I am getting more, rather than less, confused with every additional detail you are adding to your alleged explanation. But I think I get the gist of it, and we'll do everything we can to get Lt. Deveraux reanimated safely."

Ike smiled. "Thank you, sir." His smile dimmed, became more thoughtful. "Sorry I confused you with the slang, sirs. Things sure have changed a lot, back home."

"And with any luck, you'll get to see that for yourself soon enough. Now, anything else?"

"There are twenty-two other cryocells which seem to have secret access codes which were never entered. Almost all of them are marked with the crayon symbol that the Germans used to indicate pilots or plane technicians."

Newton made a dismissive clucking noise with his tongue. "The security code devices are a laugh. Put a sequential generator on any of them for a few hours and they'll open up. The locking mechanism was an afterthought, I think." He stretched. "Kind of like our getting food."

Riordan looked from one man to the other. "Haven't had any lunch?"

"Or breakfast," Ike said, as if suddenly remembering the lack of it.

"Then let's get you dinner," Riordan decided, walking back toward the entry into the mausoleum.

An hour later, they emerged into the very cool night air of Turkh'saar. Even this close to the equator, the temperature fell faster than the horizon-reddened sun.

Ike was rubbing his belly. "That's two days of real honest-to-god rations, not worm meat and low-carb fiber mush. Almost makes me feel human again—to coin a phrase."

Riordan smiled. "Where are you from, Lieutenant?"

Franklin smiled fondly. "Suburbs north of New York City. Croton-on-Hudson. Born there in 1967. Looking back, it was a pretty sweet life: private school, played football, finished near the top of my class."

And Riordan could tell from the sound in his voice that even having asked that seemingly harmless question was putting Franklin at risk of reveries that might easily turn to melancholy. So, time to redirect. "Not a lot of that prepared you for what you found here, I'll bet."

That did seem to swing Franklin around toward less homey memories. "Oh, I don't know, Commodore. I worked in an inner-city ER, jumped out of perfectly good planes into hellholes worse than this, and watched lots of *Star Trek*. Frankly, I think I was better prepared than a lot of the other folks here."

"*Star Trek*?" echoed Duncan.

Riordan, worried that the question might return Ike to intensely personal recollections, rushed onward. "Since you've been the CMO here, any advice I should pass along to our medics about this environment?"

Franklin looked down, thinking as he walked out toward the edge of the flight line and the cloudless night sky. "Tell them not to leave any wounds in contact with the ground for very long. The flora here is...well, it's nasty. Not like 'I'll bite you' nasty; more the 'get off of my property' variety. There are almost no flowering plants, so everything spreads by spores, molds, parthenogenesis, runners, budding. All noncooperative means of reproduction. So each species tends to saturate the soil with compounds that it can tolerate but its competitors can't: toxins or extremely high or low ph excretions. Most of the toxins don't care much about our bodies and vice versa. But high alkalinity or acidity doesn't require any biological compatibility to inflict damage. That's just basic chemistry. So don't leave casualties on the ground any longer than you have to, and don't lean on a gashed elbow or knee: you're likely to regret it."

"I'll pass that along," Caine assured him with a nod.

But Ike might not have heard him: he had noticed three figures sitting at the edge of the naked bedrock of the flight line, staring up into the night sky. "Well, how's it going, my Magi?" he asked.

All three men rose. From the look of their clothes,

one was a Japanese submariner, another a crewman from *Swordfish*, and the last, an older man whose turban marked him as one of the Afghanis. The first two saluted. The latter bowed, muttering almost inaudible greetings toward Franklin, but his eyes were fixed upon Riordan and Solsohn.

Franklin gestured to the trio. "They're our three wise men."

The crewman from *Swordfish* beamed widely. Not all the expected teeth were there, and many of those that remained were not in enviable condition. "As Colonel Paulsen says, we ahr the unit's sky-pilots." Seeing that neither of the newcomers understood the slang, he clarified. "We ahr self-appointed chaplains, suhs." His drawl was pronounced, an exaggerated version of what Riordan had heard when his family had travelled to various parts of the American South.

"I imagine that has been a—a very challenging calling, under these conditions."

The Japanese nodded somberly. "It is not precisely that for which the temple teachings prepare one. But all enlightenment begins in ignorance and humility. This place has been a constant instruction in both."

Riordan smiled. "I presume you are a Zen Buddhist, Mr.—?"

He bowed. "Sakai. Sakai Koetsu, Commodore."

Riordan returned the gesture. "And your companions?"

The American, a swarthy man of large frame and facial features, shoved out a meaty hand. "Seaman First Class Ronald Purcett, suh. Cook's mate. Preacher before Uncle Sam tapped me on't shoulder—an' still am, when I can get them durn boys tuh lissen."

Riordan shook and released Purcett's hand, turned to the Afghani. "And you are?"

The man—wrinkled, thin-cheeked, unblinking dark brown eyes—nodded slowly. "I am Yasuf Ali, Commodore. I must ask you a question."

Startled by the gravity in the older man's voice, Riordan nodded sharply. "Of course, Mr. Ali."

The brown eyes turned back to the stars. "Where is our home?"

"Your—?"

"Earth, Commodore. Where is Earth?"

Riordan suddenly understood the longing and pain lurking behind Yasuf's eyes. Caine turned, found the right patch of star-strewn night sky, and pointed. "There, Mr. Ali. The small star, just to the left of those two larger ones. Do you see?"

Ali nodded slowly. "Are you sure?"

Riordan returned the nod. "I am. Others have already asked the question. We confirmed the position earlier today with our celestial navigation and location programs."

Ali bowed. "Blessings upon you, Commodore." And without another word, the tall, wizened man turned, paced back to where he had been sitting, unbound and unfurled a rug upon which he prepared to kneel.

Riordan cleared his throat. "Mr. Ali, I'm sorry I did not think to inquire if there were any among you who had been waiting for this information. I would have made a point of disseminating it before sundown."

Yasuf smiled. His eyes began to glimmer in the low light; one tear escaped, made circuitous progress down his weathered cheek. "Your intentions are a gift, and no doubt please the Prophet, who will still welcome the fervor and joy of our tardy prayers. Especially now that we may face toward Mecca."

With a final nod, he kneeled upon the unfurled mat and sank forward slowly, until his forehead touched the ground. His smile, both pained and joyful, showed a partial row of teeth, which shone along with his tears as he commenced his devotions.

Chapter Thirty-Four

Yaargraukh finished his long, loping sprint to the top of the northern ridge line, went over the crest, reversed and threw himself down behind a fernlike bush, the stalks of which were sparse where they entered the ground. He stared between them, his head obscured by the thick leafy top, his body hidden by the ridge line itself. He waited.

Two minutes later, across the small glen, a silhouette disturbed the dim outline of the lower, opposite ridge to the south. The pace at which that shadow moved was relatively casual at first, but then became more hurried. And Yaargraukh knew why.

His own pace—and therefore, the distance between his tracks—had remained a walk since he had left the Flag's laager. But as soon as he had slipped over the ridge he was now watching, he had broken into a full run. His objective: to reach the more northerly ridgeline so he would see if he was being followed. Anyone tracking him would profile themselves against the early night sky as they came over the lower crest he had left behind.

Clearly, then, he was being followed. And where there is one tracker—

Another silhouette joined the first. And then a third. Their gestures were hurried, urgent: their quarry had surprised them, had dramatically increased its speed the moment it had gone behind the crest of the ridge upon which they now stood. Which meant that they had presumably been spotted and had to move quickly in order to catch up.

Fortunately, their quarry had not been able to move as carefully as he had before reaching these foothills. His long, sprinting strides had left deep imprints in the loam: an easy track to follow. Confident, they set out in immediate and hard pursuit, having little need to check for nuances in the trail that had been left.

Or so they thought.

Khaakhoz of the Moiety of Sh'ashyrkuk approached Urgluuz, his cousin, who had stopped his pursuit. As the lead, or coursing, hunter, it was Urgluuz's job to press the prey as much as possible. They did so in turns, a traditional Hkh'Rkh means of wearing down game. And fugitives.

"Why have you stopped?" Khaakhoz hissed as he drew alongside Urgluuz. Given the vocal apparatus of Hkh'Rkh, it truly was a hiss.

Urgluuz shrugged, waited for the third in their hunting triad, Sakneev, to catch up until he was close enough to hear. "See what is before us: a hunter's path. It heads to the east and the west. It is well-travelled, and the quarry slowed to a pace that blends his tracks into those of the rovers who use it."

Khaakhoz glanced in both directions, controlled

the annoyed tremor of his eyes. "This is what he was heading for. And this is why he began running so swiftly once he was out of our sight. He had enough time to reach this trail unobserved by us. Now we cannot tell which way he went."

"Assuming," Sakneev added, drawing in a great breath, "that he has not, instead, gone stealthily into the bush. Which would leave us three trails to follow."

Khaakhoz found it difficult to still his eyes. Sakneev's family was less fortunate, so he had spent some time among the New Families as a rover: the only one that Jrekhalkar was able to send with them as they tracked Yaargraukh. All the true rovers were Fringelanders: New Family scions and Warriors who lived and died by their ability to track, hunt, and leave little trace while doing so. As had Yaargraukh, for the first fifteen years of his life. "We start by seeking such a trail in the bush, from this point or ten meters along either of the trails."

"He may have put as much as a kilometer between himself and this point before he left the hunter's path."

"True, Sakneev, but if we spend the time to carefully search a kilometer in either direction, he will have gained so much on us that we may never catch him." Which the traitorous Flag Leader no doubt knew and intended. "Quickly, now: seek a fresh trail along the margins of the path."

They did—and found nothing. But another five minutes had elapsed.

"What now?" asked Urgluuz, running his forward digit over the trigger guard of his scattergun.

Khaakhoz considered. The next step in their pursuit was clear: coursers along both paths. But the choice of personnel required a delicate balancing of the exigencies of both fieldcraft and politics.

Sakneev was by far their best tracker. Up until now, that had not been crucial. Yaargraukh had started for Iarzut'thruk at a leisurely pace, then had made a gradual northward deviation, leaving tracks that a whelpling could follow. But once on this pathway, it would be difficult to stay both mindful of where he might have subtly slipped off into the trackless bush and also move swiftly enough to catch him. The path allowed one to make good time without leaving any distinctive prints. So, since they would have to split into two groups, the crucial question was: which direction had Yaargraukh been more likely to choose? Because that was the direction in which two of them, rather than one, should be sent. However, there was an additional delicate consideration: what needed to be done once Yaargraukh was located?

Khaakhoz glanced furtively at Sakneev's back. Although the Warrior's sire was Old Family, when his clan had fallen upon hard times, distant kin among the New Families had taken them in. In so doing, they had become more sympathetic to the hardships of those lower-classed Hkh'Rkh. So although Sakneev's tracking skills recommended that he be put on the path that Yaargraukh had been most likely to follow, political wisdom suggested the opposite. Because once Yaargraukh was found, he would have to be dealt with—and in a manner that disturbed even Khaakhoz's rudimentary sense of Honor.

By veering north, Yaargraukh had departed the most direct path toward Iarzut'thruk. That in itself did not prove that he intended to defy Jrekhalkar's order to place himself in the custody of Old Family Warriors in the capitol. Indeed, Yaargraukh might simply be extending his travel by a day, to press northward into the Fringelands where he himself grew up as a young rover, to visit family friends who still lived there. But it was also possible that he intended to seek refuge among those same friends, to disobey Jrekhalkar and remain at large, aided and abetted by the New Families who knew the region as if it was incised upon their four-jointed palms and who had no love of the Old Family scions and the dictates that were issued by the Clanhall in Iarzut'thruk.

But there was a more onerous possibility: that Yaargraukh meant to get to a radio, or attempt to reach the humans personally. The latter would be a difficult task, given the distance. The only breach in the thick clusterwoods between here and the raiders' forward base was the course cut by the River Kakaagsukh. But the banks of that deep, sea-rushing flow were craggy at many points, requiring detours through long stretches of uneven land choked by heavy vegetation. It was very unlikely that Yaargraukh could arrive among the humans in time if he was determined to follow the course of that river.

However, whereas the former Advocate's intent was unclear, Khaakhoz's mission was not. If Yaargraukh headed north, it was essential to presume the worst and eliminate him. Not by Challenge or anything resembling a fair fight, but by the most certain and expeditious means: assassination from ambush.

Khaakhoz did not mind being ordered to kill Yaargraukh—indeed, he welcomed the Voice's dictate—but the means gave him pause. It made him wonder if there might be something to the New Family rhetoric: that in clutching to their legacy of power and control, the Old Families were drifting further and further from the heritage of Honor and the principles upon which their authority had always been presumed to rest.

Khaakhoz's thoughts flinched away from that troubling concept. These were matters for infirm sages, not strong-thewed Warriors who had a mission to complete, no matter how ethically odious it might be. "Sakneev, you will follow the westward path alone. If he is heading that direction, he probably means to either visit or hide among the New Families of the northern Fringeland." A dubious contention, at best. "You are familiar with them and so are the most likely to be able to solicit their aid. Or at least the truth."

Sakneev stared at Khaakhoz, said nothing. He was a relatively silent Warrior. It was impossible to know whether he was simply waiting for further orders or whether his lack of comment reflected a lack of belief in his superior's explanation. At any rate, it was something less than full and ready affirmation and compliance. Which Khaakhoz found unacceptable. "Do you have a question, Warrior?"

"I do not." But Sakneev's tone suggested that he might suspect the careful considerations which had resulted in his being ordered to seek to the west: it was the opposite direction from the one Yaargraukh would have headed if his intents were traitorous. "Shall I set out?" His voice was flat—or did Khaakhoz hear a thin thread of disgust running under it?

Khaakhoz nodded. "We shall meet back at this site in thirty-six hours. If either you or we fail to appear by then, any survivor must bear news back to Jrekhalkar."

Sakneev gave a faint pony-nod. "I understand." He turned and loped off to the west, head swinging slightly from side to side as he scanned for any trail-sign that might indicate a spot where Yaargraukh had slipped back into the bush.

Once he had passed well beyond earshot, Khaakhoz turned to Urgluuz. "The urgent job rests upon our necks. If Yaargraukh has followed the trail east, he is doubling back."

"Toward the humans."

"We must presume so. And we must eliminate him as we would the *s'fet* he goes to aid. As a traitor, he is beyond Honor." Khaakhoz wished he could believe that hasty moral formulation himself: it was a vast presumption upon which to base so terrible a violation of honor among Warriors.

But Urgluuz had been chosen for two attributes: the immense size of his body and the diminutive size of his intellect. "If we find him, we shall kill him." He began rubbing his fore-digit along the curve of his scattergun's trigger guard once again. More rapidly, now.

Khaakhoz gestured toward the east. "You begin as the courser. I shall follow, watching for signs where the traitor may have left the path." Maybe, by splitting the tasks of coursing and sign-watching between them, they might conjointly approach Sakneev's wilderness skills. But Khaakhoz doubted it.

Urgluuz had turned, was sprinting away on the eastward track. Khaakhoz, talon-tip resting lightly on his assault rifle's safety, followed.

Yaargraukh watched the lone Warrior pause at the point where he had left the westward trail, furtively assess the underbrush for snares. *He has been a rover at some point in his life. So he dwelt on the Fringelands. But whether or not he is New Family, he will not be a potential ally: Jrekhalkar would have made sure of that. At most, he will be reluctant—and that is not enough for me to depend on.*

The Warrior's tail was barely raised slightly as he entered the bush, following Yaargraukh's trail; tracking in that posture allowed him to lean over further as he moved, maintaining speed even as he kept his head close to the sparse tracks. Fifty meters in, he straightened; Yaargraukh had made less effort to soften his footfalls at that point, left a clearer trail. The Warrior's tail came up and he began to run along the path, his rifle cradled in an assault carry, his long head questing after each new clue to his quarry's movement.

He began to slow as he drew directly beneath Yaargraukh. The trail led directly into a clump of tall, thick bushes. The pursuer paused, hesitant, then pushed into the undergrowth cautiously. The going was slow, both due to the density of the long, spiky leaves and the need to remain alert for an ambush; the prey might be using this blind to reverse their roles and become the predator. The tops of the foliage kept parting grudgingly, snapping closed behind him—until, just four meters shy of reaching a spot in the thicket devoid of bushtops, two meters' worth of bushes gave way. The courser fell out of sight with a shout and a crash.

Yaargraukh watched, listened. After ten seconds, he swung down from a tree that had grown up against the thicket and slipped in between the stems and stalks that his pursuer had begun parting less than a minute earlier.

He slowed as he neared the edge of the pit, the one he and his relatives had dug almost seventeen years ago to catch the largest game on Turkh'saar: *d'lyrkh*, a thick-hided, tough-gutted pack grazer that had been introduced to the planet from Rkh'yaa. The larger varieties had not survived: the volume of toxins they took in while foraging for edible plants shortened their lifespan so severely that they were not able to breed at replacement levels.

But the smaller "pygmy" *d'lyrkh* were made of tougher stuff and, having a shorter binge-then-sleep cycle, did not accumulate the same toxic load in the course of their grazing. Unfortunately, they were no more domesticatable on Turkh'saar than they had been on the Hkh'Rkh homeworld, and had been released to breed feral. Which they had done with great abandon, sheltering in thickets to sleep, either while their engorged bellies slowly digested plant matter, or when they retired there to whelp.

This trap was of a kind specially designed to dupe the *d'lyrkh*. A shelf of shallow-rooted brush topped a thin rim of soil that projected slightly out beyond the circumference of the pit. When two or three of the dense, barrel-shaped *d'lyrkh* stepped on it, the shelf gave way and dropped them down upon stakes held fast by the almost equally sharp stone spurs that lined the floor of the pit. As Yaargraukh had anticipated, the weight of a Warrior was more than sufficient to generate the same effect. He peered cautiously over the lip of the deadfall trap.

His pursuer lay sprawled, almost twenty feet below.

Maroon stains were evident on the rocks, particularly a large smear where one of the stakes had impaled his left arm and another one where his head was pushed at an awkward angle against a fang of granite. His weapon—a somewhat outdated assault rifle—lay beyond his grasp. Assuming, that is, he would ever grasp anything again.

Lowering himself over the ledge until his left foot found the first stone step that his own sire had set into the near side of the pit, Yaargraukh began his descent to ensure that his pursuer was indeed beyond grasping his weapon—or peforming any other task.

Khaakhoz slowed as he approached the effective end of the eastern path: a three-pronged diffusion into wandering game trails, none of which had been used recently. In the course of switching between courser and sweeper, he and Urgluuz had come across two sets of faint tracks detouring into the bush, but neither had been left by Yaargraukh. One had led to a three-day old hunter's camp, the other to a now-stripped *d'lyrkh* carcass; both marked the passage of rovers operating in the further Fringelands.

And now, standing at the end of the path, Khaakhoz found himself staring down a slight slope at one of the few flat, scree-littered stretches of silt along this part of the River Kakaagsukh. The gruff whisper of turbulence reached him in the night air. The light glimmering off fretful wavelets made it the brightest object in the landscape: a scattering of half-seen opals restively riding the back of a dark, undulating roadway. Which now ran across Yaargraukh's presumed path like a wide canyon. Clearly, Yaargraukh had not come this way. So he must have left the path elsewhere, or had in fact headed west. In which case, Sakneev—

A throaty report came from perhaps a hundred meters behind him; back where Urgluuz was sweeping for tracks that left the main pathway—as slowly as ever.

Khaakhoz turned and sprinted in that direction. The weapon discharge had been from a scattergun and Urgluuz had the only one. With any luck, he had found Yaargraukh lurking near the pathway, waiting for them to pass by, possibly to double back—

Rounding a large, flat spur of rock, Khaakhoz caught sight of Urgluuz: face down, with the hilt of a short-sword protruding from his back. And his scattergun was on the ground beside him. But then how—?

Khaakhoz did not see so much as feel the black mass that detached itself from the deep shadows of the rock he was passing. He spun in that direction, bringing up his assault rifle—

But before he could fully turn, he felt something slide into his body: cool at first, but then very sharp and burning. The weight behind it bore him to the ground, and his attacker used that fall to crush down upon the hilt of the blade. It had penetrated both muscle and lung-plate before stopping just within the rubbery sheath that protected the primary reservoir of the cardiosac. Struggling to draw in breath, and bring his left arm around to grab his attacker, Khaakhoz felt his body shift closer to the tip of the weapon—but too late. There was a sudden lightheaded rush that every whelpling recalled from the first tales they heard of the ancient battles: his cardiac-sac had been breached, so the flow of blood was immediately controlled to prevent or at least slow exsanguination.

That gave him maybe another thirty seconds of energy with which to fight.

But his attacker must have seen or felt the sudden rush of blood that jetted out along the blade before the contractile tissue stemmed that tide. The dark shape leaped away, just out of Khaakhoz's faltering sweep, tearing the stricken Hkh'Rkh's assault rifle out of his weakened grasp.

It was Yaargraukh.

Khaakhoz goggled. "You—How?"

But Yaargraukh, who'd left Urgluuz's shortsword in the wound, sprang forward again, rifle raised, aimed at Khaakhoz's head. The hunter blinked, threw up a protecting arm—and discovered that the aggressive move had been a feint: the calar claw of Yaargraukh's right foot came in low, spiked directly into Khaakhoz's left ankle, which buckled.

Back on the ground, Khaakhoz felt the death-surge rising: he did not have much time left. But his left leg wobbled fearfully as he rose back up, trying to ignore the pain. And Yaargraukh, who was almost a hand-span shorter than he, had backed up and showed no signs of reapproaching. Khaakhoz understood as he took one step forward and almost fell. "You meant to cripple me. So I could not reach you with my last strength."

"Yes."

"Then why not shoot me and be done with it?"

"Because one report of a scattergun will not carry so far as that of an assault rifle. Nor will it attract much attention: hunters use them frequently enough."

"Then why did you fire it at all? You killed Urgluuz with a sword."

"Yes, but I needed to bring you to me at a run,

expecting to find me dead, rather than armed. Urgluuz carried the gun, and you knew I was unarmed. Logically, if you heard the report of a scattergun, it should mean I was dead, or at the very least, was in sight and being pursued."

Khaakhoz discovered he'd sagged; the arc of his left haunch was directly supported by the ground. He had another minute of consciousness, maybe two. "You are a clever traitor, Yaargraukh, but a dead one. There's nothing but water ahead of you. And nothing but more of us true-hearted Warriors behind."

Yaargraukh kept the assault rifle trained on Khaakhoz. "You are wrong in every assertion but one. Firstly, I am not a traitor. I mean to save our people from a war that neither we nor the humans have caused, and from which neither of us would benefit. Secondly, I am not dead, literally or figuratively, since I need not retrace my steps. But you are correct to point out that there is water before me."

"And so you are either trapped here or forced to retrace your steps. And so, are dead. As I assert."

"You ignore a third possibility: that I shall travel by river."

"The banks are too rough. You may travel that way, but not soon enough to cheat the fate that awaits you at Jrekhalkar's hands, after he has finished off the humans."

"I did not say I will travel along the river. I said travel *by* the river."

"You mean—in the water? Are you mad?"

"No, I am a scholar. And I learned that, in order to understand one's adversaries, one must understand their ways. Humans are creatures of both water and

land. I easily understood their existence on land, but
not their relationship to water. So I availed myself of
that knowledge."

"You—you learned how to, to—swim?" Khaakhoz
realized he had slumped over, was on his back. The
stars above—the embers of his sires—seemed to spin,
hypnotizing him before he set upon his journey to
join them.

"I also learned how to float. And there are many
old shoots of clustertrees snagged among the rocks
lining the Kakaagsukh. I shall find a suitable one,
take hold, and let the river carry me downstream, to
the very fringes of the recent battle with the raiders.
I expect I shall arrive there even before Jrekhalkar
himself. Perhaps in time to stop this insane conflict."

But Khaakhoz did not hear the end of Yaargraukh's
explanation.

He had begun the upward journey to join his sires.

PART THREE
June 2121

CONQUEST

Aut vincere aut mori
(Either to conquer or to die)

Chapter Thirty-Five

Newly minted Sergeant Bernardo "Bear" de los Reyes pushed his helmet's visor up before making his report to newly minted Captain Christopher "Tygg" Robin. "Sir, creeper sweep confirms Wedge One's sensor results: the Hkh'Rkh did not seed the FOB with mines."

Tygg tapped his collarcom. "Wedge One, LZ is clear. You are cleared to drop and go."

Before Tygg touched his collarcom to close the circuit, the thunder of approaching turbojets became a raucous whine: they had swung into vertical mode, making any further attempts at communication pointless. Wedge One came in fast over the eastern clustertree line and bellied down aggressively into the clearing that had been the marshalling ground for the Lost Soldiers' forward operating base. As the jetwash intensified, the rotors of the abandoned Mi-8 and UH-1 began shimmying.

As de los Reyes turned his back against the cyclone, he saw Riordan's inquiries popping up in his HUD: had the tunnel complex and helicopters been swept for booby traps? Were there any anomalous EM signals, the kind that might be made by any snoop-tech that the Hkh'Rkh left behind? Was there any sign that the helicopters had been sabotaged?

He toggled the answers to each, all of which confirmed that the Hkh'Rkh had immediately unassed the area after *Puller* and Top Sergeant Fanny's MULTI had wreaked havoc upon their armor. The Hkh'Rkh hadn't even come back to reclaim their dead: a clear sign that they had not withdrawn, but routed off the field.

Dust and bits of debris—leaves, branches, wrappers— swirled around de los Reyes angrily, smacking and spatting off his resealed visor. Suddenly, they repented their blind rage and fell in mid swirl. Wedge One had landed and cut thrust. Turning back toward the transport, de los Reyes saw figures emerging from the settling dust: about half of the Cold Guard and an equal number of Lost Soldiers, mostly post-World War II Americans and Russians. They had been been the only logical candidates for direct integration with contemporary forces. Vertical assault had its own particular tempo, and while a lot of the older Lost Soldiers were pretty tough customers, most of them had a hard time getting used to the rapidity with which conditions and tasks changed in a truly airmobile operation. But what these slightly more modern troops were going to do with their old-school battle rifles with magazines in front—in front!— of the trigger guards was still beyond de los Reyes.

One of the figures emerging from the dust swiveled its head toward de los Reyes, swerved toward him at a trot. The silhouette was that of a duty suit, bulked out by a ballistic: Riordan.

The commodore popped up his visor. "Has your team cleared the tunnels?"

"Yes, sir."

"Good. I'm calling the deployment briefing in five minutes."

A dull throbbing rose in the air around them, as if they were hearing the heart of a cloud-dwelling elephant having a panic attack. De los Reyes swung his CoBro in the direction of the sound—high to the southeast—and grabbed at Riordan's sleeve, pulling him down. Many of the Cold Guard were doing the same thing.

But the Lost Soldiers stood around casually, laughing at them. "What?" shouted Emmett Owen over the rapidly cycling *whuppa-whuppa-whuppa*. "You guys never hear a helicopter before?"

Tygg shook his head. "Not much. And not like that. Vertibirds, now."

"Vertibirds?" echoed Owen uncertainly.

"Yeah. Variable-attitude turbofans or turbojets."

Owen did not look edified. "Okay, Captain Future; you tell me and I'll believe it. Now, how far out do you want the perimeter?"

But Captain Robin wasn't listening: two helicopters—twins for the pair on the ground—rattled overhead, the whine of their turbines down-dopplering rapidly. Tygg stared after them with a frown on his face, saw that Riordan was looking at him. He nodded at the commodore. "I know, sir. The Hkh'Rkh aren't heading toward the site and Melissa has plenty of security. But I just don't like it, sir."

"Frankly, I don't either. But she was dead on about why we need to get a look at that patch of dirt and derelict buildings."

Tygg sighed, visibly forced himself not to follow the

dwindling choppers with his eyes. "I know that, sir. But I won't be happy until she—until they're back."

"Me neither, Tygg. Now, get your squads deployed, *Captain*. We need to evolve to phase two within the hour."

Hearing the term, phase two, de los Reyes put up his own visor. "Is phase two 'advance to contact,' sir?"

"Not quite that aggressive, Sergeant. I want to stay well back from the Hkh'Rkh and offer minimal provocation. However, we'll establish a defensive line where the ground favors us and weakens them."

"Yes, sir. I guess I'll hear the details during Major Rulaine's command briefing."

"You will. In three minutes. Is that enough time to explain this home-brewed sensor enhancement which you mentioned to him?"

"Yes, sir. It's Private Somers's idea, actually. She's pretty much a whiz when it comes to comms and sensors. So, since we can't rely on our one satellite to be overhead when we need it, she's put together a nonorbital workaround called a ping-pong locator system. But I suspect you're already familiar with those—"

Caine stopped de los Reyes with a smile and raised hand. "I'm pretty much a newb when it comes to nonconventional field expedients."

De los Reyes started. "Sir, that's not what the scuttlebutt says."

Riordan smiled. "Let's assume that scuttlebutt is wrong. Walk me through the details of this ping-pong system."

De los Reyes nodded, hoped he didn't show his surprise. *Okay, the guy's ego doesn't get in his way.*

*Or ours. And he's not looking for medals or a promo-
tion. Damn, we just might all live through this to tell
the tale.* "Sir, a ping-pong locator system is a more
powerful version of the emergency locator grids used
during disasters where satellite communications are
lost or unreliable. In place of satcomms, an overhead
grid emulator is compiled by networking multiple transponders and comms, all of which track their spatial
relationship to other elements of the system through
range and vector confirmations. When that entire
matrix is then anchored to a prime transmitter with
a fixed location on a shared map, every other comm
can use the full index of range and vector values to
locate itself in relation to every other network element,
which allows it to be situated on the map.

"The military version—'ping-pong'—adds in all our
drones, quadrotors, creepers, your and my helmet
sensors: everything. So it's a huge grid with lots of
different data from all across the EM spectrum. It
gives us a work-around for getting coordinates, target
designation and tracking, maintaining lascom links:
almost anything normally enabled by satcomms."

Riordan was nodding as if he had actually understood. "Sergeant, make sure that Private Somers
contacts Ms. Veriden to bring her up to speed on
this ping-pong network. She should include recommendations on how best to integrate it with the feed
from the two overhead sensors we're about to bring on
line." Riordan glanced at his wrist-mounted palmtop.
"In about twenty seconds, Wedge Two will deploy a
pair of EXHALTEDs at the thirty-kilometer mark—"

"Sir, I'm sorry to interrupt, but—EXHALTED?"

"EXtremely High ALtitude Theater Engagement

Designator/director. It's legacy communications and sensor tech, but in a miniaturized platform with extraordinary loiter time, due to improvements in both power beaming and batteries. Regionally, it can do ninety percent of the work of a conventional satellite for about two weeks."

"I'll get that info to Somers immediately, sir. I should also give you some logistical updates. The big helicopters—the Jollies?—are currently dropping the MULTI systems along the rear of the defensive line you highlighted yesterday. The MISLS will be off-loaded from Wedge One before the hour is out. We're deploying them in a randomized dispersed array, but all units will have LoS command link back here and with at least two other launchers."

Riordan nodded. "Good. Anything else?"

"The Proxie anthrobot is functional and forward-deployed, sir. Major Solsohn put it through its paces. He seems to be quite the artist with it, sir."

"I'm glad to hear it. Bring it back inside our perimeter and power it down until we need it." Riordan grinned, tapped the palmcomp on his wrist. "By the way, you are now officially late for Major Rulaine's brief."

De los Reyes saluted, was turning to sprint back to the tunnel entrance when Riordan's voice added, "Good job keeping track of all those moving parts, Sergeant."

Bernardo de los Reyes hadn't heard genuine appreciation from an officer in a long time. He stopped, turned back toward Riordan. "I was just doing my job, Commodore."

"I've seen people 'just do their job,' Sergeant de los

Reyes. You give yours one hundred percent and then some. If we start butting heads with the Hkh'Rkh, your hard work will wind up saving lives. Dismissed."

The frank gratitude in Riordan's eyes stuck with him all the way back to the cave mouth.

Having completed his quick tour of the FOB, Riordan doubled back toward Wedge One. It felt wrong, not remaining with the Cold Guard: he was their CO, damn it. But then again, they had all the best gear, all the creepers and quadrotors, all the support weapons—and if he didn't get back on board Wedge One, he was holding up the one thing they still lacked: the rest of the Lost Soldiers who'd been slated for active defense roles.

Heading up the rear ramp into the cavernous maw of the delta-shaped transport, Caine wondered how they'd managed to fit as many troops in as they had during this first ferry run. The cargo bay was already jammed with the various equipment and supplies that had been left behind for the Lost Soldiers—and which they would now never need.

His collarcom chirped: he tapped it. "Riordan. Go."

"Commodore," asked Chief Warrant Officer Gaudet in her lilting Carib accent, "how much longer do you require on the ground? We are ready to lift."

"I'm on board, almost into the crew compartment. Don't wait for me to strap in. Head back for the next load."

"Very well, sir."

The bay-door klaxon droned a repetitive warning as the ramp started rising. Another alarm announced that lift was imminent. Riordan made it out of the cargo bay before Wedge One lurched upward, and then swung sharply starboard, tilting him toward the portside bulkhead. He passed the empty passenger section—eighty claustrophobic seats mounted atop lockers big enough for a trooper's full kit—and entered the forward crew section.

By the time the hatch closed behind him, Wedge One was in level flight, and he could hear the bridge chatter up ahead. "We are inbound to you, Dante. ETA: eleven minutes. Keep the next detachment back under the flightline overhang and faced toward the hillside. Landing kicks up more grit than take off."

Riordan entered the bridge—although in the wedges, it felt more like a large plane cockpit—and strapped into what would have been the assistant flight engineer's acceleration couch. Gaudet smiled back at him, as did his new adjutant: Lieutenant Commander Martin Enderle. He was the senior surviving officer from the crew of the Polish sub *Orzel,* a Czech expatriate who had fled the Reich's annexation of the Sudetenland, a translator in four languages, a speaker of seven, and a certifiable genius. He was already getting the hang of the instrumentation in a transatmospheric transport that had been built at least one hundred and seventy years after he was presumed dead in action against the Nazis.

Martin started to come to attention—some of the older, European Lost Soldiers were almost painfully formal no matter how often they were invited to relax—but Riordan waved him down. "Enjoying the ride?" Riordan asked.

"Yes, sir," Enderle affirmed, "very much so, sir. It is an honor to be—"

"Mr. Enderle, your manners are beyond reproach, but right now, I need a report on the status of Wedges Two and Three."

"Yes, sir. The two transports signal that they are in their...er...ah, final approach vector and are making a gradual descent to commence flying at, at—"

"Nap-of-Earth," Gaudet inserted into Martin's lengthening silence. "Flight Rating Nagy reports that Wedge Three is still handling sluggishly."

"I'll bet Phil Friel isn't happy about that."

Gaudet smiled, nodded. "Chief Friel has made his displeasure known. To everyone."

"Any reaction from the Hkh'Rkh?"

"Not that we can tell. Our sensors are basic compared to *Puller*'s and the EXHALTEDs have not yet synced with the integrated tactical net that Ms. Veriden is running back at Dante." Gaudet turned her head just enough that she could aim one eye back at Riordan. "Commodore, we had a pool going; most of us expected you'd assign *Puller* to the FOB, on overwatch."

"And did you win or lose?"

"I am now an even poorer woman than I was when this mission started."

Riordan smiled. "Ms. Gaudet, conventional wisdom would have us keep *Puller* up here where we can bring her lasers and railguns into direct action against the Hkh'Rkh. But *Puller* is not merely our fist; she's our brains and eyes and voice. If the enemy eliminates her, most of our communications and computing advantages go away, too. But she can still get here in eight minutes if she *has* to."

Gaudet adjusted the thruster output slightly. "Copy

all that, sir. By the way, I just received an update from Dr. Sleeman's task force. They are landing at the site now. No sign of the enemy and no difficulties. They hope to have an initial report within the next—"

Martin came erect in his seat as the navigation alert started chiming. "Wampire, wampire!" he shouted, his carefully groomed Anglo accent falling away. "Missile launch! I am uncertain—"

"Calculating," interrupted Gaudet, taking over. "Fourteen missiles. Multiple launch sites between ten and fifteen kilometers north of Dr. Sleeman's current position sir."

"Show me the plot," Riordan ordered. *If those missiles hit Sleeman's helicopters . . .*

"Yes, sir—but remember: this tub doesn't rate holographs."

"Understood," Riordan replied, as a screen over Martin's co-pilot couch illuminated and showed fourteen red bogeys leaving a trail as they headed north. *North: so away from Sleeman.* They were also well past an optimal course to engage Wedge One. *So what—?*

Riordan's hands and feet became frigid. "They've locked on to Wedges Two and Three. Order them to go NOE: now!"

"Sir, at their current speed—"

"Just send the order, my authority. They've got to hug the deck, force the missiles to go higher to reacquire lock, or at least to get a new line of intercept." He tapped his collarcom. "Karam?"

The Flight Officer was a moment responding. "Shit. Yeah; I see 'em. Railgun won't intercept in time, not at that range: too much air in the way."

"Lasers?"

"Yeah, but I won't get them all. Too much atmospheric diffusion. Heading up to engagement altitude now." Behind Karam, Caine heard Solsohn arriving on *Puller's* bridge, calling for Dora to relay telemetry to the gunnery station.

Riordan raised his voice. "Duncan, I've sent Wedge flight down to the deck. That should force the missiles higher, give you a better shot."

"Affirmative. Taking those shots now."

Riordan, Gaudet, and Enderle watched the overhead plot. One of the bogeys vanished, then two more.

"Widen the view," Riordan ordered. "Duncan, hurry it up."

"I wish I could. Atmosphere is degrading beam focus: I'm throwing joules all over each missile, not holding a single target point."

The overhead view had widened and sharpened: the EXHALTED was now online. The missiles had closed most of the distance to the two wedges, one of which was lagging further and further behind. *Damn, it's Wedge Three.* "Gaudet, are you in contact with the—?"

"Negative, sir. No direct line of sight to the wedges once they went nap-of-earth. Broadcast will have some of the same problems; the engagement will be over by the time we clean it up."

Besides, what could anyone tell Miles and Phil that they didn't already know? No doubt their own sensors showed them what Riordan's did now: that another five missiles had been eliminated. Wedge Two took a daring swerve toward the missiles. That baited all but three of the remaining bogeys toward her, at which point she maxed her thrust, discharged flares and at least one image maker, and dove so low that—Had she crashed?

Two more bogeys disappeared, Duncan cursing at the amount of time each intercept was taking. Several others lost lock, maneuvered, attempted to reengage, but had clearly fallen beyond any feasible engagement envelope. But three continued to bore in on Wedge Three.

Wedge Two reappeared—she had apparently flown so close to a sheer cliff face that the sensors couldn't separate her from it—and attempted to lure the remaining missiles in her direction.

But whether it was a live operator or an intercept algorithm, the remaining missiles' guidance had already dismissed Wedge Two as the prey that got away: they bore down on Wedge Three instead.

That craft attempted to go even lower, following along the bottom of the river valley, skimming above the rolling, froth-filled water not quite ten kilometers west of the FOB. The missiles angled into the narrow intercept aperture which the terrain forced them to adopt. One of them disappeared; Duncan emitted a satisfied grunt.

Another one chased after a brace of flares launched by Wedge Three, evidently discovered its error, tried to come back around, but the space was too tight for it to maneuver adequately: it burrowed into a hillside.

But the third only flinched in the direction of the flares before it bore back in.

"Damn it," breathed Solsohn, "that valley floor is under my arc of fire. I can't hit it."

They watched the missile close the distance, almost touching Wedge Three, then falter: it had chased so long, with so many sharp maneuvers, that it was probably close to burnout.

The missile exploded: a sudden wash of red on the plot. The icon denoting Wedge Three veered sharply, but unsteadily, eastward: toward the FOB.

"Can we get a visual?" Caine shouted.

Dora's voice answered. "Tasking EXHALTED now."

They watched the blue icon wobble like a wounded bird heading for an open field.

The overhead view from EXHALTED snapped on in place of the map just in time to show Wedge Three approach the ground, her turbofans in full counterthrust mode; they were rotated so that the ducted force was actually aiming forward. She slowed mightily, trailing smoke from her rear quarter, brought her nose up—and then ploughed into a loamy stretch of floodplain flanked by clustertree copses. She came to a stop within a long stone's throw of the river, just to the west.

"Get Wedge Three a lascom downlink from the EXHALTED," Riordan ordered. "Dora, check the Hkh'Rkh. Are they responding with air assets?"

"No, but some of their lighter vehicles have just picked up speed. They're heading toward one of the river fords, I think."

Gaudet turned back to him. "Wedge Three on lascom sir."

Caine kept his voice calm. "Chief Friel, report."

Friel sounded genuinely calm: typical Phil. "Last bogey didn't hit us directly, sir, but went for a proximity strike. Caught us with some shrapnel. I had to shut down the port main thruster and the rear portside tilt-nacelle. Damn lucky we were empty."

"Damage to the fuselage?"

"Impossible to say yet, sir. I'm seeing some yellow lights on two of the extendable landing gear, but we weren't going to be using them, anyway."

"True, but I need an immediate assessment of whether she can be made flightworthy, how long it would take, and whether she will retain pressure integrity or leak like a sieve when and if she gets to orbit."

"I'm on it, sir."

"In the meantime, I am going to send a security contingent to you."

"Sir? I'm not sure that's nec—"

"Phil, the Hkh'Rkh know you're down. They are pressing to get to you. It will be a few hours yet, but we're not going to take any chances. They might have scouts well ahead of their vehicles."

"I see. But, sir, this barge isn't going to be flightworthy anytime within the next few hours. So, if they get here before then—"

"Your job is to assess damage and start repairs. My job is to protect you while you do it."

Gaudet, off-channel, turned to look back at Caine. "Which you mean to do how, sir?"

"By advancing our line further west. To the edge of the river."

Solsohn, hearing that, switched to a private channel. "Commodore, if we move to hold the river crossings, we won't have the same advantage of terrain anymore. The Hkh'Rkh will try to roll right over us."

"They'll try, Major," Riordan responded quietly, "but we're not going to let them."

Chapter Thirty-Six

Riordan trotted down the ramp of Wedge One as a slick and a Hind dusted off from the edge of Dante's flightline. The Hind's stubby wings were heavy with munitions.

Paulsen and Rodermund were waiting at the bottom of the ramp. "They're heading toward Wedge Three," Rodermund explained. "With the better part of two squads. Once they've deployed, we'll pull the choppers back to high ground. Any sign of the snorks, and the Hind will chase 'em back while the slick comes in to scoop your people up."

"Good," Riordan answered with a nod, gesturing that the two men should walk with him. "I need two more of the, er, slicks on standby."

"Done," Paulsen answered. "What for? More troops?"

"No, we're going to use Wedges One and Two for feeding units into the defensive line along the river. The slicks will bring Phil Friel some personnel handy at fixing machines."

507

"Submariners," deduced Rodermund. "Who do you need?"

Riordan handed them a printout. "Here's a skill list. Pull folks who have any related aptitudes. They just need to be able to follow some basic mechanical instructions. But quickly, and without hand-holding."

As Rodermund strode off with the hardcopy, Paulsen scratched his ear. "Commodore, I just got word that you're moving our line down to the eastern bank of the river. That almost quintuples the amount of frontage we've got to defend. But if we keep our line on the eastern ridge overlooking the fords, the Hkh'Rkh have to come at us uphill through a narrowing pass. Most of their armored vehicles probably can't make it up that funnel."

Riordan hadn't used a firm tone with Paulsen yet—the man was probably half again as old as he was, after all—but this was the moment that proved that there was a first time for everything. "I am aware of the tactical ramifications, Colonel, but I don't have any choice. One of my primary orders is to ensure that we leave nothing behind. Nothing. But as bad as it would be to leave behind some of your gear, it would be an unmitigated disaster to leave behind a downed military transport painted in CTR colors and with naval tail numbers. That would be all the evidence the Hkh'Rkh, and others, would need to claim that this was all a prelude to a larger invasion."

"Well, damn," Paulsen solemnized. "Things really *haven't* changed much. COs are still trying to carry out impossible orders cut by suits in stateside offices." He glanced back at a platoon of Lost Soldiers waiting to load up on to Wedge One. "You're going to need all of them, aren't you?"

"Pretty much. We've got to cease loading for the extraction, anyway. Our last step would have been to break down the choppers and stow personal combat loads, but we can't do that until we know the shooting is over. I will leave a small security detachment on site, drawn from the *Swordfish* crew. Somebody's got to maintain the perimeter to protect our medical staff. I'm also designating two slicks for medevac, and we'll need to set up a field hospital just inside the cave."

Paulsen nodded. "I'll pass the word." He took two steps up the ramp, started to wave the waiting Lost Soldiers into Wedge One's bay.

Riordan put a restraining hand on Paulsen's arm before he could finish the summons to his men. "You're staying here, too."

Paulsen turned, eyes wide. "The hell I am. Commodore."

"You are." Riordan said it without affect and without emphasis. "*Puller* has got to stay out of the sky, particularly since they know roughly where she is after intercepting those missiles. Major Solsohn is driving the Proxie unit from inside her. Ms. Veriden is managing our C4I from her commo and data suite. We have to keep all the uncommitted helicopters and flight crews sheltered here on standby, along with the submariners you trained to work mission prep. And now there's a hospital to run, as well. So I need a site commander who can keep all those balls in the air, all at once, during high-tempo operations. And most important, it's got to be someone who can and will give orders if the command staff at the front is—incapacitated. So I need you here. And you know it."

Paulsen squinted, looked back toward the yawning cavern of Wedge One's open bay. "I'd keep arguing with you, if I was a ground commander, and if I knew all your technology."

"Yeah, but you aren't and you don't. And you're the right guy for this job, Pat. So get it done."

Paulsen's answering smile was crooked. He walked woodenly back down the ramp. "Godspeed, Commodore. If you want, I can rig the Cayuses as light attack choppers. Doubt you're going to want them drawing fire as observation platforms."

"See? And that's why we need you here. Prep 'em."

Paulsen tossed a salute as he turned to head back toward Dante, saw Arseniy Pugachyov waiting at the head of the next detachment of Lost Soldiers. They traded an even slower salute: somehow the gesture imparted a sense of regretful farewell more than acknowledgement of rank.

Riordan tapped his collarcom. "Chief Gaudet?"

"Yes, sir?"

"You ready for the next load of troops?"

"Ready. I will send Lt. Commander Enderle down to brief them on loading their gear and strapping in."

"Very good. I'll have them standing by." He tapped off the line, walked down the ramp. "Lieutenant Pugachyov, have your men stand ready to board Wedge One."

Riordan watched Wedge One lumber aloft through the unshielded windows of *Puller*'s bridge. Surrounded by a set of dynamically reconfigurable screens customized to allow oversight of both communications and computing, Dora Veriden was emitting a steady stream of subvocal curses. In three different languages.

"Dare I ask how it's going?" Caine wondered aloud.

"You just did. And the answer is: shitty."

"Well, you seem to have the Know-It-All working pretty well."

"Yeah, but only because I'm riding it bareback. Exceptions keep popping up. And I have to troubleshoot them in real time. Hey, Karam; get me more coffee."

"I hear and obey," drawled the Flight Officer. Who smiled and left his acceleration couch, but none too quickly.

"Well," Riordan finished, "I'm glad we've got you to run it."

"Sleeman would be better," Dora countered testily. "And I should be in the field. We're going to be pretty heavily outnumbered, according to what the sensors are showing."

"I'd say five to one. At least," Riordan agreed.

"*Mierde*, you sound awfully calm."

"I've become an accomplished actor."

Dora's responding grunt might have been her equivalent of a chuckle. "Well, at least you're not a complete disaster as a commander." She glanced at the holoplot. "I notice you've kept some units on the ridge overlooking the river."

Riordan nodded. "Our heavy weapons. Forward MISLS positions and MULTIs. The MULTIs are at the edge of their optimum engagement range, but from that vantage point, they can cover all the fords, as well as the narrows where the Hkh'Rkh might try to swim their APCs across. I'm keeping the attack choppers a klick further back, behind the ridgeline."

Dora smiled. "Did you just call the helicopters 'choppers'?"

Riordan started, grinned sheepishly. "I did. I think I've been spending too much time with Paulsen and Rodermund."

"A minute with them is an eternity," Dora muttered. Her patience for regular military types had not improved in the time Caine had known her, showed no sign that it would ever do so. *Speaking of which*—"Is Major Solsohn in the gunnery bubble?"

"Far as I know. Why?"

"I need to update him. If things don't go our way, we're not going to be able to meet all our objectives."

"You mean getting ourselves, the Lost Soldiers, and all their gear off the planet? Hell," she wondered in a richly facetious tone, "how hard could it be?"

"Yeah, and which of those objectives do we ditch if the price of success means starting the war we're trying to prevent?" Riordan headed toward the iris valve that led off the bridge, stopped, turned back. "You're doing a great job here, Dora."

"I know. So let me get back to it. Uh, sir." She looked up. "Don't worry: when there's non-family around, I'll be more official."

Riordan smiled, answered, "That's all I ask," and ducked out under the upper rim of the hatch coaming.

Once in the corridor, her comment about speaking more respectfully when there was "non-family around" almost caused him to break stride: *she's the most incorrigible person on this team, but she's also the one who most frequently refers to us as a "family."* Caine wondered what that might indicate about the inner life of the outwardly scratchy and scrappy Pandora Veriden, but didn't have time to pursue that line of thinking. He only had fifteen minutes before Wedge One returned to ferry him, and another load of troops, back to the lines.

Sitting alongside Chief Gaudet in Wedge One's co-pilot's seat, Riordan watched the setting sun rapidly shift from deep orange to vermillion as they neared the ridgeline that overlooked the river. The comm alert tone buzzed in his helmet: the identifier code was Melissa Sleeman's. He opened the line, double-checked the encryption protocol. "Riordan."

"Commodore, I have some interesting findings to report."

"Excellent, but you can save them until you get back to Dante." Sleeman did not reply. "Doctor?" Caine realized with a pulse of dread that he did not hear the incessant thrumming of rotors in the background.

"Sir," Sleeman explained, "we are not returning to Dante this evening."

Holding his temper in check—*damn; I knew this was a bad idea*—Riordan calmly asked, "Please explain, Doctor."

"Yes, sir. Conducting a general survey took longer than expected. It appears that the irregular ground we noted during planetfall was more than just impact sequelae. There are a score of excavation sites as well, most of them partially or fully filled in.

"Assessing them took time, and I was distracted by what we started finding in some of the deeper pits. By the time I returned to the helicopters, I learned that one of them had developed an ignition problem. There had been a dispute between the two flight officers whether they should attempt a repair."

"Why didn't they contact you?"

"The radios couldn't reach us at the bottom of the pits. So they sent a runner. He fell into a sinkhole—the ground here is extremely porous—and they had to pull him out. By that time, we had come back into radio contact and I ordered them to make repairs."

Riordan heard Sleeman swallow. "Sir, this is my fault. The senior flight officer warned me that the repairs might take too long, might strand us here overnight. He was right. I should have risked flying with the malfunction."

"No, Doctor, you did the right thing." *It was I who made the crucial mistake: letting you go there in the first place.* "If the malfunction is in the electrical systems, you could have a cascading failure while airborne. In which case you'd be lucky to survive. On the other hand, if the approaching Hkh'Rkh are aware of you, they haven't sent any units your way."

"How can you be sure, sir?"

"They don't seem to be aware of the EXHALTEDs Wedge Two deployed, so they're not hiding their movement. What's the repair status of the helicopter?"

"It's just about fixed, sir. There's some more work to be done, but I agree with the security officer that it's better for us to observe light- and noise-discipline now and finish in the morning, rather than risk attracting the attention of Hkh'Rkh scouts or sensors."

"I agree, Doctor. If you lay low tonight and remain unnoticed, an extra hour or two tomorrow at the site tomorrow morning should not significantly increase the chances that they'll detect you. Use radio squelch to update us, and voice communication when you have commenced your return."

"Yes, sir. And staying here overnight also gives me time to collect a few more samples from the most interesting of the pits we found."

Riordan heard the hanging tone and the edge of eagerness behind it. "What's piqued your interest, Doctor?"

Sleeman's voice changed instantly: her excited gush of information was so unrelenting that Caine found it difficult to keep up. "Firstly, our hypothesis was correct: this is not a typical impact site. The ground pattern is all wrong. Whatever came in hit at an abnormally shallow angle. Secondary impactors shook loose, cutting their own grooves as they decelerated, mostly on trajectories that angled away from the center of mass. So although it's faint, the topography clearly shows a shallow trench cut by a massive object, with secondary rills radiating outward from the primary impact point. Those rills are dispersed along a fairly narrow arc of deviation: not more than fifteen degrees from the main axis.

"But the really interesting spoor is in the pits, particularly the partially filled ones. Metal splinters, not even significantly deformed by heat. I think there may be traces of some composites as well."

Riordan managed to get in a question when she finally gasped for air. "I notice you used the term composites, not compounds."

Sleeman sounded pleased. "Yes, precisely. Not naturally occurring materials. It's all very preliminary of course. I won't be able to be sure of any of this until I get back to my—well, my 'lab,'"—her tone dripped disparagement—"on *Puller*. But I've never heard of residue like this being left by a meteor."

"Makes you wonder what's at the bottom of the filled pits."

"My thought exactly, sir. Because it is very clear that these were filled in *after* having been left empty for some time. There's also no evidence of any significant burst of heat in the area, and I don't see any major chronological variation amongst the local growth, even ranging out to thirty kilometers."

Riordan watched the sun meet the ridgeline just in front of them. "So whatever hit failed to generate much of a shockwave or a heat pulse: not enough to burn off the surrounding flora and necessitate a wave of new growth."

"Correct. I've found some evidence of superheating on small stones in the pits and along the main trenchline, but nothing more than you'd expect from a plane or transatmospheric shuttle crash."

"And the buildings?"

"Not built as habitations, sir. More like low hangars or warehouses. Wide bay doors. Each building shows modest ground compression along a lengthwise access lane. Typical of the ground effects caused by forklifts and trucks in storage structures."

"Comfort facilities?"

"Almost none. I've seen what may have been a few privies, but if so, they were field expedients. There isn't enough left of the buildings to tell if they were wired for electricity, but if so, it was very minimal. There's no plumbing or water supply of any sort."

"So, a semi-permanent facility which can house and protect a lot of objects, but not good for much else."

"Yes, sir. Like the forensics facilities we erect for the extended investigation of a crash site. Personnel live in portable housing, with portable facilities. Everything is packed up when it's over."

"Yes, Doctor, but the buildings we saw—these 'warehouses,' or maybe forensic hangars—look pretty substantial."

"They were: they have poured foundations. So I agree with what you are implying: even though the personnel facilities may have been portable, whoever worked this site did so for an extended period of time—far longer than typical crash investigators. It is more like—well, an archaeological dig."

"Yes, it seems that way. I'll be interested to hear your final report, but for now, Doctor, you need to hunker down for the night. Is there any cover near by?"

"Actually, there is. The bottom of one of the pits has a shaft—like an outsized concrete culvert—running about fifty meters into the ground at a twenty-degree angle. There's no sign of what they used it for, but they filled it in at the bottom, also."

"Probably access for smaller digging machines."

"Logical, Commodore. We're going dark now."

"We'll speak again in the morning. Riordan out."

Donna Gaudet looked over from the pilot's position. "Never a dull moment here, eh, Commodore?"

"Haven't experienced one yet, Chief Gaudet. Now, let's get this last detachment down and into cover before we lose the last of the light."

Chapter Thirty-Seven

Riordan was finishing a piece of canned pound cake when he heard a knock outside the hatch of his temporary refuge: one of the transport's four triple-occupancy bunkrooms. "Come."

The hatch opened; Bannor Rulaine leaned in. "Sampling the antique food, I see."

"Yeah." Caine waved toward the bottom bunk, scooting his knees close against the fresher's sliding door so his friend could slip past to take the offered seat. "Have you tried it?"

Rulaine stared at the collection of cans and wrappers that were the remains of Riordan's meal. "I'm not a masochist," the major replied with great, possibly exaggerated, gravity.

Caine smiled, knew from the response that Bannor had not only tried it but had probably been living on it. In a show of solidarity and sympathy (and in some cases, curiosity) most of *Puller*'s crew and the Cold Guard had swapped rations with the Lost Soldiers.

518

Who had, in turn, raved about the quality of the food from the future, and pledged to die in place of their rescuers as gratitude for the self-heating entrees that were on a par with passable diner fare. Riordan dusted crumbs off his fingers. "If we could learn how this food—how *all* these supplies—were preserved for so damned long, the terms 'spoilage' and 'expiration date' would become archaic. And there's something else I don't understand about these meals: their names."

"What? C-rations?"

"Yeah. Or c-rats, as the Lost Soldiers call them."

"What's so odd about that?"

Riordan tossed him the packaging. "Because that's not what they're labeled. See? 'MCI: meal, combat, individual.'"

Rulaine studied the tan box with the plain black lettering. "Ah, well. What's in a name?"

"I'm not taking the Shakespearean bait, Bannor."

"Pity."

"Just come to visit?"

"Mostly. Decided to bring you the day's last report in person. Might not be much time for it come tomorrow."

Riordan stared down at the empty cans, was silent for several seconds. "I don't think we're going to get out of this without more shooting. Lots of it."

"Certainly looks that way. It would have been uncertain under the best of circumstances. But with Wedge Three's damage more extensive than we hoped—" Rulaine shook his head. "It's out of our hands."

Riordan sighed, wondered if it was the inevitability of the combat or the food which made his stomach seem to turn sideways; maybe both. "How's the line looking?"

"Good as can be expected. The Hkh'Rkh aren't big fans of water, and there are only three points along the river where they can cross on foot. Even at those points, the river is fast, rough, and deep: they'd get mauled by us. Of course, they could get their APCs across easily, so, we have quadrotors and light detachments covering the fords. And I've reserved the Cayuses as fast response platforms, so we can get a small fire brigade to help hold any of the fords or any place else along the line. Or to drop off a laser designator to call in a few MISLS."

Riordan shook his head. "We can't use the MISLS to support the line: we don't have enough. The burden of defending the fords is going to be on the MULTIs and their overhead-engagement munitions. We have to reserve our MISLS for quick, decisive intervention where we don't have other, or enough, assets."

Rulaine nodded. "I'll make the change, and pull all the MISLS back behind the ridgeline. I've stationed large, mixed squads at each ford, ready to hit the Hkh'Rkh when they're at midcourse. We're reserving the Cold Guard for laser designation of vehicles and countersniper work. The EXHALTEDs have given us clean topographical data, so our sightlines are optimized. But our fighting positions are still lousy."

"You need more time?"

Rulaine shook his head. "No, we need more tools. The Lost Soldiers' abductors didn't bother to provide them with any, so we've had to work with what nature has given us: fallen trees, rock formations, every rise and hump in the terrain. Which means we're light on genuine cover, particularly overhead. I've got our spotters and snipers watching for enemy drones or

ROVs. If they have any, they'll probably send them across the river tonight, trying to plot our positions for barrages."

Riordan nodded. "If they've brought mobile artillery, we're going to have to hit them with counterbattery fire ASAP. That's why we have to keep the MISLS in reserve."

"Prudent. Also, if they do get any quadrotors into range tonight, or put scouts close enough for direct observation, we'll need to show them that we own the airwaves: jam them, keep them from relaying grid coordinates."

Riordan rubbed a finger along his upper lip. "Even undirected fire could cut lots of our people to ribbons. Particularly the submariners; they don't have the training for this kind of engagement."

Rulaine nodded. "That's why I've assigned most of them as loaders for the MULTIs on the ridge and the machine guns we dug in along the river. But we need some of those submariners in the line: we've got too much frontage to cover. They may not do a whole lot of damage with those submachine guns at long range, but if they make the Hkh'Rkh duck or slow down, that will make the real infantry's job a lot easier."

Riordan nodded. "That 'real infantry' is going to be pretty busy. If it weren't for our antique air mobility, I still think the approaching horde would be able to swarm us."

Bannor shrugged. "Those attack helicopters will help keep them at bay so long as we keep them below the treeline until we need them for pop-up fire missions."

"Medevac ready?"

"Set for relay to both the aid station at the FOB

and to the surgery at Dante, depending upon severity. Relax, Caine; we've done everything we can."

Riordan nodded. But doing everything one could did not bring much relief. Indonesia and Disparity had taught him that no matter how good a plan is, it never survives first contact with reality. "I'll be glad when this is over."

Bannor shrugged. "We all will." He paused. "This is your first conventional command, isn't it?"

"Yep. Insurgencies and unexpected skirmishes are pretty much about improvisation, limited choices, and leading from the front. This—?" He waved a hand at the world beyond the hull. "There are a lot of choices, a lot of moving parts, a lot of delegation of authority and planning: a lot that can go wrong."

Bannor actually smiled. "Or you may be overthinking this."

Riordan couldn't find any humor in the situation. "I'm not sure it's possible to overthink a situation in which your orders are going to get people killed."

"Fair enough. But so far, you've gotten a whole lot fewer killed than most, given the battles you've been in."

"Bannor, the only truly acceptable number of casualties is zero."

"Said the promising new CO. Granted: that determination to protect your troops is part of what makes a good officer. But only so long as it doesn't paralyze you. You know, of course, that no plan—"

"—survives first contact with reality. I know the axiom; I just mentally recited it to myself. And it's too damned true. But by going over the details again and again—well, it's a bit like martial arts. When you're surprised, you fight from muscle memory, from the

training and the moves that you've drilled again and
again and again. So that when the time comes, the
right response doesn't require thought. And that might
buy you enough time to grab the back initiative." He
glanced up at Bannor, who was still smiling. Sort of.
"You've done this most of your adult life."

"Damn near."

"So how do you deal with the worry?"

Rulaine leaned back. "I've seen all sorts of people deal
with eve-of-battle jitters in all sorts of ways. A lot try to
pump themselves up into a berserker frenzy. Oorah and
death unto everything—maybe even themselves—until
they're deaf and hoarse with the screaming of it. I've
seen some people meditate; I've seen some people write
letters that they never mean to send. I've seen dozens of
whacky rituals and there are probably hundreds more I
haven't seen. What you're doing isn't too unusual, but I
have seen it derail some otherwise good officers. Once
the shooting starts, they try to stick to their grand plan
even when it's broken. That's how they get jammed up.

"But if all the planning doesn't reduce your ability
to respond, adapt, and innovate, then you're probably
doing the best thing you can right now. Except it's even
better if you can get some rack time, too."

Caine nodded. "Yeah, that's the hardest part. Figuring
out when, and how, to stop trying to think through all
the angles." The partial smile had left Bannor's face.
"How do you do it—get sleep, that is?"

The smile came back, but crooked. "I didn't say I
do. I say it's best if you can. 'Night, Caine."

Caine suspected that the smile that grew on his
face was a match for the one with which his friend
departed.

Chapter Thirty-Eight

Caine was half out of bed, covered in cold sweat and with one hand outstretched for his CoBro eight-millimeter, before he realized that the sound that had awakened him—a banging on the bunkroom's hatch—was a summons, not an attack.

As his hand touched the pistol grip of the unfamiliar and unusually heavy Thompson, he remembered that his CoBro was gone, consigned to the hands of Rich Hailey, who had been one of the dozen MACV-SOG and Special Forces Lost Soldiers who'd quickly adapted to all the bells and whistles of modern weapons. And since Riordan was supposed remain at the forward HQ, not the front itself, the CoBro couldn't stay with him. It had to go where it would do the most good.

Lieutenant Commander Martin Enderle's voice was thick and his English more accented as he called through the closed hatch. "Commodore, I regret to disturb you, but the matter is urgent."

Riordan, who'd been sleeping in his duty suit,

reached over, opened the hatch, peeled down the top of the suit to reinsert the ballistic liner. "Brief me, Martin. Where have the Hkh'Rkh engaged us?"

Enderle half-entered, looked slightly disheveled; he'd probably nodded off while manning the comms. "They have not engaged us, sir." He paused. "At least, not as you mean."

Riordan noted the quizzical tone with which Martin completed his comment, glanced at the time: 0442 hours local. "Lieutenant Commander, you just cut my rack time by half an hour. Have a better reason than a riddle."

Enderle snapped straight, nodded sharply. "Yes, sir! I do, sir! North ford combat group, Dugout One, reports contact with a single Hkh'Rkh. Speaking English and asking for you by name, Commodore."

Riordan rose so fast that he didn't quite clear the upper bunk; his head struck its frame with a dull thump. The considerable pain felt distant. "How did this Hkh'Rkh contact us? Where is he now? He has to be protected at all costs."

"Yes, sir. The Hkh'Rkh came down the river, riding a pair of tree trunks that were lashed together. He came ashore and hailed the men at Dugout One. He remains in their custody."

"Did he give a name?"

"If so, Sergeant de los Reyes did not relay it."

Riordan resisted the impulse to send a helicopter, even though it was dark. "Relay the following to Captain Robin, north ford CO. The Hkh'Rkh is to be escorted under heavy guard at least two hundred meters to the rear, and then brought to the nearest overland access point to await pickup." He tore a sheet of paper from a Lost Soldier clipboard—*damned handy having so many of these around*—and commenced writing. "You will personally go to the vehicle pool, get a driver, two security, and requisition one of the two Hkh'Rkh scout cars." He handed Martin the sheet. "You will then rendezvous with the Hkh'Rkh's escort detachment and bring him back here, post haste. You are not to stop for anything or anyone. You are to treat the Hkh'Rkh as our guest, not our prisoner."

"Our guest? Why, sir?"

"Because, unless I am very much mistaken, he is a friend of mine. Now get going."

BD+56 2966 was edging over the horizon when the Hkh'Rkh scout car, its controls modified so that humans could drive it, crested the ridgeline and swerved down the back side, dust pluming up from its tires. Riordan stood away from the interactive map that showed the enemy's overnight activity, compiled from the EXHALTEDs and the creepers that they'd seeded over on the western side of the river thirty-six hours earlier.

The car slowed, the Hkh'Rkh conspicuously larger than the other passengers. He remained in the vehicle's rear jump seat until all the humans had exited, three keeping Thompsons pointed in his general direction. Riordan approached and Enderle waved the Hkh'Rkh out of the scout car. But Caine found himself wondering, *Is that Yaargraukh? How can I be sure?*

It was, he had discovered, difficult to discern distinctions in the various features of exosapient species. Individuals were relatively easy to keep separate when they were present in a group: variations in height, coloration, build, even vocal sounds, were immediate and self-evident. But when memory alone became the repository for the identifying characteristics of an exosapient, Riordan became keenly aware of how limited his perception was, having only sporadic contact with each species. No doubt Hkh'Rkh would effortlessly note and recall differences in each others' spiky tufted crests, in the distribution of their partial pelt, shape of neck and head, just the way a human would effortlessly recall a new acquaintance's hair and eye color, complexion, and other physical characteristics.

So he peered closely at the Hkh'Rkh—who was markedly small for a male—before he ventured, "Yaargraukh?"

"It is I, Caine Riordan. I am most gratified to see you again, although I wish it was under different circumstances." Yaargraukh was still dripping wet.

Riordan checked his first reflex: to invite the Hkh'Rkh into Wedge One, where he had set up his HQ and could readily display the entire salient in greater comfort. "I'd offer you a place to dry off and be at your ease, but I think my officers and troops would question my sanity if I was too hasty in my confidence and courtesies. They don't know our prior relationship."

"They would be correct in their concern, of course. After all, the last time we saw each other, we were enemies. Or rather, the powers which we serve were. The only thing that has changed since then is that I am now in your custody, not you in mine."

"But as I did when I returned to Jakarta, you have come here voluntarily. And no doubt, over the objections of your superiors."

Yaargraukh made the hoarse huffing noise that was a Hkh'Rkh laugh. "You have a gift for understatement.

Their objections made my journey here quite interesting. And uncertain."

Riordan was not sure he had understood his friend's implication. "Are you saying your superiors attempted to assassinate you before you could reach us?"

"Yes. I was deemed highly suspect. Also, seniority here on Turkh'saar is more rooted in tradition than rank. So my presence was not convenient to those in authority."

Riordan nodded. "Old Family local government?"

Yaargraukh's pony-neck bobbed once. "Whose leader is determined to destroy you, even though I attempted to demonstrate that the raiders who have now joined your ranks"—he glanced back at his guards—"were incapable of being a contemporary human raiding force."

Riordan looked at the icons on the electronic battlemap; a tide of red ones were approaching his thin, river-following crust of blue ones. "And there is no chance that he will agree to parley? Even if reparations are offered?" Bannor approached from the direction of Wedge Two.

"Reparations are acceptable when the losses are strictly military. When the losses include what you would call civilians, they become an insult."

"Because your protection of the Unhonored must remain absolute. They must be avenged. To take compensation for their deaths would suggest that their lives are commodities."

"That is how it would be seen, yes."

Riordan not only understood the internal logic of that code, but had more than a little sympathy for it. "I presume they would not be appeased by learning that the 'raiders' destroyed their initial leaders, who enslaved them and compelled them to kill your people?"

Yaargraukh studied Caine carefully. "So. I had suspected this. It *was* the Germans, the Nazis, who set the pattern of raiding. And brutality."

Bannor almost never started in surprise. He did now. "How the hell did you learn that?"

The Hkh'Rkh examined the new human carefully. "Deduction."

Bannor brought up his weapon slightly. "Or do you have hidden bugs, snoopers, seeded among us?"

"No. We do not rely heavily on such sensors, and have none here on Turkh'saar. I deduced the presence, and downfall, of the Nazis, from helmet footage and postcombat forensics."

Bannor looked still more amazed—possibly as much by the eloquent and composed response as its content. "Explain."

Yaargraukh did so. Riordan intuited that they were getting the tips of the investigatory icebergs only. But all the pieces fit.

At the end, Bannor glanced at Riordan. "So this is the one you met? The, uh, Advocate of the Unhonored?"

"Yes, this is Yaargraukh: my friend." Caine answered slowly, determined that each word should be heard in the full context of its meaning. "He is a being of great Honor." The small ring of humans who'd been gathering remained quiet, but several exchanged looks that were partly surprise, partly doubt. Riordan paid no attention to them. "Yaargraukh, in coming here, I perceive that you have made yourself an outlaw, if you remain on this world. And if you are caught, it seems sure that your life would be forfeit."

For the first time, Yaargraukh's black-marble eyes shifted away, and his pony-neck oscillated slightly: a Hkh'Rkh shrug. "That is a matter of no consequence."

"It is to me. And I would not be worthy of the Honor you have been bold enough to claim for me in the past if I ignored this matter. So I would ask that you do me the honor of accepting our offer of asylum, for as long as we are upon Turkh'saar to provide it."

Yaargraukh's eyes disappeared beneath the bony ridges that protected them, then reemerged: the "blink" indicated the depth of his surprise. "You do me much Honor," he began, "but—"

And for the first time in Riordan's experience, the Hkh'Rkh paused as if undecided. *Something's wrong: if Yaargraukh wasn't fully resolved to asylum with us, he'd reject it outright, albeit politely. But he's hesitating, he's unsure. There must be a deeper conflict of honor*—And then Caine knew: "There are others whose safety has been compromised by your actions."

Yaargraukh's pony-nod was small, grudging. "It is as you say. Shortly after dispatching my pursuers, I discovered that I had other watchers: distant relatives from the Fringelands. Among them are the last of my Moiety who remain on Turkh'saar. They had already hidden the body of the first pursuer I killed, then brought me food for my further journey. And before that, they had made their intents to assist me known to the New Family Warriors who had slipped away from Voice Jrekhalkar's Flag to bring news of the dishonorable path the Old Family scions had taken. By assisting me, and doing so openly, they joined their fate to mine."

"Then I extend asylum to them as well."

Bannor stepped forward. "Caine . . . Commodore, granted: you know this Hkh'Rkh and he's proven himself to you—but these others? We can't take the risk of—"

Riordan interrupted Rulaine: he had not taken his eyes from Yaargraukh. "My friend, do you vouch for your companions' Honor with your own?"

"I do. And they have no love for the Old Families."

Bannor stared. "Enough to go to war against them on our behalf?"

"You misperceive, comrade of Caine Riordan. They would not be fighting for you. They would be avenging their relatives, many of whom perished in the hard life to which they have been consigned in the Fringelands. The inequities our people face on our Homeworld are magnified a hundredfold here. If by fighting Jrekhalkar, they can break the callous tyranny of the Old Families here on Turkh'saar, they will now do so. They have crossed that line and have claimed themselves Hearthless, even as I now am.

"But you are wise and prudent, comrade of Riordan. So if you would put full trust in my companions, charge me with their direct oversight. We might yet be useful to you, even if we are not directly in combat with our own kind. Your northern flank is all but undefended and unpatrolled. You rightly believe that the River Kakaagsukh cannot be forded further upstream and that it is most unlikely that any of the approaching force could swing further north in time. But such a thing is only unlikely, not impossible. With your observers to monitor us, I propose to take my brethren north to watch for threats from that direction. Or I submit myself to you for confinement, as a prisoner. My brethren will follow me into captivity. The choice is yours."

Bannor shrugged, leaned toward Caine. "We could call his bluff. Put them all in the brig for a few hours. If they don't resist, then—"

"Then we will have insulted willing allies who have come to us without preconditions or expectations, Major." Riordan hated bluntly rejecting what would normally be a prudent course of action, but Bannor did not understand the cultural dynamic at work— not yet, anyway. "I not only trust Yaargraukh's word implicitly, I trust his judgment. If he had any doubt about his companions, he would not allow them to be included in our offer of asylum, much less as part of our forces for the duration of this conflict. I am also relatively sure from his remarks that he knew them all personally during his youth on Turkh'saar."

Yaargraukh lowered his head once, deeply. "It is as Caine Riordan says. I know them all, although two were whelplings, still playing 'coursers and catchers,' when I departed to commence my studies on Rkh'yaa. And now, they are the last of their families still here, the rest having left or perished from the rigors of their life on the Fringelands."

Bannor shrugged. "Understood." He glanced at Riordan. "But let me pick the force that will be monitoring them. Okay, sir?"

Riordan nodded. "With one proviso. I'm putting Lieutenant Commander Enderle in charge of that detachment."

Martin, who had been a close observer of the exchange thus far, started upright. "Sir? Am I not needed as your adjutant?"

"You are, Martin: you've picked up more about our communications and computers than any other Lost Soldier. But now you've demonstrated an even more rare talent: interacting with an exosapient without letting xenophobia or fear cloud your judgment."

"Sir, with all respect, I simply fetched him in a scout car."

"Yes, and you'd be surprised how many people couldn't even manage that. What do you think, Yaargraukh? You've observed plenty of humans. What is your assessment of Lieutenant Commander Enderle?"

The Hkh'Rkh's black eyes shifted sideways, studying the young Czech/Polish submariner. "He is extremely observant. He is somewhat talkative, but he is not excitable. Indeed, as a situation grows more serious, he grows more quiet. And his demeanor during our brief interactions was colored by curiosity, not fear or repugnance. Although I am no expert in human psychology or selection of command staff, he seems an apt liaison."

"How do we contact your companions?"

"I have witnessed your raiders' use of smoke. Do you still have red, purple, or yellow?"

Riordan glanced at Bannor. Who glanced at Martin. Who nodded.

"Excellent," Yaargraukh said. He walked toward the table; the security detachment's Thompsons came up. Riordan aimed a hard stare at them in response. The muzzles lowered.

Yaargraukh pointed at the electronic map. "Activate one purple smoke in this grid block. Precisely two hundred seconds later, follow it with yellow smoke." He moved his claw tip slightly more to the east and north. "My followers will approach in this region. They will be armed, but will be moving with weapons slung. They will wait for me to arrive before they cooperate with humans."

Riordan nodded, turned to Bannor. "Good thing the Cayuses are still uncommitted. Pass the word back to dismount their armaments, spin one up, and get Yaargraukh up to these coordinates as soon as we're done here."

Bannor nodded. "And how soon will that be?"

Riordan turned back toward Yaargraukh. "That depends upon how much our guest is comfortable telling us about the situation on the other side of the lines."

The Hkh'Rkh emitted a long, phlegm-burbling sigh. "This is a point of difference in our cultures, Caine Riordan. In most of your traditions, a change of allegiance is complete, and carries no implicit or explicit restrictions. You commit not only your fortunes, but all your information, to your new allies. Among us, it is different. What I have learned in Jrekhalkar's camp and command tent, I learned only because I was in his service. Among us, changing alliances is inevitable, but to share what was given as privileged information is considered to be among the most dishonorable of acts."

"Must make it hard on your spies," Bannor quipped.

Yaargraukh stared at him. "Their lives are usually short. They are universally despised."

Bannor nodded, evidently accepting that his humor had fallen upon infertile ground. "So, no intel."

Yaargraukh tilted his head slightly. "No specific data that were imparted to me in confidence," he corrected.

"I may, however speak in generalities about my own observations and activities while in Jrekhalkar's service."

Even in the alien voice, Riordan heard the leading tone. "So, in general, what was your role with the local military?"

"Firstly, Turkh'saar only has a poorly equipped militia. My role was as an ostensible second-in-command, but relegated to training. Which was brief and intensive."

"How brief?"

"Two days. As we travelled."

Riordan constructed a mental cause-effect timeline. "So when we appeared overhead, your leaders decided to start hitting back harder."

"Your arrival accelerated a process that had begun due to other events, the most pivotal of which was a large attack upon a town known as Ylogh. I was very nearly captured there, and my adjutant was taken prisoner. Do you have any news of him, by the way?"

Riordan nodded. "We found him caged in the cave complex back at the FOB." He gestured eastward, down the back slope of the ridgeline. Helicopters of various marks waited there, munitions, water, and other supplies stacked in readiness. Medevac crews—mostly submariners—sat on the crates, waiting just beyond the drooping rotors. "We only had time for a few quick questions. The 'raiders' left him there, to show that humans are not mindless savages, that we do not kill indiscriminately."

Yaargraukh was frowning. "When I departed Jrekhalkar's camp, either he had not reached us, or knowledge of his return had been kept to an inner circle. Did he know that your raiders were not, in fact, raiders?"

"He suspected it, and our conversation might have

confirmed that suspicion for him. But we had less than three minutes together. He convinced me to leave him behind, tranqed, so that your forces would not suspect that we had had contact."

Yaargraukh's neck tremored slightly. "He was wise to do so. I hope he has reached Jrekhalkar's camp and realized that he would only endanger himself if he asserted that you were here to remove the raiders, rather than reinforce them."

"If he didn't share that opinion, then how can he change Jrekhalkar's actions?"

"Gradually and indirectly. You do not understand, Caine Riordan: Jrekhalkar is motivated as much by personal fears and needs as by his resolve to defend Turkh'saar. He and his recently deceased father constructed a narrative that explains the presence of the raiders and keeps the colony united in its action against you. So now Jrekhalkar cannot undo the former without undoing the latter—and he cannot afford that. His life and family fortunes would eventually be forfeit to a Challenger unless he shows himself to be a decisive and successful leader now. As this colony's savior, he would be beyond ready Challenge, and would have the respect and loyalty of the advisors who could help him navigate the subtler currents of the local clan politics."

"So," sighed Rulaine, "we're pretty much screwed."

Yaargraukh's black eyes stared. "I do not understand your expression—'screwed?' This is a carpentry metaphor?"

Bannor almost smiled. "Not exactly."

"Not at all," Riordan amended. "Let's return to the questions you may answer. I'm guessing all the armored vehicles we see heading toward us were not part of your codominium agreement with the Arat Kur in this system."

"Your deduction is correct, Caine Riordan, and it further explains why Jrekhalkar cannot afford to fail. The only outcome which will vindicate his clan's, and the Patrijuridicate's, violation of the codominium agreement will be the successful repulse of invaders. It is illogical, but in the thinking of my people, victory here will be the only significant rebuttal to Arat Kur accusations of oath-breaking. The violation will retroactively be deemed essential, since it will have proven to be the indispensable means for achieving victory."

Riordan allowed himself a lopsided, ironic smile. "Your people aren't alone in that kind of thinking."

"Indeed. I have seen similar trends in human statecraft. There is a motto I recall: might makes right. It articulates much the same kind of illogic."

"It certainly does. And I suspect the hardest violation to explain will be the missiles."

Yaargraukh's eyes retracted slightly, slowly: he was becoming cautious. "It will. But I suspect that is a more tangled matter. Certainly more tangled than we might productively discuss here."

"But later?"

Yaargraukh gave two quick, full-length nods. "Most assuredly."

"And the nature of the training you provided: artillery and the tactics of maneuver? I presume that since the militia had never had much access to such systems, they did not have much experience with it."

"You are correct."

"And I presume you were also teaching them how to operate without radio coordination?"

Yaargraukh stopped, his eyes protruding slightly. "You deduced this from examining our vehicles' rudimentary communication suites?"

Riordan shrugged. "That helped, but postwar technical intelligence gave us a pretty good look at your comm systems. Your dirtside formations don't rely much on lascom, except at headquarters level. Our assessment of your operational doctrine is that you find widespread lascom too limiting, too constraining due to the prerequisite infrastructure." Enderle looked lost. Caine aimed his explication at the young Czech expatriate. "All the redundancy required, all the coordination, all the drones and renetworking to adapt to battlefield losses: it's a highly dynamic and complex asset management matrix." He turned his focus back upon Yaargraukh. "All of that delicate support infrastructure is not in keeping with your operational emphasis on simplicity and tempo. So it's logical you're willing to rely on radio wherever you can. Just talk into a microphone and go. But you can't rely on that working against us. Which is why your vehicles are not as spread out as they might be. Your crews are relying on hand signals and other non-laser line-of-sight communications. Not only are our jamming and hacking strong, but we have all your codes from the war. So I'm guessing that you gave the local militia simple, squelch-break radio disciplines and other homegrown codes which, if used sparingly, we might not break in time because they are operation-specific."

Yaargraukh nodded. "They are what you call 'burner codes,' if I am not mistaken."

"They are." Riordan turned to Bannor. "That confirms most of our hypotheses, Major. But Jrekhalkar will presume that Yaargraukh has reached us, so he'll junk the burner codes, too. However, that means the Hkh'Rkh have no choice but to keep their artillery batteries in fairly close formation if they are going to coordinate their fires upon us. And they won't be sending their fire orders by radio: we'd pick apart a grid coordinate cypher in minutes. So they'll try to use spotters with scout cars, even runners, to get occasional messages to the batteries in the rear. So their fire correction is going to be slow or nonexistent. Instead, they are likely to range in select targets or map features and then hold fire until it's needed."

"It sounds like the First World War," Bannor muttered. "So we should be able to predict where they plan on hitting us hardest just by watching their ranging fire."

Riordan shrugged. "Maybe, but I'm guessing that Yaargraukh"—he turned and nodded respectfully to his friend—"thought of that and advised them to reserve several tubes just to walk fires up and down the line, thereby obscuring the actual ranging fires within a larger number of strikes which they are conducting solely to mislead us."

Bannor glanced at Yaargraukh. Whose neck oscillated lazily: another shrug, this one almost human in its overtones of histrionic ingenuousness.

In the distance, a fast clatter of light rotors began up-dopplering. Riordan looked back toward the FOB, saw a Cayuse approaching. "Looks like our time is almost up, Yaargraukh." He turned, smiled at the hulking Hkh'Rkh. "Our conversations are always being cut short, it seems."

Yaargraukh's tongue whipped out briefly: a grin. "Yes. It has begun to feel like a law of nature." He turned to watch as the Cayuse set down only thirty yards away. It hardly looked big enough for the Hkh'Rkh to be able to sit in the passenger seat.

When the dust had settled, Riordan put his fist to his sternum and bowed, Hkh'Rkh fashion. "Honor, Yaargraukh."

Who returned the gesture with a deeper, longer bow. "Honor, Caine Riordan. I wish you success and swift victory—so swift that few of either of our species need pay a Warrior's final price."

"Me, too," Riordan agreed as his friend squeezed himself into the cockpit bubble of the Cayuse.

But I doubt it's going to turn out that way.

Chapter Thirty-Nine

Caine and Bannor watched the Cayuse swing north, staying beneath the backslope lip of the ridgeline. The Special Forces major glanced at the electronic map. "I was coming over to update you. The Hkh'Rkh only sent three drones across the river last night. Civilian models. Our snipers put them down before they got fifty meters inland. If that's an honest measure of what they have in their remote sensing golfbag, then Yaargraukh's report on them is accurate; they are definitely minor league."

"You can trust him, Bannor. Whatever he's not sharing, it's because he's Honor-bound not to."

Rulaine nodded. "Fair enough—particularly since our other observations bear out what he either confirmed or revealed. There are scores of enemy scouts hidden along the opposite bank of the river. They're stretched out along the five-kilometer stretch where all three vehicle-rated fords are located."

"Any fire from them?"

"No, but our people have been observing a lot of hand signals, a lot of movement to and from their rear area. Just like you and he were mentioning."

Riordan nodded. "The Hkh'Rkh tend to stick with the basics. You saw that in Indonesia."

"Yeah, but there it was harder to tell just *how* basic Hkh'Rkh tech and doctrine was. I figured they were just leaning on the Arat Kur for secure comms and sensors."

Riordan began studying the electronic map more closely . . . just as a half-hued red icon blinked into existence just ten kilometers away from the impact site, straddling the southern edge of the display.

"Suspected contact," Bannor muttered. "Do we retask one of the EXHALTEDs to conduct detailed surveillance on those coordinates?"

Riordan shook his head, hated doing so. "We can't. Those two sky-eyes are the only reason we've got this good a picture of enemy activity. We start zooming in here and there and we could miss a large movement, or at least see it too late to react properly. Do we have any drones down there?"

Rulaine stared. "That's completely out of the AO, Caine. Any Hkh'Rkh south of the fords can't get to us. The river is totally unfordable at that point. It's too rough for boats, even: there's a series of waterfalls that starts just downstream of our positions."

"Then why the hell are they sending a scout unit toward the site?"

Bannor's voice was reassuringly level. "Commodore, we don't know there's a Hkh'Rkh unit moving in that direction. All we've got are sensor returns indicating an enemy force *may* be at those coordinates."

"True, but we have to presume that it's an actual contact. Which means we—or rather Dr. Sleeman—has trouble on the way. And her only option is to leave, since the site is on the Hkh'Rkh side of the river." *And why the hell haven't you called in yet, Melissa?*

Bannor studied the region more closely, zoomed in on it. "It's mostly open terrain, but that enemy unit—if it's a unit—has a long walk ahead of it."

"But why go there at all unless old, embedded sensors have detected Sleeman's presence?"

Bannor frowned. "If he had a solid contact, I suspect Jrekhalkar would send more than a dozen or so soldiers ambling in that direction without support. Besides, Sleeman's team should be done repairing those helicopters long before these maybe-Warriors are within range to do anything except wave goodbye when they dust off."

"I hope you're right," Caine replied, scanning the rest of the map. "Either way, the Hkh'Rkh advance is picking up tempo. Their lead carriers could be on the west bank in a little less than an hour. Their tracks—probably artillery—could be pulling into firing positions about the same time."

"True, but the artillery is going to have to range in first. That's going to take some time, and we can hit them with counterbattery fire from the MISLS or even the MULTIs."

Riordan kept staring at the map. "All those plans are founded on an assumption."

"Which is?"

"That there are no Ktor nearby, waiting for us to misstep."

"Hell, even if they are shadowing us—and that's an

extremely big 'if'—it's not like they can expect us to follow any predictable course of action."

"Why not? Look at how we're analyzing the Hkh'Rkh, watching how their strategies are forced upon them by the limitations of their technology and training. The Ktor could be doing the same thing, observing how the Hkh'Rkh deployment shapes *our* defense, makes us just as predictable."

Bannor nodded slowly. "Point taken. What do we do about it?"

Riordan drew in a long breath and sighed. "What I wanted to avoid doing until after we had extracted the Lost Soldiers: I'm going to put in a call to Yiithrii'ah'aash."

Riordan plugged the coordinates of the Slaasriithi's commo relay platform into Wedge One's computer, according to Dora's remote, impatient instructions, which ended with, "But you know, it would be a whole hell of a lot easier if you just routed your messages back to me here on *Puller* and I lascommed it to their platform. *Puller* has better encryption, and better—"

"*Puller* needs to stay out of operations and out of sight until and unless we need to pull it in as our Sunday punch. I'm pretty sure that the number-one item on our enemy's wish list is your coordinates."

"Yeah? Well, good luck hitting us with those old-school missiles. And hell, we could even call down the PDF drones we left in orbit and—"

"Dora, why am I calling the Slaasriithi?"

The line back to Dante grew quiet. "Yeah, okay, I get it. We might be dealing with something a lot more dangerous than Hkh'Rkh tech. So go ahead.

And remember: you've got a five minute delay. So you might want to front-load all your data and questions."

Riordan tried not to smile, imagined that Dora was probably channeling her tough-as-nails granmama. Who, apparently, had also been a world-class worrier, even while denying that she gave a damn about anyone or anything. *The crab apple may not have fallen too far from the tree.* "Thanks, Dora. I got all that drilled into me during OCS, but it's always good to get a reminder."

"You call that thirty-day-wonder bullshit they pushed you through OCS? *Mierde*, Riordan, do you believe in Santa Claus, too?"

"You are stepping over the line, Ms. Veriden."

She grumbled something inaudible; if it was a comeback, she was keeping it to herself. "Yeah, so don't let me hold you up. I'll go back to being rude to Karam."

He had no doubt she would. "Thanks, Dora."

"Yeah. Sure. Whatever. Don't die." The link broke.

Riordan had already run a basic tactical update through Wedge One's encryption, but now added the more problematic details to his message:

> Repair progress on Wedge Three steady but will not be complete before Hkh'Rkh colonial militia is in position to launch full attack. Enemy rate of advance is increasing. Their probable objective is to seize or destroy Wedge Three to prevent a full extraction of the Lost Soldiers. Significant casualties anticipated on both sides. Withdrawal once engaged is likely to result in higher friendly losses. The alternative, a heavy preemptive strike against enemy units, contravenes our rules of engagement.

Lastly, the nature of the cryogenic suspension technology discovered at base camp Dante, and the suspicious timing of the Lost Soldiers' reanimation, combine to create a statistically significant threat of proximal Ktoran involvement. They may be observing events on Turkh'saar. They may also have concealed combat elements in the system.

In consideration of these variables, I request that *Tidal-Drift-Instaurator-to-Shore-of-Stars* commence its approach now, in order to facilitate timely support for either defensive or extraction operations.

Riordan

He pushed the send icon on the reconfigurable screen and settled back to eat the breakfast he'd not yet had the time to wolf down.

Six minutes and thirty-two seconds later, the incoming encryption tone chimed twice. Yiithrii'ah'aash's response began scrolling on the comm panel's primary screen:

Greetings, Caine Riordan.

All data received and understood. Agree with your conjectures. However, additional considerations influence our response.

Uh oh. What the hell does that *mean?*

Firstly, one of the microsensors we deployed into the inner system detected a stellar flare. Specific readings on the phenomenon shall be appended to the end of this message, including approximate timing and intensities. In summary, it will peak within the next six to eight hours. Catastrophic EMP effects (i.e., permanently disabled systems) are unlikely. However, near-orbit and high altitude ionization will compromise airborne command-and-control links, and will cripple any systems at those altitudes that are not equipped with sensors capable of triggering automatic shut-down protocols. Since your systems are so equipped, we recommend that you simply adopt appropriate tactical and operational contingencies in anticipation of a temporary loss of communications and sensing platforms.

A lousy weather report. And thanks for advising the obvious, Yiithrii'ah'aash.

We concur that Ktor involvement is the only reasonable explanation for the presence of the Lost Soldiers and the advanced cryotechnology with which they were moved to, and maintained on, Turkh'saar.

We further concur that the probability of Ktor combat assets being present in this system is great enough to warrant special consideration. For our ship, that means that we must remain well outside Turkh'saar's gravity well. As long as the enemy capabilities remain unknown, we cannot decrement the speed and maneuverability which enable us to avoid engagement and, possibly, destruction.

I wonder if the official motto of the Slaasriithi is, "When in doubt, prepare to flee"?

We deem it overwhelmingly likely that if Ktor elements are present in the system, some have been seeded into Turkh'saar's debris ring. Although unlikely to conceal ships, the debris can easily hide drones and observation platforms, as you have proven by employing it in just that fashion.

Well, he's got a point, there.

Consequently, shortly after you made planetfall, we dispatched several small sensor platforms and four combat drone-craft (identical to the ones you have labeled "cannonballs") to help defend against any unanticipated threat forces and to support your eventual extraction from Turkh'saar. These assets are currently in the process of making their final approach to the debris field around the planet. The sensor platforms will alert us and task the "cannonballs" in the event of Ktor activity.

We trust that this answers your current needs and concerns. We wish you all good fortune.

Yiithrii'ah'aash,
Prime Ratiocinator
of the Great Ring

Chief Gaudet returned to the large cockpit, carrying the half cup of coffee that was the last survivor of her double breakfast. For such a spare young woman, she sure could eat. "Good morning again, Commodore."

Before Caine could make a polite reply, the comm board illuminated: a red signal, indicating a non-LoS transmission, and so, susceptible to both disruption and interception. Not surprisingly, the sender was identified as Melissa Sleeman. He tapped the board. "Good morning, Doctor. I take it you're airborne?"

Sleeman's pause left the line silent—too silent: there were no rotors churning in the background. "No, Commodore we're not airborne. We ran into yet another complication."

Well, now it was beginning to feel like a real combat operation. "Please explain, Doctor."

"What was originally diagnosed as a failure in the electronics turns out to be combat damage. A key component was nicked by a stray fragment during the Hkh'Rkh attack on the forward operating base. That part has now fully failed."

"The crews that checked out the two helicopters are also the ones currently operating them. How did they miss the hole?"

"Because the penetration was inside the helicopter, sir. Apparently, one of the doors had been left open when the Lost Soldiers abandoned the base in a rush. The fragment was thin, small; it didn't leave any discernible entry aperture."

Damn it. "Can you all get into the remaining chopper?" Riordan prayed that it was the Huey which was out of action.

His prayer had evidently not been heard. "No, sir. The crippled helicopter is the Mi-8. The Huey could not have carried all of us to safety, no matter how much we lighten the load."

"'Couldn't have?' Why are you speaking about the Huey in the past tense, Doctor?"

Sleeman sighed. "Because whatever put an invisible fragment into the Mi-8 did the same to the Huey."

Oh, for the love of—"Nature of the damage?"

"Very slow fuel leak. Must have started just before we arrived here."

"Wasn't that helicopter given a preflight check?"

"Yes, right before the Hkh'Rkh attacked the FOB. The engine cowl was left up and a fragment from the autocannon fire must have seamed a fuel line. By the time the flight crew returned to the FOB, someone had apparently closed the cowling so no one knew to look inside again. The crew chief thinks the in-flight vibration is what opened up the seam and started the leak."

"And no one saw it when you landed?"

"Sir, it is a *very* slow leak. The helicopters were left at the center of the defensive perimeter, so we did not see—or smell—it until we regathered near them at the end of the day."

Riordan forced himself to breathe deeply. "Do you have a revised estimate on the Mi-8's repair time?"

"Another three hours, sir."

"Then be aware that you may have an enemy unit inbound. Its ETA is two hours. No vehicles. A dozen Warriors, at most. I am sending their current coordinates and approximate vector of approach."

"Very good, sir. I will relay those to my security chief. And will share the ETA with the chief flight mechanic: I don't know if it is possible to increase his motivation, but if anything can achieve it, this news should."

Riordan admired Sleeman's increasing calm during crisis: she had even started making jokes when her life was on the line. Surest way to preserve sanity in a combat zone. "I agree with your assessment, Doctor. I'm going to hand you over to Chief Gaudet to

give you a set of more detailed squelch-break codes
for when you update us. We can't risk voice-grade
commo again."

"Understood, sir."

He nodded to Gaudet, who jumped on the channel
as Caine snicked off.

And wondered if he'd ever see Sleeman alive again.

Chapter Forty

Idrem had arrived on *Red Lurker*'s bridge less than ten seconds before Brenlor, who therefore heard the beginning of the Aboriginal watch-officer's report: "A great deal of communication is originating from the engagement area on Turkh'saar."

"Explicate," Brenlor ordered, taking the commander's couch.

"The first communiqué is Hkh'Rkh, unencrypted, and intimates that the remaining Clanhall leadership in the capitol of Iarzut'thruk is uncomfortable with Voice Jrekhalkar's decision to take personal charge of the situation at the front. Or, if he insists on remaining there, they are concerned that he has made no mention of a succession contingency. From what we can determine, he is without issue, and all the older males of his den and clan died recently or in the late war."

Brenlor frowned. "Why do they expect him to be so stupid as to lead from the front? The Hkh'Rkh leaders did not do so on Earth, according to what I heard."

Idrem intervened. "There may be unique variables

552

pushing Jrekhalkar to take a more personal role in the coming combat. He is young and has apparently not proven himself in any conflict or duel. Consequently, without accruing respect through battle, and particularly a victory, his ability to retain both his Family possessions and his position as Voice of the colony is uncertain."

"If he dies, is his line not respected enough for vassals to come forward to protect its continuation through a regency?"

"Brenlor, from what little information we have with us on Hkh'Rkh culture, they appear not to have a legal institution analogous to a regency. If a family or clan is so reduced that it does not have any persons who possess Honor and may answer Challenges, then it has no right to continue to exist."

"And are the remainder then Extirpated and Exiled, as we were?"

"No. The Family's females and offspring are bound into the family that successfully Challenged its last Warrior. Not as chattel or serfs, but more as lowest-ranked retainers."

Brenlor frowned, spent several long moments staring at the main screen's view of the engagement area on Turkh'saar. "This, then, is dire news. The local leadership of Turkh'saar is already so heavily damaged that the objective of our intervention—to place a debt of Honor upon the local Voice—could be undone if he is killed in the engagement. Which, given his position at the front, is far too likely."

Idrem tried to inject a note of reasonable optimism. "Even if that occurs, those who inherit the position of Voice will be almost as grateful."

"Will they?" Brenlor's tone was utterly self-assured. When it came to anticipating the ruthless plots of kings and captains, he was quite competent. "The new leaderships' first order of business will be to determine who among them will succeed Jrekhalkar. Given their idiotically inefficient method for doing so—Challenges—we may be sure that it will be a week or more before they have finished slicing each other to pieces. By then, will the final Voice even be one of the Warriors who was at the battle? And why would he remember us with personal gratitude? It will not be his own position, his own reputation, which our action saves. Jrekhalkar, the direct and obligated beneficiary of our intervention, will be dead and forgotten. And there will not even be any of his family left to praise us."

Idrem was somewhat taken aback by the speed and accuracy of Brenlor's analysis. "It could indeed transpire as you foresee."

Brenlor waved an almost dismissive hand. "It is sure to, if this Jrekhalkar is killed. Our problems might not end with ensuring the compliance of Turkh'saar's new Voice. That new leader might be the member of a Clan without adequate political weight to influence the Patrijuridicate, to ensure that they shall acknowledge their Honor-debt to us for protecting their lands when they were unable to do so. In that event, the Hkh'Rkh Greatsires cannot be compelled to make our safety the price they exact for further cooperation with the Ktoran Sphere."

He stood. "Without that alliance and leverage, the resurgence of House Perekmeres cannot be achieved. We would be lucky to survive as corsairs, raiders. That is no life for a Srin, for a Hegemon. So we must bend our efforts to preventing Jrekhalkar's demise."

Idrem sensed Brenlor swinging toward the rash reactivity that the Srin often mistook for decisive action when confronted with a crisis. He moved to control the extremes of that temperament from ruining their plans. "I will have several alternatives for you within the hour."

Brenlor glanced at him. "Do not think to manage me, High Sentinel. I am not distracted by other duties, so I myself shall formulate a plan for dealing with this risk to our ultimate objective." He turned to the Aboriginal who had been waiting nervously since giving the first report. "What other communications did you detect?"

"The Terran radio squelches we detected last night do indeed originate from the unusual site south of the engagement zone. Apparently, a group that travelled there by rotary-wing aircraft is now stranded by mechanical failures. Hkh'Rkh scouts are headed toward them now."

Brenlor started. "Retask a sensor to bring that area under close observation."

"If it pleases the Srin, I was so bold as to already take that liberty, and have secured relevant information."

Brenlor eyed the Aboriginal narrowly. "Your desire to please has led you to the very brink of impertinence— but not over it. You measured the risk of your action well, this time. Now, what have you observed?"

"Two helicopters on the ground in an area that appears to be some kind of impact site where the Hkh'Rkh once conducted excavations. The number of human biosigns varies from minute to minute. I project that members of the team are exploring the excavations, causing their signals to appear and disappear as they move into the subterranean reaches."

Brenlor nodded. "You have done well." He turned to Idrem. "This further complicates matters."

Idrem noticed that both the gaze and tone of his superior were distracted. "You see a significance in this that I do not."

Brenlor nodded once. "I do. In learning about the 'assistance' we provided to the Custodians during the period when we helped them monitor the Aboriginals, I came across information about other covert operations we were able to conduct in this region of space. This site, I fear, is connected to one such operation—one the Aboriginals must not report."

Idrem rarely detected dread in Brenlor: he detected it now. "What would occur if they did report what they have now found?"

"It would depend upon how accurate their conjectures are, but if we presume—as we must—that they understand what they have seen, it would undo us. Indeed, it would make us objects of hate and targets for extermination by both the Patrijuridicate and the Sphere, debts of honor notwithstanding." Seeing Idrem's surprise, his mouth opening to ask questions, Brenlor shook his head. "There is no time to speak of the details. Suffice it to say that my grandsire knew of Turkh'saar only because there had been an earlier clandestine operation here—an operation designed to ensure the usefulness of the Hkh'Rkh when the time came to recruit them. I am certain that this site is the consequence of that operation. If it is discovered by the humans, they will deduce the nature of Ktor's manipulation of interstellar events. And they will no doubt share the evidence and their conclusions with the other powers of the Accord. Including the Hkh'Rkh. Whose resulting hatred of Ktor could well become absolute."

Idrem's reflexive curiosity tried to pull him down paths of conjecture and hypothesis, but there wasn't the time for that, now. "So whatever good we might do them here will be voided by the evidence of our species' earlier manipulations. Indeed, our current operation will be presumed to be simply one more clandestine manipulation. Which, of course, it is."

"Correct. We must now formulate a response which will both prevent this discovery and ensure that Jrekhalkar lives through the coming battle."

Idrem wanted to ask Brenlor why in the name of the Progenitors he had neglected to mention this deeper history of Turkh'saar when committing the scant survivors of House Perekmeres to their current operations. But he already knew the answer: because Nezdeh would have asserted the risk to be too great, that too many things could go wrong, that their bold grasp for victory could become a headlong plunge into the abyss. As might now occur.

Careful to suppress any sign of his anger at Brenlor, Idrem turned to the Aboriginal. "You spoke of a third communiqué. What was it?"

"One of the human transports sent a lascom signal into the suspected vicinity of the Slaasriithi shift-carrier. It was of extremely short duration. There is some evidence that an equally short reply was issued."

"Content?"

"We did not have a sufficient density of nanosensors

in the area to pick up sidescatter or intercept the beam. However, now that we have telemetry on the beam, we will send a swarm impulse so that more of the cloud will condense along that vector."

Idrem raised a cautioning finger. "Do not over-concentrate the nanosensor assets. The recent communiqués will not have been aimed directly at the Slaasriithi ship, but at a small independent relay platform that will constantly be changing position. However, the consequent telemetry change will be relatively small, so bring the cloud into that general sector, but do not concentrate them for a full intercept of subsequent signals. It is more important that we know when each side sends, and for how long. If we overconcentrate the nanosensors, in the hope of getting the content, we may miss the message entirely. For instance, what happened just before this first lascom exchange?"

The Aboriginal frowned. "The human team at the site signalled that it was stranded there."

"Exactly. It seems that this event prompted a reconsideration of plans and actions, either on its own or in conjunction with other concerns. Their communication to the Slaasriithi indicates that they consider this an event of great importance. That is crucial intelligence for us, which we might miss entirely were we to concentrate our assets too narrowly in the unlikely hope of tapping into the message itself."

Brenlor nodded approvingly. "The High Sentinel speaks wisdom that should inform all your thought. Return to your duties." He walked back toward the iris valve; Idrem knew to follow him. Once Idrem was close, Brenlor murmured, "If the Terrans bring the Slaasriithi shift-carrier into close orbit, or even geosynchronous, we are done. We would be lucky to escape alive."

"True, Brenlor. But the odds of that are low. The Slaasriithi lack the resolve to take risks. They may send drones—the ones we encountered at Disparity, for instance—but they will not endanger their shift-carrier by bringing it so close to a gravity well."

"Let us hope you are right."

"I believe we can ensure I am. We need only bring our other hulls close enough that their engine output registers on the enemy's sensors. The implied size of the craft capable of emitting such powerful energy spikes will compel the Slaasriithi to remain hidden. And we might further increase our apparent numbers and threat by emplacing image makers on *Arbitrage*'s remaining shuttles and drones."

Brenlor had begun to smile when the senior Aboriginal on the bridge turned toward them. "Long range passive sensors have just detected an approaching object, Fearsome Srin."

"Telemetry and identity?"

"Trackback indicates it emerged from the near edge of the belt, proximal to the last confirmed location of the Slaasriithi. The craft's output characteristics resemble those of an automated drone dispenser which the Slaasriithi use for long-range ferrying and deployment of independent platforms."

Brenlor examined the trajectory lines that suddenly appeared in the holoplot. "Projected destination?"

"Its trajectory will bring it very near to our own position, Esteemed Srin. However, unless the craft counterboosts more aggressively, it will pass us and decelerate to a relative stop within the debris field just beyond close orbit."

After a moment of silence, Brenlor murmured, "The Progenitors have answered our need."

Idrem did not like the sound of that. "What do you mean?"

The Srin pointed at the holoplot. "Look. The inbound Slaasriithi drone carrier will cross our line of sight to the engagement area on the planet."

Idrem was genuinely puzzled. "The Srin sees a ploy that is hidden from me."

Brenlor sounded surprised and disappointed. "Truly? Consider: what two objectives must we carry out to ensure we achieve our goals on Turkh'saar? To intervene in time to save the imbecile Jrekhalkar and to prevent the humans from discerning the true nature of the site they are investigating."

"Yes, these are our objectives."

"We may now achieve the second objective in the same stroke we use to achieve the first." He pointed into the holograph. "We shall wait for the Slaasriithi craft to come into our railgun's cone of fire."

"It is doubtful we would destroy it. The flight time of our projectiles would approach forty minutes; it would evade."

"Yes—because our enemies will perceive the Slaasriithi drone carrier to be our actual target."

Then Idrem saw the ploy, with a mix of horror, fascination, and admiration. "You intend the projectiles to strike the site."

"We must trap the humans there. The Hkh'Rkh will surely investigate and besiege them. The Terran commander will attempt to rescue his personnel and so further divide his forces and delay his departure. The Hkh'Rkh will swiftly become embroiled with the humans, sustain heavy losses, and validate our intervention."

Idrem nodded, but thought: *this is what destroyed our House. Wildly aggressive tactics that were not subjected to proper review, proper analysis. What Brenlor proposes could work, and if it does, it will pay off brilliantly. But if it does not*—"Your progenitors would swell with pride at the bold genius of the plan you propose. But it reveals us earlier than we planned."

"That hardly matters. Once we order *Arbitrage* and the tug to activate their drives, the Slaasriithi will know we are in the system."

"Yes, but they will know *Lurker*'s exact position."

"We will move to a new hiding spot, then ambush whatever drones the Slaasriithi might later release with the predeployed missiles we have floating in the debris belt. And if the Terrans dare try to rise up out of the gravity well, they will be contending with our superior weapons and targeting."

"And how do we ensure that the humans at the dig site survive our initial railgun strike so that the Hkh'Rkh may threaten them?"

"We do not need to. They will flee underground, into the excavations. And surely they will have ample warning: the Slaasriithi will detect the incoming rounds, convey that information to the Aboriginals, who will in turn alert their researchers at the site. Whose discoveries will no longer reach the Terran authorities. The Hkh'Rkh, or we, shall see to that." Brenlor stared at Idrem, at once excited and impatient.

Idrem needed to highlight the risks without challenging Brenlor's authority. "Srin Perekmeres, the Terrans have a cautionary concept: the law of unintended consequences."

"I am familiar with it. We have our own rough equivalents."

"Yes, and here is how it might apply to this stratagem. Currently, the Terrans wish to avoid combat and withdraw with the Aboriginal soldiers your ancestor left on Turkh'saar. However, if they are confronted with all the challenges you would put before them, they may change their plans."

"You mean, they would abandon the stranded Aboriginals and flee?"

"Perhaps, but I think it more likely that they might cease to avoid combat. Rather, they might elect to preemptively destroy the Hkh'Rkh forces."

"In which case we shall intervene. As per our plan."

"Yes, but we have always assumed that the Terrans would refrain from bringing their full power to bear, due to their own restrictive rules of engagement. If they set aside those rules, they could cripple the leadership of the Hkh'Rkh so swiftly that there will be no one left with a debt of honor to us, at least no one with sufficient political influence to represent us before the Patrijuridicate."

Brenlor nodded thoughtfully. "It is a reasonable concern, but not so likely as to make the plan inadvisable. We shall bear your cautions in mind as we wait for the Slaasriithi drones to come into our cone of fire. Perhaps new events shall make it inadvisable, or unnecessary to use the railgun as we proceed."

Which meant there was very little chance that the attack could be forestalled, practically speaking. But Idrem had done all that he could; he knew the set of Brenlor's heavy jaw meant that the decision had been made. "Shall I send *Arbitrage* word of our plans, and of what they must do?"

Brenlor smiled. "We shall send that message together." And Idrem wondered if the message behind the Srin's smile was, "Which will prevent you from communicating privately with Nezdeh, to coordinate an attempt to dissuade me."

Which was, of course, exactly what Idrem had hoped to do.

Nezdeh Srina Perekmeres reread the lascom transmission from *Red Lurker*, then wiped it off her screen. A moment later, her cabin's privacy chime sounded. "Enter."

The iris valve dilated; Emil Kozakowski stepped through.

She wanted to withhold her gaze but did not do so: the Aboriginal might interpret it as lack of resolve, as uncertainty of dominion. But he was increasingly unpleasant to look at. Reduced caloric intake, imposed on the Aboriginal crew both to conserve rations and to deny them the vitality needed for mutiny, had reduced his once pear-shape to more that of a simple oval. But Kozakowski had not kept up with the prescribed exercise regimen and so his decrease in weight had left his flesh baggy, flaccid. And pale, despite his claims that he spent enough time under his stateroom's health-spectrum lights.

As he always did when summoned, Kozakowski was wringing his hands. A detestable creature, his inquiry was as obsequious as had been his first, the day *Arbitrage* had been seized by the Ktor. "How may I be of service to you, Esteemed Srina Perekmeres?"

"I require an estimate of how long our image makers will be able to function aboard your primitive shuttles. They drain a great deal of energy and they will tax the electronics. You have seen the numbers I forwarded to you?"

"Yes, Srina. I have consulted with our flight technicians. If we install tankage modules in the shuttles' cargo bays, we can run their MAP thrusters in a closed cycle and generate more power. However, this is inefficient, and they will exhaust their fuel in approximately twenty-two hours. If we hold one shuttle in reserve to refuel them, we could extend this to two days. After that, the thrusters' burn rate will have outstripped our refuel rate. There would be blackouts between the exhaustion of fuel and the next visit from the tanker.

"The ability of our shuttles' electronics to handle your image makers is far more uncertain. Beyond matters of load variance and peaks, there is also a concern with rigging adequate transformers."

"Why must you rig special transformers? Certainly the shuttles' capacitors can alter the current as required."

Emil offered a regretful bow. "Feared Srina, our civilian shuttles rely on simple batteries and fuel-cell replenishment; they do not have capacitors. So they have almost no integral ability to transform current, not at the levels required by your image makers. My technical staff are completing the improvised transformers now, but until they are tested, we have no way of knowing—"

Nezdeh silenced Kozakowski with a wave. "We do not have the time for tests. The shuttles must be deployed within the hour. Failure will carry severe penalties." She held Kozakowski's evasive eyes. "Severe penalties for all concerned." Kozakowski shivered.

And now it is time to add the possibility of pleasure as an alternative to the threat of pain. "Conversely, noteworthy success warrants encouragement, so your personnel shall receive extra rations if they can keep the systems running beyond initial estimates." Kozakowski did not look particularly enthused: his desires went far beyond the creature comforts of a full belly at the end of the day. "Furthermore, I will accept a petition from you—presuming, of course, that the performance of your technicians markedly exceeds our expectations."

Emil Kozakowski's eyes fixed eagerly upon hers, suddenly bright and unblinking. "Fearsome Srina, as you have pointed out, I could never safely return to Earth as your agent so long as Ayana Tagawa might bear witness against me. I would be executed, but only after I was tortured for information about you and the *homo imperiens* of Ktor."

Nezdeh nodded. It was uncertain whether Kozakowski would be tortured—some of the Terran blocs were idiotically squeamish about employing pain as an incentive to cooperation—but his execution was a foregone conclusion. "So: speak what you wish. Plainly."

"I wish to be safe in your continued service."

Such clever, craven phrasing. If you were a Ktor—perish that thought!—you would know how to say it directly: "I wish Ayana Tagawa dead." Nezdeh affected a regretful shake of her head. "I cannot grant that at this time: Tagawa is crucial to the operation of *Arbitrage* and the oversight of many crew functions."

"I understand, Esteemed Srina. But perhaps later, when her services are no longer so essential?"

Nezdeh acted as though she was considering his request carefully, made him wait—thereby ensuring that Kozakowski would never guess that this was precisely what she wanted him to request. Because, ultimately, it was precisely what she wanted him to do.

Tagawa and the other officers who had been given command over *Arbitrage* had not been liked by the crew. They had been sent by the CTR in the wake of the war, replacing Kozakowski and his staff to guarantee the ship's loyalty to the new global order. But Tagawa had nonetheless earned the crew's respect. She was brave, capable, efficient, unflappable: all things that might make her a dangerous leader. And above all, a dangerous martyr, if she were slain out of hand by the new Ktoran masters.

But if her death was arranged and carried out by other members of the human crew, she would not become a martyr, merely a murder victim. And the blood and any resentment would stick to Kozakowski's hands, not hers.

Finally, Nezdeh nodded slowly at the obsequiously crouching human on the other side of her desk. "Yes. Perhaps later, I will deign to grant your request. If you are sure it is what you want."

Kozakowski bobbed fervently, furiously. "Yes, yes, Fearsome Srina. I want that, above all else. You may be sure of it."

Oh, I am, you spineless rodent. I am. "Very well. See to the final arrangements for installing the image makers on the shuttles. Our long wait is over. Now, we act."

Chapter Forty-One

KAKAAGSUKH RIVER VALLEY, BD+56 2966 TWO ("TURKH'SAAR")

While Jrekhalkar stared intently in the monitor, Ezz-raamar of the Moiety of Nys'maharn peered cautiously around his shoulder. Linked to one of the remote-controlled cameras that had been mounted in the tops of the clustertrees, it could not show the river itself: foliage obstructed the bottom third of the screen. However, it offered a clear view of the far shore and the slope that rose from the water and then steepened into the ridgeline that followed the river's eastern bank. It was almost four hundred meters high, whereas the more distant western ridge—almost seven kilometers behind them—crested at only two hundred meters.

That was further than Jrekhalkar had wished; the mobile mortars he had hidden in its lee were beyond their optimum range. In comparison, the multiple rocket launchers, or MRLs, alongside them were still within their prime effectiveness envelope. However, both forms of artillery were crippled by the absence of a real-time link to observers who could correct their fire. Because of the surrounding clustertrees, a

567

Warrior had to be within fifty meters of their shore of the river to observe the far bank and the lowland that stretched away from it. And of course, that would be where the enemy infantry was no doubt hiding, ready to deny a crossing.

"And the humans never mentioned having artillery of their own?" Jrekhalkar asked in a tense voice.

Ezzraamar bobbed his head slightly. "No, Voice. Although I do not think they do. Those who equipped them apparently intended for them to fight as airmobile infantry, without any other supporting arms."

Jrekhalkar's snout wrinkled slightly as Ezzraamar uttered the words, "those who equipped them." It annoyed him that his new adjutant's time in captivity had not yielded any evidence that these humans had come here of their own volition, nor had any knowledge of who might have effected their relocation. The Voice had insisted, loudly and imperiously, that clearly this was more evidence of human guile, merely an act to conceal their true origins and motivations. Ezzraamar had simply stood in a posture of ready respect when his superior made such confident, yet implausible, declamations.

A more worrisome unknown was the equipage of the most recent intruders, those who had arrived with the one named Caine Riordan. Ezzraamar had been glad for the tranqs which had made much of his brief meeting with the human vague, dreamlike, and, happily, easy to suppress. However, he remembered, and fretted over, the basic substance of it.

He didn't recall being rescued; apparently, he had almost been missed and left behind. The Hkh'Rkh had withdrawn in haste (some dared to use the word "fled") when the human ship began to destroy their vehicles, one after the other, with its railgun. He had awakened in a hastily made camp, beyond the western ridge, and was immediately carried back to Jrekhalkar. The Voice had entertained high hopes of gleaning useful information from the young squad leader, who had been the only other Hkh'Rkh with any facility in human languages and one of the few local veterans of the recent war.

What little he was able to impart was either of minimal use or was distinctly unwelcome. While it was useful to understand the approximate location and numbers of the raiders, their numbers and equipment had already been determined with reasonable accuracy. But when Ezzraamar obliquely alluded to the raiders' conversations, of their perplexity, worry, desire to break contact and cease raiding, Jrekhalkar had terminated the report abruptly. He had, instead, attached Ezzraamar as both adjutant and tactical advisor, and ordered the young squad leader not to share the details of his captivity with any other Hkh'Rkh. To speak of it would simply excite profitless rumors.

But Ezzraamar understood the real motivation behind Jrekhalkar's instructions: to conceal any information which might conflict with the official narrative about why the humans were on Turkh'saar. Significantly, Yaargraukh had been dismissed from his post with the Flag and sent back to Iarzut'thruk mere hours before Ezzraamar had arrived. The timing, which assured that they just barely missed each other, was entirely too convenient to be chance.

Jrekhalkar turned away from the screen to view the electronic battle map which had been unfolded on a field table beside his command track. Operating under radio silence and with vehicle transponders off, marshalling the Flag was as much a matter of estimate as it was intelligence. They could occasionally exchange coded squelch breaks—units confirming that they had arrived in preplotted positions, scouts reporting suspected enemy positions on the opposite bank—but any significant increase in such activity brought an impenetrable wave of jamming in response. It was always brief; the humans clearly did not want to give their adversaries an extended opportunity to analyze the method or home in on the source. However, it was enough to constrain the Hkh'Rkh's use of radio and force them into more rudimentary command and control methods. Ezzraamar wondered, with no small measure of hopefulness, if the humans would be able to extract the raiders before battle could be joined . . .

That hope died in the very moment that Ezzraamar dared to conceive it: a squelch break, and then another, crackled out of the communications carrier parked nearby. Jrekhalkar's long, heavy neck swiveled toward the operator. "Which unit?"

"The scouts near the Site, Voice. They confirm that two of the raiders' rotary-wings are present. At least one vehicle is being repaired, possibly both."

Jrekhalkar aimed a calar claw at the communications specialist. "Send the activation squelch to the following harrier troop. They are to close and engage as soon as they are in range."

"Destroy the enemy?"

"No! For now, their objective is only to render the rotary-wings inoperable." He turned to the rest of his command staff, his nostrils wide and pulsing with eagerness. "Prepare the batteries for one-round fire: all tubes except the MRLs."

The tassle leader responsible for communicating orders back to the batteries was so surprised that his eyes vanished for a moment. When they reemerged, he spread his claws wide. "But Voice, we have not yet ranged our tubes on their targets. We only have estimates—"

"And that will be sufficient, Tassle Leader. Our objective is to divide the *s'fets'* attention between two concerns: rescuing their team at the Site and responding to our preliminary attack. With any luck, they will be hasty and overreact. Watch for targets of opportunity. Bring the APCs forward to missile and machine-gun range to support our first probe across the river."

Ezzraamar watched the various friendly icons on the map—amber-colored—move toward the maroon-mauve line that estimated the humans' positions. One distant amber triangle had started moving at high speed toward the Site. Representing a half dozen scout cars and light APCs, it would join the scouts in less than twenty minutes.

"Ezzraamar."

Jrekhalkar's voice startled the young Warrior, who looked up and discovered the flag leader watching him attentively. "Yes, Honored Voice?"

"Your expression is one of misgiving. Why?"

Ezzraamar waggled his neck: an apologetic shrug. "I am probably overly cautious, Voice."

Jrekhalkar's expression softened slightly. "Perhaps. But I would hear your thoughts."

Ezzraamar's answering gesture took in the whole

of the map. "Humans do not become distracted so easily, at least they did not when fighting for their homeworld. And I worry about the technologies they might have with them which could inflict grave casualties upon us if we move in daylight."

Jrekhalkar pony-nodded. "This is well said. I have no intent to mount our main attack until the sun has set and our eyes give us the advantage. But the opportunity to strike, to compel them to divide their attention, and possibly their forces, presents itself now. If we wait, we shall not catch their team at the Site in our claws—and that is just where we must keep it, if we wish to continue to divide their forces and attention.

"Now, attend me: we are relocating to the front."

A creeper that had been steadily working its way to the western ridgeline for the past thirty-six hours, detected the distant thumps of mortars, giving Riordan about six seconds' warning.

"Cover!" he shouted and ducked back into his CP within Wedge One. All along the ridge line, there were identical cries. From the river-facing slope, like hoarse whispers riding the breeze, more warnings rose up—right before the first ragged pop sounded.

Riordan's earbud trilled Bannor command tone. "Go."

"Confirming that I keep counterbattery sensors dark until you order."

"Confirmed. If we light our arrays, they'll try to knock them out. So we sit tight and let the EXHALTEDs gather photo reconnaissance. Any useful sound-ranging data from the creeper?"

"Not accurate enough to generate coordinates. Just narrows down the azimuth."

More pops, one close enough to sound like a bang with a fade out. "Keep compiling the data. We'll feed it into the fire computer soon enough."

"Assuming their mortar carriers aren't playing shoot and scoot."

Riordan called up the feed from the dedicated EXHALTED. "I don't see any vehicles moving. Yet. This may just be one ranging round. Are they coming anywhere near our positions?"

Four more pops before Bannor answered. "Closest was about eighty meters away from MULTI number four. Almost certainly luck. They had no way of spotting it."

"Roger that. Looks like they're throwing one round per tube. Probably marking each tube's impact point."

"A single ranging round doesn't do them much good."

"Not if they were looking to hit individual targets, no. But since they can't really adjust their fires, they may just drop rounds blind all along the river. If they can keep our heads down, they can limit our ability to contest their crossings."

"Yeah, but they'll guess that we have infantry positions near the fords, and they'll shift to airbursts before they cross. And none of our guys down there have overhead cover."

"That's why we'll hit back hard with counterbattery fire before they can make the shift to airbursts."

More pops, then a few faint crumps down near the river. The EXHALTED's feed was now flagging a single suspected smoke emission from the deck of each tracked mortar carrier. "Time to get all our quadrotors and drones airborne: we need eyes everywhere at once, now."

"They're already moving, Commodore. And it looks like some of the enemy APCs are advancing to jump-off points about a hundred meters back from their bank. They're staying within stands of clustertrees, though. That's going to cut down our ability to launch overhead-engagement munitions from the MULTIs."

"Then we'll wait until we have line-of-sight on them as they approach the river."

"And if they stay there and hold off crossing until night?"

"Trickier, but with the EXHALTEDs detecting their idling engines, we can still hit them. Frankly, I'm more worried about Sleeman's team."

"Yeah. I've had Tygg on the line twice, wanting to take a helicopter out there with a team and pull them out."

"What did you tell him?"

"What the map has been telling you and me. We can't spare the air mobility assets, and if we put those flimsy old crates out over the actual battlefield for any appreciable amount of time, the Hkh'Rkh rockets and autocannons could rip them to pieces. When the heck was Melissa's team supposed to finish those repairs, anyhow?"

Riordan checked his wrist-mounted palmcomp. "Fifteen minutes ago."

Idrem had barely stepped foot back on the bridge when Brenlor pointed to an image from one of their sensors hidden in close orbit. "Now we know how the Terrans have managed to respond so adroitly to the Hkh'Rkh approach." He half-turned toward the Aboriginal sensor operator. "Enlarge on the object."

"Enlarging to maximum," the crewman replied.

The surface of the planet seemed to rush up at them, then stopped. Idrem carefully scanned the image. "I do not see what you are referring to."

"I did not either. I presumed that they could not have overhead observation, if they did not successfully seed various satellites as they began their planetfall. But I was wrong. We all were." He activated the pointer function, looped his finger in the direction of the screen: a small circle appeared around a featureless section of the image.

Or, Idrem revised, almost featureless. There was a speck at the center of the ring, almost like a gnat with a smudge to either side of it. Smudges that could have been ghostly gossamer wings. "That is a high altitude observation drone, what the Terrans call an EXHALTED."

Brenlor's jaw muscles bunched. "I do not care what it is called. We must eliminate it."

Idrem thought quickly how best to put the impossibility of that request in terms that would neither summon rage, nor a deeper display of ignorance, from his leader. "Even if we were willing to reveal our position by firing our laser, it would be ineffectual. The target's range and its depth within the atmosphere will both diffuse the laser's focal point and diminish the deliverable energy. We might—*might*—compromise some of its electronics. However, we will have revealed our precise position to their passive sensors. That will help them plot a course to avoid us, should they attempt to escape."

Brenlor's voice sounded as tight as his jaw muscles looked. "Then the railgun." But he sounded annoyed as he proposed it; he probably anticipated what Idrem was going to tell him.

"Impossible. We would need to hit an object approximately the size of a bedsheet with a warhead that will have limited steerability once it enters the atmosphere. Even if we were to use a flechette warhead, a hit would be purest luck. Not only is the railgun at a significant disadvantage against small, agile targets at a great distance, but this one is in an atmosphere, where it can bank, swerve, dive and so evade more readily."

Brenlor looked away, stared at the circled object on the screen. Then his jaw muscle relaxed and smoothed back into his cheek. "If we cannot deprive the Terrans of their intelligence, then the time has come for us to make their situation unmanageable. Ready the railgun to launch the strike against the site."

Idrem opened his mouth to speak—

"No, High Sentinel. I know what you would advise: to continue to wait. To see how the situation will unfold. But we cannot wait." He jabbed his finger at the screen. "The Aboriginals could be finishing the repairs on their helicopters as we speak. My only misgiving is that the Slaasriithi drones are not yet at the center of the firing cone; the enemy is likely to discern that they are not our actual target."

Idrem closed his mouth, not merely out of obedience, but respect: Brenlor's logic was not flawed, and he might well be right. He nodded. "Very well, my Srin. We can launch the attack immediately. You have but to give the word."

Brenlor smiled: a wolfish, predatory display of teeth. "The word is given."

Chapter Forty-Two

Caine glanced over at his new adjutant, Susan Phillips. Formerly an intelligence liaison to the Free French Resistance, she had been "lost" off the Brittany coast when Nazi sub-chasers had boxed in her ride, the Free Polish sub *Orzel*. She was a natural linguist—had learned all the different languages of the Lost Soldiers and become their unofficial intergroup interpreter—and was, so far as anyone could tell, utterly unflappable. And utterly without emotions other than those which would be proper for a young English lady to express, particularly if she aspired to become an old English dowager of impeccable reputation.

Consequently, while her *sang froid* was not surprising, Riordan still found her dispassionate calm unnerving when she said, "Commodore, we now have reports of small-arms fire from all along the line. Seeing if they can get a rise out of us. I have been asked by the commanders if they may return fire?"

"Not yet."

"Very good, sir. And I just now have Dr. Sleeman calling in with an emergency."

Great. "Is she on lascom?"

"No, sir. Broadcast, sending in the clear."

Better and better. "Pipe her through." The channel crackled for a moment, then cleared—and Caine heard faint gunfire in the background. *Better still.* "Dr. Sleeman, this is Riordan. What is your situation?"

"Not good, Commodore. Hkh'Rkh scouts are in the western treeline. I was sending up the drone to give you our estimated dust off and ETA by lascom when they hit it with small arms fire. Nothing left but rubbish. My security team is trading shots with them, keeping them at a distance and keeping their heads—well, necks—down."

"Are you ready to take off?"

"Negative. The crew chief is still trying to fix the wiring. He says he'll be done in half an hour."

"Sit tight, Doctor. We are going to clear your flank." He shifted over to the lascom that linked back to *Puller.* "Karam?"

"Here. Sue Phillips updated me on Melissa's situation. What do you need from us?"

"I need one stand-alone antipersonnel MISLS to eliminate, or at least suppress, the Hkh'Rkh unit closing in on her."

"Will do if it can be done. Let me look at the EXHALTED feed. Hrm. The threat force is pretty spread out, I think. Can't tell for sure. Wrong time of day for crisp, definitive thermals."

"Karam, give me the bottom line: do you have a target?"

"Yes, but I can't guarantee that—"

"Execute fire mission. Report results when you've got them."

"Acknowledged. One MISLS on its way."

From approximately two klicks behind Riordan, a breathy rush announced a skyward-jabbing plume of smoke: the exhaust of a Multiple Independent Stand-alone Launch System. With targeting data downlinked from the EXHALTED and oriented upon the grid established by the "ping-pong" sensor matrix, the weapon arced up, bending increasingly toward the southwestern horizon. Then, at the limit of visibility, it pitched over sharply and started down, riding a renewed gush of white exhaust.

Riordan instructed his palmcomp, "Set timer with alarm: two minutes. Start." The palmcomp emitted its compliance tone and started counting down toward the MISLS's impact.

Bannor jumped on the command channel. "What's the target?" After Caine explained, the special forces major muttered, "Karam, watch for the Hkh'Rkh to try to hit our launch point with their MRLs. They've been waiting for a target."

"Already watching," Tsaami replied. "Dora's just itching to counter their counterbattery fire."

But a reasonable window for Hkh'Rkh counterfire—forty seconds—came and went. Riordan checked the countdown on his palmtop: a minute left. "They're too smart to send a barrage at the launch point of a single MISLS. They saw do that often enough in Indonesia to know that they could be shooting at an empty clearing. But if we—"

Rulaine interrupted. "Could be coincidence, but our quadrotors and creepers are showing enemy APCs quickly converging toward the three fords. Looks like they're readying a push."

"Update me as you can," Caine replied, sending Bannor off the link. He checked his palmcomp, switched back to Sleeman's channel. "Doctor, get your people under cover. Now."

"What—oh!" Warnings were shouted in the background, then brief silence—before what sounded like a distant fire hose up-dopplered sharply and ended in a ragged blast. When Sleeman came back on the channel, she sounded both rattled and irritated. "A little more warning would have been nice, Commodore."

"It would have also risked warning the enemy. If they had a full minute to watch you scurrying for cover, that might have been enough time for them to figure out that they'd better do the same. Hold on while I get a preliminary report on effect." He switched back to the command channel. "Karam: damage assessment?"

"Too much smoke for visuals, and too many hot spots to tease out the biosigns from the fires. But the rocket went true to the approximate center of their unit, airbursted at ten meters. That should have put all of them in the kill radius. Of course, if they had overhead cover or there was a tree between them and the warhead—"

"Understood." He networked Sleeman's channel into the command circuit. "Doctor, have your mechanics finish and sky-out as soon as you can. Best guess is that the Hkh'Rkh are suppressed, possibly eliminated. But assume that any survivors will be taking you under fire as soon as the smoke clears. And there's that troop of light vehicles still heading toward you: ETA, thirty minutes. So the clock is ticking."

"Roger that, Commodore. Sleeman out." The line snicked off.

After a brief silence, Karam asked, "You think she'll make it?"

"She should. Unless something else goes wrong."

Tsaami's tone was sour. "Caine: this is a battlefield. Something else *always* goes wrong."

To which Riordan had no ready response. After all, Karam was right.

Christopher "Tygg" Robin's commbud toned, then chittered fitfully: Miles O'Garran's ID sequence. Tygg chinned the channel open. "Go ahead, Backstop Two."

"Lots of Hkh'Rkh gathered on the other side of the river, but they're staying under cover. And the APCs haven't come forward. I'm thinking their move on this ford is a feint."

Tygg nodded at no one. "It is: they've rolled north to join the forces heading toward me." He glanced at the fire team of Cold Guards behind the low stone berm they'd constructed over the past day. Four hundred meters further back and fifty meters up the river-facing side of the eastern ridge, his "Backstop" group was like the two others led by Miles and Peter Wu, respectively: a fire brigade of Cold Guard who could not only bring long-range precision fire to bear upon the ford they oversaw, but more importantly, were experienced target designators. "It looks like the Hkh'Rkh are curious to see what we've got waiting for them."

"Not one big rush?"

"Nope: three APCs."

"Any foot behind them?"

"A few, but I think they're turning back. The water's almost hip-deep on them." Tygg watched the usually stoic and determined Hkh'Rkh thrash uncertainly in the cold, strong current and then reverse their direction. Corporal Katie Somers glanced meaningfully toward the milling and exposed enemy infantry. Tygg shook his head, muttered into the pickup, "Damn, seems like the locals don't like the water much."

"They didn't mind chasing us through rice paddies in Java."

"Yeah, but that was standing water, only ankle-deep. They're not enjoying this at all. But keep an eye peeled, Chief: your ford is about a quarter meter shallower than this one. That might make them a little more bold."

"Got it. O'Garran out."

Somers was staring up at Tygg. "Lead APC is about halfway across, sir."

"Right. Listen up," he said to the team in Backstop One, "there are three APCs and three of you. Follow your target selection order and paint 'em." He chin-toggled the channel for dedicated support. "MULTI Two?"

"Ready and waiting. We have visual on the APCs."

"Watch for our laser-painting. We'll try to give you deck shots."

"Captain, deck shots mean high angle of attack. That gives them more time for point-defense fire."

"Not a worry. Our tactical intel tells us they've got militia-grade equipment. No PDF."

"Happy days, then. We fire on your mark."

The three Cold Guard were sighting down their CoBro scopes, adjusting the controls. Each weapon began emitting a laser-designation beam, cycling through various wavelengths in the UV end of the spectrum. The troopers began to call off their readiness.

"Two: target painted."

"One: target painted," confirmed Somers a moment later.

"Three: pai—ah, damnit: hold still. Um...Three: painted," said the last.

Tygg leaned toward the mic in his helmet. "MULTI Two, stand ready."

"Standing by. You sure you don't want to bring two more MULTIs in on this, hit them all at once?"

"Negative. We're not going to reveal more than one weapon location."

"Lucky us."

"You will launch three armor-piercing. Half-second intervals. Reload same. Program all for overhead engagement profile."

"Already done."

"And..."—Tygg watched the lead enemy APC enter the heaviest current, slow as it nosed in. He waited for the other two to close the distance, deforming their delta formation into more of a ragged line—"mark."

Three kilometers to the rear and four hundred and fifty meters higher, Bannor Rulaine swung his binoculars from the three APCs to MULTI Two, which was positioned on a lipped ledge about halfway between his position on the ridgeline and the riverbank. The quad-mounted cluster of seven tubes swung upward, two thirds of the way to vertical and—*thupp, thupp, thupp*—pumped out three rockets in rapid succession. The crew swarmed back around the lightly built weapon before dust from the minimal backblast had settled, reloads at the ready.

Kicked free of their tubes by a small charge, the

rockets ignited at sixty meters altitude. White plumes marked the point where their almost lazy climbs became a flashing sprint upward and then a screaming slash down toward the river—and the APCs.

The first two struck the APCs on their upper surfaces, penetrating with a sound like a pile-driver crashing through steel plate, just before internal explosions rocked the wheeled vehicles. The second one evidently struck internal munitions: a second explosion, much louder and more violent than the first, blew the top hatches off, a sudden gout of flame and smoke jetting up ten meters.

The third rocket came down on the glacis, or front, plate of its target; it penetrated, but already at a slightly skewed angle. The vehicle slewed to a stop, sagging to the left. Crew and infantry starting clambering out into the heavy current, the vehicle smoking and hissing as the cold water ran over the superheated metal and compounds that rimmed the ragged gap torn by the rocket. One of the Hkh'Rkh, stumbling from a leg wound, lost his footing in the current, hooted, reached for a comrade's cruciform hand, but was swept away. His head broke the swells once, then was buried under them again and did not reappear.

Rulaine scanned the far shore: the Hkh'Rkh who had thought to cross on foot were loping swiftly back to the positions in which they had been waiting since the prior night. He activated the laser designator in the binoculars, painted each of their fighting pits, sent the coordinates on to *Puller*'s computer, which was managing the battle from the safety of main base Dante.

Bannor's earbud, tuned to the channel linking Tygg's team with MULTI Two, became active again. "I've got about a dozen hostiles in the clear," Katie Somers was almost shouting. "Request permission to open—"

Rulaine did not wait for Tygg, in part because he wanted the troops to know the order came from the top. "Negative," he broke in. "Do not open fire. Repeat, do not open fire. That's what they want us to do."

"Sir?" Somers sounded equally perplexed and disappointed.

Normally, Bannor would have told the corporal to pipe down, or let his NCO do it for him, but the question was a useful springboard for driving home a crucial tactical lesson. "Soldier, if they had really meant to take us on this time, they would have hit us with everything they had and would have started the show with a rolling barrage. Which would not be effective at this point. They want to find our positions, particularly those of our spotters, designators, and heavy weapons. But they'll be happy to fix the location of your fighting holes, too. Which are barely deep enough to provide you with cover."

"Or a shallow grave," Rich Hailey muttered from further up the line.

"My point exactly, Captain. They know we can't dig in very deep and we have almost no overhead cover, so once they find us, they'll try to put airbursts over our positions. So we don't give them anything to shoot at: not until they've committed the bulk of their force and they're most of the way across the river. Now, MULTI Two: pop some of those old-time smoke grenades and relocate to alternate firing position one."

"Roger that, Umpire Two."

Bannor looked down at the river again. The three smoking APCs straddled the middle ribbon—the shallowest part—of the ford. Tygg had timed the strike not merely with competence, but artistry. When the Hkh'Rkh tried to come across again, they would either have to split their forces to either side of that central obstruction, and thereby move into even deeper waters, or take the time to push the wrecks out of the way—and make themselves slow, easy targets while they did so.

Rulaine lowered the binoculars, scanned the length of the now-quiet river valley. *With a healthy dose of luck, some of us might even live to tell the story of what happened here.*

Ezzraamar stood well back as Jrekhalkar, muttering oaths, viewed the dioptiscope footage that had been carried back to him. "They only exposed that one position?"

"Yes, Voice."

"Well, we shall do what we may. Get one of the scout cars and drive to the ridgeline. Signal MRL Three to put a full flight of rockets on the enemy weapon that just—"

Ezzraamar sucked the phlegm out of his snout, signifying he was taking care to ensure that his speech was perceived as respectful. "Voice, the humans will not be there."

Jrekhalkar turned on him. "What? Why do you say this?"

"I was never on the surface of their homeworld, but I processed many of the after-action reports submitted by our invading units. The weapon they used was what they call a MULTI—a Multiple Use Launch Tube, Infantry. Because it is nothing more than a reconfigurable stand, a cluster of seven hexagonally framed launch tubes, and a detachable control unit, it is easily and swiftly readied for use. It is even more swiftly broken down and relocated. On Earth, only immediate response by our air units had a reasonable chance of catching them before they disappeared. And here, we not only lack air assets but may not even use radio to communicate coordinates and direct fire." He swiveled his neck in a wide, profound Hkh'Rkh shrug. "Unless these humans are foolish enough to leave the MULTI unmoved, all we would accomplish in firing at it would be to reveal the location of our own weapons."

"Which are hidden behind the western ridge," Jrekhalkar rebutted, flinging his arm in that direction.

"Yes, Voice, but again, I must point out that the humans have extraordinary foreknowledge of our movements. I suspect they have seeded this area with small drones of various kinds, possess an overhead platform that we have not detected, or both. Consequently, even though our batteries will be out of their line of sight, I believe the humans may be able to determine their position and initiate counterbattery fire."

"Yes, but with what? These MULTIs do not have sufficient range."

"No, but consider the report we received from the light mechanized platoon that will soon arrive at the Site. Something struck and destroyed much of the scout troop that was pinning down the humans there. So our enemy has munitions—larger rockets, I suspect—that engaged a target over sixty kilometers away. It would be quite simple for them to engage our artillery at a range of ten kilometers."

Jrekhalkar looked around his council of war, seeking suggestions: none were forthcoming. They were all Warriors, but none of them had worn the livery of the Patrijuridicate, had ever fought as part of a modern army. He stared at Ezzraamar again. "What did our forces do when confronted with such problems on Earth?"

"I regret to report that there are no direct parallels. We had far more modern equipment and had ready access to the Arat Kur command and control net. However, let us assume this much: that our mortars have neither the precision, nor the striking power, to be assured of eliminating the enemy's heavy weapons in counterbattery fire." Ezzraamar paused. *Should I share this? These are my people, my own blood—but the more effectively they fight now, the more likely that the humans will not escape and so we shall be at war. But if I do not give them better plans, how many more Warriors will die?* He closed his eyes and let his first loyalties, his reflex, guide him. "Our mortars must be considered expendable, therefore. They should provide the covering bombardment for our main attack. When our forces cross the river in greater numbers, the humans will respond as they did just now, but with all the force at their disposal. That is when we must use our radio squelch discipline to call in a full MRL bombardment against any heavy weapon we can see—or suspect. For as long as we may."

"They will counterfire at our mobile rocket launchers once they have destroyed our mortars," Jrekhalkar observed grimly.

Ezzraamar allowed his eyes to recede in slow, grim, regret. "I fear that too, Honored Voice. But if we do not find a way to cross the river, how may we prevail?"

Jrekhalkar glared at the eastern shore where the humans remained quiet and motionless in whatever positions they had prepared. He looked back at Ezzraamar. "We shall do as you suggest. And we may yet surprise them with a target they may have forgotten to protect. We shall attack immediately."

Z'gluurhek straightened. "We do not wait for dusk, My Voice?"

Jrekhalkar looked at the sun; it was barely noon. "We dare not. Time is on the side of the invaders. Even though they must repair several air vehicles, they are industrious and not wholly incompetent. Should they manage to regain the use of their transport, we have no sure way of bringing it down. And once it passes behind their ridgeline, how may we hope to stop them? They can hold the fords, and then the switchbacks that lead up the eastern ridge, most of which narrow into passes that our vehicles cannot easily navigate. By the time we could dislodge even a modest holding force, the humans will have boarded their vehicles and left."

Z'gluurhek was so surprised that he forgot to be politic. "So . . . you believe they are here to merely remove their forces, after all?"

Jrekhalkar's black eyes bulged in the direction of his short-sighted ally. "I believe that whatever their initial plans, the humans see that we are too strong for them to prevail in this place. However, what they might do after leaving this region I cannot foresee. Perhaps they will fly elsewhere on Turkh'saar, biding their time until more of their invasion force arrives. Or perhaps they will simply soar over our heads and lay waste to Iarzut'thruk, where we left only a token force. So we must hold them—and defeat them—here. Now."

Growls and mutters of agreement rose up all around the circle.

Ezzraamar was glad he had fallen from their attention, so that they did not detect his silence. Or correctly construe the misgivings it concealed.

Chapter Forty-Three

Top Sergeant Matthew Fanny ducked down into his shallow hole at Dugout Four, the forward position holding the middle ford across the River Kakaagsukh. "Here it comes," he called down the line.

Several faces looked up at him in confused terror: submariners wearing painted-over Nazi helmets and clutching museum-piece submachine guns that could have been present at the St. Valentine's Day massacre. The other eight troops manning Dugout Four simply tucked their heads down with the fatalism of soldiers who've been shelled before: if your number is up, it's up—but no reason to tempt fate.

The Russian sniper—who'd been itching to use his Dragunov all day—muttered "*Svolochi*" and then shook his head. "Mortars. Always mortars."

"Wait," muttered Fanny. "You mean you can hear—?"

A high-pitched sound zoomed closer, like a tiny jet nosediving. Then a blast and the ground shook.

"Christ, that was close!" shouted one of the submariners. "They've got us ranged in!"

591

"Shut up, Harrison," Fanny said loudly, making sure his voice carried over any following explosions. "Don't give away our position. And they sure as hell don't have us ranged in."

"True," muttered the Russian, "but they are very lucky, to be so close."

Another round burst behind them, too far away for them to hear the rush of its final descent, but dirt and leaves erupted in a savaged, circular spatter-pattern, radiating out fifty meters from where an angry burst of smoke had appeared, approximately ten meters off the ground.

"And they are big mortars, too," the Russian added. "Some set for airburst."

"Airburst? Oh, shit!" It was one of the Americans who'd been in Vietnam; he wailed his outburst more than he spoke it. Next to him, a Pashtun started a sing-song mantra: "*Allahu-akbar. Allahu-akbar. Allahu-akba—*"

Then Fanny couldn't hear anything for the thunder of all the rounds rushing down and bursting both high and low. He checked his CoBro, made sure that his commbud was fixed firmly in his ear so he wouldn't miss any orders and told himself that this was just like training. Just like training. Just like training...

—while his common sense rebutted, with the perfect calm of suppressed terror—

Bullshit.

As per protocols, Riordan pulled all his CP elements back inside Wedge One as soon as the mortar rounds began falling. Not many made it more than two thirds of the way up the ridge, but there was

always the exception that made the rule. He continued speaking into his mic. "So, only mortar fire?" he
asked Bannor as he motioned for Gaudet to close the
bridge windows' blast shields.

"You'd know it if they dropped one of their rockets
on us. But they're waiting for us to start hitting their
APCs as they cross: they don't want to bring out their
big stick until they can see where our MULTIs are
positioned."

"Then let's see if we can upset their gameplan: we
hit their mortar carriers with MISLS."

"Caine, we don't have enough MISLS to knock out
all their mortars."

"That's not my intent, Major. I want them to see
us launch a *few* of our solo-stand MISLS. That might
bait them into counterfiring with their MRLs."

He could hear Rulaine's smile. "And that's when
we use our clustered MISLS to hit their MRLs with
counterbattery fire."

"Right. And that way, we ensure that our MULTIs
remain intact for defending the fords."

"Good. I just hope this damn barrage doesn't suppress our Backstop teams, or block their laser designators. If it does, it will still be tricky hitting those
APCs when they cross."

"You can't control everything."

If Rulaine still had a smile on his face, his tone
told Caine that it had become rueful. "Commodore,
once the shooting starts, you can't control *any*thing.
Umpire Two out." His comlink terminated with a snick.

Riordan watched the combined data overview—the
EXHALTED's picture integrated with the rest of the
sensor inputs from drones, creepers, and weapon

scopes—and saw that the APCs were pushing all three fords simultaneously, the rate of mortar fire increasing along with their speed of approach. He toggled the circuit back to *Puller*. "Karam?"

"Was wondering when you were going to drop the hammer."

"We're only going to drop a little hammer at first. How many solo-stand MISLS do we have left?"

"Twelve."

"Good. Use look-down guidance from EXHALTED and hit their mortar tracks at thirty-second intervals."

"Why so long a gap?"

"Because I want them to see where we're launching from."

"Huh? Oh. Yeah. So they'll detect the launch points and go counterbattery with their MRLs." He paused. "They're likely to guess the con."

"They are, but if we take out all their mortar tracks, we eliminate their ability to lay down a barrage. They can't afford to let that happen: it's their only chance of disrupting our ability to defend the fords. So they'll have to illuminate their counterbattery radars to hit our launch sites, and use their radios to communicate the coordinates."

"Got it," Tsaami confirmed. "And we'll hit all those RF emission sources with our remaining, clustered MISLS. I'm just not sure we've got enough rockets for all those targets."

Riordan thought. "In order of priority, then. Get their radars first. Then the MRLs. Ignore the radios: we can keep jamming them."

"Roger that. When do you want me to start the fireworks?"

"Commence launching in two minutes. And tell Duncan to finish suiting up to drive the Proxie. We might need him sooner rather than later."

As soon as the sensuit had tightened itself into full contact with his body, Duncan Solsohn opened his eyes and discovered that his virtual self was in a dense thicket of clustertrees. The vision of the Proxie was a close approximation of human eyes, but was flatter and lacked nuances, such as changing depth of focus when looking down into water—as he did now from his slightly elevated perch on a wooded promontory overlooking Dugout Five.

But there were advantages, too. He looked across the river, pushing the reflex that increased both focus and magnification. The mostly concealed hull of a Hkh'Rkh APC swam into view. He checked to see if prior sensors had marked it, found that a creeper had done so less than two hours ago, swung his robotic head to look along the length of the nearby stretch of river...

...and involuntarily flinched back as a brace of mortar rounds hammered down south of the middle ford, one slapping airburst fragments into the northern edge of Dugout Five.

"Dora," he muttered over the headset.

She was on *Puller*'s bridge, only eight meters away from the gunnery bubble. But it sounded and felt more like a thousand kilometers. "Yeah, what?"

"Dugout Five just got tagged. They might have casualties."

A pause. "Yeah, got the overwatch report from Little Guy in Backstop Two. No one hurt so badly that we're counting down on the golden hour. So we'll be holding medevac until we see if there are more—and worse—casualties. Now stop the battlefield updates. We've got other channels for that. Just ready your gear and wait for the call. Uh, Major."

"Roger that."

Duncan held out his mechanical hand, activated a rear-angled fiber-optic cam so he could conduct a whole-body readiness check.

The long-barreled CoBro was firmly braced on the Proxie's right arm by a command-release frame and fitted with a five-hundred-round cassette: despite the anthrobot's heavy-duty servos, the added weight changed the weapon's balance. The CoBro's hot juice was in two large, feed-linked cannisters, the kind usually provided for machine guns. Solsohn smiled: he might run out of ammunition before the end of the day, but it wasn't likely.

His left hand held the rifle's grenade launcher, now detached to work as a separate weapon. Fitted with a selectable drum magazine usually employed with vehicle mounts, it was loaded with every kind of warhead he could want, except for a stick-RAP. A triple-length system, the "stick" couldn't be loaded unless both the launcher's breech was empty and the special magazine was detached. But just in case, he had three of the small antiarmor rockets—the only three they had—in a satchel attached to his back.

Scanning the frame of his remote self was not a memorable aesthetic experience. The Proxie was homely and, while bipedal, would not be mistaken for a human at any distance, not even orbital. Its "head" was an asymmetric, well-armored sensor cluster, its torso a stick-figure with exaggerated joints and what looked like a rear-mounted ribcage: a large carrying rack, mounted atop the anthrobot's high-gain batteries. Multiply redundant lascom links extruded or flattened like mini sea-fans, ensuring constantly adapting communication links to the improvised operator rig in which Duncan Solsohn was currently standing, the sensuit mimicking his actions. Most importantly, his gear was all loaded in locations and at angles easy to reach and manipulate: whereas body movements were easy for the gunnery bubble to mimic accurately, hand controls were more difficult, particularly because there was not a perfect correspondence between the equipment on the Proxie and the matching dummy items that Duncan would handle while wearing the sensuit.

Solsohn finished by scanning his surround-HUD for yellow or red lights, saw none. "Puppet One checks out; asset ready for tasking."

"Acknowledged." Dora sounded like she was eating. And bored.

Duncan let a few seconds pass. "Now what?"

"Now you wait. Like the rest of us."

Bannor watched another wave of mortar rounds roll from the bank of the river halfway up the ridge. Before the echoes of the blasts had finished reverberating back and forth across the valley, more reports of casualties came in. Firing blind, the Hkh'Rkh weren't scoring a lot of hits, but lots of the troops in the seven river-lining outposts—the Dugouts—had no prior experience of hunkering down during a barrage: an experience famous for breaking the morale of green troops. *Any time now, Caine...*

As if in answer to that thought, the flat expanse of scattered copses and bracken that stretched behind Rulaine began emitting almost vertical missile plumes, the buzzing snarls of high-performance rockets trailing in their wake. One after the other, they sprinted into high parabolic arcs that curved tightly over and down into screaming descents as they disappeared behind the far ridgeline. Most often, a distant *krummpfff* and eventual wisp of dark smoke indicated that they had hit their targets: tracked mortar carriers. But occasionally, the blast was larger, sharper, and the smoke came faster and thicker: a likely sign that the track had not only been hit, but its ammunition had exploded as well.

Rulaine checked his helmet's HUD, selected and enlarged the EXHALTED's bird's eye view. Sure enough, three of the mortar carriers were wholly engulfed in flames, rounds still cooking off sporadically. Others smoldered sullenly, abandoned.

As he watched, the enemy's tracked MRLs rolled out of the woods, their large, enclosed missile racks elevating slowly.

"Bannor." It was Paulsen's voice; he was standing by at the electronic warfare panels with Dora when he wasn't out walking the flight-line, keeping the ground and air crews on their toes.

"Yes, Colonel?"

"Enemy radar is alive and their radio traffic is spiking. Say the word and we'll shut it down."

"We're going to wait for them to launch their missiles and give us easy counterbattery targets." Which was sort of like waiting to be hit in the face so your adversary can't stop you from hitting back even harder.

The Hkh'Rkh didn't keep him waiting for very long. Once the MRLs had raised their tubes to sixty degrees elevation, they began firing missiles. One, and then a second, each.

Bannor jumped on the main tactical channel. "All units. Missiles inbound; repeat, missiles inbound."

Up and down the ridgeline he heard cries of "cover!" Down in the valley, he could hear similar shouts, attenuated by the distance and quickly swallowed by the tapering mortar fire. Even though the MISLS had launched from behind the ridge, that did not guarantee safety for the troops guarding the fords in the valley.

The Hkh'Rkh weapons were not small and precise, like the MISLS. They were essentially fifteen-centimeter bombardment rockets. Their larger warheads not only made them more broadly destructive, but also meant they possessed the capacity to carry far more sophisticated munitions...

—Wait: more sophisticated munitions? Shit!

Bannor broke into the secure comlink, shouted for Wedge Three. It took Phil Friel two agonizing seconds to respond. "What's the—?"

"Friel. Don't talk: listen. Who do you have for PDF control?"

"On this bird? No one but me, and I—"

Damn it. Probably not more than forty seconds, now. "Spin up your turret and make it ready for remote control." Rulaine was already paging *Puller*.

"Spin up the—? But that means active arrays for targeting. If I do that—"

"The Hkh'Rkh already know where you are. You're disabled, a fixed target. Dora?"

"Yeah?"

"Karam needs to take charge of the PDF system on Wedge Three by remote control. Now."

"What? Why—?"

"No time. Just do it."

Karam's voice joined in. "Wedge Three PDF is now on my remote. I can see—holy shit! That's a lot of missiles."

"Yeah. Tighten your intercept radius to three klicks."

"Roger. Recalibrating intercept envelope. But Bannor, the chance that they're going to land an unguided ballistic rocket right on a wedge is—"

"Those aren't just dumb HE rounds, Karam. The Hkh'Rkh have overhead antiarmor systems in their inventory: drag-chute deployed, independent lookdown targeting. The rocket will unload the system over the valley and that secondary munition will find the transport and fire straight downward at it: a nine-centimeter HEAT rocket, if I remember the stats."

"Well, shit. Then you'd better spin up the PDFs on the other wedges as well."

Damn it, he's right. "Sending those instructions now."

The first shuddering downward rush of a rocket moaned over and behind Rulaine, ended in a deafening blast. The epicenter of tree-splintering ruin was within thirty meters of the first MISLS launch site: a perfectly effective counterbattery strike—except that there was nothing left to hit. Which was the whole point of setting up a number of the MISLS on solo-stands.

Then, Bannor heard a dull burst high over the valley, and the video feed in his helmet showed parts of a rocket tumbling down. However, behind and beneath them, a small parachute had opened, a dark object cradled beneath it: a secondary, target-seeking missile. "Karam—!"

But neither the Flight Officer nor the mostly automated PDF system needed the warning. As a rocket launched itself downward from the parachute's munitions sling, the tree-obscured clearing occupied by Wedge Three emitted a sound akin to a buzzsaw chewing through cinderblocks. The descending missile detonated with a flash and a bark; the tattered parachute swayed down, tumbling from wind current to wind current.

Scanning his HUD's overview from EXHALTED, Rulaine saw a dozen more exhaust trails converging on both the valley and the launch sites behind the eastern ridgeline. "This would be a bad time for a PDF malfunction," he observed solemnly.

"Damn, and I thought I was morbid," Karam muttered in reply.

"You are," Bannor affirmed. "Just keep killing missiles."

Chapter Forty-Four

When the last mortar round came down out of a sky filled with the smoke trails and thunder of missiles, Matthew Fanny was doing just what he was supposed to: making himself one with the skin-burning dirt of Turkh'saar.

That last blast was so loud it deafened him, even with his helmet sealed and its protective audio cut-off active. It also bounced him almost a centimeter off the ground as dirt jetted up all along the rim of his fragment-flayed fighting position. Had it been one of the airbursting shells, no one in the shallow foxholes of Dugout Four would have been left alive. A painful ringing in his ears, Fanny glanced down the line.

The Pashtun and the American who'd served in Vietnam were dead. Their shirts were pocked by multiple penetration wounds, as were their necks. The blood flowing down from under the Afghani's turban and the American's helmet indicated that the lethal fragments had struck both of them in the head as well, and with enough force to penetrate curved steel plate as easily as cloth wrappings.

Harrison, the submariner was half upright in his hole and miraculously, paradoxically, unscathed. He was also gaping in wide-eyed terror. He started to rise, tensed to run—

Fanny gestured at Vani, the Russian sniper, who was closest to Harrison. "Grab him," he shouted. "Keep him down."

Vani turned to Fanny. "That will be difficult," he said calmly. His right hand was clenching the stump of his lower left arm; a widening pool of blood was gathering between his knees. Harrison darted away, running wildly, shouting what might have been words or just howls of terror.

The other five in Dugout Four's staggered row of holes—one of the Cold Guard, a submariner, two Americans, and a Russian from the Sevastopol group—were unhurt. Fanny waved the Russian over, pointed to the dead American's belt. "Tourniquet," he said, pointing to Vani's left arm.

The Russian, whose name he could never remember, glanced at the corpse, followed Fanny's gesture without comprehension.

Vani nodded at the taciturn fellow. *"Pozhalusta: turniket."*

The stocky Soviet nodded and complied with admirable alacrity.

"I guess it's in the accent?" Fanny commented, referring to the nearly identical terms.

Vani tried to smile. "Evidently so."

The veteran of Sevastopol winced apologetically when he finished the tourniquet and, using a cleaning rod, began tightening it. Vani made no sound, did not change expression, but became more pale.

"Your friend doesn't talk much," Fanny observed.

Vani shrugged slightly with his right shoulder. "He has not learned any language beyond his own. Uzbek, I think. He has just a little Russian. This embarrasses him."

The silent Soviet was now strapping the cleaning rod against Vani's arm, looping another belt around it as gently as he could to hold it in place. As he did so, the last of the MISLS began whining down behind the distant western ridgeline across the river. Matthew chinned his commlink, made sure he kept his voice calm as he called in his report to Backstop Two. "This is Dugout Four, reporting two KIA, one WIA for immediate medevac, one MIA. Down to six combat effectives. Still have full laser-designation capability—"

The other Cold Guard—a Maori by the name of Akiriri—shook his head. "My designator's shot." He held up his CoBro: the scope had almost been sliced in half by a fragment.

"Correction," Fanny backtracked, "down to one designation-capable operator. Am consulting Know-It-All to confirm reconfiguration of squad. Please acknowledge, Backstop Two."

After a brief delay, Miles O'Garran came on the line. "We've got your back, Dugout Four. Are shifting three effectives from reserve group Charlie to your command. They will signal for smoke to cover their final approach. Tell your WIA to hang tight; we will medevac ASAP."

Fanny glanced at Vani, who had stopped getting

any paler, but had also stopped talking. His eyes were unfocused. Fanny tried to keep his voice from becoming impatient. "On that medevac: any idea when ASAP might be, Chief?"

There was a pause. "Not as soon as I'd like."

Riordan watched the overhead as the MISLS slammed down into the Hkh'Rkh's dispersed array of MRL launchers.

Tracking back along each rocket's flight path to the intense thermal bloom that marked its launch point, the MISLS were unerringly accurate. One after the other, the MRL tracks flared and died. In many cases, one of the human weapons flashed down into a nearly full launch rack, detonating the warheads and rocket fuel. Billowing mushrooms of flame climbed upward, transforming into expanding smears of black smoke.

"Well," commented Dora who was watching the same feed back in *Puller*, "I hope we hit them all, because we're never going to see anything down there again. Not through that smoke."

"You'd still spot engine thermals," Caine observed, "but yeah, those vehicles will be burning for the next twelve hours, at least."

"But we *did* get them all...didn't we?"

"All the ones we've seen, even a few that didn't fire. The radar tracks didn't go up with the same fireworks, but it looks like we got them as well."

"One of which must have been a comm vehicle also, judging from the amount of radio traffic that went dead when we pranged it," added Karam. "I'd say their command, control, and indirect fire capabilities are fubared."

Riordan scanned the overhead one last time. "Yes, but we're down to our last two MISLS and have taken a fair number of casualties along the line. Fourteen killed, almost three times that many wounded. And we'll have to be careful bringing in the medevacs: all their APCs are still under cover and equipped with very big, long-ranged machine guns."

"Yeah. A bit of a standoff," Karam mused. "If they come across the river, we can blast the hell out of them. But if we try to move airmobile units over our ridgeline, they can hammer at us with dozens of autocannons."

Riordan studied the map. "They could have ways of making their crossing less costly. Their APCs' smoke dispensers might have prismatic antilaser aerosols and thermal damping compounds. The first would prevent reliable laser designation, the second would keep us from seeing them until they emerge from the cloud. And both together—"

"—would suck for us," Dora concluded.

Riordan nodded at her summary. "If they get any sizeable forces across the river, we can expect to lose the upper hand pretty damn quickly. A confused, close-range firefight is their best-case scenario—and our worst. We'd lose control of the fords, and ultimately discover that night is only a friend to the sixty of us with night-vision gear: the Cold Guards and ourselves. Everyone else will be blind."

"You think they're setting up for a night attack?"

"Could be. But I think they'd prefer getting across before night and then hunting us down as dark falls."

Dora's voice lacked its customary sardonic edge. "Then we'd better get this wrapped up today."

"I agree. Any word from Dr. Sleeman?" It was an empty question: Dora would certainly have alerted him. But, just on the off chance that, with all the activity, she had not yet remembered to mention it ...

"Nada." Dora's tone was annoyed: whether at him or the situation in general was unclear.

"Change of topic. Is Colonel Paulsen there?"

The American colonel sounded like he was leaning over Dora's shoulder. "Right here, Commodore. Nothing much happening on the flight line, just now."

"That's about to change. Spin them up, Pat: I think we're going to need the attack choppers. Soon."

Bannor waited as Miles O'Garran finished talking Top Sergeant Fanny through the procedures for an airborne medevac. Most conventional militaries had turned it into a mostly automated process. But as the resistance in Indonesia, and now the engagement on Turkh'saar, proved, the automation-mania which had swept most human armies from the late twenty-first century onward was based on overly optimistic assessments of how reliable machine-directed services were on an actual battlefield. In practice, things went sideways so quickly, and in such strange ways, that robots got too confused too often to be reliable. Humans, ultimately, were vastly better at wrangling full-on chaos, with machines as their helpers, not their stand-ins.

Before Fanny signed off, Rulaine jumped on the line. "Sergeant, you did not sound reassured when Chief O'Garran asserted that Backstop Two could provide you with enough target-designation to compensate for the loss of Private Akiriri's system."

Fanny, clearly surprised that Rulaine had been listening, fumbled for a moment. "Y-yes, sir. Major. Well, it's the breeze down here by the river."

"Come again?"

"Major, the river's current is pretty strong. Pulls a cool breeze along with it. So if they hit us with smoke preliminary to an attack, you guys upslope—the three Backstop groups and the MULTIs—could be blanketed in. But down here by the river, that smoke is going to clear faster. So they could come across at us while you're still blind. And I'm the only person in Dugout Four that can laser-designate targets. One at a time might not be fast enough, sir."

As usual, the troops on the ground were aware of potentially decisive terrain or weather conditions that just didn't show on the sensors—or if it did, that didn't call attention to its tactical consequences. Unfortunately, this particular circumstance might present a more serious problem than Fanny realized: if the Hkh'Rkh were equipped with laser-defeating aerosols, then, in order for the MULTI rounds to acquire the laser targeting, they were going to have to fire single rounds, launched high, like they had last time. Each warhead would have to clear the top of the smokescreen, look down, find the phase-shifting UV pinprick projected by Fanny's CoBro, and then streak down to take out the vehicle. Per kill, that was going to take a lot more time than engaging with direct fire, and if the Hkh'Rkh planned to come across the ford in a rush, time would be in short supply. "I see your point, Sergeant Fanny. Have you been thinking of any fixes?"

"Yes, sir. Can we move any quadrotors into my

AO? Or a dedicated drone? Any platform that has a laser designator on board?"

"No, Top. We lost almost a third of those systems in the last twenty minutes, particularly the smaller ones."

"Lost them? How?"

"All the shelling. Particularly ground strikes: the quadrotors weren't any safer in the air than you were on the ground, and we had no cover under which to park them. Frankly, we didn't foresee the Hkh'Rkh cutting loose with that full-on mortar barrage without even attempting to conduct some more ranging fire. We moved a lot of the ROVs and automated systems out of the barrage by sending them up the slope, but anything that got tagged—well, you know how fragile those systems are. Except for the full-fledged drones, one shot is a mission-kill on them."

"What do we do then, Major? When the Hkh'Rkh see the smoke you're going to lay down to cover the approach of our choppers, they'll know we're moving casualties and reinforcements. It also gives them free cover from our MULTIs. I'm betting that's when they'll hammer us again. Or try coming across in a wave."

Damned if I don't agree with you, Top.

From Backstop Two, O'Garran added an optimistic note. "Well, if they do, they won't have a barrage to support them: their mortar tracks have fallen back. The ones that are left, that is."

"Yeah," replied Fanny, "but Chief, you've seen and heard all the vehicular movement on the other shore. You've seen the estimates from the EXHALTED. They've got enough infantry and heavy weapons to hammer my Dugout to pieces, or at least keep our heads down so low that I'll be lucky to laser-designate one APC before they smoke me. And the Know-It-All agrees. 'Position untenable,' it tells me."

Bannor nodded to himself: the time had come to play their wild card. "You're right, Sergeant. But I'm not sure a quadrotor or even a drone would do the trick. Either one would have to maintain a clear line of sight to the ford. Which means the Hkh'Rkh would have a reciprocally clear line of sight to shoot down those flying eyes."

"So what do you plan to do, sir?"

"I'm going to send you a pair of eyes they *can't* shoot down so easily." He prepared to toggle the link to *Puller*. "Now get ready to pop smoke and move your wounded to the evac point."

Duncan Solsohn closed the link with Bannor. *Time to get in the game.*

He brought the Proxie out of standby mode. The batteries surged, the capacitor's RPM climbed, the suit's various microwave energy receptors signalled ready—moot, since there was no MW broadcast power available.

He activated the embedded thermoflage: the Proxie's selective heat bleeding and thermionic recapture plates would be likely to keep him off enemy TI and IR scopes beyond one hundred meters. But he felt the lack of a chromaflage wrap. Referred to by the press as a chameleon suit, it was particularly useful to Proxies, since their angular outlines tended to make them more visible than humans in a non-urban environment.

But chromaflage wraps were the kind of equipment that the Rag Tag Fleet had assiduously scooped up before they had shifted out of Delta Pavonis to commence their relief of Earth. There would be none of the bells-and-whistles add-ons to which Duncan had grown accustomed during his IRIS missions.

Doesn't matter. Like the live-ops instructor told us, "Add-ons are helpful, but not essential, to a trained operator." An axiom he would now start putting to the test.

He walked backward on the movement-pad they'd installed in the gunnery bubble. The surface under him reacted to his motion, compensated, kept him centered, working like a three-hundred-sixty-degree treadmill. Despite the lack of precise motion correlation—the pad's reaction to operator movement was not absolute— the Proxie followed Solsohn's actions and walked backward out of the bushes and clustertrees crowning the rocky river-overlook in which it had been waiting.

Once clear of the foliage, Solsohn got his bearings, both visually and by instrument. He was only one hundred and fifty meters from a protected line-of-sight position that would bear upon the middle ford. And Dugout Four.

He curled both pinkies into his palms, activating the Proxie's physical amplification system. As soon as its orange warning lights illuminated, he bit down as hard as he could on the amplification intensity control sensor between his molars and jumped forward.

The Proxie, now primed to magnify the user's motions to the maximum possible degree, leaped ahead thirty meters, its onboard sensors and gyroscopic stabilizers bringing it to a sure-footed landing.

Teeth still clamped down on the intensity sensor, Duncan started jogging to his destination. The Proxie sped between copses, remaining concealed from the opposite river bank.

Ezzraamar watched silently as Jrekhalkar, bleeding from small wounds on the left side of his long head, stared at the mostly functional electronic battle map. It had only survived the strike on his command and communication track because it had been surrounded by his staff when the human MISLS wailed down and blasted it: the only vehicle that had been struck on the river side of the western ridge. The thick, muscular torsos of two of the most mathematically gifted scions of the Old Families had been between the impact point and the map-slate; they absorbed the majority of the fragments and armor spalling that might have destroyed it. The device had been retrieved from beneath their half-shredded corpses, the blood wiped hastily from its cracked screen.

What Jrekhalkar saw on that screen evidently did not please him. "How many of these losses are confirmed?"

"Almost all, Voice," rasped a wounded adjutant whose tongue was covered with fresh blood every time it emerged from his primary nostril. "Heliographic relay from the ridgeline re-sent the revised roster just two minutes ago. We have five mortar tracks left that can both fire and maneuver, two more which are capable of fire only. Only one MRL remains, but it, too, is immobile: an enemy rocket penetrated and gutted its control cab."

"And the human losses?"

"Impossible to determine with any confidence. We have seen movement in several patches of bracken and copses where we suspected they had fighting positions.

We have also heard rotors behind their ridgeline. We think that they are removing their dead and wounded, and may be preparing to replace their losses from reserves located behind the front."

"You 'think'?"

"They are obscuring their movement with smoke."

Jrekhalkar hooted in annoyed resolve. "Their movement shall determine our own, as well as our own use of smoke. Send word to gather the vehicles of the first assault wave."

"And its Warriors?"

"Not all. We shall employ Option Three, as discussed. Those APCs with rocket launchers are to have their weapons dismounted to tripods. Observers are to take careful note of the enemy heavy weapons positions, higher up the eastern ridge. The rocket launchers are to be moved to concealed positions where we may take the enemy's weapons under direct fire." He gazed around the diminished command circle. "Ezzraamar, you foresaw their tactics. You will stay with me at all times. You will share your insights. You will not be deterred by the possibility of incurring my displeasure."

Easier said than done, Ezzraamar thought while he replied, "As the Voice commands, so shall I do."

"Excellent. Now attend; we have an attack to prepare—and quickly."

Chapter Forty-Five

Matthew Fanny was about to pop smoke to cover the approach of Dugout Four's replacements when the sound of roaring motors came across the River Kakaagsukh. Swinging around, he saw three APCs tear out of the bushes lining the western bank, wheels kicking up scree as they made for the water's edge.

"Report it!" he screamed at Akiriri as he brought up his CoBro and prepared to paint the lead vehicle before it reached its three wrecked mates, still smouldering midstream. But before he could, one of the APCs jerked to a stop and emitted what sounded like a rippling pop. Small black objects flew out from tubes embedded along the top rim of its glacis plate. Comparatively slow and clearly visible, they covered about seventy meters before beginning to tumble toward the river—at which point they burst: a dull, unthreatening sound. Smoke billowed out. They each belched out two more thick clouds before they dropped into the river, sputtering.

Shit. Fanny sighted down the CoBro's scope, activating the laser designator and found that his thermals were not registering the vehicle reliably: it was more of a heat smudge than a silhouette. And the laser designator was not reporting a coherent ping-back: either the smoke was too thick, or it had a prismatic antilaser aerosol mixed in. *Just great.*

"Do you have Umpire Two on the line?" he shouted down the line at Akiriri.

"Waiting. Comchatter says the Hkh'Rkh are doing the same at the northern ford."

Damn it. "Get Backstop Two. Tell them we've got no reliable targeting here. Enemy smoke is ruining our thermal sensors and laser painting."

"Will do."

Although in all probability, the folks higher up were already aware of that. The key question was: what were they going to do about helping Dugout Four?

"Shit, I've got nothing," Miles O'Garran muttered, looking down his scope over the low wall protecting Backstop Two. The second APC crossing the middle ford had rolled to the edge of the smoke laid down by the first vehicle, and, predictably, fired its own cannisters, which reached well beyond the midstream wrecks. He chinned his mic on. "Umpire Two, I do not have targets. They're rolling the smoke forward as they come. They're creating a new base of smoke on the far shore, too. I can't get a solid lock on any of the followup vehicles." He heard revving, straining engines over the rush of the river and thunder of approaching rotors: the medevac bird had crested the ridge just as the attack started. "I think they must be trying to push or tow some of the wrecks aside before they come on. The smoke continues to thicken at midstream. Advise on response: Know-It-All is giving me options that are all bad or waste too many MULTI rounds."

Rulaine's response was immediate. "That's because it doesn't know we've reserved a discretionary asset, kept it out of the matrix. Tell Fanny to sit tight and wave his replacements in: he doesn't need to pop his own smoke anymore. Since the Hkh'Rkh are clearing the wrecks he's got an extra minute or two. Same with the medevac, but they still need to get in and out."

"Yeah, and when the APCs come boiling out of the smoke?"

"We'll have a surprise waiting for them."

Rulaine's voice was sudden and loud in Solsohn's ear. "You in position?"

"Just found good cover. I have eyes on Dugout Four and the middle ford. Well, I would if the smoke wasn't so thick."

"Can you target any of the APCs?"

"One or two. They're trying to stay smoked in, but it looks like they're running low on cannisters and are having a hard time keeping the cloud density uniform." Duncan was familiar with the difficulty: once you were inside smoke, it was damned hard to tell when you needed to add to it, to maintain sufficient opacity. "I can paint a couple of them now."

"Do it. You're networked into the MULTIs. The rockets will launch high, then go to lookdown mode to find your designation."

"Roger that. But the OpFor has laid in a third bank of smoke: they're going to roll out on our side of the river almost on top of Dugout Four."

"Then load a RAP and prepare to engage."

"Uh, Bannor, the Hkh'Rkh are going to know where I am if I do that."

"Only those who can see you through the smoke."

"Or are flanking me on the opposite bank of the river."

"Can't be helped. We need to hold Dugout Four."

"Roger that. Puppet One out." He did not bother to raise the CoBro: the Proxie had a vastly more sophisticated and powerful laser designator built into its head. He let the optic sensors measure the density patterns of the smoke, found the thinnest area, the leading APC within it, kept it painted with his laser, looked for the next in line . . .

The gunner at MULTI Three sounded very uncertain. "Umpire Two, please say again: I am to fire overhead antiarmor rounds *without* lascom confirmation of target paint?"

Bannor kept his tone level. "Affirmative, MULTI Three. A target is painted and will be visible and phase-matched once your round clears the smoke-bank."

"Very well, sir. Firing one."

Down the slope, Bannor heard a faint *thoomf* above the more distant noise of battle; one of the MULTI's comparatively short-ranged rockets leaped into the sky.

An APC—a slope-fronted box stained with mud— roared out of the mist. Fanny swung his CoBro at it, pulled the designation trigger, thought, *Peek-a-boo, you bastard*, and remained as close to the ground as he could. As long as the field of view remained unobstructed, the MULTI's fire-and-forget rockets would not just fly at, but chase, their target as long as they could see it.

But even as Fanny ducked lower, he heard a MULTI launch behind him—in vertical mode. Meaning that MULTI Three, his primary covering battery, was pointed at the sky to launch overhead attacks, not watching the near edge of the smoke. *Damn it: they won't be able to crank down in time.*

The rocket fired by MULTI Three reached the top of its arc, tipped over, activated its seeker head, sweeping the river beneath for the correctly phased UV laser-designation point that matched its targeting data. Much of its primary search footprint, or "basket," was obscured by smoke, some of which was laser-resistant. But just beyond those drifts, it caught a glimpse of the wavelength sequence for which it was searching.

Using its fins to stabilize and align itself to the target, it prepared to ignite its secondary, intercept motor . . .

Fanny kept the CoBro's laser designator on the APC, even when he flinched at the dull *krup-p-p* of its smoke launchers discharging, waited for the sound of the smoke rounds going off—

But before they did, there was a distant fire hose sound that up-dopplered swiftly: MULTI Four had swung around to cover the gap left by MULTI Three's retasking. Which meant that Know-It-All had reacted faster than humans were able to speak, even if they had opted for the same response.

The rocket from MULTI Four hit the APC at an oblique angle on its right hull. The new smoke obscured the flash, but could not diminish the crash of the rocket hitting the armor, the follow-on roar of its warhead ripping through it with a jet of molten metal. Nor could it diminish the sound of another unseen APC being destroyed out in the river, or of the more distant squeal of approaching wheels. That was the next APC in line, which would soon race on into the fog the last one had laid down, and which had rolled over and inundated the ground around Dugout Four.

"Christ, what now?" Akiriri asked at the same moment that their replacement troops threw themselves into the holes left by the earlier casualties.

Fanny was tempted to make a profoundly ironic joke about their timing—arriving just in time to die—but didn't have the heart. Or the second to spare. "Now, you and I go to dual-purpose rocket-assisted projectiles."

"Damn, will DP RAPs get through that armor, Top?"

"I sure hope so. Get ready."

Almost three kilometers upstream, at the north ford, a lane of smoke reached from the west bank to the east bank. Ezzraamar allowed that, while its tail was diminishing somewhat, the head of the multichemical cloud kept widening as the APCs neared the other side, gathering under its cover for a swift rush into the human positions.

"They are almost across," Z'gluurhek reported. His voice was dry, raspy, his open jaw cycling air rapidly as he studied the advance through his dioptiscope. Ezzraamar could not imagine what he thought he was seeing: the far bank was hidden by the gray-white mass. "Nothing can stop them now."

"They will take heavy casualties as soon as they emerge from the smoke," Ezzraamar pointed out.

"As we anticipated," Jrekhalkar agreed. "But if each new vehicle fires smoke when it reaches the edge of the screen, we will ultimately have multiple vehicles on the shore. Once our troops dismount and get among the humans, our victory is secured."

The drumbeat of distant rotors reached them over the sounds of the APC engines and popping smoke cannisters.

"Those rotary-wings are well behind the opposite ridgeline, and heading north," asserted one of Jrekhalkar's honor guard, who had left behind his *halbardiche* and carried a large, drum-fed grenade launcher: a weapon that was usually found on a vehicle mount or a tripod. Its recoil was manageable but its weight was daunting even for a large Hkh'Rkh.

Ezzraamar listened after the rotors, a mix of heavier, slower ones, and several that were lighter, faster. "At least two different kinds of rotary-wings."

Jrekhalkar, who seemed calmer and more focused, now that battle had truly been joined, flattened his crest in mild negation. "If they attempt to come over the ridge, we have adequate firepower from the APCs still hidden in our woodline to drive them back or shoot them down." His staff phlegm-warbled their agreement with his dismissal of any risk the enemy rotary-wings might pose to their crossing.

Ezzraamar did not join them.

Matt Fanny had a sliver of a second to reflect on how realistic his training had been, how well it had technically prepared him for actual combat—and how utterly inadequate it had been at readying him to be within fifteen meters of a hulking slab of an Hkh'Rkh APC. He hastily unloaded the first of the grenades in his underslung launcher: an HE round. He cycled the second grenade—a dual-purpose warhead that had some chance of getting through the enemy vehicle's armor—into the launcher's breech, heard the sound of the enemy's smoke dispensers firing: a dull, muffled sputter.

The cannisters tumbled out over the heads of Fanny's team across a ninety-degree arc, popping and gushing smoke approximately fifty meters behind them. Meaning that in a few moments, Backstop Two wouldn't be able to see Dugout Four any longer, and more to the point, nor would MULTIs Three and Four.

A missile, similar to the one that had knocked out the first APC that had loomed out of the smoke on the riverbank, streaked down the ridge from MULTI Four's position. But whatever laser designation it had been locked to must have been compromised by the growing mist. Instead of hitting the APC in the side, it struck the glacis plate at an acute angle, ricocheted off like a stone skimming on a lake, detonated someplace in the smoke drifts slowly dissipating out over the river.

Fanny rose up, snugging the CoBro to his cheek, called down the line, "Akiriri, set for IR followup." Maybe two dual-purpose RAPs, a second one following right in behind the first's IR trail, would manage to punch a hole in the armor facing them.

"Can't," Akiriri replied. "IR tracking died with the scope, Top."

Shit. Of course it had.

The commander's hatch on the APC opened, swinging forward like a shield. The hulking torso of a Hkh'Rkh was up behind it immediately, grabbing for the machine gun—damn, more like an autocannon—on the pintle mount. At this range, and at this angle, the fighting holes of Dugout Four offered almost no protection. Fanny knew that his next thought was likely his last, was surprised and disappointed at the notion of being shot like a fish in a barrel. Somehow, he'd always imagined getting his ticket punched running in the open, or in a furious close-quarters firefight. But not crouching in a shallow hole like a scared rabbit, a massive armored vehicle looming over him.

He rose up to take what was likely to be his final, futile shot—

A blur to the left of the vehicle. A bipedal figure leaped into view, having sprung out from behind a rock outcropping that bordered on the river. As the vehicle commander swung the APC's immense machine gun down toward Dugout Four, the figure landed, balancing itself immediately despite its angular and awkward appearance. It was the Proxie, its left arm already raised, mounted with the grenade launcher that was usually underslung on a CoBro rifle—but which had no magazine loaded. Which probably meant that Major Solsohn had equipped it with—

The launcher spat out a stick-RAP with a cough that became a raucous hiss as the small rocket ignited and, riding a tail of flame, drove into the flank of the APC. A bright flash—a HEAT round breaching metal—was followed by the clangor of armor being rent, punched inward—

Fanny dove, yelled, "Down!"

—just as the APC emitted a furious belch of flame and sound from the open top hatch, the figure there slumping over. Smoke roiled up out of its breached side. Judging from the shouts of urgency and pain, Warriors were exiting it from the rear doors.

The Proxie's sensors had not missed that development, evidently. It sprang—effortlessly—eight meters toward the river, now almost invisible in the smoke. Its CoBro spat in three round bursts: once, twice, then two more times. Each time, wild counterfire responded, and was hastily silenced by the rifle's next short stutter. Then, from across the river, several machine guns began chattering: tracers zipped through the mists, chewing up the ground just behind the Proxie.

Which, with deceptive ease, hopped clear over the guttering APC, landing in a crouch behind its land-facing side. It was unscathed.

Fanny looked into its eyes—well, three ganged lenses—and breathed heavily. "Thank you. Sir."

"Glad to help." Solsohn's voice was both in Fanny's earbud and crackling out of the Proxie's external speakers. "Now get ready. More are coming across."

Chapter Forty-Six

Jrekhalkar watched the last of the first assault wave's APCs roll into the River Kakaagsukh's coursing waters, then glanced around his diminished command staff. "We are making better progress than anticipated. I ask your counsel: should I gamble the second wave?" The tone of his voice told the others that he was eager to do so.

Z'gluurhek pony-nodded deeply, immediately. The others followed, some reluctantly. One, Ssrykh'oon, cast an uncertain glance at the far bank. "Voice, do you now doubt our original plan will assure of us victory once the sun sets?"

Jrekhalkar visibly labored to respond in a tone both measured and calm. "I doubt nothing. The night attack would still succeed, I believe. But there is no reason to forego seizing an even greater victory now. Their many-tubed rocket launchers on the ridge have not been able to engage our vehicles for all the smoke we have laid. The battle horns tell us our formation is ready to break free of the mists in numbers so great

624

that it is unlikely the humans will engage enough of our vehicles in time. We could carry the day, here and now, except for the fact that we held so many of our Warriors back, in anticipation of tonight's crossing. But if we were to send them across, now, even if many of them had to ride on the backs of the second wave's APCs—"

Ezzraamar bowed his neck deeply, held the position.

Jrekhalkar was not able to ignore, nor resist, the ancient posture of supplication. He interrupted himself, stood more erect. "I would hear you, Ezzraamar of the Moiety of Nys'maharn."

"My thanks, Esteemed Voice." And, now that he had Jrekhalkar's attention, how best to dissuade him from this overly bold scheme? "I counsel we wait to see how the first wave fares in its first ten minutes on the far shore. If, as you conjecture, the humans are unable to repel our numbers, we shall see it quickly enough. No doubt they will attempt to use their MULTIs to eliminate our APCs, and then, fire HE among our Warriors.

"However, doing so would occupy almost all the assets they would also need to contest the crossing of the second assault wave. So, if our first wave is even marginally successful, our second wave may cross and enter the battle without any significant resistance. If, on the other hand, our first wave does not meet with success, it will surely be because too many of our APCs are destroyed or disabled as they exit the smokescreen that is even now diminishing. If that is the case, the second assault wave will not only have to make the same crossing but, upon arriving on the far shore, will have its maneuver restricted by the wrecks littering the exit from the ford. Which would then confirm that your plan to cross and attack at night is, indeed, the correct strategy." As he heard the last words of his careful appeal come out of his mouth, Ezzraamar realized how much he had learned from his time as Yaargraukh's adjutant: not merely in terms of tactics used on the battlefield, but in the council-circle.

Jrekhalkar stared at Ezzraamar, phlegm rattling in his snout as he testily weighed this advice against his preferred impulse.

Ssrykh'oon swung slowly toward the north, his crest rising. He pointed to where the River Kakaagsukh disappeared in a long westward curve behind the steep ridge that met their shore at that point. Just downstream of the river's bend was a narrow water gap where rocky teeth stuck up from the foaming current that roared between them. "I hear—"

Before Ssrykh'oon could complete his sentence, the rest of them heard it, too: a syncopated susurration that seemed to emerge from the chaotic rumble of the upstream rapids and the currents that rushed swiftly over the wide northern ford. Jrekhalkar's immense Honor Guardian jabbed a claw at the base of their own ridgeline where the river flowed angrily around it. "There!"

Swinging around that headland, the humans' three biggest attack rotaries spread out across the width of the River Kakaagsukh, only ten meters above the white-flecked water. A moment later, the sound of their rotors became more distinct: a heavy beat, like a death drum. Slow for a rotary.

Then another, faster pulse joined theirs: sharper,

more vicious, more distinctly mechanical in timbre. Two smaller attack rotaries banked around the ridge-line, falling in behind the three larger ones. The five vehicle formation came downriver swiftly, staggered so that the two in the rear were positioned between the gaps separating the three in the lead.

Jrekhalkar jumped atop the glacis plate of his new command APC, shouted to all the hornwielders who could hear him. "Sound the command! All carriers: get to the closest shore!" Ssrykh'oon had already dived into the APC, was issuing similar orders to the radio operator, who began attempting to break squelch and send the warning. But the human jamming was suddenly absolute.

The helicopters tucked closer against the Hkh'Rkh shore as they came down the river. Ezzraamar admired the bold tactic. By angling in that direction, the humans' approach put them in an enfilade position relative to the APCs hidden in the treeline of the western bank, and so, put the rotaries out of the ready arc of their weapons. The enemy craft were also positioned to attack the left rear flank of the unsuspecting midstream APCs. With signal horns blaring, engines straining, and radios emitting nothing but static, the crews inside them had neither heard nor been apprised of the approaching rotary-wings. And although the smoke over the middle of the river was thinning, that was mostly to the rear of the APCs; the one flank they believed was safe.

Jrekhalkar was shouting for the second wave's APCs to commence firing at the approaching rotaries, but only a few of their weapons had viable sightlines: a sparse stuttering of autocannons and machine guns had no evident effect on the human craft. That would change soon, when the rotaries either turned to get back to their shore or flew on past. But before that happened—

The human craft did not launch their rockets all at once. The lead rotary fired two from its drooping, weapon-heavy wing-stubs; one fell short, the other detonated in the water between two of the APCs at the midstream point. The enemy helicopters seemed to make minute attitude adjustments and then each started firing in a slow, deliberate sequence, one rocket after another.

The net effect was a torrent of missiles of different sizes, different shapes, and quite distinctive sounds. The first two missed—

Then they began to hit. The first wave's column of half-obscured APCs, now stretched out over the length of the ford, became pockmarked with eruptions of fire, smoke, and gouts of water as the missiles slashed into its northern flank. One vehicle's fuel tank was hit: a sheet of orange flame sprang up with a breathy roar. Another—swerving, tilting, trying to head downsteam out of the line of fire—was hit by two rockets: it rolled with a metallic groan. Water rushed into the passenger compartment, snarling as it turned that protective armored box into an outsized, watery sarcophagus.

As the pace of the missile launches began diminishing, the human helicopters began firing their guns. Whereas the smaller helicopters had fired more accurate and deadly rockets, the larger ones now became the hammers that smote vehicle after vehicle. Their chin turrets roved, working along the line of APCs that were struggling to spread out, even run off the ford rather than remain effectively motionless. The heavy projectiles hammered through the flat sides of the APCs, blew out their tires, peppered the Warriors who bailed out of rocket-stricken vehicles into the water.

As swiftly as the attack had commenced, it broke off, the lighter helicopters veering off first, their smaller machine guns being of limited use against the armor of the Hkh'Rkh vehicles. A moment later, the heavier ones followed, lumbering after them at much slower speed.

This was the moment that the second wave's gunners had been waiting for. As the human helicopters swerved away, they nearly came abreast of the rough line of APCs. Their machine guns and autocannons clattered in an angry, discordant chorus, sending waves of projectiles after the withdrawing craft.

One of the big ones flared twice, then a third time, as autocannon shells tore into it. It struggled to hold a steady course, then its engine emitted what sounded akin to a long groan, and the vehicle heeled over, heading down. Another of the large ones began to trail smoke, faltered, righted, gave its fatally stricken mate a wide berth as that one ploughed into the base of the opposite ridge. A burst of smoke and flame preceded the sound that reached across the river a moment later: a sharp burst of smashing metal, followed by the longer thunder of exploding fuel.

The rockets that reached out for the helicopters from the dismounted launchers would have been far deadlier had they hit, but, designed for engaging ground vehicles and stationary targets, they were lucky to get as close as they did. One burst just near the tail of the rearmost of the lighter rotaries, which wobbled a bit, but then finished its climb up and over the far ridgeline, right behind its twin. The other two craft followed a few moments later.

The moment they were gone, one of the human MULTIs fired a steady stream of rockets, each swerving into a slightly different trajectory. Ezzraamar saw the last of the seven heading almost directly toward them, then watched it jink downward and plunge through the deck armor of one of the second wave APCs that had given away its position by firing at the helicopters. Five others were similarly hit. None exploded, but all of them smoked, caught fire, and began to burn sullenly.

"Second wave: reverse to cover!" howled Jrekhalkar, whose order was taken up along the line by battle horns and hand signals. The remaining vehicles pulled back from the woodline that flanked either side of the northern ford, one last rocket chasing after a late responder. The human weapon exploded a few meters short of the rear-rolling APC, sending up a fountain of dirt.

The engagement was over as abruptly as it had begun. The clearing smokescreen revealed eight APCs disabled or shattered along the ford itself, three more mostly submerged to either side of it. A handful of surviving Warriors struggled to return to the western bank. Unseen, unheard shots from the human side took them in the back. To a one, they flopped forward into the swift current. Only one kicked and splashed before he, too, slipped under the swells and disappeared.

On the far shore, behind the smoke that still partially obscured the head of the north ford, gunfire continued sporadically: the sound of a Hkh'Rkh fifteen-millimeter machine gun was unmistakable as it stubbornly rose above the lighter weapons of the humans. Then, from a more southerly position on the ridge, another MULTI revealed itself: two white fingers of rocket exhausts jutted down into the dissipating mists. A pair of dim flashes appeared to make the remaining smoke waver just before the sound of twin explosions reached across the water. Then silence. The Hkh'Rkh machine gun did not speak again.

"I suspect all the APCs that made it to the other bank have been eliminated," Ezzraamar observed, trying to make his voice and posture match the circumspection of his words.

Jrekhalkar burbled infuriated phlegm in his nostils, but nodded once, sharply. "You were wise to urge me to listen to my better instincts, to keep from committing the second wave."

Ezzraamar could not help blinking in surprise. His better instincts? Fifteen minutes before, the Voice's sole instinct had been to attack with all his Warriors, which would have put them all out on the ford to be slaughtered by the helicopters, had he done so.

But Ezzraamar had observed and learned well during his time with Yaargraukh. He allowed his silence to be interpreted as consent as he thought, *I am now seeing the Old Families—my Families—as Yaargraukh saw them. The instinct toward pride is stronger than the dedication to truth. The need to be right is more powerful than the duty to take responsibility. And the threat of a Challenge is always lurking in the background, ready to overcome reasonable objections with the silence of an untimely death.*

Jrekhalkar stood straighter to survey the damage. "By letting the humans believe that they have fooled and crippled us, we have managed to fool them—and lead them into false security as night falls."

Ssrykh'oon's eye-covers pinched into wrinkled masses. "We—fooled *them*?" he echoed.

Jrekhalkar was quick to reply, glancing to Z'gluurhek who nodded in agreement even before his leader's explanation was uttered. "Of course. It was a clever trick the humans used, admittedly. The helicopters obviously flew north, following behind the ridgeline on their side of the river until they were beyond the reach of both our eyes and ears. Then they came over the crest and down to follow along the river and use the sheltering bend north of us—and the sound of the rapids—to screen their approach. Clever, but predictable."

"Predictable?" Ssrykh'oon repeated, incredulous. "Voice, did you mean for all our Warriors and vehicles to die on this ford?"

Jrekhalkar turned disapproving eyes on the flabbergasted scion. "Your tone could be mistaken for insolence," he said quietly. "And of course I did not *intend* for our forces to be slain as they were. But it was part of the risk we accepted to lay the groundwork for tonight's attack, in the event that this assault did not succeed. As we feared, it has not."

He turned to the rest of his staff before Ssrykh'oon's eyes stopped blinking in shock. "I require a casualty count. Dismount all heavy weapons from the remaining APCs to tripods. Emplace them along the woodline, and establish multiple fall-backs for each. When that is complete, have the rocket launchers commence fire against the positions occupied by the human MULTIs on the opposite ridge. Our gunners are to fire two rockets, then move immediately. The humans will counterfire and they will be more accurate, since we will have marked our position."

Z'gluurhek sounded pained to raise his point. "We cannot hope to slay many of the *s'fet*, that way."

"We are not trying to kill them. We are trying to scare them out of their positions by showing them we know where they are located. They have not had the time to fortify and they do not have ground vehicles; they cannot reposition their heavy weapons easily or very far. We shall keep them moving and off balance, so that when the sun begins to set, they shall be exhausted and in less optimal positions than those in which they started. With any luck, they will not be as well organized, either. Precisely the conditions under which we wish to make our final and decisive attack." His crest puffed out briefly, putting a period on the end of his declaration, before he turned to consult the rapidly updating battlemap.

Chapter Forty-Seven

Riordan stared at the numbers again.

Gaudet murmured, "Sir, every time you do that—"

Riordan nodded. "I know. I'll be fine." But it was a lie. Or, at best, an optimistic hope that even he didn't believe.

Thirty-four dead. Twelve triaged because they were beyond saving, either due to the severity of their wounds or the certainty that the angel flight wouldn't get them to the surgeons in time. The wounded hadn't been tallied yet, but the number was well above fifty. Out beyond the open hatchway of Wedge One, a Jolly scissored its way aloft, heading back to Dante with another load of WIAs.

Hearing the rotorwash batter down at the naked dirt that rimmed the much-mauled ridgeline, Riordan couldn't keep from looking at the matériel losses that were listed alongside the casualties. They were down to one functional Mi-8, four slicks, one Hind, and two Cobras. He'd been able to keep the heavy lifters—the Chinook and the Jollies—out of the line of fire. But he wouldn't have that luxury next time.

634

He had expended all but two MISLS, most of the antiarmor loads for the MULTIs, and two-thirds of the sensors. And the Hkh'Rkh had located and eliminated all but one of the creepers and one of the quadrotors he'd hidden over on their side of the river.

He leaned back, thought about trying to eat his sandwich again, then thought he might throw up.

Gaudet turned around in her couch. "Major Rulaine on secure one, sir. And Major Solsohn, too, it seems."

Riordan nodded. "Go ahead."

The line was quiet for a moment. Then Bannor's voice, as careful as a dog approaching a moody cat: "That's a hell of a glum tone after winning a battle."

"You call this winning?" Riordan tried to keep the disgust and anger out of his voice; he knew he had failed.

"Yeah, that's exactly what we call it," Dora's voice retorted.

Riordan didn't care enough to be tactful. "Ms. Veriden, you're a trained killer—and a damned good one—but you've made it perfectly clear that you've always worked solo, like it that way, and don't want the responsibility of command. So you will kindly shut up and butt out. Solsohn, what the hell is she doing on the line anyway?"

"I asked her. Just like I asked Karam and Tina. This may be the only chance we have to compare notes, get new orders."

"Very well. Then remain in the loop, Ms. Veriden."

Dora managed to sound annoyed, surprised, and hurt all at once. "All right. Commodore."

Okay, so she was trying to be encouraging in her own irascible fashion. And maybe I'll thank her for that later on. Much later. If we live. And if she stops being such a pain. "Tina, you're keeping track of repair and refit, right?"

"Yes, sir. Best news: we'll get that big Russian helicopter airworthy again, but with reduced speed. I've got mechanics down at MULTI Two: it got pranged a few minutes ago, trading shots with the heavy weapons across the river. I don't think it's a write-off, but I'm not sure it's going to be combat ready before this dust-up is over."

"Okay, let's assume it's not. We redress the battery placement so we've still got equal coverage across the line."

"That's a lot of moving, sir."

"I know. That's why we're going to get the Chinook on the job. It's bringing up the last reserves—flight line techs at Dante—and will drop them off as it moves along the ridge line, shifting the MULTIs."

"Commodore," Bannor said cautiously, "the Chinook is big and slow and the Hkh'Rkh gunners across the river are competent and eager."

"True. And what rounds do we have in abundance for the MULTIs, Major?"

"Uh . . ." A crooked grin crept into Rulaine's voice. "Smoke."

"Exactly, which we were saving to cover our movement. Up until now, we were worried about losing sight of the opposite bank, of giving them the opportunity to reposition or mass without our having eyes on them. But if all of you are correct, they are now licking their wounds even more than we are. So this seems like the moment to screen our line with heavy smoke and shift assets using the Chinook and the Jollies. We've got weapons and people to move into new positions. Speaking of which, can we make any use of the machine guns on the Hkh'Rkh APCs?"

Bannor sounded surprised. "Well, I—I don't know, sir, but the Lost Soldiers don't have experience with anything that heavy."

"Well, this will be the time for them to learn. Find any remaining submariner who was trained to crew their deck AA guns. Give them a helmet and a crash course on operating Hkh'Rkh gear with human hands. We'll either dismount the weapons to tripods—there should be one in every enemy vehicle—or our gunners will have to man it from the commander's hatch of the dead APC. We'll build up what cover we can for them. Which reminds me: do the APCs have pioneer tools?"

"Uh, not sure, sir."

"Well, find out. And if they do, get the Dugout teams started on digging in deeper and improving their positions. From what I've seen, those fighting holes didn't do the job, not when the APCs got close to them. We lost more people that way than any other, even the shelling."

Duncan's caveat was quiet, reflective. "We would have lost even more if we hadn't given all the armor liners to the Cold Guard that were assigned to the Dugout positions. It did a fair job against the shrapnel."

"Except we didn't lose anyone down at the south ford," Karam muttered. "They didn't even probe us there, much less attack."

Rulaine sighed. "Yeah, that was odd. And it worries me."

Riordan frowned. "You think they were doing

something other than massing forces to have better odds at the two fords?"

"I don't know. Could be. But they didn't even test us. Not a single shot, other than the general shelling. They're not even trying to duel with our MULTIs there."

Riordan frowned. "Those exchanges are still going on?"

"Yep. They hammer a few rounds at us. Our MULTI takes a shot at them. They fire at the launch bloom. Repeat, ad nauseam."

"Pass the word to our MULTIs: don't take the return shots."

"Sir, that really rattles troops, taking incoming without firing back."

"I'd rather have them a little rattled by highly inaccurate long range fire than us launching HE rockets across the river on the off chance that we tag them before they move their weapon to a new position. Anyhow, a few minutes after we finish here, there's going to be a big wall of smoke between our side of the river and theirs: that should give our troops a much-needed break. Besides, we can't risk losing any MULTIs. They're going to be our backbone in the next fight."

"What do you mean?" asked Dora.

"I mean that we've expended almost all of our other purpose-built antiarmor missiles and munitions. All we have left are the MULTIs and the dual-purpose RAPs from the underslung CoBro launchers."

"The helicopters—" began Karam.

"They're almost entirely out of antiarmor rockets and they aren't modern vehicles," Caine interrupted.

"And if the Hkh'Rkh come across at night, the helicopters are useless: they were created before night vision was a built-in feature."

"The Lost Soldiers still use flares, I'm told." Tsaami sounded stubborn, but less than fully convinced in the efficacy of his assertion.

"They do, and it might come to that, but in a ground fight, that will help the Hkh'Rkh more than it will us. In darkness, their vision is about the same as a dog's, which means if you give them a little light, their vision will improve more than ours will."

"Sounds like the next attack is shaping up to be low-tech night fight," Solsohn said slowly.

"I'm betting on it," Riordan affirmed, "although I'm wishing for anything else. Between their vision, their armor, and the power of their individual weapons, the Hkh'Rkh will tear our people up at night. Except for the Cold Guard, but they can't be everywhere. Dora, has Know-It-All given us recommendations on optimal unit reconfiguration for a close infantry engagement?"

"Yeah," she answered glumly. "You want the short version or the long version?"

"Short, please."

"Okay, here it is: the difference in night vision screws us. Know-It-All keeps trying to compensate by shifting our positions into the trees, to hide until the enemy is so close that our weapons and difference in night vision no longer really matters. But then if you add in the variable that the Dugout positions cannot be abandoned, it starts making what seem like random choices and 'advises the operator' to expect eighty percent casualties. Or more."

Karam's snicker was decidedly sardonic. "So much

for the genius of assistive automation. Sounds like we just need to put everyone we can on the line."

Riordan exhaled slowly. "We have. Flight line support is down to four men. I've even agreed to allow two of our doctors, Lieutenants Baruch and Franklin, to come forward. Everyone who can fight is going to be fighting."

Susan Phillips turned around from her comms board. "Is that an absolute directive, sir?"

Riordan nodded grimly. "I'm afraid it is, Ms. Phillips."

"Well, then," she said standing swiftly and smoothing her clothes. "I will leave the communications in Chief Warrant Officer Gaudet's capable hands, for now. I think one of the recently wounded radio operators from *Scorpion* would do nicely as a full-time replacement."

"Ms. Phillips, what are you talking about?"

She was halfway to the exterior hatch. "I am following your directive, Commodore. That everyone who can fight must fight. That includes me."

"Ms. Phillips, we need you here."

"Sir, I would never think of showing disrespect for your rank. But if you were not my superior, my reply would be, 'what nonsense!' I will have you know that I was hiding in cellars, bombed-out buildings, and concealed dugouts with the French Resistance for the better part of two years while evading and killing Nazis. I am rated an expert marksman with both rifle and pistol and it is high time I put those skills to use again. Now, if you'll excuse me, I'll need to report to Wedge Two for equipment. I believe that's our *ad hoc* armory, yes?"

That was the moment that Riordan discovered that he'd adopted an archaic form of chivalry toward the women among the Lost Soldiers. It was as if he had, as a matter of cultural courtesy, changed his interactions with them to mirror the expectations and standards of their own epoch. With an effort, he forced himself to reconceive Susan Phillips through a contemporary lens, to simply see her as a soldier—hell, a commando. He nodded. "Then, godspeed to you, Ms. Phillips."

"And to you to, Commodore," she said with a small smile. She stepped primly, briskly out the hatchway.

Damn, thought Riordan. *Just when you think a day can't get any stranger—*

Bannor's comment was low and dark. "I'm just hoping they don't get enough APCs across and overrun our lines. If they do, we're going to be in serious trouble. Although, if what Tygg reported holds true when they attack again, they might not have enough infantry with them to exploit a breakthrough."

Riordan felt himself frowning. "What did Captain Robin report?"

"Apparently, most of the APCs at the north ford had less than half their maximum infantry complement in them. I'd have thought they would want to have them fully loaded, so if any one of their vehicles made it, they'd deliver enough of a force to secure a toehold."

"That is odd," Riordan agreed. Then stopped: it wasn't the only odd, even inexplicable, data point they had observed. There was also the Hkh'Rkh's conspicuous failure to even probe the third and southernmost ford. Could there be a link between the two?

If so, it was hard to see. Not attacking the third ford was explicable, if dubious: if they didn't have enough APCs to press all fords sufficiently, they might have decided to concentrate their forces against two.

But if that was their logic, then it made absolutely no sense that they would underman the vehicles they had clustered at the other two fords. Why conduct a mass attack with less than half the mass you can bring to bear? But, by reducing the amount of infantry carried by each APC, that's exactly what they had done: undercut their own attack.

Or, to think of it from another angle, what objective was served by that choice? A choice that spent their vehicles far more freely than their foot soldiers.

Foot soldiers...

Riordan glanced at the map, saw the line of dull red rectangles that traversed the northern and middle fords: the carcasses of over a dozen APCs at each site. And nothing at the southern ford... "Dora, I need you to confirm something: the south ford is the longest, but also the widest and the shallowest of the fords, correct?"

"Yeah. The river spreads out just upstream, so the force of the current drops. That's probably why you've got all that sediment there."

"Which should have made it the easiest for the Hkh'Rkh to cross."

"Yeah," Dora said slowly, dubiously.

"What are you thinking?" asked Bannor, who had probably learned what it meant when Riordan started asking strange questions in a distracted tone.

Riordan looked at the map again, gathered his thoughts. "I think I know what they're planning. Look at what they've done in the past hour. They've located almost all our support weapons, shelled us, then tried rushing across two fords with three quarters of their APCs, most of which they lost, left behind as wrecks along the ford. But the ford that would have been easiest to cross they leave alone. And it turns out that they only have a fire team in each of the APCs they sent across, rather than a full squad. On the surface, it's crazy, right?"

"It's crazy down beyond the surface, too," Dora affirmed.

"Yes, it seems to be—except the Hkh'Rkh aren't crazy. They know the way to beat us: to close and get into a firefight, preferably at night. But they tried a day crossing and left most of their vehicles behind in the worst, most treacherous currents of the river."

Solsohn's voice was suspicious. "What are you getting at, sir?"

Riordan paused before explaining. "Maybe the outcome of their last attack was exactly what they were planning on. Think about it: knowing what they do about our technology, and what sort of antiarmor capabilities we were likely to have, what was the likely outcome of their assault?"

"That we would hit their APCs with everything we've got, to keep them from getting a toehold on our side," Solsohn replied.

"And what was going to happen when we did that?"

"A graveyard of vehicles is what was going to happen," snorted Dora derisively. "Just like what they've left behind."

"Yes, exactly. A long parking lot of wrecks. Which traverses the river right on top of the two most treacherous fords. Which the Hkh'Rkh can now navigate more easily on foot, using the vehicles as handholds, taking cover behind each hull as they leapfrog their way to our shore. At night."

The comm channel was quiet. Then Karam breathed, "Damn. You think they'd sacrifice all those APCs just to put a—a set of stepping stones across the river?"

"Sure they'd sacrifice the APCs: they planned on it. That's why they didn't send full infantry teams in each vehicle. Just enough to hold a beach-head if, by some chance, their APC attack got across and started making inroads against us. My guess is that if we check their fuel tanks, we'll find they were at most a quarter full, to minimize losses and keep the chance of a catastrophic explosion low. And let's not forget that every one of those stepping stones is also a little pillbox with a heavy weapon mounted on top. Built in fire support for the Warriors crossing on foot." There was a long silence.

"*Merde*," muttered Dora, swearing in French for a change. "When you put it that way, we really do need to wrap this up before nightfall."

Caine discovered he was nodding at the comm panel. "I agree."

"Just one little problem," Karam drawled. "*How* do we wrap this up by nightfall?"

"I think I've got a plan that should—"

"Commodore!" Gaudet's voice was sharp. "Incoming comm on secure two."

Secure Two? That means . . . "The Slaasriithi?"

Gaudet turned. "Yiithrii'ah'aash himself, sir."

"Something going sideways?" Bannor wondered aloud.

"Don't know, but I'll update you all soonest. Riordan out." To Gaudet: "Switch me over."

A pause, then, "You're on-line, sir."

"Ambassador, Riordan here. Have you been monitoring the situation?"

"Up until the last hour, yes, relatively closely. But since then, I have not had the time for anything but general updates, Caine Riordan."

Riordan felt his stomach sink slightly. "What happened an hour ago, Yiithrii'ah'aash?"

"There were two separate, but I believe related, events. Firstly, we have detected new ships in the system. Three, possibly four of them."

"They just shifted in?"

"No, there was no sign of shift. We began detecting their powerplants at extreme range, further along the track of the asteroid belt in which we are still hiding."

"So, have you taken steps to—?"

"Attend, Caine Riordan: the second event is even more dire."

Great. "Go on."

"Forty-two minutes ago, we detected a very brief energy spike amidst some of the heavier debris orbiting just inside Turkh'saar's geosynchronous track. There were no subsequent anomalies of note. It was too brief to get a very detailed fix on the source, and we did not wish to reveal the presence of our own orbital assets.

"However, that caution was evidently moot. Just four minutes ago, the drone fighters we slipped into orbit to support your extraction operations detected extremely small high-speed objects closing on an intercept vector."

Riordan's stomach sank further. "Railgun projectiles?"

"Yes. We maneuvered our drone fighters out of their path with very little time to spare."

"So, the Ktor are here. As we feared."

"Yes. But that is not the most urgent news, Caine

Riordan. The railgun rounds that bore down upon our fighters did not actually miss, because their vector only *appeared* to be focused on those craft."

Riordan felt the hair on the back of his neck start pricking upward. "Then what was their real target?"

"Turkh'saar itself. Specifically, the site where Dr. Sleeman is conducting her field survey."

Chapter Forty-Eight

KAKAAGSUKH RIVER VALLEY AND
CLOSE ORBIT, BD+56 2966 TWO ("TURKH'SAAR")

Riordan's initial surprise lasted less than a second. *If the Ktor are here, they've been watching. So of course they're going to strike the site. They can't afford* not *to.*

"Caine Riordan, are you still there? Are you still receiving my signal?"

"Loud and clear, Ambassador. How long until impact?"

"We estimate nine minutes, presuming the projectiles do not have an independent means of altering course. I regret to report that we did not realize their actual target point until they had moved past the intercept range of our drone fighters."

"Can your drone fighters engage the Ktoran craft that fired them? We have our own assets in orbit. Together, they might be able to—"

"Caine Riordan, we do not have the location of the enemy craft and would reveal the position of our orbiting drones and sensors if we attempted to hunt for it. And we might yet require those assets to deal with the ships we have detected, two of which are producing energy emissions consistent with shift-capable vessels. The other two probably do not have that capability, but could still be warships of considerable size. It is possible that one or more of them are decoys, but until that is determined, it would be imprudent to compromise our position or assets. I profoundly apologize that we cannot come to your assistance."

So, we're on our own. Again. And logically, that was also how it had to be. "Ambassador, I understand and concur: until you've got those ship signatures sorted out, you're effectively paralyzed. We'll keep updating you on the situation down here. Riordan out."

Caine did not wait to hear the Slaasriithi's farewell, glanced at Gaudet, whose hand was poised to open the secure channel to Sleeman. Riordan shook his head. "No, send in the clear."

Gaudet's eyes grew round. "Sir, do you really want to take the chance that the enemy will—?"

"It doesn't matter who else hears us, as long as Dr. Sleeman does, and as quickly as possible. But get Karam back on secure one and tell him I want our last two MISLS launched at that enemy unit approaching the site. Same procedure as last time."

"Roger that, sir. Dr. Sleeman is on, sir."

Riordan did not waste time on pleasantries. "Doctor, pay close attention to what I am about to say. You need to get your people under cover. I will be using two MISLS against the light armored platoon that is approaching your position."

"Good; we shall, as Tygg says, 'hunker down,' and—"

"Melissa: for now, just listen. Hunkering down is not going to be enough. There's more inbound than the MISLS."

"Oh? What?"

Riordan told her, during which time Gaudet gave him a thumb's up: the MISLS were on their way.

After several seconds of silence, Melissa said, "If we are the target of a railgun attack, then we probably will not be able to communicate after I sign off this time. The portable radio will not last that long."

"That's probably true."

"Then I shall relay all additional data now. And if something, well, happens to us, I will be carrying a sample container. In it, you will find physical evidence to support each of my conjectures."

"Dr. Sleeman, there's no reason to assume—"

"Commodore, there is *every* reason to assume that I will not survive. But the box surely will. And if you understand my conjecture, you will be able to make sense of its contents.

"Firstly, we ran sensor sweeps at the bottom of one of the half-filled pits, got some solid returns, dug up markers. Written in Hkhi. They are age estimates, corresponding to the sediment levels at which they were found. Problem is, I think their estimates on the age of the crash site are wrong. By a whole order of magnitude. At least."

"Why?"

"Because while the sedimentary layers in which the debris was found are consistent with the age the Hkh'Rkh assigned to it, the micro remainders of what actually crashed there just don't look like they've been in the ground that long."

"Why? And please tell me you're moving with the radio, right now."

"I am moving, but the radio's battery is almost finished; we had no way to recharge it. So. Do you remember what we found in the soil? The splinters and fine-grain composites that were torn away from whatever object came down here?"

"Yes. That's what convinced you it was a ship that crashed, not a meteorite."

"Correct. However, the soil level where we found those residues and signs of scorching dates to about five thousand years ago. Or more. But the residues themselves haven't been there more than a few hundred years. At most. They haven't oxidized enough, haven't been significantly deformed by earth movement and all the other geological effects that leave their mark on even the hardest materials."

"Well, how the hell—? Wait: are you saying this ship crashed in a *predug* hole?"

"If you have any other explanation, I would love to hear it. But yes: that is exactly what I am proposing. Nothing else makes sense. On the other hand, a ship crashing in a prepared hole makes a great deal of sense if we assume that the crash was not an accident, but was staged."

"Staged? You mean—?" And then it all made sense to Riordan, almost as quickly as Sleeman rolled out the details supporting her conjecture.

"I believe the ship or object was brought down into a preexcavated hole to make it look like it had crashed here much longer ago. The impact was enough to obliterate any evidence that a hole had been dug, but not enough to fully destroy the ship. So some parts were still intact, enough to be of interest. That is what the Hkh'Rkh must have found, removed, and catalogued. And which led them to decide it was worth protecting the site with an extensive automated missile system.

"Whoever selected the location of this hole was quite crafty. This site is one of the few patches of ground on this planet that has not experienced glaciation in the past half dozen millennia or so. If it had, it would be more obvious that a hole had been dug. There would have been marks where they cut through the geological features left by that glaciation, which would have defeated any attempt to fake the actual age of the crash. So whoever staged this chose a spot where there was no such record to give away their charade."

Riordan ran a hand through his hair. "Could the Hkh'Rkh really miss all those clues, do you think?"

"Sadly, I think they could, particularly if their interest was not primarily archeological. If they were after artifacts of immediate use to them, there is a good chance that they would have ruined a lot of their own forensics. Which is not an area of science in which they are particularly advanced." Her voice seemed to get more hollow, with a hint of an echo. "We are heading down the deepest dig shaft now. I think I can hear something overhead."

"Those are the MISLS. Stay safe. We'll try to get you out of there just as soon as—"

Gaudet shook her head at him. "Signal lost, sir."

Riordan stared at the dead comm indicator—and suddenly realized that with Ktor in the area, he hadn't been thinking far enough ahead. "Get the command staff back on secure one! Right now!"

Idrem rarely invoked the Progenitors, even silently— *the dead are dead, after all*—but he was tempted to do so now.

Brenlor Srin Perekmeres was poised over the holo-plot, watching the white lines of their railgun projectiles arc down toward the site at which the human survey team was stranded.

"Ninety seconds," announced the senior Aboriginal on *Red Lurker*'s bridge.

"And you say that the Terrans launched two missiles at the Hkh'Rkh unit approaching the excavation?"

"Yes, Fearsome Srin. Their missiles just impacted. The vehicles seem to be destroyed or disabled, but there are survivors."

"And the Terrans launched the missiles minutes after concluding their new lascom transmission to the Slaasriithi?"

"Yes, sir."

"Content of message?"

"Marginal reception only, Dominant One. Without more, we cannot begin to attempt code-breaking."

Brenlor frowned, glanced at the estimated results of the Hkh'Rkh's main, two-pronged attempt to press across the river separating them from the humans and the still-inert transport. The attackers had paid a fearsome price; by comparison, the humans seemed largely undamaged. "I fear that the Hkh'Rkh are no longer in control of the battle," he grumbled. "Do you disagree?"

Idrem could not do so, even if he had wanted to. If the outcome of the Hkh'Rkh's most recent engagement was part of some greater, subtle plan, it eluded his ability to construct what that might be. "No, my Srin."

Brenlor nodded. "Having thrown back the Hkh'Rkh so decisively, the Terrans may be correct in presuming that as soon as they complete repairs to their transport, they can extract and escape without impediment. We must convince them otherwise."

"How?"

"By putting our thumb upon the scales." He smiled. "Well, two thumbs. Gunner!"

"What is your command, Honored Srin?"

"The rearmost kinetic warhead and the rearmost fragmentation warhead in our volley; are their steering systems still reporting full function?"

"They are, Srin Perekmeres."

"Then give them a little more lift. I wish to move their impact point seventy kilometers further downrange."

"Yes, Fearsome Srin. Calculating the extension of their descent tracks now."

Idrem glanced at the new impact point for the two rounds, then stared at Brenlor. "If this strike does not finish the Terrans, we must hope that the Hkh'Rkh will do so swiftly."

"They shall. Retarget the two warheads as I instruct. Bring them down on the eastern side of the river, just there." He pointed to the five-kilometer stretch where Hkh'Rkh had attempted, and failed, to cross.

Using one massive, bloodstained cruciform hand to clutch the crumpled and multiply-rent wheel-guard of his crippled light APC, Troop Leader Nezhvaagk, scanned what was left of his column: twelve Warriors, including the severely wounded who still insisted that they could fight. His command vehicle—essentially a hybrid between an APC and an armored car—was immobilized but its engine still functioned. Which meant it still had power to traverse its turret and fire its twenty-five-millimeter autocannon.

But there were no targets visible, other than the two abandoned rotary-wings. Had the humans left, after all? Had they abandoned their—?

A crackling emanated from the cloudless sky, as if something was being seared and roasted up beyond the blue-green vault overhead.

Scanning, he found find the source of the peculiar sound—and froze. He felt his narrow jaw sag open, did not care that he no longer presented an imposing figure of stern authority to his Warriors.

Angry, actinic, yellow-white spears were rushing planetside, drawing closer with incredible speed, burning their afterimage onto his retinae. Their crackling approach turned into a shuddering series of sharp booms, through which a building scream rushed down, threatening to roll over him like a wave of multi-toned sound—

"Cover!" he yelled at his Warriors. Several were already diving to the ground.

As he dropped, he saw four of the eye-burning objects burst, still a hundred meters above the ground, and a kilometer away. Each of those lances of fusion-bright fire became a screeching hail of flechette-sized splinters that arrived at the site a moment before the following, solid warheads slashed into the ground with bright bursts of light and titanic eruptions of dirt.

The ground came up to hit Nezhvaagk before he had fully fallen. The shock wave tossed him back up momentarily, tilted one of his chassis-crippled vehicles, knocked down several of the trees that the human missiles had already weakened. Then two more of the warheads passed overhead, tearing apart the air—*krk-krk-krakk!*—as they streaked further north.

Nezhvaagk rose slowly, realized that he could not hear anything through the ringing in his ears, discovered he was bleeding from two of his three nostrils, saw that most of his men were suffering the same effects. Hefting his assault rifle, and favoring his injured left foot, he peered around his battered light APC.

Eight hundred meters away, the helicopters were still visible, but transformed. The smaller one, equipped with skids instead of landing gear, had been thrown over on its side by the near impact of one of the solid warheads. Its fuselage was in tatters, as if a whole Host of Warriors had spent the better part of a day using it for target practice. The other vehicle was still upright, but sagged on its flat tires, one of its rotors broken and trailing like the wing of a crippled avian. The rest of the rotors were pitted and pierced, akin to wood so well-eaten by worms that even they had forsaken further interest in it. The fuselage was similarly holed and rent, and seemed to be bowing outward, as if the weight of the top-mounted engine could no longer be borne by the structure of the body.

Nezhvaagk turned, gestured to one of his Warriors. "G'skodrun, get into my vehicle. The radio still works. Use squelch breaks to make report to Jrekhalkar. Tell him—what we have seen."

"And if I cannot break through the human jamming?"

"Then return to the scout car that survived the missiles and begin the drive back. The Voice must know what has happened here."

Riordan ran out of Wedge One to both greet Steve Rodermund and get him under cover. The colonel hopped down casually from the Cayuse that had brought him from Dante, its rotors still churning and whining. "When I said we needed some extra manpower, I didn't mean you, Colonel."

Rodermund smiled. "What? Aren't you glad to see me?"

"Yes, but I didn't want anyone flying right now. We could have incoming—"

In the south, a sudden roar quickly up-dopplered into a sky-wide scream. Riordan turned, saw a sharp, blinding light bearing down on them, almost riding along the ridgeline. Using one hand to slap his collarcom open—"Cover!" he shouted—Caine used the other to grab Rodermund's sleeve and pull him down.

The sound hit a shrill peak as it swept overhead, then down-dopplered into a short moan as the firebolt neared the tops of the clustertrees about seven hundred meters behind and a kilometer north of their position. A sharp blast transformed the bolt into a zipping, whining torrent of incandescent slivers, sleeting down into the foliage further along its flight path. They cut a sudden, wide fan of devastation among the clustertrees: for almost a kilometer along the round's trajectory, trunks were severed, tops splintered, bushes and ferns shredded.

"What the hell?" Rodermund gasped.

"Railgun," Riordan coughed out through the dust in his throat.

"Rail-what?"

Riordan rose, helping Rodermund up. "I'll explain later. I just hope that's the only—"

An identical eye-searing pinpoint came streaking out of the south at a similar angle, but on the other side of the ridgeline. The sound, like a hypersonic transport magnified, was deafening: it soared, became shrill—just as the glowing warhead sliced into the ground at a shallow angle, burrowing a massive trench along the river-facing slope as it went.

The soil jetted up like water behind a high-speed water-skier. Rocks and trees were caught in the mix like leaves in a northbound windstorm. The sound was unlike anything Caine had ever heard, as if a titanic rock saw was ripping through a granite cliff.

MULTI Three, perched on a small rocky overlook, was directly in the path of the north-burrowing munition. The entire rock formation flew apart in a howl of splintering stone and a sparking blast of light gray dust. Riordan, rocked backward by the shockwave that crested the ridgeline, knew they would never find any remains of the crew or the weapon.

As the fire-tipped gash seamed open the slope with the speed of lightning, it cut through one of the clustertree copses that had been the cover for two squads of reserves ready to reinforce the Dugouts defending the north and middle fords. Tree trunks, flung up and to either side like shredded twigs, landed in what was left of the covering growth, even as the shockwave flattened it.

One of the Jollies, returning upridge after collecting wounded from the north ford's staging area, tried sweeping higher up the slope to get out of the path of annihilation. Light debris flew past it on either side, but then the bow of the shockwave hit. The massive helicopter was slung around sideways at a drunken angle, the rotors deforming—right before the pressure-peak of the wave slapped it down against the side of the ridge. The overlapping shrieks of fuselage ripping apart, motor shredding itself, rotors cutting through trees and each other, was drowned out by the following thunder of the railgun round.

Which sliced into a massive rock outcropping, splitting it in two: the sharp crack of the impact was like an audial exclamation mark, declaring that the warhead had come to a stop, that the destruction was over. The downslope half of the ruined outcropping slid, then crumbled into a rockslide, the last thunder of the devastation settling into a silence so heavy that it seemed as though the sound itself was too exhausted to continue.

"Jesus H. Christ," muttered Steve Rodermund hollowly. "If they—whoever they are—do that again—"

Riordan exhaled. "I don't think they'll take that chance. Besides, I don't think they'll want to."

"Why?"

As his collarcom started paging wildly, and desperate shouting rose up from several points downslope, Riordan pointed across the valley at the far shore. "Because the Hkh'Rkh know we've just been torn up, and that our comms are going to be jammed as we try to assess damage and restructure our defenses."

"So you think they'll come across right now?"

Riordan shrugged. "If I were them, I wouldn't give my enemy any time to recover." He started toward the hatch that led back into Wedge One and the communications panel in the bridge.

Rodermund's hand closed on his arm, held him back. "Look, Commodore: having Pat Paulsen and I both back at Dante was command-grade overkill. He's the best guy for managing the flight line and interfacing with your folks in *Puller*. Me? I'm not comfortable moving pieces on a map in the rear. Which is why I got my overaged ass shot down over Laos. Which is why I'm here, now. So, what I can do to help?"

Riordan considered, moved a step beyond Rodermund's reach. "Stick with me. There's going to be a lot of work to do and not a lot of time to do it. And start learning how to work with the Know-It-All system."

"You mean that commander-in-a-can you guys trust? No thanks: that's not really my styl—"

"Steve, if you want to help, you'll have to hold your nose and work with Know-It-All. Not take orders from it, but allow it to help you choose—quickly—between different options, and also to understand the ramifications of all the technologies that will be under your control." He started walking into Wedge One. "You coming?"

Steve Rodermund sucked on his teeth. For a moment, Caine was able to imagine him standing in a cornfield, warily eyeing a new-fangled tractor, one hand still on the bridle of the mules that pulled his plow. "I guess I am."

"Good. We've got a lot of work to do."

Chapter Forty-Nine

Ezzraamar stared at the dust hanging in the air on the other side of the river, obscuring the northern half of the ridgeline, from middle of the slope to the crest. It was beginning to drift downhill, as well.

He started when Jrekhalkar clambered swiftly up the handholds on the side of the *de facto* command APC and gestured to his junior *halbardicher*. The young Warrior let his assault rifle fall loose on its sling; he produced a large horn—the Voice's Summons—and blew a long, sharp peal.

As its long wail began to taper, an answering sound rose up behind it: a collective hooting. Some tones were long and sonorous, others shorter, higher, excited. The reply to the horn continued to grow, both from upstream and downstream: the Warriors were responding to the ancient call for readiness, for impending battle.

Z'gluurhek emerged from the APC's interior. "The other tassle leaders report they can commence an attack in two minutes. It will take that long to start their APCs, organize their troops into assault waves,

660

and give new instructions to the crews manning the heavy weapons."

"And the need to lead with APCs: they understand this?"

"They understand the need to once again furnish the first wave with a rolling smokescreen across the ford. Although this may be difficult to do at the north and middle fords: they are already choked by wrecks."

Jrekhalkar turned to look at Ezzraamar. "What does your training indicate as the appropriate course of action for the north and middle fords?"

Ezzraamar considered. "Warriors carrying smoke cannisters should move forward and enter each wreck. Most are merely disabled, not destroyed. The Warriors shall reload the launchers from what they are carrying or from the vehicle's magazine. They will fire a full spread of cannisters. They will repeat this as they move across, from each wreck to the next, thereby advancing behind the smokescreen. Under which cover the rest of our foot will advance."

Z'gluurhek turned the claws of his free hand downward. "But if the engine is disabled, the launcher will not function. Its ignition is electronic."

Ezzraamar raised a single claw. "There is a hand-crank which may be used to charge the vehicle's battery for low-power operations. It was included for just such uses as this. Then, as the infantry makes its crossing, the remaining APCs should swim the river, just upstream of each ford."

Jrekhalkar's voice was constricted, rasping: angry. "We do not have the same equipment you enjoy in the formations of the Patrijuridicate. Our APCs have no auxiliary hydrojets for propulsion."

"That is not the only means of crossing water," Ezzraamar replied quietly. "You may spin the two rear pair of wheels to make slow headway. And if the current is strong and moves you downstream, well, that is why you are crossing upstream. When the wheels are pushed into contact with the lip of the ford, the traction will allow the vehicle to continue crossing."

Z'gluurhek's eye-flaps concentrated in two masses of tight wrinkles. "And what will keep the humans from targeting these even slower, swimming APCs, driven by Warriors who are unfamiliar with the task?"

"The humans will be busy repelling the full measure of our attack: they will not be able to engage all our vehicles. But, although it sounds grim, it is even more prudent to hope that the advance of our APCs will draw enemy fire away from the infantry. The majority of our Warriors will be traversing the fords on foot, and in full sight of whatever heavy weapons the humans have left near the shore. Better that the Terran MULTIs spend time trying to hit vehicles hull-down in the water rather than firing airburst munitions at our troops, struggling through the currents on foot."

Jrekhalkar leaned down toward Ezzraamar. "So even the military doctrine of the Patrijuridicate formations would recognize this as the best moment to cross the river and resume the attack?"

Ezzraamar knew he had to choose his words carefully. "I believe different Patrijuridicate commanders would have different opinions on what that tactics would be most appropriate in these circumstances. But, if it were provable or likely that the enemy command and control was seriously compromised by the strike we just witnessed, then yes: I believe this would be seen as an opportunity that should be exploited."

If Jrekhalkar had noted the distinction between Ezzraamar's phrasing and his own—"an opportunity that should be exploited" versus "this is the best moment to cross," he gave no indication of it. Instead, he rose as tall as he could, lifted his own rifle high, and spoke-hooted, as if translating what the peal of his horn of office had meant: "The Warriors of Turkh'saar do not wait for night: we cross now!"

And as the rest of the Flag took up the shout, Ezzraamar wondered, *Am I the only one wondering* where *that strike came from? And why?*

As Gaudet continued to talk Phil Friel through the procedures for securing Wedge Three against external attack, Riordan toggled Wedge One's lascom connection to *Puller*.

The speaker crackled slightly, then: "*Puller* here."

"Dora, this is Riordan. I need a fast update on what the EXHALTEDs are showing us."

"I was just about to call you about that. The Hkh'Rkh are gathering near the fords. All of them. And really quickly. I can relay our look-down so you can see for yourself."

"No, don't do that. The demands on your lascom capacity are about to go into overdrive, so you have to reserve it for critical systems. I've sent two of our remaining quadrotors up high to continue feeding us an overhead view. That should do."

"You're going to rely on quadrotor broadcasts? That means a crappy signal and crappier security."

"We can live with it. The Hkh'Rkh are already too

busy to look for little quadrotors in the sky or play hacking games. I'm more worried about restoring our local comm net."

"You should be. That damn railgun attack took a big chunk out of our airmobile lascom relay assets. The shockwave knocked down a third of what we had left, and the remainder are still trying to find each others' LoS footprints through the smoke and dust."

"Understood. That's why you're going to issue a set of my commands by secure broadcast."

"The Hkh'Rkh will break the encryption eventually."

"Yes, but not before this battle is over. So once I give you the orders, you're in charge of getting them to the COs who need them. I don't know who's left or reachable right now. Some positions have been offline since the railgun strike."

"Yeah, and here's some more cheery news. The EM surge from the flare is starting to hit. Radio is going to be unpredictable. At best."

"So you've got to get these orders out ASAP. First, have all remaining MULTIs hit the head of the south ford with all the FASCAMs we've got. Then—"

"Wait: FASCAMs? What the hell are tho—?"

"FAmily of SCAtterable Mines: the MULTIs launch cannisters that deploy them from the air. If we saturate the south ford with mines, that might slow the Hkh'Rkh enough that they won't be able to establish a solid beachhead and mass for a breakthrough.

"Next, I need all transport choppers except the Chinook to head downslope, scoop up all the rear-rank reserves, and ferry them directly into the front line. After they're done with that, the Hueys and the Jollies are to be armed for strike missions."

"That will take time, Caine, and it will cut their troop carrying capacity by more than half."

"Understood, but once our troops are all on the line, I think the airmobile part of this fight will be over."

"So what should I tell the Chinook pilot?"

"Tell him he's to go north and pick up Yaargraukh's team, as well as Lieutenant Commander Enderle's. I need them back here."

"Not worried about a northern infiltration anymore?"

"Not enough to leave any forces up there. And I need Yaargraukh on hand to better understand our enemy—and maybe to talk to them.

"Lastly, contact each Backstop team and instruct them to move up to a support position no more than one hundred meters to the rear of the Dugout directly blocking their ford. Each Backstop will convert one CoBro to a heavy-barrel machine-gun configuration. They are to hold it in reserve for long-range engagement and defense against overrun attacks against that Dugout. Riflemen are to laser-paint any vehicle that comes across the river. And if an enemy heavy weapon can't be engaged by laser-designated munitions, the Cobras and Hinds have standing orders to pop up and hammer it down."

"Should I order the Cayuses to be rearmed?"

"No, I have other plans for them. But since they're near me here on the ridgeline, I'll give the orders in person."

"Got it. After the orders are sent, I'll get out there myself and—"

"Negative. You and Karam are our aces in the hole and Duncan has to keep driving the Proxie.

So all three of you have to stay put. Tina, too. If anything breaks on board *Puller*, we need her to fix it yesterday."

Dora's tone had become surly. "Anyone else you want held back from the lines?"

"Actually, there are some folks I need pulled *off* the line. That includes all of our security team from *Puller*. Except Peter: he has to stay in overall command near the south ford. Also, expect Bannor to grab about a dozen Cold Guards and Lost Soldiers out of our reserve units."

"Why?"

"Special operation. Details to follow."

"Okay. You're the boss, Boss." Dora's pause was long. "Did I really just say that?"

"Yes, you really did."

She muttered something under her breath that sounded like it might have been profane self-recrimination. "I'll let you know when I've got all that sorted. *Puller* out."

Bannor wondered if something even worse than the railgun strike had occurred: Riordan came through the hatch of Wedge Two wearing an expression most commonly seen in funeral processions. Steve Rodermund, following behind him, merely looked somber.

Riordan stopped, nodded. "Major."

Bannor frowned. "Commodore." So was the formality for Rodermund's benefit, or was there something else going on? There was enough hitting the fan that Riordan didn't need to walk along the ridgeline just to convey a message.

Riordan drew up a little straighter. "Major, I—I don't know any good way to say this, so here it is without preamble—"

My god, what's happened? Who's been killed?

"—I need you in the field. Colonel Rodermund is taking over as Umpire Two."

Bannor almost laughed. "Is that all—sir? After pushing buttons and hovering over the comms panel, it will be a relief to be in the field."

"I'm not sure you'll agree when you learn more. But, for right now, I need you to bring in all *Puller*'s security personnel for pick up. Except Peter: he stays as CO at Backstop Three."

"Yes, sir...but 'pick up' how? With what?"

"With the Cayuses. I also need you to select six of the Cold Guard with the best marksmanship ratings and best record for independent operations."

"Yes, sir. You are looking for a background in small team ops?"

"No, Major. In solo or two-man teams."

Okay, when you said independent ops, you weren't kidding.

Riordan had not finished. "I need you to contact Rich Hailey to choose six Lost Soldiers who have the same skills at comparable levels. I need all of them to be armed with CoBros or the best rifles in the Lost Soldier inventory. All are going to need duty suits with balllistic inserts."

"Commodore, surely you're aware we're going to come up somewhat short on that equipment."

"No, we shouldn't. I had Duncan's and Karam's gear brought out two hours ago. And I'm giving up my own."

Well, this sounds more serious with every passing second. "I see, sir. Anything else?"

"Yes. I believe you've got the short-duration EVA shells for the duty suits here aboard Wedge Two?"

Huh? "Yes."

"You'll need those on hand as well. And as much ammo as you can carry."

Bannor nodded. "Sir, this is an unusual load for defensive operations."

"Yes, it is."

When working with Caine, Bannor was used to being the laconic one. This was an unnerving switch. "Sir, allow me to ask a more specific question. The operation for which you're drawing these forces and equipment: is it a *defensive* operation?"

"Yes. In a manner of speaking."

Peter Wu waved to the Cold Guards who were setting up Backstop Three's CoBro heavy barrel, motioned for them to bring it a meter further back from the treeline. The change of position barely reduced its arc of fire but greatly increased the amount of concealment afforded by the trunk-spanning mosses.

A helicopter clattered closer, attracting a predictable response: the Hkh'Rkh greeted it with jackhammering autocannons. The rotors pitched higher; the slick dropped down swiftly, angling away from the streams of enemy fire as it maneuvered toward the copse just slightly to the rear of the one in which Backstop Three was preparing to provide support for Dugout Seven.

As the autocannons tracked after the helicopter, more rotor-sounds rose in a distant chorus. Back near the top of the ridgeline, rising over the slowly settling fogbank of smoke and dust that had drifted southward along with the breeze, a Cobra and a Hind tilted down to face the far shore. Their chin guns chattered; missiles streaked overhead and sped across the river. Explosions of dirt and stone marked the approximate site of the now silent Hkh'Rkh weapons. Peter could not tell if they had been neutralized or simply elected to cease firing. If the latter, it was a prudent decision: the two human attack helicopters sank back down beneath the ridgeline.

Soon, the only rotor sounds were the slower *whuppp—whuppp—whuppp* of the grounded slick, which was simply keeping the engine at the ready while it disgorged its load of troops. After which, the rotors sped up again. As it rose into the air, approximately twenty crouching figures raced toward Backstop Three.

Either the Hkh'Rkh were cowed or too busy readying for an assault, but Wu's polyglot reinforcements drew no fire during their approach. Peter scanned them quickly: submariners and Russians from both eras rounded out a contingent that was mostly comprised of AK-armed Viet Cong. Except, on closer inspection, one of the World War II-era Russian infantrymen was not Russian. Or a man, for that matter. "Ms. Phillips?"

"How nice of you to still recognize me in this outfit. A bit bulky, to be honest, but quite adequate. Now, would you be so kind as to suggest the safest route of approach to Dugout Seven, Lieutenant Wu?"

"Dugout Seven? You intend to go there?" He glanced at the weapon she was carrying: a scoped Lee-Enfield. "Ms. Phillips, given your weapon, I suspect it might be best for you to remain back here, providing long-range support fire."

"That's very prudent advice, Lieutenant, but I'm afraid I can't take it."

"Why not?"

"Because I'm commanding this detachment, of course. Lead from the front, as the Army chaps say. Now, there really isn't time to waste, so do be a dear and show me the suspected positions of the snorks' beastly machine guns."

Peter Wu, resisting the urge to shake his head in a mix of wonder and rue, commenced to point out the locations she had requested. Out of the corner of his eye, he noticed faint signs of movement on the far bank. "And I recommend you move to Dugout Seven at the trot, Ms. Phillips," he finished.

"Very well. But why?"

He pointed. "Because the enemy is coming. Now."

Chapter Fifty

Through his dioptiscope, Ezzraamar watched the Warriors at the north ford wade out to the nearest APCs, keeping low in the water. Even so, the Hkh'Rkh were not comfortable in that element and rose up more often than they should. The largest Warrior stood before he was fully concealed behind one of the blackened and still-steaming APCs: he quivered, then fell limp, face-first, into the water. Given the range and the profound lethality of their rounds, he had almost certainly been hit by one of the human liquimix rifles.

Being heavily muscled, Hkh'Rkh did not float unless their lung-sacs were full of air. As Ezzraamar grimly expected, this Warrior did not bob back to the surface. The others continued to remain in a shoulder-down crouch until they reached the rear-bay of the vehicle. Once there, a pair of them pried open one of the doors, struggling against the push of the current. A third Warrior slipped inside.

Half a minute later, the APC's forward-angled

smoke dispensers coughed faintly: small black spots arced away from the wreck. As they began to curve back down to the surface of the river, they spat out smoke in several tightly sequenced discharges. Within two seconds, the billowing white clouds had become thick enough to prompt a platoon of Warriors to rise up from concealment near the head of the ford and race down toward the restive currents. If the humans saw their movement, they gave no sign of it.

"And so they will advance, across the river," fluted Jrekhalkar, who was beside Ezzraamar, observing. As he spoke, the first of the APCs rolled swiftly down to the bank of the river, approximately twenty meters upstream from where the troops were entering the water. The far shore remained silent and, to Ezzraamar's eyes, brooding.

He turned his head slowly southward. The scene at the middle ford was similar. The long, irregular column of burnt-out APCs now had Warriors moving amongst them, the leading teams already invisible in the smoke laid down from the tubes of the nearest wrecks. The first of the new, smaller wave of APCs were already in the water, struggling across, their noses aimed slightly upstream in an attempt to offset the force of the current by angling into it.

Further southward, the activity at the southern ford was markedly different. With only three APCs crawling along the downstream side of the ford—and therefore easy to push off if hit and disabled—they had already generated a thick, high bank of smoke. It was well-advanced across the river, which rippled energetically wherever the ford ran less than half a meter deep. Rather than approach the furthest edge of the smoke cloud, cautious Warriors probed forward, signalling when the lead APC was nearing that point. Still wholly obscured, that APC fired a veritable barrage of smoke cannisters as far forward and as high as possible, before vehicles from the rear advanced past it. Behind them, several hundred Warriors were ready to rush the shore, when the word came.

The enemy MULTIs were already defending their bank of the south ford, but rather futilely, Ezzraamar thought. Almost all the rounds were coming apart without any discernible explosion. Only a few, reached out over the ford itself, airbursting, causing no small number of casualties. But for every two Hkh'Rkh that went down, one of them rose back up and resumed their advance. And for every one that did not rise, three more were entering the river, swelling the attack force.

Jrekhalkar's gaze had followed Ezzraamar's own—whether by chance or intent, he could not tell. However, the Voice and Fist had become increasingly attentive to the young scion's observations and speculations, albeit without conferring any special rank, position, or privileges upon him. If he had, it would have been as good as admitting to his own scant knowledge of military procedures and practices. It was an irrational embarrassment that Ezzraamar had now observed frequently this day among Old Family Warriors: that their lifetime of preparation for combat did not also ready them to function well on battlefields. Fighting and war, while related, were two very different endeavors, a truth that the New Families and the humans not only realized, but took to heart in their planning.

Jrekhalkar emitted a triumphant hoot, then let the phlegm roll long and contemptuous in his snout as he pointed to the human artillery. "Apparently, their recent losses and our actions have disrupted the *s'fets'* coordination and aim. They are only sending their rockets against the southernmost ford, and are unable to reliably target our force. If they were any more inaccurate, they would be hitting their own positions, just back from the water."

Ezzraamar inclined his head faintly but said nothing. The human bombardment was puzzling, but he was unsure that it indicated incompetence or inadequate coordination. Indeed, he deemed it unlikely that the human aim could be so poor as it seemed, even though the great majority of the rockets seemed to be disintegrating before they cleared the far bank, while others were landing in the water and exploding. But he could not imagine nor conjecture what intelligent intent might be behind such strange performance, and knew that, without something more concrete than vague misgivings, he could not profitably mention the matter to Jrekhalkar.

He aimed his dioptiscope at the slopes above the far bank of the ford, wished its magnification was sufficient to show him more of what was happening there, just as he wished he knew more about the human combat technologies and doctrines. But in his preparation for the disastrous invasion of Earth, that had not been his area of expertise.

As another score of Warriors rushed into the current, Jrekhalkar's voice was thick with the assurance of impending victory. "Soon we shall repay these invaders for what they have done to us today, and for all their months of raiding."

Ezzraamar just kept watching the rockets that disintegrated without apparent effect over the far bank, hoped to see some evidence of why they were all failing. Or what they might actually be achieving.

Matthew Fanny swept his scope across the narrow pathway that joined his bank of the middle ford to the far one. There were no more exposed Hkh'Rkh to bring down. The humans had hit almost a dozen so far, but now the smoke was too thick and fewer of the enemy were careless. If the Hkh'Rkh had had any doubts regarding the superior range and accuracy of the human weapons, they had evidently put that behind them. Which only underscored the logic of their simple but effective tactics: to close as much as they could with the humans, where their heavier weapons and greater numbers would offset the various technological and performance advantages enjoyed by a small but decisive percentage of the opposing forces. Or, to be more specific, he and the rest of the Cold Guard.

One of the many casualty replacements in Dugout Four, Boris Ilizarov, a private from Sevastopol, scanned the smokescreen while hugging his AK-47 tightly. "Maybe they have stopped advancing, hey?"

Ilizarov's comrades groaned at his optimism before Fanny could turn what he hoped was a sobering gaze upon the youngster. "Private, be sure of this: they are coming. They wouldn't waste time and resources to get two-thirds of the way across the river and not attack."

As if to underscore Fanny's assertion, a covey of smoke cannisters flew out of the cloud like a scattering of oversized clay pigeons. Fifty meters beyond the former limit of the screen, they began bursting, emitting a mist that rapidly grew in density. They were spent before they hit the river.

Ilizarov swallowed, his eyes wide. He was among the youngest of the Lost Soldiers, and had enjoyed the protectiveness that older soldiers sometimes—rarely, but sometimes—extend toward that youngster in their ranks who reminds them of some kid in their own town. Some kid who never got into serious trouble, but just enough to prove he had some spunk; who did not excel in school but tried hard and rarely failed; who loved his parents and siblings and was not particularly wise in the ways of the world; who would grow up to marry his fresh-faced sweetheart and happily propagate the next generation that would emulate all his homey values and innocence. Most of the salty old veterans never quite figured out why they even took risks for this innocent on the battlefield, and never, ever understood that—as long as he was alive—so too were their memories of, and belief in, their own little town that had no war in it and to which they longed to return.

The expressions on the other faces in the slightly deeper holes of Dugout Four could not have been more different from Ilizarov's. Where the first team in Dugout Four had been a mix of actual infantry, insurgents, and submariners with tommy guns, this new group had not merely replaced his casualties, but had swollen his oversized squad to a full section. Mostly seasoned U.S. and Soviet troops who had been held in reserve as airmobile fire brigades, they had been choppered in only ten minutes earlier, and were now in their fighting positions, cool, calm, collected. The appearance of which was, of course, a learned behavior, a mixture of resolve and familiarity with fear: a demon that never stopped haunting them in combat, but with which they had made their accommodations, if not exactly their peace.

Most of them were armed with M-14s, a few with Dragunovs and scoped bolt actions. Upon arriving, they had set to digging deeper holes and grenade sumps with the slow, focused determination of professionals. Until, that is, the Hkh'Rkh autocannons started chattering three minutes ago. It was intermittent fire, and woefully inaccurate, but an extra centimeter of cover wasn't worth the risk of staying exposed. So they had stopped, spread and laid upon the ponchos, shelter halfs, and plastic wraps that they had brought forward from Dante.

Fanny heard faint helicopter sounds from behind the ridgeline to the north. They grew more distant, possibly moving up toward the north ford, or Dugout Two, just a bit south of it.

"Flanking attack against the north ford?" one of the Americans from Vietnam wondered out loud.

Fanny shrugged. If it was, he hadn't heard anything about it. But then again, with their commnet half gone, and the flare-related static growing steadily, he wasn't in the command loop anymore. Assuming, of course, that there was still anything vaguely like a command loop left to be in.

Only local comms between the Cold Guards were reliable, and only when the officers and NCOs were in a configuration that allowed their lascoms to be integrated by Know-It-All into a mini-server and command net. Which was obviously the case presently:

Backstop Two's primary target designator, Private Yehuda ben York, muttered, "I've got a clean sight picture on the lead APC that's coming across. Want I should paint it?"

"No," replied Captain Hasseler, who had taken over for O'Garran as CO. "Let them get closer. Don't engage until they're within five meters of the shore."

"What?" York was so surprised that he forgot to add, "Sir."

The captain was not worrying about formalities just now. "It will be easier to paint once it's in the shallows, starts rising out of the water. There's more hull to hit. And it's better to have them all in the water and wallowing toward us before we create a traffic jam of wrecks just north of the ford."

"Yeah," added Fanny. "Besides, the MULTIs aren't done dumping FASCAMs down at the south ford, and we can get some flanking designation from the Proxie, just like last time." He glanced over toward the gutted ruin of the APC that had been the high water mark of the last Hkh'Rkh assault. The anthrobot was gone. "Damn, where's the Proxie?"

Captain Hasseler sounded convincingly calm. "Don't worry, Top. He's just back up in the overwatch copse."

Fanny shifted to their command channel. "How do you know, sir? I didn't hear you order him off his post."

"He got orders from the rear, came back, and refitted from our stores."

"Refitted for—?"

Hasseler interrupted. "Eyes forward, Fanny, and on your scope. There are thermals in the smoke. They're coming into range."

⋄   ⋄   ⋄

Duncan Solsohn, chafed by the sweat-slick sensuit as he waited in *Puller*'s gunnery bubble, heard the tones indicating that secure command channel one was active in his headset. The link was scratchy, distorted, but Riordan's voice was clear, steady, slow: probably a conscious effort to ensure that his message got through.

"I don't know who's receiving this. We still don't have communications with all senior commanders. We also don't have enough assets to keep a full lascom relay net in place. Flare intensity is increasing, so broadcast—any wireless signal—is going to be subject to interference. Bottom line: as our comms degrade, so will our coordination.

"So, fight the holes you have. I leave it to the local COs whether you want to try to shelter behind and hold the wrecked APCs on the banks of the northern and middle fords. However, they must be rigged with *hardwire*-demolitions, in case the enemy takes them. It's crucial that you deny the Hkh'Rkh any cover at the head of the fords. Also, don't hold back from using your command detonated grenades: your signal could fail at any time.

"All Backstop COs: keep your counterattack teams hidden as long as you can, and update Know-It-All every time you take casualties. Most importantly, follow your own instincts if the command net is lost. But, if instinct isn't helping you, it's better to follow Know-It-All's advice rather than spend half a minute doing nothing."

The signal rapidly degraded, becoming only partially audible. "And remember, if the Hkh'Rkh breach just one ford, and some of their troops reach Wedge Three, we can't make a complete extraction. Protecting it is our primary objective. Do what you must to achieve it. Good luck."

Duncan stared out of the Proxie's eyes over the River Kakaagsukh. He chinned the channel to MULTI One: not the closest to his position, but the one least likely to be retasked to give direct fire support to the southern ford. "MULTI One, this is Puppet One. Are you just about done laying down FASCAMs at the southern ford?"

"We're still working on that, Puppet One. That's a long reach for us, even as indirect fire."

"Roger that, MULTI One, but I'm going to need airbursts when I get the go signal from Umpire One."

"Major Solsohn, sir, with all due respect, I received my fire orders directly from Umpire One half an hour ago. I've got to conduct that fire mission for the south ford until my FASCAM ammo boxes are dry."

Well, the gunnery officer was following command protocols, just like she should. But protocols were layered for a reason. "Sergeant Ippolito, I presume you were also given an override code by Umpire One?"

"Uh...well, yes, sir, I was."

"Then here it is: Foch One. I am overriding your fire order, shifting your targeting to the middle ford."

"Yes, sir, I acknowledge the override code. What's my new fire mission?"

"You will fire one HE round, set for twenty-meter airburst, over each one of the five preset fire coordinates you used to repel the first Hkh'Rkh crossing. I will then need rounds, fire-for-effect airburst, when and where I call for them. I may be using coordinates; I may be laser-designating."

"Sir, you could also be danger close. In fact, you're likely to be."

"That's the idea, Sergeant. Stand by to fire on my mark."

Bannor Rulaine, riding the flimsy skid of an ancient observation helicopter as he held on to the open hatch of the cockpit bubble, thought, *This is insane.* The vehicle sped toward the river, only five meters off the ground: behind it, the other Cayuse and a Huey followed the same, tight nap-of-earth flight path.

With a sudden lurch that made Rulaine glad for the improvised lanyard that kept him on the helicopter, his vehicle snapped higher, then banked sharply toward the right. Some weapons fire tracked along, far in the vehicle's wake. *Someone really ought to teach that Warrior how to lead a target.* But he was glad for his enemy's ignorance, was glad they were up against colonists with little or no military training. Had they been up against the Patrijuridicate forces he'd encountered in Java, that combination of equipment and training would have made their defense of the river impossible. This way, given the numbers, it was *almost* impossible.

The Cayuse dropped down behind a high stack of shrub-weeds joined by barbed runners. The other choppers tucked in behind. Men started jumping to the ground. Others, already waiting in the bushes, parted two shrubs, waved them into the thicket. Bannor watched his team go in, one by one. When he got a thumb's up from a large figure deeper in the underbrush—Tygg Robin—Rulaine nodded, jumped down, gave the same sign to the flight leader.

Nodding, the chopper jock returned the gesture, juiced the rotors. The small craft rose up, started turning to head back up the slope—

Gunfire from the far shore, muffled and indistinct as it fought through the noise of the rotors and the rolling rush of the river, seemed to startle the Cayuse. Its upward progress stopped with a hard jerk, then it tilted slightly. The rotor head began to shimmy. The pilot, fighting his controls, waved frantically for Bannor to clear the landing zone.

Rulaine leaped into the brush. He heard as much as saw the rotational armature shake apart, one of the rotors cartwheeling viciously in his direction.

He hit the dirt, flattened, felt something shriek over him, scything the air—and wondered if this was his last moment of consciousness, of life.

Chapter Fifty-One

Watching through his scope's thermals, Peter Wu saw a faint rectangular outline emerge out of the smoke-filled visual light spectrum like a slowly materializing ghost: the lead APC, still about fifteen meters back in the mixed smoke. Probably preparing to send another volley of cannisters up beyond the ford and well onto the shore. Unacceptable.

Wu chinned into the local net. "Private Baker."

"I see it, Lieutenant Wu. Want me to hit it with a DP RAP?"

"On my mark. I'm setting for IR followup."

"Roger that, but you'd better hurry, si—"

"Mark!"

A rocket-assisted projectile rushed out of the central hole in Dugout Seven's irregular cluster of positions. Wu's scope, now set to detect any friendly round, automatically centered on the sudden exhaust bloom; Peter squeezed the trigger.

As Two-Gun Baker's RAP hit the APC—an abrupt, blinding glare in the thermal sights—his own was already halfway downrange, aligning itself to follow the thermal path left by the first. It slammed into the same impact point, and this time, the flash was different. The initial pulse was more intense, but less widespread: Peter's dual purpose warhead had breached the armor where Baker's had weakened it. A much brighter flash followed, accompanied by a roar. A rush of heat jetted out of the evidently open top-hatch: probably a mixture of flame from the rocket-propelled grenade's warhead, and onboard munitions cooking off. Not enough to blow the vehicle apart—that kind of catastrophic hit was rare—but certainly enough to start fires.

The Hkh'Rkh response was immediate. Before the sound of the explosion had faded, a horn sounded near the head of the ford: an angry howl. It was joined quickly by several others and a loud, multi-toned hooting that Peter had only heard in one other place: Java, right before Hkh'Rkh launched an all-out attack.

He chinned into the general channel. "Ready on the line. Watch your zones and time your reloading." Then he selected a HUD feed, the last to which he had access: a bird's-eye view from one of the two quadrotors Riordan had positioned well above the river.

There were hundreds of Hkh'Rkh streaming across the southern ford, the smoke having dissipated from midstream back to their shore. As he toggled the tactical circuit, trying to reach the MULTIs, Wu heard small explosions rippling like strings of firecrackers, just beyond the limits of the smokescreen. Thermal ghost-Hkh'Rkh twisted and died there, singly and in bunches: they had entered the FASCAM minefield. Too small to be easily detected during the heat of combat, the smoke that the enemy had rolled forward now made the antipersonnel devices practically invisible.

As the explosions continued, one Hkh'Rkh staggered out of the mists. A Thompson stuttered at the Warrior, who, already wounded, went down. And although the mines continued to explode in the smoke, and phantom enemies continued to fall, they showed no sign of retreating.

Wu's earbud toned, indicating that it had finally connected. The audio he received sounded more like an ocean squall than a human voice. "MULTI Five; go."

"This is Backstop Three, requesting fire mission at coordinate set delta. HE, airburst at twenty meters. Two rounds per coordinate. Fire for effect."

Back on the dust-misted ridgeline, Peter heard the *throof—throof* of the first two rockets he'd called for. At the same moment, four more Hkh'Rkh stumbled out of the smoke. M-14s barked sharply at them. Three went down, two lying motionless. The one still on his feet looked for targets, swung in the direction of Dugout Seven—just as Baker's CoBro spat and dropped him, the round emerging from the Hkh'Rkh's spine with a misty exit spray discernible even at one hundred meters. The one who had been dropped but was still moving rose to the four-legged running stance that Hkh'Rkh sometimes used for short bursts of speed—but two Thompsons hammered him back to the ground. Where he remained.

Wu took a moment to appreciate the small arms fire sequencing being orchestrated by Know-It-All, which was cannily making recommendations that preserved the ammunition of the most important weapons, before the sound of descending rockets distracted him.

Above the ford, visible just above the top of the smokescreen, two angry bursts of smoke appeared like abrupt, lethal asterisks: the first two airburst rounds. Wu glanced at the overhead view in his HUD. Although lined by static now, the effect was noticeable: almost a score of the Hkh'Rkh sprawled into the water; most did not get back up. A few, limbs waving weakly, struggled to remain upon the ford but the current carried them off. They disappeared downstream, the tips of their snouts marking the points where they finally submerged and succumbed.

Two more rockets sliced down and detonated. The massacre moved closer to midstream; coordinate set delta had five grid points that walked the fire from the near shore to the far. But, as with the mines, the Hkh'Rkh kept coming, and many of those who seemed dead at first stirred and rose again.

The horns had been blaring the whole time. Some fell silent and then were sounded anew. Hkh'Rkh picked them up from the fallen and winded them, much as human troops had caught up and carried flags across corpse-littered fields in the bygone days of infantry charges. Then, without warning, silence—

—before they came charging out of the smoke en masse, gaps blown in their loose ranks by mine after mine.

Which, if anything, made them charge faster, firing as they came.

Top Sergeant Matthew Fanny swapped in a new bottle of hotjuice as Private Akiriri, the other Cold Guard in Dugout Four, popped up to drop two Hkh'Rkh who'd reached the sagging remains of the

APC that had made it to shore during the first attack. Its blackened sides weren't worth much in the way of cover anymore. Since being disabled, it had been repeatedly hit from the far shore by rocket launchers that had been dismounted from enemy carriers. That had compelled Fanny's troops to retire from their de facto pillbox at the head of the ford. Only Major Solsohn's Proxie had been able to stand the heat and the fragments and hold that position.

But the Proxie had withdrawn now, was lurking in the tree-cluttered overlook just thirty meters downstream, waiting for god-knew-what. Fanny only knew that they could have used its help any time now, thank you very much.

The enemy smokescreen at the middle ford was now so heavy that the MULTIs were not able to hit the later carriers that had been swimming across, although the first half-dozen had all been struck by overhead antiarmor missiles from MULTI Four. Now clogging that part of shoreline smooth enough for APCs to roll up out of the river, the six smoking wrecks had compelled the others to finish crossing elsewhere. Their options: either cut across and land on the rugged downstream side, or steer alongside the upstream rim of the jammed ford, clinging to its side as they made for land. However, the now scratchy and half-clouded images from the on-site quadrotor made it difficult for the human defenders to know which of the alternatives the remaining APCs had chosen.

Almost a dozen Hkh'Rkh infantry emerged from the smoke near the scorched and sagging sides of the gutted APC. Not as disoriented as the earlier groups, they quickly swung toward Dugout Four and laid down fire. One raised a grenade launcher. Its cough sent a projectile arcing overhead—it was not rocket-propelled—but it then diverted downward sharply to land among their holes: a terminal correction charge, apparently.

The spray of fragments riddled Ilizarov's legs, blasted the stock of his AK-47: the young Russian gasped, then started screaming. An American, Rollins, moved to roll from his hole into Ilizarov's, but Fanny shouted, "Fight your holes! Return fire!" and hated himself as he did so: he had probably condemned poor Ilizarov to bleeding out.

More Hkh'Rkh managed to exit the smokescreen and survive, sheltering behind what little cover the APC offered. Fanny popped his head up, saw that the enemy Warriors were clustered just where he'd buried the last four of his command-detonated grenades. He ducked back down, grabbed for the detonator, and twisted the activator as large-bore rounds raked the air above him.

Nothing.

Shit. Weak signal? He lifted the detonator so that its transmitter would not be obstructed by the side of his fighting hole, tried again, despite enemy fire that came perilously close to his hands.

Still nothing.

Okay, either a grenade malfunction—damned unlikely to affect all four at the same time—a comm malfunction, or solar flare interference. Impossible to tell, and right now, not important. Because all that mattered was that the Hkh'Rkh were continuing to accumulate at the head of the ford. Support fire from Backstop Two was chipping away at them, but Dugout Four was now almost completely suppressed. Two men—one Russian, one American—crept upward to fire, staying mostly prone: it didn't matter. Bursts from the Hkh'Rkh's large caliber assault rifles literally shredded them, ripping through their torsos like heavy machine-gun rounds.

In fact, if Captain Hasseler didn't take a chance and call for MULTI Four to saturate the head of the ford with HE—and at danger-close—Fanny really wasn't sure how much longer they could hold—

Over the lip of his fighting hole, Matthew Fanny saw a blur of motion in the distance: a vaguely anthropomorphic object that seemed to be jumping through the air, was about to disappear into the smoke.

The Proxie.

As it soared through its long leap, its back-mounted munitions dispenser coughed twice. Two bombs—similar to mortar rounds—arced in, heading for the rear flank of the oblivious Hkh'Rkh who had collected in the vicinity of the ruined APC.

Fanny ducked down just as the bombs landed with twin roars.

As his thirty-five-meter running broad jump brought Duncan Solsohn's point of view into the smokescreen, the Proxie's superior thermal vision showed him that he was on course to land on the deck of the next wrecked APC. He had plotted its position during his first attack and so had simply instructed the Proxie to leap to those coordinates, as soon as Riordan's go signal had come through.

As he prepared to land, Solsohn swung the grenade launcher on the Proxie's left arm toward an APC that was trying to roll up on the shore, one set of wheels gripping the upstream side of the ford, the other set still churning the water. At a range of seven meters, he aimed a dual-purpose RAP down at the vehicle's lightly armored deck doors, firing as he overrode the minimum arming and motor ignition distances. The weapon rocketed off his arm, scorching the end of the launcher with a backblast that would have incapacitated a human but which had no effect upon the Proxie. The round burrowed through the armor, exploded inside, sending one of the long, rectangular doors flying up over his head as he landed on the wreck he'd selected.

Duncan scanned his surroundings: approximately forty enemy troops, milling uncertainly in the smoke. Luckily, the drifts did not have as heavy a mix of antithermal agents as the Hkh'Rkh had used during their first attack. Two more APCs were trying to copy the example of the one he'd just destroyed: to follow along the upstream rim of the ford and thereby get to land by going around the wrecks clustered where the water was shallowest. And further on, in the smoke that stretched out beyond the middle of the river, he saw—

A solid wall of thermal signatures, like a crowd on a broad city sidewalk. He chinned the priority circuit to MULTI Four, one of the few batteries still reachable by lascom. "This is Puppet One. Commence override fire order; authorization Foch One."

"Received and executing, Puppet One."

Duncan located three more ruined APCs that were sequential stepping stones across the ford. Each one was within the Proxie's standing broad jump range of the next. Before leaping again, he targeted the deck of the next semi-swimming APC and fired: the round hit obliquely, caromed off. *Well, shit: I guess I'd better improve that angle.*

Solsohn jumped, waited until he was almost staring straight down at the back of the APC, instructed the launcher to fire at the same aimpoint, minimal arming and ignition distances overridden. Another rocket-propelled blur drilled down at the enemy APC. This explosion wasn't quite so dramatic, but the vehicle swerved off the ford, began to drift and turn in the current. A mission kill.

Just before Duncan landed, he took a shot at the last active APC he had spotted. This RAP went low, but some of the fragments burst two tires and crippled their suspension: the vehicle started spinning pointlessly, like a rowboat with an oar on only one side. *Good enough*, he thought as he landed and the airbursting MULTI rounds began slashing down and detonating behind him. *Yep: time to jump again.*

Duncan's next leap carried him beyond the back edge of the smokescreen. Beneath him, the snout-like heads of dozens of Hkh'Rkh stared upwards, too surprised to act, for a moment.

But only for a moment. Assault rifles tracked him in his arc, none of the fire coming particularly close. But, as an experienced Proxie operator, Duncan knew their aim would improve as he came closer to landing. It was hard to gauge a target passing quickly overhead, but the closer it dropped toward the horizon, toward a lateral engagement vector, the more accurate fire became. However, Solsohn had paced his crossing with that in mind, as well as the flight time of the airbursting HE rockets fired by MULTI Four.

As the Hkh'Rkh swung their weapons and snouts

skyward, missiles exploded twenty meters above them. The Warriors went down in windrows, clutching ruined skulls, trying to staunch gushing neck and shoulder wounds, arms shredded by fragments.

Duncan landed, counted off two seconds as the next section of Hkh'Rkh Warriors saw him, raised their weapons—and over their heads, dirty blossoms of downward-jetting death bloomed. Before leaping, Solsohn scanned their thinned ranks for spots of heavier density, called the coordinates in to Sergeant Ippolito at MULTI Four.

Her response came after a brief pause. "Major, don't these rounds constitute a danger to the Proxie—and your mission?"

Duncan jumped again. "Negative. The fragments can't penetrate the Proxie's armor." *Of course, they can still take out subsystems or external stores, but I'll live with that risk.*

As if to prove that the universe never misses an opportunity to chastise human overconfidence, the next airbursting round went off only twelve meters behind the Proxie. As the shockwave tumbled the anthrobot, Solsohn felt a transmitted impact on his back. He scanned his system readouts, saw the munitions bay for the back-mounted dispenser change from green to red, jettisoned it just before it exploded.

Which tumbled him again. Realizing that instinct would not handle the new change of vector and attitude in time, he triggered the automatic correction system. Below, he saw the snoutlike faces of Hkh'Rkh staring up at him as the Proxie went through a contortionist's combination of rolls and tumbles to reorient for an optimal landing.

It was still awkward. He missed his footing on the next APC, skittered over the edge of the back deck, fell into the water on his left side.

The half-dozen Hkh'Rkh that were sheltering there overcame their surprise within a second: they brought up their weapons—

—as Solsohn turned the Proxie in a semicircle, the flashing rifle on its right arm sweeping across them like the blade of a glittering buzzsaw. They fell in a ring. Duncan stood and jumped again as more missiles airbursted along the column behind him.

This leap carried him over the enemy troop concentration at their end of the ford, gunfire following the arc of his progress. He landed in a small clearing he'd spotted between three clumps of clustertrees. He hopped immediately for a larger clearing behind it, where, at last, he would begin to run instead of jump.

The clearing had signs of being a bivouac site for troops, but none were present, other than a few wounded, some of whom moved feebly toward their weapons when he landed. He began running—long, loping, six-meter strides—and checked the status of his grenade launcher. It was fine, but an orange damage sensor had come on for his left knee joint, the part of the Proxie which had absorbed the primary impact of his awkward landing.

He ran into a flood plain, mottled by copses and stands of sapling-sized weeds which roughly paralleled the river, and sped north for seven hundred meters. If there was any pursuit close behind him, there was no sign of it. He consulted the overhead view—he had access to both the feed from an EXHALTED and one of the quadrotors—and found the heavy weapon emplacements that Dugout Two had spotted earlier in the day. He swerved in their direction, bringing up his grenade launcher.

He stopped two hundred meters behind the weapon sites, scanned for thermal signatures, found two clusters roughly where he expected them. He chose those coordinates, selected two HE and one smoke round for each site, and then let the Proxie do the shooting. The anthrobot positioned itself in what an external observer might have perceived as a squatting boxer's stance and pumped out two HE rounds at the first target, then another two at the second. Sequential explosions flashed among the clustertrees in which the heavy weapons were hidden. Many of the thermal signatures began fading. The others' biosigns were prone and stationary.

The Proxie swiveled back to its first orientation, thumped a smoke round into the first smoking weapon site, and then another into the second. Twin plumes of dense white billowed upward and outward like ground-spawning cumulus clouds.

Duncan turned and began sprinting directly away from the river, moving swiftly toward the higher, less trafficked ground at the foot of the western ridge. He chinned the link to *Puller*'s bridge, eight meters away from the gunnery bubble in which he was controlling the Proxie. "Dora, I have completed phase one. Crossing point has been cleared and obscured. Now moving toward waypoint two."

"Okay. Confirming target coordinates for phase two."

"Received. Proceeding to search for phase-two target."

Duncan Solsohn—wishing the sensuit wasn't so hot and sticky, wishing he had the time to stop and get a drink of water—continued running, angling southward as well as west until his direction indicator centered on his target:

The last remaining broadcast hub of the Hkh'Rkh, located approximately six hundred meters back from the west bank of the middle ford.

Peter Wu was no stranger to combat, much of which had been at less than one hundred meters range in the streets and jungles of Java. But never before had he seen over a hundred Hkh'Rkh appear all at once, charging straight toward him as a hooting mob.

The real problem was that, long before they reached him, they would swarm over the positions of Dugout Seven, whose defenders were emptying their various weapons into the oncoming horde. Some flowed around its far flank, threatening to break into the gap between Dugout Seven and the much smaller Dugout Six. Wu pointed them out to the crew of the CoBro heavy-barrel, currently configured as a cassette-fed machine gun. "Target right: engage," he shouted.

The gunner swung the weapon to lead the leakers, squeezed the trigger, and the Hkh'Rkh began to go down. Wu shouted above the stuttering reports, "Fire Teams One and Two, protective fire for Dugout Seven. Remember your zones." He didn't need to finish by saying "Execute." The remaining troops of Backstop Three were already firing into the pack of Hkh'Rkh who were bearing down upon Dugout Seven.

Wu saw Phillips give up trying to rally two of her troops who would not rise to fire; one a young Vietnamese who could not have been older than seventeen, another a Russian who was perhaps a year older. And

Wu could not blame them: the storm of fire that swept along the low rims of their fighting holes was heavy, ceaseless. Two of the defenders had already been killed outright; several others were fighting back despite grievous wounds. And the Hkh'Rkh, despite casualties that would have paralyzed any human unit that Wu had seen or heard of, came on with a mounting fury so intense that it made "resolve" or "courage" needless. Their desire to kill had overwhelmed any self-preservation instinct that might have still existed under their rage.

The CoBro machine gun next to Wu finally fell silent. He glanced quickly at the weapon's kill zone: the Hkh'Rkh leakers were either dead or disabled, the last few survivors crawling toward the concealment of low, irregular bushes. "New target," he shouted. "Swing left. Clear all enemy within fifteen meters of Dugout Seven. Set weapon for automated engagement. Execute." He chinned the comlink to Two-Gun Baker, hoped it was still working. "Baker? If you can hear me, stay down: we are employing autoengagement."

As the machine gun started the strangely irregular chattering characteristic of the automated engagement setting, he heard Baker's static-lined reply, "Damn straight I'm staying down!" He saw a Hkh'Rkh leap toward his position, saw his CoBro's long barrel clear the lip of his fighting hole, saw its muzzle twinkle. Baker's attacker fell limply, halfway in his hole.

Many other Hkh'Rkh started falling as well, and even at one hundred meters, the wounds inflicted by the machine gun were visible. The expanding rounds fired by the CoBro heavy tore open their armor, exited their heavily muscled bodies with puffs of dim maroon mist. The gunner walked the weapon's field of fire slowly down the line defended by Dugout Seven, her finger holding down the trigger the whole time. But rather than generating a steady stream of fire, the weapon's sensor-computer controls assessed every new object that occupied the center of its sighting scope, determined if it was friend or foe, and spat a four-round burst. Sometimes it ran across three targets in the course of a single second, sometimes only one, which created its eerie sound: a broken staccato that nonetheless had intervals of regularity nested within it.

Of the two dozen Hkh'Rkh who came close enough to the linked fighting holes to angle their fire down at the sheltering humans, only three survived long enough to unload their own weapons. The Hkh'Rkh either fell back from, or toppled down upon the humans they had killed.

In the brief lull that followed, Wu tried to reach Two-Gun Baker again—the other Cold Guard in Dugout Seven was either dead or wounded—but a wave of static was the only reply he received. He scanned the position; at a guess, half of Dugout Seven was dead or so badly wounded that they were incapable of fighting on. Of those still firing, maybe half could truly be called "combat effectives"—and even that was a generous estimate.

Tactics and humane action required the same response. Wu turned his head, began shouting orders. "Heavy barrel; reposition three meters left. Then swap cassettes and prepare to resume fire. Fire Team Two, prepare to reinforce Dugout Seven. Fire Team One, provide cover fire. Teams: execute!"

As the machine gun's crew moved the weapon to

a new position that would—hopefully—throw off any imminent enemy counterfire, Fire Team One began sniping at the next wave of Hkh'Rkh, choosing any who seemed to be trying to train their weapons on the three sprinting figures of Fire Team Two.

But more and more Hkh'Rkh were emerging from the smoke. The FASCAMs had done their work, but the Warriors had evidently carved a path through them, paved by those the mines had slain. Several at the front of the new horde, at the flank closest to Dugout Seven, did not press on with their charge, but kneeled, aimed at Fire Team Two—

And were hit in the side by a fusillade from Dugout Seven's fighting holes, only fifteen meters away from them. Susan Phillips had risen, along with Two-Gun Baker and several GIs and Soviets. Their sudden wave of fire rocked the kneeling Hkh'Rkh back: several rolled limp, several fell, tried to rise up. Phillips, having abandoned her scoped Lee-Enfield for a Thompson, vaulted to the top of her hole and charged at them; the mobile defenders of Dugout Seven followed without pause.

Wu, speechless, breathless, realized that her distraction just might enable Fire Team Two to survive their sprint to Dugout Seven.

The more pressing question, he discerned as his team's heavy-barrel machine gun began to speak again, was whether Susan Phillips and the rest of the defenders would still be alive by the time they got there.

Chapter Fifty-Two

Jrekhalkar moved his civilian-grade dioptiscope higher back on his unusually long head. "I would have your assessment, Ezzraamar Laarkhduur of the Moiety of Nys'maharn: where shall I show my *halbardiche*? At which ford should the Voice and Fist of Turkh'saar make his personal crossing?"

Which, Ezzraamar knew, was code for: *where shall we commit our last reserves to break through?* Because the contests were close and fierce at all three crossing points, it seemed wisest to concentrate their remaining resources to forcing just one.

Ezzraamar pony-nodded. "To advise, I must assess more closely."

Jrekhalkar flung his hand, claws stretched, in the direction of the river: a gesture of permission that Ezzraamar might do as he pleased.

Ezzraamar snugged his military dioptiscope over his eyes, adjusted the magnification to respond to sustained ocular fixity, and watched the river as it swam into and out of focus for a moment. The current was diminishing slightly, which meant that far downstream, in the bay into which it emptied, the tide was probably at its peak. The resistance of the rising water took time to register upstream, slowing the current but also causing more chop. By nighttime, the effect here would be at its greatest: the water would be calmer, but already slightly deeper, even though the tide in the bay would be running out by then. Would that impact the outcome of the battle? Unlikely, since it was still many hours to nightfall. But if the combat was not resolved by then—if, for instance, the Warriors of Turkh'saar had secured a foothold on the far shore but had been contained there by enemy forces—then the slower current would make for an easier night crossing. It would be both safer and easier to send enough Warriors across the River Kakaagsukh to force a breakout from whatever pocket in which the humans had them hemmed.

He swung his head northward, but paid more attention to the faint, erratic hisses and frying sounds in his earpiece: the radio degradation from the flare was continuing to build. With any luck, it would force the humans to ground their rotary aircraft. Usually, engines were not as sensitive as communications or computing equipment, but flares were unpredictable, and the consequences of an in-flight failure were usually final.

He steadied his head so that it was aimed in the direction of the northernmost ford. The image swam, grew, resolved.

There wasn't a lot to see, other than the masses of infantry crouched among the ruined APCs on the ford, a line which disappeared into the still-screened far shore. It was impossible to make out the weaponfire from here: the thundering exchanges at the middle ford—barely three hundred meters away—drowned out all other sounds. However, the amount of infantry that seemed to be waiting, rather than moving, among the wrecks on the northern ford was not promising. It indicated that whatever else was transpiring there, the pace of the assault, and the speed with which forces were securing a foothold on the far bank, was quite slow. And in attacks such as this one, a slow pace tended to favor the defender, not the attacker.

He moved his view southward, scanning the stretch between the northern and middle fords for some sign of the activity that had drawn his attention to the area earlier. The dioptiscope showed no activity on the human side, only a faint wisp of smoke where helicopters had arrived to either drop off or pick up troops near the river. Their purposes had not been clear. But the militia's machine guns had brought down one of the smaller rotary-wings, its rotors suddenly askew, one of them tearing through a patch of underbrush that ran down to the water. The other aircraft had not tarried, but sped away shortly afterward.

Ezzraamar's view swam back, reducing the magnification, as the dioptiscope grazed across the middle ford. It had been the site of the worst losses to date, worsening further when, just a short time ago, a human robot had come leaping out of the tower of smoke on the far shore, bounding from one ruined APC to the next like a whelpling using conveniently spaced rocks to hop across a stream. Covered by a devastating barrage from the humans' MULTIs, the robot had single-handedly broken the attempt of a second wave of APCs to skirt the wrecks on the ford and support the assault. It had then bounded into the clustertrees behind their side of the ford and apparently attacked and suppressed the heavy weapons that had brought down the human rotary-wing between the north and middle fords. Jrekhalkar had sent a full troop in pursuit of the mechanical monster but, so far, they had reported no luck in finding it.

Ezzraamar finally swung his head toward the south ford, where the largest mass of Warriors was moving swiftly across the shallows, disappearing into the smoke on the other side. The roar of gunfire and explosions from beyond those thick, billowing drifts was fierce and relentless. Still, if only a fraction of the Warriors pouring on to the far shore were surviving to secure a foothold, it was by far the most promising of the three assaults.

Ezzraamar pushed back his dioptiscope. "I agree: the southern ford. But I am concerned that the human robot is still on our side of the river. It has the power to disrupt our forces, our plans."

Jrekhalkar's answering gesture was dismissive. "We have over fifty of our best Warriors tracking it. They will find and destroy the abomination."

Rather than offer his opinion regarding their ability to carry out that mission, Ezzraamar approached the topic obliquely. "The automaton is very fast and is no longer engaging us directly. It may be difficult to hunt."

Jrekhalkar did not seem concerned. "Most likely it is looking to locate and eliminate our heavy weapons. We shall continue to pursue it, but concern with it must not undermine our commitment to the current attacks. Actually, I would rather have it on this side of the river than over there, fighting to turn us back from the far shore."

Ezzraamar saw the wisdom of that, but also saw the

danger the device might pose operating in their rear. However, Jrekhalkar's opinion was well-founded in one regard: they did not have much "rear area" left to protect. All their assets had been brought up to the line to carry out the attack. The few mortar carriers which had not been eliminated were now almost as likely to hit Warriors as humans, so their moment had passed.

Jrekhalkar turned to address the rest of his staff, who had already given their opinions on where to invest their last, sizable reserves. "It is decided. The *halbardiche* of the Voice shall cross at the southern ford. Move our reserves into position." Two runners left at a trot, heading back to the command APC, two hundred meters further back at the Flag's command post. He gestured to most of the others. "You shall await the outcome at my command vehicle, and shall coordinate and manage communications among us as best as you may. Ezzraamar, Z'gluurhek, G'Ken, and Odokhaas: you and my bodyguard shall make for the southern ford immediately. We shall show our Warriors the way across the river, the way to victory!"

Jrekhalkar had no doubt meant his words to be stirring, and it had some of the desired effect upon the other Warriors he had summoned to work as his immediate retinue in this, their finest hour. But Ezzraamar turned his eyes back into the forest behind them, where a human killing machine was still wandering unchecked.

Bannor Rulaine used his thermal goggles to scan for hidden Hkh'Rkh. Resolution was lousy at this time of the day—early afternoon, when the sun had imparted considerable heat to most objects—but biosigns still stood out a bit.

Happily, in the copses and scrub-thickets surrounding the small stand of clustertrees in which his team had come ashore, there were no such signatures. There were hot spots aplenty, mostly exposed rock faces, but almost no active thermal emanators, and those few that he saw were consistent with animals. Cowering animals, judging from their stillness and the incessant thunder of gunfire and explosions.

Tygg Robin crawled past him, surprisingly stealthy for so large a man, two small quadrotors following him like obedient, airborne puppies. Currently slaved to home in on his transponder, it reduced the need to furnish them with active control. Behind him, the rest of the team was still shrugging their way out of the light pressure helmets and life support packs that they had swiped from the duty suit EVA shells to effect their underwater crossing of the River Kakaagsukh. The Lost Soldiers who had been recruited for this mission—four Americans, two Soviets—had demonstrated reasonable competence for the apparatus and staying on the ROV-deployed guide-line. But even so, one of the Soviets had gone missing during the crossing. Whether he had mistakenly detached from the line, had a technical failure, or would show up later, far downstream, was anyone's guess.

The Soviet—a crack shot named Grisov—had not been the only casualty before the mission began. One of the Cold Guards and one of the American GIs—a sniper who'd managed to live through the Battle of the Bulge—had both been killed when the Cayuse's rotor had spun away from the stricken helicopter, slicing through the brush and their torsos.

Now the question was whether the team was large

enough to complete the mission—or rather, any of several missions with which Riordan might task it. It was equally uncertain how they'd be signalled: by lascom (if they had the line of sight when needed), radio squelch (if it could get through the solar activity) or signal flare from the far shore (if the were looking in the right direction when it went off). The operational status of the remaining team—Bannor, Tygg, O'Garran, Rich Hailey, Alexander Shvartsman, five Cold Guards, one Soviet, and three Americans—had now been downgraded to "marginally sufficient," according to Know-It-All's review of the various missions with which they might be tasked.

The senior Cold Guard, de los Reyes, scuttled over to Rulaine. "What now, Major?" Others heard the muted question, turned in their direction; several hunched closer.

"As soon as Captain Robin has finished slaving the quadrotors to our group lascom net, we'll move inland and then south. With any luck, they won't have seen us slip into the water when we started crossing."

"Is that why the Proxie took out the two weapon sites just across the river from us?"

"Yes. That had to happen anyhow—to take out the only enemy units likely to see us—but after they shot down the Cayuse, the Proxie's attack will seem like a countervalue strike, not random destruction." He couldn't see the Cayuse's crash as a lucky break—lucky breaks didn't kill three sibs-in-arms—but Duncan's attack was now explainable in terms of a logical combat response, which made the Hkh'Rkh unlikely to question why the marauding anthrobot had diverted northward to knock out the two weapons and their crews.

"Why are all these flying egg-beaters with us?" asked

Owen, staring dubiously at one of the quadrotors that was hovering within arm's reach.

"To maintain comms and security," Rulaine answered. "The commodore gave us almost a third of the remaining small-scale assets. Some of them are lascom equipped, and with our own local version of Know-It-All to coordinate them, they're going to keep us in communication with each other. That, and the underwater crossing, were the reasons we had to have all of you in duty suits; we need their embedded transponders. The quadrotors will keep track of them and furnish Know-It-All with overlapping surveillance of our collective footprint. That way, even though we'll all be separated by a hundred meters or more, Know-It-All will be aware of our relative positions and the approach of any Hkh'Rkh."

Owen frowned. "It can do all that?"

O'Garran smiled broadly. "If it wasn't for this damn solar flare and all the drones we lost, it could do a hell of a lot more."

Rulaine nodded. "This way, we won't get too close to each other, and won't wear ourselves out having to watch for bad guys. I'm not suggesting you try to take a quick nap when you stop moving, but Know-It-All has your back. From two or three points of view, usually." Tygg signalled that all the quadrotors were ready to move autonomously.

Owen shrugged. "Okay, so what's the op, Major?"

Bannor rose into a crouch. "To get to where we'll be needed."

"And where's that?"

"I'm not sure yet—but I'll tell you when we get there. Now, on me: we're moving out."

❖   ❖   ❖

Duncan Solsohn forgot for a moment that it wasn't he himself leaping through copses of clustertrees; he put up a hand to deflect a stray branch that he was flying past, three meters off the ground.

It happened sometimes, that Proxie operators got so comfortable "driving" the anthrobot that they got lost in the experience. Understandable, but not the right frame of mind during combat operations. And definitely not now.

He was closing on the enemy transmission coordinates, which had remained steady for the past twenty minutes, reconfirmed by the remaining battlefield sensors that were still linked by lascom.

Solsohn's next bound brought him to the edge of a copse of trees that the view from EXHALTED indicated as the closest cover to his target. He crouched down, and reached out with the anthrobot's sensors.

Standard visual spectrum revealed what he'd expected: a loose laager of Hkh'Rkh APCs. Thermal showed that they were starting to shed heat, mostly accumulated from the sun, some from modest engine activity a few hours earlier. Enhanced by motion cueing, guidons pointed out those hot spots that were walking about: fewer than he and Riordan had expected. Wasn't this the enemy command post? Had they taken the precaution of separating their leadership from their comms nexus? According to Riordan, the Hkh'Rkh hadn't even taken that step during the war on Java, where they had had far more reason to suspect that their C4I assets would be detected and selectively targeted by both insurgents and main-line units.

His broadcast sensors imposed radiant, out-flowing rings upon one of the two centrally located APCs: new transmissions. And now that he zoomed in to 300x magnification, Duncan saw telltale signs of a hull-embedded dispersed aerial: a dedicated communications vehicle. Probably not the best they had: more likely a standard model that had been factory upgraded with an auxiliary comms package.

The out-spreading rings faded: the radio signal had terminated. A moment later, four Hkh'Rkh exited the vehicle, collected under a small tarp that had been pitched like an awning, rigged to the side of one of the other vehicles. Most of the Hkh'Rkh were older, judging from the color and shape of their manes, and they were gathering around what looked like a map table. *So: the command staff—or some of it. But where's the guy in charge?*

Duncan scanned that group closely for any sign of the large, archaically equipped Warriors who would be the commander's ceremonial and actual bodyguards: the *halbardichers*. There was no sign of them.

Well, no time to wait or to waste. Solsohn painted each one of the APCs, starting with those protected at the center of the laager and working outward. He brought up the automatic grenade launcher controls, detailed two DP rounds for the comms vehicle, and one for every other. Sufficient, but it meant he would run dry of DPs. He activated the autoattack mode, turned his attention to the targeting screen for the CoBro mounted on his right arm.

Without his controlling it, the Proxie's left arm came up and starting firing RAPs at the vehicles clustered just over one hundred and fifty meters away. The very first grenade sailed right through the open rear hatch of the comms APC. Flame and smoke jetted out of every hatch and firing port.

By the time the fifth grenade hit its target, the Hkh'Rkh had not only spotted its source, but were laying down withering fire. One long stream of heavy projectiles shredded the clustertree next to which Solsohn had parked the Proxie; audio track-back indicated a source outside the laager, up on a small, bush-crowned knoll. He swung his visual sensors over to it: a dismounted autocannon. *Hell, even at range, that could actually hurt me.*

He switched to the CoBro's scope, zoomed in to 40x resolution for a good sight picture, and, after selecting exploding rounds, he activated the Proxie's auto engagement system. The rifle on his arm started spitting out rounds fitfully; the Hkh'Rkh manning the weapon started thrashing and falling, small flashes marking where the rounds were hitting and detonating.

But before the last one slumped over the autocannon, a long row of angry divots stitched their way along the ground leading to Solsohn, walked right up into him. The view from the Proxie shuddered; an orange light came on. The left knee joint, again. And the light was pulsing now. Damnit: imminent failure.

Duncan glanced back at the laager of vehicles. Except for one that was lumbering away with one tire flattened and its wheel askew, they were all motionless, sending up black curlicues of smoke. Scattered among them, Hkh'Rkh were firing at him, helping wounded comrades, trying to work around his flank.

Which, if he didn't move now, would be what he would die defending.

The experts told you never to leap when you have a damaged leg: the force of landing was too great, was likely to break the appendage before it failed on its own. But Solsohn had learned in the field that actually, if you jump and make sure to land with your weight on your good leg, that actually extended the remaining time you had in the bad one. Assuming you were good enough to manage to stick an imbalanced landing.

Duncan smiled, jumped.

And, yes, I am that good, damn it.

In Wedge One, Caine watched the overhead map update—sluggishly in some places, not at all in others. The full impact of the flare's communication disruption was being felt, although there were indications that the peak had been reached. Perhaps, in another ten or twenty minutes, the helicopters could resume operations, but for now, they were still grounded. Which meant that his attack choppers could not defend the fords, that the chopper carrying Newton Baruch and Ike Franklin from Dante had grounded five klicks shy of the ridgeline, and that Yaargraukh and his team were stranded where the Chinook had put down, still ten kilometers away.

"Commodore, report coming in from Colonel Rodermund—er, Umpire Two," Gaudet said over her shoulder.

Steve Rodermund had taken over gathering battlefield updates. Without reliable radio, and with the drones grounded because they were just old enough to be vulnerable to the flare, the colonel and two of the other fixed-wing pilots from his era had stationed themselves on the ridgeline with scopes and binoculars, gathering what information they could through direct observation.

Caine nodded for Gaudet to link him. "What's the sitrep, Steve?"

"Damned uncertain. There's still a lot of dust in the air from the railgun strike, so we're getting temporary glimpses at this point, not steady visuals. We did get some radio reports from Sergeant Ippolito, who took over the north ford from Captain Robin. The wrecked APCs on the shore have become the local equivalent of the battle for the barricades. It's close-quarters combat, up there. Five meters and less at times."

Riordan rubbed his eyes. When combat shrank to those ranges, casualties were always high, no matter how much cover or technological superiority you might have. And it was no surprise that there was now a pitched firefight under way to control the wrecks. Being armored, they were the best and only cover near the ford. For the humans, that cover meant having a reasonable position from which they could mount effective fires out upon the ford itself, a secure spot from which they could mow down the wading Warriors. Conversely, for the Hkh'Rkh, the wrecked APCs signified a means of getting a toehold on the shore, which also provided a slim but crucial shield for the forces struggling to get across. "Steve, do you know if Dugout One had enough time to finish rigging the APCs with demo charges?"

"They did, but they can't blow them."

"What? Why? Didn't they run the hardwire detonators?"

"They did, but they tested negative just a few minutes ago. Best guess is that the wires were severed, probably by fire."

"Then they've got to send out a team to find the break and repair it."

Rodermund was silent for a long second. "That will be—expensive, sir. The wire crosses exposed ground and the Hkh'Rkh have managed to get small flanking toeholds to either side of the ford."

Caine forced himself not to close his eyes as his stomach lurched against the words he had to say. "Understood. But you are to relay those orders, nonetheless. And they must carry them out ASAP. That is mission-imperative." He wondered how many men he had just killed with that order. They'd be submariners, mostly. Men who had been snatched from the jaws of death in the Sea of Japan, carried off in cold sleep to a world twenty-one light-years away, awaking one hundred and seventy-eight years later—just to die checking exposed demolition wires on a minor colony world during a firefight spawned by stupidity and chance. Riordan flinched away from any further reflection on that grim fate—and that he had condemned them to it. "Word on the other fords?"

"No words, but like I said, a few glimpses. Your remote-control robot broke the momentum of the attack on the middle ford. It seems to be building again. I can't see midstream, but my guess is that the enemy recovery is pretty wobbly: they don't seem to be getting ahead of their casualty rate. What does EXHALTED show?"

Riordan glanced at the bird's-eye view, saw no change. "EXHALTEDs are blind on the middle ford. The new burning APCs, in addition to the old ones set on fire by the MULTI strikes, have completely blocked the overhead view. But I've got another way to direct the fire, if you think another salvo from our tubes would drive them back."

"I do think that. But the real problem is the south ford. That's where the snorks have committed their remaining forces. They've almost overrun Dugout Seven two times, now. And I think they're about to try it again. If it wasn't for the FASCAMs, they'd have gone through us already."

"And the support from MULTI Five isn't enough?"

"Not so far. Every time MULTI Five has to stop and reload tubes, the snorks get another platoon into the beachhead. But one of the Hinds could turn that situation around pretty quickly, I think."

Riordan glanced at the readouts on the flare: still too dangerous to fly. "Can't send one yet. Recommendations, Colonel?"

"If you believe in the power of prayer, you might try that."

"Steve, I'm serious."

"So am I. Every other asset we have is tied up. Dugout Six tried a flank attack to relieve Dugout Seven, got mauled. We can't retarget MULTI Four to help out; it's essential to holding the middle ford. The only hammer left unswung is *Puller*."

Riordan heard the hanging tone. "Steve, if I put *Puller* in the air, I jeopardize everything. If the Hkh'Rkh have any missiles left, that's probably the target they're waiting for. And I've got no way of knowing if the ship that launched the railgun attack has closed in enough to try to hit us from orbit. Either way, damage to *Puller* could compromise whatever central comms we have left, including the links to Bannor's team and the Proxie."

"Then I guess it's a race between how long Wu

can hold on at the south ford and how soon the flare fades to the point where you can risk putting our choppers back in the air."

And if we can keep our strung out comm links patched together, and keep both the netcentric and local versions of Know-It-All running long enough. But what he said was, "Tell me, Steve: do *you* believe in the power of prayer?"

Rodermund was silent for three whole seconds. "Haven't for years. But I might give it a try today."

And although he didn't intend it as an invocation to a deity, Riordan thought: *Amen to that.*

Chapter Fifty-Three

Matthew Fanny popped his head and arms out of his fighting hole, sighted on two Hkh'Rkh running toward Dugout Four. They were using the apelike, four-legged run they occasionally adopted when they weren't carrying long arms. Which meant that they were going to try to get into grenade range. Again.

His CoBro set for four-round bursts, Fanny tapped the first, who went down. That prompted the second to stop, rear back, grabbing one of their soft-ball sized grenades off its equivalent of web gear. The Warrior's torso filled the sight picture in the rifle's scope; Fanny squeezed the trigger.

The Hkh'Rkh slumped, went down atop the grenade— which had evidently been armed: two seconds later, an explosion blew the corpse almost two meters off the ground. What landed was missing more parts than not.

Suppressing the shakes—sergeants didn't have the luxury of getting the shakes, particularly not tops—Fanny glanced to his left. The two fighting holes closest to the ford had been hit by enemy grenades. Now scorched and irregular in shape, there was no trace left of the soldiers who had manned them. Hkh'Rkh grenades massed almost three times human varieties and didn't leave much behind—at least not when they landed alongside you in a hole, two at a time.

Fanny felt sweat trickle down the back of his neck. The ballistic inserts of a duty suit weren't going to keep out shrapnel from a monster grenade snugged up against his butt. And once they got his hole—and with it, the last fully functional CoBro on the front line—the Hkh'Rkh would be ready to make an all-out assault to take Dugout Four. Unless Captain Hasseler sent another Cold Guard up to reinforce—

Motion caught the opposite corner of his eye. Fanny turned toward the river, kept turning until he was looking slightly upriver. There, floating in between drifts of smoke like a cloverleaf of pie plates, was a quadrotor. And it had an edge-on view of the ford.

Fanny chinned the secure channel in a panic of desperation and relief. "Captain Hasseler, we've got eyes on the ford, I think."

For a moment, Fanny was afraid that now—of all times—the local net had finally broken down, now when deliverance was hovering in sight out over the choppy waters of the River Kakaagsukh. Then: "Roger that, Matt. Its feed just came up on my system. Umpire One must have reassigned it directly to our local net."

Which meant that the entirety of the engagement was now being monitored by one quadrotor: a considerable risk, but at this particular moment, Fanny cared a great deal less about the big picture and a lot more about his little piece of hard-fought and perilous ground. "Captain, I'm down to fifty percent combat effectives, and the two holes closest to the head of the ford can no longer be manned. If you're planning to send a fire order back to MULTI Four, I'd be grateful if you did it quickly."

"It's already in, Sergeant. In a minute or two—"

But that might be too late, Fanny realized as a wave of shadows appeared at the near edge of the smokescreen and broke through: at least two score of Hkh'Rkh, charging straight for him.

"Captain, I need defensive fire—right now!" He turned to the remaining defenders of Dugout Four. "Commence firing! Shoot 'til you're dry!"

Because if you don't, he added silently as the machine gun and CoBros of Backstop Two started dropping the onrushing Warriors, *we won't still be here by the time the rockets arrive.*

Duncan Solsohn stopped checking the multiple sightlines long enough to enjoy the view.

From the top of one of the tallest clustertrees in a copse midway between the middle and southern fords, and three hundred meters back from the river on a small rise, the valley stretched out before him like a panoramic mural. For just a moment, he consciously ignored the sights and sounds of the conflict that raged along it, and tried to appreciate the view.

Except, he decided, it just wasn't that beautiful. Almost all the flora and fauna were dull variations along a few very common themes. Duncan could not imagine missing this world, but could easily imagine forgetting its particulars.

He checked his top-down map: Bannor's team was drawing abreast of his position, but was deeper inland.

Their individual separation was good, and, according to EXHALTED's minimized sensor abilities, they were not drifting closer to any Hkh'Rkh.

The enemy forces were, if anything, less mobile than before. That was hardly surprising: having lost their theater-level comm center to send occasional coded squelch breaks through the shuddering surges of interference, it was now impossible for them to coordinate movement or action beyond the level of horns, heliograph, or hand signals—all of which he'd seen them employing on a local level. But given the now-obvious commitment of their reserves to the assault on the southern ford, that loss of coordination would probably be less keenly felt: the Hkh'Rkh commander had cast the die. All that remained was for them to take the ford or fail, to win or lose. It was strange, he reflected, how despite the complexity of twenty-second-century warfighting tools, a battle could still boil down to the conclusive clash typical of the ancient and medieval epochs: a final charge to pierce the defender's line.

But before that last act, he might have more work to do. Duncan shifted to improve his view of the middle and south fords—and almost fell out of the tree: his left knee, now totally unresponsive, swung out of the crevice in which he had lodged it, almost pulling him out of his sniper's perch. He reached down and pulled the free-swinging leg back up into a crook just below the branch upon which he sat.

Reinforced against any further wobbling, Solsohn scanned the near side of the middle ford, checked ranges, painted a few pretargeted spots. He turned toward the south ford, was somewhat surprised to see hundreds of Hkh'Rkh still waiting under cover, back from the edge of the river. If Riordan didn't do something to help turn back that tide—

Peter Wu, reloading his CoBro with an extended heterogeneous magazine, saw the thermal ghosts of another wave of Hkh'Rkh nearing the edge of the smokescreen. An invisible APC popped yet another flurry of cannisters onto the bank from deeper within the cloud. They had evidently run out of thermal damper cannisters: Wu could make out heat signatures much further into the obscured area at the head of the ford. But he was down to thirty percent ammunition and couldn't afford to shoot at targets upon which he could not get a positive lock—not anymore.

Wu turned, watched the machine-gun crew swap in their fourth tank of hotjuice. He'd lost count of the cassettes they'd burned through: the pile of empties was waist-high behind them and there were only four fresh ones left.

A few Hkh'Rkh emerged from the rethickening smoke, crouch-running toward Dugout Seven, keeping pace with the leading edges of the cloud. Wu swung his CoBro in that direction, surveyed the site with his scope; there were eight, maybe nine people left manning those holes, counting his own Fire Team Two. Phillips had managed to pull most of her people back from the diversion that had covered their approach, but the withering fire of the advancing Warriors was continuing to take its toll.

The troop mass building within the smokescreen was arguably the largest one yet. Too much for Dugout Seven to resist if it didn't have more firepower on the line. Which meant there were two possible options for holding the ford.

Wu chinned his lascom link; nothing. He switched to encrypted broadcast. Faint, scratchy snippets of conversation; probably bleedthrough from the stronger transmitters on one of the wedges.

Wait: the wedges. He switched the channel to Wedge Three. After a short delay, Phil Friel's voice answered, garbled but readable, "Wedge Three, here. Peter?"

"Yes. I need information quickly. Are you still in contact with Wedge One?"

"Only if I go all bands in the clear. The ship comms can piece a message together from the bits and pieces it gets from each—"

"Good enough. Get this message through to Riordan: We need a helicopter gunship strike on the southern ford. We can't see it, so we can't call in or correct fire from MULTI Five. Laser designation is impossible."

"Why not just try hitting the prior coordinates?"

"Because MULTI Five is running low. By my count, they probably have less than a dozen HE warheads left. Each one *has* to be effective."

"I'll try to get through to HQ. Stay on this line."

As if I can reach anyone else. Five seconds passed.

"Peter, I got through to Rodermund. The gunships are still a no-go. But if the flare continues to fade at the current rate, they might be able to get airborne in ten minutes. Can Dugout Seven hold out that long?"

Peter Wu had lived a generally positive life, always trying to put the best foot forward, and the best face upon any situation. But he was out of patience and out of time. "Without help, Dugout Seven will be gone in two minutes. Wu out."

Well, that left one alternative. It was tantamount to suicide, but huddling next to the almost reloaded machine gun wasn't much better. He stood, turned to the gun crew. "Cover us. Fire as long as you can." Then he looked down the line, yelled, "Fire Team One, on me!" and charged toward Dugout Seven.

There was movement up ahead in the fighting holes toward which he and three of the Cold Guard were now sprinting: troops moving the wounded or corpses to make room for the reinforcements.

If they got there. Twenty meters away from Dugout Seven, horns sounded yet again—and nearly a hundred Hkh'Rkh broke from the smokescreen. They came as a single wave, weapons in assault carry, firing as they came.

Wu resisted the urge to go prone and return fire: if Fire Team One did not push on and get to cover, they were as good as dead. "Follow me!" he shouted and ran harder than he had during the first eighty meters, if that were possible.

Warriors spotted them, dropped to their knees to train their weapons upon the four advancing humans— and sprawled: Phillips was directing fire against any who stopped long enough to aim at her reinforcements. A moment later, the heavy machine gun in Backstop Three added its lethal firepower to the effort, the gunner taking her targeting cue from Phillips.

But the Hkh'Rkh did not stop coming, nor did the rate at which they were emerging from the smoke abate. They had clearly been gathering for this and they smelled weakness.

Wu was about to leap into the rearmost of the fighting holes when the leading edge of the Hkh'Rkh

reached the forward holes of Dugout Seven. Three
Viet Cong, two still armed with AKs, another wield-
ing a fallen American's M-14, rose quickly to engage
the Warriors. They were immediately battered into
pulp by a wash of point-blank enemy fire and then
disappeared as the large aliens swarmed into and past
their fighting position.

Wu changed his mind, leaped over the fighting
hole he'd been trying to reach, pressed on to Phillips's own, central position. He almost stumbled as
he landed: the bodies of the dead and wounded were
two deep in most places. Without stopping to speak,
he raised his CoBro, thumb snapping the selector
switch to lowest RPM stream fire: two hundred fifty
rounds per minute. He didn't bother with the scope:
at fifteen meters range, the dozen Hkh'Rkh closing on
them were easier to track with iron sights. He swept
the staccato-barking weapon across the first rank of
attackers: half fell. The remainder went down under
a mass of fire from tommy guns, M-14s, and a lone
Dragunov. A second group started to emerge from
cover—from the fighting holes they had so dearly
won—but the machine gun at Backstop Three drilled
down the first two who exposed their full torsos. With
any luck, Wu had perhaps ten seconds to coordinate
actions with Susan Phillips.

Who was looking at him, a small but genuine smile on
her face. "Well," she said, "it's about time, Lieuten—"

Wu heard the report—a Hkh'Rkh assault rifle—the
same moment that a red hole punched through her
shirt near her appendix. Phillips, eyes wide, fell back.

Wu swung around, saw his target: one, no two,
Hkh'Rkh firing prone over the lip of the forward fighting

hole. He went to scope, increased the magnification and reduced the juice feed with a single combined thumb motion. As he squeezed the trigger, he felt the vastly decreased recoil, saw the unprotected snout of his first target explode into a maroon-mauve ruin as he edged the weapon sideways and fired at the second Warrior. Whether he hit him or simply drove him back, he never learned: from the edge of the fading smoke, a ragged chorus of scatterguns roared and and rounds hammered into his torso.

At that range, his ballistic liner prevented penetration— just barely. But as the impacts drove him back, Wu saw that the next wave of Warriors was readying itself to break free of the smoke. Soon they'd join the others who were in the forward positions of Dugout Seven, were sheltering near the scant remains of the ruined APC, or prone behind the heaps of their own dead. And once they started working in concert—

The time had come for his final and unacceptable contingency. "MULTI Five, come in."

"Here."

"I need fire support."

"We still don't have visuals or designation for the ford—"

"Copy these new coordinates." Wu rattled off the numbers. "Fire for effect. Immediately."

The Hkh'Rkh started emerging from the smoke, firing as they came.

The voice that answered Wu was jittery; "Lieutenant, those coordinates—that's worse than dangerously close. That's nearly on top of your posi—"

"I am calling a Broken Arrow; I say again, Broken Arrow." Behind him, Wu heard Phillips groan, then curse in a most unladylike fashion. But the battery commander at MULTI Five was making hesitant sounds—and hesitation was the one thing Peter could not afford. "MULTI Five, I confirm I am calling coordinates which overlap Dugout Seven. Fire all remaining HE. Airburst only." Wu saw Phillips trying to rise, dragging up the tommy gun.

"Airburst?" said the voice in his earbud. "Lieutenant Wu, that's suici—!"

"You have your orders. Execute."

Wu turned, grabbed Phillips, who was considerably taller than he was, and shouted down the line. "In your holes, now. Cold Guard on top of Lost Soldiers. Airbursting munitions inbound." He pulled Phillips to the bottom of their position, dove on top of her, saw Hkh'Rkh silhouettes loom near—

—and heard the up-dopplering downrush of the first rockets from MULTI Five.

Even through the thick canopy of the clustertrees, Bannor Rulaine both saw and heard the explosion behind the smoke obscuring the eastern bank of the northern ford. Dirt, scree, and debris jetted up almost a hundred meters; the long thunderclap reverberated down the valley, rebounding between the ridges.

His comm monitor toned: an incoming local lascom from de los Reyes, the closest of all of Bannor's well-scattered team. "What is it, Sergeant?"

"Major, what the hell was that explosion? That didn't sound like any vehicle going up. It sounded more like a demo charge. And a big one."

"That's what it was."

"So . . . that was us?"

"Yes, Sergeant. Dugout One. Executing a contingency plan." *A plan which tells me just how close-fought this battle has become.* It was not an unexpected event, but it was sobering. In the extreme.

Bear de los Reyes wasn't finished. "So, sir, have we won?"

"No. It means we haven't lost. Yet. It also means that we should be going to phase two shortly."

"What's phase two, Major?"

"Engaging the target. We're waiting for that signal."

"Sorry, sir, but engaging what?"

"Target selection will be part of the signal. Now, give it a rest, Sergeant: you'll be one of the first to get the word, when the word comes down."

"Yes, sir. De los Reyes out."

Bannor heard the channel close, was glad that de los Reyes had not asked for how, exactly, that signal was to be received, since the radio was now almost useless. *Which could leave the time and the target up to my judgment. Without access to updates or any wider view of the battlefield than this hunter's blind in which I'm stuck.*

Great. Just great.

Riordan, standing on the ridgeline with a set of modern binoculars, was still trying to make out the enemy movement across the river when his earbud toned: secure one. He tapped his collarcom. "Steve?"

"No, sir. This is Chief Nagy, sir, pilot for Wedge Two. Colonel Rodermund walked down the line to the Cobra helicopters, sir. After we sent the mechanics into the line two hours ago, he's the best qualified to tell if their electronics are flight worthy or not."

After what that flare did, Rodermund's recommendation to ground their birds had been the right—and eminently prudent—course of action. "Okay, but next time Umpire Two leaves the clubhouse, he needs to tell me."

"He tried, Commodore. That was right when the last surge hit. So this is both his notification to you and the battlefield report I've been collecting."

Time to face the music. "Go ahead, Chief Nagy."

"Yes, sir. Fair warning: there are a lot of holes. Comms are just now starting to come back, and I think a lot of the old sets must be fried."

"I'm well aware of that, Chief Nagy." In fact, it was probably Warrant Officer Nagy who didn't understand just how badly degraded their communication and data sharing was. It had been almost an hour since lascom—and therefore, signals to and from the EXHALTEDs and *Puller*—had been reliable. Although lascom was not as sensitive as broadcast equipment, it was still subject to automated, protective shutdowns when the astrometeorology algorithms didn't like the flare patterns. Between that, and the excessive data load, the Know-It-All had ceased to have a netcentric reach: it was running in local modes, only. And that, in turn, meant that communication to and from field commanders had been uneven and the link to Bannor's team effectively lost. "Give me the sitrep you have, Chief."

"Yes, sir. Sergeant Ippolito at the northern ford finally got through about five minutes ago, confirmed she lost control of the APC barricade there."

As if everyone in the valley hadn't figured that out after she blew it up.

"She demoed the wrecks, as ordered. The concussive effects of the blast stunned the Hkh'Rkh who'd taken up flanking positions. Using reinforcements from Backstop One and Dugouts Two and Three, she cleared those pockets and is now in full possession of the ford on our side of the river."

Riordan made sure to keep his voice level, calm. "And the demo team?"

"Two survived long enough to find and fix the wire, sir. But they weren't able to get far enough from the charges before the Sergeant had to—well, they're gone, sir."

The Warrant Officer hurried on with the rest of her report. "Shortly afterward, the Hkh'Rkh either ran out of smoke cannisters or stopped launching them: the screen cleared. That allowed Sergeant Ippolito to call in fire from MULTI One again. She laid down standard HE among the ruined APCs in the river. Not completely effective—the Hkh'Rkh used the wrecks as shelters—but they pulled back once they realized they'd lost their beachhead."

So, the north ford is solidly in our hands. Thank god for small favors. "And the middle ford?"

"A stalemate, sir. The MULTIs broke up whatever forces they were trying to muster for a decisive push, particularly those near our side of the ford. Also, their remaining APCs could not make it ashore due to the wrecks jamming the banks. When their remaining vehicles started turning back, their infantry attack lost whatever momentum it had left.

"However, they've still got troops sheltered among the wrecks from midstream back to their side. We can't dislodge them and don't have the weapons to try."

Okay, so we're holding the middle ford not because we defeated the Hkh'Rkh, but because we exhausted them. "And the southern ford?"

"Hard fought, sir. Heavy casualties. Dugout Seven was partially overrun on three separate occasions. Lieutenant Wu had to personally lead a counterattack into point-blank range, and then called in a MULTI strike on the position itself while enemy forces were less than five meters away from him. That broke the attack. It also broke our position at Dugout Seven."

Riordan's throat tried closing as he asked the fateful question. "Lieutenant Wu?"

"No word yet, sir. But most of the personnel alive at the time of the Broken Arrow strike survived. The Cold Guard had armor inserts in their duty suits and protected the Lost Soldiers with their bodies. The Hind you cleared for operations arrived about three minutes later and rolled right up the Hkh'Rkh column, from our side of the ford to midstream. The enemy had almost no cover there, sir, just the three APCs that had been sent to advance the smokescreen. The Hind expended all its ordnance. I'm told it was a pretty gruesome scene, sir."

"And the Hind?"

"Got back, but with more holes in it than cheese-cloth, sir. They couldn't make it up the ridge, so they landed four hundred meters behind Backstop Three. Those old-time Russians sure swing brass sets. Sir."

"They certainly do, Chief. Who's in charge at the south ford right now?"

"Lieutenant Thon, who ran all the way down the hill with her MULTI team to reinforce the line there. She's asking for more troops."

Riordan called up a mental image of the last map update he'd seen. "Send Thon the crew of the Hind, and have it dismount its doorguns to add to their firepower. Also, Yaargraukh and his team are airborne again, and only five minutes out. I'll send them to join as an allied autonomous force, but not on the line. They'll provide fire support from Backstop Three."

The Warrant Officer was silent for several seconds before she hazarded a question. "Sir, are you sure it's safe to insert Hkh'Rkh into the defensive positions on *our* side, right now?"

"No, Chief Nagy, I'm not certain it's safe. But I am certain that we can't afford to leave the south ford insufficiently defended. About which: once Rodermund gives it a clean bill of health, get the first available Cobra over to the ridgeline to support the south ford. Send the first airborne Huey to the north ford and pull half of Backstop One out for relocation to Backstop Three."

"That will leave north ford a little light, sir."

"That's okay. The Hkh'Rkh pulled all the way back, there, and we'll have the second Cobra ready to intervene."

"Yes, sir. Anything else?"

"Did any enemy leakers get to Wedge Three?"

"Two, sir. About a squad of them got ashore from an APC that swam the river upstream of the middle ford. We didn't see it because we'd pulled the shore watchers in Dugout Four to replace the troops from Dugout Three that got sucked into the battle for the north ford. Apparently a second enemy vehicle tried to swim across but got swamped and went down midstream.

"The APC that made it to our shore landed four hundred meters north of the middle ford and headed north toward Wedge Three. Backstop Two saw them, inflicted a few casualties, but could not keep them engaged because they had to remain in their position to support Sergeant Fanny. But when the surviving Hkh'Rkh—five, we think—got within seventy meters of Wedge Three, they were detected by ground sensors and Chief Friel engaged them with the transport's PDF system."

"Engaged, not neutralized, them?"

"Sir, until we have the time to sweep the bush, we really can't be sure. The PDF system—well, sir, it doesn't leave a lot of remains. If you take my meaning."

"Yes, Chief Nagy, I take your meaning." Riordan had seen the twenty-five-millimeter hyper-velocity autocannons in operation. "Any word from Major Rulaine?"

"None, sir. We might hear from him if he were to transmit on one frequency constantly, and in the clear. But he can't try the same. He's got to stick with the automated freq hopping and encryption that his local Know-It-All package is running. Anyhow, the current EM activity makes it unlikely that we'd get more than small pieces of his transmissions. So even if all is well, we wouldn't hear about it."

Any more than we'd hear if they had all been hunted down and killed. Riordan's stomach was so hard that it was becoming intensely painful.

Chief Nagy asked cautiously, "Anything else, Commodore?"

Riordan bit his lip. *Yes, Warrant Officer Nagy, there is one other thing. I'm wondering if you could tell me how many of my friends I've killed today?* Bannor,

Tygg, "Little Guy" O'Garran, Wu: they'd all saved his life at one time or another. In some cases, more than once. And today, he'd managed to toss them all on the chopping block. Because, after all, wasn't that what friends did to friends? But all Caine said was, "That will be all, Ms. Nagy."

Riordan tapped out of the circuit, stared down into the valley where dozens of smoke columns clawed up toward the sky. A Cobra clattered past, two hundred meters behind him, angling away on a course that would carry it over the ridgeline and down toward the south ford, where the casualty count was sure to be highest.

Someone shifted their feet, just behind him. Another person cleared his throat carefully. Riordan turned, too weary to be surprised.

Newton Baruch and Ike Franklin stood two meters further down the backslope. They both nodded, murmured "Sir," or something that sounded like it.

He returned their nods. "Just off the chopper?"

"Not exactly, sir," Newton answered, keeping his eyes lowered.

"We hoofed it the last five klicks, Commodore," Ike said frankly. "We heard what was going on out here. We didn't want to—to miss out."

Riordan smiled. He knew what Franklin had meant to say—"to help out"—but admitting to overt altruism wasn't the parajumper's style.

Baruch glanced at his companion, then at Riordan. "I'm sorry we didn't get here in time, sir."

Riordan shook his head. "Not like you two had any choice in the matter, Newton. The flare made the decision for you. But I'm glad you're here now. I've got work for you to do."

They looked up; if anything, Franklin looked too eager.

"Lieutenant Baruch, you are going to assume overall command of a special security detail that will be formed to gather at the south ford."

"Yes, sir, but why there?"

"Because, unless I am much mistaken, that is where we'll next be encountering the Hkh'Rkh—either in battle or parley."

The two spoke as a chorus. "Parley, sir?"

"Gentlemen, I've been at victories and I've been at defeats. This isn't either one. They didn't get what they want—to destroy Wedge Three—but we're no longer in a condition to mount a safe extraction. There are still too many loose ends." Melissa Sleeman's face swam up into his consciousness: *add one more friend I've possibly killed today.*

"What about me, sir?" Franklin asked, stepping forward, eyes bright.

"You, Lieutenant Franklin, will give me your perspective on the Hkh'Rkh of this planet. Every bit of information, every nuance, could prove crucial during negotiations."

Franklin winced. "Damn, you mean now we're going to have to *talk* to them, sir?"

"Yes, Lieutenant, that's just what we'll be doing in a couple of hours. If we're lucky."

PART FOUR
June 2121

PRIDE

Contritionem praecedit superbia
et ante ruinam exaltatur spiritus
(Pride goeth before destruction,
and a haughty spirit before a fall)

Chapter Fifty-Four

Rodermund, Ike, and Newton squeezed into Wedge One's bridge, which was really just an outsized cockpit. With Yaargraukh seated—or rather, perched—in one of the seats, the compartment felt not merely small, but shrunken.

Steve Rodermund stared at the Hkh'Rkh. Either he could not keep the hostility out of his eyes or did not bother to try. "So what's the word, Commodore: do we have to kill some more of them, or do we get to leave, now?"

"Not sure, yet," Riordan answered. "But they're willing to meet."

Newton frowned. "Sir, are you certain that's a good idea?"

Riordan shrugged. "It is if we want to see Melissa Sleeman and her team again. The Hkh'Rkh leader, Jrekhalkar, has forces at what they simply call 'the Site,' enough to find and wipe them out before we could get there."

Rodermund frowned. "Look, Commodore: they're not

735

running radar and we've still got air assets. If we were careful, I'll bet we could be down at the Site before they realize it. Hell, we've still got the ability to jam all their radio signals. So if we got moving right away—"

"There's another problem with our negotiating position," Riordan sighed. "A rather large problem, actually."

"How large?"

"Two hundred kilotons large, to be precise."

Ike's eyes widened. "They have a nuke?"

"Yes. Here. In the valley."

Newton sat, his frown deepening. "And they would be willing to destroy themselves along with us?"

Yaargraukh nodded slowly, as if he were trying to imitate the subtly different human gesture of affirmation. "Even those Warriors who felt Jrekhalkar unwise to bring this fight to you would now be Honor-bound to stay. They have not lost the battle so long as they have not retreated from where it was fought. Similarly, they have not driven you from that ground either. As long as their Honor is at stake, it is immaterial to them whether they die resuming their attack or by a nuclear blast that destroys us all." Yaargraukh spread his claws out flat as if pressing air down against the deck. "If this were part of a larger, longer campaign, if it were conceivable that they could ultimately triumph by ceding this field today, then Honor would not be an issue. But Jrekhalkar's entire Flag was mustered with the sole purpose of driving you out, of avenging our Unhonored dead. So for them to allow you to escape, or for them to admit defeat, is to turn their backs on avenging both the Unhonored and the Warriors who died here."

Rodermund had been growing increasingly redder during Yaargraukh's explanation. His retort came out in a blistering rush. "So what the hell is this, then? A war or a—a vendetta waged by battalions instead of gangs?"

Riordan glanced at Yaargraukh. If the Hkh'Rkh responded with equal heat, the conflict could escalate right here on the bridge of Wedge One.

But Yaargraukh's reply was as calm as his first comments had been. "Even for us, the difference between a war and a matter of Honor is often hard to distinguish. I understand your impatience, your frustration, Colonel. We of the New Families often have similar reactions. We rarely have the luxury of allowing pride to dictate unwise political policy. We lack the power, the resources, to survive very long if we did so.

"So like you, I find the rituals and traditions now driving Jrekhalkar and the other scions of the Old Family both aggravating and counterproductive. But they shall not be dissuaded from them. Certainly not by you or me."

Newton folded his hands. "So if the Hkh'Rkh hold our team at the Site hostage, and have the equivalent of a nuclear fail-safe in this valley, how did you get them to negotiate, Commodore?"

Riordan shrugged. "We hold all three fords. Even if they could muster another attack, it would be so costly that they'd be unlikely to carry the day. Besides, when they upped the ante by putting a nuke on the table, I matched them."

Ike frowned. "With what?"

"With the nuke our superiors would be likely to

drop on Iarzut'thruk if Jrekhalkar used one here in the valley."

Ike blinked. "What superiors? What nuke?"

Rodermund was grinning. "Have you played poker, Lieutenant?"

"A few times."

Rodermund's grin widened. "You bluff much?"

"Er... as I said, I've only played a few times."

Rodermund almost chortled. "Then I recommend you don't play with the Commodore."

"Yeah, okay, I get the tactic. Sir." Franklin replied testily. "But the Hkh'Rkh know we don't have a fleet in orbit, sensors or no sensors."

Riordan shook his head. "They may know we don't have a larger force in orbit around this planet, but they can only *suspect* we don't have one in this system. And when the cost of calling my bluff could be the very colony they're trying to save... well, little doubts can start to loom very large. For instance, they *do* know we didn't arrive in any of the wedges or *Puller*, so where is our shift-carrier? And what else is it carrying? And what are our rules of engagement?

"When it comes to warfighting, we're as much a mystery to the Hkh'Rkh as they are to us. For instance, on Earth, it puzzled them that, once we got the upper hand, we did not slaughter all the invaders immediately. To them, the concepts of fighting to achieve an armistice, or a limited war, are not merely confounding: they are meaningless. Conquest is their way of war because it is their way of life. The only time a truce occurs is when both sides are so vulnerable that other powers might be able to pounce and grab all their property, and so, destroy that Family."

Franklin stared. "So, if there's a border clash between a couple of hotheads who don't know how to back down, they go to war over it?"

Yaargraukh's long head oscillated slowly. "Not always, no. But far more frequently than your nations do. It is why our history is so marked by wars. Three of them all but smashed our civilization." He let a long, quiet monotone echo out of his snout: a deep Hkh'Rkh sigh. "Seven thousand years have given our traditions not merely the power of law, but the semblance of inevitability, as if our Honor-culture is inherent, unalterable. What you call the Industrial Age has arisen on Rkh'yaa on three separate occasions, because until the most recent iteration, it was also the harbinger of an apocalypse. We had no way, no social mechanisms, to arrest the eventual fall into total war."

"And what was different this last time?"

Yaargraukh glanced at Ike. "More power was consolidated in a smaller number of Families, making them more akin to your states. Before, we had been largely feudal and decentralized. But with the dawning of the current epoch, the balance of power—and redress—shifted to the greatest family of each alliance. In time, the relations between different Families, between suzerains and vassals, became less fluid, more permanent and deeply invested. This reduced the chance that incidents between smaller states could expand into full-blown war, since the leading families could make their displeasure felt swiftly and decisively if a vassal was behaving too aggressively toward the clients of another great power."

Franklin nodded. "But otherwise, the old ways haven't changed."

Yaargraukh's neck oscillated more dramatically. "That would be a hasty conclusion, Lieutenant. Certainly, the intransigence of this colony's Old Families invites that conclusion. But whereas war was historically waged solely between Warriors, the onset of machines changed that. As in your own history, the factories that created more and deadlier weapons ultimately became the primary targets of those same weapons. Ultimately, the targeting expanded to include the workforce that labored in those factories. Or produced food. Or worked in mines. Or enabled mass transport." Another Hkh'Rkh sigh. "Our codes of Honor arose to protect the weak from the strong, from the trained Warriors. Now, the Unhonored are spared the horrors of war only when doing so does not overly inconvenience their leaders."

Rodermund leaned forward. "Okay: enough history. Let's get back to current events. The situation in this valley is a Mexican standoff. They can't beat us, but if we try leaving, they hit this valley with a nuke. Which, with a nominal yield of two hundred kilotons, will pretty much wipe out everything between the two ridgelines."

Riordan nodded. "Meaning the entirety of the extraction force and over ninety percent of the people we came to extract will be gone. Along with Wedge Three."

Newton nodded. "And eliminates our ability to minimize any signs of our presence."

"Yeah," Rodermund agreed, "once a nuke goes off, policing up our gear and rubbish is pretty much a moot point. To say nothing of the fact that we wouldn't be capable of doing it anymore."

Or of getting those Ktoran cold cells back to Earth, which is too important to pass up. But Riordan didn't want to bring that up just yet. "So we have to figure a way out of this, er, this 'Mexican standoff.'"

"And how are you going to do that?" Newton asked.

"I'm not entirely sure, yet. But I'm going to meet with the Hkh'Rkh Voice—and Fist—Jrekhalkar to discuss possible solutions."

"Where did you agree to meet?"

"On their side of the river, a little downstream of the southern ford."

Rodermund rolled his eyes. Ike stared hard at Riordan. Newton shook his head slowly. "Sir, if you do that, there is no way to provide you with adequate protection."

Riordan nodded. "I understand your concern. But Yaargraukh has assured me that Jrekhalkar's Honor—and that of everyone under his command—would be forfeit if he were to harm me after I travel to his side of the river to parley. And they will not come to our side."

"Oh?" Rodermund's suspicion was barbed with sarcasm. "And I wonder why they won't come to us, if their offer to parley is on the up-and-up?"

"It's doesn't indicate an intention to double-cross us, Steve. Actually, it means they are near-certain that *I* would double-cross *them.*"

Ike Franklin evidently detected Caine's emphasis on the singular pronoun "I." "Wait a minute. Commodore, are you saying that the Hkh'Rkh have reason to doubt your honesty—your *personal* honesty?"

"That is correct, Lieutenant. At the start of the recent war, a...a good friend of mine, Trevor Corcoran, and I were escaping their sneak attack at Barnard's Star. Our ship was making a surprisingly successful getaway: more successful than it should have been. When the enemy craft closed in on us, we fired. What we were not aware of at the time was that the ship was running under a diplomatic transponder."

Rodermund leaned back. "Shit. So you fired on them when you were showing a white flag."

Riordan nodded. "So my reputation is not exactly in good standing with the Hkh'Rkh, even though we provided proof that we were unaware of the diplomatic transponder. Then, at the end of the war, while present in their headquarters under diplomatic credentials, events conspired to make it appear as though I was carrying out sabotage."

Newton's eyes did not blink as he asked, "And were you?"

"No, but there was an object that had been secretly embedded in my arm which was specially designed to infect their command and communications network. They didn't believe I was unaware of it, and I'm not sure I blame them. At any rate, as far as the Hkh'Rkh are concerned, I'm not trustworthy."

"Not *all* Hkh'Rkh believe that, Caine Riordan," amended Yaargraukh.

Caine smiled. "Maybe not, but those are not the Hkh'Rkh we're facing across the river today, are they?"

Yaargraukh's black, snakelike tongue darted out briefly: a polite, maybe wry, smile. "Alas, they are not."

Rodermund leaned forward, as though he might try grabbing Caine to shake some sense into him. "Then why the hell are you putting yourself on the same side of the river as a horde of creatures"—he glanced at Yaargraukh, worried and embarrassed—"I mean, of *beings*, who want to stick a knife in you?"

"Because no one else can go, Steve. They know I'm in charge. To send a subordinate would be both an insult and a show of cowardice, in their code. I'm also the only human on this planet who's ever dealt with Hkh'Rkh except over the barrel of a gun. I'm no expert on them, but I've studied a bit of their culture and know a few words in their language."

"And I shall accompany him, returning to my role as Advocate of the Unhonored, as at the Convocation where we met."

Rodermund's stare all but spoke what was clearly in his mind: *Assuming Yaargraukh won't sell you out to score some political points.*

Caine chose to ignore the stare. "But the final and definitive reason that I have to be the one to go is because this is my command, Steve. Doesn't matter who did what, or how we all got to this point: I'm responsible for what happens on my watch. And that's not subject to interpretation or debate. Now: any more questions?"

"Yeah...Commodore," Ike replied. "Once you're there, what are you going to do? They don't trust you and they can't back down. How do you even start the conversation?"

"Well, it's their world and we trespassed, even if we were trying to undo crimes we didn't commit. So I'll start by listening."

"Won't that make you look weak?" Rodermund's voice was surprised, sharp, unpleasant.

"What it does is get me information about what they're thinking, what they see as a positive outcome.

And I don't really care what they think of me if I can get our people out of here. And keep from killing any more of theirs."

"You taking volunteers?" Ike asked.

Riordan managed to suppress showing his surprise. "For what?"

"For coming along with you."

Riordan hadn't given the matter of human companions any thought—until now. "Lieutenant Franklin, as a doctor, you have more than enough work to do back here."

"With respect, sir, that's not true. Most of the cases who made it off the battlefield are getting good care back at Dante, as good as any we can give them. They have more surgeons and attendants than they need. I know because I checked. So I'm free as a bird, and you said you wanted my perspective on the Hkh'Rkh of this planet. Well, I'll be there to give it to you."

"Maybe, but flying with me could be suicide, Ike."

"Maybe, but you shouldn't be alone—I mean, the only human—when you're standing toe to toe with the Hkh'Rkh. And I want to see them up close, for myself. And make a difference. If I can."

Riordan shrugged, watching peripherally for a negative sign from Yaargraukh: none was forthcoming. "Okay, then, Ike. Welcome aboard."

Newton steepled his fingers. "Commodore, what if they want you to be the one to start talking?"

Riordan shook his head. "Very unlikely. Yaargraukh informs me—and it matches what I've seen—that Hkh'Rkh establish, assert, and maintain dominance by taking control of conversations. If their leader was more shrewd, like First Voice was on Earth, I would be a bit more concerned. But this Jrekhalkar is impulsive and insecure about his position, so I think he will try to grab the reins of the discussion right away. And I intend to let him—and learn what he's thinking while he does. If he doesn't give us anything to work with, I'll slip a prearranged signal into the conversation and keep him talking as long as I can."

"While we do what?"

"Evacuate as many people as you can from the valley. Wedge Three may be ready to lift by then. If we talk until dark, or agree to resume talks tomorrow, we'll send a nighttime raiding force to attempt to grab Dr. Sleeman and her team. And we'll just have to hope that Bannor and his team are still intact, possibly to hunt down and neutralize that tacnuke."

"And how will we get that, or any other, order to them, sir? Hunting down a bomb wasn't one of their contingency orders."

"No, it wasn't. But radio is improving and we're working to reestablish lascom. We'll also bring one of the EXHALTEDs closer to the ground once night falls."

"If they give you that long, sir."

"Yes, Lieutenant Baruch, that's the great uncertainty in all this."

"I think there's another uncertainty, sir."

"Which is?"

"Let us say this all works out somehow, and the Hkh'Rkh allow us to load the transports and boost towards orbit. It seems as though we have trouble waiting there, too: Ktor, from what Karam and Dora were telling us back at *Puller*."

"Yes, that is indeed how it seems. But if the Ktoran threats to *Shore-of-Stars* were genuine, we'd all know it by now. Once they tipped their hand with the railgun attack, they had no further reason to play coy. Unless, that is, they don't have as much strength on site as they'd like us to believe. So I think a little aggressive reconnaissance by Yiithrii'ah'aash is in order."

Newton nodded. "One last thing, sir: any idea why Jrekhalkar has asked for the meet to be south of the ford? It's a bother, from a security standpoint."

Riordan smiled. "I think that's why he wants it there. He certainly doesn't want anyone from our side charging over the ford to join a dispute. And he didn't want to meet us in plain view of our prepared positions, either."

Newton shrugged. "It's not as if we won't move our security assets to an overwatch point across from your meeting, sir."

Riordan nodded. "Which I'm sure they expect. But they want to make it as inconvenient and costly as they can. Besides, we have a few hidden variables to add to the overall security equation. Such as Bannor's team." *If they are still alive.* He turned to Rodermund. "While we're on that topic of a few hidden variables, Steve, pass orders to the troops at the middle ford that I need them to pop a few flares..."

Bannor Rulaine, seeing the first red flare, watched for and saw the second as soon as it cleared the woodline just south of the middle ford. *So, we know the south ford is our next waypoint,* he thought. *Now, what's the mission?*

But no more flares rose up from the opposite side of the river. Rulaine continued to watch for three minutes, then gave up. The order had evidently been aborted. The maximum interval between the second and third flares—those designating the waypoint and the objective, respectively—was ninety seconds: twice the time that he had waited for them.

Bannor's earbud paged: secure one, local channel broadcast. He chinned the line open. "Rulaine here."

It was Tygg that spoke, but his comms monitor showed Rulaine that two others were active on the circuit: Rich Hailey and Alexander Shvartsman. "Major," Tygg said in a tightly constricted voice, "what the hell was that? Do you think there's a team of Hkh'Rkh on the other bank? That they hit the signals team while they were sending up the flares?"

"Possible, but I doubt it, Tygg. The fords are clear. Only one APC swam across and its troops took a lot of casualties right after landing. So I don't think the signals were interrupted due to enemy action."

"Then why the hell did they stop signalling, sir?"

Rulaine didn't respond; he was too busy trying to think up some reasonable answer to that troubling question.

It was Alexander Shvartsman who answered, speaking slowly, as if feeling his way along the explanation as he went. "I agree with Major Rulaine that enemy action is not reason why flares stopped. So I am thinking: what if flare code we saw is exactly what signallers intended?"

Bannor was not sure whether he was misunderstanding Shvartsman's imperfect English or the concept he was trying to convey. "What do you mean, Alexander?"

The Russian's voice imparted the sense of a shrug. "What if Commodore Riordan wishes us to be at south ford, but none of our contingency missions are what he wishes us to carry out once we are there? What if plans have changed so that old objectives are no longer relevant? Perhaps we are simply to go there to observe and then—what is it Americans are fond of saying?—use 'personal initiative' to decide upon our course of action?"

Rich Hailey chuckled. "I like the way you think, Alexander."

So did Bannor, who glanced back at the fading arc that the flare's smoke trail had drawn across the late afternoon sky. "You may be right, Alexander," he murmured. "And, since I can't think of any other way to interpret that signal, that's how we're going to proceed. Pass the word: we are making for the south ford, ASAP."

Chapter Fifty-Five

As the whining rotors of the slick faded back across the River Kakaagsukh, Riordan stared at the approaching Hkh'Rkh and thought: *I forgot just how big they can get.*

Yaargraukh, at two meters, was actually something of a runt for his species. Of the three Warriors approaching from the thickets ten meters from the water's edge, two were over two-and-a-half meters, their immense torsos made larger by hide-and-laminate breastplates. The third, a shorter and more narrowly built Hkh'Rkh, was wearing the synthetic and far more effective Patrijuridicate armor that had been typical among the invaders of Earth.

At the sight of that third Warrior, Yaargraukh stopped short. "It is Ezzraamar, who was my adjutant here on Turkh'saar. This is a helpful happenstance."

"And it looks to be getting more helpful," added Ike. "They're sending him forward first."

Yaargraukh's voice was thick; Riordan heard his esophogeal plates clack together lightly. "That is not a

749

positive sign," he corrected. "They send him forward because they do not wish to be soiled by contact with me if they can avoid it."

"Because you are being seen with us?"

"And because of what that implies," Yaargraukh explicated. "If I am with you, trusted enough to be unrestrained, they will assume that I am your ally, or at least, have forsaken the defenders of my own world to consort with its invaders. Whatever my reasons for doing so, standing unfettered alongside you is damning."

Franklin shook his head. "Man, you come from some hard-assed folk, Yaargraukh, that they'd kick you to the curb just for showing up in the same chopper we landed in."

"It is not my own fate that concerns me, Isaac Franklin."

Riordan glanced at his Hkh'Rkh friend. "The New Family scions. You're worried that if Jrekhalkar believes you to have committed treason, your guilt will spread to them?"

"Not immediately, but in the long run, any soiled by a blood connection to me will be the targets of endless Challenges from Old Family scions. Until the last of my kin and friends are gone."

"And because the Voice will ultimately learn that some of them rallied to your side and travelled to meet us, he might not merely accuse you of treason, but of fomenting insurrection. Even though it was they who came to you."

"That would be consistent with the political climate, yes. But let us not assume the worst without first learning where we stand. I shall go forward to meet with Ezzraamar."

Yaargraukh spent less than fifteen seconds chatting with his adjutant before returning.

"Well," Riordan commented as he came back to stand with the two humans, "that short a conversation is either a very good omen or a very bad omen."

"The latter, I fear. Ezzraamar was sent forward only to establish my status: whether I had taken formal allegiance with you on one extreme, or on the other, was your prisoner on parole. Naturally, my answer was that neither extreme applied. This satisfied Jrekhalkar, albeit barely."

Franklin frowned. "Satisfied him how?"

"That I am not fully a traitor. If I was, he could not stand in a conversation with me."

"You mean, he'd need to shun you?"

"No. He, or another of his retinue, would be Honor-bound to Challenge me."

Franklin looked away, muttered, "Damn, this honor crap is getting pretty thick around here."

Ezzraamar had finished making his report to Jrekhalkar and his equally large companion; all three of them were coming forward now. As they did, almost a score of Hkh'Rkh emerged from the trees behind the thickets and spread out into a half-circle. They halted when both groups of parleyers were centered between the curved arms of their formation.

Riordan turned to Yaargraukh, spoke loudly enough for the other Hkh'Rkh to hear. "Having no Honor, I must ask you, Advocate, to address my greeting to the Voice of Turkh'saar."

Jrekhalkar waved Yaargraukh to silence, gesturing for him to interpret, instead. "The one you call Yaargraukh is now barely more than you in our eyes, human. And if, as tales tell it, First Voice deigned to suffer direct speech from you both at Convocation and upon your homeworld, then I shall not fail to follow his example. But at least you and he had matters to discuss, uncertainties to navigate. Here, there are none such. Creatures of your world violated this one. You have come in support of them. Our Unhonored, our defenseless whelplings and females, have been slain by you, as have more than a thousand of our Warriors in this past day. What is left to discuss? How shall we walk away from this field of battle with anything less than your corpses to avenge them, to appease us? I agree to meet with you for one reason only: that perhaps you shall discern an alternative that I do not. A means whereby that final battle may be averted. For if we fail in the test of arms, we are Honor-bound to destroy you with the bomb we have hidden here in the valley. Before I condemn so many scions of so many Families to death, and leave their dens without Warriors to answer Challenges and see to their welfare, I will entertain your speech, though it is sure to be filled with lies. For your name is known among us, Caine Riordan, as are your perfidies against our people in the war. I smear my honor by conferring with you, in the hope that something you say shows me a way to save the lives of my brothers."

Caine nodded. "Firstly, I thank you for the honor of addressing you directly." Riordan felt the urge to spit as he recited that formula, but if there was to be any discussion with Jrekhalkar, it had to be followed. "Secondly, I wish to clarify that my ships and my troops did not journey here to support the humans already on your world, but to remove them."

"A quibble that changes nothing. The first of your

kind on this world were murderers and raiders. Theft and killing was their only interaction with us. You have not arrived to punish them, or to turn them over to us for that purpose, but to escape with them: to ensure that they might flee the scene of their crimes, to fly further than our justice can reach. This we cannot permit, and this motivation marks you as no better than them."

Riordan swayed his head slowly from side to side, so that the Hkh'Rkh might see in it their own gesture of negation. "Not so, Voice. We arrived uncertain of what we would find or the actions that we would need to undertake. We deemed it quite possible that we would find hardened criminals who would not submit to our authority, who would not consent to be removed from this world or repent their deeds. If that was what we had found, we would have taken all necessary steps to take them prisoner and hold them accountable before the law."

"Human law, argued in human courts," Jrekhalkar countered. "You do not respect our territory or our rights, even when you claim to be agents of justice. But that is moot now, since you have evidently decided that, despite the hundreds they have killed and robbed, the humans you have found here are beyond reproach, are guilty of no crimes. If the hundreds killed on Turkh'saar were before you now, how would you answer their demand for justice and vengeance?"

"I would begin by insisting that justice and vengeance are different. Vengeance is often blind to reason: all it can see is the object it hates. Conversely, justice is blind to our preferences and prejudices; all it may see are the deeds and the conditions under which they were carried out."

"And your justice sees no blame in these humans who killed hundreds of defenseless colonists, living and working on their own world, harming no one?"

"Our justice sees blame, respected Voice, but its stain is upon the hands of those who forced these others to act under threat of death, and before that, upon those who brought them all—unwilling and forlorn—to your world. It was the malice of their impressors that led to the deaths of your colonists."

"And so where are these guilty parties, that we may punish them, that we may have our vengeance upon them?"

"Those who were left here to be the masters were slain by those who remain. Hundreds of these brutal masters were killed; hundreds died to kill them and bring their reign of terror to an end. Those who brought all the humans here did so long ago, before there was even a colony upon Turkh'saar."

Jrekhalkar's tongue whipped out briefly. "How improbably convenient. And how impossibly foresightful: that nonhumans brought slumbering humans to this world even before the first Hkh'Rkh settlers arrived. And how timely that they just happened to awaken immediately after a war that could not have been anticipated by either of us—since we did not know of each others' existence when this bizarre plot was ostensibly set in motion. What other fantasies do you have to share today, Riordan?"

Caine sighed: this tack was not making any headway. Time to try something a little more radical—and unsettling. "I tell no fantasies, but I share your incredulity at all the coincidences that, to a sane mind, can hardly be accepted as coincidences. So perhaps you might explain something to me: how is it that you come to have a nuclear device, Voice? Granted, your colonial forces have shown just how profoundly your former leaders were willing to violate the terms of your armament limitation agreements with the Arat Kur, but a nuclear warhead? That is so grave a violation that it will warrant deep investigation—an investigation that will no doubt insist on discovering where it came from."

"It came from our armory. Where else?"

Yaargraukh conveyed Jrekhalkar's evasive tone by mimicking it as he translated. Riordan suppressed a smile. "So your armory was furnished with a nuclear weapon, but without the means to deliver it? That's odd—unless it was never intended to be a weapon. Maybe it was a demolition device, something to remove obstacles. Or evidence. Specifically, I wonder if it was originally buried at the Site you so pointedly avoid, that is still defended by missiles, and that still has autonomous sensors that were able to detect us."

"I did not remove any such device from the site," Jrekhalkar claimed with an excess of defiance.

"I am not suggesting that *you* did, Jrekhalkar. But I cannot help but wonder which of your sires did, perhaps because they considered its original purpose a past worry."

From the corner of his eye, Riordan noticed that Yaargraukh's one-time adjutant, Ezzraamar, was becoming alarmed: his nostrils were dilating and his eyes were protruding further and further from their protective brow shelves, almost as if they were on stalks. Clearly, Riordan was coming close to the ragged edge of what was permissible with Jrekhalkar.

Whose esophageal plates contracted as he posed a phlegm-growling question. "Do you actually believe that this line of speculation shall help us find a way not to kill each other, human?"

"In fact, I do, respected Voice. Consider: you are not to blame for the removal of the nuclear weapon from the site. You have not been Voice, or Fist, long enough to undertake such an action. And I perceive you did not know all your late sire's secrets."

"You perceive—or you were *told?*" Jrekhalkar glanced sharply at Yaargraukh.

"I have asked Yaargraukh of the Moiety of Hsraluur no questions that would violate his vow of allegiance to you." *Of course, since he didn't take issue with any of my many conjectures, I'm pretty sure they were accurate.* "At any rate, I am confident that you are not the architect of the removal of the bomb, and that it was not originally put here with the consent of most of the colonists. Nor has its existence been known beyond a select few, since then."

"And your point?"

"That many of us inherit situations that are not of our doing, yet we are tasked to deal with their consequences. You and I are both inheritors of someone else's dubious or illegal decisions. Should I then hold you directly responsible for the bomb that is now in your possession? Conversely, should you hold me responsible for the presence of these humans on your world?"

"And yet you have come to actively seek them, remove them."

"True. And you brought your bomb to this place to ensure a particular outcome regardless of the means whereby you might achieve it." Riordan elected not to push the legal and ethical comparisons any further: he could tell from Jrekhalkar's slower responses that nuanced thought was not a constant or welcome companion to his moment-to-moment consciousness.

Jrekhalkar reared back into a more erect posture. "For all I know, you are lying, intending to dupe us with these words, with false comparisons. But even if you did not, even if your current words are not lies, what may we do? You will not leave these humans behind to satisfy our just vengeance, and we will not allow you to abscond with them." He looked wistfully at the far shore. "Among my people, in times past, when such impasses were encountered, two beings of Honor, two Warriors, could avoid needless bloodshed of thousands by agreeing to a Challenge whereby they would settle their disagreement."

Caine almost sighed in relief: he had been worried Jrekhalkar would not open that door, that pathway to a solution.

But before Riordan could make the proposal he had been maneuvering to bring into the conversation, Yaargraukh stepped forward, shoulders pushing ahead. "The destruction of this conflict has already become an obscenity, far outstripping the violations it was meant to correct. Caine Riordan has confirmed what I told you days ago: that the initial raiders were compelled by threats of execution and starvation by the humans I identified as Nazis. And that their savage reign was ended by a rebellion of those who remain. Had I been allowed to contact the extraction team when I asked, this waste of the blood of the brave would never have occurred.

"But since battle has been joined and blood has been spilled, and since we must find a solution that satisfies Honor, I shall stand for Caine Riordan, to enable a legal Challenge. As Advocate of the Unhonored, none may do so as logically, or with better right, than me."

Jrekhalkar reared back as well. Dwarfed by the large Voice, the comparison between them magnified the courage—and danger—of Yaargraukh's offer. "And so the collaborator takes up the cause of the liar. What a surprise." The tongue of Jrekhalkar's large companion came writhing out of his central nostril, but he was otherwise silent. "You would have the best claim to standing in for the human—if the *s'fet* had any Honor of his own to defend, and if yours was not so deeply suspect. Have a care, Yaargraukh: as it stands, you will be called before the Council in Iarzut'thruk to account for your actions. Many associate your name with the words 'treason' and 'traitor' already. The most lenient call for your banishment."

"Even among the New Families?"

Jrekhalkar made a dismissive huffing noise. "When contemplating how to punish a traitor, I do not consult the kin of the accused."

"Less than a third of the New Families of the Fringelands are any kin of mine."

"As your own people have it, 'all New Families are kin.'"

Yaargraukh's posture changed subtly: his legs tensed, one claw twitched. Riordan wondered, horrified, if he was about to leap at Jrekhalkar. But the stance faded almost as quickly as it had arisen, and, instead, Yaargraukh made an abbreviated pony-nod and stepped back. "Let it be noted by all present that I offered myself to serve the needs of Honor for all who have fallen this day—and was refused."

There were murmurs of assent from the semicircle of Warriors that faced them. Jrekhalkar affected no notice of their response, which had been demanded by tradition: an even greater authority than he.

Riordan felt the opportunity latent in a Challenge slipping away, stepped forward into the spot that Yaargraukh had vacated. "Since you will not accept the Advocate's offer, then perhaps you will accept mine. You may deem me a liar and an enemy, but that should not deter you: I am under no suspicion as a traitor, which was your only objection to Yaargraukh's proposal."

"You are not a person. You cannot possess Honor."

"And where is that written in law?"

Jrekhalkar shook his head; his crest puffed out as he finished the convulsive gesture. "It need not be written in law; it is our tradition."

"You will forgive my persistence, but I have read the main points of your Honor Code. It is not merely tradition, but written: those of your own society who are legally labeled as the Unhonored are to be protected from harm and abuse by being excluded from combat and confrontation. This is the very reason that Honor and Challenge exists. Do you deny that this is the law, the written law, of the Patrijuridicate?"

Jrekhalkar's nostrils pinched slightly. "I do not. It has been thus for millennia. It is the bedrock of our civilization."

"Now, what is written of alien species?"

"You are not part of our social structure. So naturally, you are Unhonored."

"I am not asking you what seems logical or natural. I am asking you a different question: where is it *written* that we are Unhonored?"

Jrekhalkar's feet shifted; his similarly-sized companion glanced at him. "I am sure that the Patrijuridicate has crafted some document concerning—"

"In fact," Yaargraukh interrupted, "they have not. There were some among the Families who pushed for such a written declaration, but the Allsires, the Patrijuridicate's highest court, declined to do so. And their reasoning was thus: among us, the Unhonored have other rights that we do not extend to aliens. Whelpling males become Warriors, so it is evident that some Unhonored may grow to accrue Honor. But not all: the weak and the infirm are spared the onus of that rite of passage. Due to these and other inconsistencies, it was therefore deemed unwise to designate aliens as Unhonored. The Allsires foresaw that aliens would require special conditions and exclusions, and so, be a formal class unto themselves.

"However, debate on the specifics were tangled and not deemed particularly urgent, at the time I departed Rkh'yaa. So, for convenience sake, humans—and the other species of the Accord—have all been treated as Unhonored, simply because none among them have had Honor conferred upon them."

"But there is nothing in the law that says you may *not* do so," Riordan said before Jrekhalkar could reply. "So although what I propose is not addressed by your tradition, it violates no law. And if you wish to avoid detonating your nuclear device in this valley, and ensure that my superiors above do not retaliate in kind upon Iarzut'thruk, then this may be the one path by which such outcomes may be escaped. And if later Voices question your bold decision to break with tradition, they cannot call it either illegal or imprudent. Indeed, you would be remembered as a Voice whose first concern was for the welfare of his Warriors and the Unhonored whom they—and you—are sworn to protect."

Caine saw Jrekhalkar start when he uttered the words "bold decision" and then again upon hearing "you would be remembered." And so Riordan knew to remain silent, to let the seeds of those new and wholly unforeseen possibilities take root and germinate in the Voice's mind.

"This," Jrekhalkar said slowly, "is an interesting concept."

Riordan imitated the Hkh'Rkh pony-nod; it necessitated moving the top half of his torso, to generate the same effect. "I hoped it would be. Given the losses on this field of battle, I presume that, as commander of my forces, I have proven myself a worthy enough opponent to be given the provisional status to put the contest between us, personally. And if my actions here are insufficient argument on my behalf, I remind you that I led insurgents against your Warriors on Earth. Certainly, none will criticize you for deeming me a sufficiently worthy opponent."

The Voice stared at Caine. "So you are willing to face me personally, then?" He exchanged a sidelong glance with his large lackey, then looked Caine up and down: it was a brief look. "I would welcome this." He began to move forward.

Riordan held up a hand. "No. My terms were clear from the outset. This is not simply a personal contest. It must be a full Challenge."

Jrekhalkar's head jerked backward. "That cannot be. Even if I consent to a personal contest with you, that does not mean you have Honor. I am simply accepting the outcome of our contest as the means of settling the dispute we would otherwise be settling through battle."

"And that is the problem, Voice. Having no Family or Honor, promises made to me need not be kept. I am not protected by the laws that hold you to your word."

Jrekhalkar's eyes contracted slowly. He clearly wished to deny this, but, with Yaargraukh—and possibly other New Family—scions in earshot, he could hardly claim that the Old Families always kept their word even if they did not have to. The history of the Hkh'Rkh whose clans and moieties had been destroyed—the Hearthless—was a tapestry woven from the broken promises of the Old Families.

"So," Caine concluded carefully, "for me be to assured that you will keep your promise, our contest must be a formal Challenge."

"So argued by the chief liar of a race of liars. I am unwilling to abase myself by Challenging you. I will, however, consider a Challenge from you."

"That will not be sufficient." *And you know it.*

"What do you mean?"

"I mean that you could later claim that regardless of the language I used, there was no legal Challenge because I did not possess Honor. You could then claim you simply killed me for having the temerity to *presume* to possess it. However, if you Challenge me, there is no question that you have recognized me as a true being, that I possess Honor. Otherwise, you could not Challenge me at all. And then I know you will keep your word."

Jrekhalkar stared down—far down—at Caine for a very long time. He looked away. "Very well. I Challenge thee, Caine of the Family Riordan."

Riordan swallowed, managed not to stammer as he said, "I accept."

Chapter Fifty-Six

Yaargraukh stepped between Riordan and Jrekhalkar. "This is a formal challenge, in all its particulars?"

"Of course. Stand aside."

"Before I do, Voice Jrekhalkar of the Moiety of Gdar'khoom, speak the terms of Challenge so all gathered here may witness it, as is required by law and tradition."

The Voice's jaw—low on his head, like a sperm whale's—opened; a slow whine of air came out. Caine was left with the impression of exasperation, was relatively sure that if Hkh'Rkh could have rolled their eyes, that he might have at this moment. "I, Jrekhalkar of the Moiety of Gdar'khoom, do issue formal Challenge to Caine of the Family Riordan, and pledge my possessions and Honor as escrow of my intent and upon the outcome of this contest."

Yaargraukh nodded solemnly to Caine. "Now you must speak the same phrases, except you use the word 'accept' instead of 'issue.' You must speak it in Hkhi, so that the witnessing of the declarations is binding. I will provide assistance, if you require."

764

Riordan nodded. "Thank you. I might need some coaching: I didn't recognize all of the terms." Caine started, stammered over a few uncertain words, started again. Ultimately, Yaargraukh had to intervene four times.

While Riordan struggled with the unfamiliar words and sounds that were almost impossible for a human throat and mouth to replicate, the Warriors that half-ringed them listened carefully, solemnly, their eyes extruding further and further as Riordan neared the end of his declaration. They also leaned forward, as if they were preparing to witness some impossible feat—and in their minds, Caine reflected, that was probably how this was striking them: they were watching the unthinkable occur.

When Riordan stuttered out the last syllable of his declaration, Jrekhalkar began to remove his dioptiscope, lighten himself for personal combat.

Isaac Franklin stepped forward before Riordan could speak again. "Wait a minute, wait a minute!" He looked back at Caine. "Commodore, are you sure—*sure*—you want to do this?"

Damn it, don't mess this up, Ike. "Absolutely." *Besides, there's no going back now.*

But Ike wasn't done: he turned quickly toward Yaargraukh. "Look: isn't there some kind of ... well, agreement? You know, the terms of what happens if the Commodore wins—or Jrekhalkar?"

Yaargraukh shrugged. "It is not necessary. The terms, as you call them, are absolute. The victor decides the fate of all those whom his opponent commands."

"All of them?"

Yaargraukh's gaze rested patiently upon Ike for a second before he emphasized. "All of them."

Franklin turned back to Caine, shook his head, and as he resumed his place behind his commander's left shoulder, muttered, "I sure hope you know what you're doing, sir."

Riordan turned, showed him a crooked smile. "So do I, Lieutenant. Now stand ready. Things could start going off-script any moment now."

"What do you—?"

But Riordan turned back toward Jrekhalkar, who was waiting, legs tensed. He spoke over his shoulder to the Warriors of his retinue. "This will not be long, I think." He was answered by a chorus of coughing laughs and a bevy of black tongues that danced in and out of nostrils. Riordan bent over to start preparing for the contest.

When Jrekhalkar turned back to Caine, however, he stopped and his crest rose slightly. "Human, what are you doing?"

"Removing my boots."

Jrekhalkar's choking laugh seemed to expel most of his tongue in a panicked spasm. "My curiosity is too great to set aside, and if I do not ask you now, the answer will die with you: how does removing your footwear help you to prepare for combat?"

"It doesn't. But it certainly helps me prepare to swim."

Jrekhalkar's black-snake tongue went back into his snout with an audible *zzzippp!* "Swim? You mean to fight me in the water?"

Riordan straightened, set his boots aside. "The Challenged has the right of choosing the nature of the Challenge. That is Hkh'Rkh law, not merely tradition. As was explained to me when I first met your race at Convocation. As the Challenged, I choose that our contest will be one of swimming."

Jrekhalkar stomped forward. Riordan did not move as the Voice roared, his words streaming out so quickly that he had to fully rely upon Yaargraukh's translation. "You are an imbecile. It is traditional that the champions of opposing hosts are to settle their dispute with combat."

Thank you for making my point. Riordan shrugged. "You said it yourself, Voice Jrekhalkar: that is the *traditional* method of settling the dispute, but it is not law. And there are exceptions. According to your history, one such exception occurred within living memory, when Uungsk'srel of the Moiety of Gaat'vynakh, cousin of your First Voice, won the Ninth Zh't'Zhree Dispute by besting his Challenger in the completion of a quadratic equation." Jrekhalkar stood utterly still, made no response. Riordan shrugged. "I can cite others, if you wish."

"I have no doubt that you can, liar. Very well, state your Challenge."

"The Challenge shall be a race to the far shore. Do you accept?"

Jrekhalkar glanced at the river, then at the distance to the ford. Several of his Warriors moved restlessly behind him: if the Voice did not respond, it was the same as if he had declined the Challenge, and so, forfeited the contest. "The Challenge is unfair. It is as if you were to challenge me to be the first to count to five on the fingers of one hand." He held up his four claw-tipped fingers, spread wide in a menacing cruciform. "You may not choose a form of Challenge that you can perform, but that I cannot."

Riordan nodded slowly. "I have read your laws. That

is why I did not choose a game of chess, or a test involving language: you could rightly refuse based on the lack of common knowledge. But swimming is not beyond your capability. I believe that in the heroic lay of V'shaath'ur, the hero swims across a monster-ridden river to rescue his whelpling. It was slow and dangerous for him, but it *is* part of your culture. In fact, it is a hero-deed, one which your elite forces must accomplish in order to earn their place in what you call your Hadakhurakh: First in Battle. It is one of the supreme tests of their courage to swim a mile in water that is deeper than they are tall."

Riordan did not take his eyes off Jrekhalkar but peripherally noted that almost all the long heads of the semicircle of warriors turned toward the Voice.

"He is well within the laws of the Challenge," Yaargraukh observed mildly.

"Yes, no doubt due to your careful counsel," Jrekhalkar shot back through a snarl—a true, animal snarl.

"I did not advise Caine Riordan in how best to prepare for this moment."

"No? You seem unsurprised by his ploys."

"Caine Riordan is capable of researching the references we provided to his species at Convocation, and his inventiveness is not to be underestimated."

Riordan was always gratified, and surprised, by how well Yaargraukh avoided possibly indicting facts without lying. He had certainly not advised Caine, but had answered no small number of queries about Hkh'Rkh law and history in the hour before the Huey had dropped them off on this shore.

It was difficult to discern whether Jrekhalkar believed Yaargraukh, or even cared: his eyes were rigidly set in their protective folds. He nodded slowly at Riordan. "I agree. He who reaches the far shore first shall be the victor. You may commence when you are ready, human."

Riordan managed to suppress his surprise: he had expected more debate. He spun on his heel and ran down to the river, checking that the smart-collar on his undersized duty suit was as snug as the memory-fibers would permit.

He sprinted to a ledge hanging over a small pool, scalloped deep by the back-swirling current, and dove deep into the water.

Ezzraamar was momentarily disoriented when, instead of charging down to the water—on land, Hkh'Rkh were much faster than humans—Jrekhalkar simply turned to him and said, "I require your weapon and ammunition, Troop Leader."

Too surprised to inquire why, Ezzraamar complied.

Checking the assault rifle's action and then its active-targeting sights, Jrekhalkar began to walk toward the river. "Attend me," he ordered without bothering to turn around. The group did as he bade.

Yaargraukh, who had been careful to give no hint of the closer bond he and Ezzraamar had forged during their brief service together, moved ahead of Jrekhalkar, staring at the weapon. "What do you mean to do?"

The Voice stopped when he reached the rough, scree-covered bank beside the upstream flank of the rocks from which Riordan had dived into the water. "Is it not obvious? If the human never gets to the other side, then I can take my time—to build a bridge across this river, or even walk around this world—and still reach the far bank before he does."

Yaargraukh looked in disbelief. "Riordan's meaning was clear."

"Was it?" Jrekhalkar made sure that the assault rifle's selective fire switch was set for semiautomatic. "The human's words were not vague. He mentioned nothing of the tools with which one may meet the Challenge."

Yaargraukh blinked. "What you hold is a weapon, not a tool. And he specified a race."

"True, and he did not dispute my terms when I qualified what he meant by a 'race': to be the first to reach the far shore. And he did not preclude any tool, not even one capable of being used as a weapon. But even if he had, this is not combat, so this is not a weapon. This is merely a tool."

Yaargraukh's voice was so loud, so forceful that the Voice's ring of retainers advanced, tightened in around them. "It is a tool with which you are trying to attack him. That makes it a weapon."

Jrekhalkar's tongue licked out briefly. "That is a matter open to interpretation. I am merely attempting to block him from completing his journey. If I could accomplish that end by using blankets, I would. But, since that would not work, I am simply choosing a different tool to achieve the same end."

Yaargraukh's claws were reflexively cycling through the open-closed sequence consistent with Hkh'Rkh fury. Homicidal fury. "Your choice is a—a perversion of the rules."

Jrekhalkar's neck wobbled diffidently as he scanned the river: still no sign of the human Riordan. "You are welcome to present your objections to the Council Ring in Iarzut'thruk, although I suspect they shall have an interpretation similar to mine." Next to him, Z'gluurhek's tongue wiggled in dark amusement.

Yaargraukh calmed himself, reared back. "This 'choice' of yours: it was made when Riordan was not present. He has the right to be made aware of it." Yaargraukh stepped toward the shore aggressively.

With terrible, practiced swiftness, Jrekhalkar swiveled his gun around so that it was centered on Yaargraukh's chest. "Are you Riordan's second?"

"I am not. How could I be? He could not request that of me until he had Honor, and he did not have it until you accepted his Challenge."

"Correct. So, at this moment, you have no duty to him, and I forbid you to share any report of my words or actions with him until this Challenge is resolved." Jrekhalkar nodded Z'gluurhek over to cover Yaargraukh, lifted his rifle and walked down to the edge of the water. "The human wishes to walk the path of Hkh'Rkh Honor? Very well; he—and his race—shall learn the caution with which one must enter that domain. He should have been more careful in his words."

Seeing Jrekhalkar move down onto the smaller scree that lined the beach, the human Isaac Franklin turned toward Yaargraukh, eyes wide. "What the hell is going on?"

Yaargraukh translated their debate for him.

Franklin's eyes examined the set of the weapon in Z'gluurhek's arms, saw its meaningful angle toward Yaargraukh. "I see. Well, I guess I'll see how this all turns out, then." He turned, began to scan the water. If Z'gluurhek had understood the nature of their exchange, he gave no sign of it.

Ezzraamar looked after Ike Franklin, followed him closer to the water and found himself at a fork in his own path of Honor. What was the greater failure: to neglect to alert the Voice that Franklin now had a full understanding of what was soon to occur? Or, given Jrekhalkar's insupportable interpretation of the rules of the Challenge, to remain silent and let Franklin do what he might to rebalance the scales of justice?

Assuming such a feat was possible.

Caine did not strike out directly nor strongly for the far shore. Rather, he used the current to carry him along, measuring it and assessing the temperature: not bad, given that he had taken the precaution of adding a cold-weather liner to the EVA rated duty suit, and had chosen a smaller size so that it fit snugly around his neck, wrists, and ankles. Nowhere near as good as a wetsuit, but a hell of a lot better than swimming in sodden clothes.

Before he became too eager for air, he gave a final kick and allowed himself to drift closer to the surface, rolling on his back as the light grew around him.

As his face breached the surface, he sealed his nostrils against the steady slapping of the wavelets. It took a few moments to get his bearings, and then a few more to make out what was going on back at the parley site.

Jrekhalkar was not in the water. He was holding something. An assault rifle. *An assault rifle? Well, shit*—The Voice's big lieutenant was holding a scattergun pointed more or less in Yaargraukh's direction. Yaargraukh's former adjutant—Ezzraamar, if memory served—had evidently given his gun to Jrekhalkar and was not looking enthusiastic about the unfolding developments. And Ike Franklin—

—Ike Franklin had been almost forgotten by the Hkh'Rkh, who were scanning the river carefully. Fortunately, even Ike wasn't looking far enough downriver. But that mistake—of not understanding just how fast the current was, or how quickly a reasonable swimmer could move when kicking along with it—was not likely to last for very long.

Riordan exhaled, ducked his head, scissor-kicked down, careful not to break the surface—and angled back toward the Hkh'Rkh side of the river: the last place they'd look, at least for a little while longer.

Since he was working mostly with the current, the swim wasn't particularly taxing, but Riordan was resolved to hold his breath as long as possible to prevent leaving a bubble trail. As he neared the shore, the light increased, the stony bottom elevated slowly toward him and the muted burble of water over rocks rose in his ears. He stopped in a meter of water, lifted the right side of his head to get a glimpse of his surroundings.

Sparse brush littered the sight-line between him and the Hkh'Rkh, now about one hundred and fifty meters upstream. There was no sign that any had left their leader to scout the shores and river yet, but that was only a matter of time. He edged his mouth out of the water far enough to take in slow, deep, measured breaths while he assessed the downstream course.

According to what the EXHALTED's overhead images had shown him, the River Kakaagsukh broke its watery back over rapids and a few small waterfalls about four hundred meters further south. There were no particularly dramatic drops or jagged boulders, but it was not navigable by boats and was presumed unpassable by swimmers. Maybe an expert, well prepared, could make it, but he was neither. It was bounded by steeper, rocky ground and had a bed that was so irregular in depth and composition that it could not be crossed without great risk.

So, he couldn't simply cruise slowly down the river for a kilometer or more, staying mostly underwater until he was out of the effective range of Jrekhalkar's assault rifle. And he couldn't get too close to the rapids: the speed of the water and strength of the current increased briskly, there. Consequently, he couldn't afford to slip more than another two hundred meters downstream: still well within the range of a Hkh'Rkh assault rifle's active sights.

But it wasn't as though he could simply hug the western shore for two hundred meters and then hang a left and cross straight over. The current was too strong, would be pushing him all the way. So instead of a two-part journey—downstream and then across—it would be wiser and far less taxing to start swimming across here, but without fighting the current. That would take him across to roughly the same spot by using a diagonal course.

A single rifle report surprised him, made him flinch. A small jet in the water, sixty meters upstream and toward the center of the river, marked where Jrekhalkar had evidently believed he'd seen something.

But bellowing hoots from his Warriors warned Riordan that several were now moving in his direction. *Damn it; barely made a splash when I flinched, but they still heard it.* Hardly surprising, though: many of the Hkh'Rkh of Turkh'saar put food on their table by hunting. Riordan sucked in a deep breath, aimed himself directly at the far shore, and slid under the water in a long, shallow dive.

The light diminished and then held steady as he levelled off at about two meters' depth. There, he had enough visibility to stay roughly oriented and to compensate for any unexpected currents or surges from an uneven river bottom, since anything that pushed him too close to the surface was an unacceptable hazard.

The current was carrying him downstream at a considerable rate, away from a direct crossing: just what he wanted. What he did not want to do was come up for air, but it was better he do so a bit early rather than wear himself out and burst through the surface, desperately gulping in great wracking breaths. Anything that attracted attention to his location was the greatest danger.

Riordan scissor-kicked upward and pulled water past him, but ceased moving his arms or legs as the surface brightened above him. His head came up into a noticeable breeze—he had entered the swifter midcourse currents—and he breathed deeply and slowly, head turned toward the Hkh'Rkh shore, but at right angles to the chop running downstream. After several seconds, distant cries reached him over the water: Franklin, warning him—a moment before the lieutenant was interrupted by two sharp reports from the Voice's rifle and then silenced by a blow from other large Hkh'Rkh. Fighting every trained and instinctual reflex he had, Riordan kept his head above the rushing current, kept drawing in air.

Ten meters upstream, two bullets cut divots in

the water. Riordan took the time to pull in one more deep breath, turned, gauged how far he'd been pushed downriver—about seventy-five meters—and dove sharply. Jrekhalkar's initial marksmanship would be the worst: every subsequent shot was sure to be closer, more likely to hit.

Halfway through his dive, Riordan heard a brief, muffled frying sound: bullets slicing into the water. Probably very close to where he'd been. Not bad marksmanship, shooting without a proper scope at a human head bobbing up and down in the water at a range of two hundred thirty meters. Riordan levelled off and began pulling at the water and kicking hard as he crossed the cooler midstream current. As soon as felt the strength of the current diminish, he began to kick with it: to have done so earlier might have carried him too far downstream.

This time he swam as briskly as he could until his lungs felt ready to burst. He kicked for the surface, breached more suddenly than he would have liked, but it had been a necessary risk. This time, his objective had been to open the range between himself and Jrekhalkar and also to move downstream further and faster than the Hkh'Rkh was likely to predict.

His strategy had worked: it was at least five seconds before he heard a flurry of reports, borne faintly by the southward breeze. He dove as he heard the bullets peppering the water, widely dispersed and most of them well upstream. He levelled out again, this time only a meter down, to make better speed for his own shore. As he began to pull the water past him with cupped hands, he was struck by the physical inevitability of the dilemma his actions had posed

Jrekhalkar. Riordan had known—from what he had read and seen in Java—that the Hkh'Rkh were slow and awkward in the water, but until this moment, he had not considered how profoundly unsuited to it they really were.

Fingers arranged in a cruciform, they could not cup the water with any efficiency. Being digitigrade, long, scissoring kicks were impossible. Their usually enviable muscle-to-fat ratio guaranteed that they would swiftly sink unless their immense lungs were filled with air. During heavy exertion—such as swimming—they relied upon breathing through both their mouths and nostrils, but their mouths were located well back on the underside of their neck. So in order to breathe, they had to rear their heads out of the water, as if struggling to expose their collarbone.

Caine pulled swiftly, surely through the water and realized that, despite being a fair swimmer, he had never fully appreciated how much human beings were still sea creatures. Not until now.

He swam briskly, gladly, for the nearby shore.

Ezzraamar was no less stunned than Jrekhalkar at just how much further down the river Riordan had moved in such a short span of time. The sequence of the Voice's shots was too rapid to allow much reaiming between them. He was clearly growing more desperate, more despairing of hitting a target he had presumed would be far closer and far easier to track.

Z'gluurhek expressed his annoyance in a rough, phlegm-warbling shout. "Is the human a sea-worm?"

Yaargraukh, who was helping Isaac Franklin to his feet, huffed slightly. "Compared to us? Yes."

Ezzraamar glanced at the human. Unlike those whose skin was lighter, blood on him did not appear red, but as a black gleam. "Is Franklin severely injured?"

"I should have killed him," Z'gluurhek grumbled. "His offense warranted it."

Yaargraukh glanced at Z'gluurhek's scattergun as he countered, "Riordan has bound himself to the laws of a Challenge; Lieutenant Franklin has not."

"Then he should not be here."

"I require silence," Jrekhalkar said over his massive shoulder.

"Yes, Esteemed Voice," Z'gluurhek replied. And then immediately violated his compliance: "Should I send some of the Warriors further downsteam, that they might—?"

"I must do this myself. And I shall finish the race soon, now."

Even Z'gluurhek had to look away when Jrekhalkar called his attempt at assassination a race.

Yaargraukh took his hand from Franklin's arm when the human was steady—they bled profusely when struck in the face, Ezzraamar noted—and walked slowly toward a vantage point that put him abreast of Jrekhalkar. The muzzle of Z'gluurhek's scattergun followed him.

"You cannot succeed," the former Advocate said quietly. "Riordan is—"

"—is not a fish, whatever else he might be." Jrekhalkar kept scanning downstream, but actually, Ezzraamar realized, more at the opposite bank than the river itself. "He must emerge eventu—there!" Jrekhalkar snapped the weapon up to his shoulder. He fired twice as Riordan—a distant figure in a dark blue duty suit—staggered up out of the water near a rocky outcropping on the far shore, almost three hundred and fifty meters away. Dust arose from the rocks. Either Riordan fell back, or dove back, into the water.

Yaargraukh hooted in alarm and surprise, grabbed the Voice by his left arm, was up against him so quickly that Z'gluurhek could no longer intervene without risking hitting both of them with the scattergun. "Enough!" The smaller Hkh'Rkh's angry, suppressed hiss was the kind reserved for sneaking about on battlefields or in the brush. "This madness is over. He has reached the far shore. You have lost."

"Your vision is deficient." Jrekhalkar shook off Yaargraukh's grasp. "His lower legs are still in the water." He hastily swapped magazines, raised the weapon again.

This time, Yaargraukh grabbed him so forcefully that Jrekhalkar's finger slipped inside the trigger guard: a report, a stray shot zipped across the river. "This goes beyond twisting the terms of the Challenge. Cease. Now."

The Voice looked at Yaargraukh's straining hand. "You have touched me without permission. Twice, now. Both times, you have interfered in the conduct of th Challenge. You give me the right to Challenge you, possibly petition for your execution."

"I interfered because your conduct of the Challenge is now not merely in error; it is inarguably duplicitous. Firing at Riordan as he swam could, at best, be construed as a momentary—and desperate—lapse in judgment. But that moment is past. For you to fire again is to break every code of Honor we know."

"And if I disagree? I will Challenge and kill you next. And that will settle the matter."

Yaargraukh spoke louder, ensuring that his voice

would be heard by the surrounding retinue. "I wonder. Will those around us agree to this? If you Challenge or execute me because I have signaled and borne testimony to so obvious a foul, what must they do?"

Jrekhalkar glanced back at his retinue, and his eyes told him what Ezzraamar—and apparently Yaargraukh— already knew he would find there. Not all would support the dishonored ex-Advocate, maybe not even most of them. But enough would feel compelled to assert that the Voice had violated the contract of the Challenge.

"What must they do?" Yaargraukh pressed.

"Whatever they choose." Jrekhalkar shrugged off the former Advocate's hand with one powerful churn of his left shoulder, aimed back at the downriver rock outcropping—just as Riordan appeared again, apparently trying to swim his way around the stony spur but failing, pushed back by the speed of the current there. Jrekhalkar snapped the selector switch on the assault rifle and, holding the weapon firmly, emptied the entire magazine in one long burst. Dust, fragments, and water sprayed in a wide pattern: at well over three hundred meters range, automatic fire was notoriously inaccurate. It was impossible to tell if Riordan had been hit or had dived down again.

None of these uncertainties deterred Jrekhalkar, who calmly ejected the spent magazine and loaded another.

Four hundred and twenty-seven meters away in a treetop to the northwest, Bannor Rulaine chinned the local secure channel. "Enemy gunfire is confirmed. Weapons free. Watch the quadrotor feeds; the Hkh'Rkh will try to find and flank us." Rulaine ignored the chorus of affirmations—some relieved, some impatient, some eager—as he leaned down to peer into his CoBro's scope once again. He snapped the safety off—

"Great Voice of our colony," Ezzraamar asked, suppressing the fear and disgust that would have otherwise put a thick buzz in his voice, "how long do you intend to continue with thi—?"

"As long as it takes, Adjutant." Jrekhalkar did not even bother to glance at him. "Fetch more ammunition. The human, if he is still alive, could remain hard to hit if he stays sheltered near—"

Riordan rose up from behind a line of low rocks located slightly more upstream, dove toward the shore. Jrekhalkar sent another stuttering stream of fire at the distant figure, ejected the emptied magazine. Yaargraukh flinched forward. Z'gluurhek's scattergun came up—and four dark craters appeared on the back of his armor: maroon blood jetted out so far from his chest that Ezzraamor could see it from behind.

Jrekhalkar, in the middle of swapping in another magazine, turned sharply, his eyes running over Ezzraamar and then his own retinue, scanning for traitors, at the same moment that a short, faint tattoo of distant rifle fire finally reached them. The reports—a human CoBro at maximum power—was unmistakable. "Humans!" screamed Jrekhalkar "Behind us! We are betray—!"

As the Voice turned to face the invisible threat, he was hit by so many rounds, and in such close sequence, that Ezzraamar could barely count them: at least a dozen, possibly more, blasted through his torso, legs, and neck.

As his leader fell, Ezzraamar rushed forward to grab his weapon—unsure what he would do with it when he laid hold of it—but a hand intercepted his: Yaargraukh's.

"No," his former commander hissed. "Leave it or be killed."

"Then what—?"

But the older Hkh'Rkh was pulling him another direction: toward the water. Behind them, staccato bursts of human and Hkh'Rkh weaponfire were now contending with each other. Franklin was already diving into the same pool in which Riordan had begun his race. Ezzraamar pulled back. "But I cannot—"

"I will help you swim," Yaargraukh assured him as they ran over the small ledge and Ezzraamar saw the perversely still water appear beneath his airborne feet. "We shall embrace this Hero-deed together."

Then, with a rush of cold that ran along his body and up his snout, the water was over and inside of his head.

Chapter Fifty-Seven

Brenlor continued to stare at the overhead of the battlefield. Idrem had not seen him blink in over a minute. An orange triangle on the human side of the river touched down briefly near the south ford, then moved further eastward, traversing the now-settling dust that had been raised by the railgun strike.

Brenlor folded his arms. "Is that the last human helicopter?"

"It is, Fearsome Srin," the senior Aboriginal present answered.

He nodded once. "So, the Hkh'Rkh have lost control of the battle, as we surmised."

Idrem silently amended that "have lost control" was a decidedly charitable characterization of what they had seen over the past sixty minutes. After eighty percent of their mobile assets were disabled or destroyed during two failed attempts at crossing the river, the Hkh'Rkh had apparently lost rear-area security as well. An hour ago, a number of what were evidently small unit strikes had taken out several heavy weapons and additional APCs on their side of the river, including, apparently, the backup command and radio vehicle. Since then, only weaker signals had been detected, and only on a local level.

Shortly after that, a large ambush had eliminated almost half a platoon of Hkh'Rkh that had gathered beneath the south ford. Human helicopters then streamed across the river to that site, from which several other short strikes had been conducted against two nearby clusters of vehicles. Now, the last of the human assault teams had evidently been withdrawn, back to their side of the valley.

In short, the Hkh'Rkh had not merely lost control, had not merely lost the battle: they were no longer a force in being. At best, they were a splintered rabble of a thousand, maybe less, hunkering down or roving about on the western side of the river, without any centralized control.

Brenlor turned to look at Idrem. "Do you see any option other than direct intervention?"

Idrem shook his head. "No. It is that, or leave." Idrem did not add that, had Brenlor not insisted on launching the railgun strikes, the Hkh'Rkh might have waited for night and forced a crossing at one or more of the fords. But that outcome only existed in a parallel universe, now—assuming such theoretical places existed.

Brenlor did not bother looking at the Aboriginal communications specialist. "You have the frequency and cypher for the colonial capitol, the place they refer to as Iarzut'thruk."

"I do, Potent Srin. Although it may be difficult for them to reply to our signal."

"Why so?"

"*Red Lurker*'s broadcast equipment can easily push aside the Terran jamming. However, the Hkh'Rkh transmitters may be unable to do so."

Half a year ago, no crewperson would have dared relay such disappointing observations to Brenlor, for fear that they would become the target of his frustrated fury. But Brenlor had learned since then, and if the role of Srin and *de facto* Hegemon of House Perekmeres still did not sit easy or natural upon him, neither did it chafe so much as it had.

Brenlor simply nodded his understanding. "Attempt to contact what the brutes call their Clanhall."

The Aboriginal complied, listened for a response, began to shake his head. "A response, sir. But—"

"Yes?"

"I do not think the signal's source is in Iarzut'thruk."

"Then locate it!"

"I cannot do so definitively, Great Srin. They are switching between several transmitters. It is possible that none of them are colocated with the actual source. But they are waiting on the line."

"Very well. I will speak with the colonial representative."

The Aboriginal nodded that the channel was open.

Brenlor raised his chin. "I am—the ally who assisted you with orbital strikes against the Terrans. I wish to speak with Jrekhalkar, senior leader in the government of Turkh'saar."

There was a long pause on the line, then: "Jrekhalkar of the Moiety of Gdar'khoom is no longer the Voice of Turkh'saar. He has lost his own and his Family's possessions in a Challenge."

"He lost them? To whom?"

"He lost them to a Challenger, who has since made the New Families' Collective the proxy government. I am the spokesman for the New Families on this world."

"Then it is to you that I shall speak. Be assured that I would be pleased, and have sufficient power, to avenge and reclaim your compromised honor, to end the human scourge upon your planet. I stand ready to destroy their forces and to intercept their craft should they attempt to flee to orbit."

The pause was long. Brenlor exchanged worried looks with Idrem before the unnervingly calm voice replied, "Before we Hkh'Rkh incur an Honor-debt, we are in the habit of asking to whom we shall owe it. Also, as the spokesperson for Turkh'saar at this time, it is legally incumbent upon me to ask you to identify yourself."

Brenlor and Idrem had both foreseen this. The Srin straightened slightly. "I am Brenlor Srin Perekmeres of the Ktoran Sphere. Our peoples were allied in the recent war. I would rid you of our common foe: the humans infesting your world."

"Do you refer to the raiders who have been plaguing us for months, or the representatives of the Consolidated Terran Republic, who arrived more recently?"

"Both, since both trespass upon your world and make war upon your people. Seeing that your offensive against them has encountered difficulties, we would be honored to eliminate them for you."

Another, even longer pause. "That is an interesting offer. However, you misperceive the circumstances of the present conflict. The first humans did indeed raid our settlements and caused much loss of life. The

Terrans arrived and brought these depredations to an end. They discovered that it was not—indeed, could not have been—their contemporaries who deposited the raiders on Turkh'saar. Whoever stranded them here did so more than a century before Terra achieved interstellar travel. Furthermore, the raiders were left behind in cold cells of unusually advanced design, more advanced than anything the Terrans possess now.

"Of course, considering the rumors I have heard regarding the true physical nature of the Ktor, this suggests a troubling explanation for how the renegade humans came to be stranded here at a time when Earth itself lacked any capacity for interstellar travel. It could also explain why you are so eager to intervene now, when evidence of this past wrongdoing on Turkh'saar might easily fall into either our hands or those of the Terrans.

"However, if these conjectures and the rumors are baseless, if Ktor are in fact the very alien species they claim to be, then that can be easily proven. You may safely land in any of our communities, that we might discern your true form for ourselves."

Brenlor terminated the link. "Our gambit is lost."

"Srin, we may yet—"

"No, Idrem. We may inflict losses upon our foes, could possibly wipe them out, but still, we shall lose. The political leadership of Turkh'saar has changed and with it, so have our fortunes. And it might have been otherwise, had I not been intemperate."

"With respect, Srin, it was impossible to foresee all the variables put into motion when we were compelled to disrupt the Terran investigation of the Site."

"That was not the failure point, Idrem. It was at

the inception, the concept, of the plan itself." Brenlor shook his head. "I should have realized that some of the Ktor who seeded the Aboriginals here must also have known of the Site, probably helped in the creation of the sham. Both projects *had* to be close to the region where the Hkh'Rkh were most likely to found a colony. For the contents of the site to influence the brutes, it had to be placed where they were sure to find it. Similarly, for awakened Aboriginals to cause a political incident, they had to be placed close enough to discover and raid the Hkh'Rkh. This one miserable patch of ground was too thick with the tendrils of our forefathers' plotting for us to avoid becoming snared in them ourselves."

"My Srin, you could not know—"

"True: I could not *know* it—but I should have suspected it. I should have recoiled from the complications and convolutions of my plot, rather than being mesmerized by the victory that would have been ours had everything worked as we wished." His face grew grim. "As if the universe is ever congenial, even to the simplest plans." He turned haunted eyes upon Idrem. "I am not oblivious to your, and Nezdeh's, trepidation when I announce a plan. You fear the same intemperate risk-taking that spawned the Doomsday Rock or the Site below us, or the disastrous outcome on Disparity. And you were right to do so; see what I have wrought here." He stood straight. "No longer. No more great gambles for high stakes. From this day forth, the strategies of House Perekmeres shall be fashioned so that its fortunes improve incrementally, are not perilous gambles for great gains."

Idrem nodded, but thought, *that is a most welcome*

development. Presuming we survive long enough to put your new resolve into practice.

Yaargraukh leaned away from the communications panel in *Puller*. "I seem to have been cut off." The narrow tube that was his tongue whipped out and in again. "A technical malfunction, I am sure."

Riordan grinned, as did most of the others on the bridge. Except Dora, who kept eyeing the Hkh'Rkh warily. Caine nodded at her control panel. "Ms. Veriden, please keep at least one of your eyes on the passive sensors we left in orbit. I want to know when the Ktoran ship leaves and on what vector." *Although I think I've got a pretty damned good idea where they're going to head.* He turned to Yaargraukh. "So, how does it feel to be the dominant landowner on Turkh'saar?"

"I do not know, Caine Riordan. The elders in the Clanhall will not recognize your transfer of property to me."

Bannor Rulaine frowned. "Well, we've got it on tape. And it was witnessed by the same scions who agreed to the truce and the return of their wounded from our side of the river. So it can hardly be said they lacked the authority to make agreements that are binding upon the colony."

Yaargraukh spread his claws open, pointed them downward. "I do not disagree with you, Bannor Rulaine. But in my culture, when tradition is challenged by law, the law is often twisted, construed, and reconstrued until it can be made to conform with tradition. I believe your word for this is teleology: where a result is decided before the process of debate or discovery is initiated."

O'Garran snorted. "Fancy word for saying, 'they're going to have it their way, no matter what.' And your people, the New Families, are going to let them get away with that?"

"It is not so simple as you make it sound, Miles O'Garran. The would-be jurists among the Old Families will claim that Caine Riordan's interpretation of our law was in error, that Jrekhalkar never had the right to offer Challenge since a human cannot possess Honor."

Tygg Robin frowned. "But your own people have agreed that the Challenge was fairly made and accepted. Hell, even Jrekhalkar admitted that the law was silent on whether humans—or any alien—can possess Honor."

Yaargraukh's neck oscillated once. "Yes, but the elders here, and ultimately, back on Rkh'yaa, are likely to argue that where the law is silent, one must first seek the guidance of tradition before acting freely. It will not aid their case that the Old Families themselves have frequently done otherwise and have had their deeds upheld in court. But then, the Old Families control the courts and will ignore any precedents that are inconvenient."

Karam sucked in a breath through a rictus-smile. "Damn. Sounds just like home."

Bannor stuck to his original point. "Yes, but until then, you hold the property here. In just a year's time, you could make huge changes—"

"You misperceive, Bannor Rulaine. The Old Families will not relinquish their hold upon their property and then hope to reclaim it. They will deny our legal right to it until they may bring the matter before the Allsires on Rkh'yaa: a court where the jurists are their peers, possibly their relatives."

Dora looked up from the sensors. "So when Cai—when the Commodore formally presented you with the spoils of the Challenge, and all the scions agreed, that was all just meaningless theater that will accomplish nothing?"

Yaargraukh's ears flattened and he made a cutting gesture with his left hand. "No, but what it accomplishes will be registered in minds, not legal documents. The Old Families will wish this incident to be buried, to be forgotten. The lengths to which Jrekhalkar went to legitimate a Challenge that he then twisted and violated in an attempt to secure victory are alarming, even for the most opportunistic members of the Old Families. They hold their power because of tradition, and with us, the core of all tradition is Honor. They have now shown themselves to be so completely faithless and self-serving that it will not only galvanize the New Families' resistance to them, but create doubt and dissension in their own ranks. For every Old Family scion who is willing to bend or break the rules of Honor to serve their own ends, there are nine who frown upon such degeneracy."

Riordan folded his arms. "So if it is a foregone conclusion that the Old Family elders here on Turkh'saar are going to ignore the outcome of the Challenge, and that the Patrijuridicate on Rkh'yaa is going to back them up; then why did you accept my offer of all of the property of Jrekhalkar's Family? Isn't that going to put you in their crosshairs?"

Yaargraukh's tongue emerged and wagged fitfully. "As if I am not already? The scions who agreed to the truce and transfer of spoils were relatively young and stunned by both the battle and the reversal of the Challenge. But in time, they, and the elders, will recall and recount and amplify my involvement in these events. I shall be branded a traitor and either exiled or executed. I shall save them the trouble of making that decision, if you will be so kind as to take me from this place."

Riordan stared. "Are you officially asking for political asylum?"

"I am. You will note that I did not accept the spoils of the Challenge personally, but in trust for the New Families of Turkh'saar. However, the issues of property will not be solved simply because I have departed. They will remain a contested matter as long as there are any New Family leaders here to contest them."

Duncan Solson nodded. "And are those leaders the same Warriors that accompanied you when you joined us?"

Yaargraukh expelled a long, tired breath. "Unfortunately, no. I must presume that my fate shall determine theirs. If I am branded a traitor, so shall they be. So I must ask if not just I, but also those who followed me here, may seek asylum with you."

Riordan felt the eyes in the room turning toward him: *Puller*'s crew was accumulating diplomatic responsibilities and hot potatoes at a prodigious rate. But even peripherally, he could tell that their gazes were expectant, rather than alarmed. "Yes. Of course. But what do you plan to do, once you have left the Patrijuridicate?"

Yaargraukh neck-wobbled. "To work, to teach those of you who wish to learn our ways, and to help find and repatriate our battle-brothers who still hide in the jungles of Indonesia. If your government will allow us to do so."

Duncan nodded. "That shouldn't be a problem. Similar terms were offered to any of your POWs who'd be willing to help us end the fighting on Java. Last I heard, that offer had not been rescinded."

Riordan was still troubled. "But Yaargraukh, what happens to the New Families when we're gone? If they keep publicizing what happened here, keep pushing for their property rights, won't the Patrijuridicate start to lean on them? Hard?"

"Possibly so. It has happened in the past. But this time may be different. This is our most productive colony world, but not widely settled by New Families because we could come not as owners, or even homesteaders, but as serfs. If, on the other hand, the New Families were to keep the property rights you conferred upon them today, that would change their attitudes entirely. We have never had so clear and strong a case to make, with so much power to gain if we win. So the Old Families may indeed pressure us, but this time, I suspect we will press back. And that is overdue." He paused. "Frankly, my greatest concern with accepting the spoils of your Challenge, Caine Riordan, was the consequences that it might visit upon *your* people."

"My people? You mean Earth? How does my giving you this property endanger us? Hell, wouldn't it have been worse if I had tried to hold on to it?"

"Yes, undoubtedly. However, let us conjecture how the Patrijuridicate will perceive—or at least represent—your role in this. Will they not say this outcome—of Old Family property transferred into New Family claws—was what your government intended from the start? That the raiders and then your arrival and the subsequent battle were, collectively, all parts of an elaborate ploy to provide the New Families with enough power—or legal outrage—to incite a civil war among the Hkh'Rkh? And thereby, neutralize one of Earth's enemies in the last war?"

Caine considered. "And wouldn't they have said that anyway, even if I didn't give you the property? Even if there were no spoils or I elected not to claim them?" Yaargraukh nodded. "So then, will the events here hurt Earth or the New Families any more than it would have, simply because we legally gave you the spoils of our success? Will that cause any to believe the conspiracy theory who would not already have believed it?"

Yaargraukh's neck tremored slightly. "Probably not. I suspect that from the moment your Lost Soldiers began raiding our settlements, all the damage that has followed was inevitable. Which is, I suppose, a testimony to the perfidious inspiration that caused the Ktor to place this interspeciate time bomb where they did."

"While we're on the topic of time bombs: what about Ezzraamar? He's Old Family, but he's very closely associated with you. Does he want to stay or go?"

"I think he would stay, if he could. But he cannot."

"Because he fears reprisals?"

"No, not initially. What he fears is that, as the Warrior who had the most contact with me, he will be pressed to bear false witness against me. And against you humans."

"Against us?"

"Of course. Consider his brief exchange with you when he was a prisoner in the forward operating base. And even more, what he heard his captors discussing when they had no suspicion that he understood their words. For him to tell the truth is to further implicate Jrekhalkar and the Old Family scions in the willful suppression of that information and of substituting lies in its place. It would mean disgrace not only to Jrekhalkar himself, but to his colleagues and his sire.

"So Ezzraamar has a choice between following the path of Honor and telling truths which will result in his ostracization and possible exile, or he may lie and become the cherished tool of the Old Families—and lose his true, private Honor in the process."

"So he's opting for choice number three: asylum."

"Correct. If you will have him."

Caine looked around the group. When no one made any response other than replying with a wry smile, Dora threw up her hands. "Sure. Why not? The more the merrier."

"Ezzraamar will be honored to travel with you," Yaargraukh said solemnly. "Besides, now it will be possible for me to keep my promise to him."

"Which is?"

"To teach him how to swim."

Dora's face seemed to twist around her nose. "And you couldn't do that here? Seems like you've got plenty of water around."

"Water, yes, but for us, it is safest to learn in a natatorium."

"In a what?"

"Ah. A pool. We have none here, and there are, I believe, only four on Rkh'yaa. Mostly for special operations training."

Riordan nodded, turned toward Bannor. "Speaking of special operations, what's the final status of the tactical nuke you secured?"

Bannor stared at him. "It's broken."

"I know it's disabled; I got the report right after you were extracted from their side of the river. What I'm asking is, how badly broken is it?"

Bannor did not blink. "It's *really* broken."

"Bannor: I need to know if it is still transportable."

Now Bannor blinked. Twice. "Sir?"

"You heard me: I want to know if it's safe to move."

"Why?"

"Because we need to take it with us."

Chapter Fifty-Eight

The room grew more quiet than Caine had expected.
Then again, being tasked to move a potentially unstable
nuclear warhead was not generally considered welcome news.

Bannor scratched his head through his thinning hair.
"Well, I *think* we can move it. More or less. But it
was a pretty hot warhead to begin with. Can't say I
think much of Hkh'Rkh engineering." He glanced at
Yaargraukh. "Sorry . . . eh, Advocate."

"I am no longer an advocate: merely Yaargraukh.
And do not be sorry for your frank speech. Until we
Hkh'Rkh are free to make similar comments, we shall
not improve."

Bannor frowned. "You have laws against criticizing
your own technology?"

"No, nothing formal. But the Old Families have a
profound insecurity regarding our technological acumen.
It is considered disloyal to praise the accomplishments
of another race. Or to criticize our own."

Riordan leaned back. "So, what do we need to do to secure the warhead?"

Bannor looked quizzical. "Do you mean for transport or for use?"

"Transport. We need it as evidence of just how profoundly the Patrijuridicate violated the Turkh'saar nonmilitarization pact with the Arat Kur."

Bannor looked relieved. "So you want to use it as an extra poker chip for our side in the blame game that's going to storm up around this whole 'incident.'"

"If it comes to that. I'm hoping this particular poker chip is so big that it will convince the Patrijuridicate that they'd be better off not starting the game at all."

Duncan Solsohn rubbed his chin. "Caine, you don't actually think that anything we do will be enough to smother word of what happened here, do you?"

"No, but we could make sure that the Patrijuridicate is informed, through unofficial channels, that it would not be in their best interests to pursue the matter too aggressively."

Bannor nodded. "So having the bomb doesn't stop the shouting; it just ensures that it doesn't get so loud that we have to go to war over it."

"That's what I'm hoping. Karam, are we ready to boost for orbit?"

"Just about. There's still a lot of reshuffling going on in the wedges."

"Bringing in all the banged-up chopper parts?" asked Dora.

The room got quiet. "No," said Caine. "The wounded." He glanced at Duncan who, after losing the Proxie two hours earlier, had taken over the grim duty of processing the casualty count. "Do we have final numbers?"

Duncan nodded tightly. "One hundred and eleven dead, fifty-four wounded. That's just the Lost Soldiers. We had five KIA and eight WIA among the Cold Guard."

Karam leaned far back in his acceleration couch. "Damn, that's pretty lopsided: usually it's far more wounded than dead. I know the Hkh'Rkh weapons are powerful, but—"

"It wasn't their weapons," Duncan broke in. "It wasn't even the railgun strikes or front-line losses, although the casualties in the Dugouts were awful. Mostly, it was our inability to keep up with the mede-vac calls, particularly after the stellar flare grounded our choppers. More than half of our dead could have been saved, but their golden hour came and went before we could get the angel flights started again."

The room was quiet. Riordan glanced at Yaargraukh, who was sitting in the relaxed squat typical of his spe-cies. No one had counted the Hkh'Rkh dead, and the remaining Warriors had no way to recover them all. There were more bodies to collect than ambulatory Hkh'Rkh left to collect them. But, by all the estimates Caine had seen, their losses had been almost an order of magnitude greater than the humans. What that meant in terms of the colony's ability to continue to provide for itself was beyond his reckoning and too sensitive a topic to bring up with Yaargraukh.

Riordan looked up. "So how many survivors are we loading?"

Duncan glanced at his dataslate. "Three hundred and eight all told."

Caine nodded, managed to resist the urge to hang his head. Three hundred and eight. There had been four hundred and thirty-two survivors remaining when they had commenced planetfall. And yet everyone—the Lost Soldiers most of all—were calling this a victory. *A victory*. For a moment, Riordan feared he might laugh out loud. Or vomit. Maybe both. "And Dr. Sleeman?"

"They just found her and dusted off, sir. ETA twenty minutes."

He turned to Dora, whose expression was a little less hard-bitten than usual. "How much site cleanup are we really going to be able to manage, Ms. Veriden?"

She frowned, appeared not to want to make her report. "I'm sorry, Commodore: there's simply no way to sanitize the battlefield. Or the Site. It would take weeks combing the undergrowth just to find all the spent brass, all the medical disposables, all the busted parts that fell off crippled helicopters. But even if we did all that, there's a lot of material evidence we just can't get to without excavating equipment—or a company of coroners."

Riordan understood her reference to the excavating equipment—the railgun strikes had buried bodies and equipment under hundreds of tons of debris—but: "Coroners?"

"The Hkh'Rkh dead, sir. It would be pretty difficult to retrieve all the expended rounds and shrapnel lodged in their bodies."

Riordan's stomach knotted: he hadn't thought of that. Maybe because he hadn't wanted to. "Okay, Dora. Just have our people collect the largest pieces of debris and load them up. We'll report we did our best. If Downing isn't happy, he can come out here with a broom."

"Okay, but one last item, sir."

"Yes?"

"The mass grave, sir. That alone holds eighty-six Nazis and almost eighty of the Japanese. And then there are the other Lost Soldiers who were killed before we arrived. You'd hoped we'd be able to exhume them, maybe bury them at sea, like we're going to have to do with today's dead..." Her voice trailed off.

When she stopped talking, Riordan realized he'd closed his eyes. He'd been responsible for disposing of bodies in Java: you didn't command insurgents without suffering casualties, sometimes a lot of them. But not on this scale. And it didn't really matter that many of the bodies in the mass grave truly deserved to be there. It was simply the size of the butcher's bill, whether it had accrued on his watch or not. Caine opened his eyes, looked at Yaargraukh. "The soil here: will it reduce them quickly?"

The Hkh'Rkh nodded. "Yes. Most of the dermal irritation caused by contact is from high levels of acidity or alkalinity. Given how long they have already been in the ground, it is a certainty that they have been reduced to bone. In another four months, there will be no identifiable remains."

Riordan nodded. "Then we leave the mass grave as we found it. For the Lost Soldiers who died during operations before we arrived, I'll leave that up to their officers. If the survivors want to take the time to exhume them, we'll give them that time—if the Ktor let us."

Bannor's voice was quiet, almost gentle. "And what about the Cold Guard? Can we still take their bodies back if we don't take those of the Lost Soldiers, too?"

Riordan resisted the urge to close his eyes again. "Yes. Those men and women still have families who remember them, and there will be inquiries. Besides, we brought them and we have the capacity to take them back home. But the Lost Soldiers—" He waved his hand in the direction of the River Kakaagsukh. "There are just too many of their dead. We can't take them all. We can't." He stopped before he repeated himself again.

Karam broke the silence. "Well, there's one piece of happy news: the Ktoran craft that fired the railgun rounds is now accelerating out of orbit."

Tygg smiled. "Nice to see them running scared."

"More like running to catch the last ride home. It seems the advancing Slaasriithi recon drones spooked the four Ktoran signatures out near the belt. They're moving off."

Riordan nodded. "I'm pretty sure the two weaker signatures will prove to be decoys, probably mounted on shuttles and fueled by a portable reactor."

"Shuttles?" Miles O'Garran echoed. "Why are you so sure they're on shuttles?"

Before Riordan could figure a polite way to respond, Karam chose a far more direct approach. "Because, genius, unless you were asleep during the recent radio exchange, the bad-guy-in-chief identified himself as Brenlor Perekmeres. Ring any bells?"

"Can't say it does—asshole."

"Stow that." Riordan looked up at the two of them. "If you two have something to settle, you can take it outside. Later. As in, when we are out of the shit. Which we aren't. Not by a mile. Fast version, Miles: we've heard the name Perekmeres before—well, those of us who read the intel briefs compiled after we were ambushed on Disparity. One of the clones the

Ktor commandeered from the *Arbitrage* survived, and that was one of the names he gave us. Brenlor was the leader of House Perekmeres, a bunch of Ktoran renegades."

"Renegades? What did they do?"

"The clone didn't know. Didn't know much of anything, actually."

O'Garran rocked back in the chair he'd snagged from the common area. "You mean those bastards have chased us to hell and back just to screw with us again? Here?"

Riordan shook his head. "No, that doesn't add up. If they've still got the *Arbitrage* in tow, they can't hide too well. So there's no way they could have trailed us into our own space, to Delta Pavonis Three, and then here. I'm thinking that they came here directly because someone in their crew knew about the Lost Soldiers."

"Okay, but why? I mean, how does it help them to wake up a battalion of old-timey Earthers their grandaddies snapped up back in the day?"

"That's an excellent question," Caine affirmed with a nod, "but we don't have the time, or data, to answer it now. But since they didn't simply grab the Lost Soldiers as recruits for their own ranks, I'm betting that this was a play for some kind of political leverage." He stood. "Unfortunately, we're not done dealing with these Ktor. We have to chase them. It's still possible that the more distant ships could double back, and, in conjunction with the one in front of us, threaten the *Shore-of-Stars*."

"And what if they turn and fight?" Dora asked. "If they're in the same ship they hit us with at Disparity, they're going to kick our ass just as badly. All over again."

"Not if we bring along all our toys. We left Slaas-riithi PDF drones and some of our own missiles on station in the near-orbit wreckage."

"Yeah," drawled Karam, "and they probably did, too."

"Yes, which is why we're going to flush them out before we start to boost. In addition to the drones and missiles, we left sensors topside. When we hid *Puller*, we lost lascom contact with them, but now we can use them to sniff out whatever the Ktor left behind."

"And if the Ktor don't bite?"

"It's not the Ktor themselves who will or won't bite: it's the AI on board their automated platforms. If the Ktoran ship keeps crowding gees to rendezvous with the *Arbitrage* and its shift-tug, their communication lag time is going to be too great for effective remote control. So those robot brains are going to be in full autonomous mode, not sitting fat, dumb, and happy until they're compromised."

Karam pouted agreeably. "Makes sense. And hell, it's going to be another few hours before we can boost for orbit, anyhow."

"Exactly. We'll let our sensors flush out the game, and then let our attack platforms—and the new ones the Slaasriithi sent to help us—overwhelm them. One at a time, if possible. And we don't have to hunt them all down. We just need to clear a vector that allows us to get spaceside and hard on the tail of the Ktoran ship."

Dora was frowning. "Do you really think that, even with Slaasriithi PIPs and fighter drones—and the *Shore-of-Stars* and *its* fighter drones—we'll be able to take on all those Ktoran ships?"

"Firstly, Ms. Veriden, there are only two Ktoran

ships: the one we're chasing and the shift-tug the Slaasriithi first spotted at Disparity. Secondly, the *Arbitrage* is slow. A lot slower than us or the Slaasriithi. And if she has to run away from Slaasriithi recon platforms, it's going to take her a while before she can maneuver to mate with that tug. So the clock is on our side. And the more time we have, the more force we'll be able to concentrate against them."

"Yeah," Dora persisted, "but the ship we'll be chasing can outrun *us*. That gives them the ability bring all their force together, too."

Riordan smiled. "Not if we play our cards correctly, Ms. Veriden."

As *Puller* reduced thrust after its initial boost to orbit, Duncan Solsohn found himself floating in the gunnery bubble, working to remove the last of the emergency wiring that had been required to convert it into a control chamber for the now-junked Proxie. He had just tethered himself to a handhold when the thrust resumed, but not quite as strong as before.

"We don't get much of a break, do we?" asked a voice from the bubble's entry. Riordan.

Duncan smiled. "Not in the job description, so far as I could ever tell."

"Can you use a hand?"

"Sure," replied Duncan. Who knew all too well that Riordan had more important things to do than help rewire the gunnery bubble.

After familiarizing himself with the basic tasks, the commodore didn't waste a lot of time maintaining the charade. "You know, on our way up out of the gravity well just now, we got a chance to do something

we couldn't do on the way in. We ran active sensors.
Showed us a lot more of the debris field. And in
more detail."

Uh oh: here it comes.

"Seems that there were a lot of big structures in
orbit here when the Slaasriithi raiders came through.
Some were almost as big as those ruined tank farms we
saw off the shoulder of the gas giant in orbit seven."

Duncan feigned moderate interest, nodded encour-
agingly. What the hell else could he do?

"There must also have been a hell of a lot of traffic through here, as well. Now that we know what to
look for, and can run detailed 3-D rotations of all the
wreckage, it turns out that Turkh'saar was a crossroads
in more than name. Most of the debris is from station
components, docking collars, maintenance frames, orbital
tugs. Even munitions launchers. The disposable kind
carried by Hkh'Rkh warships. Destroyers and larger."

"You don't say?" Even to Duncan, his own response
sounded like a bad line delivered by a third-rate actor.

From the corner of his eye, he saw Riordan smile.
"And I suspect if we were to run similarly detailed
scans out at the gas giant, we'd find the same. Just
lots more of it. Enough to account for a whole fleet's
infrastructure. What do you think?"

"Sir, no disrespect intended, but why are you asking me?" Although Duncan knew perfectly well why
Riordan was asking him.

And judging from his smile, Riordan knew that
Duncan knew. "Because I looked back at the scans
we performed when we first arrived in this system,
particularly as we played hide-and-seek for keeps with
the killer drones the Arat Kur and the Hkh'Rkh left

behind near the gas giant. When I did, I discovered that you accessed those sensor results repeatedly while the rest of us on *Puller* were still semi-comatose, recovering from having been jolted awake to get our hands dirty for the Slaasriithi."

Damn it. Caught.

"I also noticed that you were running orbital projection software, particularly for the bits of the tankage farms that didn't have a lot of damage or tumble. Which, by logical extension, were the ones that only received glancing blows, or maybe weren't even hit directly: just bumped by a few pieces of light debris. Their orbits wouldn't have been altered too much, certainly not so much that you couldn't back-calculate what the original orbits were.

"Seems they were in very sensible orbits for refueling, actually: they moved in a sequence that always put one of the big tank farms near each of the three primary transfer points. Strange thing, though. When you run the simulations backward, it turns out that inserting all those structures into all those orbits required quite an orbital ballet. The Arat Kur and the Hkh'Rkh had to follow a precise order of placement, largely determined by the periods and positions of the gas giant's natural satellites and rings. And the latest they could have started that placement schedule was just over five years ago."

Solsohn smiled although he thought he might get sick. "When did you find that out?"

"On the way up to orbit. The active scans started me thinking."

Rule one: never start Riordan thinking. Not unless that's going to help you. "So you know."

"Depends what you mean. I know that two years ago, we hadn't even been invited to the Convocation that introduced us to the Arat Kur and the Hkh'Rkh—who attacked us only five weeks later. So, by deduction, I also know that the Arat Kur and Hkh'Rkh didn't scrape together their invasion force because of what happened at Convocation. It was already here, in this system, prepared and waiting to go. That's the only way they could have reacted so quickly: they had been accumulating forces here for at least two or three years. Which means that their mutual cooperation and collusion to invade Earth was ongoing before the Hkh'Rkh were even invited to Convocation. And I'm guessing that's what you were *really* sent out here to determine."

Duncan shook his head. "Not just that: the raiders—the recordings of the radio chatter that Yaargraukh sent to us from Turkh'saar—that was job one. But it also gave us a chance to look at the system itself.

"Downing suspected there was something hinky about the timing between Convocation and the first attack on Barnard's Star: like you said, it was just too close. And when we started looking at the star maps, and working the numbers backward—how long it would have taken them to get a fleet together, given the shift-ranges and the locations of the Arat Kur and Hkh'Rkh systems—well, all the deductive arrows pointed at Turkh'saar."

"So you were sent to confirm that this was where the Hkh'Rkh readied their part of the fleet."

Duncan shrugged. "We were pretty sure about that. My job was to see just how duplicitous they and the Arat Kur had been." Riordan looked puzzled. "It's like this: the more haphazard everything looked here, the more reasonable doubt there was about just how far in advance the Arat Kur and Hkh'Rkh planned the invasion, and the more likely it was something that they'd thrown together in the last few months, or maybe a year." Solsohn shook his head. "But this degree of infrastructure, which was clearly built up over the course of several years? No. Both species knew that they were getting ready to go to war, and against whom."

Riordan folded his arms. "Actually, the Arat Kur, or at least some of them, had to be in collusion with the Hkh'Rkh for even longer, for five or six years. Their fleets were too optimally balanced for it to be chance. The Hkh'Rkh ships were mostly troop transports and ground attack craft; the Arat Kur were mostly spaceside combat platforms and carriers for the Hkh'Rkh troop ships. The two races had worked out their respective invasion roles even before the Hkh'Rkh started moving all their assets into this system."

"It sure looks that way, Commodore."

"So what's the second part of your job: to cover up what you found?" Duncan heard the real question behind Riordan's tone: *So, are you going to keep humanity in the dark about what's really been going on, about why we were invaded?*

Solsohn shook his head. "The way I see it, my job is to make sure our planet doesn't launch itself into a war that could destroy it. Literally. You know how people back home would react to this: that Convocation was a sham, that the only reason we were there was to be set up for a sucker punch, with the Hkh'Rkh and Arat Kur fists already cocked and waiting."

"Yes, that's how they'd see it. And they'd be right."

"Yeah, and that's the problem: because knowing they're right means there'd be no stopping them. And if we get into a war right now, we will get greased. And you know it. Because who are we going to have to fight? The Arat Kur? We've arrogated half their best hulls and could destroy Homenest any time we please. The Hkh'Rkh? They can't reach us without Arat Kur shift-carriers to carry them. So who would we be going to war against?"

Riordan glanced away. "The Ktor. Of course."

"Of course. And then you add the whole Lost Soldier story into the mix. War heroes taken hostages taken by aliens—aliens who are also humans bent on conquering us?" Solsohn pushed the reconfigured wiring back into the wall, replaced the panel. "Earth's billions would be screaming for war, and they'd probably get it—and get conquered in the process."

Riordan's collarcom toned: he was wanted back on the bridge. "We're coming to the point of our trajectory where we have to call in our on-station assets and flush out whatever the Ktor left behind. And then straight into a stern chase."

"I suspect we'll have plenty of time to debate this later."

Riordan, halfway out the hatch, turned and smiled. It was a rueful expression. "With any luck."

Chapter Fifty-Nine

Riordan moved against the thrust, got abreast of his acceleration couch, slid into it. As he fastened the straps, he asked, "Status, Karam?"

"We are on course and sternchasing the Ktor. All three wedges have lifted successfully and are on widely divergent trajectories to frustrate any attempts at a multiple intercept. The Slaasriithi automated fighters and PIP drones are in the process of matching course and speed with us. We'll have them aboard or affixed to the hull within two hours, assuming our recon platforms don't flush something out of the debris before then."

"Bet that they will, Flight Officer. Dr. Sleeman, they won't give us much warning, so keep a close watch on sensors. And welcome back."

"Good to be back, sir."

"I assume you have a final report on your findings?"

"Still working on the samples from the Site, sir. For final determinations, I'm going to need access to the small lab in the medical annex of our cryomod, back at *Shore-of-Stars*. But I suspect the results will be worth the wait."

"I daresay they will." The hatch dilated behind him. Riordan turned. "Major Solsohn?"

Duncan started as he entered. "Yes, sir?"

"You will be running remote ops again. Assume that the Ktor have left behind semi-automated platforms that are far swifter and better armed than the Slaasriithis' and certainly better than the missiles we seeded in orbit. However, we'll have two advantages. Given their distance from the controlling hull, they have to deal with lascom lag time as they exchange data with their operators. And we're bringing a much greater number of platforms to the fight."

"Yes, sir. Sounds like the battle will resemble bear-baiting."

"It will if we're doing it correctly. And one other caveat: if we have to take any losses, I want it to be to our—to Terran-manufactured—systems."

"Sir?"

"I know it's protocol to preferentially preserve our own assets, but we have to keep the best units functioning as long as we can. And the Slaasriithi fighters and PIPs are are the best we have." *And damn near the only ones, now.*

Duncan nodded, muttered, "That might change if we could get a close look at them."

Riordan smiled. "I'm working on that objective, too, Major."

Veriden looked up. "Slaasriithi communiqué. Encrypted, high compression squeak.

"They're proposing telemetries for rendezvous and are also giving us permission to take direct control over the drone fighters that are closest to us, since our new electronics have that capability."

"Advise them that we must decline both recommendations at this time."

"We *don't* want to rendezvous with them?" Dora was too surprised to sound surly.

"Not yet. I want to give the Ktor two widely divergent threats from which they must continue to withdraw. That cuts down their maneuver and evasion options."

"Okay. Sending reply—"

Duncan spoke quickly. "Belay that for a moment, Ms. Veriden." He turned to Riordan. "Commodore, I understand not rendezvousing with them, but declining to take direct control over their drone fighters? That reduction of our lascom lag time will give us more of an advantage when the Ktor platforms come popping out to ambush ours."

Riordan nodded. "I am aware of that. But I have my reasons. Decline both recommendations, Ms. Veriden. Major, I trust your expertise will give us the edge we need in dealing with the enemy drones."

Solsohn's response was almost a grumble, but not quite. "Yes, sir."

Karam, surveying the piloting panel in front of him, reported, "If the bogey continues on its present course, and if we maintain thrust and heading, we will overtake it in approximately seventeen hours."

"Very good, Mr. Tsaami." Riordan leaned back, studied the intercept vectors that the holotank beside him was painting between the friendly and enemy icons. "Hold course and speed. And be sure not to exceed *Puller*'s original specs for thrust or energy output. No exceptions."

Karam turned, caught Riordan's eye, lifted a quiz-zical eyebrow. Caine simply smiled. Karam's other eyebrow lifted, then he shrugged and returned his attention to his instruments.

Caine settled back, wished he could catch a quick nap, knew he couldn't afford to be away from the bridge when and if the Ktoran drones came out of hiding. And besides, he needed to make sure that, in every particular, *Puller* performed the way it had at Disparity.

Down to the very last detail.

Idrem rose and stood aside from the command couch when Brenlor entered the bridge. "The Aboriginals are very determined. They hold course and speed."

Brenlor, skin still slick from an hour of physical training, glanced at the holosphere. "They are also over-confident." Idrem did not nod or offer any other sign of agreement. Brenlor noticed. "You do not concur?"

Idrem squinted at the plot also. "I am uncertain. Everything is proceeding as we might expect from a competent adversary. The human ship gathered its drones—and the Slaasriithi's—to it, but not before forc-ing ours to reveal and spend themselves suboptimally. In return, ours only eliminated human sensor drones."

Brenlor nodded. "Yes, which reduces their ability to use a stand-off active sensor to put a target lock on us."

"I agree, my Srin, but in whatever engagement we might envision as imminent, that is unlikely to be a decisive factor. If we were destined to engage them in a debris field, or even an asteroid belt, ours might have been a worthwhile exchange of playing pieces. But they have surely assessed our course and speed and deduced our objective: to rejoin our ships as soon as possible to dock for out-shift. Which means we are bound for open space, where nothing may hide. And so, why would they place a high value upon acquiring a target lock with a stand-off sensor? It still does not allow their ship to remain undetected or even untargeted."

Brenlor frowned. "Very well: so they were willing to sacrifice their sensor platforms."

"Yes, if that allowed them to preserve their remote combat assets: the Slaasriithi automated fighters and PDF drones. Which is precisely what they managed to do."

"Let us assume you are correct. Still, they come toward us like a *krexyes* in rutting fever, blind and incautious. Their overconfidence is laughable. That is a Wolfe-class corvette. We faced one such vessel at Disparity. Had we not been fighting three foes simultaneously there, we would have vaporized it." Brenlor frowned, called up the latest sensor results to scroll down in midair, alongside the holoplot. "In fact, as Nezdeh pointed out when we discovered that the Slaasriithi shift-carrier was the same one we ambushed at Disparity, this might be the same corvette, as well. We were unable to discern that, given the range. But now, it should be possible." He turned to the Aboriginal manning the sensors. "Quickly: call up the thrust and energy profile recorded during our engagement with the Wolfe-class corvette at Disparity. Compare that profile with the emissions of the warship pursuing us. Report the results."

Idrem was unclear what insight Brenlor hoped to derive from that data. "And if it is the same ship?"

"Then we know two things we did not know before. First, it means that our adversary was heavily damaged and has been repaired recently—and perhaps too hastily. Which could be an advantage."

"Forgive me, my Srin, but how do you come to that conclusion?"

Brenlor seemed surprised. "By consulting the calendar. It seems a surety that the *Shore-of-Stars* returned to Aboriginal space, since they arrived here with three Aboriginal transports and a reasonable amount of infantry."

Idrem reflected that they could also have retraced their steps to Sigma Draconis, where the Terrans still had a sizable occupation fleet, but allowed that this was less likely. Tlerek Srin Shethkador's *Ferocious Monolith* was almost certainly still there, and the Slaasriithi would have been sure to give it a wide berth: their aversion to the Ktor was profound. "Very well: let us presume they returned to Aboriginal space before journeying here."

"If they did, we can also project how long they were there, based on the shift intervals we observed while shadowing the Slaasriithi ship: a maximum of fifty or sixty days. That presumes their journey was to the nearest facility capable of repairing a Wolfe-class corvette. And what is the likelihood that, as the Aboriginals still recover from the recent war, that this small ship received priority attention in their overtaxed naval yards?"

Idrem frowned, was about to point out that there was an alternative: that the Slaasriithi had managed to repair the human corvette during the course of their travels to Terran space. But even he had to admit that was a highly unlikely scenario. The Slaasriithi were notoriously reluctant to share or exchange their technology, and the possibility that they would have been able to effect repairs on a ship so different from their own—well, it could not be ruled out, but there was also nothing to suggest that the Slaasriithi would be disposed to do so, any more than there was evidence that they were particularly inventive or versatile engineers. So: "Yes, your conjecture is quite logical."

Brenlor nodded, not merely satisfied but gratified, turned back to the sensor operator. "Results?"

"Just completed now, Terrible Srin. The corvette's drive output is almost identical: less than that observed at Disparity by one-half to one percent."

Brenlor looked triumphant.

"However, the thrust signature is different. The model may be identical, but it is not the very same engine."

Brenlor managed not to look crestfallen as he leaned his chin upon his fist. "So, a different corvette of the same class, then."

"Yes," Idrem agreed, "and so, without the weaknesses we might have hoped for, had it been hastily repaired. But it might still be the same group of Aboriginals manning it: those who survived Disparity."

"What leads you to that conclusion?"

"I offer it as a possibility, not a conclusion, my Srin. Because the Aboriginals are restricting exosapient contact to personnel with high security classifications, it is likely that a second mission with the Slaasriithi would be given to a crew that had already been in contact with them. More significantly though, it is unusual to encounter two human groups which routinely employ such unorthodox solutions."

Brenlor frowned. "Explain."

"I will as best I may, my Srin. These reasons are difficult to quantify because they do not emerge from deduction but instinct. And instinct is a very unreliable source."

"But one that often enables great leaps of insight. Continue."

"Very well. Consider how the humans on Disparity used deception to make us believe their corvette was dead in orbit. For almost two weeks. I also suspect it was they, not the Slaasriithi, who had the foresight to destroy the antimatter facility in the near belt, thereby preventing us from commandeering the fuel supplies we needed for free operations. And we never did learn how the humans stranded on the planet defeated the assault team we sent to eliminate them: we had no communications and so, no updates. But what we knew of them and their equipment told us that our victory should never have been in doubt. Instead, despite having a traitor planted among our adversaries, our forces disappeared without a word or a trace."

"And you see similar activities here?"

"Not similar activities, but a similar habit of mind. Call it a ready embrace of unconventional methods. Their tactics on Turkh'saar were, as best we could discern, professional and competent. But the synthesis of their disparate personnel into an effective fighting force is no mean feat, particularly when achieved so quickly. And their ability to lure out our orbital drones and eliminate them while only giving up their sensor platforms in return: that was shrewdly played."

"Very well: I concede there may be parallels. But how does it impact our plans?"

"In just this one way, Srin Perekmeres: that these

Aboriginals are not merely capable. They are inventive, unpredictable. And their greatest weapon, again and again, has been deception and misdirection."

"Idrem, if I did not know better, I would say you admire them."

"That would indeed be overstating the case, my Srin. But I suspect that at least some of them would make interesting contributions to our genecode."

"You may well be right." Brenlor shrugged, leaned back in the commander's couch. "A pity we must kill them all."

Idrem was considering the practicality of getting a meal when Brenlor, who had been brooding since their last exchange an hour ago, leaned toward the Aboriginal at the helm. "Course change: thirty by three-twenty, vector-relative. Execute."

Red Lurker lurched; Brenlor watched the holoplot carefully, ordered, "Sensors, track and time the enemy response. All enemy elements, not just the corvette."

Idrem, thoughts of food forgotten, began to rise. "My Srin, what troubles you?"

"Watch the Slaasriithi drones; tell me how they behave."

Puzzled, Idrem complied—and saw, even before the sensor operator reported it, that despite their vastly greater performance, the spherical Slaasriithi remote fighters lagged well behind the Terran PDF drones in their response.

Brenlor had seen it, too. He glanced up at the crewman manning the sensors. "How far behind were they, in their response?"

"Almost three seconds, Potent Srin."

Brenlor turned toward Idrem. "So. They are not under Aboriginal control. The Slaasriithi are still masters of their own drones. Which means that our enemies will have trouble coordinating any attacks involving those remote fighters."

Idrem experienced a twinge of misgiving at that hasty conclusion. "Your foresight in anticipating that the distant Slaasriithi retain control of their combat platforms is masterful, Srin Perekmeres. But let us test and make sure that it is not an artifact of some other circumstance."

"Such as?" Brenlor sounded almost truculent.

"Such as flawed communication protocols between Terran and Slaasriithi technology, to name just one possibility. What we witnessed might be caused by a lack of compatibility between the corvette's and the fighters' electronics or computers."

"Very well: how do we test that?"

Idrem thought. "Let us deploy a small cloud of nanosensors behind us. Presuming that the human ship continues to stern-chase us without deviation, it will pass through them in roughly four hours. When it does so, *Lurker* should once again maneuver sharply. If the drone fighters are in fact under direct Slaasriithi control—"

"—then the nanosensors will detect lascom control links from the Slaasriithi. Only after that will their remote fighters conform to the course changes made by the platforms under the corvette's direct control. Yes, excellent: do so."

Four hours and three minutes later, Brenlor nodded at the helmsman. "Execute the maneuver."

This time, *Red Lurker*'s heavy particle thrusters flared at maximum, pushing the patrol hunter onto a trajectory toward *Shore-of-Stars*. A second later, the Wolfe-class corvette made a matching course correction, her directly controlled PIP drones following closely. Almost four seconds later, the nanosensors detected a lascom transmission from the shift-carrier. Finally, the spherical Slaasriithi remote fighters changed telemetry to match.

Brenlor nodded. "Either the Slaasriithi refuse to give the Aboriginals direct control over their platforms, or the low-breed control systems are unable to interface sufficiently with those of the drone fighters. It makes little difference: in combat, that lag could be decisive. Helm, resume our prior course."

But Idrem was still watching the larger tacplot. "My Srin, I recommend you examine the reaction of the Slaasriithi shift-carrier."

Brenlor grabbed at the peripheries of the holographic navigational display, shrank it, sought the icon denoting the Slaasriithi shift-carrier. "They are—accelerating?"

Idrem nodded. "In response to our feint at closing with them."

Brenlor frowned. "They are Slaasriithi. Logic and experience dictates that they should be reversing thrust, trying to maintain distance."

Idrem nodded again. "Yes. But the data before us indicates the opposite."

Brenlor studied the holoplot more carefully. "This only makes sense if they mean to tempt us into chasing them, to make intercept."

Idrem stuck a finger into the holosphere, uttered the words, "Computer: sample plot."

"Sample plot engaged."

He turned toward Brenlor. "Consider what happens if we move to engage the Slaasriithi ship." He tapped its icon. "Computer, plot intercept for this object, given current telemetry." The computer drew glowing trajectory lines, *Red Lurker* angling sharply toward the larger craft, and in so doing, moving dramatically further away from the pursuing corvette.

Brenlor nodded. "The corvette will follow, come in behind us. Our position would not be optimal. When using our railgun or main keel-laser, we would have to tumble to engage the Slaasriithi to our bow and then again the Aboriginal to our stern. But we can defeat that ploy by approaching the Slaasriithi less directly, keeping them both to spinward of us."

Idrem shook his head slowly. "You presume that their plan is to bracket *Red Lurker*. I suspect a different stratagem, one that also explains why the human craft has been expending so much of its limited thrust to overtake us."

Idrem advanced his index finger again, touched the orange icon denoting the enemy corvette. "Computer; project this object's intercept trajectory to *Uzhmarek*."

The holoplot—which was not scaled minutely enough to show the whole system—zoomed back dramatically. The apparent distance between *Red Lurker*, the Slaasriithi, and the human corvette shrank until they had all contracted into a smallish, irregular triangle. Then the computer projected a vector that, with little modification, sent the Terran corvette off in the direction of a distant pair of green icons, moving outsystem from the far side of the belt that lay between the orbits of Turkh'saar and Planet Seven.

Brenlor leaned back. "So, the Slaasriithi acceleration is a ruse. If we were to rush after their shift-carrier, we would be leaving the corvette an uncontested path toward our other ships." He frowned. "But that makes little sense as a stratagem. The human ship is too small, too weak, to do much damage to our tug, and it is unlikely to be able to cripple, let alone destroy, *Arbitrage*."

Idrem stepped away from the holoplot. "All true, my Srin. But I do not believe the Aboriginals are eager to damage our ships; they are eager to harry *Arbitrage* so that it cannot mate with the tug, and so delay our ability to commence preacceleration toward shift."

Brenlor glanced at the plot again. "So when they saw us move aggressively toward the Slaasriithi—"

"—they did not realize that was simply a feint. Rather, it encouraged the enemy shift-carrier to start a run toward our larger ships. Which would have ended as soon as we had committed ourselves to intercepting it. Once on that heading, we would have been unable to prevent the corvette from reaching *Arbitrage* and *Uzhmarek*, disrupting their docking operations, and so delay our ability to depart this system."

Brenlor started. "Is it possible that the ship Nezdeh detected making out-shift four days ago could have been one of theirs, is summoning in a response that could trap us in this system if we were delayed?"

Idrem shook his head. "No. The ship that Nezdeh detected could hardly be any ship other than our own. But that is dire enough."

Brenlor nodded. "If Shethkador hears of, or deduces, our presence and actions here, he will certainly take steps to eliminate us. And since we are Extirpated, he will be within his legal rights to instruct his Autarchal ship to undertake such a mission."

"Exactly."

Brenlor glared at the orange icon signifying the corvette. "So their apparent imprudence in pursuing us so hotly was just another form of misdirection, to invite us to misstep."

"So it seems."

"And now that we have resumed our original course and speed?"

"They still show no change in their own."

Brenlor smiled. "We shall see how long they intend to keep up their charade. A Wolfe-class vessel cannot afford to expend fuel so lavishly, and her engines have less than twenty-five percent the efficiency of ours. If she continues at this rate, she will not be able to retroboost swiftly enough to engage us effectively. But we, at any point, can commence a four-gee counter burn and let her go past us. We can then catch her between ourselves and our own drones, summoned from the *Uzhmarek*. By the time the enemy shift-carrier reaches the area, the human ship will be gone. At which point, I predict the Slaasriithi will lose their atypical boldness."

Idrem was relieved at the prudence of Brenlor's plan: he had feared the Srin would wish to turn and attack the humans immediately. This, instead, forced hard choices upon the human commander, who, if he or she was not cautious, would doom themselves by overreaching. "An excellent response, Brenlor. Let us see what choice they make. I suspect that, since we have resumed our first course, they will realize we

have seen through their ploy and will relent on their
unsustainable approach."

"Yes. I suppose they will," Brenlor grumbled. "But
I wish they wouldn't."

Against all expectations and likelihood, Brenlor got
what he hoped for. Eleven hours, two meals, and an
all-too-brief period of sleep later, Idrem reentered
the bridge. Brenlor pointed into the holoplot and
announced, "They are mad. They continue pursuing us
at the same thrust and on the same vector. Except for
recalling both their drones and the Slaasriithi's—perhaps
for refueling—their behavior remains unchanged."

Idrem frowned. "It makes no sense." He walked
over to stand at the edge of the holosphere, positioning
himself so that he looked down directly at the orange
delta icon. "With such an inferior acceleration rating,
they must know what will happen if they continue
onward. They should have tumbled and started coun-
terthrusting twenty minutes ago, lest they overshoot
us and make themselves vulnerable."

Brenlor nodded. "Instead, they continue to chase
us at full speed."

"As I said, their behavior is odd."

"Their behavior is idiotic. Not only will they be
unable to protect themselves adequately from us when
they fly past, but even if they were to start braking
now, they would be in danger of overshooting our
other ships, particularly if they have burned through
as much fuel as we project. Indeed, they may not
have enough left to come to a full stop—ever."

Brenlor stared angrily at the orange icon. "Still, if
they do have fuel left, they might hope to navigate

close enough to complicate our preacceleration vector. It might become a running battle, all the way until we effect shift."

Idrem leaned forward, stared into the holoplot. Something was amiss here. Either the humans were resorting to a highly uncertain strategy, or they were grooming a far subtler one. But if the latter, it eluded Idrem's detection. Frustrated, he straightened. "I can see no other possibilities."

"Then we either wait and hope that fortune does not favor them, or we engage the corvette now and dispatch it. Once that is achieved, the Slaasriithi will be on their own, and we are at liberty to turn upon them when and as opportunity or necessity dictate."

With a nagging misgiving, Idrem replied, "I believe so, my Srin."

"Then that is what we shall do. Helm, come about. The low-breeds seek a fight. Let us not disappoint them."

Chapter Sixty

Despite short watches that allowed for catnaps, *Puller*'s bridge was a subdued environment of boring routines and unchanging readouts—until the automated klaxon began pealing.

Riordan rubbed his face briskly, keeping his hands far enough apart to manage to demand, "Status."

"Bogey has tumbled and is counterboosting at four gees," Melissa Sleeman said a little too loudly. She looked as though she was on the verge of nausea from being jarred out of her near-stupor so abruptly.

Karam's voice was less drowsy than it had been during his last helm update, nine minutes ago. "Looks like they're coming about to have a go at us."

Riordan looked at the holoplot and agreed. "It certainly does, Flight Officer. Cut thrust."

"Cut—?"

"Do it. Now." Riordan started tapping his way down the different commlinks. "Engineering?"

Tina Melah sounded like she'd just awakened from a good night's sleep: Riordan had noticed that the ability to sleep anywhere, anytime, was not uncommon among the Navy folk in his crew. "Here, sir."

"Soft deploy all remote platforms. Release mooring clamps on Slaasriithi remote fighters."

"Aye, aye, sir."

"Ms. Veriden?"

"Yeah?"

"Enter the override code Yiithrii'a'ash gave us nine hours ago."

"Done. Slaasriithi drone fighters are now under our direct control."

"Very well. Remember the drill, Dora: every time we give our drones an order—"

"—I wait approximately four seconds to send it to the Slaasriithi 'cannonballs.' Until you say otherwise."

"Exactly. And pass the word: all crew strap in, seal duty suits, helmets ready for autoseal in the event of pressure loss." He selected the direct line to Engineering. "Phil?"

"Friel here."

"In less than twenty minutes, I'm going to need *full* power output at a moment's notice. Can you do that without destroying the plant?"

"I think I can get to full output in under fifteen seconds, Commodore. This Slaasriithi powerplant is—well, it's pretty feckin' amazing. Er, sir."

"Duncan?"

"Already in the bubble and in the sensuit. How do you see this going down, Commodore?"

Riordan watched the distance between *Puller* and the Ktor patrol hunter diminish rapidly. "They'll cut their lead over us until they are confident that we are still out of effective laser range. Then they'll start using their laser to pick off our remote platforms. They might use their railgun against us, too, or even some missiles. But they'll want to eliminate all our other pieces from the game board first."

"So my job is...?"

"You're going to start with low-velocity railgun rounds. Flechettes set for widest possible dispersal. I want to complicate their maneuver options, create some deadzones."

"Commodore, I know you know this, but—space is a mighty big place."

"Yes, I do know that. I'm not looking to box them in: there's no way to do that in free space. But I want our computers to choose some of their more likely maneuver alternatives and then know our target won't go there. That makes our predictive algorithms just a little bit better. And right now, I'll take every advantage I can get."

"Anything else?"

"Yes. When you get the word to start firing, put one kinetic penetrator round on target every fifteen seconds."

"It will be blind luck—or more likely, an enemy malfunction—for any of those to ever hit."

"I know, but I'm betting that they'll tackle intermittent attacks with PDF laser fire; they won't bother to evade."

"Then what are we achieving?"

"You—and the new computer—are going to get a good long look at their laser-emanation points from a variety of different angles. Because the first thing I'm going to ask for you to do with our laser is to see if you can put one of their blisters out of commission."

Solsohn's response was preceded by a low whistle. "That's a pretty tough shot, sir."

"You forget, Major: we're working with all Slaasriithi systems, now. If we don't give the Ktor any reason to alter their course or attitude, your first shot should have maximum accuracy, based on multiple observations."

"And after that, you'll want me to saturate them will railgun rounds?"

"Yes."

"Missiles?"

"Full spreads, one after the other, until we're dry."

"Got it. Gunnery is ready, sir."

Riordan looked in the holotank, watched the distance numbers race toward zero, glanced around the bridge.

Yaargraukh, who had apparently entered while he'd been busy coordinating the coming action, looked back at him steadily.

Riordan nodded toward him. "Do you have any suggestions on the coming engagement?"

"No," the Hkh'Rkh replied calmly. "But I have a question."

"That might be even better. What is it?"

"Why?"

Riordan, his mind speeding down preset grooves of tactical and technical orchestration, bumped to a rough halt. "Why what?" he repeated.

Yaargraukh waved a claw toward the holograph, kept his voice low. "Why this pursuit? Why an attack in which you are willing to expend all your remaining munitions—to achieve what? They are fleeing. They are beaten. What is your purpose in this?"

Hkh'Rkh speech inflections were profoundly different and the subtleties of their body language and facial expressions still eluded him, so Caine was uncertain whether his friend meant the question as a simple inquiry or subtle remonstration. Whichever it was, however, Riordan's answer was the same: "Mostly, because the ship in front of us is the Ktor's last combat-capable resource, and until we've disabled or destroyed it, I do not consider us safe.

"But secondly, this particular Ktoran ship and its crew hunted us down to the very doorstep of the Slaasriithi homeworld in an attempt to assassinate us before we could complete our mission as emissaries. I don't know why. When they failed in their first attempt, they landed on the planet where we crashed to try to destroy the survivors. Again, I don't know why. But here they are again, apparently behind the abduction and impressment of hundreds of people from Earth. And I still don't know why, although I can imagine strategies underlying all their actions.

"But there's one thing I *do* know: they are ruthless, perfidious killers. They infect children with terminal diseases so that they can manipulate their parents with the promise of a cure. They literally backstab noncombatants"—he pushed down an image of Elena Corcoran's face—"after they have given their promise of surrender. They let loose a mix of desperate and sociopathic soldiers upon Turkh'saar to kill civilians, all in the hopes of reigniting a war." Riordan leaned forward. "I hunt them now to stop them, Yaargraukh, to stop them the only way that I know how, given their own habits."

"You mean, to kill them."

"Yes."

Yaargraukh considered, pony-nodded once, deeply. "I

understand. I would do no less, having seen what you have. An enemy so inscrutably determined as this one must be destroyed when the chance presents itself."

"I'm glad you feel similarly," replied Caine, who meant it, but also knew that whether the Hkh'Rkh—or any one else—agreed with him was, ultimately, moot. Whether by chance or intent, these Ktor had put a crosshair not just on his back, but on his friends, his comrades, his loved ones. And that had to end. Now. "Dr. Sleeman, how long until the bogey reaches its laser's observed effective range?"

"Three minutes to our drones, seven minutes to us."

"Ms. Veriden, I want a two-tier formation of our drone assets. The Slaasriithi PIPs in the lead, the remote fighters three kiloklicks behind them. All sensors out to the peripheries."

"You want them to get active target locks, or—?"

"No, Ms. Veriden. I want those sensors ready to function as a phased array. I want maximum resolution and precision of targeting when we start using our laser."

"The Ktor will start smacking them down, Caine."

"I'm counting on it. And I'm willing to absorb those losses if they're inflicting them with their laser. But if they try to take them out with railgun munitions, use the PIPs to defend the sensor platforms."

"And if they try to take out our PDF drones?"

"That's when we use the Slaasriithi cannonballs to provide PDF cover for our more forward assets."

"And if they go after the cannonballs?"

"When they get that close, we'll give them something else to think about."

In the holoplot, the forward screen of Slaasriithi

PIPs and human sensor drones were arrayed in a rough disk; behind them, a smaller disk of Slaasriithi cannonballs followed: it looked like a salad plate trailing behind a dinner dish. To the rear of them all was the icon signifying *Puller* herself. The red mote that was the Ktor arrowed in like a knife, determined to drill through the center of the stack.

"Ktor have illuminated active sensors," Sleeman said. "Targeting our PDF drones."

Riordan nodded. "Evasive maneuvers for our drones, Ms. Veriden."

"Complying—but you know that won't save them."

"I do. But I want the Ktor to work for what they get—and give us a lot of time to look at their laser while they work."

The PDF drones began altering their vectors and thrust, which slightly diminished their rate of general advance, but eroded the ease with which the Ktor would focus a laser beam on any one point of their external ablative armor, and ultimately, the hull underneath. As the range decreased, and the focal intensity of the beam increased, this would become pointless: a hit would be a kill. But, like any prudent commander, the Ktor was taking enemy pieces off the table while his opponent was still powerless to mount an effective counterattack.

Caine smiled. *Just keeping shooting at them, asshole . . . .*

Dora looked up. "One gone."

Riordan nodded. "Dr. Sleeman, what sort of luck are our sensors having?"

"Modest, at best, sir. The Ktor hull seems to be coated with some kind of material that not only breaks up, but actively absorbs our sensor emissions. But I'm not seeing a corresponding increase in heat."

"High efficiency thermionic materials," Riordan muttered. "Converts heat directly into electricity."

"Also a great stealth tech," Sleeman added irritably. "Damned hard to get a lock on them, except when they're firing."

Riordan nodded. "Let's change our remote sensor configuration. Break them into three smaller, more widely separated phased arrays. Then aggregate the results of each."

Sleeman nodded. "Like a multitiered parallax system. That should clean up the targeting, but I think we'll need to get closer before we can depend upon that alone for a lock."

Riordan couldn't entirely suppress a smile. "Don't worry, Dr. Sleeman; we'll be getting closer."

Veriden looked up as he said it, a worried look on her face. "The second of our PIPs is gone. And they're shifting their laser over to the cannonballs—or trying to. They're also dodging railgun rounds, sir."

"Cannonballs are to evade and combine fires with our remaining PIPs to deflect the railgun rounds. Time until *Puller* enters the outer envelope of the Ktor's laser range?"

"One minute, sir."

In the holoplot, one of the cannonballs registered a hit, but was moving fast enough that the focal point of the enemy laser smeared across, rather than drilled into, its surface: minor damage, which was quickly tended to by the fighter's self-repairing systems. The human sensor and Slaasriithi PIP drones spread further out, the cannonballs pulling forward into the space

they vacated: the two disks became one, the smaller
one advancing to occupy the center of the larger
one. "Computer: plot effective range band of *Puller's*
original laser." A silver line glittered out from *Puller's*
blue icon, reaching halfway to the approaching red
icon. Which meant that the Ktor was almost within
the new laser's engagement envelope.

Pandora Veriden's voice was tight, irritated. "If you
have any plans for these cannonballs, you'd better use
them soon. We are less than one hundred seconds
from contact, and I don't know how much longer the
evasion subroutines and I are going to be able to—"

"Miss Veriden: all cannonballs, maximum thrust
toward the bogey, employing evasion pattern echo-nine.
All their weapons systems: continuous fire. Our PIPs
sole job is now to keep the railgun rounds off them."

"Caine, maximum evasion undercuts accuracy and
effectiven—"

"Just do it, Dora. Dr. Sleeman, I want the integrated
data from our sensor-ring slaved to Major Solsohn's
targeting routines in the gunnery bubble. Engineering?"

"Friel, here. Go."

"I need that power now."

"Pushing it to the red line, sir."

"Karam, let me know when you have enough power
for three gees of thrust."

Karam half turned. "Five seconds."

In the holoplot, one of the Slaasriithi cannonball
icons was limned in yellow, then orange, then disappeared. He scanned the remaining ones. "Dora, drop
Cannonball Two back a bit from the others."

"Done."

"We are at full power," Karam reported.

Riordan leaned far back, tried to relax. "On my mark, boost three gees for the bogey. Duncan, shift over to rapid fire on the railgun, but leave enough energy for the laser to discharge at full power. Dora, all cannonballs: continue firing, but cease evasion. Instruct them to ram the bogey."

"Ram the—?"

"Ram. That will keep their laser busy for a few seconds. And . . . mark."

The almost stately, predictable scene in the holoplot became a frenzy of dramatic, abrupt changes. The three remaining cannonballs ceased shimmying their way toward the Ktor, raced for it like heat-seeking missiles. The Ktor launched a flurry of missiles at them, along with streams of railgun rounds. The PIPs sent out reciprocal streams to counter them: the Ktor laser-blisters split their fire between the PIPs and the cannonballs. Despite appearing overwhelmed by foes, it was clear that, within seconds, the tremendous firepower of the Ktoran ship would overwhelm all the other systems—and needed to, lest the close range of the cannonballs' lasers or their collision courses bring the battle to an abupt and decisive end.

But strangest of all was to watch *Puller*'s glowing blue delta leap forward almost as fast as the cannonballs themselves. For a moment, there was no response to this dramatic change in the tactical picture—then the Ktor tried maneuvering briskly, reversing its four-gee thrust to diminish the rate of closure between the ships, and also, change its own vector.

But as it did so, the outward drifting scatter of faint sunflowers that marked the slowly expanding clouds of fragments seeded by the flechette rounds from *Puller*'s railgun impeded the Ktoran ship's ability to maneuver freely. It wasn't a profound effect, may have only cost the enemy a second or two, but given the speed with which events were unfolding, those seconds were crucial. The Ktor labored to find a path whereby it could open the range to the unprecedentedly swift corvette, buy time with which to bring its otherwise busy weapons to bear upon this sudden threat...

Riordan saw the silver ray indicating the limit of *Puller*'s original laser graze the enemy icon—"Duncan, do you have a counterfire solution on their laser?"

"Good as I can expect."

"Fire laser at full power—and launch missiles right after."

The last of the Slaasriithi PIPs flared amber and disappeared. Another of the cannonballs coded orange, began tumbling, its power indicator dark...

The deck seemed to hum under them, as if a giant tuning fork was vibrating along the length of *Puller*'s keel. Riordan looked to the mainscreen, saw nothing. Only if the Ktoran ship exploded would it be visible at this distance—and then, only as the brief twinkle of a new, quickly dying star.

But Melissa Sleeman told him what he had hoped to hear. "Hit on the bogey. Laser fire has dropped off. Outgassing detected. Cannot determine if it is atmosphere or fuel. Power output constan— Another hit. More outgassing."

Riordan glanced at the holoplot: the ship icons—his and the Ktor—were almost on top of each other. "Time to intercept?"

"Thirty seconds. Our missiles are nearing detonation

range. Bogey launching missiles—at us! Locked! Closing!"

Riordan started rapping out orders as fast as he could. "Cannonballs divert from ramming; commence counterboost. Laser to PDF mode. All excess power to railgun. Kinetic penetrators, maximum rate of fire at the bogey. Karam, continue accelerating; open the range once we pass. Dora—"

"I'm hitting the bogey with laser fire from the last two cannonballs. But the bastards have diverted some of their missiles to—"

On the screen, impossibly, Riordan saw a small speck winking at the far starboard edge: the enemy ship, evidently tumbling—whether as part of a maneuver or a consequence of the laser hits and outgassing, he could not tell. And then it was past. Riordan glanced at the holoplot, saw a small red pinprick—an enemy missile— lying atop *Puller*'s own icon. He tried to interrupt the stream of his own orders, to shout a warning—

Puller seemed to body block him from the rear, despite the fact he was strapped into an acceleration couch. The rear of his head throbbed in response, and his vision was blurry as, briefly, sound seemed to diminish and fade. Then it, and his vision, surged back: damage alarms blended in with the battle stations klaxon, and the world came back into focus. The rest of the crew had been similarly affected: they were reaching groggily for their controls. "Engineering," he yelled into the comms pickup. "Report."

There was no reply.

Shit. "Engineering, report your status."

A sudden burst of static, then Tina Melah's voice. "Melah here. We're okay, but—"

He cut her off—hated doing so, but first things first. "Dora, have the cannonballs cover us as we open the range. Melissa, status of bogey."

The picture in the holoplot matched what she described. "Two of our missiles detonated within effective range of bogey, but no contact hits. All others were destroyed. Two of our railgun rounds hit her aft: effect unknown. However, their energy output has dropped to twenty percent and they have begun to drift."

"Our drones?"

Dora shrugged. "Cannonball Two is the last one functioning. It has retroboosted and is closing on the bogey once again."

"Karam, how much thrust do we have?"

"Pretty much all of it. Avionics, too. I'm good to go."

"Duncan?"

"Our laser—well, I should say the Slaasriithi laser—and the PDF system knocked down all of their missiles. We were so close, they didn't get a chance to build a lot of delta vee. But one came pretty close."

"Yeah, I think we all felt that. Systems?"

"Good to go. I'm looking at full function across the board."

That was the moment that Riordan realized that his armpits were not merely damp; they were dripping. *Okay: next step, then.* "Dora, bring Cannonball Two to within five hundred kilometers of the bogey and commence sustained laser fire into her engine decks."

Riordan felt several pairs of eyes turn upon him. "Sir?" asked Dora, too surprised to remember to be flippant or disrespectful.

"I don't want to destroy that ship; I want to neutralize it. No power or maneuver capability."

Karam turned around as far as his straps permitted. "Yes, sir, but—five hundred kilometers? At that range, if they've got any offensive capability left, just PDF fire control, they'll be able to—"

"Five hundred kilometers," Riordan said sharply, staring at Dora and then Karam.

Both of whom shrugged. "Cannonball Two firing during approach. Closing to five hundred kilometers. As ordered."

Riordan leaned back. "Thank you. Duncan?"

"Sir?"

"If the bogey attacks our cannonball, I suspect it will be a lot easier to hit the PDF system that takes it under fire now."

"Of course, sir. The ship is drifting and—and they're engaging now."

In the holoplot, Cannonball Two, still at a range of thirty-seven hundred kilometers, registered two hits by one of the Ktor's laser blisters, albeit at vastly reduced power. The small green spherical icon became orange.

Dora spoke through an exasperated sigh. "Cannonball Two is now offline: damage to maneuver and weapon systems."

Riordan smiled. "Very good. Major Solsohn, please be good enough to scan the Ktor and eliminate any remaining laser blisters."

Even Duncan sounded perplexed. "Yes, sir. Accessing. Engaging." There were a few seconds of silence. "Done, sir. I'm getting some scatter on my targeting scans, sir: she may be outgassing more energetically now."

Sleeman nodded. "Confirm that, sir. And her powerplant is dead. From what I can tell, she's running off capacitor or batteries."

"If our guesses about Ktoran technology are at all accurate, it will be the former, and then the latter when the capacitor is drained." Riordan sat forward slightly. "Flight Officer, keeping to the bogey's aft, commence a gradual approach to Cannonball Two."

Karam turned and stared. "Sir, with all due respect, did you misspeak? Are you sure you want—"

"Cannonball Two," Riordan affirmed crisply. "I am not in a rush to conduct a boarding action against a Ktoran wreck. I'm happy to let them outgas, get cold, wear down their suits' life support. And while we wait, it's time for us to rendezvous with Cannonball Two."

"For repairs?" Sleeman asked.

Riordan smiled. "No. For salvage." He glanced at Dora. "You said number two went dark, correct?"

"Yes, sir," Veriden said, a slow sly smile pushing up one corner of her mouth. "That is correct. No power. And no transponder signal either, if that's what you're thinking."

Riordan nodded. "It is indeed. Now: let's go grab the technology that I strongly suspect Yiithrii'ah'aash meant to slip us under the table."

"What?" Sleeman's query ended on a very high note.

Karam had started smiling, too. "Yeah, he'd have never offered us direct control over the cannonballs unless he meant for us to arrange a 'lost' fighter that's intact enough for us to examine. Shame it had to be splashed by the Ktor, first."

Riordan shrugged. "There was no avoiding it. It had to go offline legitimately. What happened to it after that—the 'catastrophic failure' that vaporized it—was tragic. Wouldn't you agree, Dr. Sleeman?"

She looked and sounded thoroughly unamused.

"Utterly tragic. Now, do you want me to raise the Ktoran vessel, Commodore?"

Riordan smiled again. "Yes. Please do."

Idrem touched the faceplate of his pressure helmet to Brenlor's. "All but two are dead in engineering. The coolant line severed by the Aboriginal railgun has emptied and vented; there is not enough left in the system to attempt a restart. Also, cryonics is completely unusable."

"Cold sleep is no escape from this." Brenlor's voice was constricted: the blood running from both his nostrils was very dark, and he would not take his hand from the wound just beneath his clavicle: debris had pierced him there. If he was bleeding from that wound, it remained inside his suit.

Idrem collected himself. "I do not convey the condition of the cryonics because I think it would be advisable to use them. I am simply making a complete report. Which I resume. All six laser blisters have been either destroyed or disabled. We cannot power our active sensors, our external communications, or charge our railgun. Our lascom array is gone, as is our primary radio dish. We could launch missiles, but have no way to target or control them. We have lost seventy percent of our atmosphere. If we restrict our access to the bridge, the ready room, and its fresher, we have approximately fifteen hours of life support remaining."

Brenlor laughed in response to that—and surprised himself by coughing up a massive, dark blood clot, followed by a rush of bright red. "You see," he said, sputtering, "I am not concerned by our remaining life support. It will be more than sufficient for me."

"My Srin—my Hegemon, you are not—"

"I am clear-headed enough to know that I am dying. I was uncertain of that up until this moment, but I—and you—may be assured of my fate." He let his hand slip away from the fragment that was protruding from his breastbone: where it cut into his spacesuit, it curved wickedly downward. Toward the heart. "I am unable to effect sufficient vasoconstriction, Idrem; I suspect because I do not have sufficient blood pressure remaining. I am growing lightheaded, but I can feel wetness all along my body. I suspect I am swimming in my own blood: only the smart collar is keeping it out of my helmet."

Idrem nodded. "So this is why you bid us seal our suits, even once we stabilized life support—so the crew could not see how badly wounded you are."

"Partly, but the main reason was that we may speak, helmet to helmet, with our radios off. That was essential."

Idrem understood. "Yes. Our crew, the Aboriginals, would rebel—even at the risk of their own lives—if they knew what must occur now."

"Precisely. The Terrans will want to seize our technology. Do you believe we can last long enough to bait the enemy ship alongside?"

Idrem shook his head. "Brenlor, the Terran commander is no fool. And he does not presume that we are. He will not come so close that we can ensure their destruction through our own." *And you will not live long enough to see it.*

"Then how do you intend to do it?"

Idrem thought. "The unlaunched missiles in the magazine that feeds the ventral rotary launcher. I shall remove one of the warheads, access the detonation circuitry, and trigger the charge with a simple battery pulse." He thought of Nezdeh as he said it, realized that if he thought of her again, he might lose his resolve. He only needed four or five more minutes of discipline. He could keep from thinking about her for that long. He believed. He hoped.

He stood. "I shall scuttle the ship now. Every moment is an opportunity for fate to thwart that plan in some unforeseen fashion—which would convey Ktor technology into the hands of the Aboriginals. That must not happen. Farewell, Brenlor Srin Perekmeres. It has been my honor to—"

Brenlor reached up, grabbed his shoulder: Idrem was startled by how weak his grasp had become. "Can you not rig a remote destruct device—or a timer, to ensure that you, at least, might escape? Surely, you do not wish to die. Surely, you and Nezdeh, together, could bring back House Perek—"

Idrem pushed away, drifted out of Brenlor's faltering grip. "No, my Srin, that path is not open to me. *Arbitrage* and *Uzhmarek* cannot return for me. And if they could, they must not. Our remaining ships are now outclassed by those of our foe. Clearly, the Slaasriithi *did* repair the human corvette we encountered at Disparity, using their own systems." *And I was a fool for persisting in the assumption that they would withhold their technology. Instead, they furnished the human craft with more than double its former thrust and five times as much power for its laser.* "Therefore, who is most likely to rescue me?" He pointed beyond the hull of *Red Lurker*. "The Aboriginals.

"Let us be reasonable and acknowledge that given

enough time, even if they must resort to truth-drugs, they can derange me to the point where I will babble, not knowing reality from dream. And what might I say in such a state? But moreover, what will my own DNA tell them?" He tapped his chest. "We are *homo imperiens* because of what is resident here. Shall we give that to them? Shall I be known as the Ktor who feared death so much, despite a lifetime of preparing to face it, that I forfeited our greatest advantages—our genetics and our technology—to our most dangerous adversaries?"

Idrem straightened. "No. I am no coward. And I shall not risk living with that shame—and of having Nezdeh learn it of me."

Brenlor's reaching hand fell, limp. Even through the visor of his helmet, he was clearly very pale. "You honor me, and all of us, Idrem Perekmeresuum." He coughed, nodded weakly. "And you are the better Ktor, of the two of us."

Idrem looked down at the dying Srin and replied, "Yes. I know." Then he kicked off the deck, drifting toward the ship's magazine.

Chapter Sixty-One

Nezdeh Srina Perekmeres saw the green chevron that signified *Red Lurker* fade from the faux 3-D plot on the bridge of the *Arbitrage*. She waited, long enough to be sure that the icon had not momentarily blanked as the hologlobe refreshed its data, then closed her eyes for a moment. She let the sounds of the bridge fade away, then fade back in, and thought: *this is what the universe sounds like, feels like, when I know that Idrem is no longer in it.* It was not a pleasant feeling, but she had been accustomed to it in the years before she had met Idrem. She would get accustomed to it once again. Resolved to and assured of her self control, she opened her eyes.

Beside her, Zurur Deosketer had bowed her head slightly. "They are gone."

Standing across the tacplot, Tegrese Hreteyarkus pounded her fists down on the rim of the electronic chart-table. "It cannot be."

"It is," Nezdeh replied.

"The destruction of the ship does not mean the destruction of all its crew," Zurur said calmly.

Tegrese's eyes widened. "Exactly! It is likely that at least Brenlor and Idrem found a way to escape. A rescue will be difficult, but—"

"It will also be pointless: they are dead."

"How do you know?" For once, Tegrese sounded wounded and desperate, rather than contentious.

"Because," Nezdeh explained through a sigh. "I received a message from Idrem just after *Red Lurker* was first hit."

Tegrese frowned. "And he knew then that the whole crew was doomed?"

"That was not the nature of the message. It was a single-character code. Its meaning was, 'I shall take care of you.'"

Tegrese frowned. "And how did you become the beneficiary of this message?"

"How else?" Nezdeh gestured toward jur-Omrethe, the huscarle who was manning the comms.

"Allow me to rephrase, Srina. How is it that you and Idrem had a private battle-code at all?"

Nezdeh straightened, stared at her. "He and I arranged it beforehand. Of course."

"Without the knowledge of the Srin who was to have become our Hegemon?"

"Again, of course." *It would not have been of much use otherwise, you dolt.* Watching as anger began to displace the fear and pain in Tegrese's face—*a common substitution among the emotionally stunted*—Nezdeh leaned across the table, made her voice sharp. "So tell me, what if *Red Lurker* was not destroyed, but merely dead in space, as it was for minutes before it was clearly scuttled? What would we have had to do then?"

"Why, rescue the Srin and Idrem!"

Nezdeh shook her head. "You miss the point. We would still have had to journey to *Red Lurker*—and risk our own destruction doing so, even if we knew that the whole crew had perished."

Zurur nodded. "We would have had to destroy the equipment. And the ship itself."

"Correct," Nezdeh affirmed loudly. "We cannot allow our technology to fall into the hands of the Aboriginals. That is what Idrem meant by his signal, 'I will take care of you.' He was indicating that he would scuttle the ship and destroy all the technology aboard."

"You mean—they killed themselves? What madness is—?"

Nezdeh put her hand on her sidearm. "There is no madness here, except the risks you take with your life by accusing your superiors of incompetence, Tegrese Hreteyarkus. My patience is at an end."

"You would execute me?"

"Or challenge you, if you prefer." Nezdeh shrugged. "It makes no difference to me; you would be dead in either event. But in either event, it would be a loss we cannot afford. It is bad enough our enemies continue to diminish our numbers; let us not do it to ourselves."

Either the logic of Nezdeh's words or her indifferent certitude in asserting that further insolence would result in Tegrese's death caused a change in the posture of the woman facing the last Srina of House Perekmeres. Tegrese's shoulders slumped slightly. She frowned, nodded.

Nezdeh carefully managed her breath in the second that followed, felt a silence building, partly out of the grim shock of their suddenly changed circumstances, partly out of the uncertainty of what to do or say next, and partly out of their collective awareness that no one had lost more than Nezdeh.

Idrem's face—beside her, across from her, under her, over her—played like a collage of images before her mind's eye, which she shut. Hard. *No time for that now. No time for it ever, perhaps. The First Breedmothers' warnings are true. Emotions like love make us vulnerable to disappointment, to loss, which in turn weakens the will to power and the determination to persevere. So, you old hags of myth, perhaps you are right about the pain love may bring. But you are wrong in your prediction that its loss slays those who knew the piercing of its sharp joys. I am stronger than that, than your finger-wagging fears. I am Nezdeh, last Srina of House Perekmeres, and I shall lead us forward.*

As if putting that resolve to an immediate test, Zurur asked, "What is your plan, Nezdeh?" Her tone held much curiosity but no fear.

They always think I have a plan for every eventuality. Even this. Which was why Idrem had observed, on multiple occasions, that although the fortunes of the House were marginally better with Brenlor alive, they would not be significantly harmed by his demise. *Ironic that it came from Idrem: only now do we see that it was he whom we—and I—could not readily do without.* But he had been correct in asserting that the few remaining Ktor of their House looked to Nezdeh for stability, cleverness, thoroughness. When Brenlor announced a plan, they were excited, but that was simply because those announcements meant action. As soon as that excitement passed, their eyes always drifted toward Nezdeh, because if she evinced calm confidence in that plan, then they did as well, all doubts assuaged. And she had to play that same card now, to bring them through this dark moment.

Nezdeh took her hand from her sidearm, folded her arms as she thought out loud, but carefully, slowly, so that she would not need to revise any of her words. This was to be, ultimately, not so much a brainstorming session, as a proclamation. "The first question we must ask is whether there is even a chance for the House to be restored, without Brenlor. The answer, technically, is yes. We all know it is more common for Breedmothers to hold supreme power in a House, even though its male Hegemon remains its official ruler. However, there have also been women who sat in the Hegemon's Chair." Naturally, the Breedmothers always advised their best protéges to resist the temptation to strive for that place of political dominion. Males were useful figureheads, frequently because it ensured that they were the ones who ended their days encountering Fate's headsmen. If they held a slight edge in the day-to-day authority they exerted, they were effectively inconsequential when it came to the continuity and duration of a House's true power. Both genetically and strategically, even the smallest Family depended upon its Srinas and Breedmothers. The alternative had been proven several times within living memory: when governance and inter-House diplomacy was left to the aggression-maximized males, the Ktoran Sphere fell to bickering, lost cultural and political coherence.

Tegrese sounded awed, surprised, and envious all at the same time. "Are you claiming the Hegemon's Chair for yourself, then?"

She hadn't meant to—exactly—but there was no alternative. "I do—because I must. The remaining male Evolved among us, Vranut and Ulpreln Baltheker, are promising, but only that: they are young and unproven. Only I carry the rank of Srina. And Brenlor named me his successor." She smiled. "But I see no Hegemon's Chair in my future, Tegrese. The irony—to style myself a ruler when in fact I am now little more than a pirate baroness—is too great for me to bear, or for you and others not to laugh at. I wish neither. So I will not take the title of Hegemon, though I may exert that authority, until our wanderings are over and we have a home again."

"That could be a long time," Tegrese muttered.

"It might be," Nezdeh agreed. "But first we must live through the coming days and weeks." She straightened to her full height. "So, the stratagem that brought us to this system is beyond recovery. Consequently, flight is our only option. We must mate the *Arbitrage* to *Uzhmarek* as quickly as possible and then commence preacceleration immediately. And we must presume that the Slaasriithi and Aboriginals will pursue us all the way."

"And to where shall we shift?" Zurur asked.

Nezdeh's glance took in their last Intendant, Sehtrek, who was at the helm. Fearing what might be unfolding as *Red Lurker* came under attack, she had cleared the bridge of Aboriginals: no reason to let them see that Ktor could, in fact, be defeated. "We have little choice: Sigma Draconis."

"Sigma Draconis?" Tegrese was halfway to shouting it before she remembered either Nezdeh's threat, or her childhood lessons about mastery of one's own demeanor leading to mastery of others. "Tlerek Srin Shethkador is there," she finished more coolly.

"Indeed. And that is why it is our destination."

"You would treat with the offspring of the architects of our Extirpation?"

"I would if he is our last option, and right now, he is."

"And what can we offer him of value?"

"Advance knowledge of what happened here, and how, and why. The humans and the Slaasriithi have won. They will report these events, and other clues they found in this system, soon enough. I suspect they will be heading to Sigma Draconis also, to share that knowledge. I suspect that Shethkador would find it useful to know what news they might be bringing and when. We can tell him that, and he can take steps to destroy the bearers of that information. For if he cannot silence the Terrans and their new allies, his situation may become untenable."

Sehtrek stood. "If the Srina will allow—"

"You are allowed, Sehtrek." *Fate, by this time next month, we may be assessing you for Elevation. Which, admittedly, is overdue.*

Sehtrek approached the plotting table. "How does the information from this system make Shethkador's situation untenable?"

"Tlerek Srin Shethkador was a Ktoran agent on Earth, passing among the Aboriginals as one of their own kind. It was his responsibility to ensure that the war there went according to the Autarchs' plans. Obviously, it did not. He was to be retrieved from Terran custody when *Ferocious Monolith* reached Sigma Draconis, one shift after we hijacked *Red Lurker* and struck out on our own. Since no ship has passed through Turkh'saar bearing news of a final peace settlement, I suspect he is still present in that system, awaiting, and possibly trying to influence, the resolution of those negotiations.

"When he learns what has happened in this system, of how it reveals the Ktoran Sphere's interference in local affairs not just recently, but for centuries, he will lose whatever political cachet he may have retained and built over the course of the armistice talks between the humans and the Arat Kur. He will have failed in his mission, and there will be flagrant violations of the Accord for which he will be held accountable."

Sehtrek nodded. "Yet, he was not the architect of those violations, the ones of which we bear news."

Nezdeh shook her head. "That will not matter. You must embrace the full link between success and dominion, Sehtrek, if you hope to Elevate. In short, Tlerek Shethkador had the title and the power to dictate the actions of the Ktoran Sphere in this region of space. It does not matter which Family or House actually perpetrated the violations: he will be held accountable. Just as he would have accrued all the honors had he succeeded. The absolute connection between highest rank and full responsibility ensure that our leaders are vigilant and cunning. And if the Terrans succeed in bringing evidence of what they uncovered in this system to Sigma Draconis, he will be held responsible by our enemies, and by the Sphere itself.

"So, the earlier he is made aware, the greater the chance he might be able to intercept the humans and Slaasriithi. And destroy them."

Sehtrek frowned. "That will create quite an incident in itself."

"Yes, it will," Nezdeh allowed, "but far less than if he does not. He can justify his actions by manufacturing some incident, some case of mistaken sensor readings that compels him to destroy the enemy ships. But if he does not act, there will be no explaining away the reports the Aboriginals will bring: of lowbreeds who were taken hostage on Earth more than a century and a half ago, of the crash site placed on Turkh'saar by the Sphere, or of the aftermath of our failed attempt to neutralize both the kidnapped lowbreeds and Terrans sent to recover them."

Tegrese folded her arms. "So. What would you hope to get from Shethkador in return for this warning?"

"At worst, extra fuel and safe passage—for right now, we lack both. At best, influence and interest in cooperation."

"Cooperation? With him?"

"Yes, with anyone whose interests coincide with ours, at the moment. And if his situation in Sigma Draconis becomes untenable, he too may need to flee."

"And we would take him on as a renegade?"

"I doubt he would come without significant protection, without some ship of his own. But yes—if that's what it took for him to fuel us and ready us for departure before he lost his authority."

"And then what?" Zurur asked quietly.

And then, Zurur, I shall pause and I shall think: long and hard, Nezdeh answered silently. The huscarles who brought the *Uzhmarek*—Omrethe, Karsekot, Mnarethem, Jelkrethuun, Haddesh—would, like Sehtrek, need to be Elevated, even though great deeds should precede such recognition. Once that was accomplished,

House Perekmeres' total population would amount to four females and seven males. Including its Srina.

And once your ranks have swollen to such a host, what world shall you conquer first? What alliances shall you deign to make? What armies and fleets shall you deploy to compel the Autarchs to restore your House? Nezdeh did not allow herself the bitter smile she felt pushing forward from behind her clenched teeth. What Srin or Srina who still held the title had ever been faced with such enormous challenges as these, such daunting odds? None.

But of course, that was also an immense opportunity. What Srin or Srina, let alone Hegemon, had ever fought their way up from such dire beginnings to claim true dominion? Again, none.

Very well: I shall set the new standard. I shall be the one of whom they write tales. I shall succeed—no matter what I must do.

She let herself smile, saw the others around the plotting table stare at her—because she knew her smile was no longer bitter, but terrifying.

As it should be.

Chapter Sixty-Two

OUTER SYSTEM, BD+56 2966

Caine, backed by Bannor, Melissa, and Yaargraukh, was waiting at the bay doors on *Tidal-Drift-Instaurator-to-Shore-of-Stars* when they finally opened. But instead of moving inward, Riordan had to stand back: Lost Soldiers and Cold Guards alike, minor wounds wrapped with gauze or, in some cases, rags, burst out, carrying stretchers. The second stretcher was being paced by Peter Wu, despite that fact that his left thigh was splinted. Riordan smiled, relieved to see Wu, discovered he wasn't even looking up: his eyes did not leave the figure on the stretcher.

That figure, Susan Phillips, waved weakly with her left hand. "I'm afraid I can't give you a proper salute, Commodore. Right arm is a bit scraped up."

Riordan smiled. Her injured arm was not merely scraped: it was thickly wrapped and strapped tightly to the side. More extensive dressings around her midriff were spotted with fresh blood. He placed a gentle hand on her left shoulder. "Carry on, Ms. Phillips."

She mumbled something in response as her head

sank back against the folded fatigue jacket that was her pillow.

Peter met Riordan's gaze, nodded somberly, resumed walking on. Then he stopped, turned, let the stretcher get a little further ahead as he stared at Caine. "Just in case, so you know—she was magnificent."

Riordan sought for words, nodded when none came.

Peter turned and followed her stretcher.

"My God," Riordan breathed, stepping aside as the stretchers continued to pour into the Slaasriithi ship.

Bannor stepped closer. "You're looking a little pale, boss."

"I should. I gave the orders that led to . . . to this."

"I was right there, giving the orders with you, Cai—"

Riordan cut the air with his hand. "My command, my calls, my responsibility."

"It's not that simple, Caine."

Riordan turned to look at him as the last of the stretchers passed. "Isn't it?"

Melissa Sleeman folded her arms. "It's not your fault, sir. You were doing your job. And we're alive to talk about it."

"Not all of us, Doctor. Not by a long shot." Caine shook his head. "Besides, it's not a question of what we did right or wrong. It's about the weight we feel—we *should* feel—when the orders we give cost lives. It's about the weight of those dead. On our backs. For as long as we live."

Yaargraukh breathed out slowly: a faint tone accompanied his words. "We Hkh'Rkh know this feeling, have a special word for it that does not translate well into any of your languages. 'Memorial haunting' comes closest: that we must carry the spirits of those who died in our command with us until we, ourselves, die. They make our lives heavier not because of any flaw in our deeds or our orders, but because *they* died following them. And the life we live afterward must make us the . . . the worthy vessels of their honor." Yaargraukh's fluting undertone became an annoyed phlegm-rattle. "I have not explained it well."

"Sounds pretty clear to me," Bannor mumbled. "And pretty familiar."

Riordan nodded, watched the last of the troops file off Wedge Two. "We're late for the meeting. Let's not keep Yiithrii'ah'aash waiting."

Yiithrii'ah'aash concluded by pointing to the mauve-colored spindle that represented the now-mated *Arbitrage* and Ktoran shift-tug. "And because of their vector, we feel confident that they will be shifting to Sigma Draconis, thirty-six hours ahead of us."

"How do you come to that conclusion?" Bannor asked.

Yiithrii'ah'aash extended a tendril, circled the end of the projected preacceleration track: a white ring appeared around the terminus of the glowing golden line. "This is the space-time region where this system's superstring connection—or you might prefer 'entanglement'—with Sigma Draconis is most susceptible to the transmission you call 'shift.'"

Yaargraukh leaned toward the Slaasriithi translator with which he had been provided: he spoke slowly, carefully. "Could the Ktoran course be a ruse, so that we might believe we are following them to Sigma Draconis but once there, find ourselves to be deceived?"

Yiithrii'ah'aash let two fingers trail through the air

like calming streamers. "Possible, but unlikely. The increased energy costs to shift to other locations from this point will reduce their range—and therefore, their destination options—dramatically. Unless they mean to wander along a sequence of systems that have no appreciable populations or facilities, they would either be moving deeper into Arat Kur or Hkh'Rkh territory. And after what you discovered on Turkh'saar, I suspect they will not willingly follow such a course."

Melissa shrugged. "Sigma Draconis is Arat Kur space, too. The very heart of it."

One half of Yiithrii'ah'aash's bifurcated tail curled then drooped. "Yes, it is. But it is also the site of much political activity, presently. So I would be quite surprised if the Ktoran shift-cruiser last present there, *Ferocious Monolith*, has departed; if it has, I presume it has been replaced. In either case, they may be fleeing there to seek the assistance from their own kind. But if they do not travel to Sigma Draconis, then we shall have arrived at a most propitious location to commence a search. Even if a truce has been concluded, your own fleet will still be there in strength. And I am sure Arat Kur shift-carriers could be tasked to assist."

Bannor folded his arms. "The Arat Kur and the Ktor were allies in the last war, Ambassador."

"So they were, Major, but that was before the Ktor revealed themselves to be another branch of humanity, the one that almost wiped out the Arat Kur, more than ten millennia ago. I suspect the Arat Kur may be willing to cooperate in light of that changed context."

Bannor smiled, glanced at Caine.

Who had been careful to say nothing, was waiting to hear Yiithrii'ah'aash close his part of the meeting.

Because when he did, when he had no more items to cover, it would mean that Riordan's guess had been correct: that the Slaasriithi ambassador had indeed wanted his Terran allies to squirrel away the wreckage of Cannonball Two, which they had reported as having been reduced to "inconsequential debris."

Yiithrii'ah'aash waved all his tendrils in the air as if miming rainfall. "I have finished. What, if any, topics do you wish to discuss?"

Okay, so we get to keep the remains of the cannonball and dissect its secrets. Let's move along to a very different topic, then—"Yiithrii'ah'aash, we're curious about how Turkh'saar figured into Accord policy before now. But we are uncertain about how, or if, we may go about asking our questions."

"What is the cause of your uncertainty?"

"Well, according to the Fourth Accord, it is unlawful for any species to share information about any other species. But when it comes to Turkh'saar, every race is already involved. The Custodians were responsible for overseeing the system originally. It was first explored by the Arat Kur, but they left it for the Hkh'Rkh to develop. Which is a pretty confusing detail, since that means the Hkh'Rkh were already in a codominium arrangement with a member of the Accord before they were invited to a Convocation. Then, your people struck at military targets here during the late and undeclared war, which would constitute a double territorial violation. And now you've returned with us so that we can extract humans from Earth, but who were placed here even earlier by Ktoran trespassers."

Yiithrii'ah'aash's reply was a rippling purr: amusement? "It is a most atypical situation, and so is one of the few matters that have been approved for open discussion by the Custodians. You may freely share what you know or conjecture about other species in regard to the political irregularities of Turkh'saar. As may we."

Riordan nodded gratefully. "So, since the Custodians oversee 'protected species' that have not attained interstellar travel, they must have known when the Hkh'Rkh were preparing to journey here, and were about to encounter the Arat Kur."

"You are correct, although the Custodians were not present for the first encounter. The Arat Kur had previously been enjoined by the Custodians to permit the Hkh'Rkh to build a refueling facility so that they could return to their home system when they eventually explored BD+56 2966. The Custodians were surprised, and pleased, that the Arat Kur instead offered to make the system a codominium. The Slaasriithi Great Ring was pleased as well, although some of us had misgivings."

"You being among them?"

"No. That transpired in the lifecycle before mine. But the Arat Kur have never been known for spontaneous generosity. And we had some knowledge of the Hkh'Rkh through reports, enough to know that they were the most aggressive and predatory intelligent species that had ever been encountered. The more cautious of our leaders on Beta Aquilae considered the Arat Kur offer to make this system a codominium to be uncharacteristic. In the extreme."

"And that's all you know about it?"

"It is."

"Then, with your permission, Dr. Sleeman would like to share some of her findings with you—and with

Advocate Yaargraukh. They may alter the understanding of what happened here on Turkh'saar in the past."

"I have no objections," Yiithrii'ah'aash assured him with a blithe cascade of tendrils.

"Nor I," Yaargraukh followed more cautiously. "Although I can no longer be titled 'Advocate,' I think."

Riordan nodded, looked at Sleeman. "Doctor?"

Sleeman tapped her palmtop: the Slaasriithi holo-projector summoned several floating images into existence. Sleeman reached toward one, twisted her wrist: the image enlarged, stood forth from the others and began to turn slowly. The bright parts of it appeared to be a scattering of debris, like pieces of a broken plate, several of which retained some of the curve of their original shape. The rest of the image was layers of gray, fading down to charcoal black.

"When my team and I took cover from the railgun attack at the crash site, we chose the deepest tunnels, which were clustered near the start of the impact path. They had not yielded much in the way of useful samples but, having nothing to do other than wait and hope for the best, we used our time there to conduct the densitometer scans which you see before you now. I should point out, Ambassador, that our densitometer technology is very crude, so the resolution of these images is vastly inferior to your own.

"As it turns out, it was fortuitous that fate conspired to send us into the deepest reaches of these tunnels, and for long enough to complete several focused scans, which we have since integrated to give a more reliable, composite picture. Otherwise, we would have never found these." She touched the bright, curved pieces of debris. "As you will note from the scale at the bottom, the largest dimension of some of these fragments is a bit over seven meters. They are the deepest of all the pieces, with most of the smaller debris clustered above them. Judging from the angle of probable impact, this supports the hypothesis that this is the hull of a space-craft which brought its nose up at the last second to land flat along its keel. The curved pieces are ventral hull sections that stripped off and were embedded in the ground. The lighter wreckage is probably from the decks above, which were subject to extreme compression, since they were mostly empty, air-filled spaces filled with lightly built components."

Bannor rubbed his chin. "What a mess."

"It certainly looks that way, but in fact, a ship made of such heavy materials as these should have hit harder and made a much bigger mess. Instead, the degree and pattern of damage, and length of the impact trail, do not indicate that the craft was traveling at high speed. Our best estimates project that it was unpowered at the time it came down, that it did not fall from a height of greater than four hundred meters, and that its attitude was normative during its descent."

Yaargraukh sounded hesitant. "The data you postulate, if accurate, more closely describes a descent on a controlled glide, not a 'crash.' And a controlled glide, along with the craft's immense size, suggests it was built for atmospheric flight only, not space operations."

Sleeman nodded. "That is exactly what we thought, and why we doubted our initial hypothesis. Until, that is, we conducted a scan even further back along the impact path. Where we discovered this."

Sleeman swung a hand at the image, pushed at another with a turn of her wrist: the current image fell back and stopped rotating; the new one expanded and moved forward, starting to spin as it did so. In this image, there were fewer bright objects and many more charcoal-black masses. Sleeman grabbed one of the bright fragments off the corner of the rotating image. It grew, and as it did, it became more angular, finally appearing like the junked leg of a robot. But, given the scale, it would have been close to eight meters long, if it had been fully extended.

Sleeman folded her hands. "That is a landing leg. Upon confirming this, we knew we were looking at the wreck of a spacecraft of some kind."

Bannor gestured toward the image. "One that apparently lost control while trying to land."

"Actually, no. What you see here—part of the aft port strut—was still within the periphery of the hull debris which was just a bit below it. So at the time of the crash, the leg was still folded in the undeployed position."

"I do not understand," the Slaasriithi objected mildly. "You project a spacecraft. You project that its velocity at the time of impact was no greater than what it would have accumulated during a descent from four hundred meters, at a shallow angle, and with enough control to bring up its bow just prior to hitting the surface. Yet it made no attempt to extend its landing legs. Could it have suffered a complete power loss?"

"We wondered that, too, Ambassador. So when we got to *Puller*, we did a little research on that topic. What the math tells us is this: if a craft this heavy lost all electrical power, as well as thrust, at an altitude of four hundred meters, it should not have been able to maintain a steady attitude or make a controlled crash. Even if its hull was a lifting body, which might provide it with some glide potential, it would need either physical controls like flaps, or active control like thrust, in order to make a smooth descent. This is true for any technology we have seen to date.

"Besides, there's another problem with the 'failed landing' scenario. Even the largest aerodynamic hulls we know of are not meant to land on planets. They are streamlined so that they can skim the upper atmosphere while deploying subcraft, as well as maintaining stable flight during close approaches to the edges of a gas giant while trailing a refueling drogue. However, many such ships *are* equipped with extendable landing legs for use on worlds with thin or no atmosphere. So while the landing legs would be consistent with their construction, an attempt to land on the surface of a larger planet such as Turkh'saar is not within their operational envelope.

"There was also a finding which suggested the wreck might be of Arat Kur origin. One of the soil elements we discovered at the bottom of two tunnels at the rear of the impact path was peculiar in both its complexity and novelty. Specifically, we detected trace elements of an advanced composite that human science did not even know existed just two years ago. It is a material that the Arat Kur use in the capacitors with which they store the energy they bleed off from their shift-drive. A layered wafer of ultraconductors and advanced thermionic materials, it is not as advanced as your own analogs, or the Ktor's, but far beyond anything we knew how to make."

Yiithrii'ah'aash's tendrils became suddenly motionless. "And, since you found this at the very beginning of the trough, and since the craft crashed tail-first, you conjecture that the deposition of this composite occurred when the engineering section was driven into the ground."

"That's what seems most logical to us, Ambassador."

Two of Yiithrii'ah'aash's tendrils snapped rigid. "I am aware of only one class of ship which is this large, which is streamlined to enter an atmosphere, and which has a shift-drive."

Sleeman nodded. "An Arat Kur shift-cruiser. We ourselves produced one ship like that for initial exploration—the *Prometheus*—but she's still in service. We obviously know it was not Hkh'Rkh. We have too little knowledge of Ktor and Dornaani ships to eliminate those possibilities, but from what we have been able to observe, the materials used in the construction of this one are well below either of their technological capabilities. And lastly, we must presume it is not yours because you seemed as surprised as we did when we discovered it. So, after that process of elimination, we decided to run forensic comparisons between the precise shape of the curved hull wreckage and that of the various models of Arat Kur shift-cruisers. And that resulted in our high-confidence identification of the wreckage.

"As it turns out, the Arat Kur have only lost two streamlined starships. Their first, prototype shift-ship was streamlined so that it had descent options if it was stranded in a distant system. It was, however entirely different in shape and dimensions from what we found on Turkh'saar. The curved sections of wreckage did not conform to it in any way.

"But the other lost ship was one of the Arat Kur's

earliest shift-cruisers, built approximately four hundred years ago. After only thirty years, it was declared obsolete and relegated to border surveys. During which service it was lost without trace."

Phlegm rolled slowly, reflectively, in Yaargraukh's long nasal passages. "Perhaps it was lost here, en route to an exploratory mission?"

"That was our first guess. But the Arat Kur records, both of their activities in this system and of the ship they lost, point to a different answer. The Arat Kur have maintained active, and then more recently, passive monitoring here ever since they discovered FTL. This system is a neighbor to their own homeworld. They learned shortly after their first interstellar mission— which was to this system—that the Hkh'Rkh homeworld is also adjacent. This became a major concern to the Arat Kur, who were inducted into the Accord within months of reaching Turkh'saar."

Yiithrii'ah'aash touched two tendrils together lightly. "This is true. If anything, it is an understatement. They were greatly disturbed by the fact that this system was the only one that was listed on the permitted paths of interstellar expansion for two species: theirs and the Hkh'Rkh. At the time, the latter was still a protected species without any immediate promise of achieving starflight. However, the Arat Kur foresaw difficulties in having to share the system, when the time came. But I am curious regarding one of your assertions, Dr. Sleeman. Specifically, how do you know that the ship on Turkh'saar was not, in fact, lost in this system as Yaargraukh suggests?"

Sleeman smiles. "The Arat Kur are as dedicated to keeping records and chronicles as your species is indifferent to them, Ambassador Yiithrii'ah'aash, and those records show that the ship in question was lost far away from here. It's also particularly well documented, since the disappearance of this ship—the *Katek Hud,* or *Far Journeyer*—cost the Arat Kur Homenest one of its favorite daughters: an explorer who opened more worlds to their species than any other, before or since. She was the captain when it was lost."

Yiithrii'ah'aash's tendrils, flat against the tabletop, rippled. "You have unusually complete records on your small ship, Doctor."

Sleeman steepled her fingers. "After the war, our intelligence services had access to the complete data-banks of approximately half the ships of the Arat Kur invasion fleet. Establishing the reliability of that data was among the first postwar intelligence tasks undertaken on Earth. The coherence and lack of inconsistencies left the analysts with no doubt as to its authenticity. And since Commodore Riordan's mission involved venturing into a system that was partly owned by the Arat Kur, our superiors deemed it prudent that we had all the data."

"Yes, but that data seems to be leading to con-jectures that are at odds with those implied by your first findings, Doctor. Specifically, before the railgun attack, you reported that the ship had apparently been crashed into a waiting hole, or trough, in the ground. You conjectured that the purpose of this might have been to make it seem that the wreckage had been there for much longer than it actually had been, since it would be discovered at deeper sedimentary layers than those which dated from the time of its actual descent. But now you reveal that the ship can be almost conclusively proven to be one of Arat Kur manufacture, which crashed only three and a half centuries ago. If both of these assessments are accurate, then it seems that the Arat Kur attempt to disguise the actual date of the crash was extremely incompetent. Suspiciously so."

Sleeman nodded. "Yes. But there is another alternative: that the Arat Kur are not the ones who staged this 'crash.'"

Yaargraukh's eyes extended slightly. "Please explain, Doctor." He sounded somewhat—tense?

She nodded. "Firstly, let us set some context. Whoever staged this crash had no ability to control or predict precisely how or when it would be discovered, and so, had no way of knowing how carefully the site would be conserved during the process of excavation. It is entirely likely that, had the Hkh'Rkh who discovered it sunk just one or two more exploratory shafts, the all-important landing leg might have been found and removed. Similarly, had they been thorough enough to remove all the larger fragments, we would have seen no curved hull remains now. Take away those two evidentiary pieces, and this crash site would have been a forensic dead end. So, perhaps the incompetence is less profound than it seems to us.

"Secondly, let's assume, just for a moment, that the Arat Kur are not the ones who staged the crash. As you say, if they were behind it, they certainly would not have left such a profound contradiction in their own records."

Yaargraukh's neck wobbled around its resting axis. "That is reasonable."

"Then the question becomes, if the persons who faked this crash hoped its true nature would be obliterated when it was discovered, then why would they bother to make it look like the Arat Kur were behind it?"

Yaargraukh's answer was immediate and sharp. "Plausible deniability."

Riordan glanced at his friend, said nothing. *You have a fine mind; I hope it isn't too distressed by what's coming.*

Sleeman was nodding at the Hkh'Rkh's quick insight. "Precisely. And that changes our process of elimination. We now conjecture that the Arat Kur are being false-flagged."

"By whom?" Yaargraukh pressed.

Sleeman shrugged. "Neither we nor the Hkh'Rkh had the capability to reach this system at the time at the time of the crash. So unless this is all part of a Slaasriithi scheme"—she smiled as she mentioned that patently absurd alternative—"that leaves only two possibilities: the Ktor or the Dornaani, in their capacity as Custodians. And while I have it on good authority that Dornaani have been known to scheme, false-flag operations are not in keeping with their ethics. The Ktor, on the other hand—"

Yiithrii'ah'aash's sensor cluster dipped slightly. "Yes. The Lost Soldiers. We would never have needed to come here if the Ktor did not routinely use the misdirection of, as you call them, 'false-flag' conceits. So you project that the Ktor captured the *Katek Hud*, brought it to Turkh'saar, prepared the crash site with the hope that those who discovered it would presume it to be an object of great antiquity due to the apparent date of its impact. But also, to include elements of a plausibly deniable second scenario for those who might discover the inconsistencies of the first."

Riordan was pretty sure he would not have been able to summarize so multifaceted a hypothesis so succinctly. Sleeman simply nodded again. "Yes, that's what we believe."

Yaargraukh's tail had been moving restively as the explanation had become more detailed—and convincing. "I see no other reasonable scenario," he said through a long exhaled breath. "But although you have satisfied me regarding *how* it was done, you have offered no hypothesis as to *why*. The scenario you have proposed entails immense costs and considerable political risk. What did the Ktor hope to achieve, given that expense?"

Sleeman stiffened, glanced sideways at Riordan. He nodded, turned toward Yaargraukh. "They wanted you as allies in the coming war. This was how they made sure you were ready."

The room was silent for a very long moment. Yaargraukh's tail fell still. He leaned forward. "Caine Riordan, I do not understand. Please expand upon your assertion."

"It is our belief that the Ktor have intended to start a war for some time. Centuries, in fact. We suspect they saw the cycle in which your history had been trapped—one of perpetual rise and fall—and reasoned that if you ever did get to a period of stability long enough to enable your first slower-than-light interstellar journey, that it would reinforce that stability if you found clues that led you quickly to building an FTL drive. So they decided to leave you those clues on Turkh'saar, at an apparently ancient crash site." He paused. "They set you up to become their footsoldiers. Against us."

Chapter Sixty-Three

Riordan watched Yaargraukh carefully as the large exosapient processed those assertions. His pupilless black eyes retracted slowly but steadily into his protective eyefolds. Which ultimately closed. "I would hear you posit the Ktoran rationale," he said quietly.

Riordan did not try to keep from frowning. "Not all of this will be flattering or easy to hear, my friend."

"I do not expect any of it will be. All the more important that I hear it. Whether I ultimately place the same faith in it that you do is a separate matter."

Caine nodded. "Fair enough. Our thinking is that the Ktor looked at the patterns in the Patrijuridicate some centuries ago and compared your probable timeline of advance with ours. They concluded that we'd be the first to achieve interstellar travel and, ultimately, FTL. That meant we were on track to be brought to Convocation long before you.

"Conversely, the Ktor had seen you smash yourself back to a preindustrial state numerous times. If nothing was done to break that cycle, you could not be

872

of use to them, either politically or militarily. Without interstellar travel, you were not going to get invited to Convocation, and therefore, would remain a protected species, rather than a member of the Accord."

"And why were we so important to them, do you think?"

It was Yiithrii'ah'aash that answered. "I have not heard Commodore Riordan's and Dr. Sleeman's surmises before this, but I will hazard an answer, based on what I have observed of the Ktor at Convocations and what I suspect of them given the fragments of earlier history which we retain.

"Like your own species, Yaargraukh of the Moiety of Hsraluur, the Ktor are conquest-oriented. That was to be the basis of your understanding and alliance. Shared visions of victorious battles and new possessions would not have required deceit on the part of the Ktor, merely selective self-representation. You were likely to have deemed them kindred spirits. Using that cultural leverage, I suspect the Ktor planned on having—and may yet have—considerable success manipulating your species to do what they wish, even though it will seem like a partnership. Indeed, they have already achieved this: the Hkh'Rkh delegation's umbrage was fundamental to ensuring the dissolution of the abortive Convocation at which both your species hoped to receive an offer of membership."

Yaargraukh thought for several seconds before asking, "But this is a puzzlement: if the Ktor are in fact humans, why would their efforts not be bent toward securing the alliance of Earth?"

Riordan leaned back. "Because we were infected with the rot of pluralism, to paraphrase the lecture

Tlerek Srin Shethkador gave us when we exposed him at the end of the war. That's why the Ktor tried to drop the Doomsday Rock on us forty years ago: to reset us. Probably in the hope that by the time we were ready to emerge into space once again, they would have done away with the Accord, possibly the Dornaani as well. That would have left them free to conquer us and impart the 'correct' cultural shape to what remained of our nations and institutions."

Yaargraukh sat very still. "And we were to be tools in that process?"

"My guess is that they foresaw various ways to use you, had various contingency plans for the Patri-juridicate."

"All of which end with us in unwitting thrall to them."

Yiithrii'ah'aash's body was as quiet as his voice. "I do not think that would be your end."

Yaargraukh's nostrils widened slowly. "What do you mean?"

The Slaasriithi ambassador repositioned himself in the squat-seat that his species used in place of chairs. He interlaced his tendrils. "I mean that the Ktor, despite their willingness to destroy ten or more centuries of progress on Earth to make its population more—manageable—are, paradoxically more interested in them than they are in other species. Markedly so."

Yaargraukh leaned forward like a hound on the scent of prey. "Ambassador, I would be grateful for words that are direct, rather than oblique. I do not fear what you have to say."

Yiithrii'ah'aash's split tail stirred, switched—annoyance, or distress? "Very well. Plainly spoken, then. The Ktor are proven genocidalists. They are almost certainly responsible for the near extermination of my species approximately fifteen thousand years ago, at the end of the last cycle of history in this stellar cluster. Shortly afterward, or possibly before, they attempted a similar annihilation of the Arat Kur. They did so again two years ago by nearly convincing the Terran counterattack fleet to infect Homenest with a lethal plague. I fear, Yaargraukh, they would treat your race no differently.

"If our fragmentary understanding of the Ktor is in any measure accurate, they are instinctively distrustful of all others, including their own peers. By extension, then, the existence of another species foretells a war of genocide that has yet to occur. Their strategy is to preempt that inevitability by exterminating competitor races when they may, minding only the political price they might have to pay."

Phlegm rolled harshly in Yaargraukh's nostrils. "So, at such time as we ceased to be of use to them, they would have eliminated us."

"I fear so."

Yaargraukh pulled his long head upright. "So, you posit that as their rationale. It is sound. What of their process, the plans they carried out and executed? Logically, their objectives should be reflected in their methods."

Sleeman leaned forward again. "We gamed it out from their point of view. The first constraint was that there was no way to seed the wreck on your homeworld. Being a combat-intensive environment at the time they carried out this ploy, they could not conduct any activity on Rkh'yaa without a high probability of being detected. Also, there would have been no way for them to make the crash look like a millennia-old event, given how thoroughly your own planet had been explored and charted. Lastly, it would have been suspiciously convenient for you to discover the remains of FTL technology on your own planet.

"So, looking at it through the Ktor lens, the next most sensible spot to put it was someplace in your own solar system. But again, the chances of being spotted while planting it were still unacceptably high. There was the further problem of making the staged crash highly discoverable without making the wreck so well-preserved that it raised suspicions.

"So, moving out from your solar system, the next best spot would be the first star to which you were likely to mount an interstellar mission: Turkh'saar, the closest to your homeworld and furnished with a green world, as any probe or even a first-generation phased-array telescope was certain to show. And during their tenure as assistant Custodians, the Ktor had legitimate cause to put their ships get very close to this part of space."

Yiithrii'ah'aash raised a single tendril. "This conforms to the timeline you proposed during your presentation of the physical crash evidence, Dr. Sleeman. The Ktor commenced their duties as assistant Custodians just over four hundred years ago."

Sleeman nodded her thanks while continuing. "So the Ktor seize the *Katek Hud,* bring it here, dig the trench, stage the crash, and leave. And during those operations, some of them get a good look at this region of space, the coming political sensitivity of the system, the probable utility of being able to ruin Earth's reputation with its relative neighbors, and begin to conceive of false-flag plots which ultimately lead to their depositing the Lost Soldiers here, more than two centuries later. The years pass. New soil piles high upon the wreck, covering it." She glanced at Riordan. "The Commodore has a better grasp of the relevant history, so perhaps he should take it from here."

Caine nodded, turned toward Yaargraukh. "If I recall correctly, this would all be occurring early in your Third Industrial Age, which, like your first one, progressed slowly due to your constant wars. And while war sparks innovation for the Hkh'Rkh, it does not seem to do so as dramatically as it does for us."

"That is an accurate assessment," Yaargraukh said quietly.

"So after several centuries, you are just starting to resume spaceflight, are just returning to what had been your prior peak achievements, when you detect radio signals from outer space. Ours."

"Correct. In many ways, it transformed our culture. And not always for the better. It marked a distinct move to power centralization. The Patrijuridicate, which began as a council for adjudicating disputes between Families without restoring to war, quickly evolved into an oligarchic governing body. Our wars with each other decreased; a significant amount of that energy was diverted into preparing to defend ourselves against creatures from other worlds."

"Logical, particularly given what you heard and saw in our broadcasts. In fact, it was as if only our very worst events ever reached you—or at least, did so disproportionately."

Yiithrii'ah'aash's inquiry was a rough purr. "So, you suspect that the Hkh'Rkh did not actually receive your transmissions, but rather, signals that were selectively boosted or retransmitted by the Ktor?"

Riordan smiled. "It's certainly possible, and consistent with their penchant for misdirection."

"Yes," Yiithrii'ah'aash agreed in a similar tone, "it is. It is also significant that this change in the Hkh'Rkh culture disrupted the Accord's projections for when it might become ready for first contact. Until their rapid centralization just over one hundred and fifty years ago, we estimated that they would be called to Convocation in three hundred to five hundred years. This was predicated upon the assumption that there would not be another crippling internecine conflict."

Yaargraukh's long spine straightened. "Yet we sent out our first interstellar mission only ninety years later. Well, the first one that succeeded."

Riordan nodded. "That was about 2040 by our calendar, and that mission had a forty-year round trip. But you launched your very next one just eight years after the first one arrived at Turkh'saar, in 2051. Which was pretty surprising. It meant, given the light speed delay on communication, the Patrijuridicate launched that followup mission only three years after receiving the first one's initial report."

Yaargraukh pony-nodded. "It remains one of our proudest feats. But I hear the suggestion underneath your words, Caine Riordan: that the first mission had found the wreck on Turkh'saar and understood the scientific gains that might be extracted from it. Secretly."

"Yes. And it would have been easy enough to account for that urgency by other motivations: the confirmation of a green world and the need to press outward as quickly as possible to ready yourself for contact with the warlike aliens."

Yiithrii'ah'aash unlaced his tendrils, raised them in a wave. "This matches the timeline we witnessed in the Accord. The Custodians reported slower-than-light missions from Rkh'yaa to Turkh'saar in your year of 2040, then 2059, and again in 2064. The Arat Kur became increasingly agitated during this time, although the Custodians prevailed upon them to refrain from contact.

"The first Hkh'Rkh mission returned to their home-world in 2091: Nineteen years later, after two failures, they tested their first successful shift-ship. Shortly after that, the Arat Kur explained that after a chance meeting with the Hkh'Rkh, they had agreed to the standing plan of making the Turkh'saar system a codominium. And so we began to make preparations for the most recent—and disastrous—Convocation."

Riordan smiled. "It's interesting how 'random' events came together to ensure that the Hkh'Rkh perfected their FTL drive only five years after we did. And how the disputes over introducing both our states in the same Convocation delayed the Custodians from convening it for another eight years."

Yaargraukh's voice was harsh, bitter. "Enough time for us to build a fleet. Enough time to learn that Turkh'saar was not so inviting a world after all, but that it was also the best we could reach. So we had the means for expansion but no place worthy of that goal. And the Patrijuridicate and Old Houses became restless."

Bannor raised his chin. "For conquest?"

"Always, for conquest. But that was, as you would say, the carrot. There was also a stick: the tremendous investment it took to mount such a vigorous

interstellar program, to develop our shift-drive. It
was largely funded by the greatest of the Old Families, who needed a return on their investment, and
quickly, if they were to avoid default and war." He
paused. "This also explains why, in the past decade,
our leaders became so fiercely defensive regarding our
technological acumen, particularly in comparison to
aliens that we had not yet encountered. Because they
alone knew that our scientists had not discovered the
shift-drive on their own, but had copied it, purloined
it from the wreckage of an alien ship."

"Makes sense," Bannor agreed. "And it shines some
additional light on why they left missiles at the site
and planted a nuke there, as well. They didn't want
anyone to learn what they'd found and excavated there,
least of all their own people. But I'm guessing that
someplace along the line, that directive was lost, that
the leaders of Turkh'saar forgot they were supposed
to safeguard the site."

Yaargraukh shook his head vigorously, like a pony
trying to shoo a fly. "Bannor Rulaine, you forget:
Turkh'saar is the planet of my birth. The directive did
not fade from memory: it was *meant* to be forgotten.
A secret such as that one? Even an Honor-bound
people such as mine share secrets, given enough time
and opportunity. Remember: I spent my adult life on
Rkh'yaa. I grew up in the shadow of the towers of
the Patrijuridicate. So believe me when I say I know
how they think: their intent would have been to bury
the secret along with the missiles and the nuclear
device. And it must have a very special clearance
requirement attached to it, since I never learned
of it, even though I was on the First Voice's staff."

He considered. "If there was a person on Turkh'saar entrusted with that secret, it would have been the Great Voice of the colony, and it would be passed as a Familial honor and obligation. Which is subject to errors and abuse. As we saw."

Riordan frowned. "But no matter who does or doesn't know about the truth of the Site on Turkh'saar, the Patrijuridicate and Old Family Sires know. So they are going to be even more upset by our incursion than we originally guessed."

Yiithrii'ah'aash's tendrils frizzed outward from his "palms": alarm, surprise. "Yes. They will rightly conjecture that you found the Site and shall, or already do, discern its full significance."

Riordan nodded. "Which includes knowing that the Patrijuridicate has hidden it for years and pushed the cost of that interstellar program increasingly upon the backs of the New Families." He smiled, didn't mean it to be bitter, but conceded that it probably was. "A perfect outcome, so far as the Ktor are concerned."

Yaargraukh turned to look at him. "What do you mean?"

"I mean that if we reveal what we've found, that could be the spark that ignites a civil war between the New Families and the Old."

"Yeah," agreed Bannor, "and it also means that a lot of Old Family patriarchs might be happier if First Voice stayed lost. If he returns, his cronies can't be sure what he might decide to do upon coming home: maintain the cover-up or pull the skeletons out of the closet—both to get ahead of the political fallout and as a display of good faith to the New Families."

Yaargraukh's voice was low. "That revelation would

forever change the dynamic between New Families and Old, would embolden my people."

Bannor nodded. "Which means the Old Family patriarchs might stick a knife in First Voice the moment he stepped off the shuttle."

The quiet that followed was long and somber. Yiithrii'ah'aash's sensor cluster finally elevated slightly. He asked, "I have one last question, Dr. Sleeman."

"Yes, Ambassador?"

"I received word that you also brought some biota on board from Turkh'saar."

"Yes. Mostly animals. Some are native to Turkh'saar, but a number of them are species that the Hkh'Rkh brought with them and released into the wild."

"And how do they bear upon your research of these issues, if at all?"

Sleeman glanced away, sounded evasive. "I don't know the answer to that yet. But I will keep you updated on my investigation, Ambassador."

"Please do. Now let us attend to your wounded together. We have nine days before we make shift to Sigma Draconis."

Bannor frowned. "A day and a half later than the Ktor, damn it."

"Yes," Yiithrii'ah'aash agreed as he stood. "That could prove—inconvenient."

PART FIVE
June 2121

SNAKES

Anguis in herba
(A snake in the grass)

Chapter Sixty-Four

OUTER SYSTEM, SIGMA DRACONIS

Thirty-seven hours after the *Arbitrage*-tug kludge made shift to Sigma Draconis, Yiithrii'ah'aash warned his passengers that they should strap into their couches: transition was imminent.

Waiting on the bridge of *Puller*, Caine enjoyed the moment of silence waiting for the shift which, on Slaasriithi shift-carriers, was so subtle when it occurred that he thought he might have nodded off.

But the view in the screen had changed. "*Shore-of-Stars* has completed shift," announced Melissa Sleeman. "Getting sensor feed from their bridge."

"Position?"

"Confirmed in Sigma Draconis. Approximately two light-seconds above the ecliptic, relative bearing. Just beyond the fifth orbit."

"Any sign of *Arbitrage* and the tug?"

"Yes, sir. About six light-seconds to low trailing, relative bearing. They are at full stop."

Hmmm... "Any comms emanating from them?"

"No, sir. But the Slaasriithi passive array is showing

a small craft—exhaust makes it one of *Arbitrage's* shuttles—heading in toward the fourth orbit. Currently decelerating."

Hmmm. Someone getting called on the carpet? "Any other signatures?"

"No—yes, sir! A bogey heading out...no, *coming back* from the heliopause. It appears to have been preaccelerating and has just recently aborted that run by tumbling and counterboosting at four gee with a huge energy spike. No precise mass reading, but she's about the size of a large freighter or a destroyer. I'd hate to be behind her: judging from the heat and the rads, I think she's running on antimatter."

Dora screwed up her face. "Antimatter? For thrust? Can that be done?"

"I guess we've just seen it," Riordan answered.

"Yeah," Karam agreed. "There's no reason you can't. It was originally considered as an alternative to fusion for an STL drive. But antimatter is so expensive, and in such demand for shift-drives, that we've never seen it used for standard propulsion. Until now, I guess."

"Yeah, because whoever's in that ship has antimatter to burn. Along with millions upon millions of unis."

Duncan looked up. "Something tells me they're from a place where our credits aren't any good."

Dora glanced at him. "You think?" But her tone was friendly sass, not snark.

So, some improvement there, thought Caine, as he felt a faint tremor run through *Puller*. "Are we under way, Dr. Sleeman?"

"We are, sir. Yiithrii'ah'aash just sent word that we are maneuvering insystem. But it looks like the

Arbitrage and the enemy tug have commenced acceleration, also, sir. On an intercept course. A leisurely one. Matching *Shore-of-Stars*'s acceleration."

Well, of course they are. He reached for the restraints hanging down on either side of his acceleration couch. "I don't know if the tempo is going to be slow or fast, but I think we're about to dance. Stand to your stations and strap in."

Shethkador stared out the narrow bridge windows of *Ferocious Monolith*'s sole remaining patrol hunter, *Doom Herald*. Barely visible at two hundred kilometers, the archaic shuttle from the human commercial shift-carrier *Arbitrage* twinkled, the only star in the black velvet of space that did so: she was slowly rolling, changing the pattern of the light she reflected.

"Is their craft disabled, Great Srin?" the lictor at the helm wondered aloud.

Shethkador kept his voice low. "Although this is your first assignment, the ignorance you display is barely acceptable."

The back of the man's neck darkened. "My apologies, Fearsome Srin. I am unfamiliar in the protocols for this kind of rendezvous."

"That is only one of the two ignorances that will be fatal to you, should you display either one of them again."

"I crave your pardon, my Srin, but, so I do not risk arousing your wrath once more, what is the other ignorance I must correct?"

"The assumption that I am here to instruct you. Ask the lokagon who commands your section. He will, I hope, use a lash to improve your attentiveness and memory." *Dolt. Of course the shuttle was not in distress.* Although still at two hundred kilometers, Nezdeh Perekmeres was prudent—and right—to be concerned that stealthed boarders in assault capsules could have been launched at her small craft, might be inbound as they spoke. If so, a rolling ship was notoriously difficult and time-consuming to board, even if it was not making any headway.

"Incoming signal on lascom," announced the autarchon manning the comms.

"I will be in the commander's ready room," Tlerek said as he pushed off the deck and drifted through the smaller of the two iris valves on the bridge. "Secure channel, double encryption."

"Yes, Potent Srin."

The screen flashed on as he guided himself into the seat behind the ready room's desk. The face of Nezdeh, formerly of House Perekmeres, appeared, calm and collected. She inclined her head slightly. "Tlerek Srin Shethkador, I thank you for meeting me as I requested."

"I was uncertain whether I would, but curiosity trumped both justice and vengeance. At least temporarily."

"You assured me that I could approach with safety."

"And you swore an oath to serve the Autarchs years before you arranged to have members of my crew murdered, then mutinied and seized control of *Red Lurker* while it was on detached duty in system V 1581. I find it amusing that you think yourself in any position to lecture me on duplicity—or anything else."

"I do not presume to lecture. And I understand why our House was Extirpated. But Extirpated or not, we remain Ktor in our instincts and ambitions. We grew up with the Progenitors' words in our ears, would have been disgraces to them and ourselves had we not kept faith with their exhortation that all Ktor must seek dominion. And if one relents on securing the freedom necessary for that search, one is as good as dead. And should be made so."

"The very words of the Progenitors," he agreed, and had to admit that he liked her frankness and courage. It was a pity she would have to die at some point—sooner rather than later, probably—but caution stayed him from making too hasty a commitment to her demise. She might yet become useful in any number of ways. "You promised me valuable information. You had best have it, Houseless Nezdeh, or I shall have the pleasure of destroying you. This very minute."

"I understand. But once I have provided you with that information, I believe it would also benefit you to hear my projections and my entreaties."

"About what?"

"About the way the information I have shared could influence both coming events and survival."

"Yours?"

"And my crew's. And perhaps even your own, Srin Shethkador. So, the information. You will of course wish to know what transpired on Turkh'saar as soon as possible."

"Will I?"

"Most assuredly. Otherwise you would not have had a destroyer lurking there. And if you did not consider the intelligence vital, you would not have been redispatching it back to that system when we arrived. According to my calculations, it was only nine hours away from completing its preacceleration and making shift."

"Eight hours, actually. Make your report."

"I would secure guarantees first."

"That request is not worthy of your intelligence nor your experience, fallen Nezdeh. I have dominion here, not you. You are seeking my favor. Yet you insult me by thinking that I would give you any guarantees on the sheerest possibility that you might have something of interest to share with me. And you insult yourself by thinking that I would honor those guarantees if you have no means of making it worthwhile for me to do so."

Nezdeh smiled. "So. We understand each other."

"I understand you. Your actions indicate you do not understand me."

"I must differ on that point, Srin Shethkador. Because I understand very well why you were concerned with the events that transpired on Turkh'saar, and why it was important for you to have access to that information as swiftly as possible—and without the Aboriginals knowing you have received it."

"Our lascoms are secure."

"Secure from conventional interception and decoding, yes—but the Aboriginals had much time to seed this system with free-floating monitors before *Ferocious Monolith* arrived. If I had not journeyed to you in this shuttle, but had instead initiated communication between our distant vessels, they would likely have detected that activity, and presumed that I reported to you and so would hold you responsible for what I shall report. At our current proximity, however, our sensors assure us that there are no micromonitors near enough to even detect the low-power lascoms carrying these signals."

"So what is this urgent news you bear from Turkh'saar?"

Nezdeh told him the long, and possibly complete, story of what had transpired there. "I am sending a full report by secure squeak on channel two," she finished.

Shethkador was careful to control himself before he spoke. What she had revealed was very grave for the interests of the Ktoran Sphere—and himself. "You bring me news of folly compounded upon folly. What possessed the former leaders of your House to adopt such an outlandish scheme of impressing Aboriginals for use on an alien planet?"

"The purposes and plans of my forebears shall remain forever unknown to me, but I suspect they were moved by desperation and a paucity of resources."

"House Perekmeres was of considerable weight before its Extirpation. How were they desperate or wanting for resources?"

"Understand that in answering you, I am not arguing their case; they were rash to take the gambles they did, here and at Home, at Earth. However, I deduce that they were convinced that the more gradual course of reconquest agreed upon by the Autarchs and Hegemons was dangerous, afforded the Aboriginals enough time to mount a more credible resistance."

Shethkador waved a dismissive hand. "Had Perekmeres not decided to accelerate the process with what the Aboriginals call the Doomsday Rock, the low-breeds would likely still be poking aimlessly about their own solar system. It was the panicked response to that asteroid threat which finally invigorated what had been, up to then, their indolent expansion into space, and ultimately, the stars."

"As I said, Srin Shethkador, in this particular, my

own opinions match yours. But the Hegemons of House Perekmeres perceived otherwise. And having limited access to this part of space, they planted the seeds of incidents that, in their mind, would either profoundly set back the Aboriginals, or would accelerate the onset of general war when and if they became members of the Accord. Clearly, my forebears' decision to sequester sleeping Aboriginal soldiers on Turkh'saar was meant to ensure the latter."

"And you were foolish enough to believe that this would be in your interests, also."

"Again, the plan was not mine."

"But you did not disagree."

Nezdeh straightened, as if steeling herself to something that she had to say for the benefit of others. "In the wake of our failure to destroy the Aboriginals' diplomatic mission to the Slaasriithi homeworld, our choice was either to make a bid for power that would allow us to return to the Sphere, or to accept a life as outcasts, welcome in no place where our species is known. Our only resources were the ships in our possession, their contents, and this one sleeping asset that we might leverage to secure the help of the Hkh'Rkh to return home safely."

Shethkador raised one eyebrow. "Your Srin was foolish and rash. It was known of him. A pity he eluded attempts at Extirpation."

He had meant that comment to press her, to see how far she would subjugate her House loyalty, and herself, to his will and opinion. He did not expect her reply, which was frank and calm—maybe almost a relief to her. "I agree. Brenlor was rash. And if his plans contained sparks of inspiration, they were invariably undermined by his disregard for adequate analysis and review."

Perhaps she could be useful after all. "Strange you did not assassinate him and take dominion for yourself."

She seemed to suppress a sigh. "We were few in number and drawn from disparate branches of our former House—"

—"Former" House? Is that truly her outlook now, that their bid to restore their House is at an end? Or is that simply what she wishes me to think?

"—so strife among ourselves was fatal to our enterprise. We needed numbers and coherence."

Shethkador smiled. "Brenlor would never have been able to see the wisdom of that, had your positions been reversed."

"And that is the impetuousness which doomed House Perekmeres."

"On this we are agreed. Very well, having advance knowledge of what transpired upon Turkh'saar allows me to plan both denials and deceptions that may be used during the discussions that shall arise with the Aboriginals. But it is barely valuable enough to be worth your life. You must have, and want, more than that."

Nezdeh's nod was slow, grave: *so unlike the ungovernable* krexyes *that had been her cousin, the Srin.*

"What I want," she said, "is to be given the opportunity to refuel and flee unmolested. What I have to offer is cooperation in eliminating the Slaasriithi and the Aboriginals who are the only witnesses to, and possess the only evidence of, what transpired upon Turkh'saar."

"And how would you help me achieve that?"

"My help would be twofold. Firstly, your ship and

the destroyer are both more than a day's journey from where the Slaasriithi shift-carrier has just appeared. If your enemies have all that time to maneuver as they choose, they will be difficult to catch."

"Difficult, but hardly impossible. Given the vastly superior performance of our ships, we shall have them soon enough. Well less than a week, I estimate."

"I agree, but what will happen during that week? Will the Aboriginal fleet sit idle? Will they accept your account of what then transpires, even before the witness of their own eyes: that a pair of Ktoran vessels hunted a Slaasriithi ship with humans aboard, until it was brought to heel and destroyed?"

"And what alternative do you offer?"

"My ships are less than six light-seconds from the newly arrived enemy. Although the *Arbitrage* is slow, my tug the *Uzhmarek* is not. Using the two, I can impede their freedom of movement, shepherd them in such a way that *Ferocious Monolith* and your destroyer may converge on them from two other points and box them in. I estimate that it will take less than forty-eight hours to trap and destroy them."

"That would be preferable to a week-long chase. But you promised that your cooperation would provide me with *two* advantages."

"I did. The second is plausible deniability. You can record a communiqué from me in which I claim that the Slaasriithi craft is chasing mine, that they attempted to destroy us when we stumbled upon their transgression of Arat Kur and Hkh'Rkh territory. So naturally, it becomes fully explicable that you would come to our rescue and assist us in destroying these hostile vessels."

Shethkador suppressed a smile. *She is good.* "And if the Aboriginal fleet commanders do not believe the story, or if the truth of what occurred on Turkh'saar is relayed to them by the Slaasriithi ship before they can be destroyed?"

"Firstly, if no physical evidence is relayed, it will be my word against their word. Inconclusive. But, in the event that the recently arrived ships from Turkh'saar are somehow able to provide compelling evidence at a distance, you may disavow me, may explain that you were unaware that my ships had gone rogue. And to prove that, you will have the recording of me, deceiving you by claiming that my ships had been under attack, and were still under your command."

"That will do my own fortunes no good in the eyes of the Autarchs. Dominion must be absolute. Even if the Aboriginals can be misled, the Autarchs will know that I failed to maintain both the semblance and the fact of mastery over all Ktoran assets in this salient."

"I cannot disagree, Srin Shethkador, for I know what you say is true. However, it may not come to such a pass. Revealing our status as a rogue unit is a worst-case contingency plan, only. But more pertinently, while it may do your reputation no good among our superiors, it is far better than the alternative. Consider: if the Aboriginals make a complete report before you can chase and destroy them, you will surely have precipitated the war you rightly damn my forebears for being too eager to start."

Shethkador nodded. "So, in two days, with your help, we will have trapped and destroyed the Slaasriithi ship. Which means that my two warships will also come close enough to your tug and lumbering

Aboriginal barge to obliterate them." He pointed at her. "And so, I shall eliminate the loose ends that might later betray me, or might threaten to reveal the truth at some later date." He smiled. "Come now, you have considered this. And you must have provided yourself with insurance against that outcome. Or you are not anywhere near as clever as you seem, Houseless Nezdeh."

Her responding smile was as mirthless as he imagined his own must be. "Of course. My insurance is that I possess one other thing that I know you want."

"And what could that possibly be?"

"An Aboriginal who you, or one of your closest agents, suborned: the captain—well, megacorporate factor—of the *Arbitrage*. He possesses two characteristics that I am sure will interest you keenly."

"Be explicit and succinct: I am not in the mood to guess." *Then again, I never am.*

"The Aboriginal may be the most highly placed CoDevCo executive who remains unpurged by the government of the so-called Consolidated Terran Republic. That is conjecture on my part, of course: my knowledge of the state of affairs on our estranged homeworld is almost a year out of date, now. However, at last report—"

"You have made your point." *Happily she does not have current information, or she might well have tried to press for more concessions.* During the most recent of his tiresome Reification-contacts with the Autarchs, the senior Autarch, Davros Tval Herelkeom, had asked Shethkador to assess the same situation. Tlerek, obeying both prudence and practicality, had answered with the simple truth: the network of agents that had been so laboriously constructed on Earth was gutted and in complete chaos. The words of his recommendation came back to haunt him: *"We must slowly but steadily reestablish our presence on Home under more direct control. Our proxies in the megacorporations proved both unreliable and unprofessional. It will be more difficult to achieve, though, now that the Aboriginals know that we may walk among them."* A high-ranking CoDevCo executive, for whom a backstory of heroic resistance against renegade Ktoran pirates could be created without fear of contradiction, would be an excellent asset upon which to build such a campaign of reinfiltration. "What is this Aboriginal's second interesting characteristic?"

Nezdeh shrugged. "It is not so much a characteristic as it is a consideration of what would occur if this individual were to be released directly to the Aboriginals. If he must curry favor with the governments of Earth, the very knowledge that makes him a useful foundation for rebuilding our covert network there becomes the very weapon with which they can further hunt down and destroy what is left of it. And you may be sure, if threatened with execution or torture, he will not only expose the agents that remain, but also provide the Aboriginals with all the cultural insight they need to understand who and what we really are—and why any hope of peace with Ktor is at best a grave miscalculation, and at worst, a delusion."

Shethkador affected airy disinterest. "The Aboriginals already suspect as much. In actuality, a few know it outright, but were sworn to secrecy." But if the human to which Nezdeh referred was able to make this information more widely known...

Nezdeh clearly knew she was on solid argumenta-
tive ground. "The Aboriginals do not have specific
information about our lifespan, about how we think,
about our social ranks and classes, about how intoler-
ant our society is of weakness or of ethical and moral
delusions. Brenlor was incautious in the presence of
this Aboriginal; what was not explicitly revealed, he
has surely deduced. If anyone can paint a picture
that will terrify the cattle of Earth and unite them
resolutely against us, it is this low-breed."

"And you would do this to your own kind? Would
undermine the rise of *homo imperiens* and, I daresay,
homo transcendens?"

"I would, if given no other choice. And you are
correct in your conjecture, Srin Shethkador: I, too,
am *homo transcendens*."

Shethkador suppressed any reaction but quickly
recalculated the risks and benefits of making any agreement with her. Since she was also capable of effecting Reifications, she was both a tremendous danger
and a tremendous asset. The trick was in finding the
leverage that nullified the danger while preserving the
benefit. But time and unfolding events would dictate
that. "So where is this Aboriginal?"

"I shall show you."

The picture changed; a new visual feed had been
swapped into the channel. It revealed a male Aboriginal,
sitting morosely in a featureless chamber. A moment
later, his sagging pear shape and fishlike eyes kindled
a memory: Emil Kozakowski. One of Shethkador's best
and most obsequious agents within the human megacorporations. He had not met the man personally—he
had minimized all personal contact while among the

Aboriginals—but had communicated with, and had read reports by and about, him. In the proper hands, Kozakowski would be a singularly effective asset; handed over to the Aboriginal authorities, he would be a singular disaster.

When Shethkador did not react immediately, Nezdeh spoke over the image of the collaborator. "As you may remember, Srin Shethkador, I was a communications officer while aboard the *Ferocious Monolith*. So I know channels—back channels—to the journalists embedded with the Aboriginal fleet."

"Yes. Your point?"

"My point is that you have no way to eliminate this Aboriginal before he is delivered to them. You do not know where to find him. The Aboriginal military will not know where to find him. But, when and if the time comes, the Aboriginal press will know where to find him."

As she spoke, Shethkador made sure that the return feed to Nezdeh only showed his face. He scrawled on the bridge-linked tablet in front of him: *Communications: find the source of the signal from which we are receiving the picture of the Aboriginal.* As Nezdeh finished, the comm officer's reply scrolled in: *Impossible. Image is being sent via lascom from the tug Uzhmarek. We have no assets on site to determine whether the tug is the source of, or merely a relay for, the signal.*

So, it was not possible to follow a trail of signals to Emil Kozakowski's actual location. No surprise, really: Nezdeh did not seem to be sloppy. Consequently, the Aboriginal might be located in a room on her ship, or on a life-support pod sequestered almost anywhere that her vessels—including the shuttle she was presently on—had passed near. And with a situation unfolding this quickly, and in a system held by the enemy, he would never find the Aboriginal in time on his own. "Very well," he admitted, "it seems you do have something I want, after all. But I cannot simply allow you to refuel and depart. It must be made to appear that you fled without warning. We shall achieve this by explaining that we have put a prize crew aboard the *Uzhmarek* and are removing you for questioning and possible discipline. The Aboriginal fleet's sensors will show them that our crew boarded the tug, oversaw the refueling, and apparently took off a number of crewpersons."

Nezdeh nodded. "And then, just before shift, your remaining crew shall exit the tug and we shall be free to go on our way."

"No, that is not possible. The tug must remain in our possession. The Ktoran Sphere cannot risk the political crises that would arise if we were to leave you as a free-roving raider in Aboriginal space, for that is surely what you would do to survive. Similarly, you and I both know you cannot return to the Sphere: your lives would be forfeit upon first detection."

"Then what do you propose?"

"I do not propose, Houseless Nezdeh: I decree. The tug will apparently shift you homeward but shall covertly deposit you in the Epsilon Indi system, instead. You will retain the *Arbitrage* and her various assets, which can be modified to blend in with the machinery and craft that the Aboriginals expect to see there. Of more particular interest, there is an ill-defined combination of piracy and rebellion brewing in that system, possibly aided and abetted by the survivors of a Hkh'Rkh commerce raider that the Arat Kur dropped off there: the *Relentless Hunter*."

He leaned back. "It will not be an opulent life, but you may hope to dominate the lesser beings who resist the Terran Republic in that place. That provides you with freedom of action and the possibility of achieving dominion among the criminal and revolutionary elements in Epsilon Indi. And for me, there is the assurance that you are contained and that your own survival depends upon your remaining incognito. Because if the Aboriginals learned your actual identities, they would spare no expense hunting you down for intelligence purposes."

Her eyes were cold and her mouth a thin line. "This is a hard life to which you condemn us."

"It is your own actions that condemned you. And perhaps, if you distinguish yourselves enough by disrupting the Aboriginal interests in that system, your remaining genelines will become too prized for purging. You might well earn your survival in other Houses by merit. It is one of the recurrent themes of our history."

"I suppose we have little choice."

"You have *no* choice."

"Very well. I accept your terms. I shall commence the return to my ships and instruct them to obstruct the movement of the Slaasriithi shift-carrier."

"Excellent. Establish a lascom link with my subordinate aboard *Will Breaker*, the destroyer heading insystem. It is less likely that the enemy will detect communications you send to it. He will keep me informed of your status: the link between true warships is harder for them to detect." *Or to assert as evidence that there was direct collusion between me and you. Because, Houseless Nezdeh, unless you are very skilled and prove very valuable, your reward shall still be death.*

He closed the link.

Nezdeh Srina Perekmeres leaned away from the communications console. "The die is cast," she muttered.

Beside her, Zurur Deosketer was still staring at the archaic flatscreen. "Do you think he will keep his word?"

Nezdeh shrugged. "He will certainly work with us long enough to destroy the Slaasriithi ship. He cannot allow their report and evidence to reach the Aboriginal authorities. Then he will destroy us."

"Can he afford to do that? What if they suspect collusion? And will they not doubt his claim to the contrary if he has also conveniently destroyed the only ones who might reveal otherwise? Namely, us?"

"Do not forget that he will also have apparent evidence that we deceived him: the recording of the communication I shall send soon. So we become his scapegoat, and the Aboriginals will have no evidence to the contrary."

Zurur leaned away, frowning, doubtful. "Would anyone, even low-breeds, be so ingenuous to believe such a tale?"

"Remarkably, yes. Their power to believe what they wish, if not given incontrovertible evidence to the contrary, is rather astonishing. And if he implicates us in the attack at Disparity, that makes us not only prime suspects, but proven renegades."

"So you will only reveal Kozakowski's location after we are safely away?"

"Unfortunately, the only point at which we will be safely away is when we make shift. And his prize crew on the *Uzhmarek* will never let us depart until we have shared Kozakowski's location."

"But the moment it is shared, the tug's crew shall separate our ships and leave us stranded—until Shethkador's warships arrive to eliminate us."

"Yes. That is why we do not have one Aboriginal hostage as assurance, but two."

"Two? Who is the second one?"

By way of answer, Nezdeh activated the lascom to the *Arbitrage*. "Haddesh?"

"Yes, Srina Perekmeres?"

"Ready another isolation pod."

"Yes, Nezdeh. For whom?"

"Ayana Tagawa." Nezdeh turned back toward Zurur. "She knows too much: in some ways more than Kozakowski."

"But how—?"

"In the same breath that we reveal Kozakowski's location, we shall inform Shethkador that Tagawa has also been positioned for discovery by the press, and that we shall send them her coordinates unless he instructs his prize crew to abandon the tug. And so we shall make good our escape."

"And you intend to send him Tagawa's location in the moment before we shift?"

Nezdeh could not stop the smile that curved one side of her mouth. "Perhaps."

Chapter Sixty-Five

OUTER SYSTEM, SIGMA DRACONIS

Riordan stared at the holoplot. "Yiithrii'ah'aash, this does not look promising."

"No, it does not," the voice of the ambassador agreed in his earbud. "The Ktoran tug is almost as fast as we are, and when we make challenge by counterboosting, it simply retreats again."

Riordan nodded. "There's no use in following that tactic anymore. It's just costing us time. And they're not going to risk letting that tug get too close, not as long as you keep those two cannonballs out behind us."

"Agreed. Additionally, their constant operation is draining their fuel and energy reserves. And despite having left our homeworld with a double load of the remote fighters, we only have four left. The operations at Turkh'saar were costly."

Maybe more costly than they had to be, damn it. And that's on me. I didn't see this coming. "Have you had any luck raising our fleet?"

"None yet, but it has only been two hours: it is

not unlikely that their response has yet to reach us, given the distance-delay."

Riordan looked at the passive scans of the expanses to starward. Inward from the third orbit, radiant energy signatures marked the presence of larger warships and shift-carriers, almost all of which belonged to the Consolidated Terran Republic. None of them were at significant velocity; they would be able to respond quickly, since little counterboost was required. But sensors showed no ships of size on any deep patrols, at least not in their region. Which meant that help was probably about three days off. And without having some idea of the vectors by which that help might approach, it was impossible to plot a course that was both optimized for the earliest possible rendezvous and also confounded Ktoran attempts at interception.

Riordan checked the clock. It had been almost three hours since they'd arrived insystem. By now, their in-shift signatures would have been seen by fleet sensors, which would no doubt have already been aimed in this general direction. The tug's in-shift a day and a half earlier had no doubt resulted in detection, tracking, and hails—which might or might not have been answered.

Ultimately, that choice depended upon which face the Ktor had elected to show. If they were trying to act as though the long-lost *Arbitrage* had finally returned to known space on her own, they'd have members of the human crew communicating with the fleet, deflecting any offers of help. If, on the other hand, the Ktor elected to ignore fleet hails, then the fleet had probably already formulated a response and had given up further attempts at communication. *Unless* . . .

Riordan tapped his collarcom; its annoyed double-chirp indicated the circuit to Yiithrii'ah'aash was open. "Ambassador, are you sure there's no current jamming of the broadcast frequencies?"

"Quite sure."

Well, nothing definitive there. It was possible that the fleet had tried using broadcast to contact the *Arbitrage* when she had first shown up—and then gave up if the Ktor had jamming capable of shutting them down. Which, given some of the tricks he'd seen the Ktor pull, would not be out of the realm of possibility.

He looked up. Only Karam and Sleeman were on duty, and it was duty in word only. With *Puller* still docked to *Shore-of-Stars*, all the piloting and sensor operations were being handled by the Slaasriithi. Time to give one of the two remaining bridgecrew a rest—and to consult with the other. "Dr. Sleeman?"

"Yes, Commodore?"

Riordan smiled. "Now that we're just the team again, you can call me 'Caine.'"

She smiled back, weary but relaxed. "Only if you start calling me 'Melissa,' Commodore."

"Okay, Melissa. Why not get a few hours sleep? We'll be sure to wake you if something interesting happens."

Without protest, Dr. Melissa Sleeman was on her feet and heading for the main hatch. "Thank you, sir."

Riordan simply nodded and worked at keeping the smile off his face until she was off the bridge. With Tygg aboard, he suspected that sleep might not be her first priority. He turned toward Karam.

Who was looking at him. "So, we're alone. Whaddya want?"

"Am I that transparent?"

"Not usually, but sometimes I can read the bulk-head lettering right through you. Like now. Obvious you wanted to have a private confab."

"Yeah. Here's the thing: they ran me through an OCS crash course at the Pearl, so I'm anything but an old hand when it comes to communications protocols, or even doctrine—"

"So you want to know if you followed proper procedures when you aimed our lascom pings at the automated network's check-in sites." Karam nodded. "You hit the right coordinates, so far as I could tell."

Caine glanced at the clock. Three hours, four minutes since they'd arrived. "Well, then maybe something's wrong with the relays. We should have received a ping back about a minute ago."

Karam looked at the clock, too. "Damn. So either the doggo net is malfunctioning—"

"Or it's been fried."

"Yeah. Hey, you're in intelligence: isn't there some kind of backup?"

Riordan shook his head. "That's the sort of thing that Navy SIGINT handles, not IRIS. But I think I know someone who might have the answers we need."

"Oh? Who?"

Riordan smiled, tapped his collarcom. "Major Solsohn to the bridge, please."

Riordan watched Duncan examine the coordinates they'd used while trying to link into the automated lascom system that the Navy had set up in Sigma Draconis. "Yeah, you followed the proper protocols," he concluded with a nod.

"Okay, then how else do we get in touch with the fleet?"

Duncan shrugged. "Oh, that's easy." He nodded to Karam, who'd taken over the comms when Melissa had gone off duty. "Go to buoy channel seven."

Tsaami tapped a few tabs on his dynamically reconfigurable screen. "Done."

"Send the following message: 'Sample rate Hidden Mirror.'"

"Broadcast and encrypted?"

"Broadcast, yes, but in the clear."

As Karam typed the code in, he frowned. "You know, I've been piloting covert ops for more than ten years, but I've never seen this. What is it?"

"Hidden Mirror is a cache of encrypted values embedded in navigational buoy signals. The term 'sample rate' is a coded command for 'send us the cache.'"

Riordan wondered why Solsohn just didn't explain the whole system at once. "And once we decrypt those values, they give us—what?"

Duncan stared at Riordan as if disbelieving that his question was serious. "Spatial coordinates for micro lascom relays. Of course."

"Micro relays? You mean there's a backup network?"

"Yeah. Seeded into star systems where Fleet thinks our presence is uncertain. Accessing it will require a password."

"Which is?"

"For us? The Operations Order reference code."

Riordan turned with a smile. "I don't have that. I noticed that it had been redacted from my order packet. But I'll bet Downing gave you a complete copy of the OpOrd, didn't he?"

Solsohn reddened slightly. "Yeah. I'll do it." He moved to the helm.

Karam leaned aside, raised an eyebrow in Caine's direction. "Spooks," he said.

Riordan rolled his eyes. "Don't start." He turned to Solsohn. "And now?"

"And now we wait for the photons to reach the buoy and then get sent back to us."

Riordan looked at the clock; another three hours and four minutes of waiting.

By which time, their pursuers would have cut down even more of their running options.

Three hours and seven minutes later, the incoming comm tone sounded on *Puller's* more populated bridge.

Dora looked up from her board, surprised. "Caine, this incoming message is voice grade."

Well, that was fast. Riordan signalled to send it through. "This is UCS *Puller*, Commodore Riordan speaking."

There was a delay of several minutes. Then a wry, Oxbridge-accented voice jocularly remonstrated, "You needn't try to pull rank with me, Caine. I knew you when."

"Richard?" Caine almost shouted.

"Downing?" Duncan whispered, eyebrows raised.

After another seemingly endless wait: "Yes. Currently in an advance base, closer to your position. I came out here when we saw the *Arbitrage* shift in almost two days ago. We've been trying to las-ping the *Shore-of-Stars* since she shifted in, but no luck. Mostly because it hasn't been holding a steady course: makes it impossible to aim a lascom ping at your anticipated position an hour and a half ahead of time."

"Yes, Yiithrii'ah'aash has been trying to push back

the *Arbitrage* and the tug by intermittently changing vector toward them. Keeps us from getting herded toward whatever intercept point they have in mind."

"Understood. But we had no other way to reach you. When *Arbitrage* arrived, the Ktor rendered our broadcast useless: we can't get through their jamming. Then they mucked about with our independent lascom net. We've only just reestablished ship-to-ship comms. And not a moment too soon: there are some serious problems to solve."

"And people tell me *I* have a talent for under-statement."

"Well, Caine, in that regard, I have a distinct advantage."

"Which is?"

"I'm English."

Had the communication delay not been so great, and had he not been on a bridge, Riordan might have groaned. "Fine. So which tactical problem do we tackle first?"

"A timely rendezvous. What's your current intended course?"

Riordan got Yiithrii'ah'aash on the line, who relayed the combination of feint and flight that he had plotted for the next twelve hours.

The pause on Downing's end of the line was very long. "Received and understood, Ambassador. Stand by to receive recommended course changes. These will reduce the time remaining before you rendezvous with our two closest ships, the destroyers RFS *Pokryshkin* and TOS *Mato Grosso*."

"I think we may need a little more help than two destroyers, Richard."

"You do have a knack for attracting trouble, Caine."

"You have a knack for putting me where trouble congregates, Richard."

"*Touché*. Eighteen ships are following after the destroyers. Just to make the Ktor see reason."

"I hope those numbers are sufficient, Richard. We saw how effective our ships were—or rather, weren't—against the Ktor just before I left on the envoy mission with the Ambassador."

"Fair enough, but we know a little bit more about what to expect, now, and there will be a few arrogated Arat Kur craft along with us. They're not up to Ktor standards, but ton for ton, they're much better than our own. And lastly, if the Ktor do decide to try cases with twenty of our ships, they're no longer managing an incident. They're starting a war, which they don't seem eager to do."

"Maybe not, but they're making four gees to engage. Richard, I don't mean to rain on your optimistic parade, but our computers have just double-checked the numbers: your twenty ships are not going to get to us in time."

"Not for the start of the engagement, no, but certainly in time to make them pay handsomely if they make good on their threat. Also, as *Ferocious Monolith* continues to accelerate on her current vector, she loses the ready ability to divert resources to make unanticipated intercepts. Pursuant to that, we have quite a collection of deep system resources— drones and missiles lying doggo near asteroids or debris—that *can* reach you in time. We'll send them your way, just as soon as *Ferocious Monolith*, or any platforms she might send out, are unable to revector enough to interfere with them. When our platforms are close enough, reach out to them with the secure codes we are sending you now. They'll transfer to your direct control."

Yiithrii'ah'aash spent almost a minute thanking Downing. Then, apparently sensing that the humans wished a moment of privacy, he disconnected. Riordan sighed. "Richard, for just one moment, I need you to stop the pep talks."

Richard's voice, almost buoyant until now, came back subdued. "Very well."

"I may not have experience commensurate with my rank, but I don't give us much chance of surviving, let alone winning. Not even with the automated assets that you say will get here before the fight starts. So I need you to promise me something."

"If I can, I will, Caine."

I wonder if your full name is Richard Caveat Downing. "I want Trevor Corcoran designated as Connor's legal guardian. Record that as a codicil to my will."

"I'll have the captain of this ship witness my receipt of your request. Which is certainly understandable."

"And you have to promise me that you'll find Elena and bring her home."

This time, the pause was longer than could simply be explained by the comm delay. "Caine, I—I can't make that promise. As the director of IRIS, I—"

"To hell with IRIS. Quit it, if you have to. She's your goddaughter and she spent almost as much time on your knee as her late father's. You owe him, and her—and *me*—that much. And don't worry: if I do get out of this, I'll go find her myself."

And abandon Connor yet again? Watch what you

swear to, Riordan. But there wasn't enough time to think through the details: only enough to speak the human truths that needed to be spoken. "At a certain point, Richard, you have to let governments and organizations find someone else to do your job. When only you, her father Nolan, and a handful of others knew that there were exosapients waiting for us beyond the solar system, maybe then you had no choice. Maybe there was no one else who could do the job, given how fate had put you in that place, and in that time.

"But you're not there anymore. Even the best-intentioned state will drain us dry, if we let it. There comes a time when you have to say 'no more,' and do your best not for the many, but for the few: the few people in your life who are bound to you by love, for whom you would and should do anything. That's what Elena deserves from me. But if I'm not there to do it, it's what she deserves from you. Now: promise me."

An even longer pause. "I will not rest until I bring her home. Downing out."

Riordan leaned back, became suddenly, and uncomfortably, aware of the carefully averted eyes of the bridge crew. *Well, time to get back to business—which will make all of us more comfortable, anyhow.* "Dr. Sleeman, what's the countdown clock on the bogeys?"

Her look told him that, just over the course of his conversation with Downing, it had gotten worse.

Much worse.

Chapter Sixty-Six

Well, Riordan thought, *if the fight goes against us, at least we're all going to die better rested and better fed.* Since arriving in Sigma Draconis a day and a half ago, there'd been little to do except watch the symbols of ships and drones creep toward each other in the holoplot: a deceptive depiction of events, since many of those craft were pulling maximum gees.

The notable exception was *Shore-of-Stars* itself. Her best plan was to conserve power and not overcommit to any given vector, a tactic that had taken almost thirty minutes to explain to those officers among the Lost Soldiers who had wanted an update on what was occurring. In particular, it was counterintuitive to them that superior speed did not always translate into the surety of escape. Instead, constant application of maximum acceleration along a given vector made a craft's future movement infinitely more predictable, more plottable, and consequently, more susceptible to intercept—particulary when three comparable ships were closing from entirely different directions.

Riordan reflected that the Lost Soldiers, and particularly the pilots among them, had not really been slow to understand the concepts; they had been unwilling to *accept* them. There was a species of fatalism to the unfolding of deep-space maneuver that unsettled them, that ran counter to their expectations of dogfights in which quick wits and clever piloting could enable rapid reversals in position and outcome. Not so in deep space. There, the cold equations of vector, thrust, and enemy applications of the same created what was essentially a predestined outcome. It was not so much a matter of what was going to happen, but when.

And that certainty, combined with the past thirty-six hours of waiting for the inevitable, was what the Lost Soldiers had found the hardest to cope with. There had been plenty of waiting in their experience of war; hence one of the Americans' favorite rueful colloquialisms for explaining the tempo of military life: "Hurry up and wait." But at least that waiting was often leavened by glimmers of hope, of the possibility that some unexpected event might occur and the outcome would be better than anticipated. That was not the predominant mindscape of deep-space warfare; everything was in sight and everything had plotted motion. Unless one or more units were called away or had mechanical failures, the time and place of meeting, of combat, were fundamentally preordained.

And now, that preordained moment was nearly upon them. "Dora, crew to their posts."

"You calling for battle stations?"

"Not yet. But I want people awake and ready: no one in bunks or in the galley. Dr. Sleeman, what's the latest estimated time to engagement?"

"About three hours, sir, depending upon how much advance fire they want to commit to with their railguns."

"And what's the ETA on the remote assets that Downing sent our way?"

"Varies from twenty-seven minutes to four hours, assuming they match vector and velocity with us before we commit them to engagement."

"Let's assume that the platforms arriving more than three hours from now are not tasked to match our vector and velocity. How does that change their ETA?"

"All of them would be on hand for the battle, sir. But the later ones will be passing through quickly, since getting them here on time means little or no counterboost before the engagement."

I doubt they'll survive long enough for that to be an issue. "Very well. Mr. Solsohn, start sending the control codes to the remote platforms. We're going to want to have the earlier ones forming up on us."

"You mean on *Shore-of-Stars*, sir?"

"No, I mean *Puller*. We'll be detaching in a few minutes." He tapped his collarcom. "Ambassador Yiithrii'ah'aash?"

A pause, then: "Commodore. Have you reconsidered my suggestion?"

"I must continue to decline, Ambassador."

"If you wait ten more minutes, your ship's new engines will help you escape the imminent battle. The enemy will be at pains to intercept your ship, having committed to courses predicated on *Shore-of-Stars*'s thrust limitations."

"Yes, Ambassador, that is true. But we will not turn our backs upon you or our personnel aboard the wedges." Even if Riordan had wanted to, there simply wasn't enough room on *Puller* to evacuate even a quarter of the Cold Guard or Lost Soldiers. "Besides, our fleet's first wave is only eight hours away. They'll start counterboosting as soon as they're in range and will throw out a lot of firepower before they pass us. After them, smaller squadrons will join us, decelerating so as to match our trajectory and stand in the battle. And if *Puller* detaches now, and we have the fleet's remote assets form up on us, that will complicate the Ktorans' tactical picture, should cause them to slow down somewhat."

"Yes, it will slow them. But not enough. We have run those scenarios through our computers several times now. The outcome is always the same: your destruction."

"There are variables, such as when the Ktor decide to commence firing—"

"Which could be happening very soon, sir," Sleeman interrupted. "*Ferocious Monolith* has launched independent platforms. They appear to be PDF, sensor, and attack drones. They have been deployed with railgun on a reverse vector."

Which meant that although they were moving away from *Ferocious Monolith* now, they would ultimately begin to overtake her as she continued to counterboost. "I presume they will arrive concurrent with *Ferocious Monolith*, Doctor?"

"About ten minutes ahead of her, sir. Just in time for all their weapons to achieve effective range simultaneously."

But of course. "Very well. Ambassador, you need to de-spin *Puller*'s berthing arm so we can detach and take up station alongsid—"

"New contact!" Sleeman shouted as the automated emergency klaxon began to wail its call to battle stations.

What the—? Riordan glanced at the holoplot: a white delta—an unidentified craft—had appeared approximately two light-seconds away. It was directly between them and the approaching Ktor shift-cruiser. "Dr. Sleeman, where the hell did that come from? And what the hell is—?"

"It came out of nowhere, sir. Getting transponder and cross-sectional scans now, sir."

"On the main screen."

Sleeman complied; a slightly drooping delta shape appeared, similar to, but much smaller than, the shift cruisers of the Arat Kur, or even the Ktor. Which meant—

"Contact identified as Custodial shift-cruiser *Olsloov*, Commodore." Sleeman sounded distracted as she reported it, was leaning even more intently over her sensors.

Dora scowled. "Senior Mentor Alnduul hailing on secure one, sir. And the bastard already seems to have our encryption."

Big surprise, there. "Put Alnduul through, Dora."

"He's on line, sir."

Riordan raised his voice enough so the general mic would catch it. "Alnduul, this is Caine Riordan. We are always glad to see you, but this time we're a little happier than usual."

"We are gratified to see you as well, Caine Riordan. I apologize for our rather sudden appearance—"

—Yeah, "sudden," as in, "out of thin air." Or vacuum, I guess. Wonder how long you were lurking near us?—

"—but the deployment of remote weapons by the Ktoran cruiser made it essential that we make our presence known immediately."

"And you've remained in this system since we started on the diplomatic mission to the Slaasriithi homeworld?"

"We have. With ongoing interactions between all the Accord states and protected races focused on this system, and affecting several nearby, it was the most central location. I trust we did not startle you too much when we disengaged our hull's active energy-absorption matrix."

"Well, frankly, we've never been so happy to be startled—"

"Commodore," Sleeman muttered, "a word. Please."

Riordan glanced at her: she was staring at him. Hard. "Alnduul, your appearance has made it necessary to discontinue a few of our prebattle procedures. I will return to this channel in less than a minute."

"I understand. I shall wait."

"Thank you." Caine turned toward Sleeman. "Doctor, you have sixty seconds."

She nodded. "Alnduul's lying, sir. Or at least, I think he's not telling us the full truth."

"In what way?"

"Commodore, there was an anomalous sensor return when the *Olsloov* appeared."

Riordan nodded. "The first time we encountered a Dornaani ship, the one that picked us up for Convocation, the sensors got a strange froth back when they encountered its energy-absorbing hull."

Sleeman shook her head. "No, sir. It's not that anomaly. But my return does match an earlier one you detected on that same occasion. Specifically, when that first Dornaani ship shifted in, it had an atypical shift signature: fewer photons and heat, more cosmic rays, and something that looked like mesons forming out of subquantal junk. And it all arrived a moment *after* the shift was completed, like a stern wash." She nodded at the image of *Olsloov*. "That's what I saw just now, too."

Riordan stared at the Dornaani ship. "So are you telling us that the *Olsloov* hasn't been tagging along with us unseen, but shifted in? Right beside us?"

"It looks that way, sir. I don't see any particle trails that match its current vector."

Dora scowled. "So the *bastardos* lied to us. They weren't in this system the whole time we were gone."

Riordan could feel his frown deepening. "Actually, they might have been."

Solsohn's question was slow, almost cautious. "What are you getting at?"

Riordan gestured in the direction of the holoplot. "If they just in-shifted from another system, then how the hell did they know exactly where we were? Either they have invisible sensors which can instantaneously communicate their readings across any distance—"

"—or they can shift *within* a system." Karam finished. "So maybe they aren't limited to making single large shifts. Maybe they can—well, perform microshifts."

Caine nodded, remembered the strange sensation he'd experienced the last time he'd been on a Dornaani ship while it was shifting. It had been the sixteen-light-year hop—unprecedented, in itself—that had carried him from the disastrous Convocation at EV Lacertae to Barnard's star. Conducted without preacceleration, it had taken Caine by surprise, but not so much so that he didn't recall that the sensation was different from the sharp, occasionally profound disorientation that persisted for a moment or two after a typical shift. On the Dornaani ship, it had felt more like his mind was shuddering, teetering at the edge of unconsciousness without ever slipping all the way into it. And then they were at Barnard's Star, and far closer to their destination than any human navigation system could have achieved.

Dora was clearly more interested in deeds than she was in physics. "So did they lie to us or not?"

Riordan shrugged. "We can't be sure. But I've never known Alnduul to tell an outright lie. However, I have seen his role as a Custodian force him into situations where he tells partial truths, leaves out details he's not at liberty to share. That could be what's happening here. Dora, let's talk to Alnduul again."

"As you wish," she muttered. "Mic is live."

"Alnduul, my apologies for the delay."

"Apologies are unneeded, Caine Riordan. During the elapsed time, I have been in contact with *Ferocious Monolith*. They assure me that they meant only to defend *Arbitrage*, which signaled that they were in imminent danger of destruction from a pursuing Slaasriithi shift-carrier."

"Hmm. And did *Ferocious Monolith* happen to explain why *Arbitrage* was brought here by a Ktoran tug? Or why that tug isn't running a transponder?"

"No. They also failed to explain how or why a ship of the Slaasriithi Great Ring—statistically and inherently the most peaceful of all the species of the Accord—was pursuing a human craft with intent to destroy it. I think we may safely conclude that the Ktoran ambassador Tlerek Srin Shethkador is not being entirely forthcoming in all his communiqués." Riordan could easily picture Alnduul's characteristically Dornaani expression of irony: a half-twist of his everted lamprey mouth.

Sleeman announced the practical consequences of Alnduul's communication with the Ktor. "Both *Ferocious Monolith* and the destroyer are sheering off, sir: they are no longer closing to engagement. They are recalling their independent platforms."

Riordan nodded his acknowledgment. "So what now, Alnduul? I expect the Custodians should be apprised of what we found on Turkh'saar."

"Indeed. It will also be imperative for us to learn why the Slaasriithi broke the Fifth Accord by violating the territory of the Arat Kur and the Hkh'Rkh, and why you accompanied, and possibly assisted, them as they did so. I am assuming it has to do with the human transmissions that were reported to us as emanating from that system."

"It did. And we received a summons from Advocate of the Unhonored Yaargraukh to assist him in addressing the source of those communications."

"And were they indeed human communications?"

"They were. And Yaargraukh has returned with us, although his status among his own people is now uncertain."

"I am sad to hear this. He is a most gifted diplomat and would have been of great value to the Patrijuridicate. I hope he shall be yet. At any rate, we shall all commence a journey back to Homenest."

"Very well, although Richard Downing has yet to order us to commence travel to that destination."

"I have also been in contact with Mr. Downing. He agrees that a discussion of the events that transpired on Turkh'saar is prudent."

"And who proposed that discussion? You?"

"Oddly, no. The Ktoran ambassador. He was most adamant."

Caine couldn't help smiling. *Damn, but the Ktor had a brass set.* "Well, that figures: Shethkador is always looking to tell a few more astute lies."

"Actually, he said that, in this case, helping the Ktoran Sphere was of second importance. His primary objective was to help you."

"You mean, the Terran Republic?" *Is he trying to set a new record for "most outrageous lie?"*

"No. I believe he was talking about the entirety of your species, Caine Riordan. And he may even have meant it."

Which, in some ways, was an even more disturbing prospect.

Tlerek Srin Shethkador bestowed upon Olsirkos Shethkador'vah, master of *Will Breaker*, the supreme courtesy of listening to the entirety of his utterly flawed assessment of how the Ktoran ships might still productively engage their enemies, even with the arrival of the *Olsloov*. It had been sadly fascinating, hearing how a mind as narrowly gifted as Olreknas's could brilliantly assess the particulars of each aspect of tactical combat, while remaining mostly blind to the strategic ramifications. Moreover, he was wholly insensate to the greater diplomatic consequences. "Your summary of operational alternatives was most thorough, Olsirkos."

Charles E. Gannon

"The Great Srin's opinion of my efforts is a source of pride and encouragement for me."

We'll see if you still feel that way after I show you how pointless it all is. "However, despite the detailed accuracy of your assessments, it would be counterproductive to proceed as you recommend. Indeed, it would be disastrous."

There was a prolonged silence on the secure channel. "I regret and apologize that I have wasted the Srin's time."

Me, too. But Shethkador said, "It is only a waste if you learn nothing from it. Tell me: why do you project I am refusing to take action against our foes?"

A shorter pause. "Uncertainty of the outcome."

As an answer on a test, it was passing—barely—but far from astute or even promising. "Let us deal with those uncertainties first, although they are not the reason I elect against combat. Superficially, your contention that their Slaasriithi shift-carrier and Dornaani shift-cruiser would not fare well against the combined power of our cruiser, destroyer, tug and the *Arbitrage* has some merit. We have the advantage of position and flexibility of multiple assets. And your point is well taken that all four of ours, even the *Arbitrage* and the tug have decisive weaponry, insofar as their navigational clearance lasers have power and range sufficient to function as the equivalent of military spinal-mounted beam weapons.

"However, this is where your analysis begins to show its flaws. Firstly, the Custodial ship appeared in a position which put it within firing range of the *Arbitrage*. How long do you expect that engagement would have lasted?"

"Honored Srin, I did offer the caveat that I anticipated it would have been brief."

"It would have lasted five seconds—if that. While it is
true that Ktoran craft have not tried cases with Dornaani
for centuries, that is no excuse for lacking familiarity
with our enemy's last-known weapon systems. Which
are so powerful and so accurate that the human craft
would have been reduced to debris in the first attack.
But for the Extirpates' human shift-carrier to have any
value in the coming battle, it had to inflict significant
damage against the *Olsloov* before it was disabled. And
what, do you think, were the odds of that outcome?"

"Low, Esteemed Srin."

"Nonexistent, 'vah. You should acquaint yourself with
the energy-absorbing characteristics of the thermionic
and ultraconducting matrices embedded in the Dornaani hull. The Aboriginal navigational laser would
have been lucky to score a significant hit: the rate at
which it deposits energy is unlikely to overcome the
absorption limits of the matrix before the speed of
the Dornaani ship shifts the aimpoint to an adjacent
part of the hull.

"So now it is only three ships to two, and our tug
will have to flee before the Dornaani to not be lost
similarly. Granted, its navigational laser is far more
powerful, and its structure far more robust than the
primitive Aboriginal starship, but it is hard to imagine
that the outcome would be much different. At most, the
Dornaani vessel might now have accrued some damage.
But consider: even with the Dornaani damaged, the
enemy now has the advantage in hulls. Furthermore,
Nezdeh, head of the Perekmeres Extirpates, shared
sensor data that indicates that the otherwise negligible

performance of the Aboriginal Wolfe-class corvette has been significantly enhanced. Enough so that we must figure it in our equations. It is also unknown how many drone fighters the Slaasriithi shift-carrier has in its bays. According to the sensor recordings of the battle in Turkh'saar, they apparently lost four. But that does not tell us how many they have left. That is a significant variable. As are the thirty remote platforms that the Aboriginal fleet sent ahead to aid the corvette.

"However, let us assume that the Slaasriithi have none of their drone fighters left and that the Aboriginal remote platforms are easily defeated. Let us also assume that we fare well in a long, hard battle against the enemy ships—a contest in which we might easily find ourselves overmatched. Let us happily assume we defeat all our enemies. How then shall we deal with the hordes of Aboriginal warships heading our way? Although nowhere near as technologically advanced as the Slaasriithi craft, these vessels are built expressly for war. Their armament is lavish and their speed, particularly over short distances, is not inconsiderable. Would we destroy many of them? Undoubtedly. But by the end of our battle with the *Olsloov*, the *Shore-of-Stars*, and the corvette, how damaged will we be? How extensively have we expended our own missiles and drones? How much damage will we have suffered to our drives? Will we be able to escape them? And if not, will we still have enough control over our own hulls to be sure of scuttling them before the Aboriginals commandeer them and thereby gain access to technology that they would quickly reengineer and so become dangerous rivals within a decade's time?"

Olsirkos sounded chastened. "The Srin's wisdom once again instructs my own."

As it had better. "The arrival of the Dornaani ship changed all the assumptions upon which our original estimates of victory were based. To have continued with our attack would have endangered the technological edge enjoyed by our entire race. This is how strategic thought must instruct tactics, Olsirkos, if you hope to move beyond your status as 'vah."

Shethkador told himself that he should really take the time to instruct his subordinate in the finer diplomatic points which bore upon the current situation. Yet, on the other hand, even an unpromising 'vah should be able to foresee that once the Custodial ship arrived, all hope of plausible deniability evaporated. The *Arbitrage*'s dubious claim that it was in imminent danger became moot: the Custodians had arrived to ensure a nonviolent resolution. An attack would have triggered a Custodial response in kind and a rekindling of general hostilities— exactly what Shethkador had been sent to this accursed region of space to prevent. It was imperative to calm the roiling postwar waters and preserve an interval of peace, during which Ktor could ready itself for a now-inevitable confrontation with Earth—a confrontation the Aboriginals had not yet foreseen.

"My Srin," Olsirkos began after a long silence, "I understand that you had no choice but to accept the Dornaani instructions, but why did you say that you were 'happy' to comply?"

"Because, in all truth, I was. As I explained to their tiresome Senior Mentor Alnduul, recent events are bringing too many of the species of the Accord back to the brink of war. If we are to arrest that slide into the abyss, it is imperative that we speak with the 'Terrans,' since an understanding between us is the key to building a lasting peace. So we must meet with them—and them alone."

"But to what actual end do you intend this meeting?"

"To reassure them, to calm them, to placate them if necessary. All to buy time for us."

Olsirkos sounded perplexed. "I did not foresee that. I shall set course for Homenest, then."

And here's something else you didn't foresee. "You will not. Nor shall *Ferocious Monolith*."

"Terrible Srin, I thought you said—"

"I said I would go to a conference with the humans. I said nothing about our ships. I will take *Doom Herald* to Homenest. You will be in command of all our craft and refuel. You will also take my place upon *Ferocious Monolith* and bring over personnel from *Will Breaker* to spend time in the cruiser's full-gee rotational habitat. When I signal that I am returning, you shall arrange transportation delays so that there shall be at least two watches from *Will Breaker* aboard *Ferocious Monolith* when I return."

"Imposing Srin, any exchange of crew between our House destroyer and an Autarchal ship such as *Ferocious Monolith* is technically prohibited. Having so much crew loyal to a single House—even our own—aboard your shift-cruiser is a serious violation."

"Duly noted. We shall take steps to assuage any concern. Have the galley prepare double rations for the crew on that day."

"The Srin is most generous."

Shethkador smiled. "The Srin is most cautious." *And has good reason to fear the worst.*

Chapter Sixty-Seven

Riordan, escorted by two ursine door-kickers from the 75th Ranger Regiment's Transatmospheric Assault Battalion and a small pack of defense and sensor drones, found Richard Downing waiting in a domelike chamber that was irregular and rough-hewn. The director of IRIS nodded to the two guards, who saluted him, then Riordan, then marched back the way they had come. The drones stayed, joining about a dozen others and four black-garbed soldiers in combat armor, visors down, and without any unit markings.

Richard put out a hand. "Quite a trip, down here, isn't it?"

Caine put his own out to shake Downing's briefly. "Took a similar one when I was here yesterday. Can't say I'm liking it any better this time." He looked for any code, or writing on any of the walls. Nothing. And there never seemed to be. "Hard to imagine how they live in these tunnels."

"Well, with any luck, your meeting with Darzhee Kut yesterday might get us one step closer to exchanges which might provide some answers."

Riordan shook his head. "Not going to happen because of me. I got the information I needed about the prewar period and that was all."

"Well, by any practical measure, your visit was a success."

"Maybe, but I'm not welcome here. And never will be."

"Even though it was you who kept them from getting exterminated. Rather ironic."

"That's one thing I've noticed about war, Richard: there's always more than enough irony to go around. Where's Vassily?"

"Consul Sukhinin is on his way. His security precautions are, you will appreciate, somewhat more elaborate than ours. Now, any final questions?"

"No, I think we're on the same page. We certainly spent enough time coordinating, yesterday."

"True enough. I suspect—" Downing paused, listening.

A full squad of Spetsnaz filed into the chamber quickly, sweeping it both with naked eyes and a variety of sensors. After it was deemed clear, another squad approached and stopped just outside the entry. Vassily emerged from their ranks, headed straight toward Riordan. "Caine, the *dvulichniye* Ktor just can't seem to kill you, hey? Not as though they don't try." He took Caine's hand in both of his and shook it warmly. He looked worn. Working as the senior human political authority in the Sigma Draconis system, and thus, in charge of finalizing the peace agreement, had apparently not been easy duty.

"It's very good to see you, Vassily. When will they let you out of here so that the Ktor can start trying to kill you, instead?"

Sukhinin chortled. "I have missed you, *parnishka*. And to answer your question: soon. I think. We were ready to finalize and ratify the agreements this week. Then you showed up, bringing trouble and disruption as usual. Bah. You have no consideration for an old man."

"Hm. Well, when you become an old man, I'll start having appropriate consideration."

Sukhinin smiled. "It is a kind lie you tell. I am getting older faster than ever: a week for every day I am here, I think. It is a new kind of relativity. Come: let us get this over with." He walked to the wall directly opposite the entrance, rapped on a smooth rock that protruded slightly from the otherwise craggy, inward-sloping surface.

The rock made a soft grinding noise, then began to recede.

Caine looked at Sukhinin, who shrugged. "We are meeting in what the Arat Kur call a secrecy room. It is specially constructed to be impenetrable to any sensors, has no electricity or mechanisms in it. And none are allowed. Leave your palmtop and collarcom with my adjutant."

Caine did so, looked around. "I thought there would be Arat Kur present, to oversee the process."

Sukhinin nodded. "Usually, there are."

"But today—?"

Vassily sighed, turned his baggy eyes upon Caine. "But today, you are here and they will not come."

Riordan had nothing to say for a moment. "They're dropping their security just because they'd have to have contact with me?"

"Trust me; their security is here. They may not be present in this antechamber—there are several which

lead into any secrecy room—but they are watching
and could deal with us very easily if we violated the
protocols. You cannot see their sensors, or their remote
weapons, but they are all around you."

Riordan looked at the cave walls again, once again
felt the sensation with which he had entered the
tunnels an hour ago. *It is as though I am descending into a dungeon. No, a pit. And at the bottom is
a monster. A monster named Tlerek Srin Shethkador.
A monster that tried to kill me in Jakarta. And may
have killed the woman I love and the mother of my
son, if the Dornaani haven't been able to heal her.
In a more honest world, I would be carrying a torch
and a sword, not going in empty-handed to duel with
words.* "I can't believe that Shethkador actually thinks
we believe his rhetoric about finding a path to peace."

Downing shrugged. "I rather expect he knows we
don't believe it. But he could hardly speak honestly,
could he? It's bad diplomatic form to begin an exchange
with, 'I'd like you to meet me apart from the other
races, so I can lie about our involvement without
having them present to contradict me.'"

Vassily rolled his eyes as he waited in front of the
hole that the receding rock had left in the wall. "We
shall be lucky if those are the only lies we shall have
to hear today."

Riordan saw a dim light begin to grow in the low,
meter-wide opening before them. "Well, at least Alnduul will be there to keep him from distorting the
truth too much."

The big Russian lowered himself into a crawling
position; Riordan felt a pang of sadness, watching
how much he favored his knees. "Alnduul and his

Custodians are not such a help as you may think, *parnishka*. They do not take sides, even when one side is speaking truth and the other is speaking nothing but lies."

Richard crouched down as well, started crawling into the hole after Sukhinin. "Alnduul is limited by the mandate of the Custodians, Vassily. If other powers of the Accord lie, that has to be proven."

"And with any luck," added Caine, "that's exactly what we'll do today." He got down on his hands and knees and started scrabbling through the narrow passageway after the two older men.

As Caine emerged into the secrecy room, he noticed that the light was dim and oddly diffuse. Looking around for the source, he discovered that it was coming from almost all points of the ceiling and walls: a bioluminescent mold that emitted a greenish-yellow glow.

Standing near the center of the chamber was a single, short figure with a top-heavy teardrop-shaped head and bottom-heavy teardrop body: Alnduul. The Dornaani's large, apparently pupilless eyes turned upon Caine; their nictating lenses cycled once, slowly. "It is good to see you again, Caine Riordan. I trust you are well."

"I am. And it is good to see you also, Alnduul. Is it customary here that the, well, I guess the moderator of a discussion arrives in the secrecy room first?"

"It is."

"And did you choose for us to enter after you?"

"No, the sequence of entry is determined by protocols. Usually, the order in which the interlocutors enter is determined by a random process. Traditionally, each party tosses five rocks which are marked on one side. The greater the number of rocks that show the marking when they settle, the earlier in the order that party enters."

"Heads, we win," murmured Caine.

"However," continued Alnduul, "today, there are circumstances that take precedence over random determination. Any party with a member that has never entered a secrecy room before has priority."

Riordan shrugged. "So, that would be me."

"Indeed. Before we bring in the last interlocutor, do you have questions?"

Caine nodded. "Are there other protocols about which I should know?"

"An excellent question." Alnduul gestured at the bare stone floor, moved to seat himself. As he did, his heavy robe made a faint sloshing sound: evidently it was a very primitive, heavily lined saturation suit. At home in higher temperatures and humidity—or immersed in water—Dornaani that were in air for an extended period of time wore the equivalent of light-duty environmental protection suits. Low humidity damaged their skin; low temperature led to torpor and respiratory constricton. However, Caine had only seen them wearing highly advanced and very light-weight protective gear before now. This unpowered model was a great deal more bulky. Alnduul used his four-fingered hand to protect what seemed to be a dorsal reservoir from getting caught behind him as he finished seating himself.

His small, protuberant sucker mouth flattened in frustration as he smoothed the suit and made sure it wasn't doubling over on itself before continuing. "There can be no implements or artifactures in this room of any kind, other than our clothes. And even that is a concession that the Arat Kur make for exosapient visitors: they attend completely unadorned. The primary reason for this is to ensure that no being brings any external advantage of any kind into this chamber. This is not to equalize a potential conflict; it is to serve as a constant disincentive to violence, as well as a reminder that physical confrontation of any kind is expressly forbidden in a secrecy room.

"The room itself is surrounded by solid rock fifty meters in all directions. No water or power conduits of any kind are located anywhere within one hundred meters of its center. Interlocutors in a secrecy room may leave whenever they choose, but they may not reenter. Violations of the rules have consequences which range from never being allowed in a secrecy room again, to banishment to the surface of Homenest. While this would not be a hardship for us, this was considered a fate worse than death to the ancient Arat Kur." Alnduul settled himself more comfortably in the folds of his saturation suit. "If you are ready, we may bring in the other interlocutor now."

Riordan forced himself to remain still as Shethkador entered: alone and in loose-fitting clothes that might have been suitable for travel in a desert or on safari. Evidently familiar with the traditions of the secrecy room, he settled himself to the floor, the last point of an equilateral triangle formed by the three separate parties.

Alnduul's inner eyelids nictated sharply, twice. "You are ready to proceed, Ambassador Shethkador?"

"I am. Although I remain surprised that you were able to prevail upon the Arat Kur to allow us this private conversation. I had expected there to be a representative waiting for me when I arrived, chittering remonstrations and clamoring to be included."

Caine replied before Alnduul could open his mouth. "Frankly, the Arat Kur made it perfectly clear to me yesterday that they did not want to be in the same room with you. Or with me, for that matter. And they have no desire to interact with humans in a shared space." *Damn it, I'm too jumpy. I've got to calm down.*

Alnduul was already interceding. "Although Commodore Riordan speaks with undue emotion, it is true that the Arat Kur have signaled their desire to avoid contact with both of you, individually."

Shethkador smiled at Caine. "A bond of common experience, at last."

Sukhinin leaned forward. "Enough of your poisonous small talk. You have much to answer for, Ktor."

Shethkador's smile broadened; he reclined, leaning back on one elbow as if lounging beside a pool. "You will not even offer me the courtesy of a title, *Ambassador* Sukhinin? Brutish, of course, but I find your hatred refreshing. There is so little frankness in diplomacy."

Sukhinin did not take the bait. "The list of crimes committed by your state, and by your own crew, are extensive. And I am only counting those you committed during your time in this system as the diplomatic representative of the Ktoran Sphere."

Shethkador nodded. "Let me see if I may anticipate the items on that list. It would begin with murders of various persons in your fleet, as well as sabotage of several of your craft, all so that two saboteurs could be placed with your envoy to the Slaasriithi. Then there would be the seizure of your megacorporate shift-carrier, the *Arbitrage*, in system V 1581, the slaying of her security forces and command staff, and the abduction of her crew. I suppose the next item would be the violation, by the *Arbitrage* and tug *Uzhmarek*, of numerous Arat Kur and Slaasriithi systems as they trailed your envoy to system BD +02 4076, which the Slaasriithi call Disparity. Where, if what I have been told is correct, your delegation and the Slaasriithi ship carrying it were attacked and many casualties were inflicted, including a number during an assault upon the planet itself. And finally, there are the late events in the system you designate as BD+56 2966, where the same Ktoran-led group inflicted casualties both on the planet Turkh'saar and in the nearby regions of space." His smile had not faded. "Does my list match yours? Is it sufficiently comprehensive?"

Downing smiled back. "It is helpful that you have agreed to this list of infractions without debate, Ambassador. That will shorten the process of resolving the grievances."

"Mister—Downing, I believe? I did not claim responsibility for these acts. I simply recited the list I believe you would have recited to me, probably with far more details than were needed."

Sukhinin frowned. "You said yourself that Ktor were involved in all these acts."

"They were. But not upon my orders."

"Ridiculous. They—"

"There is nothing ridiculous about that assertion, either as a fact or an extenuating circumstance that absolves the Ktoran Sphere from direct culpability. However, there is the further matter of violations by other members of the Accord, including your own, which certainly problematize your presumption of unilateral guilt. Those violations include two separate species attacking your own homeworld, your subsequent counterattack into Arat Kur space, culminating in an attack upon this system, at which point you threatened to unleash a viral plague that would depopulate their homeworld, and perhaps their entire polity. And recently, your forces trespassed in Arat Kur space and attacked Hkh'Rkh forces on Turkh'saar in the course of extracting a band of human renegades who had been raiding and pillaging that planet. And let us not forget the unsettled matter of your colonizing 70 Ophiuchi, a system that you were not permitted to claim, according to the permitted pathways of settlement established by the Accord."

"Of which the Terrans had no knowledge," Alnduul amended. "Also, in this matter, and the others you cite, they are still not members of the Accord and so, are not bound by it."

"True, but they *are* a protected species. And whose job, ultimately, is it to ensure that they were properly informed regarding 70 Ophiuchi? Who was to be the guarantor of their behavior toward other powers while a protected species?"

"The Custodians, as you imply. But your implication ignores other, crucial facts. If we had been given a clear mandate for first contact when we asked for it, we could have informed the Terrans in a timely fashion. But the Accord refused to give us that mandate."

"That is hardly our affair."

"Yet it is your doing. Timely first contact was prevented due to objections mounted by the Ktoran Sphere and the Arat Kur Wholenest. In any event, the failure was not the Custodians': we were prevented from making contact when we advised. And the other violations of which you accuse the Terrans were direct responses to being attacked by another protected species—the Hkh'Rkh—and two member states: yours and the Arat Kur's."

"We did not attack the Terrans."

Riordan felt his face grow hot. "You attacked *this* Terran. Fired a rod into my back and damn near killed me. You, personally, Ambassador. And then you followed up by doing the same thing to my—to Elena Corcoran. All perpetrated after you had surrendered along with the Arat Kur headquarters staff. And let's not forget the CoDevCo executives you suborned, who unleashed their battalions of clones against the population of Indonesia."

Shethkador smiled. "All of which has been explained. Advising other species or your world's corporations is not a declaration of war, Captain—oh, it is Commodore now, isn't it? And my attacks upon you and Ms. Corcoran were, as I have already explained, in response to what I perceived to be imminent threats upon my life. I was surrounded by your soldiers, after all."

The more Shethkador lied, the easier Riordan found it to remain calm. "Those lies change nothing, Ambassador. Your dubious diplomatic privilege notwithstanding, you interfered in the affairs of a protected species by advising, aiding, and abetting military operations against it. So far as the Accords are concerned, it doesn't matter whether you were holding a weapon yourself or not."

Shethkador's smile dimmed slightly. "Which actually brings us back to the silent enablers—or should that be architects?—of all this misery: the Accords themselves. A set of agreements which have now been violated so many times in such quick succession that their unsuitability is more nakedly evident than ever before.

"And whose fault is it that the Accord is so flawed? Its crafters, the Dornaani." He leaned back further, smile restored to its full ironic width. "Unless I've missed somebody, we now have accusations of violations and duplicity leveled against every known intelligent species. What wonderful Accords: the one thing they have achieved is to establish that everybody is guilty of something."

Downing nodded. "Very well. So let us resolve these violations. Let us have each one delineated and brought before the courts of the species whose laws were violated."

Shethkador had clearly not expected that response, deflected it with a dismissive wave. "An ingenuously quixotic suggestion. If we started down such a path, we would spend decades trying cases for which we do not even have a common basis in law."

"I'm not talking about a common basis in law: I'm saying let each species decide upon who, finally, is responsible for the violations they purport to have suffered."

Shethkador's sudden impatience seemed to be motivated, in part, by a desire to get off the topic. "You are prattling about something that cannot be done. The Accord, as flawed as it is, recognizes the futility of such actions. That is why there is no provision for it. Rather, the Ninth Accord indicates that all such disagreements must be submitted to the Custodians for arbitration—which would no doubt be resolved in your favor." His sidelong glance at Alnduul lasted no longer than his pause. "However, you remain a protected species. You are thus protected against aggression and trespass, but only so long as you constrain your own actions to those permitted by the Accords." Shethkador smiled. "But you have not constrained your actions accordingly. So legally, the Custodians may not protect you any longer."

"Preposterous," replied Downing. "Our settlement of 70 Ophiuchi was to be a mediated matter. But before it could be, two members of the Accord attacked us and brought another protected species, the Hkh'Rkh, along for company."

"So, according to your own admission, your violation at 70 Ophiuchi was what triggered the subsequent violations against you. You cannot claim protection when you yourselves began the sequence of violations."

Caine couldn't help laughing. "There's a specious argument if I ever heard one. We unwittingly violated the pathway of permitted expansion before we knew you or any other exosapients existed. We were party to no contract at that time. Only once we attended Convocation were we informed that we were a protected species and what that entailed. And a few weeks later we were attacked. But we had to see to our own defense while we waited for the legitimate protection forces to arrive." Riordan looked at Alnduul. "Sadly, those forces never did arrive, at least not in the form we were promised. And they haven't shown up to handle the aftermath, either."

Downing nodded. "With the exception of our friend Alnduul, we can't even get the Custodians to respond to our inquiries right now. So does that mean we're supposed to put up our weapons and return home?"

Shethkador was no longer in a pose of sybaritic ease. "There is nothing that legally validates your continued presence here or in any systems other than your own."

Riordan had had enough. "We waited for the rules to work for us once, and it almost cost us our world. Don't count on us being that optimistic, or gullible, again. So when it comes to Turkh'saar, we had a pretty stark choice: either wait for the Custodians, who still haven't shown up to confer with us about the first violation of our protected species status, or deal with the situation ourselves. Thankfully, the Slaasriithi helped us, in the interest of trying to avoid another war."

"Even so, a violation is a violation. And you violated the territory of two other species when you interfered at Turkh'saar."

"By that logic, spitting on the sidewalk is as great a crime as mass murder."

"Law is neither coherent nor reliable if it excuses some crimes while punishing others. I repeat: a violation is a violation."

"Happily," interjected Downing, who placed a restraining hand on Riordan's arm, "the Accord's arbitrations assess each deed in the context of the extenuating circumstances, and then assign fitting penalties if it is, in fact, held to be a violation. If the Accord were not capable of making such basic juridical distinctions, then we would have no interest in becoming part of it."

Shethkador's smile returned. "So, we return to my

first assertions: that the decisions—and therefore, the problems—of the Accord ultimately rest with the Custodians. Who are now in the uncomfortable position of having to punish all, none, or only some of the violators. And if they choose the latter, it will be incumbent upon them to explain how that is anything other than favoritism."

Alnduul stirred slightly. "I cannot speak for all the Custodians, but in every case that has come to us for arbitration, the severity and multiplicity of the infractions guides our decisions. And never have the proportions of blame been so uneven as in this case."

"And there's another factor to be considered, Shethkador," Riordan added. "Your violations weren't simply mistakes, or even opportunistic. They were premeditated, with malice and aforethought."

Shethkador smiled. "I should like to see you prove it."

Riordan's answering smile was wider. "Okay: I will."

Chapter Sixty-Eight

Tlerek Srin Shethkador's smile faltered. "If you are speaking of the actions I listed earlier, I once again disavow them. They were the crimes of a rogue group, members of a House that the Ktoran Sphere identified as dangerous both to itself and the interests of interspeciate amity. That is why we Extirpated them."

Downing frowned. "I'm sorry: you did what to them?"

"They were Extirpated." When Downing still stared at him, uncertain, Shethkador continued, agitated. "They were removed, excised, exterminated. What word will make it most clear? We are not weak or irresolute in correcting a wrong once it is detected, and our methods are final."

Riordan stared at him. "Not final enough, it seems. But it's not their deeds that damn you: it's your own. Specifically, you repeatedly claim that you weren't behind the war that the Arat Kur and Hkh'Rkh waged upon us, that you were simply a friendly party called in to give advice."

"That is true."

"No, that is a lie. And we found the proof in the Turkh'saar system, where all three of the powers that attacked us probably hoped it would remain hidden. Because what we found there indicates that the attack on Earth wasn't caused by the events of the last Convocation. Rather, it appears the disastrous outcome of that meeting was actually carefully orchestrated by you and the other species to provide a pretext for war."

Riordan glanced at Alnduul to see if there were any signs of surprise. The Dornaani not only appeared unruffled but serene. *Of course, maybe this is exactly the revelation you've been hoping for but couldn't unveil yourself, lest it look like, well, favoritism.*

Riordan shifted his attention back to Shethkador. "We surveyed the debris in the BD+56 2966 system, particularly around the gas giant in the seventh orbit and Turkh'saar itself. The Slaasriithi did not merely destroy normal interstellar infrastructure: they stumbled upon and eliminated the logistical apparatus for the invasion fleet that struck us at Barnard's Star about a month after Convocation ended. Which means that the facilities were already there long before Convocation was convened. Which in turn means that the Arat Kur and the Hkh'Rkh were using the system as a joint staging area. From which they would have had to be advancing *before* word of the outcome of Convocation could have reached them. In summary, both species went to Convocation with the intent of starting a war that would commence immediately afterward—because their forces were already in motion."

Shethkador's smile was a great deal less natural, now. "And what if your delegation had agreed to abandon your illegal settlement in the 70 Ophiuchi system? That would have meant these forces were invading without cause. Which makes your entire hypothesis flawed and ridiculous."

"That criticism conveniently leaves out a few key facts. First of all, it was established by the Accord, not us, that our delegation had no power to make policy: we were there to observe and represent our species. And that was all. So we *couldn't* offer to withdraw from 70 Ophiuchi and the Arat Kur knew it: they were assured that they'd still have an axe to grind with us after the Convocation had concluded.

"But if, by some quirk of fate, the matter had been settled, one look at a star chart shows what the contingency plan must have been. Given their shift limitations, the Arat Kur fleet elements already had to be in 61 Cygni as the final jump off point; it's the only system from which they can reach Barnard's Star.

"Of course, 61 Cygni can also be reached in one shift from EV Lacertae, quickly enough to call off the invasion in time. But the only ships which can reach it in one shift are *Ktoran* ships. Neither the Arat Kur nor the Hkh'Rkh have sufficient range. So in the event that the Dornaani had allowed us to make a last minute concession to all the Arat Kur demands at Convocation, there was only one way to prevent the fleet from making its final shift into battle: a Ktoran courier. Or to, put it another way, your material support was a key part of their invasion plans."

Downing leaned forward. "Of course, all of that is just the tip of the iceberg. Fleet logistics, such as those the Slaasriithi destroyed at BD+56 2966, don't get built overnight. And the strategic decisions behind them—such as delegating all ground operations to the Hkh'Rkh and all spaceside combat to the Arat Kur—take a while to work out, to optimize. Each side has to ready itself for its role in the coming war. And that is the work of years, not weeks or months. Or would you assert otherwise, Ambassador Shethkador?"

"I will make my rebuttal when I have heard this fabulation through in its entirety." Shethkador's tone was nowhere near so bold or dismissive as his words.

"Very well. As it turns out, we were alerted to the problems in Turkh'saar by Yaargraukh, one of the members of the Hkh'Rkh delegation to the Convocation. While he did not speak for the Patrijuridicate, he opted to contact us by back channels to see if it wasn't possible for us to intercede in the matter of a human incursion on the planet. Naturally, you know what we found there." Downing plainly waited for Shethkador to object to that assumption; when no interruption occurred, he continued. "However, what we did not anticipate was that Yaargraukh would be compelled to seek asylum with Commodore Riordan and return with him."

Shethkador's eyes opened slightly wider, but he did not respond otherwise.

"Consequently, we have gained a rather unique perspective on the probable timeline that must have been involved in the war preparations. In short, between his intimate knowledge of the politics and projects of the Patrijuridicate during the period in question, and Ambassador Yiithrii'ah'aash's detailed recollections of the concurrent proceedings of the Accord, we learned that the Arat Kur and the Hkh'Rkh actually came into contact 'unintentionally' in 2111 and determined that Turkh'saar was to be a nonmilitarized codominium."

Downing shrugged. "However, given the nature of the wreckage that we found in the system, it is quite clear that this agreement was a sham, concocted to mislead the other, unsuspecting members of the Accord. We've run orbital backtracks on a variety of small, mostly intact platforms, all of which indicate that they were inserted into their orbits sometime between 2114 and 2116. As much as five years before Convocation."

Alnduul shifted so that he could stare at Shethkador.

The Ktor waved a dismissive hand. "And what do we have to do with the connivings of two alien species? Is there any evidence that we were present, that we helped ready them for this invasion?"

Caine leaned forward. "Not recently, no, but I wonder who made sure the Hkh'Rkh were ready to participate?"

"You are deaf or obtuse, Commodore Riordan. I said we were not in the system at that time."

"If there's anyone being obtuse, Ambassador, it's you—and willfully so. I'm not talking about your actions in the system recently; I'm talking about three and a half centuries ago. Give or take a decade or two. But I'd lay odds that your ships were in the BD+56 2966 system within ten years of the disappearance of the Arat Kur shift-cruiser *Katek Hud*. We found its wreckage on Turkh'saar, along with evidence that it was the means whereby the Hkh'Rkh achieved supraluminal travel: a prerequisite for them to be a useful partner in the invasion of Earth."

Shethkador stretched. "So you found a missing Arat Kur starship on Turkh'saar. And the Hkh'Rkh found it before you and derived the principles of the shift-drive from its remains. Again, what does this have to do with the Ktor?"

"Perhaps a great deal, since the *Katek Hud* disappeared in the Ross 508 system, over forty light-years from where it crashed on Turkh'saar. Or should I say, was brought down in such a way to make it *appear* to have crashed. There's a file waiting to be distributed to *Ferocious Monolith* and *Olsloov* as soon as this meeting is over. In it, you'll find all the forensics establishing the circumstances of the *Katek Hud*'s descent and hard landing—because you can't really call it a crash. Interestingly, there were no Arat Kur remains or artifacts at the site, not even their grooming and other domestic implements. The ship was improbably bare when it came down on Turkh'saar."

"And so this 'proves' Ktoran involvement?"

"No, not on its own. But it is interesting how certain members of House Perekmeres were familiar with the Turkh'saar system, how they knew ahead of time that almost eight hundred Terran abductees had been planted there sometime in the last century or so. Which begs the question: who planted them there to begin with? And how were they familiar enough with the system and the planet to do so? Which leads us back to the identity of those who placed the wreck of the *Katek Hud* on Turkh'saar, which, by process of induction, is no longer so mysterious. Because whoever put her there obviously passed on knowledge of the system—and her presence—to those who later planted the Lost Soldiers nearby.

"That was a mistake, of course: too many clues in so small a plot of ground. But the placement of the wreck: that was extremely clever, and subtle. BD+56

2966 was obviously the first system the Hkh'Rkh would explore when they achieved sublight interstellar travel. Not surprisingly, they noticed the 'crash site' and immediately found and developed the shift-drive technology. And so they were ready to play an indispensable role in the invasion of Earth: an invasion that the Arat Kur could not hope to have carried off alone, given their distaste for above-ground activities in general and combat in particular."

Shethkador was not smiling, but did not appear rattled. "An interesting set of hypotheses, Commodore—but hypotheses, just the same. In your legal parlance, they are supported by circumstantial evidence alone."

"Well, I suppose that's true—presuming we don't find some Arat Kur and Hkh'Rkh to corroborate our suspicions."

Shethkador sat a little more erect.

"You have excellent intelligence sources inside our fleet, so you no doubt know I was conferring with highly placed Arat Kur yesterday. And you no doubt know that if First Voice is discovered alive, and is apprised of your deeds, he will be likely to share what few know: that both his government and the Arat Kur Wholenest were coordinating with the Ktoran Sphere years in advance of the invasion."

"The last is pure conjecture, Commodore."

"No, I merely lack evidence. That's not quite the same thing. But thank you for indirectly confirming what the Arat Kur and Hkh'Rkh leadership has, or will, tell us about your prewar involvement with them.

"Frankly, I suspect that the Patrijuridicate will not want First Voice to be found. During my time with him, I found him a balanced leader and not entirely comfortable with the role in which he had been cast: the face most associated with the invasion of Earth. Yaargraukh has long been convinced that he may have been talked into cooperation with you by the more hard-line Old Families, who publicly claimed that the war was the *outcome* of Convocation. That lie will unravel as soon as they have access to the data on the wreckage near Turkh'saar: the average Hkh'Rkh can reconstruct an obvious timeline as well as anyone else.

"Yaargraukh also suspects First Voice would have been willing to call off the assault if the outcome of Convocation had been better. Which makes it interesting to wonder if he was among those who were purposely misled. Perhaps only the Arat Kur and the Ktor conspired to orchestrate a bad outcome and so, ensure the progression to war."

Shethkador shrugged. "Your prewar accusations are without conclusive, objective evidence. So a senior Arat Kur or First Voice of the Hkh'Rkh decide to accuse Ktor of collusion: what of it? Do you suppose that only Ktor's leaders lie? Your own recent history is filled with evidence to the contrary.

"And as far as the more recent violations are concerned, I reiterate that they are not the doing of the Ktoran Sphere, but of a group of traitors whom we spared because we believed they were redeemable. A bitter error, on our part."

Downing perched his chin upon his palm. "I must confess that I admire the unmitigated gall it takes to try to float such a fatuous collection of denials regarding Ktor's involvement. If you would have us believe that you are truly innocent of a misdeed, such as the attempt to wipe us out with the Doomsday Rock forty years ago, then you need to start by explaining why you didn't come clean on it in the first place, the moment we were introduced at Convocation.

"But I suppose that would be rather difficult, since then we might press you to explain why you were on Earth itself during the prior century, in violation of the Accords. And why you have since been advising other races in their campaigns to attack a homeworld, the most serious of all possible violations? Because if we start down that path, then we will demand to know the source, the origins, of those transgressions within the Ktoran Sphere. In each case, someone gave orders, those orders were obeyed, and consequences followed. So tell us: who gave the order that you, personally, should go to Earth in disguise? Who gave the orders to infiltrate our corporations? Who gave the order that your entire race should conceal its true speciate identity, thereby violating the Accords in the very act of applying to them for admission?"

Shethkador shrugged. "You do not understand the impossibility of what you ask, because you do not know how political decisions are taken in the Sphere."

"No, but I understand this: without accounting for the historic violations to which you admit, you have no reason to expect that we will take your word that the Ktoran Sphere was uninvolved in the ones perpetrated most recently. From our standpoint, only now—when you have nothing to gain by keeping the earlier violations secret and denying their very existence—do you admit that there are, in fact, flaws in your organization, that you don't have complete control over all your personnel." Downing shrugged.

"Perhaps those admissions might have mattered before. They are pointless, now. They simply underscore how utterly opportunistic you are: if you believe you can get away with something, you elect to keep it secret, or to blame someone or something else, for as long as you can."

Shethkador leaned forward. "You call my admission pointless, but in so saying, you acknowledge that they are admissions. You thus concede the real possibility that we, the Ktoran Sphere, had no direct hand in the events that took place surrounding the seizure of the *Arbitrage* and all that followed therefrom."

"It's possible, but no longer important."

"It is urgently important, and I will illustrate why." The Ktor sat straighter. "If some group of your people were to go rogue, should we hold Terra accountable for their infractions?"

"Yes, you should, particularly if it takes us almost forty years to admit our people made a mess of things, having known about it all along. And since you were one of the powers watching our system at the time this House Perekmeres pushed the Doomsday Rock at us, you can hardly claim you didn't know."

Sukhinin sliced the air with his heavy hand. "Enough, Richard. We know he and his breed are guilty, and he has made it clear that they will not admit it. This is now a matter for the Custodians, to whom we have provided the evidence of our accusations." He looked at Shethkador as if he was a hatrack. "It was you who asked for this meeting. What do you want?"

Shethkador shrugged. "I want to prevent our people from going to war."

And it sounded like he meant it.

Chapter Sixty-Nine

"We have never wanted to fight you," Shethkador continued. Which sounded somewhat less true.

Sukhinin seemed less willing to pursue the nuances in Shethkador's responses. He scoffed. "Yes, you wanted to rule us without fighting. It is as you pointed out just after we discovered that you were human—more or less. You would have been quite pleased if Hitler had won World War II. That would have made your job easier for you." Sukhinin, whose family was said to have suffered horribly in his nation's Great Patriotic War against the Nazis, wore a smile that was more reminiscent of bared teeth.

Shethkador's reply was almost casual. "Of course we would have preferred that outcome. You would have been preacculturated to our ways."

Downing raised an eyebrow. "So Adolf Hitler is your idea of an *ubermensch*?"

"Hitler? A superior being? Fate, no. Do not mistake our approval of the ethos of a regime for admiration of its leader. Hitler was a weak, superstitious amateur whose profound insecurities and absolute inability to perceive himself accurately ultimately caused the downfall of his project."

"How so?"

"Is it not obvious? Firstly, he surrounded himself with those like himself; fanatics who were also cranks, individuals whose personal derangements or need for rationalizing their own inferiority led them to a psychopathic projection of their own failings onto others. The true object of their exterminations was what they most feared and loathed in themselves; weakness, insufficiency, flaccidity, cowardice. They could not admit this, of course, so they protected the roots of their self-hatred by ensuring that these traits were not the overt criteria upon which their social extirpations were based. Rather, they demonized specific groups and then attributed these traits to them, thereby amplifying the political appeal of their movement by invoking traditional prejudices and stereotypes through suitably crafted propaganda."

Riordan folded his arms. "Actually, their methods sound almost as devious and well-rationalized as your own."

Shethkador waved a hand at Caine's comment as if it were a pesky insect. "A jibe that reveals how little you understand. Ktor breeds strength and power through pitiless self-knowledge: that is the natural purpose of any healthy organism. Hitler and his cabal subsumed their personal psychoses of self-loathing and need for rebirth by projecting all that destructive energy outward, so it could never rebound upon them. The immense social and physical monuments they then built to discharge their own psychoses demonstrates how just profound their weakness was."

Downing nodded. "Indulge me; cite one such moment of weakness."

"The Wansee Conference. The so-called Final Solution and the deathcamps."

"But wouldn't that be the ultimate expression and assertion of one's mastery over others?"

Shethkador seemed to flinch backward. "Ultimate? Perhaps—but so grotesque and wasteful that the desire to construct it can only be interpreted as a crippling weakness in any leader who would embark upon such a project.

"Consider: how many did Hitler kill? Six million? What if he had simply held his genocidal bigotry in check, had sought suitable recruits from among that immense throng? Even if only ten percent were emotionally, psychologically, culturally, and physically fit for service in his armies, that would have furnished him with slightly over six hundred thousand additional troops. Then consider all the security forces required to maintain and operate the machinery of genocide: the guards, the train security, the detachments tasked with rounding up those to be detained, the intelligence assets dedicated to investigating who did and did not belong in the camps. It was an immense undertaking. Let us be conservative, though, and assume that it was achieved with no more than sixty thousand personnel. So, all together, Hitler wasted the manpower of forty-four divisions of fifteen thousand men in his insane scheme. Then add in the cost of constructing the camps and shuttling detainees to and fro, often at the expense of adequate logistical support for his army. In short, Hitler's maniacal focus to destroy select subcultures on the Eurasian landmass may very well have cost him the war, and ultimately, his life. Had these persons been carriers of a literal plague, then maybe such actions would have been valid. But the priority he gave the Final Solution was out of all proportion to his strategic objectives. Hitler had a war to win but, in fact, his psychosis ensured his own defeat."

"If you mean to teach us that insanity is a weakness," Sukhinin smirked, "then here is a lesson for you: good instructors do not teach the obvious."

"They also do not labor to teach the ungifted, but I shall make an exception for you, given the importance of this discussion. So I will provide an example in which the weakness is not so much a byproduct of psychoses. To wit: consider Hitler's idiotic impatience to achieve his objectives. Consider his bloodless European acquisitions throughout the 1930s and the profound appeasementist attitudes in England, France, and Russia as the swastika came to fly over Vienna, then Prague, then Copenhagen, then parts of the Ruhr and the Saar. What if he had done what any sane individual would have done: pause and consolidate?

"It would have been easy to do: the other powers were still exhausted from World War One, did not wish to mobilize. And these early acquisitions were an immense adornment to the growing Nazi industrial complex. Given a five-year program of war preparations, during which he could have utterly obliterated any resistance in these territories, their addition and integration could have made Hitler all but unstoppable.

"But he was not the master of himself, of his drives. His vision of, and personal need for, self-assuring success overwhelmed strategic prudence. It is a similar species of ego—his ardent desire to be seen as a great war leader—that led him to consistently contradict and countermand the advice and plans of his own supremely capable general staff. And had he won, who was then to stop him from selectively demobilizing his armies and ensuring that the members of the groups he wished to exterminate never returned home, but were led to remote places where they could be disposed of? Who would have remained to contest his forces when they came for the families, back in their homelands?"

Sukhinin sneered. "And who would want to hear you talk so much, about a topic that has nothing to do with preventing war between us?"

"But that is where you are mistaken, Consul Sukhinin," Shethkador objected. "It has *everything* to do with preventing war. It is important—imperative—that you understand us. Note I do not say it is urgent that you like, or even accept, us—but that you understand us."

Riordan stared at him. "You mean, understand you to the extent you deem it safe and useful."

"Of course I meant that. It would be absurd to propose that we are potential friends, or even disinterested states. But for you to make prudent decisions dealing with the Ktoran Sphere, you must understand that our power structures do not work the same way yours do. We are not founded on nations, but Houses, and while our self-interest is united and absolute, our political will is concentrated in far fewer hands that are resolved to act with vigor and dispatch. We are not the Nazis: we are not a monolith, nor are we subject to the whims of leaders like Hitler, whose actions are just as often motivated by suppressed insecurities and phobias as they are by prudent statecraft."

Downing rubbed an index finger under his lower lip. "And how do you propose this should guide our interactions with you—to prevent war, as you said?"

Tlerek nodded. "Actually, we require only one thing: that you do not reveal the existence of the Aborig—the Terrans you have labeled the Lost Soldiers."

Downing blinked. "And what would you suggest we do with them?"

"Whatever is necessary. I suspect you will wish to maroon them somewhere, possibly return them all to cryogenic suspension. Such a solution reveals the weakness of your system: your delusions of sympathy, of justice, of ethics, are ultimately just fetishes you worship in the hope that you shall be the beneficiaries of similar treatment. It is a ritual of self-reassurance, no different than those practiced by Hitler, except that his were global in expression and, according to your value structures, more egoistic and barbaric."

Downing's reply was slow, which often meant he was struggling to control his reaction. "I see. And you would not maroon the Lost Soldiers?"

"Of course not. They, and the other personnel who encountered them personally, should be eliminated. That is the only way to be sure that a secret shall be kept: that there is no one left to keep it."

"*Virodok!*" exclaimed Sukhinin, who sounded short of breath. "Do you monsters hold nothing dear beyond yourselves?"

"No, we do not, and that is the source of our power: to reject the delusion that any human, any-where, at any time, actually does anything or feels anything that they believe is not, at some level, in their own interest."

Riordan nodded. "Okay. So let's presume that we refuse to put the Lost Soldiers into cold sleep or on a module headed into the sun. What do you fear as a result?"

"It is not a fear, but a certainty, of what shall occur next. Your people will hear their story, the narrative of their rescue, and come to understand that it was the Ktor who put the Lost Soldiers on Turkh'saar. They will thus learn that we have been on Earth at various times in the past one hundred and fifty years. Immediately, our hand will be seen behind every war, every disaster, every misery your race has ever inflicted upon itself. In the wake of the recent invasion, your terrified populace wants a common enemy to hate, so they are singularly primed to declare us the source of all of Earth's woes."

Sukhinin's lips pulled back in a snarling smile. "So far, I am enjoying this picture you are painting."

"That is because you are foolish, Consul Sukhinin. Within mere hours, after your governments have been flooded with inquiries about our interference, the rumors about the ruins you found on Delta Pavonis Three will suddenly arise again, but as much more than scientific curiosities. They will become mute answers to the questions of your people. The Ktor can walk among you because we *are* you, because you and we were both in the stars long ago, servitors to the more advanced races that came before us.

"I must believe you see what follows, just as every domino flawlessly foretells the fall of the one after it. This revelation will spawn all manner of outcry among your unruly population—itself a classic illustration of the inadvisability of conferring political power upon lesser beings. That shall bring immense pressure to bear upon every level of government. There will be demands that you disclose information that you do not even possess, and your best attempts at transparency will be disbelieved. There will be increased suspicion among your population, a veritable witch hunt of 'Ktor sightings' that will fuel both fear and viciousness. It shall particularly impact your commercial entities, even those we did not suborn, resulting in significant physical damage and fiscal disruption. And since the government of Indonesia joined the megacorporations in inviting the Arat Kur and Hkh'Rkh to land as guests, a new purge will sweep Jakarta, and Indonesians in other countries will be in daily fear for their lives.

"All across your globe, and the worlds beyond it, your *hoi polloi* will be up in arms, will fawn over the ragged handful of bewildered captives who have returned with memories of abduction from the twentieth century, and before long, you will have questions about the Doomsday Rock that you will not be able to deflect."

"Tell me how our people would be wrong to wish to know such facts."

"Consul, this is not about facts; this is about outcomes. If you wish descent into a war that cannot be stopped or limited, allow what I foresee to happen. Your rabble's one unifying cry will be that there must be retribution. Most will call this 'justice.' A few of the most intemperate will also be the most honest; they will call it 'revenge.' And once they learn what the Accord really is, and understand its power, and

962   *Charles E. Gannon*

understand that the Custodians could have defended
them against the invasion that we are accused of having masterminded, they will press your governments
to ask for another Convocation, so that Terra may
enjoy the protection of being a member state and be
avenged upon the perfidious Ktor. It would all have
operatic sweep, I am sure. And in the course of this,
the other powers of the Accord will ineluctably be
made aware of the true speciate identity of Ktorans,
proven beyond doubt by the various pieces of evidence
you now possess."

Sukhinin nodded. "Again: overdue."

"And again, not the point. But please do persist
with your myopia; please do allow the question of our
speciate identity to come to the floor of the Accord's
next Convocation. You will have no problem pushing
the agenda. We are already censured and cannot stop
you. You are 'victims.' The Arat Kur hate us, the
Slaasriithi fear us, and the Dornaani have felt us to
be their antagonists for millennia."

Downing lifted his chin. "Do be good enough
to tell me how any of those attitudes are unjust or
inaccurate."

"Again you miss my point. If what you want is war,
simply follow this path I am charting. Have us branded
liars in the Accord, and probably voted out. You are
the Dornaani's lapdogs, and they will be happy to
admit you, perhaps make you the Custodians."

"God forbid."

"That is a wise aversion, Mr. Downing, but it avails
us not in the matter we are considering currently. To
conclude: the Accord will charge us with five millennia
of misrepresentation, of knowingly breaking one of the

fundamental Accords: the Second, which insists upon a race's accurate self-representation. Even the listless Dornaani and the ineffectual Slaasriithi will affirm this sustained crime warrants more than censure, for the Second Accord is quite explicit as to the penalty: loss of membership. And so we will be expelled."

Shethkador leaned forward. "Now this is the part where you must pay particularly close attention, because this is where understanding Ktor will show you why you do not wish events to follow the path I have just outlined. If the Sphere's senior leadership should learn that our speciate identity is revealed, and we are no longer members of the Accord, it is overwhelmingly likely that they would not seek restitution of membership, but would instead pursue their terrestrial ambitions without further diplomatic engagement."

"They would attack us?" Sukhinin shouted. "That would be suicide: the Accord defends its members against external aggression."

"Yes, it does. And that is why the Ktoran Sphere would have full freedom of action, because attacking Earth would *not* be external aggression."

"But you have said that Ktor would no longer be a member state."

Alnduul leaned forward. "You will appreciate that we now come to the part of the conversation that made me concur with Ambassador Shethkador regarding the attendance at this conversation. Specifically, that with the exception of myself as the necessary Custodial referee, no other species should be present, because this was solely a human matter." Alnduul turned toward Riordan as he uttered the last two words with a slight increase in emphasis: it was a *human matter* ...

Riordan's hands and feet suddenly became very cold; the prickling on the nape of his neck suggested that the hairs there were standing straight up. "The Fourth Accord," he said through a gulp.

"What?" Downing asked.

Alnduul's eyelids nictated once and closed.

"The Fourth Accord's first sentence states . . . uh, it states . . ."

Alnduul supplied the text from memory: "'The Accord and its individual member states are expressly and absolutely forbidden from interfering in the internal affairs of any member state.'"

"But they wouldn't be," Sukhinin protested as Shethkador smiled. "We are separate states. *Bozhe moi*, that's why they attacked us!"

Riordan shook his head. "I'm sorry, Vassily, but you're wrong. Read the Accords closely. The words 'race' and 'state' are used interchangeably. Otherwise, do you think the Ktor would be represented by just one 'state' in the Accord? Why wouldn't each of their Houses strive for membership of their own? Why wouldn't our own blocs do the same?"

Alnduul let the fingers of one hand raise and droop. "I am sorry that I must confirm Commodore Riordan's interpretation. For instance, if you were to read the Nineteenth and Twentieth Accords in sequence, you would see that the terms 'race' and 'state' are indeed interchangeable."

Downing's stare at Alnduul would have been lethal, if it had been a weapon. "Then why doesn't it bloody say so explicitly?"

Alnduul's fingers drooped again. "Some of this stems from difficulties in translation. The original document, written in our language, uses a term which specifically refers to an *entire species* as a discrete political entity with innate powers of, and rights to, self-determination. This is distinct from your word 'state,' which usually refers to political subdivisions within, or at least without regard to, the speciate whole. So, in order to ensure that the full implicit meaning was conveyed to all parties, it was agreed to use both terms at different points in the document, but in such a way that their interchangeability was made inescapably clear."

"Then, in this case, the Custodians failed," Sukhinin grumbled. It was a dangerous sound.

"As they so often do," Shethkador added brightly.

Riordan was aware of the exchange, but most of his mind was busily rearranging the assumptions with which he'd entered the secrecy room. He had begun by wondering if Alnduul might actually have believed that Shethkador truly wanted to ensure peace between the Ktoran Sphere and the Consolidated Terran Republic, or if he was hoping to patch together enough of a detente to reweave the frayed threads of the Accord and thereby save it. But now his real purpose was clear: if each race was only entitled to one seat on the Accord, then, by definition, any struggle between members of the same species was internecine—and according to the dictates of the Fourth Accord, there was no legal way for any other Accord power to intervene.

Shethkador was showing the others how the remaining dominoes were sure to fall. "So let us walk through the inevitable steps. You reveal our identity. The evidence proving it is brought before the Accord. It is accepted. We are now entitled to one seat, between us. Of course, this raises the unprecedented question

966 	*Charles E. Gannon*

of whether you are still a protected species. In the event that you are, it will necessitate a tortuous juridical explanation of how that is valid, when in fact, our dispute is now, by definition, a human matter to be resolved amongst ourselves. Meaning that the Custodians must stand aside."

Downing frowned. "Perhaps, but not the Dornaani, or other individual powers. As we are not a full member of the Accord, we are not necessarily protected from their 'interference,' or rather, 'alliance.'"

Shethkador inclined his head. "There is nothing to stop them from aiding you, of course. On the other hand, there is no longer any guarantee that they, or anyone else, will help you against us. And we have a reputation for being fearsome foes. Indeed, the only way in which becoming a member of the Accord changes your circumstances is that you will have knowingly renounced your protected species status. Which means that the prohibitions of the Fourth Accord must take full effect, and none may come to your aid, or ours, in any struggle that might arise between us."

Alnduul lowered his head slightly. "If you decide to retain your protected species status, you may reasonably claim that all your actions before this moment were predicated upon the presumption—and assurances—that the Custodians would protect you from any harm. Furthermore, you may not legally be invited to assume the mantle of membership for your species until the Ktor are deemed to have lost theirs, which will be determined in the next Convocation. In any event, you cannot be expected to suffer the consequences that might arise from the misleading speciate information they provided you, in violation of the Second Accord.

So you may continue under the protection that you presumed, until you take the voluntary step of joining the Accord as a full member."

Shethkador's infuriating smile had returned. "You see? You may always trust a Dornaani to bore a loophole through a solid law, given enough time and juridical creativity. But then what a fine organization the Accord is: two states remain voting members—the Dornaani and their Slaasriithi lapdogs. Two are censured and in a probationary status until our final fates are determined: ourselves and the Arat Kur. And two more had their bids for membership arrested at a stalemated Convocation, and who now are either not permitted or not willing to be reconsidered for membership in the near future: the Hkh'Rkh and yourselves. I suspect that the Accord will either enter into long-term paralysis or realize that rigor mortis is already setting in. Only time will tell which we are witnessing." He turned his smile upon Sukhinin, whose scowl had deepened. "So, let us presume that Ktor is expelled from the Accord. What will occur, do you think?"

"We will eye each other over a border with unremitting hatred."

"If only it were to stop there. Although we are quite superior to your sub-breed, we are both still 'human,' still the same race. What will the Custodians press you to do, if we, alone, threaten the Accord?"

Riordan saw where Shethkador was going. "They will urge us to clean our own house. After all, once you are out of the Accord, you are not protected."

"Precisely. I do wonder if we would then be part of the same protected race as you. But that would be inconvenient for the Custodians, so I suspect they would find some clever juridical language to show that we should not be so categorized.

"So in actuality, they'd push you toward a conflict with us, but not too hard or too fast. They know that coming after us right away would be your undoing. They could always provide you with support, or at least promise to do so—but you've seen how that worked out when your planet was invaded. As you said, you are still waiting for them to show up. At best, then, I predict that they might give you the power needed to persevere, but not to prevail. And if that occurs, the only outcome of which we can be sure is mutual despoliation on a scale that has not been witnessed in almost twenty millennia."

Downing raised an eyebrow. "Do you find that so terrible a prospect? You don't seem the peace-loving type, Ambassador Shethkador."

"Indeed, I am not. The fact that you tell yourselves that *you* are peace-loving, when you are not either, is a different debate for a different day. But here is what I am: a being too smart to invite apocalypse when I cannot be sure of benefitting by it. Ktor will have its dominion, but alas, not this day."

Riordan leaned back; Shethkador had waxed just a bit too histrionic. "No. Your dominion isn't being delayed by your stand-off with the Custodians, or even the Accord. It's threatened by internal politics. *Your* internal politics. The Perekmeres' rogue status isn't unique; it's indicative of broader discord in the Sphere. So when it comes to war, you're not just uncertain of winning; you fear you might lose. Entirely."

"And you are not? You have less than one million persons outside of your home system and are busy trying to resupply the nations of Earth with electricity.

You think we fear so crippled and immature a threat as you present now?"

Riordan smiled. "Why yes, Ambassador, I think you do. Because if you didn't have problems in your own house, you wouldn't have been trying so hard to burn ours down around our ears."

"There is a limit to all things, including my willingness to endure these moronic barbs. I offer a path to peace, and in return I require only one thing: that the Lost Soldiers are not allowed to return to Earth."

Sukhinin's chin came up. "And if we refuse?"

"Then I cannot assure you what the leaders of the Ktoran Sphere will decide to do. Logically, you cannot conceal the Lost Soldiers' existence indefinitely. With every passing day, it is more likely that some word of them will leak out; no secret is eternal. So I suspect that my leaders would decide to act preemptively: if not by attacking, then aggressively preparing for a conflict. And once that martial leviathan is set in motion, your tardy compliance is unlikely to halt it.

"Once the so-called Lost Soldiers are allowed to leave this system, it will rapidly become impossible for you to provide the Sphere with sufficiently convincing verification of their elimination. Here, they are all together and have not come into contact with other humans except their rescuers. Once they have travelled from this place, how can we know if the soldiers you say you have eliminated to preserve the peace, have, in fact, been eliminated?"

"So, in fact," Vassily said, "all your fine-sounding words are merely a veil draped over an ultimatum: that we do away with the Lost Soldiers or else."

"I suppose I cannot keep you from perceiving it as

an ultimatum. I simply see it as a prediction of what my superiors would do in response. There is, of course, another way, a way that would solve all these problems, end all these impasses, and would save countless millions in the coming decades, even centuries."

"And what is that?"

"Charting a course toward cooperation. Beginning now. Slowly, carefully."

Sukhinin was the first to recover enough from his surprise to ask, "And you would ally with us?"

"Would you believe me if I said yes?"

"No."

Shethkador's smile became slightly sad. "Of course you wouldn't. You already know what we intend. Subversion, seduction, co-option: it is how we have attempted to conquer you thus far."

Downing sprayed saliva with the force of his rejection. "And are you actually deluded enough to believe that this appeals to us? In any way?"

Shethkador reclined again. "I hoped the eventual outcome might be more palatable if it was gradual and voluntary: that I might be able to entice you with the carrot, rather than threaten with the stick. Because Ktor certainly has enough sticks to beat your sub-race into submission."

Sukhinin stuck out his sizable chin. "You are not ready for war. You have said so yourself."

"I could throw your so-called Republic into turmoil without firing a shot, Consul."

"Oh, and how would you achieve this?"

"By giving a single, simple order to the crew of my ship. This very second."

"It has remained at the fifth orbit, Ambassador. I

think even your weapons would find it difficult to target us at that range."

Shethkador shook his head. "I only require them to send a coded signal to devices we managed to secret on this planet. Perhaps we emplaced them over the course of our many attendances at the peace process, or perhaps long before. After all, the Arat Kur have no doubt claimed that we sent emissaries here before the war. If so, it would have been simplicity itself to conceal a liter-sized dispersal unit with the viral plague that you yourselves identified. Our visits have given us ready access to various biological samples, and we are vastly superior to you at decoding and manipulating exogenetic materials.

"If you suspect I am bluffing, why not challenge me to see if my claim is genuine, whether in fact I have the stick with which I promise to punish your noncompliance? And do not mistake this as an idle threat, or even as an arbitrary display of power. If you are determined to resist us, my superiors will not allow you to have the Arat Kur as your assistants in industrial production and technological tutelage.

"Do not stare, Ambassador: that would be a logical evolution of cooperation between your species. And while the virus might do nothing more than devastate Homenest, that will be sufficient for our other purpose: which is, to blame you for the plague. We will deny any involvement. After all, you are the invaders, have been on the surface repeatedly, visiting and inspecting various parts of their planet over the past year. Consequently, you would have had far more opportunity and access than we ever did or of which we availed ourselves."

Downing exhaled slowly. "You truly are a bloody monster."

"Am I? So much more than you? Think of the fate to which you are condemning your own race by dismissing any possibility of cooperating with us. Your defeat is inevitable. Yet I am giving you the choice to save millions of lives by managing the process. And after all, its outcome will not come to pass in your lifetime."

Downing's stare and voice were those of a horrible fascination. "And what about my children, or grandchildren?"

Shethkador shrugged. "At least they would be safe." He turned toward Riordan. "Yours, too."

Riordan managed not to blink. What had started out sounding like a general, historical assurance had taken on a personal tone. *Is that a promise? And if so, is there a flip side: is that a personal threat? Either way, it doesn't matter.* "I've seen how Ktoran promises work out. One of the operatives the Perekmeres seeded into our mission to the Slaasriithi homeworld was working for them to save his daughter from a disease they induced in her. But he learned that her cure probably wasn't permanent. That's how you bastards keep the people you've suborned on the hook." He spat on the floor between them. "So you can go to hell." Sukhinin and Downing nodded slowly, solemnly.

Shethkador rose. "I had hoped, and am under orders, to avoid bringing war to your world, Commodore Riordan, But there is nothing that stops me from bringing war to you."

"You've been trying to kill me for years now. So why should I see anything new in that threat?"

Shethkador smiled. "As you live, so shall you learn. Until we meet again, Commodore." He bowed to the others and began to back out of the secrecy room.

Chapter Seventy

Tlerek Srin Shethkador exited his cabin aboard *Doom Herald*, his finger still tingling from where he had contacted the Catalysite that made it possible for him to effect a contact Reification that linked him with the Autarchs some fifty-five light-years away. But while the tingling in his finger diminished, his brow was growing increasingly moist with the sweat of uncertainty. And fear.

He had known the final report on the peace treaty would not be received well, but the Autarchs wanted it as quickly as possible. He also knew that they would wish to learn that the various troubling incidents that had plagued Ktor's—which was to say his—operations in the region had been caused by a renegade band of House Perekmeres: renegades who should have been purged instead of made Arrogates and reassigned to an Autarch hull. And the Autarchs had been sure to demand his assessment on the amount of time remaining before the Aboriginal leadership revealed that the Ktor were in fact their speciate relatives. But none

of those had been the reasons that Shethkador had
sought privacy and the altered state of a Reification
so swiftly upon his return to *Doom Herald*.

He had needed to know the degree of danger in
which he now existed.

Only one Autarch would communicate that to him,
of course: his own relative Kromn Tval Shethkador,
who could not share such information overtly. Rather,
as Tlerek was receiving the markedly terse and unen-
thusiastic farewells from the other Autarchs, the one
uttered by Kromn was in fact a code-speaking. The
second word of the Tval's last sentence was a cypher
that indicated the degree of danger Tlerek now faced;
the next to last word in the same sentence conveyed
House Shethkador's advice for how to respond to that
danger. He had hurried to his chambers to decode
the messages.

The first code came back as the highest degree of
danger. This indicated that the Autarchs had compared
notes on the magnitude of his ostensible failure and
deemed it was best for the interests of the Ktoran
Sphere that his command should be terminated. Permanently. In such cases, the usually anonymous vote
stipulated that the commander in question was to
be given over without warning to undisclosed loyalty
officers (usually lictors) among the crew. The appre-
hension would be carried out as soon as the signal
could reach them. In the case of *Ferocious Monolith*,
that would occur when next she contacted another
Autarch ship. Probably captained by another Aware
such as himself, who had received the termination
order via Reification.

The second cypher had been the surprise. It was a

code that translated crudely as "exile, with our blessing."
Normally contradictory terms, this combination signified
that despite being on his own—he could no longer be
recognized by House Shethkador officially—they were
willing to take him back if he performed deeds that
would make him worthy in enough Autarchal eyes to
accept him once again.

Tlerek had not thought that old Kromn Tval Shethkador was either adventurous or devious enough to
mislead the rest of the Autarchs so profoundly: to
overtly agree to the assassination and then covertly
encourage him to flee and redeem himself. Because
the only way for Tlerek to do that would involve taking
steps against his fellow Ktor. In short, he could not
escape, could not pursue deeds and fortune worthy
of reinstatement, without a ship. And the more ships
he could count under his banner, the more bold his
actions could be.

As he approached the iris valve to the bridge, it
dilated, grinding faintly. "Has Senior Tagmator Olsirkos
Shethkador'vah of the *Will Breaker* sent a reply yet?"

"Less than five minutes ago, Potent Srin. We have
just finished decryption."

Tlerek nodded. "Put it through to my ready room.
Access restricted to my code."

"At once, my Srin."

He paused at the threshold of his open ready room.
"When this hatch seals behind me, wait thirty seconds,
then engage thrust as before."

"Three gees thrust, Srin. Any course change?"

"None." He let the hatch whisper shut.

Shethkador moved quickly to his seat, activating
the information center as he did. Strapping in with

his left hand, and tapping in his access code with his right, he experienced the strange, if grim, thrill of knowing that lowly Olsirkos's response would be more determinative of his ultimate fate than any of the exchanges that Tlerek recalled having with the various Hegemons and Autarchs who had held some measure of power over him.

The screen of the information center brightened. Olsirkos's face loomed close in view. "Honored Srin, I have received your communiqué and have executed the orders you gave therein. Two watches from *Will Breaker*, drawn primarily from engineering and security personnel, are now aboard *Ferocious Monolith*, One is currently exiting the full-gee rotation modules, the other ostensibly preparing to enter. They have been given access codes to the armory and stand ready for action."

The world seemed to tug him backward; *Doom Herald*'s full cruising thrust had resumed.

Olsirkos's report continued without delay.

"The double ration distributed to *Ferocious Monolith*'s own, recent watches—both the one standing down and the one standing up—has been drugged and infected as you instructed. My medical officer aboard *Will Breaker*—who has spent time in the ur-precincts of your own sire, the Hegemon of House Shethkador—confirms that the delaying buffers in the drug will cause it to take effect in two to three hours, resulting in profound drowsiness and probable sleep. He estimates they shall be incapacitated for four hours. During that time, the intestinal virus that was also introduced into their meal will take effect. Upon waking, the dosed crew will begin to experience severe nausea and symptoms consistent with acute gastroenteritis. However, as you instructed, the viral strain employed cannot be communicated among the crew other than by shared foodstuffs or utensils, so there should be little or no spread beyond the target population.

"Refueling is nearly complete for all vessels, and the running crew sent to *Uzhmarek* has taken command of that hull and awaits your orders, as do we all. Indeed, the crew of my own *Will Breaker*, which has necessarily become aware of your imminent usurpation of full dominion, is eager at the prospect. They bear little love for the servitors of the Autarchs." Which was hardly news; to serve under the Autarchs was to be Houseless, or so low in stature as to merit nothing more than contempt.

Olsirkos hesitated a moment, as if uncertain of the words he would utter next. "Tlerek Srin Shethkador, I fully understand the danger and desperate nature of moving against the Autarchs, of commandeering their ship and taking it for your own. Almost all hands will be turned against us, and most others shall not be extended in friendship, but in the expectation of premium payment for illegal services.

"And yet . . . and yet the prospect of this enterprise excites me, puts renewed energy into every step and action I take. It was an honor to serve under you as agents of the Autarchs, but now it shall be a daily challenge to undertake the things of which legends are made. I am not so skilled with words to be able to fashion a statement of my gratitude any better than this, but know, Terrible Srin, that, even if you were not Srin, I would be with you to the end." Olsirkos's image faded.

Shethkador leaned back. Of all the emotions he had never expected to feel toward Olsirkos, gratitude was near, if not at the very top, of the list. But that is precisely what he felt now. And not merely for the 'vah's loyalty, but, equally paradoxically, for his limitations.

Olsirkos Shethkador'vah's greatest failing to date, as an aspirant to make his final ascent into the ranks of the Evolved, was imagination and versatility, traits necessary for an excellent commander. But they were also the traits that tended to fuel ambition, that encouraged those who possessed them to relentlessly consider how the universe might be shaped more to their advantage. In short, it made them more opportunistic, more willing to not merely abandon one role for a better one, but to consider if they stood more to gain by simply departing their current position, or by betraying those whom they served under or with. After all, an agent on the inside of a rival organization was always worth more, operationally speaking, than a loyal servitor in one's own.

For the first time, therefore, Olsirkos's greatest failing—a lack of imagination—became his greatest virtue, and Shethkador saw that their new ventures together would actually confirm his subordinate in those tendencies, rather than encourage their erosion. Olsirkos worked best in stable environments where the expectations upon him were clear, predictable, and aligned with his greatest skills: those involving the handling of ships and troops in combat. His penchant for tactics and understanding the details and greater implications of different martial technologies was the reason he had risen as high as he had.

Now, if they succeeded in what lay before them, he would necessarily have accrued an impressive list of battlefield successes, certainly enough to assure him of final Elevation. Indeed, the steepest bar of necessary achievement was now before Tlerek himself: his deeds against the enemies of the Sphere would have to be truly momentous, if he was to be reembraced in spite of mutiny, murder, and his failures at Earth and Homenest.

But a question remained: to whom might he turn for counsel? It was always a difficult choice for a Srin. Any Evolved who was useful as a counselor was also likely to have ambitions of their own, and the more closely they served a powerful leader, the more they tended to aspire to that power for themselves—often through the agency of a timely knife in the back.

But in the current circumstances, that was not Shethkador's problem. It was, rather, the paucity of likely candidates for such a position. *Ferocious Monolith* was, for all her material power, a barren desert insofar as potential counselors were concerned. The only Evolved on her were, as Olsirkos was, loaned from their respective Houses. It was a posting that usually indicated that their talents were so modest or limited that their House felt it no great loss to offer them as a form of living tithes. It fulfilled the House's obligation to the Autarchy, and gave their less-promising 'vahs some hope of distinguishing themselves enough to complete their Elevation. In the thirteen months he had now spent aboard *Ferocious Monolith*, Tlerek had assessed all her Evolved, and found them all wanting in ability and oversupplied with personal ambition and loyalty to their respective Houses. Therefore, they would be among those who would never recover from the digestive malady that was, judging from the communication delay of Olsirkos's message, even now upon them.

The crew of *Will Breaker* had good officers, Sheth-kador'vah's all, but were either much younger or even less promising than Olsirkos. And even if Tlerek was willing to risk a run into the heart of the Sphere, hoping to recruit the sons and daughters of distaff Families of declining Houses, it would be a task of such difficulty, and requiring such delicate and careful planning, that his attempt might prove a fatal enterprise. So it seemed he had no reasonable hope to find a suitable counselor...

The idea—or rather, the madness—that rose in answer to that sad conclusion caused him to physically start before he pushed it away as the chimerical thought that it was. But, with the slow patience of dog returning to a neglectful master, the idea repeated:

Nezdeh.

Fate, no. In all probability, she wishes my death more than that of any other living being. And in her place, I would have the same wish: mine was the House most active in securing not merely the downfall, but the extinction, of hers. Other Hegemons, and many Autarchs, had been willing to simply Exile Perekmeres, but not my sire. He wanted an Extirpation that purged their House starting at the top, rather than an Exodus, which would have disintegrated them from the bottom before sending the remainder on a slower-than-light journey into the Scatters. And I have been vocal in my support of that choice. Surely, no blood would be sweeter for her to shed than my own.

And yet . . .

Nezdeh.

Of course, it was not as though she deserved anything other than an agonizing death, cast naked into the frigid, airless void of space. It might have been Brenlor who led the Perekmeres renegades, but it was doubtless she who had been the intellect, the energy, and the spirit behind their actions. And, cumulatively, those actions had sealed Tlerek's own fate. They had shown his regional control to be incomplete, even over his own forces, and had ultimately driven the Aboriginals and Slaasriithi closer together after the bungled attack at Disparity. And now, unquestionably, their interference at Turkh'saar had set in motion waves of Hkh'Rkh anger, directed both externally and internally. Those already unruly and unpredictable allies were now just that much more uncertain, particularly if they discovered the truth of the Aboriginals' assertions: that the Ktor had been grooming them as expendable allies for centuries, had all but led them into the recent war like kittens following a saucer of sweetened milk swayed under their noses. None of that had been the Perekmeres' intention, of course: Brenlor's plans had achieved the opposite of the effects he had sought. But Brenlor was dead, the Perekmeres were ghosts, and the Autarchs needed a scapegoat: Tlerek Srin Shethkador, for whom several already nursed the peculiar, jealous hatred which impotent age often focuses upon promising youth. By all rights, he should wish death upon Nezdeh, even more than the Aboriginals who had repeatedly thwarted him.

And yet . . .

Nezdeh.

Nezdeh had every trait he sought in a counselor, in the mind that would assess his plans for weaknesses, would detect ways to accentuate their strengths, provide the fresh perspective that promised new solutions. She was clever, resourceful, resilient, multitalented, charismatic, both bold and brave—for those were not the same things—and ruthless. Yes, utterly, remarkably, fabulously ruthless.

But therein lay the great problem and uncertainty: that she would *not* strike at him quickly, that she would *not* seek a swift advantage. Rather, she would work to suborn his own personnel and allies, to make the fruits of his victories her own before she struck at him in the most unforeseeable fashion, at the most impossible moment.

Shethkador was doubly glad he was presently alone, not just because the quiet helped him think more deeply, but because no other being saw the sudden, sharp shiver that shook him from his neck to his feet. It was a bold thing, if he did it. Truly, the stuff of legends. It was the equivalent of taking along a sapient viper for a traveling companion. That serpent was a potent and subtle weapon, but it would be a constant danger and challenge to keep sufficiently fed and sufficiently cowed so as not to turn on and slay its owner.

Ultimately, it was the extraordinary nature of that challenge, as well as the extraordinary qualities Nezdeh possessed, that decided him. Yes, he would extend his hand to Homeless Nezdeh to share his fortune as fellow outlaws, who, if they could manage not to kill each other, could serve each others' ends. He reached out to activate the comm circuits, to begin giving the orders that would set them on their new path. Why, he could even foresee a conclusion that did not end in Nezdeh's death.

His hand stopped in mid reach. Surely, that fleeting notion was merely a distraction in this moment of supreme exigency.

Surely.

Chapter Seventy-One

Last to emerge from the seemingly limitless subterranean warrens of the Arat Kur, Riordan squinted up at the sun, then, eyes adjusting, at the alien landscape around him.

Sigma Draconis was, frankly, beautiful. It was not particularly reminiscent of Earth, not the way DeePeeThree, or reportedly Zeta Tucanae, were, but it was furnished with a rich diversity of biomes, in which flora and fauna teemed. And almost all of it was untouched. The Arat Kur's subsurface existence had led some xenotheorists to speculate that they would consider the surface of their world little better than a dumping ground and protein factory. They were sorely mistaken. Living underground had taught the Arat Kur, better than any other species, the dangers of unmanaged wastes. It had also made them careful accountants of resources, of assessing the costs and benefits of every choice they made. That spirit of thrift and conservancy had informed their approach to the surface of their world every bit as much as it had defined their use of its bedrock. Sigma Draconis Two was, to all appearances, as pristine a planet as humanity had ever encountered.

Downing turned back toward Riordan. "Taking in the view, are you?"

Caine nodded. "And to think that, just a year ago, we were thinking about bombing all this into radioactive slag—and that that was the less dire of the two options before us."

Sukhinin shrugged. "*Da*, but they admitted that, if they were allowed to survive and given the chance, they would have returned to Earth and done the same to us."

Alnduul pulled his sloshing robe closer around him. "That is why the Accords are necessary, Consul Sukhinin. They encourage all species to pause, if only for one more minute or hour, before they act upon such impulses. They gave you pause, after all, at that pivotal moment."

Vassily jerked his head in Caine's direction. "They gave *him* pause," he amended with histrionic impatience. "He is young—well, younger—and idealistic. Which is to say, foolish."

Alnduul turned toward Sukhinin, saw that the big Russian was smiling. His eyes nictated rapidly. "Ah. A joke. At times, despite the many decades I have spent in the study of your species, your humor can still surprise me."

"Possibly because some of our humor is only partly a jest," Downing speculated. High overhead, there was a crack of unnaturally sharp thunder.

The security personnel, who had preceded them out of the tunnels and arrayed themselves in a loose perimeter, looked up. Their leader announced, "Shuttle inbound. ETA: nine minutes."

Alnduul opened his arms in a gesture that included the three humans closest to him. "It has been gratifying and illuminating to associate with you all. However, I suspect that I shall soon be called away from here. With the signing of the peace treaty scheduled for tomorrow, I am needed elsewhere."

"Earth?" asked Riordan. Hopefully.

"It is difficult to say. Very little has gone as the Custodians or the Dornaani Collective foresaw. And I do not mean this simply in terms of the events among your species, but among my own kind."

Downing nodded. "Differences of opinion regarding how to proceed?"

Alnduul traced a downward slope in the air with two fingers. "More so than you might imagine. Perhaps, at this stage, more than you *can* imagine. Suffice it to say that you are not alone in voicing frustration at the Custodians' continued lack of direct presence in your home system. And more than that I may not say."

Riordan nodded. It was no secret that Alnduul had been deeply frustrated with his own government's alarming passivity in the recent war and in its aftermath. Earth's pundits were fond of crafting alarmist editorials asserting that the Dornaani had knowingly misled the delegation that attended Convocation, that the Custodians' support had been all talk without any intent of actually backing it up with force. But having known Alnduul for almost two years now, Riordan and others who had spent much time in the presence of the Dornaani, had detected signs that the problem was far more complex, that his species was deeply divided over the degree and nature of their involvement with others, and that the Custodians had been almost as surprised as the humans when more assistance or direct diplomatic overtures had not been forthcoming from their own race. "I understand that what you may share with us is restricted. I felt that factor intrude on the meeting in the secrecy room several times."

Alnduul looked up at him. "Explain, please."

Riordan smiled: it was becoming a ritual with them. The human conjectured; the Dornaani either corrected the conjectures or remained affirmatively silent. If Alnduul had had an actual nose, Caine imagined he would often have laid a conspiratorial finger alongside it. "You couldn't urge us toward any course of action. You could only point out the consequences of pursuing membership in the Accord versus remaining a protected species. But it was pretty clear which alternative you would recommend."

"Is it?"

Downing smiled. "Of course it is, Alnduul. You never offered an opposite opinion when Shethkador asserted that the Consolidated Terran Republic is simply no match for the Ktoran Sphere. Which is to say, they enjoy immense advantages in terms of technology, resources, interstellar expansion, knowledge, and practical experience fighting interstellar wars."

Alnduul's mouth twisted slightly to one side: the equivalent of a faint, and mostly suppressed, grin. "It is true that I did not disagree with the Ambassador's statements on such matters."

Riordan smiled. "Which means that you want us to keep the true speciate identity of the Ktor under wraps long enough for humanity to be able to fight back effectively. And maybe to take the place of the Ktor as Associate Custodians."

Alnduul looked up in the sky again, his inner lids half-closing over his eyes. "There is much logic in such a conclusion."

"Logic is not always the engine that drives human politics," Sukhinin grumbled. "Since the Dornaani were not especially prompt providing help in the last war"—Riordan doubted that even an alien could miss Vassily's broadly sardonic tone—"there is no great eagerness to help them, in return. It has even reduced support for joining the Accord."

Alnduul inclined his head. "Such matters are not decided in weeks or months, but years or decades. Or longer. Be patient. In five years, much will have changed."

"Yes," Downing added, "and in the meantime, since we are not in the Accord, we can continue ignoring the 'allowed pathways of expansion' and run around the stellar neighborhood, nicking whatever systems we choose. I'm sure our flag-planting expeditions aren't very popular back home, eh?"

Alnduul turned to consider Downing somberly. "No, they are not popular. But as I counseled Consul Sukhinin, there is time enough for everything. Even for 'nicking' systems, to use your idiom."

Riordan and Downing exchanged glances. Had Alnduul just given tacit permission for the Consolidated Terran Republic to go on grabbing star systems unclaimed by other species? Granted, it made a certain kind of sense. If the Dornaani hoped Earth to be the source of the new Associate Custodians, and perhaps take on the full job one day, then they had to become members of the Accord first. And the moment they did, they'd probably have to fight the Ktor. Which meant they'd need something approaching parity in terms of resources and military capability. And how were they going to achieve that in the foreseeable future without more worlds and more people living on them? Riordan cleared his throat. "That's a—a most provocative comment, Alnduul."

"Is it? I simply observed that there is time for all things."

Yeah, sure you did. "Well, you must be right: it certainly worked out that way with the Arat Kur."

"It did indeed," agreed Downing with a smile.

Sukhinin turned to look at them directly. "You are speaking of their willingness—finally—to sign the peace treaty?"

"Not exactly," Downing mumbled.

Sukhinin's considerable eyebrows descended like a silver-and-gray stormfront running in over his eyes. "Richard, no secrets. You know my clearance."

"I do, old boy, but I'm afraid in this case, your position as Consul made it imperative *not* to tell you ahead of time."

"Tell me what?" the Russian insisted, with steadily growing volume.

Riordan stepped closer to him. "Vassily, the Arat Kur have been refusing to sign the peace treaty for months because they wanted proof that it was the Ktor—and only the Ktor—who were the Great Destroyers of their myth, that although we might make mistakes, we would never prefer xenocide as a solution."

"Yes, and so they finally saw sense and relented. They have come to know us. Is this what Alnduul means by all things happening in time?"

"No, because it wasn't getting to know us that made them relent. It was having, finally, the opportunity to hear the Ktor admit to their past atrocities—and their willingness to perform them again."

For a moment, Sukhinin stared at Riordan without comprehension. Then his eyebrows rose, the storm of imminent anger lifting away with them. "Do you mean when Shethkador spoke of threatening to exterminate the Arat Kur? But—but it is a secrecy room. The Arat Kur could not hear and we had no recording devices. And they will certainly not believe us."

"They don't have to, because, well, not all secrecy rooms are really all that secret."

Sukhinin's eyebrows descended again, but this time in twisted perplexity. "*Shto?*"

Downing finally succumbed to a grin. "Vassily, the Arat Kur may not be a particularly warlike race, but that doesn't mean they don't have their fair share of power struggles. So naturally, some of them found ways to eavesdrop on what goes on in supposed secrecy rooms."

"How?"

"All secrecy rooms must be hollowed out of stone, without any access other than the entry tunnels from the antechambers. But some were purposely built to lie athwart different veins of rock. That gave the Arat Kur the opportunity to leverage the different ways that sound travels through different kinds of stone. If you were to look at a cut-away cross section of these not-so-secrecy rooms, you'd discover that under them is a column of variegated rock, most natural, but some added by the builders. The acoustic properties of the layering are really quite ingenious. The columns of mixed rock, if you will, work with each other to carry vibrations, and the solid rock that surrounds this 'eavesdropping column' is always a substance that is particularly good at insulating the column without absorbing any of the vibrations itself. Essentially, it's a protective tube which preserves the signal integrity."

Sukhinin did not look convinced. "All very good. But fifty meters of rock is fifty meters of rock. What sound can go through it?"

Riordan smiled. "Very faint sounds. Sounds that we can't hear, and most machines can't detect. But that's where a special kind of Arat Kur enters the picture: a far-listener."

Sukhinin crossed his arms. "I have endured almost thirteen months of negotiations with the Arat Kur. I have learned all their castes and subcastes. I know much of their history. I have never heard of this kind of Arat Kur."

"And you probably wouldn't unless you were reading one of their medical references. A far-listener is actually a term for an Arat Kur with a congenital defect: they are so attuned to sound and vibration, particularly in solids or liquids, that they must be kept in specially soundproofed environments. However, if they are put in direct contact with the other end of the shaft of rock I mentioned, they can make out the sounds being emitted in the secrecy room. Quite clearly."

"This seems—most improbable."

Downing stuck his hands in the pockets of his duty suit, glanced up at the sky in response to the distant sound of approaching turbojets. "Actually, there are human analogs, Vassily. But since our primary sense is sight, that's where we encounter the more recognizable analogs. A far-listener is the equivalent of a human who is so sensitive to light that they spend their lives half-blinded. And just as they often have vision advantages in low light, so the far-listener has advantages with faint sound."

Alnduul glanced up at Caine. "I wish to ask you about a related ethical irregularity, Caine Riordan."

Now what? "Certainly."

"When the Ktoran ambassador entered the secrecy room, he expressed glad surprise that there were no Arat Kur present. To which you responded, 'they did not want to be in the same room with you. Or with me, for that matter. And they have no desire to interact with humans in a shared space.' At least, I believe that is what you said."

"It is."

"Granted that your statement is technically honest in its specific claim—that the Arat Kur did not want to be in the same room with humans—it seems to me that you counted upon the idiom of speech to mislead the Ambassador, to invite him to presume that they were not interested in hearing your discourse."

Riordan shrugged. "Guilty as charged. But there is a big difference between lying and using language that will trick the incautious. More importantly though, if the Ktor are going to wholly ignore the rules of fair and honest communication, then I'd say we're on pretty firm ethical ground if we simply decide to play by the letter, not the spirit, of those rules. Furthermore, it was the Arat Kur who not only suggested this ploy, but that we use this particular secrecy room. When I expressed concern over whether it was really the right thing to do, they replied that they made their proposal 'without compunctions or misgivings.'"

Alnduul's eyes closed slowly. "Then I am satisfied. It was ultimately their affair. And now that they have heard the Ktor admit to their past deeds and threaten to reprise them, they are satisfied that signing the treaty is in their best interests. Although I have heard that they are not pleased with the terms, and feel no better about being forced to interact with humanity." He turned toward Sukhinin, who seemed ready to take umbrage. "Yours is still the race that almost destroyed theirs, out of caprice, so far as we may tell. It does not matter that the culprits were a deviant subspecies: they fear you as the source, the rootstock, of that crime, even though you were not the perpetrators. To change that will take time."

He stared up at the approaching shuttle. "But again, there is time for all things. Even that."

Nezdeh reached over and tapped the hatch release; Zurur Deosketer entered calmly, but her complexion was slightly darker, betraying her anxious excitement. Nezdeh felt a tinge of pity. *She is so accomplished at controlling her reactions to emotions, but she has not been able to master the blush response. It is difficult: impossible, for some.*

Zurur sat next to Nezdeh, who leaned back from the communications console. She did not speak.

Nezdeh offered a small smile. "You are quite patient."

"I have to be, living with this ridiculous blush response."

Nezdeh's smile widened before she could control it. Zurur was not brilliant, but she was clever, frank, and was becoming an excellent adjutant. Although that would soon change. Technically. "My conversation with Shethkador resolved in an unexpected manner."

"Indeed?" And that was all Zurur said.

Well, she truly can master her eagerness. "We are not going to Epsilon Indi after all."

"No? Then where?"

"Gamma Leporis."

Zurur stared. "But Gamma Leporis is a training world, and a Wilding preserve, as well. If we go there, we will be sure to encounter the more promising 'vahs and young Elevated of other Houses. They will be sure to see us, report us."

"All true. But we will not be alone."

"No?"

"We are going with Shethkador. We are going as a flotilla. Of outlaws."

Zurur was silent for several seconds. "You are not joking."

"How often have you known me to joke?"

"Never, which is the only reason I can believe that you are not doing so now. Nezdeh, what has happened? He is a Srin of one of the greatest Houses and progeny of its ur-primogenitorial line. Why would he undertake such a journey with us?"

"It is we who are journeying with him; he has *Ferocious Monolith* under his dominion. It is no longer an Autarchy ship. His family's destroyer *Will Breaker*, and its own jump tug, have signed to his colors as well."

Zurur looked out the windows at the distant gas giant in the fifth orbit. "I am not easily stunned. But I am now."

"This development had the same effect on me." However, Nezdeh had not only suppressed any sign of surprise when Shethkador had told her, but had coolly yet respectfully conjectured why the Srin's fortunes had changed. He allowed that she was correct in her surmises, was impressed when she further hypothesized that he had acted with the speed he had because, in the long run, it was better to be accused of piracy and treason against the Autarchs, than to be declared a failure and to have his geneline stricken from House Shethkador's ur-primogenitorial list. This way, should he manage to redeem himself, he would only have the present crimes to answer for—the commission of which handily preempted the Autarchs' resolve to officially derogate his professional abilities and downgrade his genecode.

Zurur continued to look out into space. "So I presume he gave you a choice that was no choice: to accompany him or die?"

Nezdeh shook her head. "Strangely, no. He was wise. He allowed me to choose."

"And you chose to join causes with a sworn enemy of our House?"

"I did. But only because it was the better alternative, Zurur. Think of it: we shall be in a system where we may recruit more to our banners, may hope to gather more assets."

"Yes—before we must flee the inevitable reprisals."

"We will have ample warning to flee, for they will be send investigators first if we manage to prevent rival ships from leaving the system once they in-shift. And with *Ferocious Monolith*, we might reasonably hope to do just that."

"And then where?"

"The Scatters, I suppose."

"To what end?"

"To craft a force that we will use in the coming war."

"War? Have the Aboriginals been foolish enough to declare war upon us?"

"No, but they will. They would not agree to eliminating the abductees we activated on Turkh'saar."

"The mere presence of Aboriginals on Turkh'saar does not prove it was a Ktoran plot."

"No, but the fools who buried that false-flag operation either lacked the time, technology, or foresight to ensure the destruction of the cryopods after the abductees were awoken."

"Fate, that puts our fingerprints on them, and all but proves our true species. But Nezdeh—you call our sires 'fools'?"

She turned toward Zurur. "I do, because what else may I call them? See what they have wrought for us, their offspring. Our legacy is one of ruin and shame, thanks to their incompetence and impetuosity. No, Zurur Deosketer, be glad your name comes from one of the subsidiary Houses. I for one, have no desire to be a Perekmeres any longer."

Zurur leaned back. "You cannot mean this."

"I have never meant anything more. I am done with this futile attempt to salvage a legacy and a family which is best left buried. I will make a new House of my own."

"The Breedmothers will not support that."

"Then they may go inseminate themselves with the seed of helots, for all I care. Too many of us have paid too great a price chasing the glory of a name that shed any worthiness or proud reputation centuries ago. And if my reaction seems to run against our traditions—for not many women have founded Houses in our history—I would remind you of the Progenitors' words: 'Battles are lost because a combatant stops fighting too soon; wars are lost because a combatant does not stop fighting soon enough.'" She leaned toward her adjutant. "We have been fighting this losing war too long, Zurur. We must stop fighting before all of us are dead. Your lines—all those with us—will be honored and kept at the same level of regard that they had in House Perekmeres—but you will swear new loyalty, to a new name, and a new Hegemon."

Zurur seemed ready to blink in surprise. "I doubt Shethkador is likely to be pleased at this, your latest resolve," she commented drily.

Nezdeh managed to suppress her smile. "He would not be pleased—if he knew of it. But for the foreseeable future, I shall simply be his lieutenant."

"He will not trust you. He may try to kill you."

"Trust me? Never. Kill me? Only if I become unnecessary. And I intend not to let that happen. When we depart, or usurp his place, it will be at a time and place of my choosing."

"Leave? You would let him live, rather than exact vengeance?"

Nezdeh stared at the communications board. "That is an interesting question. I am slow to make a resolve on the matter, even to myself. Does he deserve death? Most certainly. But is it prudent? That I cannot know until we see how this new venture unfolds. He holds the great majority of the power in our relationship, but what we bring is not inconsiderable: excess Aboriginal crewpersons who can be awakened from their cold sleep, as well as several companies of clones that, with proper training, could be turned into better warriors."

"Their equipment is—archaic, Nezdeh."

"And that is one of the reasons we shall travel to a training world that is also a preserve. In that place, the clones' rudimentary technology will make them a suitable force for returning gods. Such as we shall be."

"By the gray locks of the Progenitors, you are bold, Nezdeh. But there is a matter wanting resolution."

"What is that?"

"Kozakowski. He is still adrift in the pod. Shall we leave him, or—?"

"No. We will need him now. Retrieve him at once."

"And Tagawa?"

Nezdeh smiled. "Her we will leave."

"At last, you shall be rid of her. Should I auto-evacuate the air from her pod?"

"I said I would leave her, not kill her."

"But to what end?"

"To the ends of vengeance, of bringing war against the Houses and Autarchs who Extirpated House Perekmeres with such glee, such greed and caprice. And to the ends of our own success, for the sooner war comes, the sooner they shall have need of outlaws who have experience fighting Aboriginals along our borders."

"And how do you mean to use Ayana to that end?"

Nezdeh smiled, which she allowed since it was not an expression of amusement. "You still have the covert access channels to the journalists we suborned in the Aboriginal fleet?"

"Of course."

"Send them the coordinates of Tagawa's lifepod, just before we out-shift." She smiled more broadly. "I shall be disappointed not to witness the beginning of their feeding frenzy—and the war that will consume the Aboriginals. And, with any luck, will also cripple the Houses that Extirpated ours. Cripple them enough for us to finish them off."

Chapter Seventy-Two

"Detaching from *Shore-of-Stars* in three, two, one . . . and mark." Karam Tsaami tapped a dynamic control: a hum overhead announced the retraction of the mooring ring that was the last connection between *Puller* and her cradle on the Slaasriithi starship. "We're away."

"Time to start heading for our ride home," Caine Riordan said, stretching. Frankly, it felt good to relax back into the casual bridge banter of *Puller*'s polyglot crew. And if Yaargraukh, who was currently still on *Puller*, was disturbed by the lack of military decorum and proprieties, he gave no sign of it. "Make for the shift-carrier *Intrepid*. Zero point two gee constant from the HMAP thrusters, Karam."

"Easing into it now, Caine."

Melissa Sleeman looked up from her sensors—and they truly had become *her* sensors. "Wedges One through Three following us out of their cradles. Forming up."

He smiled his thanks, started thinking about Connor, and how he would juggle becoming a true parent for

999

him with finding some way to get Elena back from the Dornaani—and stopped. *No, not yet. There will be plenty of time to think about that on the way home. For now, stay focused on the tasks at hand. You're not out of the woods until you are actually out of the woods.*

And besides, there was a quiet pleasure in savoring these last moments for themselves. He had spent the better part of a year with these people, had lost fellow travellers along the way, had come too close to dying too often with them. But when they got back to Earth, their tight-knit community would dissolve, like willowy spindles of overripe milkweed scattering away from the pods that had bound them together, and that had now ceased to have the power or reason to hold them. Caine never imagined that returning to Earth, to home, to his loves and his life, would impart a feeling of melancholy as well as joy and relief. But it did.

Dora, who had been unusually taciturn for much of the past day, frowned. "I've got an incoming signal. From Downing." She looked up. "Secure Two. Special encryption."

Curious glances ping-ponged between the bridge crew.

Riordan shrugged. "Okay, put him on."

Downing appeared on the main screen. The background was nondescript, and he was alone. "Caine, I see you've cast off and are headed back."

"That's correct, Richard." *And since when have you started keeping track of* Puller's *routine maneuvers?* "What can I do for you?"

"Just wanted to send a few course changes to you.

There are some new arrangements for your various rides home."

"Mr. Tsaami is ready for the new helm data." *Wait a minute.* "What do you mean, 'various rides home'? Aren't we all going back on *Intrepid*?"

"You and the crew of *Puller*, yes. But the wedges are being vectored into a holding box, alongside the arrogated Arat Kur shift-cruiser, *Mimic*."

Riordan frowned. "Why?"

"Protocols from upstairs. Reacculturation assessment for the Lost Soldiers. That sort of thing." Downing looked away. At nothing. In a bare room.

Riordan discovered that he was more than curious: he was becoming wary. "Richard, why is it you who's contacting us, instead of Fleet or port authority? And why have *us* send the coordinates on to the wedges? Why not do it directly? Hell, *Puller*'s the only ship that *isn't* changing course, according to those orders."

"Caine, I'm hardly at the top of the chain of command, as you well know, so I'm afraid I don't have all the answers. So be a good fellow and—"

Riordan stood. When Downing started waffling, when he started with the forced, archaic affability of "good lad" or "old chap" or even "stout fellow," then something was wrong. Caine had learned, someplace along the way, that while Richard did a lot of lying in his line of work and did it very well, Richard wasn't very good at lying to *him*. Never had been. And he wasn't doing any better this time. "Richard, what's going on? Are the Lost Soldiers not coming back on the same shift-carrier that we are?" Which objectively, should not have been a significant detail in the grand scheme of things, but suddenly, it seemed very important. Crucial.

"Caine, if you must know, then at least let's make this conversation private. I'll wait until you've relocated to your ready room before I—"

"I'm not going to the ready room. I'm staying right here. Whatever you have to say to me, you can say to all my crew."

"Caine, without meaning to be rude, I must point out that you don't all have the same clearance levels."

So this casual relay of a course change has suddenly become a beyond-top secret discussion? "Richard, my crew has spent extensive time with the Slaasriithi, with the Hkh'Rkh, with the Lost Soldiers, witnessed Ktor attacks against us, and has seen and examined concrete evidence of Ktor technology—their cold cells—that was used to abduct people from our planet over one hundred and fifty years ago. I don't know what their old clearance levels were, but I think they've pretty much hit the top of the bar, don't you think?"

Downing was silent for several very long seconds. "Well, if you must have it, have it then. Your team, and Major Solsohn, are cleared for immediate return to Earth. But the Lost Soldiers present a far more complicated challenge, one for which we do not have adequate contingencies."

Riordan glanced at Solsohn, whose face was screwed into a tight, perplexed frown. Seeing Caine's look, he shook his head and shrugged. And although it was possible that Duncan was faking it, Riordan didn't think so: this turn of events was catching him as much by surprise as everyone else. *So, either you were kept in the dark about this, or it's a new development. Let's see which it is.* "Richard, the Cold Guard and Lost Soldiers are split between all three wedges. It sounds like you're going to need us to re-dock with *Shore-of-Stars* to effect a redistribution. We should be able to get all the Cold Guard on Wedge One, the Lost Soldiers on Wedges Two and Three."

Richard's countermand came too quickly, was pitched a little too sharply. "No need of that, Caine. They can continue on to us as they are."

"Hold on: the Cold Guard aren't coming home with us either? But they were cleared for high-sensitivity ops. Surely you had all necessary contingencies in place for *their* return?"

Solsohn's frown didn't diminish, but he nodded approvingly.

Downing's response only made Duncan's frown deepen. "Things have changed since you left Delta Pavonis, Caine."

Just great. "I didn't think we'd been gone long enough for another interstellar incident to arise."

"One hasn't. This change is coming straight from home. From Earth."

Riordan glanced at Dora. "Ms. Veriden, could you please try to clean up the audio? I couldn't make out Mr. Downing's last transmission."

She had foreseen his request for privacy. "Audio is cut."

Riordan turned his back to the screen; he didn't put it past Downing to have lip-readers available. "Dora, do you have live lascom with the wedges?"

"All three."

"Good. Order them to perform the following tasks in precisely this order. They are to deactivate broadcast and lascom simultaneously, and watch their systems for embedded codes that reactivate those systems autonomously. Then they are to reverse course toward *Shore-of-Stars*, on vectors optimum for redocking. They are to disregard any orders to the contrary, and treat all approaching craft other than *Shore-of-Stars* and *Puller* as potentially hostile. They are to execute their orders immediately."

Solsohn leaned back in his acceleration couch as Pandora sent the orders. "What are you doing?"

Riordan turned toward Melissa. "Dr. Sleeman, I need a tacplot ASAP. Specifically, I need all ships running CTR transponders to be coded as potential threat contacts. I need to see which hulls are in position to attempt what kind of intercepts."

Bannor Rulaine cleared his throat. "Caine, are you sure—?"

"I am. Dora, now I need you to power down our broadcast receiver."

"Done. Lascom?"

Riordan shook his head. "We've got to keep it."

"Why? So that *pendejo* Downing can keep lying to us?"

"No, because we have to learn more about what's going on, and lascom is the safest pipeline."

"Yeah, well, it's not *totally* safe."

"I know. That's why you've got to get in touch with Tina in Engineering. I want all our systems run by her computer, not the main-brain. For now, auxiliary control has the lead on all ship functions. Isolate the mainframe. Pull physical connections if that's what it takes."

Karam half-turned his head. "Controls are going to be sluggish."

Riordan nodded. "Understood. Can't be helped.

It's more important that we don't leave open any backdoors for them to take over our systems. Dora, tell me when you're done."

"Finished."

"Excellent. Restore audio." Riordan turned to face Downing.

Who was standing with his arms crossed and his face set in hard, straight lines. "This is very unwise, Caine."

"I can see how you'd think so."

"And your crew? What do they think?"

"Well, I haven't had any signs of mutiny over here, so I guess they're willing to play along for now. Speaking of my crew, we'd all like to hear a bit more about why the Lost Soldiers and the Cold Guard aren't coming home with us." Riordan glanced at the tacplot. "And while you're at it, you can also explain why seven Federation and Commonwealth destroyers that seemed to be in their docking cradles aboard their respective carriers two minutes ago are now detached and on intercept courses. At high gee."

"The answer to your second question is the same as the answer to your first question: because the Interbloc Council of the Republic has given these orders. The destroyers are authorized to enforce those orders in the event that you did not understand, or agree with, the need to control contact between both those groups and the population back home. It could be highly destabilizing for them."

Riordan nodded. "What you really mean is 'highly destabilizing for the Republic.' So, we're giving Shethkador what he asked for, after all. We're keeping the Lost Soldiers under wraps."

"Caine, there is no scenario in which your crew is cleared to know the contents of the diplomatic exchange with the Ktoran Ambass—"

"That argument only matters if I give a damn about your orders and I don't. Not anymore."

"I think you are overlooking the seven destroyers which will compel your compliance, Caine."

"Not in the least." He turned to Karam. "Mr. Tsaami, maneuver to obstruct the oncoming CTR bogeys."

"And if they fire, sir?"

"Then we squeak-broadcast the contents of this conversation and my operation logs. I'm sure Mr. Downing will find it a challenge worthy of his skills to try to control that kind of information pollution."

Solsohn stared around the bridge. "I don't like this any better than you do, Commodore—but I didn't sign on to become a marty. Or a mutineer."

"I don't expect we'll go down as either, before this is done, Major. But then again, you also didn't sign on for this crew at all: you were assigned. You will be free to choose between staying with us or going with Mr. Downing, without fear for your safety or prejudice against you. But I counsel you to consider the consequences of that choice first. Very carefully."

He turned back toward Downing. "Richard, I'm pretty sure that you don't approve of the orders under which you are operating. And I'm pretty sure that the people who gave them anticipated that and are listening in."

Downing replied slowly, choosing his words with great care. "Our exchanges are being recorded. The new protocols stipulate that there is to be full accountability for all aspects of all IRIS operations."

A new protocol that shows up at the very same time that the CTR's first Proconsul, Ching of the DWC, starts giving direct orders having to do with operational contingencies and procedures. Except... Ching is a moderate, a Shanghai globalist, not a Beijing cultural protectionist. So... "I'm sure that there was some initial resistance to these orders at the Council level. Out of curiosity, how did Proconsul Ching respond to that resistance? Maybe his perspectives will inform our own." *There, Richard: now you can brief us—and even express unpopular opinions as coming from the other blocs, not from you.*

Downing nodded slowly. "If that will help you come to a more prudent decision, I will be happy to comply." Having dispensed the necessary disclaimer for why he would discuss politics with a noncompliant operative, Richard relaxed slightly. "Proconsul Ching's home government—and the Developing World Coalition bloc in toto—feel that they have been systematically excluded from IRIS. Consequently, the DWC's representatives prevailed upon what it characterizes as IRIS's controlling eurogenic triad—the Commonwealth, Union, and Federation—to adopt new policies of complete transparency and shared authority."

Riordan wondered just how much nausea that diplomatic doubletalk had stirred in Downing's gut. IRIS had been a predominantly Commonwealth operation—the old Five Eyes upgraded with ties to select partners in the European Union, the Russlavic Federation, and Japan—because too many of the world's intelligence services were too porous, too incautious, or too subject to external leverage to be trusted. Beijing's intelligence services did not fall into any of those categories, but had a different set of problems: namely, it was split into multiple internal domains that frequently pursued their own interests at the expense of their nation's. Furthermore, the competition among China's rival intelligence chiefs was aggravated by a three-way doctrinal split between the globalists, the protectionists, and a third, more nebulous group: the careerists, who treated all political fracture lines as zones of opportunity for their own enrichment.

But Beijing both denied that reality and insisted on full equivalence in IRIS. Anything less was an undeniable and (understandably) intolerable loss of face in the global community. So, the protectionist hardliners had no doubt threatened to break ranks with Ching if he failed to force IRIS to comply at this critical juncture, thereby proving to themselves and the rest of the world that they were truly an equal power. And if they didn't get their way, that posed a more harrowing threat than merely causing rifts in the still-fragile bonds holding the Consolidated Terran Republic together: failure to suppress word of the Lost Soldiers could mean renewed war with the Ktor, as per Shethkador's prediction.

Time to find out just how easily the rest of the consuls had swallowed this bitter pill. "And the other blocs happily went along with this?"

The corner of Downing's mouth pinched in irony. "There was, as diplomatic parlance has it, a frank and stimulating exchange of views. Significantly, the matter could not be settled until the military representatives of the blocs were excluded from the discussion, particularly those of the Commonwealth and the Federation." Downing paused. "Particularly them."

Riordan nodded; Downing nodded back. *Okay; that's*

good to know. And not surprising. It also meant that the Commonwealth and Federation destroyers that had just been scrambled to enforce the will of the CTR might be filled with sympathetic crews looking for any excuse to interpret their orders in the most liberal possible fashion . . .

Okay, time to give Downing some plausible deniability in helping us defy the Republic's dictate. "Look, before I can discuss standing aside and surrendering custody of the Lost Soldiers and Cold Guard, I have to know where they're going to be taken."

Downing answered, "I can't tell you."

"What, more clearance issues?"

"No. The political representatives on site haven't told me. Or Ambassador Sukhinin."

Which strongly implied that Vassily wasn't any happier about this development, and that he might have communicated that to his bloc's naval commanders. Specifically, those who were at the cons of the oncoming Federation destroyers. Caine shook his head. "I'm sorry, Richard. I won't—I can't—turn over these people without knowing what's going to become of them."

"And I have no way to get those answers for you. God knows, I tried to get them for myself, Caine. I was told I am not on the 'need to know' list."

"Sounds like you don't much like these orders, either."

Downing's face and voice were carefully expressionless. "We are all subject to the chain of command."

"Only if we choose to be. And I don't, not this time. I don't want to make trouble for you or decline to follow a direct order, but I will if I have to—and in a very public way."

"That presumes you *can* go public, Caine."

"So does that mean you've also got orders to muzzle us? Or impound us? Or worse?"

"Caine, your team is not at risk. You were all cleared for top secret operations involving exosapients. So while we have protocols for controlling public exposure, they do not include forcibly silencing you."

"I'm sure we'd be well cared for. Perhaps living for years like canaries in gilded high-security cages, or in subterranean vaults. To keep us from leaking what we know, what we've seen, voluntarily or otherwise."

Downing folded his arms. "All I can say is that your safety is assured. And that I very much regret not having any information on the intended disposition of the Lost Soldiers or the Cold Guards."

Dora crossed her own arms. "Our safety is assured only if we assume you're telling the truth."

Downing reddened. "I am not lying to you."

"Maybe not, but how do you know *you* haven't been lied to? Because if you have, then"—she freed one hand to draw her index finger across her neck—"we get to join the others. So it seems there are only two reasons those approaching destroyers might not open fire on us: they might hit or offend the Slaasriithi, or we might send what we know out on broadcast."

Downing frowned, looked over at Riordan. "And would you betray Earth that way, Caine?"

"No. Not unless my own government betrays me."

"Caine, don't be ingenuous: a government frequently has to change its objectives, its orders. That's what is happening here, not betrayal."

"Really? Then what is it when leaders lie to their followers? Because that's *exactly* what has happened here. My team, the Cold Guard, and the Lost Soldiers all took oaths to serve, mostly to governments that are still in existence. Having kept their oaths, there is simply no justification for handing them over to another power for imprisonment, exile, or execution. What's their crime? Doing their duty?"

Downing cut the air with the side of his hand. "Caine, neither of us has a choice in this matter. The orders must be obeyed. The full truth of what you found, of what your troops know and can testify to, is too destabilizing. It's a delicate time, Caine. You, more than anyone else, should understand that."

"I do understand. I understand that the time has come to stop managing information and concealing the truth."

"Even if revealing that truth condemns us to starting a war we can't win?"

"That's one possible outcome. But only that: a *possible* outcome. At some point, we have an obligation to share the facts so that our people can decide for themselves whether or not they should trust these Ktor bastards."

Downing shook his head. "You heard what Shethkador said. His government is likely to see any sharing of the Lost Soldiers' true identity as a prelude to war, a war in which the Accord might not be able to help us."

Riordan folded his arms. "Richard, at a certain point, we can't control, or worry about, what the Ktor might think. If we are to keep alive the premise of plurality, we have to keep its basic promise: that the citizens of the CTR are competent to handle basic information and exert their political will. Otherwise, our governments become no different than mandarin star chambers, and political process becomes just so much theater. We have to keep our promises. That means I have to keep my oath to the Lost Soldiers, and implicitly, to the Cold Guard: that I will not turn them over to anyone else without concrete guarantees for their safety and fair treatment. You've given me neither."

"That sounds very fine, Caine, but tell me: how is keeping this secret any different from the other secrets you've kept?"

"I haven't liked most of the secrets I've been tasked to keep, but they've never been at the expense of our own people. That's what you're asking this time, and that's why I won't stand for it. So, excepting those Lost Soldiers or Cold Guard who want to go with you—with full knowledge of the conditions under which they are doing so—I cannot comply with your requests. Unless, that is, we figure another way out of this."

Downing nodded slowly. "You have a proposal for how we might come to a peaceful agreement?"

"I might. I need to confer with my officers and put the matter before the Lost Soldiers and Cold Guard. And in order to do that, Wedges One through Three are going to need to redock with the *Shore-of-Stars*. As will we. So call the hounds off, Richard."

Downing smiled faintly, gestured off screen. In the holoplot, the seven yellow chevrons denoting the CTR destroyers began slowing: they were counterboosting at maximum thrust. "How soon may we hope to hear from you again, Caine?"

Riordan shrugged. "It depends."

"Upon what?"

"Upon just how outraged the people on my side of the equation feel by their homeworld's betrayal of them. Riordan out."

Caine turned toward Duncan Solsohn as soon as Downing's image had faded from *Puller*'s screen. "Major, I need direct answers to some very blunt questions."

"I expected that."

"Good. Did you know this was coming?"

Solsohn shook his head. "No. I knew there was some political infighting over our mission to Turkh'saar, but nothing like this. And I still find it hard to believe that Mr. Downing is standing there telling us to give up our own people. That's just not like him."

"You mean, he's not quite that big an asshole?" asked Veriden.

Solsohn cut an unfriendly glance in her direction. "He's not an asshole, Dora. But he does have a shitty job. I just didn't know it had gotten *this* shitty."

Riordan folded his arms. "So when you joined us, you didn't know about these new protocols governing IRIS?"

Solsohn shook his head. "I can't believe that Downing did, either. He would have briefed me differently, set out more detailed contingencies. Hell, he wanted to put you and your team directly in the loop on our suspicions regarding BD+56 2966, but the politicos nixed it."

Riordan frowned. "Which politicos?"

Duncan smile was crooked, rueful. "Developing World Coalition, with some scattered support from TOCIO."

Riordan nodded. "The same powers that resented being kept in the dark about the existence, let alone operations, of IRIS. So, the handwriting was on the wall even before we left Delta Pavonis. And while we were gone, they've flexed their muscles, made their cooperation contingent upon shared control."

Duncan shrugged. "And can you blame them? IRIS was rolling the dice for the fate of the world in the years leading up to the war and then all the way to the end of it."

Riordan sighed. "No, I don't blame them. IRIS should have come clean, at least about its existence and operational mandate, to the rest of the globe's leaders right after the Parthenon Dialogs."

Bannor scowled. "Jesus. That would have been one God-awful mess."

Riordan tried to smile. "You mean compared to the mess we have on our hands now? I think we'd be in better shape to handle this crisis if IRIS had bitten the bullet earlier, rather than later."

Karam scratched one homely ear. "Guys, none of that helps us get out of this situation."

Riordan smiled. "Actually, it might, at least insofar as there are government players who don't like their current orders any better than we do. Richard has just about come to the end of his tether. And I suspect Vassily Sukhinin is already there."

Dora frowned. "And how does that help us?"

"It means they, too, want to find an option that doesn't involve us turning over the Lost Soldiers and Cold Guard. Or being destroyed for refusing to do so."

Peter Wu's voice was very quiet and level. "I like the sound of that."

Riordan's smile broadened. "Me too. So let's find them that option."

Chapter Seventy-Three

Lieutenant Brill, senior communications officer aboard the battlecruiser *Lincoln*, appeared on the screen in the intel center. Before speaking to him, Richard Downing held up a long, slim hand, thereby cutting off the torrent of position statements being delivered by Mr. Bentley Awan, the senior attaché of the Developing World Coalition observation group that had arrived at Sigma Draconis three weeks earlier. "Yes, Mr. Brill?"

"Commodore Riordan on encrypted lascom one, sir."

"Very good, Lieutenant. Please pipe it down here. Private channel."

"Yes, sir."

Downing folded his arms, glanced at his assistant, Gray Rinehart, who had been conferring with the COs of the seven destroyers suspended halfway between the capital ships of the squadron that had been sent on this mission and *Shore-of-Stars*. Rinehart nodded faintly, surreptitiously. *Good: so everything's in readiness.*

"Let us hope Commodore Riordan has elected

to see reason in this matter," Awan said, folding his hands behind his back.

Downing nodded, wondered how the DWC liaison really felt about his job. He had arrived minutes after the first exchange with Riordan, his shuttle having pulled four gees in an attempt to get him into the conversation. The DWC power brokers, for whom Awan was the public factotum, had remained well back from engaging with any of the other senior CTR personnel in system. They had not even allowed Awan to attribute comments to any of them individually. In Downing's experience, that was a sure sign that they were unwilling to be held personally accountable for anything that might occur here, which in turn suggested that they expected outcomes that might be quite messy.

The screen blanked momentarily, then reilluminated, showing Riordan and most of the bridge of *Puller*: it was full.

"This is most irregular," Awan muttered. "We should not be speaking of policy matters in the presence of—"

"Commodore," Downing said loudly, drowning out the attaché, "there is some concern on this end regarding the persons witnessing our exchange on your end."

Riordan nodded. "I am not surprised, Mr. Downing, but since the decisions about to be made will affect everyone you see, it is our unanimous decision that all of them must be present. Otherwise, there will be no discussion at all."

Awan was hissing something about blackmail as Downing returned Riordan's nod. "I understand. We accept those conditions." *I expected them, anyway.* "Have you come up with an alternative to our current impasse, Commodore?"

Riordan continued to match Downing's formality: theater for the benefit of the DWC representative. "We have. We propose a trade."

"You have nothing to trade," Awan asserted over Downing's shoulder. "You are agents of the state. Whatever you have belongs to the Consolidated Terran Republic."

Riordan raised an eyebrow. "Mr. Awan, is it? That kind of talk might play well in Beijing and Islamabad, but I think you will want to bear in mind that the recording of this exchange will also be heard in Washington, London, Brussels, Moscow, and Tokyo. And Shanghai. Be careful not to sow discord where you are working to build cooperation."

"Do not school me in my job, Commodore. I represent interests that have long gone without representation. We are asserting our rights, which include a frank expression of how we view the affairs of the Republic and its servitors."

Riordan smiled. "As you wish. In the meantime, let me acquaint you with a practical view of how negotiations like these work: possession is nine-tenths of the law. And we have something that you want. Very badly."

"This is not trade; this is extortion!"

Downing turned. "Mr. Awan, firstly you have not even heard the Commodore's proposal. Secondly, assuming he does have something we want so badly, how does your outburst get you any closer to possessing it?"

Awan leaned back, looked away. Downing spent a moment assessing him: he was angry yes, but not just at Riordan. Was it the whole situation? Did he resent being the errand boy for the anonymous puppeteers from the DWC, sent to be the voice and face that would be forever associated with the decision to put aside the Lost Soldiers and Cold Guard in a safe place? A place that might ultimately prove to be a mass grave or deep space? If so, he might be eager for an escape from his role. "Commodore, what is it that you have that we want?"

"The Ktor cold-cell technology that we discovered on and extracted from Turkh'saar. Their systems—and we have now identified sixteen different types—are immeasurably more advanced than our own. Once they have been studied and reverse-engineered, the broader implication—rapid human colonization with essentially zero mortality risk from cold sleep—is strategically greater than all the exosapient drive, energy, and weapons technologies that have been accrued to date."

Well played, Caine. Now, let's underscore the urgency of the matter for the myopic politico in the room. "Commodore, I think you overestimate the value of that technology. It certainly cannot compare to the political authority, and unity, of the Consolidated Terran Republic, which is what you are asking us to sacrifice in exchange for these cold cells."

Riordan smiled. "Firstly, Director Downing, the technology in question is so profoundly beyond ours that not all the systems are actually 'cold' cells. More importantly, it is at best ingenuous, and at worst duplicitous, to ignore the profound changes that this will bring within even three years time. For the CTR to compete successfully, it must move population offworld rapidly. This technology removes the largest impediment to that: the mortality risks of cold sleep, which has been, since the beginning of our interstellar expansion, the fear that keeps most people from considering emigration. That has, in turn, forced most blocs to provide waking transport, which, per kiloliter, enables the relocation of one-tenth the number of persons who could be moved if they were in cryogenic suspension. With the technologies we found, these problems would come to an abrupt end.

"Now factor in the coming changes in shift-range. I understand that reverse-engineering of captured Arat Kur shift drives have now demonstrated ranges of nine point four eight light-years. That dramatically redraws the interstellar map, cutting months off of the travel times to the colonies of the Green Mains. And with the Slaasriithi engineering that has or will soon be added to that, we can expect even better performance in five years time.

"The combination of zero-risk cold sleep and drastically reduced travel time will change the current trickle of colonists to a flood. Now add in the postwar attitude: people are scared. The invasion eliminated the belief that staying on Earth meant you were in the safest possible place; it is now perceived to be in the crosshairs of various hostile exosapients. But we have to expand, to make sure that we don't have so many of our eggs in one vulnerable basket. Now, we can accomplish that. Easily.

"So when you have to vindicate this trade to whoever might be overseeing this matter, they will understand that you were right to guarantee the safety of the Lost Soldiers and Cold Guard in exchange for the Ktoran cold-cell technology. And you can blame me for forcing that choice upon you."

"And if I do not agree to those terms?"

Riordan shrugged. "Then you will not get access to that cold-sleep technology."

"You would destroy it?"

Riordan leaned back. "If you can give me a guarantee that the Lost Soldiers and Cold Guards won't be permanently disappeared, then I will be happy—relieved—to guarantee you that we will not destroy the Ktoran cold cells. We would merely—misplace them—until our people are safe. So, can you guarantee the safety of our people, Director Downing?"

Richard looked over his shoulder at Awan. *Moment of truth, old boy.*

Awan, eyes shiny, would not meet his gaze, blinked a few times. Then he shook his head, his jaw clenched.

Downing turned back to Caine. "I am unable to provide you with the guarantee you seek."

"Then we cannot give you a guarantee either, Director."

"In that event, you leave me no choice; I must agree to your terms."

Awan stepped forward rapidly. "Downing, you cannot—!"

Richard interrupted him with a hard stare. "Mr. Awan, we discussed this: are you authorizing and instructing me to use lethal force to compel Commodore Riordan and his team to comply?"

Awan went pale. Downing waited. *And here are the wages you must pay in order to climb the political ladder, you foolish sod. You've got to do the dirty work that others have ordered. I've done it out of dubious patriotism. Let's see if you'll do it out of blind ambition.*

Awan glanced away again. "You are authorized and instructed to use lethal force."

Downing turned back toward Caine. "I must inform

you that if you do not comply, we will take custody of the personnel that must be remanded to us, as well as take possession of the technologies you have extracted, through the use of force."

One or two of the bridge personnel around Riordan exchanged worried glances: most did not. "I am surprised to hear that you are willing to start a war with the Slaasriithi over this, Director Downing. They are our only allies, after all."

"I have my orders."

"And I have mine," announced a new voice. "This is Admiral Ira Silverstein. By what authority are you making that threat against our allies and our own personnel, Mr. Downing?"

"By the authority vested in Senior Attaché Bentley Awan, representative of the DWC team to the Bloc Integration Oversight Committee, which is currently aboard the WCS *Pyongyang*. I was under the impression that this was a secure line, Admiral," Downing concluded, savoring that lie.

"No line on this ship is opened or remains so unless I have access to it, Mr. Downing. My hull, my rules. Is Mr. Awan with you right now?"

From the corner of his eye, Richard saw Awan shrinking into himself. "He most certainly is, Admiral. Do you wish to speak to him?"

"I most certainly do. In my ready room."

"Admiral," Awan objected cautiously, "I am unable to comply with your request. I cannot interrupt the ongoing negotiations, which are actually in direct violation of—"

"Mr. Awan, I did not make a request. I issued an order. Or an ultimatum, if you prefer. Which you will obey immediately, or I will have you escorted off this ship posthaste."

But Awan wasn't without a measure of spine: he couldn't have risen so far in the diplomatic ranks otherwise. "Admiral, I must protest that ultimatum. And I must point out that, according to the chain of command, the DWC Oversight Committee was given full authority to use any means necessary to ensure that on this occasion, the operational caprice of IRIS does not violate the constraints that have now been placed upon it by the Interbloc Council."

"Mr. Awan, if the head of your oversight committee wants to formally, and in person, present me with a written directive to that effect, I will comply. However, I must warn you that it will not help you much, at this point."

"I do not understand, Admiral. Seven destroyers should certainly be force enough to ensure compliance of Riordan and his team."

"Not if all seven destroyers are currently fully powered down for drive maintenance, Mr. Awan."

"But you deployed them just five hours ago—"

"Yes, I did. And since it seemed we were going to sit here navel-gazing interminably, I gave orders to their captains to get their hulls back up to spec."

"Admiral, this is highly irregular."

"It might have been if I hadn't cleared it with the senior political officer in system before I gave the orders. But Consul Sukhinin thought it was a fine idea. As a standing member of the Federation Navy, he was happy to pass along the word to the Russian destroyers himself. Now, Mr. Awan, why aren't you in my briefing room already?"

"Sir, we have only been speaking for two minutes."

"Then you are already five minutes late. Get up here or get escorted off my ship. Your choice."

Awan sped out of the room without a backward glance.

Downing turned to Riordan. "I think we can speak freely now."

Riordan smiled. "I guess we can." He raised his voice slightly. "Thanks, Ira."

Silverstein's voice was now avuncular. "My pleasure. These damn Lost Soldier orders have disaster written all over them. My senior JAG, Lieutenant Commander Phalon, can jam them up procedurally for at least half a day. And I'll keep Awan waiting two hours at least. In the meantime, you might want to thank Mr. Rinehart for organizing the maintenance snafu and Vassily Sukhinin for playing along."

"It's good to have friends in high places."

Silverstein's voice became more somber. "It can be, but you know how this game works, Caine. We can explain away this one irregularity. No one can prove this wasn't a comedy of errors. But if we tried it again—"

"I understand. I've played my last trump card. Ira, thanks for the help over the years. I hope our paths will cross again."

"Me, too. Now don't waste time talking to me. Settle this hash before the politicos can stir the pot again." The connection snicked off.

Downing sighed and sat. "Let's get the particulars settled, Caine. But I won't agree to anything that is likely to sabotage the deal further downstream."

"I won't be asking for anything that would. Firstly,

we're taking the Lost Soldiers and Cold Guard into the far reaches of Terran space. They've volunteered to go back into cold sleep for at least five years time, subject to assessment by our overwatch personnel."

"And who would those be?"

Riordan smiled. "If I tell you, then you know who to look for."

Downing scowled. "I'm not coming looking for them, Caine. Surely you must realize that."

"I didn't say you'd come looking; I said you'd know who to look for. And I'm not going to put you in a position where you'd have to withhold that information and get yourself court-martialed—or my people discovered."

Fair enough. "How do you effect their transport?"

Riordan gestured behind him. "The *Shore-of-Stars*. Yiithrii'ah'aash is willing to help us so long as he has our permission to do so."

"Caine, I'm not sure I can."

"Richard, you don't have to do anything. As far as Yiithrii'ah'aash knows—formally speaking—I still have my diplomatic credentials and rank. And the mission profile for Turkh'saar provided for the possibility of our requiring him to provide transportation back into CTR space. That's what I'm invoking. And that's why he's not going to be taking your calls. Comm problems, you see."

"Of course. Comm problems. Just the way all seven destroyers needed maintenance at the same time. During a potential combat operation."

"Yep. Just like that. So with the Slaasriithi doing the hauling, there will be no need to falsify any records or manifests on CTR ships that would have had to take our people . . . wherever. So you've got a clean slate: no contamination, not even the odd antique uniform or piece of technology. It gets boxed up with them and moved to the far end of nowhere."

Downing frowned. "Do you mean to say that none of the Lost Soldiers or Cold Guard elected to go back home?"

Riordan shrugged. "Eight of the Cold Guard wanted to, badly. But they're not stupid. They know there's no way they could be allowed back into the general population right now, and that there's a significantly better than zero chance that they'd be put in cold cells that would soon suffer a tragic 'collective malfunction.'"

Downing nodded. He didn't want to admit it, but that outcome was all too possible, particularly after what he had seen this day. "So those eight Guards will be in cold cells, too?"

"Yeah, with three-year timers. They're willing to risk that the current situation will have blown over by then."

"And the rest of the Guards?"

Solsohn leaned forward. "They want out, Mr. Downing. Having to barter for their safety like this—it's really spooked them."

Can't say I blame them. "How are you going to provide cold cells for the others and for the Lost Soldiers?"

Riordan smiled. "We do have a lot of *Ktoran* cold cells, Richard."

"Now see here; you promised those to us—"

"You'll have every cold cell we don't require. And when we're done with the ones we're using, you'll get those back, too. Although let's be frank, Richard:

you'll still be getting close to four hundred units. You'll also have dozens of each variety, even though two examples of each would be enough to run the trials and analyses for reverse-engineering. And since you can doctor the report indicating how many Lost Soldiers there actually were originally, and therefore, how many cold cells there were, no one else will know that you didn't get all of them right away."

Downing nodded. "And that keeps the government from immediately looking for your people in cold sleep. After all, where could you have come up with hundreds of cryocells and not leave a paper trail a mile wide?"

Riordan nodded. "That's the idea. But we have other precautions against government attempts to find or meddle with our cold-sleepers. One that you should share with Mr. Awan, or whoever is holding his leash, if they do learn that we're keeping everyone in cryogenic suspension."

"I'm sure they're going to love this."

"I'm sure I don't care." Riordan leaned forward. "I've had enough contact with the press to know not to trust it, but even at its worst, it has its uses. In this case, if any of the Lost Soldiers or Cold Guards are abducted, interfered with, or attract undue attention, the overwatch will relay a story to the media detailing the events on Turkh'saar and here. And in the event that some eager field agent gets the bright idea to grab all the overseers first, that same exposé will be sent out automatically when our people fail to reset a countdown clock."

Downing nodded. "So the incriminating evidence is linked to a delayed deadman switch. If your personnel don't get to it within a set period of time, it is sent to the press. And I'm guessing it's not just one file package, but a multipart transmission distributed across multiple servers and multiple formats. Making it damned unlikely that counteragents would be able to stop all of them."

Riordan smiled. "You trained me well."

"Too well, it seems. Now, what about the government equipment in your possession? I don't think the CTR is going to overlook missing ships and boats."

"Nor do I. The wedges will be dropped off at a distant system before *Shore-of-Stars* departs human space, along with all the remaining gear."

"What about *Puller*? And her gear?"

Riordan shook his head. "You're going to transfer *Puller* to us as a detached vessel, provided to my team in consideration of their services and to facilitate further action on behalf of the CTR."

"Caine, I don't have the authority to do that."

"No, but Silverstein does and Vassily will sign off—and you know it. Besides, *Puller* was reported as heavily damaged back at Disparity, and there was no official update on her status before you sent us on to Turkh'saar. So, as far as the record is concerned, she was a write-off that someone found a way to make fly again."

"Very well, but even if you decide to keep her in mothballs—which I doubt—having a ship costs money. Lots of money. And I notice that you haven't talked about funding yet, so I imagine this is the segue?"

Riordan nodded. "It is. And the solution to this is also the solution to providing you with with a plausible basis for disavowing us, from the start of our mission to Turkh'saar."

Downing felt himself frowning, as he often did when he concentrated hard. "Of course. The fiction would be that I sent you under a letter of marque."

"Right. As it is, three people on my team had no connections to IRIS or the military. So by definition, the mission retained free agents."

Downing nodded. "It's simple enough to shift most of you into that category retroactively, that you were no longer directly employed by or operating under a service oath to the CTR. Once we've made that change to the record, your actions would have required that you were in possession of a letter of marque. Which we shall create promptly." Downing sighed. "A slim legal fig leaf, at best, but better than complete nudity."

"Exactly. So, since I have been operating with a letter of marque, I can approach you for funding or payment. Or, since we'll be turning over almost four hundred examples of advanced Ktoran cold-sleep tech today, prize money. And it will have to be in cash, before *Puller* leaves with *Shore-of-Stars*, because any electronic banking will reveal my team's location."

"That's all quite inspired, Caine, but there's one small problem: the politicos are going to strip you of your command and position as soon as you walk into custody. And your letter of marque will be immediately revoked. You must know that."

"Yes, that's likely. But it's not true right at this second."

"Then if it's going to be undone, what's the bloody point, except, as an excuse to get paid?"

"Well, last I checked, if you're living incognito, you need cash. But you're also going to include my XO of record as successor and deferred co-holder of the letter of marque: namely, Major Bannor Rulaine. Who has had no hand in making the decisions that led up to this situation. Who is a bona fide war hero, both in the defense of Earth and during the extraction from Turkh'saar. And who will have someone with him who reports directly to you: Duncan Solsohn."

"They're both IRIS. They will be subject to having any orders issued by me rescinded. They will have to comply, to turn around and come home, if they're still on the intel grid."

Riordan shook his head. "Not if you accept their retirement now, effective immediately, and rehire Duncan as an independent contractor. And not if their letter of marque is also signed by Vassily and Ira. And if *Puller* leaves—before you get any orders to the contrary—under a communications blackout."

The two men Riordan had named exchanged long stares, then nodded soberly at Downing. Who knew what both of them were thinking: better an uncertain future than the certainty of living in a safe house for years. Or what might be worse. If the secrecy protocols surrounding Turkh'saar became a matter of heated interbloc debate, some powers might be eager to tie off all loose ends. Even if that meant violating an ally's safe house to preemptively silence persons who had seen what they should not have.

Downing was silent for several long seconds. "They can't retire from IRIS; it doesn't officially exist. That means they—and any other IRIS personnel who want to follow the same path—must retire from the services and agencies from which IRIS borrowed them."

Bannor spoke loudly so the mic would catch his reply. "I mustered out on your orders more than a year and a half ago, now, Mr. Downing. I'll be more than happy to add a completion bonus from IRIS to my retirement pay, thank you very much."

Solsohn was slower to respond. "Mr. Downing, you know my record. You know where I carried out my field ops, and against whom. I'm guessing that my career with the CIA is going to be, well, politically awkward now, given some of the folks who will have access to my dossier through IRIS. So, rather than get stuck in an unmarked cubicle in an unnumbered room in a basement that no one knows about, or getting cashiered—or worse—I think I'll get out while the getting is good. If you take my meaning."

Downing sighed. "I do. And I wish I could disagree with you, but you might be right. If you hadn't been on Turkh'saar, I suspect your earlier career could have been ignored for the sake of interbloc cooperation. But inasmuch as you will now be intimately associated with this act of defiance, you could become a scapegoat."

"Yes, sir, that's pretty much what I was thinking."

Downing watched the rest of Caine's team nodding in agreement. "I presume you have discussed this with the Lost Soldiers?"

Riordan sighed. "At length. Hell of a homecoming for them."

Downing frowned. "And for you. You know, of course, that you're finished. You'll either have to be brought all the way inside the intelligence community and disciplined, or pushed out for good."

Caine smiled. "Is that second option a threat or a promise?" His smile faded. "Besides, I have a son to raise and a fiancée to locate."

Downing steepled his fingers. "Without your status

as an IRIS operative, I can't guarantee how fast, or even if, transportation can be arranged to the Dornaani Collective. There is still no normalized exchange between us."

Riordan shrugged. "Well, either Elena is awake or not. If she is, then the Dornaani are not telling us, which means they are no friends of ours and they probably intend to keep me away from her permanently. If she's still in surgical cold sleep, then time is not passing for her and she couldn't be in safer hands or safer technology. So I'm going to be measured about this, not allow myself to be driven by impatience. I'm not going to get her back tomorrow or the next day or next month. I have to make the right moves to get the right result. And I have to be there for my son. Which I haven't done yet."

Downing sighed. "Mr. Rinehart, how likely is it that Commodore Riordan's staff and attached personnel can remain undetected by intelligence sweeps?"

Gray Rinehart shrugged. "Every secret has a shelf life, sir. But if the political infighting among the blocs results in new personnel additions to IRIS, it's a safe bet that the restaffing effect won't reach the further star systems until long after *Shore-of-Stars* has deposited the Commodore's people. And our current operatives will be willing to look the other way or not look at all. Bottom line: I give Major Rulaine and the rest three years, four at the outside, before they're detected."

Downing revised that estimate to thirty months, maximum. By which time, hopefully, other, more urgent matters would relegate any loose ends from Turkh'saar to the bottom of the action list. "In that event, Caine, I accept your terms. Without further debate."

Riordan did not often look surprised: he did now. "Really?"

"Yes, really." The solid wall of stunned faces looking at him from the screen irked Downing; had they really been so naive to believe that his actions had ever been an expression of his own preferences, his own sense of morality? "I'm responsible for all of us being here. So I'm responsible for setting things right. That means agreeing to your proposal, since it appears to be the only way to ensure the safety of literally hundreds of innocents."

Caine was shaking his head. "Richard, you shouldn't be the one to take the fall for this. It wasn't your decision that the Lost Soldiers and the Guards had to disappear; you weren't the one who created this impasse."

Downing smiled. "So I should fall back on the old 'I was just following orders' excuse? No, Caine, I helped put all these pieces in place. And it's not just the Lost Soldiers and the Cold Guard that are at stake; it's all of us. When we start forsaking our own, then we've started down the path of undoing the values that make us who and what we are, that make us different from the Ktor. This is my line in the sand, and I will not cross it."

"Richard, you could lose your job over this."

He smiled. "To paraphrase you, is that a promise or a threat? Either way, we'll see, won't we?" He leaned back, felt simultaneously nauseous and better, cleaner, than he had in years. Decades, maybe. "There will be a shuttle coming by to collect you within the hour, Caine. Downing out."

Chapter Seventy-Four

Riordan stared at the screen a long time after Downing's face faded away.

Bannor Rulaine cleared his throat. "Boss, about your going back...I don't trust them. Downing, yeah, maybe, but—"

Riordan shook his head. "Bannor, we don't have any choice. Right now, you've got freedom of action. You can live your lives—sort of—and plan for the next step. I doubt you can remain together: you'd be too easy to locate. But you can stay in touch and keep tabs on each other, be each others' safety net. And I've got a son to raise and a—I hope—wife to retrieve from the Dornaani."

"Yes, but can you *trust* them? Will they even allow you to search for Elena, or be with your son?"

Riordan kept staring at the screen. "Downing clearly doesn't like what the politicos tried to do here. And he's not alone: Vassily has drawn his own line in the sand, and that line will run right down the middle of the World Council. If they try to bring more pressure to bear on Richard, I think he'll buck them. And if he doesn't, Elena's own family—her brother Trevor, in particular—will come down on him like a ton of bricks. I think the worst case scenario is that I'll be shown the door without ceremony or thanks while Downing calms the powers that be. And he'll still be in a position to give me advance warning if they plan to try to put me in the bag."

"Assuming they don't discharge him first."

"I don't think that can happen very quickly. Even if Downing eventually gets the boot, he's got a lot of debriefing to do, and I don't know that IRIS would allow itself to be turned over to a whole new crew of controllers. I'm guessing the next director will be from either the Russian Federation or the European Union: a transitional figure. That means that Downing should still have enough of an intel pipeline to be able to give me warning if some nation or bloc has decided that I need to be removed from the equation."

Duncan nodded. "Besides, you presented at the Parthenon Dialogs; you were the voice that announced the existence of exosapients. If you have an 'unfortunate accident,' the press would be all over that."

Bannor shrugged. "Even so, you're still balancing on the edge of a razor, Caine. And now, none of us are going to be around to lend a hand."

Riordan nodded. "Which is as it should be. You've got to get far away from Earth and get lost. It won't be hard if you go to the further systems first, and then split up. With you divided into small teams, overseeing containers full of sleeping Soldiers and Guards, you should be able to stay way under the radar."

"Not all of us," Bannor pointed out. "I'm going to

have to play mercenary commander, in order to keep up the whole 'letter of marque' charade."

"It might not be a charade, ultimately," Riordan mused. "And it will certainly seem authentic as long as you've got a freelance liaison to IRIS." He turned to look at Solsohn. "Assuming you really *have* retired from the Institute."

Duncan shrugged. "Look, if they let me stay on as a private contractor, I'd be a fool not to take it. It gives us more intel and clout if we need it. But that's just the official story. I'm with you guys, now—all the way." He smiled. "But I won't tell IRIS if you won't."

Riordan didn't try to suppress an answering smile. "Deal. And good to have you aboard."

"Yeah," Dora echoed in a voice that was anything but enthusiastic, "we'll be throwing you a welcome party real soon. Like, in fifteen years. Assuming you don't double-cross us the first chance you get."

Duncan turned to her. "Look, I get that you don't like me and that you don't trust me. But if you think this is all part of some intricate scheme, then you're just plain nuts, Dora."

"That's not what I'm worried about. I'm worried about you going back to IRIS like a dog to its master, just as soon as you can bring them some tasty info on us, tasty enough so that they'll let you back in the pack."

Duncan shook his head. "Caine has my dossier. I'm guessing he's shared it with Bannor. Maybe they should share it with you."

"Why?"

Solsohn looked up, his blue eyes pained. "Because I've got nothing to go back to. The job saw to that.

And if you look at my field work, you'll discover a really unfortunate trend: I was involved in half a dozen violations of sovereign borders. Care to guess where those borders were?"

Dora folded her arms. "Scattered throughout the Developing World Coalition bloc?"

"Guilty as charged. And that's just how the DWC is going to see it: once an operative against them, always an operative against them. And whatever powers, old or new, are driving IRIS, they're not going to want any uncomfortable reminders of the not-so-good old days." He leaned back. "I'm done, Dora. Even if I didn't want to be."

Riordan nodded. "We all are. And I wish I could be there to take the next steps, find the next path, with you." He looked at Rulaine. "But Bannor's going to be the one in the best position to blaze a new trail, such as it is."

He nodded. "Yeah. Duncan and I will be two-thirds of the team that won't be staying under the radar. We can't, if we're going to make good on our letter of marque."

Sleeman leaned her fine chin into the palm of her long-fingered hand. "And where will you be?"

"Epsilon Indi. There's a lot of postwar turmoil there. Local raiders—call them pirates, if you like— were joined by megacorporate renegades, all of whom have reportedly made common cause with Hkh'Rkh stranded in the system."

Tygg took his hand from Sleeman's shoulder. "Hkh'Rkh? In Epsilon Indi? I didn't know any invaders got that far."

A new voice answered from the open hatchway.

"It was our furthest advance, and probably unwise."
Yaargraukh entered, Susan Phillips leaning heavily on
his immense left arm and balancing more delicately
upon Peter Wu's right. "Our smallest shift-carrier,
Relentless Hunter, was carried there by a larger Arat
Kur ship. Its tactical mission was to conduct commerce
raiding and challenge your control of the system. Strategically, it was a ploy to occupy those fleet elements
we believed you had stationed in the Green Mains,
to prevent them from relieving Earth." He helped
lower Susan into an acceleration couch. "Obviously,
our strategy was profoundly misguided."

Bannor nodded; Duncan goggled. "And you're coming along? To—help us?"

Yaargraukh pony-nodded. "I would be foolish to
do otherwise. As per the axiom of our Ghostsires, 'If
my claws guard not your back, then whose claws shall
guard mine?' Besides, I and those with me have no
way to enter cold sleep; the Hkh'Rkh body is wholly
incompatible with your cold cells. So we shall function as liaisons."

Bannor nodded. "It's a logical cover. They could
even become a crucial variable in settling the conflict
in Epsilon Indi. One of the problems is that no one
can talk to the Hkh'Rkh stranded there, and who, by
all accounts, refuse to believe that the war is over.
That gives us a cover story for Yaargraukh and his
followers: that they have come of their own accord
to convince the survivors of *Relentless Hunter* that
there's an armistice and that the Patrijuridicate has
sued for peace."

Riordan nodded. "And Epsilon Indi is an excellent
system from which to send all-clear codes."

"All-clear codes?" Tygg asked.

Riordan nodded. "You can't depend upon distance and low profile to hide from the politicos who might want to find you. So we had to set up a code that would allow any of our groups, in any system, to signal that they are either safe or possibly compromised."

Susan Phillips smiled. "A pretty rum trick, actually. A modification of the old 'weather report' signals we used in the Foreign Office. Expected temperatures and rain and so forth: all code for different events and developments."

Karam nodded. "Except in this case, it's even more subtle. Our code is based on the orrery of each system in which we have a group overseeing the cold cells. Caine, or Bannor, depending upon who receives any given communiqué, will compare the sidereal date in each system with embedded comments about which moons can be seen when, and from where. It will sound like regular conversation, but if there is any deviation from the actual projected time or position of the objects in the system, we know something is off. And the nature of the error—time, position, et cetera—will tell the recipient which one of a handful of trapdoor codes are being used to hide the actual message in the rest of the message."

Riordan shrugged. "So if Bannor or I don't get the right coded message from the right people at the right time, we'll know that something is wrong. And at that point, we can decide what course of corrective action to take—including threatening to spill the beans about Turkh'saar."

Duncan nodded vigorously. "Excellent. So all we need to do is assign the overwatch teams to the different systems in which we're going to hide the Soldiers and Guards, and we're set."

Susan Phillips shook her head. "No, I don't think that's prudent. Not here; not now."

Veriden crossed her arms. "Look, *chica*, no offense, but why the hell are *you* at this meeting anyway?"

Susan smiled faintly. "I was invited. I thought it would be rude to decline."

"Invited? By whom?"

"By Peter—er, Lieutenant Wu. And Major Rulaine. Oh, and Commodore Riordan was nice enough to ask me to be here as well."

Wu leaned forward. "Ms. Phillips—actually, that is *Captain* Phillips—was an intelligence officer for the British in World War Two. Undercover in various Foreign Service offices from 1937 until 1940. In 1942, she oversaw the supply and organization of several French Resistance units for Britain's Special Operations Executive, supporting their, er, direct action against the Nazi occupation forces. When the Ktor took her, she was on her way to be inserted by sub into Vichy France as senior counterintelligence liaison to the de Gaullist cells there."

Veriden's frown had been deepening throughout Peter's recitation of Susan's credentials. "Okay, so the old lady has some experience. But why shouldn't we set up the teams and overwatch systems now?"

"Because the Commodore is an unacceptable security risk." Susan turned apologetic eyes toward Riordan. "Now that you have established the codes we will use to communicate our status to you, we must exclude you from any further inclusion in our planning, sir. You understand, I am sure."

Caine had not foreseen this consideration, which, in retrospect, was embarrassingly obvious. "Yes. Yes, of course." And in that moment he discovered another sensation he had not foreseen: desolation. He suppressed a strong desire to glance around the bridge, to take in and commit to memory the faces he had lived with for the better part of a year. This group might or might not endure and continue onward together, in one form or another, but it would be without him. Yes, he was finally going home to Connor and to commence the uncertain quest of recovering Elena from wherever she was secreted within the Dornaani Collective. But he also felt a sudden pang of regret at doing so, at leaving behind persons that he would never have met if it had not been for the vagaries of war and crisis—and in whom he had vested more confidence and more trust than any others.

Riordan stood, summoned a smile that he hoped was convincing. "Well, it will be a pleasant change not to be keeping track of all the secrets."

Phillips smiled tightly at him, sympathetic yet prim. "Secrets can be a terrible burden, sir."

He nodded. "They can. Which is why I never wanted this job." He turned to Bannor. "Major, I suspect this is the last time I will be saying this: you have the con."

Bannor nodded somberly. "I say three times, I have the con, Commodore. If I may ask, where are you off to?"

"My quarters. To pack my bags. Carry on."

Riordan secured the smart seam on his duffel and looked around his stateroom. *Puller*'s accommodations were far from luxurious; they were barely sufficient. But they had been home for the past thirteen months. They had been the site of urgent consultations, bitter loss, and unexpected levity, both in the heat of battle and the long, dull hours that had been the lot of navy personnel since humans had first conceived of venturing over far horizons aboard the self-contained communities known as "ships." And now, suddenly, it was his home no longer. He picked up his bags and went through the hatchway quickly, careful not to glance behind. What was past was past; new challenges, now.

A few dozen steps and he'd be in the airlock at which a Federation shuttle had docked a few minutes earlier. A few dozen steps and his life would veer in new directions that were equally promising and perilous. He turned the corner to the airlock—

And stopped: the narrow passageway—there were no wide ones aboard *Puller*—was lined by people. By his team.

Bannor, standing next to the airlock door, snapped to attention. "Captain on deck!"

The others—all of them, from pint-sized Miles O'Garran, to towering Tygg Robin—snapped to as well, offering the different salutes of their different services. Even Dora lifted a slow hand to touch her brow and held it there. And, ever so faintly, smiled.

Bannor, eyes straight ahead, used his barracks-room voice. "Commodore Riordan, it has been an honor to serve under you, sir."

Caine realized that his bags were hanging limp in his hands. He dropped them, snapped a salute back, focused on the ritual rather than the maelstrom of emotions that this simple but timeless gauntlet of honor summoned, unbidden, from someplace directly behind his sternum. "The honor, and the privilege, has been mine." Riordan, who secretly prided himself on never being at a loss for words, felt himself ready to stumble into inchoate, burbling testimonies of friendship, of recollections, of hopes for the future—all impossibly maudlin. He held the salute, hoping, waiting, for an inspiration that would save him from this impossible moment—

The airlock paged and auto-opened, revealing four Russlavic Federation Marines, a short man in civvies, and a woman in Commonwealth Navy blue. The man surveyed the scene, a faint smile fading as he did. "Commodore Riordan?"

Caine did not look at the man, but looked at the faces of his team, looked at each pair of eyes and did his best to commit them to memory. Then he lowered his salute. "I am sure other commanders have felt this no less than I have, but that makes it no less true: no captain has been so fortunate in the persons of the crew with whom he served. If I were to find myself confronted by peril and dire purpose once again, I could find no finer companions with which to face it, to share it." He turned to the woman in Navy blues. "I am Commodore Riordan."

She snapped a salute. "Lieutenant Commander Lorraine Phalon, sir. JAG and legal witness for Fleet, sir."

"I am not in your custody?"

"No, sir. This is a civilian matter. The Russian marines and I were assigned to expedite it and assure you that your removal from command has been duly processed and to confirm that you must recognize the authority under which it is being presented, sir."

As Riordan nodded, the small man stepped forward,

smiling. Smugly. "I am Junior Minister Robert Bwaanji. You are to accompany me back to the fleet for final disposition."

Dora and Miles started forward at that worrisome choice of words. The Federation Marines made no move to stop them. Bwaanji stared at their lack of reaction, motioned them forward. Phalon's brow lowered slightly as he did.

Like steers being forced forward into a tight, dirty paddock, the Russian marines raised their weapons into an assault carry and took up positions around Riordan. One produced handcuffs.

Riordan stood as straight and tall and defiant as he could. "State the specifications and charges."

The Marine sergeant suppressed a small sympathetic grin, glanced at Phalon, who shook her head. He looked at Bwaanji. "The crime, sir?"

Bwaanji chewed his lower lip. "I was not informed."

"That is because I am not accused of any crime," Riordan said crisply.

"That, Commodore, is simply a matter of time. Security detachment, escort the Commodore into the shuttle."

Bannor stepped forward, moved a hand cautiously toward the Marine sergeant's battle rifle. "Are the guns absolutely necessary?"

The big Russian pouted, shrugged in Bwaanji's direction, who replied, "They are indeed necessary."

"Why?"

"Commodore Riordan is deemed a flight risk."

Dora snorted so loudly that Bwaanji flinched. "A flight risk?" She flung her hand at the bulkheads. "And just where the hell is he going to flee to, asshole?"

Phalon failed to suppress a grin.

Bwaanji's chin came up. "The Commodore refused to comply with the fleet's initial instructions. We must assume that he may offer other resistance." He waved a hand toward the airlock door. "Commodore, if you please."

"Caine," said Dora, her eyes quickly assessing the Marines, measuring distances, "this doesn't look right. They could be planning to—"

"Ms. Veriden, stand down." Caine hadn't intended to use his command voice: it had come out as reflex. He turned toward her, added, "Dora, this is how it has to be."

"Commodore, no one said anything about taking you into custody," Tygg pointed out. Phalon looked away. "And they should have, if they intended to."

"I'm aware of that." He glanced around the group. "But we got what we asked for: you and the others are free. If they want to perform a little security theater when they come for me, that's a small price to pay."

Bwaanji once again motioned into the airlock and the shuttle beyond. "I think you underestimate the full costs of your actions, then, Commodore."

Riordan grinned at the others, started forward with a confident stride. "More theater," he joked as he walked through the yawning portal. "There's no reason to be worried. I'm not."

Not much.

The airlock door closed behind him.

Appendix A
Dramatis Personae

Ayana Tagawa: Former XO of SS *Arbitrage*; senior impressed crewperson aboard *Red Lurker*

Bannor Rulaine: Major, U.S. Special Forces/IRIS; crew of UCS *Puller*

Caine Riordan: Commodore, IRIS/USSF; crew of UCS *Puller*

Christopher "Tygg" Robin: Lieutenant (later Captain), IRIS; crew of UCS *Puller*

Dora Veriden: crew of UCS *Puller*

Duncan Solsohn: Operative (later Brevet-Major), IRIS; crew of UCS *Puller*

Emil Kozakowski: Former master of the SS *Arbitrage*; (former) employee of CoDevCo

Karam Tsaami: Pilot and Flight Officer, CSSO; crew of UCS *Puller*

Lorraine Phalon: Lieutenant Commander, JAG, USSF

Melissa Sleeman: Advanced science and technology expert; crew of UCS *Puller*

Miles O'Garran: Master CPO, SEAL/IRIS; crew of UCS *Puller*

Peter Wu: Lieutenant, IRIS; crew of UCS *Puller*

Philip Friel: Chief, Engineer, USSF/UCAS; crew of UCS *Puller*

Richard Downing: Director of IRIS, Caine Riordan's handler

Tina Melah: Chief, Engineer, USSF/UCAS; crew of UCS *Puller*

Vassily Sukhinin: Chief negotiator and Deputy Director of IRIS, Sigma Draconis; CTR Consul

The Cold Guards

Two-Gun Baker: Private, USMC/UCAS

Bernardo "Bear" de los Reyes: Corporal (later Sergeant), U.S. Army Ranger/UCAS

Bjorn Hasseler: Captain, Canadian Army/UCAS

Charles (Chucky, "the Hammer") Martell: Private, USMC/UCAS

Donna Gaudet: Chief Warrant Officer, CARICOM/UCAS

Yehuda ("Sundog") ben York: Private, Canadian Army/UCAS

Katie Somers: Lance Corporal, British Army/UCAS

Matthew Fanny: Top Sergeant, U.S. Army/UCAS

The Lost Soldiers

Alexander Shvartsman: First Lieutenant, Soviet Ground Forces

Carlisle Hansell: Commander, CO of USS *Swordfish*, USN

Emmett Owen: Sergeant, MACV-SOG, US Army Special Forces

Isaac Franklin: First Lieutenant, Pararescue Jumper, USAF

Ivan Zhigarev: Lieutenant Colonel, RKKA/Red Army

Martin Enderle: Lieutenant Commander, Executive Officer of *Orzel*, ORP/Free Polish Navy

Patrick Paulsen: Colonel, USAF, CO of the Lost Soldiers

Richard Hailey: Captain, MACV-SOG, US Army Special Forces

Robert Lane: Sergeant, MACV-SOG, US Army Special Forces

Steven Rodermund: Lieutenant Colonel, USAF

Susan Phillips: Captain, Special Operations Executive, UK

The Ktor

Brenlor Perekmeres: Evolved and Srin; Captain of *Red Lurker*

Idrem Perekmeresuum: Evolved; Second Officer of *Red Lurker*

Nezdeh Perekmeres: Evolved, Aware, and Srina; Executive officer of *Red Lurker*

Olsirkos Shethkador'vah: Evolved, Tagmator; Master of *Will Breaker*

Sehtrek: Intendant; crew of *Red Lurker*

Tegrese Hreteyarkus: Evolved; crew of *Red Lurker*

Tlerek Shethkador: Evolved, Aware, Srin, and Ambassador to Earth/CTR; Captain of *Ferocious Monolith*

Zurur Deosketer: Evolved; crew of *Red Lurker*

The Hkh'Rkh

Ezzraamar Laarkhduur of the Moiety of Nys'maharn

Jrekhalkar, Fist (later Voice and Fist) of the Great Clan Gdar'khoom

O'akhdruh, Silent Voice of the Great Clan Gdar'khoom

Uzkekh'gar of the Great Clan Gdar'khoom

Yaargraukh Onvaarkhayn of the moiety of Hsraluur, former Advocate of the Unhonored

Z'gluurhek, Scion, vassal of the Great Clan Gdar'khoom

Other Exosapients

Alnduul: Senior Mentor of the Custodians of the Accord, Dornaani Collective

Yiithrii'ah'aash: Prime Ratiocinator of the Great Ring, Ambassador to Earth/CTR, Slaasriithi

Appendix B
Glossary

Allsires: The ten highest Greatsires of the Patrijuridicate. They constitute an oligarchic supreme court, but have no greater legislative power (officially) than the other Greatsires.

anthrobot : An anthropomorphic machine that may be anything from fully autonomous to fully operator controlled.

bracer: Slang for a palmcomp wrist-adapter.

C4I: Command, Control, Communications, Computers, and Intelligence.

chromaflage: "Active" camouflage that blends into the visual background; a "chameleon suit."

creepers: Small semi-autonomous reconnaissance robots, shaped like spider-centipede hybrids.

Greatsires: Family heads that are the legislators of the Patrijuridicate and bring legal cases to the attention of the Allsires.

EXHALTED: EXtremely High ALtitude Theater Engagement Designator/director. A miniaturized lightweight reconnaissance platform with extraordinary loiter time.

halbardiche: Hkh'Rkh weapon, translated to reflect its fusion between a halberd and bardiche.

Know-It-All: A nearly homophonic bastardization of the acronym NOAH-ITAL (Network Overseen Automated Helper-Independent Tactical Augmentation Link). This is a purpose-built military variant of the NOAH, the most sophisticated form of autonomous personal helper.

LITI: Light Intensification/Thermal Imaging.

LoS: Line of sight.

MISLS: Multiple Independent Stand-alone Launch System. Also deployable in clusters for ease of collective control, these are untended missiles equipped with a light, disposable launch stand that may be left and fired from anywhere within the operator's range of control.

MULTI: Multiple Use Launch Tube, Infantry. A cluster of seven hexagonally framed launch tubes on a reconfigurable launch stand, firing ten-by-seventy-five-centimeter missiles.

Patrijuridicate: The combined legislative and judicial body comprising the Hkh'Rkh government; also an interchangeable term for the entirety of the Hkh'Rkh state.

prophotabs: Prophylatic tablets for both males and females.

Proxie: A nearly homophonic bastardization of the acronym PROXHAE (Platform, Remote-Operated, eXtreme Hazard, Autonomy-Enhanced.

RAP: Rocket-Assisted Projectile. A small (25-30 millimeter) rocket-propelled warhead.

Rectorship: The Hkh'Rkh equivalent of the Russian Academy of Sciences. It is funded by the Patrijuridicate and overseen by a board of Greatsires. Since most educational institutions among the Hkh'Rkh are intra-Family in nature, the supreme importance and prestige of the Rectorship is magnified by its identity as the only true state/inter-Family locus of higher education and, particularly, research.

thermoflage: "Active" camouflage that blends into the thermal background.

ur-primogenitorial list: Those in the core family of a House (the primogenitorial line) who are included on its "ur-list": products of a string of unions that meet extraordinarily rigorous selectivity criteria.

zhyzh'hakz: Hkh'Rkh ritual stimulant, formerly a combat drug.

Appendix C
The Accords

1. The Accord is a democratic council comprised of politically equal member states. Membership is conferred through a process of mutual assessment and determination. Attendance at all Convocations of the Accord is mandatory; absences are treated as abstention and warrant the censure of the Accord. Accord policy and arbitration outcomes are determined by simple majority votes. However, changes in the accords themselves (additions, deletions, emendations) require unanimous approval (abstentions are construed as rejections). Issues addressed by the Accord include:

   • Accord policies and actions toward non-Accord powers, races, objects, or phenomena;

   • interpretation and application of the accords;

   • proper procedures for administering the Accord, including first contact, meeting, and communication protocols;

- reassessment and periodic alteration of the current pathways of allowed expansion for Accord member states.

2. A member state's membership in the Accord requires, and remains contingent upon, truthful self-representation in all disclosures of data or statements of intention: lies of omission or commission are expressly forbidden. If it is found that a member state misrepresented itself upon application for membership in the Accord, its membership is annulled.

3. One member state of the Accord is designated as the Custodian of the accords. The Custodians are charged with ensuring that all member states comply with the accords, that lack of compliance is corrected, and that disputes are resolved by arbitration commissions.

4. The Accord and its individual member states are expressly and absolutely forbidden from interfering in the internal affairs of any member state. The only exception to this is articulated in the Twenty-first Accord.

5. All entry into another member state's space must comply with territorial transit agreements negotiated between the member states in question. If no such agreements exist, a member state may declare any intrusion into its territory as illegal and may require the Accord to convene an arbitration commission to seek redress. The race designated as Custodians are excluded from these constraints when acting in their capacity as Custodians. However, they are expected and enjoined to use all

possible restraint and to secure prior permission wherever and whenever possible.

6. No violence of any kind or on any scale is permitted between the races of the Accord.

7. No espionage is permitted between the races of the Accord, nor are other clandestine attempts to subvert or circumvent the autonomy, prerogatives, or secrecy constraints of another member state.

8. No agreement (legal or personal) made between individuals or collectives from two (or more) member states may ever explicitly or implicitly encumber or abridge the absolute indigenous autonomy of any of the parties to the agreement. Therefore, any member state (or inhabitant thereof) may terminate any agreement with any other member state (or inhabitant thereof) at any time for any reason, contractual obligations notwithstanding.

9. Disputes between member states and violations of these accords may only be resolved by a Custodian-appointed arbitration commission. Member states involved in a dispute may not serve on arbitration commissions convened after the commencement of their dispute until said dispute is resolved. All arbitration commissions are chaired by Custodians, and must follow the same determinative protocols as the Accord itself, as outlined in the First Accord.

10. Member states which are found to have violated an accord are instructed by the finding commission how to make amends for this violation. If the member state finds these instructions unacceptable, they may propose an alternate means of making

amends, may request a reconsideration, or may appeal for clemency or exoneration (if there are suitably extenuating circumstances).

11. Member states which flagrantly or willfully violate one or more accords forfeit their membership in the Accord. The same applies to member states which choose to ignore or reject the final determination of arbitration commissions. Former Accord member states may reapply for membership.

12. Members of the Accord must agree to restrict their use of interstellar-rated microwave and radio emissions to dire emergencies (such as distress calls, or in the event that all other communication systems have malfunctioned).

13. All Accord ships must be equipped with a transponder that, upon inquiry from any other Accord ship, will relay its member state of origin, its name or code, its master, and any special conditions under which it is operating.

14. All Accord ships must be furnished with multiple crewpersons who are conversant in the Code of Universal Signals and, if requested, must use this Code to initiate and respond to any and all communiqués.

15. All member states must maintain strict compliance with the Accord-prescribed pathways of allowed expansion. A single race may petition for a revision of its own expansion pathway: this is handled as an arbitration.

16. New races are contacted by the Accord only when they achieve routine interstellar travel, whether of a faster-than-light or slower-than-light variety.

17. The time and method of contacting a new race is determined by the Custodians of the Accord. Prior to contact, new races are designated as "protected species."

18. Monitoring of nonmember intelligent species is the responsibility of the Custodians. Routine supporting tasks may be assigned to one other member state that possesses sufficient technological and exploratory capabilities.

19. An outgoing Custodian member state selects the order in which member states are invited to succeed it. FTL travel is the prerequisite for Custodianship. The minimum duration of Custodianship is 24.6 Earth years. Minimum advance notice of resignation from Custodianship is 4.1 Earth years.

20. If no race is willing to accept Custodianship, the Accord is considered dissolved, as are all agreements previously made and enforced under its aegis.

21. Extraordinary circumstances: the Custodians are to intervene as soon as is practicable, and unilaterally if that is most expeditious, if:

- any member state's or protected race's homeworld is invaded or otherwise attacked;

- if any member state or protected race takes action that is deemed likely to result in the destruction of a planet's biosphere.

The Custodians may undertake this intervention without soliciting Accord consensus, and may, if necessary, violate other accords in order to ensure that the intervention is successful.

DID YOU KNOW YOU CAN DO ALL THESE THINGS AT THE
BAEN BOOKS WEBSITE?

* Read free sample chapters of books

* See what new books are upcoming

* Read entire Baen Books for free

* Check out your favorite author's titles

* Catch up on the latest Baen news & author events

* Buy any Baen book

* Read interviews with authors and artists

* Buy almost any Baen book as an e-book individually or an entire month at a time

* Find a list of titles suitable for young adults

* Communicate with some of the coolest fans in science fiction & some of the best minds on the planet

* Listen to our original weekly podcast, The Baen Free Radio Hour

Visit us at www.baen.com